PAWN IN FRANKINCENSE

PAWN IN FRANKINCENSE

DOROTHY DUNNETT

C

CENTURY
LONDON   MELBOURNE   AUCKLAND   JOHANNESBURG

Copyright © Dorothy Dunnett 1969

All rights reserved

First published in Great Britain in 1969 by
Cassell & Company Ltd

This edition published in 1983 by
Century Hutchinson Ltd
Brookmount House, 62–65 Chandos Place
London WC2N 4NW

Century Hutchinson Australia Pty Ltd
PO Box 496, 16–22 Church Street, Hawthorn, Victoria 3122, Australia

Century Hutchinson New Zealand Limited
PO Box 40–086, Glenfield, Auckland 10, New Zealand

Century Hutchinson South Africa (Pty) Ltd
PO Box 337, Bergvlei 2021, South Africa

Reprinted 1986

ISBN 0 7126 0064 7

Printed in Great Britain by
Redwood Burn Limited, Trowbridge, Wiltshire.

CHARACTERS

On board the Dauphiné

FRANCIS CRAWFORD OF LYMOND, Comte de Sevigny

JEROTT BLYTH, his captain, a former Knight of St John

ARCHIE ABERNETHY, his serjeant-at-arms, former Keeper of the French King's Menageries

SALABLANCA, a free Moor in his personal service

MAÎTRE GEORGES GAULTIER, usurer and horologist, of Lyons and Blois

MARTHE, a protégée of the Dame de Doubtance

PHILIPPA SOMERVILLE, young daughter of the mistress of Flaw Valleys, near Hexham, England

FOGGE, her maid

ONOPHRION ZITWITZ, a Swiss household official

M. VIÉNOT, Master of the *Dauphiné*

Other characters, in order of their appearance

THE DAME DE DOUBTANCE, an astrologer, of Lyons and Blois

SALAH RAIS, Viceroy of Algiers

OONAGH O'DWYER, a captive Irishwoman in Dragut's household, and mother of Francis Crawford's son, Khaireddin

LEONE STROZZI, of Florence, Prior of Capua in the Order of the Knights Hospitallers of St John

ALI-RASHID, camel-trader, Mehedia

KEDI, nurse to Khaireddin

THE AGA MORAT, Turkish Governor of Tripoli

GÜZEL, mistress to Dragut Rais, the corsair

SHEEMY WURMIT, a Scots dragoman

MARINO DONATI, Venetian merchant of Zakynthos

MÍKÁL, a Pilgrim of Love

EVANGELISTA DONATI, sister to Marino Donati

GRAHAM REID MALETT (Gabriel), Grand Cross of Grace of the Knights Hospitallers of St John

PIERRE GILLES D'ALBI, a scholar

PICHON, his secretary

TULIP, a child of tribute, boy-page to Philippa

GABRIEL DE LUETZ, Baron et Seigneur d'Aramon et de Valabrègues, French Ambassador to Turkey

ROXELANA SULTÁN (Khourrém), wife of Suleiman the Magnificent

SULEIMAN THE MAGNIFICENT, Sultan of Turkey and Lord of the Ottoman Empire

NÁZIK, a nightingale-dealer, Constantinople

ISHIQ, boy to the Meddáh, Constantinople

HUSSEIN, Chief Keeper of the Royal Menageries, Constantinople

JEAN CHESNAU, French Chargé d'Affaires at Constantinople

CONTENTS

The Mediterranean in the 16th century

boundaries of the Holy Roman Empire

boundaries of the Ottoman Empire

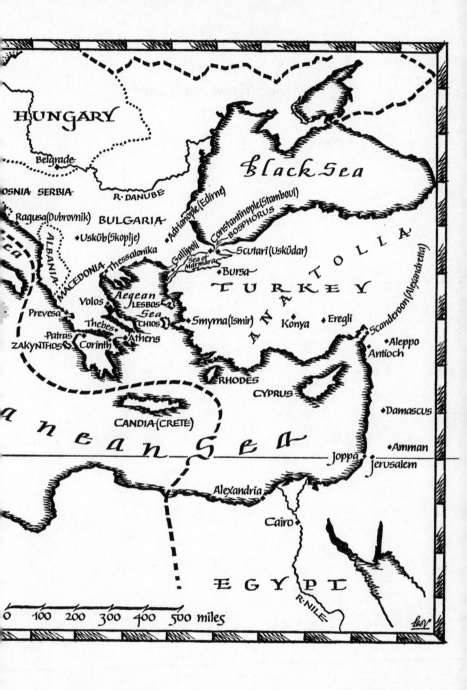

HUNGARY

Belgrade

BOSNIA SERBIA

R. DANUBE

Ragusa (Dubrovnik)

ALBANIA

MACEDONIA

BULGARIA

Usköb (Skoplje)

Thessalonika

Adrianople (Edirne)

Black Sea

Constantinople (Stamboul)

BOSPHORUS

Gallipoli

Scutari (Usküdar)

Sea of Marmara

Bursa

TURKEY

Volos

Aegean

LESBOS

Sea

CHIOS

Prevesa

Thebes

Athens

Patras

Corinth

ZAKYNTHOS

Smyrna (Ismir)

ANATOLIA

Konya

Eregli

Scanderoon (Alexandretta)

Aleppo

Antioch

RHODES

CYPRUS

Damascus

CANDIA (CRETE)

anean Sea

Amman

Joppa

Jerusalem

Alexandria

Cairo

EGYPT

R. NILE

0   100   200   300   400   500 miles

Leo V

For Ninian and Mungo

1

BADEN

The bathers of Baden in summer were few and fat. Winter was the best season, when everyone came home from the fighting, and the baths public and private were filled with magnificent men, their bodies inscribed with the robust holograph of the sword.

The pretty girls came also in winter; the unmarried with their maids and their chaperones: the matrons bright-eyed and dutiful; eager to furnish their lords with an heir.

The rule was mixed bathing. The great officers of the Church went in winter, smoothing off in the sulphurous water the ills of a summer's rich feeding; and rested afterwards sweating in bed, the warm bladders under their armpits, dreaming of Calvin. Noblemen from the Italian States and the Holy Roman Empire; from the France of Henri II and the uneasy England of Edward VI came to Switzerland for the hot baths of Baden: noblemen, soldiers and merchants, lawyers and physicians and men of learning from the universities; courtiers and diplomats; painters, poets and leisured connoisseurs of the human experience.

To trace one man in Baden at the turn of the year was a strenuous but not a disagreeable task. Neither was it impossible, even if the man were international in tongue and appearance, and had no knowledge of, or desire for, your presence. Jerott Blyth and his companion, having crossed half Europe pursuing their quarry, tried four Baden inns before locating the Engel, the largest and most high-priced of all, with the armorial bearings of all its most notable patrons studding the snow-covered front.

Among them, neat, fresh and obliging, was the familiar blazon of Lymond and Sevigny. Their journey appeared to be over.

With Jerott Blyth, innkeepers never shirked the proper discharge of their duties. To the doggedness of his Scottish birth, his long residence in France and his profession of arms had lent a particular fluency. He was black-haired, and prepossessing and rude: a masterful combination. Coming out of the Engel in five minutes flat, he swung himself up on his horse beside the rest of his retinue and led them through the slush and over the square to the far side, where the snow had been swept from an imperial flight of white steps, at the top of which was a pair of carved double doors. Jerott Blyth looked down at his companion. 'He's in there,' he said. 'In the baths. In the public baths. In the public mixed baths. You're too young to go in.'

'I'm fifteen,' said Philippa bleakly. She would have lied about that, except that Fogge, the family maid, was on the pony beside her. She added, 'The stable-boys swim in the Tyne.'

'In waist-cloths?' said Jerott. 'Philippa, Baden isn't the same as the northern counties of England.'

'In nothing,' said Philippa. 'I know.'

She got in, as she had persuaded Jerott Blyth to bring her half across France, by force of logic, a kind of flat-chested innocence and the doggedness of a flower-pecker attacking a strangling fig. Then, followed by a pink, sweating Fogge, they climbed to the gallery which ran at first-floor level overlooking the pool.

The spectators walked there, eating and drinking in their clean velvet doublets and listening to the lute and viol music which ascended in waves through the steam. The discreet abundance of steam and the powerful stink of bad eggs were the first things which Philippa noticed. The next was the size of the pool beneath, and the fact that, unlike the private baths of the hostelries, it had no central partition segregating the sexes: merely an encircling bench divided modestly underwater into pews for each bather.

They were full: so full that in the centre of the pool twenty or thirty of the displaced frolicked or swam or floated, comatose in the warm and sanitative water, beneficial for worms, colic and melancholy; and a certain cure for barrenness in young wives. Beside Philippa, an elegant visitor in shell-pink satin leaned over the carved balustrade and cast a little garland of bay leaves and gilded nutmegs into the water. Two nuns, hesitating on the edge of the pool in their long peignoirs of lawn, flinched and stepped back, but a pretty black-haired woman sitting submerged just below them looked up with the flash of a smile, and the elderly man seated beside her, his paunch bared to the waist, followed her glance with a scowl. Beside Philippa, the gallant smiled back, muttering under his breath; and fishing inside his doublet for the second time, pulled out a preserved rosebud, rather tattered, and took aim again, with rather more care. Philippa followed his eyes.

Women; pure, handsome and pert; with hair curling about their ears and their fine gowns afloat in the water around them and filming the cheerful pink of their shoulders and breasts. Men, sick and stalwart, athletic and obese: the churchmen with tonsure and crucifix lodged on the broad, naked chest; the wealthy served by their retinue, the small floating trays drifting among them bearing sweetmeats and wine, and a posy to offset the fumes. Of soldiers there were fewer than usual: the war between France and the Emperor Charles had dragged on, that winter, in the Low Countries and Italy and the beautiful men this time were otherwise engaged.

Then the steam shifted and Philippa saw there was one suavely muscled brown back, stroked here and there with the pale scars of healed thrusts and the raw marks of an encounter more recent. One gentleman of the sword, just beyond the lady of the pretty black hair and the smile; who was amusing himself with a stiff game of bouillotte, played on a light wooden board drifting between himself and a large and roseate person of no visible rank.

Of the identity of the gentleman-soldier Philippa had no doubts at all. The arching hands, dealing the cards; the barbered yellow hair, whorled and tangled with damp, could belong to only one person, as could the two deferential servants in blue and silver and red, waiting uneasily damp at his back.

'*There he is*,' said Philippa quickly, just as the limp rosebud thrown from beside her touched the bather's bare shoulder, and he flicked round, glancing upwards, and trapped it.

For a moment Philippa saw him full face: a printing of blue eyes and pale, artistic surprise. Then, rose in hand, the bather leaned further round. Behind him, the two nuns still stood, nervously hesitant, while beyond the bouillotte game two seats had become vacant. With dreadful grace, the yellow-haired man got to his feet and, reaching up, presented the rose to the elder of the pair of shy nuns, bowed, and handed both ladies down the wide shallow steps and into their seats. Then he sat down in a gentle lapping of water, and picked up his cards.

'He didn't see us,' said Philippa, disappointed. The gentleman in shell-pink, retrieving his upper torso from the reverse side of the balustrade, sighed and observed, 'How wasteful of Nature. You know him, madame?'

Jerott saved her from answering. 'We knew him in Scotland. He commanded a company of which I was a member.' He gave a sudden, malevolent grin and said, 'I think you'd have better luck with the lady.'

Shell-pink, ignoring that, pursued his inquiry. 'His name? He is alone?'

'His name is Francis Crawford of Lymond. He has the title of Comte de Sevigny,' said Jerott. 'As for being alone: I don't even know who he's playing with.'

'Ah, that is simple,' said shell-pink. 'That is Onophrion Zitwitz, the duke's household controller: one of the best-known officials in Baden. Perhaps, when you greet your friend, you will introduce me also?'

Jerott's eyes and Philippa's met. 'When I meet my friend,' said Jerott Blyth carefully, 'there is likely to be a detonation which will take the snow off Mont Blanc. I advise you to seek other auspices. Philippa, I think we should go down below.'

'To swim?' said that unprepossessing child guilelessly. 'I can stand on my head.'

'Oh, Christ,' said Jerott morosely. 'Why in hell did you come?'

The brown eyes within the damp, dun-coloured hair inspected him narrowly. 'Because you need a woman,' said Philippa finally. 'And I'm the nearest thing to it that you're likely to get. It was very

3

short notice.' She stopped short on the stairs and said, in the voice of discovery, 'You're afraid of him!'

Jerott's expression was affably menacing. 'And you think that because he's an old friend of your mother's he'll spare you. He won't.'

'Nonsense,' said Philippa. She wasn't actually listening. They arrived at ground level and took up their stance behind an arrangement of towels, from which they had an excellent view both of the pool and of the man known to most people, briefly, as Lymond.

Francis Crawford had seen them. What he thought about it was unlikely to be visible, through a long-practised sophistication of response. His voice, conversing softly with the controller, did not falter, nor did his hands, dealing the cards. The game drew to a close, in Master Zitwitz's favour, and a pile of gold gulden changed hands. The older of the two nuns, sitting beyond the controller, made a shy comment and the fair-haired man answered, his hands busy with a fresh game. The cards flipped. His nationality, which was Scottish, showed in neither his face nor his voice, which he had raised a little to carry over the noise of laughter and music and splashing: he detained the board and held it steady as two girls, pursued sluggishly by an elderly senator, curvetted past.

The farther nun, the plain one, leaned forward and said in Spanish-accented English, 'We were two years, sir, in Algiers before we escaped in October. Our sufferings may be imagined. Moors, corsairs, heretics cast out of Spain. . . . Turkish Spahis strut in the streets and because the Pasha is a puppet of that accursed of God, Sultan Suleiman, Christian prisoners are treated like hogs. Have you seen——'

A handful of gulden slipped, sparkling, into the water and there was a wallow as several hands urgently sought them. They were now playing passe-dix, and the black-haired lady's husband had joined them. The black-haired lady suddenly giggled. Righting the board: 'Banker's share, I believe,' said Crawford of Lymond courteously. 'I beg your pardon, Sister. You were saying?' Gold—a large amount of gold—changed hands.

The colour was high in the plainer nun's face. 'I was saying—have you ever been at a ganching? Seen a man's feet roasted black in his shoes? Needles driven into his fingers? Have you ever seen a friend flayed alive with such art he took three hours dying, and his skin then stuffed back to its life-shape with straw? Have you ever seen half a man cauterized on a red hot brass shield so that he lives a little time longer? Medicinal baths!' said the older nun bitterly. 'What can hot baths do for *our* scars?'

Her voice, at the sharp pitch of hysteria, carried even to where Jerott and Philippa stood. The decorative lady, paling, recoiled into the arms of her husband, and her husband, a stout soap-broker

4

from Munich, expressed his displeasure. 'There are women present,' he said.

'So there are,' said Francis Crawford gently, and throwing a ten, passed the dice into the capable hands of the household controller. '*Not* a fashionable topic. Why not come back after dinner?'

Onophrion Zitwitz, arrested, the dice in his fingers, put in a question. 'You speak of horrible tortures. But women and children surely were not subject to these?'

The young nun answered. 'They have other uses for them,' she said bitterly. 'I was a slave in the corsair Dragut's own palace. I saw his women—Spanish, French, Italian, Irish. I was at the branding of all his poor children. To some women, degradation like that is the worst sort of torture.'

There was a small silence, in which Philippa's epiglottis popped like a cork. Beside her, Jerott's breathing faltered in the same moment and resumed, shallowly, as he went on straining to hear. The steam drifted, lazily, and there was a little fuss as an old lady was carried out, overcome by the fumes. The viol, which had paused for its rest break, resumed softly, some distance away. Lymond, who had received some gold coins from both Zitwitz and the soap-broker, was counting them. The soap-broker's wife stretched her legs idly under the water.

After a long moment: 'She might have been Queen of Ireland, she told me, that black-haired Irishwoman,' said the young nun sulkily. 'And the golden child on her knee.'

There fell a weighty silence again, filled with the rattle of dice. A small crisis in the passe-dix arrived and departed. The soap-broker threw, followed by Zitwitz, followed by Lymond, who still appeared to be abstractedly considering his money. He threw less than ten, and confronted by the controller's outstretched hand, turned to the younger and prettier nun who had last spoken. 'I'm sorry, *mi bella*, but I need my loose change.'

The nun flinched. The older sister, leaning over her, exclaimed, 'Sister Anne has no money! What are you saying!' The soap-broker looked outraged.

Francis Crawford's voice was quite peaceful. 'That she has twenty gold pieces trapped under her foot.'

Master Zitwitz suddenly said, 'Ah!' Both nuns had gone patchily scarlet and white. The older one said hoarsely, 'You are baiting us! I shall appeal to the Cardinal!'

'No need,' said Lymond. And bending, he caught Sister Anne by both ankles and hurled them up over her head.

Whether she had purloined coins under her feet was not at that moment immediately evident. Her shout, and the tidal wave which went with it, brought each flaccid bather horrified to his feet. As Sister Anne floundered: 'Now, by God!' said the broker, and lunging, tripped over the large form of Master Zitwitz who, head dripping, had come up for air. 'You were right, sir!' said the household controller. 'She had stolen——' Then the broker's shin cracked on his neck, and the waters closed over Master Zitwitz again.

The merchant's wife suddenly giggled and Lymond also broke water, smoothly. The older nun, her feet pulled from beneath her by some unknown agency, disappeared likewise in a whirl of steam and a blizzard of water. Combers, running from side to medicinal side of the pool, overturned trays, wine, food and the more sportive bathers: the merchant, who had discovered why his wife giggled, advanced on Lymond through the water with dreamlike slowness, a pewter jug in his hand.

Lymond ducked. An attendant, running behind, seized his upflung arm, and Lymond, bending smartly, somersaulted him into the pool. He dodged another and watched, admiringly, as the controller, a majestic figure rising mother-naked from the depths, seized another by the liveried waist and delivered him into the arms of a Cardinal. Someone seized the soap-merchant's wife, who was now laughing incessantly, and there was the sound of cloth tearing as she passed down the length of the pool.

Water leaped and spewed over the tiles unheard in the clamour of voices. Forms, pink and uninhibited, appeared and disappeared above the boiling arena: the viol, screaming, disappeared in a fountain of spray. Lymond, ripping out timber partitions from the seats and using them alternately as weapon and shield, was upholding his rights joyously against soap-broker, attendants and Church, Master Zitwitz aiding him stoutly, when he saw that the two nuns, struggling through the many-tongued steam, had found their way to the steps.

Philippa and Jerott Blyth saw them too. Standing, restrained by Jerott's arm, not knowing whether to screech or to squeal with shocked laughter, Philippa saw the older nun climb out of the pool first, terror stark on her face, her draggled cotton clutched fast about her. She glanced at the dark-haired man and the girl, once, and then made for the robing-room like a sack of hysterical turnips.

Sister Anne was not quite so agile. As she clambered after, Lymond's strong hand closed on her ankle, and she stopped, gasping, and turned.

Against the swirling fogs of battle behind him, Lymond's lustrous blue eyes surveyed her with an air strictly practical. Ignoring the hubbub approaching, he changed his grip, pinning her hard with her back to the ladder, and, lifting finger and thumb to her chin, ripped the thin cotton bathrobe in two pieces from collar to hem.

They sagged sodden apart, while the blue stare slid over her. The nun said nothing. Then Francis Crawford, grasping her arm, looked up and straight into Philippa's powerful stare.

'Oh, bloody hell,' said Lymond. And the nun, twisting herself from his arms, clambered over the top of the stairway and bolted.

For a moment in time, Francis Crawford halted, looking at Jerott, arrived at Philippa's side. Steam, exquisitely apt, coiled round all his bare body, and the twist of linen encircling his waist. 'Did you see that?' he said.

'Yes,' said Jerott.

'Good. Come and see more,' said Lymond, and shot off after the nuns to the robing-room. Philippa followed, slowly, her lips pressed together to stop her chin wobbling, until Jerott told her to stay where she was.

Afterwards she remembered that Lymond had flung open the door of the women's changing-room just as some old woman pelted out, screaming. Then everyone went in, except herself, and there was a lot of shouting, and after a time an enormous pink man, whom she recognized as the card-player called Zitwitz, dressed in a white muslin chlamys, emerged and crossed to her. 'You are Philippa Somerville. Let us sit down.' They sat, beside the ruins of the pool, on a cold, marble bench.

'I,' said her large and unusual companion, 'am Onophrion Zitwitz of Basle, controller of gentlemen's households. You may address me as Master Onophrion. There has been a sad event, and your friends have asked me to stay with you until it is settled. The two unfortunate ladies are dead.'

After a glottal interval: '*Dead!*' exclaimed Philippa. 'How?'

The well-groomed, large-featured head inclined thoughtfully. 'How, by a knife. The throat of each had been cut. By whom, it is not known. The rooms were empty, but there are several doors. The woman who found them had just come in by another.'

'Why?' said Philippa, asking her last question; and the controller stroking his august nose, eyed her before answering.

'As to that . . . it is known that the poor ladies were masquerading. They were not, for example, nuns.'

A faint radiance, beginning at the nose, slowly began to inform Philippa's face. 'Then perhaps Sister Anne really purloined the money?'

'She did.'

'They were thieves?'

'They were more.' Master Zitwitz the household controller gave a brief cough. 'Under the robes, I must in all fairness inform you, both the young lady and the older one were *painted.*'

'So *that's* why . . .' said Philippa, and seizing her drooping, mud-coloured hair, tied it briskly together under her chin. 'But how did Mr Crawford suspect?'

'I gather,' said the controller austerely, 'that their toenails were orange. In greater detail I did not feel it necessary to inquire.'

7

He chatted to her, for which she was grateful, until Jerott returned and took her back to their inn.

*

It was some time later when Francis Crawford was able to leave the scene of the turmoil, and later still when, by arrangement, Jerott and Philippa arrived at the Engel to dine with him.

Crossing the lamplit snow, Jerott was silent. He led Philippa upstairs, knocked on Lymond's door, and shoving it open demanded grimly, 'How many batzen did it take to smooth over that little incident?' Philippa, smiling at the big Moor Salablanca who came to slip off her cloak, knew his anger to be defensive. Her feet were cold. She smoothed down the creased folds of what had been her best farthingale, and wished the buckled hemline showed less, where it had shrunk.

Lymond, standing totally dressed in front of the fire, waited until the door had closed behind Salablanca and then spoke with precision to Jevott. 'You are not here, I take it, because you have palsy, running gout or worms in the belly, but to interfere in my affairs. When I wish to be followed like a bitch in season, I shall tell you so.' The arbitrary blue gaze switched to Philippa. 'And where does your mother imagine you are?'

Only three months since, back in Scotland, he had called her his friend, although she was English and he Scots. That was when he had matched his wits against the man called Graham Reid Malett, whose nickname was Gabriel. And although he had prevailed, Gabriel had escaped and fled overseas. Philippa said, temperately, 'My mother thinks I'm with Lord Grey's wife in London. I was, but I got to Guisnes, and Mr Guthrie took me to Nantes, and Mr Blyth brought me here.'

'How benign of them,' said Lymond. 'I understood that, in my absence, Mr Guthrie was mustering my company at Sevigny and that Mr Blyth was taking it to the French camp at Hesdin. I have, after all, accepted the King's hire and paid you to fight.'

Jerott Blyth pulled out a chair. 'Sit down,' he said curtly to Philippa. Below the smooth tan, his skin was carnation-coloured from the obstinate jaw to the fall of his splendid black hair. 'Unless, of course, your mother's dear friend is proposing to throw you out in the snow.' Erect and hostile, he faced Francis Crawford. 'The company is already on its way to Hesdin under Alec Guthrie and Adam Blacklock. By my own request I was relieved of the command.'

'I am enchanted to hear it,' said Lymond. 'You are now free to take the girl back to Hexham, starting tomorrow. If you will ring the bell nearest to you, I believe they will bring us some food.' He wore dark velvet over dark, toning satin, and a ring of some price on one hand.

Jerott made no move to the bell. 'We are surely agreed,' he said, 'that Graham Reid Malett must be found, and when found, must be killed. He's evil; he's dangerous. He'll never forgive us for what we did to him in Scotland. He will certainly kill you if he can. . . . You know what else he can do. I demand,' said Jerott staunchly, 'to take my share in the execution. I am staying. And if you think you can make Philippa go back to England, good luck to you. It's more than Guthrie or I managed to do.'

Francis Crawford of Lymond, Comte de Sevigny, walked slowly towards them. He lifted the small brass bell from the table, rang and replaced it, allowing the unflattering stare to move from Philippa's unwashed brown rats' tails to Jerott's prickly splendours. 'But I'm not going to kill Graham Reid Malett,' said Lymond. 'So you might as well pack your godly emotions into your bronze chariot and get back to Malta, don't you suppose?'

'And that's a bloody lie. You're going to kill him all right,' said Jerott Blyth. 'Unless he kills you first. He found you today, didn't he? Or his agents did. They could hardly help it with your coat of arms painted all over Baden. . . . You were meant to believe those nuns and go to Algiers, weren't you? Are you trying to tell me that wasn't Gabriel's work?'

'Oh, Graham Malett arranged it,' said Lymond. 'Through our ardent friend in shell-pink, I believe. The nuns were killed when he saw their little deception had failed.'

'And a fine death you'd have met in Algiers if you'd fallen into the trap.'

'Yes. Expensive, of course,' said Lymond. 'After all, if he could have the two nuns killed, why not simply cut my throat here? Think of all the wages he'd save.'

'No,' said Philippa reflectively. She hadn't meant to speak aloud; and scarcely knew indeed that she had done so: it was a problem which interested her. 'Having to fly from Scotland meant a frightful loss of face for him, surely. After all, he used to be a Knight Grand Cross of Malta fighting for Christ, and now he's a renegade without standing in Malta or Scotland. He's a lot of old scores to wipe off before he kills Mr Crawford. If I were Gabriel,' said Philippa, her brown eyes accusing, 'I'd want to *humiliate* him first. I'd taunt him: I'd shame him. And *then* I'd kill him, I think.'

She looked up. Above her, Lymond had come to rest by her chair and, arms crossed, was studying her face. 'Pigged, I see, with a full set of teeth,' he observed. And, echoing Jerott, 'So why in hell have *you* come?'

Philippa's gaze, bright and owlish and obstinate, held his to the end. 'To look after the baby,' she answered. And disconcertingly, after a second's blank pause, Francis Crawford flung back his damp head and laughed.

*

Opening the door after tapping three times, Master Zitwitz, the duke's household controller, was a little put off by that laughter. He coughed, sonorously, and banged again on the door since, although he was inside the room, none of the three already there appeared to have noticed him. Then Lymond turned, and recognized him at once. 'I beg your pardon,' he said. 'We were having a little reunion. It's Master Zitwitz, without whose powerful defence I should have lost my virtue to a soap-merchant's lady. Sir, you fought like Zeus demolishing Titans: I am your debtor.' There was a shadow of amusement still in his voice. Philippa, a pain in her middle, sat watching them both.

'M. le Comte, it was a privilege. I have seen many gentlemen enjoying themselves with a game of cards or a fight, but never a performance of both so *aristocratic*,' said Onophrion Zitwitz. Below the opulent features, hairlessly moulded in pink marzipan, the controller's large body was dressed in sober brown short coat and breeches, with the smallest curled feather in his flat, matching cap. His voice, a musical light tenor surprising in that solid, Swiss bulk, became modestly hesitant. 'In fact, my winnings being something considerable, I have ventured to show my appreciation. The dressing of meat in this inn is better than in most, but I should not call the roasting-shop proprietor a genius: he needs to be supervised and he is prodigal, *prodigal*, with the inferior spices. So I took the liberty . . . you have not yet dined?'

As in a trance, his three auditors shook their heads.

'Good. I have taken the liberty of preparing your supper myself. This afternoon I chose the butters, the meats and the cheeses; I have made the bread and prepared the pastries. You have not tasted, I think, the roast venison we make in the castle, just moistened with wine, and with our black cherry sauce? The duke, I sometimes think, does not fully appreciate it. He is an old man. I choose his wines and select his clothes and make up his herbs and his physics, but my talents, I fear, are not used to the full. Not at all stretched.'

'No. You cook? How magnificent,' said Lymond breathlessly.

Master Onophrion Zitwitz opened the door. Instead of discomfort and anger and scathing voices, the room became filled with trestle tables, linen, platters, beakers and a file of subdued-looking inn servants bearing trays covered with napkins. The smell of choice foods and wines made the pain in Philippa's middle increase.

'I am not a gentleman,' said Master Onophrion Zitwitz. 'I do not serve. But I control all the practical aspects, you understand, of His Grace's household. For this it is necessary to know whether a thing is being done well or badly, and why. I may claim, I think, to be an expert in most if not all of the domestic arts. This is no boast: I have documents to say so from noblemen I have served all over Europe.'

He surveyed the smoking tables and the servants melting in orderly decline through the door.

'Yes. I am correct in saying, I think, that your supper would have been eatable, but not memorable. I have made the sauces a little sweet, for madame's taste. Permit me to leave you to enjoy it.'

Ten years had dropped from Jerott. He looked at Lymond, and Lymond said, 'But we are utterly overwhelmed. I cannot imagine why you should have felt any obligation towards us, although I cannot help being happy that you have. But having prepared this inestimable feast, surely you will give us the pleasure of sharing it with us?'

'That is not my place,' said Master Zitwitz. He looked pleased. 'At the baths, yes. But being in service, one does not eat in gentlemen's rooms. If you will permit me, I shall call later. I wish to have your views on the custards.'

'You disappoint us,' said Lymond. 'But we shall look forward with pleasure to dissecting the meal. . . . Until later then, Master Zitwitz.' The controller smiled, favoured them with a correct bow, and withdrew. The door closed.

As if released by a string, Jerott, his shoulders trembling with laughter, dropped among the pasties and started to splutter. Lymond's seraphic expression, surveying the feast, did not alter. Philippa, her hands screwed into her skirt, said, 'Why did you laugh?'

'I didn't laugh,' said Lymond. 'It's Jerott's childish sense of humour assaulting the eardrums. For God's sake let's sit down and eat: he's inhaled the cherry sauce three times already.'

'Why did you laugh when you knew why I meant to come with you?' said Philippa, and Jerott put his hand on her arm.

To look after the baby, she had said. A subject none of them mentioned: an affair so private and painful that you pretended it didn't exist. Unless you were Philippa Somerville.

Last year an Irish mistress of Francis Crawford's had been captured by Dragut Rais, the Turkish corsair. Lymond had been told that she had died. Only when his adversary Gabriel was defeated and begging for his life did Lymond learn that the woman Oonagh O'Dwyer was alive, and had given birth to his son.

Gabriel had escaped, taking with him the secret of the whereabouts of mother and child. He had done more. He had made it clear that their safety depended on him. And that any attempt to interfere with his life or his liberty would result in the death, wherever he was, of the child, Lymond's son.

So Graham Malett had vanished, and shortly after that Lymond himself had disappeared, to be run down in this costly Swiss hostelry, taking the waters in his own inimitable fashion and in no mood, it was clear, for unwanted company.

11

So: 'Why did you laugh?' demanded Philippa, and shook Jerott's hand off her arm.

'Oh, that?' said Lymond. 'But, my dear child, the picture was irresistible. Daddy, afflicted but purposeful, ransacking the souks of the Levant for one of his bastards, with an unchaperoned North Country schoolgirl aged—what? twelve? thirteen?—to help change its napkins when the happy meeting takes place. . . . A gallant thought, Philippa,' said Lymond kindly, sitting down at the table. 'And a touching faith in mankind. But truly, all the grown-up ladies and gentlemen would laugh themselves into bloody fluxes over the spectacle. Have some whatever-it-is.'

Philippa's eyes, stiff, brown and unyielding, stared unwinkingly at his face. 'Then where are you going?'

'I wondered when someone was going to ask that,' said Lymond; and Jerott, pressing Philippa into a seat, sat down quietly himself, his appetite gone. 'Tell us,' Jerott said. 'Bearing in mind, if you can, what Philippa has done for you.'

Lymond laid down his knife. 'I thought,' he said, 'of going to Brazil. An expedition under de Villegagnon is leaving fairly soon. It might be less tedious than some. I had a long talk with de Villegagnon, by the way. He has given me a little more written proof of Sir Graham Malett's defection. Added to what I have already, it makes certain at least that Gabriel can never set foot again either in France or in Scotland.'

'And that is enough for you?' said Jerott. 'He may gather men, money and power and range himself where he pleases: with the Emperor, with the Sultan, with the enemies of Scotland and the Faith, and you mean to do nothing? He can pay an employee to trap and chastise you, and you talk of clearing off to Brazil?'

'I said I thought of it,' said Lymond. 'For God's sake, eat the custards at least. We'll have Gargantua back in a moment expecting a consumers' opinion. . . . Then I called on Henri II of France, His Sacred Majesty, the abstract and quintessence of all honour and virtue, to hire him my small but excellent army. He also—*seid fröhlich, trinkt aus*—hired me.'

'Oh, *Christ*, what as?' said Jerott.

'As a lackey, my lords,' said Lymond. In his voice, light and absent, there was no warmth whatever. 'An ingenious Frenchman called Gaultier has devised a hideous novelty: a clock combined with a spinet and covered with every sort of automata which does all but fry fish. I am to collect this achievement from his workshop at Lyons. I am to take the machine, with M. Gaultier to preserve it, on board one of His Grace's galleys in the Mediterranean and deliver it, with trumpets, hautboys and dried neates' tongues and marmalade to the court of Allâh's Deputy on Earth, the Lord of Lords of this world, the Possessor of Men's Necks, the Majestic

Caesar, the Prince and Lord of the most happy Constellation and the Shadow of the Almighty dispensing Quiet in the Earth . . . Sultan Suleiman the Magnificent.'

'You're sailing to Constantinople?' said Jerott.

'As the King of France's special envoy.'

'And Sir Graham Malett?'

'Is in Malta.'

Jerott Blyth sprang up. Watching the skin tighten on the prominent bones of his face Philippa felt her own stomach waver once more. Malta was the home of the great Order of Chivalry to which Jerott himself had belonged, as well as Graham Reid Malett, this unique and brilliant man, whose chances in Scotland Lymond had just destroyed. Malta was the home of the Knights of St John whom Gabriel had tried to betray to the Turks after failing in his hopes of acquiring the highest power, the Grand Mastership, which would have given him control of all the Mediterranean. Because the Grand Master was himself a cunning and powerful man, with the support of France's rival, the Emperor, Gabriel had been unable to achieve the foothold he wanted and had left to try his fortune in Scotland instead. If he was back, it meant only one thing.

'The Grand Master of the Order is dying,' said Lymond. 'Gabriel hopes to succeed him.'

Jerott made a sudden, theatrical gesture. 'After selling them out to the Turks? After what he did to seize power in Scotland?'

'How should the Order know about that? Malta's a long way from Scotland.'

'You have all the proof you were talking about. Take it to them,' said Jerott, aghast.

'Don't be an ass. Grand Master de Homedes would place me in hell or in hop-shackles, and burn all the papers. He's the Emperor's minion, remember, and he's not dead just yet. As far as he's concerned I'm a cat's-paw of France, and any papers I bring are all too likely to reveal his own double-dealing.'

'Then *I'll* take them,' said Jerott.

'Same story,' said Lymond. 'You're not only suspect, you've opted out of the Order. I can see them flinging out their favourite Knight of Grace on your advice.'

'I see,' said Jerott slowly. 'You've thought it all out.'

'That's what I do,' said Lymond. 'I sit on my brood-patch and think. I'm going to Constantinople. You're going to Flaw Valleys, England, with Philippa. Graham Malett is going to be Grand Master of the Order of St John.'

'Graham Malett is going to die,' said Jerott mildly. 'And I'm going to kill him.'

There was a silence. The perfumed meats, congealing on their platters, soured the cold air with their smells. Through the thick

13

shutters the sound of bells and the rumble of horse-sleighs troubled the air and were gone. Voices sounded below from the public parlour, protesting as the pot of *Schlaftrunke*, the last of the night, was put down. Lymond said, 'No one is going to kill Graham Malett.'

Jerott faced him; still and quiet. 'I am. There are a hundred places on Malta where a small boat can land. I can't perhaps bring him to justice. But I can kill him.'

'No,' said Lymond.

'I'm not asking your permission,' said Jerott. His plate, piled with irrelevant food, still lay untouched on the table. 'I don't want your help. Or maybe you don't think you need help? Maybe you're hoping to rouse Islam to crush the Knights for you, Gabriel included?'

'Settle down with a harem at last? What a skittish fancy you do have,' said Lymond. He stood up slowly, the long oversleeves sliding; the shoulder-buckles gold in the candlelight, and moving across to the stove picked up a billet of wood and began rebuilding the fire. His hands, performing their exact office, drew Philippa's aching attention as how often before to their form and their strength. 'No,' he said at last, shutting in the new fire and, rising, turned round. '. . . Oh, God: all this bloody food. Where can we dump it?'

'There's a place,' said Philippa suddenly. 'If you open the back window, there's a rubbish-dump underneath. The snow would cover it quite fast.' Lymond walked to the window.

'Well?' said Jerott. Alone of the three he had stayed where he was, waiting. 'You don't want Gabriel dead. Supposing you tell us all why?'

'Oh, *Jerott*,' said Philippa. She turned, a trembling green jelly in one hand and a bowl of soup in the other, and her nose had begun to run because she was crying inside her eyes. 'Because if anything happens to Gabriel, the little boy has to die.'

'But . . .' said Jerott, not adjusting and loathing it. 'But . . .?'

'But how amusing,' said Lymond, admonishing. In a shower of almond blancmange, the last of Master Onophrion's light supper went shooting into the yard and, closing the shutters, Francis Crawford walked back into the room and laid the platter carefully back in its place. 'You heard. The policy is one of strict laissez-faire for a very good reason. If anything happens to Gabriel, Daddy's little bastard will die.'

Soon after that, Master Onophrion Zitwitz arrived. Shivering, in spite of the newly filled stove, Philippa barely heard Lymond's smoothly turned compliments, or the controller's satisfied acceptance of them. In her ears were Jerott's guarded apologies, and the light ruthlessness with which Lymond had silenced him.

More clearly now than when they had entered the chamber that

14

evening and met the first shock of his anger did she understand why Francis Crawford found their presence in Baden insupportable. Jerott, she knew, would not join Lymond now. Nor would she presume to scratch the gloss of his mission with her juvenile presence. . . .

A long time afterwards, she was to remember what an excellent chess-player Francis Crawford was. And that, whether romance existed in him or not, sentimentality had no place at all.

But at the time she arrived only so far in her thinking; and then was drawn out of her abstraction by Master Zitwitz's voice saying, 'But, M. le Comte, I cannot tell you how sensible I am of the honour. I shall serve the embassy with my life.'

'What?' said Philippa hoarsely to Jerott.

'It's recruiting day,' said Jerott in a murmur. 'He's asked Master Zitwitz to leave the duke and travel with him as household controller to the Ambassador's residence in Turkey.'

Philippa Somerville blew her nose sharply. 'On the strength of his sweet cherry sauce?'

'On the strength, I think, of that handy right uppercut,' said Jerott. 'I've said we'll ride with them to Lyons, and then I'm taking you back home to England. If you agree.'

'I think,' said Philippa mutinously, 'I want to go to Brazil.'

*

It was dark on the stairs when they left, and the taper Jerott's manservant carried hardly lit the bare steps outside Lymond's closed door. Moreover, the woman waiting at the first bend who slipped past them, averting her face, and ran up those same stairs was cloaked and heavily veiled. But Philippa recognized her, none the less, in a puff of bean-powder and chypre, as the soap-merchant's wife.

Jerott's hand increased its grip on her arm. 'He is an island with all its bridges wantonly severed. What hostage to evil,' said Jerott, poetic in his thumping displeasure, 'will *this* night's business conceive?'

'I don't know. But they're both nice and clean, if that's anything,' said Philippa. And led the way philosophically down.

The lady from Munich left, with equal discretion, just after two o'clock in the morning. Some time after that, after listening outside Lymond's door for a moment, Salablanca, his personal aide and his friend, laid down a candle and, entering noiselessly, crossed in near-dark to the bed.

Lymond was asleep, his hands outflung on the pillow-mattress; the sheets twisted about him. Satisfied, Salablanca moved from his side and in a few moments, soundlessly, had set the disordered room to rights and was repairing, softly as a hospitaller, the wreck of the bed.

15

Just as he finished Lymond half woke; and with a faint smile for Salablanca, turned his head fully away.

'*Lo siento, señor.*' The words were no more than a breath; and already, having said them, Salablanca had retreated without sound to the door, when Lymond spoke. '*¿ No duermes?*'

'*Duermo y guardo.*'

'There is no need,' said Lymond in Spanish and lay, looking, as Salablanca bowed his head and withdrew, closing the door on the dark.

2

LYONS

It was raining in Lyons when they got there. The journey, a remorselessly eventful one, took just under three weeks; and after three weeks in Lymond's company—longer than she had ever spent in the whole of her life—even Philippa's iron nerves were vibrating.

They were attacked three times in the course of it: once in the forest of Jurthen by the local brigand Long Peter, which they expected; and once crossing the gorge bridge near Nantua, which it appeared only Lymond expected. Because of the size of their cavalcade and its quality, the fighting in both these cases was brief, and they suffered no damage.

Philippa, used to thief-infested journeys at home and to trees with strange burdens, was not unduly disturbed. What shook her, lying under the lee of a waterfall, behind a thornbush and once, by mistake, on an anthill, was Lymond's articulate and nauseating power to command. To form an escort of even minimal size for Ambassadorial dignity he had hired men-at-arms, swiftly and rigorously chosen, on leaving the French Court. From St Mary's, his company now lent to the King, he had taken only three men: two grooms and general servants from Midculter, and the Moor Salablanca whom the year before he had freed from slavery at the castle of Tripoli. Now, in addition, he had Jerott with his two or three men, Philippa with her elderly Fogge, and Master Zitwitz with his small staff as well.

Through Onophrion Zitwitz's eyes, and through those of Jerott, Philippa witnessed the reduction of this multilingual mob, smoking, to a compact troop of precisely drilled servants. As Solothurn gave place to Berne, and Berne to Fribourg; as they passed Romont and Lausanne and skirted the Lake of Geneva to the Weisses Kreuz at Rolle; as they passed from the bearpit and the German cooking at the Falken to the Croix Blanche and the Bois de Cerf where Onophrion made them burn all the sheets, she commented, blithely, on what she saw and shared, frequently, in the scourge of Francis Crawford's disparaging tongue.

On other matters no one spoke. It was accepted, it seemed, that possessing this talent, Lymond should be exercising it on a parcel of peasants while his own massive command operated without him at Hesdin, and for no better reason than that he wished to travel in state as a Special Envoy to Turkey. It was accepted that Graham Malett, whose hunger for power was greater, perhaps, than that of any other man then living, was to remain undisturbed by Lymond to do what harm he might please on Malta. It was accepted that the mistress, alive or dead, and the son, alive or dead, whom Graham Malett claimed to have hidden as hostages when, three months before, he had bartered his life, were to continue in life or in death, untroubled by Francis Crawford; who balked at publicly beating up Europe in pursuit of a one-year-old byblow.

At the beginning, belligerent, Philippa had tried to discuss it with Jerott. 'He could at least find out if the baby's alive. He could at least hurry. If he'd left Scotland when Gabriel did and got to Malta first, he might even have rescued it.'

'Good God,' said Jerott. 'You don't suppose Gabriel's keeping them on Malta?' They were at Coppet at the time and leaving early, by Lymond's unalterable edict, because Calvin was preaching. Jerott had wished to hear Calvin. 'The bloody child's not on Malta; it's in the corsair Dragut's harem with its mother, if she's still alive. If Gabriel's issued orders to kill it, then it's dead, and Francis couldn't have stopped it. How could he? He couldn't sail for a week after Gabriel had gone, and even if he'd known where to look, Graham Malett would have got there before him.'

'But if it is dead, then Mr Crawford is free to kill Gabriel,' remarked Philippa, her mud-coloured eyes ingenuous in her very plain face.

'Quite,' said Jerott. 'Which makes it seem very possible, doesn't it, that it is in Gabriel's own best interests to keep the baby alive?'

'But inaccessible,' said Philippa thoughtfully.

'But inaccessible.'

'So why are you going to Lyons?' said Philippa. 'It's not on the way back to England.'

Jerott eyed her austerely. 'For protection.'

'It seems to me,' said Philippa prosaically, 'that on the whole we run more risks *with* Mr Crawford's protection than *without* it.'

The following week, within sight of Lyons and its frieze of occupied gibbet and wheel, they became involved, not accidentally, in a Protestant-baiting, despite all Lymond could and did do. The crowd came upon them suddenly, and with them a masked dummy, borne on a hurdle with its limbs dangling, broken in ritual to represent a heretic condemned but so far uncaught.

In a narrow faubourg, without possibility of retreat, Lymond's party reined in single file and stopped on command: no one spoke. No one knew how, in passing, the rag-filled dummy was freed from its hurdle and slung over the saddle of one of Master Zitwitz's servants whose horse, taking fright, bolted off through the throng, maiming with its hoofs as it went.

In a climate sulphurous with religious dissent, it was more than enough. The crowd, a rabble of four or five hundred, turned on the cavalcade in their midst. Philippa had time to see the reddened faces, the open mouths, the upflung hatchets and pikes; and then her horse, hauled round by Lymond's hand on the bit, turned and raced off by the way they had come, a detachment of Lymond's armed men surrounding her and her maid. From the shouting behind, she knew that Lymond himself, with Jerott and the rest, was momentarily holding the road.

She shouted then, but the men-at-arms round her wouldn't let her stop. Instead, they brought her in a broad sweep to the river they had been about to cross over, bargained swiftly, and when, a moment later, Lymond and the rest of the company appeared, riding hard, she was already in the ferryboat and half-way across, her horse swimming alongside. Kneeling in the boat, screaming encouragement, she saw them one by one launch into the water, stones splashing about them, until finally they were out of reach of the bank and the crowd, still yelling, began to disperse.

Standing safely on the opposite bank with her dry maid, her dry escort, and a company of streaming horsemen, Philippa said scathingly, 'That's men for you. Cover the lady's retreat, the book says. A hundred years ago, maybe. And what stopped you from coming with me just now? I can swim, you know.'

Onophrion Zitwitz, as so often, materialized at her side. 'M. le Comte,' he said, his face less than rosy under the sad strands of his hair, 'hoped, without success, I fear, to save that poor ill-advised servant of mine.'

'Oh, Christ, it wasn't his fault,' said Lymond. Unclasping the dead weight of his long cloak, he slung it to Salablanca and remounted as he was, his bare head darkened and rivulets from his chain mail drenching leathers and saddlecloth.

'Was it staged, then?' Jerott, also remounted, rode alongside. Lymond said, 'Don't be a fool, Jerott,' and turning, continued with the string of orders he had begun when interrupted. Philippa said patiently to Jerott, 'All right. So you were gallant. And how did you persuade four hundred people to let you ride after me in the end?'

'It's easy if you know how,' said Jerott. 'Francis emptied his purse on the street as we went.'

'Oh,' said Philippa. 'Tonight we sing in the streets?' She waited, and then said, 'What's wrong? It's not just Master Zitwitz's servant? You know I'm sorry about that.'

'You perhaps didn't notice my crack over the knuckles just now,' Jerott said. 'That was because three men were picked off and killed altogether back there in the street. One was the servant. The other two were the men Lymond himself brought from Midculter. Quite a coincidence, yes?'

Philippa drew a deep breath, and found relief in expelling it. 'Do you think,' she said carefully, 'that someone is going to be goaded into doing something soon?'

There was a long pause. 'I think,' said Jerott at length, equally carefully, 'that someone is going to the court of Sultan Suleiman the Magnificent, and someone else is going to Flaw Valleys, England, to Mother.'

Which summed it up, Philippa supposed, with regret.

For their stay in Lyons, Onophrion had hired a house, on Lymond's instructions. As with every domestic arrangement on the entire journey, the controller's dispositions were perfect. The house, in three chic carved wooden storeys with its own courtyard, was well staffed and admirable. Even more admirable was the discovery that the clothes, the household linen and even the mattresses packed under Onophrion's direction for the sumpter-mules had survived their swim in the Rhône quite intact.

The food, it became obvious, was Onophrion's dearest care; but his search for the finest tailors and cloth-makers was meticulous, and soon his special task, that of suitably dressing the men-at-arms and attendants of a Special Envoy of France, was on its rich and orderly way. Only just in time did the Special Envoy, leaving the house with Jerott, catch and stop Onophrion on the verge of purchasing ells of cramoisy velvet, violet satin and cascades of gold bullion to be made into clothing for the Special Envoy himself. 'No! No. The prayer of Job upon the dunghill was as good as Paul's in the temple. I shall choose what I want for myself.'

Master Zitwitz inclined his head. 'I have gone too far. Forgive me. I wished only to save time. If I have the best—only the best—cloths and laces set out for you, would you give yourself the trouble of choosing? I shall appoint the tailors to come as you wish. Also, M. le Comte may require jewels?' It was a sore point that, whatever Lymond's possessions might be, Salablanca had charge of them.

'Do I require jewels?' asked Francis Crawford, of the air. 'Let us ask M. Gaultier.' His eyes wide, he turned, catching Jerott's sour grin. 'Think!' said Lymond. 'Breeches! Bangles! A Hairy Alpenrose in dimity ruffles! . . . Don't you wish you were going as well?'

'I wish we were going to Gaultier's,' Jerott said evenly. 'We'll be late.' And waited while, smiling, Lymond finished buckling his sword, flung a cloak over his right shoulder and slithering downstairs, crossed the courtyard to join him.

The rue Mercière, Lyons, where rested the unique horological spinet, the King of France's gift to the Sultan Suleiman, was not far away. With the spinet was its maker, Georges Gaultier, usurer, clockmaker and dealer in antiquities, who in pursuit of his fortunes had several establishments the length and breadth of France, in two of which he had had the doubtful pleasure of entertaining Francis Crawford before.

Jerott knew this. He also knew, from sources in Scotland, a little more than Lymond would expect about Georges Gaultier's permanent house-guest. Crossing the narrow threshold in the rue Mercière he viewed without enthusiasm Maître Gaultier's fleshless frame, sallow skin and general air of liberal neglect, not helped by his attitude of qualified interest. Egypt, Syria, Armenia, Arabia Felix or otherwise, were to him as familiar, Jerott gathered, as the castle at Blois. He made only cursory mention of his previous meetings with M. le Comte de Sevigny, and betrayed no excitement over the present one. He settled a date for crating the spinet, now finished, and a further date on which the crate, accompanied by himself and assistant, would join M. de Sevigny—or did he wish to be called M. de Lymond?—to sail by river from Lyons to Marseilles.

Lymond said pleasantly, 'Let's keep the title until we have to impress somebody. I should also like you and your assistant to call on me at least a week before we embark. We shall be together for a long time. You should meet the rest of my household. And there may be purely domestic matters to settle.'

It was agreed but not, Jerott noted, with any great readiness. Why? Great sums of money—prodigal sums—had passed hands over this spinet. As the maker, Gaultier's name, already familiar, would be famous. Surely the journey alone, all expenses paid, was an inducement, no matter how often the dealer had travelled before. Or had the old creature upstairs objected?

Alert to every pulse in the air, Jerott heard Lymond say, 'And may we have the pleasure now of inspecting the instrument?' But to his surprise, this time the old man made no demur. There were two doors to pass and enough in the way of bars, bolts and keys to inhibit a woodworm. But finally the inner workshop was there, and a smallish freestanding object from which Georges Gaultier smoothed off an ancient striped bedgown masquerading as dust-sheet.

Jerott gasped.

There was a long silence while they looked, the reflected candle-light blinding their eyes. Then the dealer said softly, 'M. de Lymond? Will this please the Turk?'

'My dear Gaultier,' said Lymond. 'It will send the Shadow of God into transports. I suppose I've seen objects more grisly before, but it doesn't spring to mind where. . . . Twenty-four-carat gold, Jerott. Look. And studded with rubies like fish-roes.'

'Yes. I think he'll be pleased,' said Georges Gaultier. For the first time satisfaction, animation and even cheerfulness rang in his voice. 'Sickening, isn't it?'

Jerott wasn't sickened. He stood in silence and worked out the cost of the square Gothic cabinet whose double doors of jewels and marquetry opened on a pillared façade of Gothic fantasy plastered with gold leaf and beryls and ivory and crowned by a clock. Among the paintings, the niches, the cupboards inside the cabinet was the drawer containing the keyboard and strings of the spinet, which Gaultier pulled out as he and Francis Crawford, in the closest amity, explored every unfortunate inch of the instrument.

Jerott stood by while it struck, chimed, tinkled tunes and shot representational articles, on ratchets, in and out of suitable orifices. Presently Lymond said, 'Does the revolting thing play?' and sitting on the edge of a box, ran his hands up and down the keyboard. Then he lifted them and said, 'Yes, it does,' and rising, strolled to the door.

'Yes,' said Gaultier placidly, following him. 'She insisted on that.'

There was a pause. 'Is she upstairs?' said Lymond at length.

Maître Gaultier nodded. 'She is waiting to see you. Of course. And Mr Blyth also.'

Lymond said, 'I should prefer to meet her alone. Do you mind, Jerott?'

The tone was perfectly and familiarly final. Gaultier ignored it. 'I'm sorry,' he said. '*With* Mr Blyth. Or the lady regrets she cannot give you an interview.'

'If it's something personal . . .' Jerott said helpfully, but not too helpfully. It was something personal all right. He'd heard of this woman. The Dame de Doubtance, they called her: a madwoman and a caster of horoscopes. Gaultier gave her house-room and men and women came to her from all the known world and had their futures foretold—if she felt like it. She had given some help once to Lymond, on her own severe terms, because of a distant link, it was said, with his family. Plainly, a crazy old harridan. But if she was going to tell Lymond he ought to find a nice girl and marry her, Jerott wanted very much to be there.

Gaultier did not come with them. Abandoning him to the spinet with its double-locked doors, Lymond with Jerott hot on his heels followed an elderly manservant to another part of the house, and up a small, winding stair. There they were led through a thick velvet curtain and left, in absolute darkness.

Jerott, after feeling about for a moment, encountered something sharp and stopped trying. The atmosphere was dire, composed largely, he concluded, of dust and dry rot and very damp textiles. Lymond, presumably somewhere in the room also, said nothing. Through a faint crack of light in the far wall voices muttered: the old fellow must be announcing them. Then the crack widened, and a voice whose sex he could not discover summoned them in. Jerott looked round once, quickly, for Lymond and found him disconcertingly at his elbow, his expression politely withdrawn. Jerott, who knew that look, suddenly felt his skin crawl. Then they were in.

The Lady of Doubtance, Jerott observed, was of the older variety of witch who liked a theatrical smack to her necromancy. The bedroom, or whatever it was in which they now stood, was lit with a single wax candle, so placed that it illuminated only the face of their hostess—that of a woman of considerable age, whose bush of dead yellow hair was dressed in the style of high Saxon romance, its plaits bristling under the long, sagging chin. She was seated in a tall canopied chair, its feet lost in darkness; and of her body, too, nothing could be seen but a glimpse of archaic, unravelling robes, and two hands burdened with rubies, which lay like insects on her lap. The mouth opened, black in the seamed, underlit mask. 'You are welcome, gentlemen. Come near. I rejoice in comely people around me. You note, Mr Blyth: your exquisite companion is sulking.'

From a distance of four feet, with the hair standing out on his skin, Jerott, wide-eyed, gave a stiff smile. How Lymond's dignity had stood up to that kick in the teeth he did not know; nor did he mean to look round and find out. But Lymond's own voice said instantly, 'You misjudge me. I was projecting, I thought, a strong impression of patience. Kneeling like a drunk elephant at the feet of the Blessed. Melodrama makes Mr Blyth uncomfortable.'

The lightless eyes switched to Jerott. 'Does it? Yet what more melodramatic than to join a militant order of monks because one rather commonplace young girl died of the plague? Balance your own accounts, Mr Blyth.'

'I have,' he said. Hell: how did she know about Elizabeth? 'I have left the Order of St John.'

The old harridan gave a leer. 'A blundering Popistant?'

'If you like,' said Jerott; and again the shadowy eyes creased.

'I neither like nor dislike: I merely record the truth. And that is not the truth,' said the Lady of Doubtance. 'You left because you found corruption and intolerance against which your own faith was inadequate. You also left because of the fall of Sir Graham Reid Malett, that great Knight of Grace. What a sorry marriage you would have had of it,' said the detached voice airily, 'had he been christened Elizabeth.'

No one had ever been able to call Jerott Blyth a submissive young man. Violent in love, in hatred and in all his enthusiasms, he heard those words in a rising passion of outraged disbelief. Also, what was worse, Lymond had heard them. White-faced with rage in the darkness, Jerott opened his mouth; and suddenly heard in his head the lady's cool words of a moment ago. *I neither like nor dislike: I merely record the truth.* He did not speak.

Waiting, the other two people in the dark room were aware of a long silence. Then Jerott Blyth said, 'Then you must put on record that once I loved a girl and wished to make her my wife; and once I loved a man and wished to make him my leader. I shall never do either again.'

Beside him, Lymond did not move. In front of him, the shrewd old eyes under the grotesque Saxon wig stared unwinking at Jerott.

Then the Dame de Doubtance said, 'These are words I have waited to hear. You are adequate to your fate, Mr Blyth. You need no help from me to find it.'

And, surprisingly, it was Lymond's voice which said sharply, 'You cannot debar a human being from love!'

The old face, undisturbed, turned to look at him. 'It is easy. Who should know better than you? But what Mr Blyth has been engaged in was not love, my dear Francis. It was romance, a thing to which Mr Blyth has been very prone; together with melodrama. Whatever made you think that melodrama makes Mr Blyth uncomfortable? He revels in it.'

'A figure of speech,' said Lymond. 'But now, perhaps he might be permitted to leave?'

'Why?' asked the Dame de Doubtance, and settling herself in her chair, smoothed out her thick skirts with one bezelled claw. 'Dear Francis. Do you wish to ask me something so private?'

In a moment, Jerott knew very well, Lymond was going to lose his temper. Mortally relieved to be himself out of the firing-line, Jerott was looking forward to watching him do it. 'About bastardy, perhaps?' added the Dame de Doubtance placidly.

In all the dark room, there was no sound. Then Lymond drew breath. 'No,' he said. 'Nor about anything else. We must not tire you. . . . Jerott?' He had turned, without haste, on his heel.

Jerott stayed where he was. 'What *about* bastardy?' he said.

The dewlapped, colourless face smiled at him. 'Ah, Mr Blyth. *You* are not afraid of ridicule, it appears. What a pity that Oonagh O'Dwyer should have been Francis's mistress and not yours.'

To Jerott, everything suddenly became exquisitely clear, including Lymond's motive for privacy. 'You cast horoscopes,' said Jerott Blyth quickly to the withered face in the gloom. 'Can you tell us the child's?'

'If you can repress for a moment your spinster-like longing to meddle in my affairs,' said Lymond cuttingly, from the door, 'I am waiting to go.'

Ignoring this: 'I might, if I were paid in a little courtesy,' said the Dame de Doubtance to Jerott. 'There is no hurry, Mr Blyth. Francis will not leave while you are still here. . . . What is the child's name?'

'He doesn't know,' said Lymond, answering for him. 'He knows nothing. He is one of nature's matrons, oozing arch curiosity. You can tell he's a wood-nymph by the cow's tail under those long, snowy robes. He wants to ask about Oonagh's baby, so tell him. For God's sake, tell him. Then he and the bloody girl can find and burp it together. If it's alive.'

'Oh, it's alive,' said the Dame de Doubtance quite calmly. 'Vows made on Gabriel's altar are not lightly regarded. Son and father will meet.'

Afterwards Jerott was not certain if the word 'where?' was spoken aloud. He knew only that it sprang to his lips, and that, silenced suddenly, Lymond framed it as well. Within the golden hair, the grey eyebrows rose. 'How quiet we are,' the Dame de Doubtance said. 'It would not be good for you, I think, to be certain where. The woman, of course, is in Algiers.'

'Oonagh?' Slowly, Lymond had re-entered the room. A shadow in the dark, he passed Jerott and reaching the Dame de Doubtance's old, slippered feet, dropped quietly to one knee, all caprice gone from his face. 'Shall we meet?'

The ancient, powerful face looked down. 'You will see her.' A yellow nail, strongly curved, followed the line of his cheekbone. 'You were a pretty boy; but ungovernable. You are right not to trust me. . . . You will see her. But your father's two sons will never meet in this life again,' said the Dame de Doubtance, looking at Lymond, the candle-flame in her round, predator's eyes.

And under them, Jerott saw the fluid posture of the other man stiffen; and his stretched gaze in turn hold the woman's, stare for raw stare, until the Dame de Doubtance laughed shortly and said, 'Ah, Khaireddin. Of course. That was the child's name,' as if she had just been informed.

Your father's two sons will never meet in this life again. Jerott, listening, scowled. Lymond had only one brother—Richard, third Baron Culter, at Midculter in Scotland. Richard, the well-loved and reliable family man who held the family title and administered the family estates and who shared his home with his widowed dowager mother. Lymond said, smoothly, to that grotesque and brooding face hung above him: 'Promise me that Richard will be safe.'

And the Dame de Doubtance, glibly, repeated his words: 'Richard will be safe;' while Jerott, at last, was brought to regretting the childish sentiment which had inspired him stay and to force this queer confrontation to an inhuman issue.

'Put the next question,' the Dame de Doubtance said lightly, but Lymond said, still quietly, 'I have no more questions to ask. You wished to make Jerott your witness?'

'How quick you are,' she said, mockery in the thin voice. 'You don't ask the date of your death? *I can tell you.*'

It was suddenly too much. The old bitch, thought Jerott, falling back dazed through the boundaries of rank common sense. The crazy, senile old bitch. She ought to have a stall at a fair. And here we are, two grown men, crediting her . . .

She had moved; and, bending forward, was holding out that rheumatoid claw to be taken and kissed. Rising, Lymond held it in his and said slowly, 'Then I think it had better be soon.'

And the Dame de Doubtance, smiling, shook her head as he bent over her hand. 'Despite everything, not soon enough.' And as he straightened: 'You and I will not meet again. You do not know it, but I have loved you. Mr Blyth . . .' Jerott moved slowly forward. The jointed fingers snatched, and the little pearl crucifix he wore still, loose over his shirt, lay in her ruinous palm. 'I tell you this, Mr Blyth, from my stall in the fair, senile though I appear. I tell you by this cross and by all you still believe that what I foretell will come true. Be my witness.'

He stood still, without speaking, his crucifix still in her hand. She had read his exact mind: he had nothing to add. But Lymond, in the unchanging quiet voice, said, 'You have been kind, by your lights. For what you have done in the past, and what I think you believe must be done now, I am thankful. . . .' He stopped, and said, 'You have said nothing of Graham Malett. It may not matter.'

'Evil matters. So does love. So does pity. My pilgrim,' said the Dame de Doubtance gently, 'you have still three bitter lessons to learn.'

For a moment she stood, the little cross flickering in the dim light in her hand; then she let it slip so that, swinging back on its chain, it found its home again on Jerott's broad chest. Then she addressed Lymond. 'What Mr Blyth needs is a large drink and some bawdy conversation, as quickly as possible. Can you arrange that, do you think?'

'All Mr Blyth's friends can arrange that,' said Lymond gravely, and bowing, steered Jerott out and downstairs into the street. There, looming miraculously before them, was a familiar figure.

'Oh, *Onophrion*,' said Lymond, and Jerott, who had seen his face only a moment before, wondered at the pleasant, familiar pitch of his voice. 'Onophrion, where with safety and propriety do you consider that Mr Blyth and I might go to drink ourselves senseless?

And Onophrion, of course, knew.

*

In the event, the spinet took three weeks to crate and prepare for the journey. In the interval, Master Zitwitz finished outfitting the Comte de Sevigny's party and failed finally to do the same for the Comte de Sevigny himself. And Philippa, whose sardonic brown eye had been the first to greet Jerott on his aching return from that night-long carousal, found that Mr Blyth was not after all to escort her to England. When she discovered why, her reaction was wholly characteristic. She waited until Lymond, Jerott and Onophrion Zitwitz were all safely out of the way, and then, with maid and bodyguard expostulating behind her, marched off to the Dame de Doubtance's house.

This time it was daylight. The shutters were flung back in the shabby big bedroom and the ancient lady, whom Philippa reached with extreme rapidity, passed from servant to servant indeed like a familiar but insalubrious parcel, was sitting in a morning gown before a crackling fire, drinking something hot from a cup. 'Ah, yes. Philippa Somerville. You're early,' said the Dame de Doubtance. 'I have underestimated Mr Blyth's capacity. Sit there.'

Philippa sat. Clearly seen, the daffodil wig Jerott had told her about was soiled and chased, here and there, with grey fluff. But the bold, bony features were far from senile, and so were the shrewd black eyes. The Dame de Doubtance said, 'My cousin will bring you some *qahveh*, which you will dislike until your taste is formed. Then we shall be very pleasant: three women together. Men,' said the Lady of Doubtance, rolling the words, 'I find at times tiresome. Tell me: do *you* like melodrama?'

Philippa, her hands clamped hard in her lap, sat like a ramrod. 'I think there's more than enough in the world,' she said, 'without anyone adding to it.'

'What!' said the old lady. Her wrinkles deepened. 'An unromantic woman at last! You would not have your fortune told even if paid for it?'

Philippa drew a deep breath. 'Mr Blyth says you can read people's thoughts,' she said. 'So why ask me?'

'So that you may ask yourself. What a silly question,' said the Dame de Doubtance. 'So Mr Crawford is setting off for Constantinople, and Mr Blyth has now announced that he will accompany him? But why not? It is an amusing prospect. Francis makes austere company at present, but he will improve. And another will come, surely, to take you back home.'

'Archie Abernethy is coming from Sevigny. One of Mr Crawford's men. The one who used to tame elephants.' She waited, but as the old woman made no comment on that, she continued. 'That doesn't matter. What matters is that Mr Crawford and Mr Blyth are going to Constantinople by way of Algiers.'

'Well?' The Dame de Doubtance was interested.

'Because you said Oonagh O'Dwyer was there.'

'What an *extraordinary* fuss there has been,' said the Dame de Doubtance raspingly, 'about that irresponsible Irishwoman and her improper child. The woman has paid her price and Francis his. She has not the slightest need of him now. He will find that out soon enough in Algiers.'

'The nuns we met in Baden were paid to send him to Algiers, too,' said Philippa; and met the yellow, considering stare with a brown, obstinate one of her own.

'I see,' said the Dame de Doubtance at length. 'I see. It occurred to you that I too might be an agent of Gabriel's. Francis, I am sure, would avenge your death very prettily; but I am not. There is a trap awaiting him in Algiers, placed there by Graham Reid Malett: Francis knows this very well. Algiers is a town run by proscribed men, refugees, criminals and corsairs, paying tribute to Turkey. He knows this too. If he wishes to see Oonagh O'Dwyer he has certain odds to overcome, that is all. Ah, here comes your *qahveh*.'

Behind her, a woman had come into the room, silently, in a swirl of musk and some thick, hot scent which Philippa could not identify. Her dress, unlike the Dame de Doubtance's, was rich and new: a black silk velvet trimmed with sable, and with a girdle set with jewelled enamels. Philippa, expecting a contemporary of her hostess, saw instead a clear olive face, vividly defined with black brows and heavy, coiled black hair; a long, straight Greek nose and reddened lips, cut softly and full. 'My cousin,' said the Lady of Doubtance, watching Philippa's face as the young woman, advancing, laid a small tray before her and sank smoothly into a chair. '. . . Whom you may call Kiaya Khátún.'

The cousin wore, Philippa saw, turquoise earrings like pale blue sparrow's eggs, and baroque pearls in rayons all over her black velvet slippers. The family was, of course, in the business. Accepting a cup of hot liquid mud from the ringed hands, Philippa said, 'Thank you, Kiaya Khátún.' It smelt of burnt nuts, and pepper, and toffee, and tasted quite awful. She drank it all, including the silt at the bottom, and returned her relentless brown stare to the other two women. Kiaya Khátún, she observed, had orange palms and painted her mouth. '. . . And has Oonagh O'Dwyer's son paid its price, too?' inquired Philippa.

'O England,' said Kiaya Khátún. Her voice, mellow and strong, held an accent or a mingling of accents Philippa was unable to name. 'O England, the Hell of Horses, the Purgatory of Servants and the Paradise of Women.' She turned her splendid eyes on the soothsayer. 'She will be like Avicenna, and run through all the arts by eighteen.'

'. . . The baby, I gather, doesn't matter,' said Philippa, keeping to the subject.

Settled back in her tall chair, the tarnished brocade cast about her, the Dame de Doubtance brought her attention back to the girl. 'Is it not enough to discover the mother? The child is safe, so long as Graham Malett is unharmed: is this not sufficient? I need not remind you of the ridicule his father would suffer—and rightly suffer: you have discovered that for yourself when you renounced so nobly your plan to accompany him as dry-nurse. But what you have not considered, in this so-called practical head,' said the Dame de Doubtance dryly, 'is that the trouble of rearing this inconvenient and foreign-born byblow will fall not on Francis Crawford but on Richard his brother. Hardly a suitable companion for Richard's son, the heir to the title. And hardly a suitable return for all Richard has already endured on Lymond's behalf.'

'His mother . . .?' began Philippa.

'The Dowager Lady Crawford will not live for ever.'

28

'Then Mr Crawford himself . . .'

'After the child Khaireddin is found,' the Dame de Doubtance said calmly, 'Francis has to meet and kill Graham Malett.'

There was a silence. Then: 'What you are saying,' said Philippa slowly, 'is that the child Khaireddin would be better unfound?'

The Dame de Doubtance said nothing.

'Or are you saying,' pursued Philippa, inimical from the reedy brown crown of her head to her mud-caked cloth stockings, 'that you and I and Lymond and Lymond's mother and Lymond's brother and Graham Malett would be better off if he weren't discovered?'

'Now that,' said the Dame de Doubtance with satisfaction, 'is precisely what I was saying.'

'How can I find him?' said Philippa.

In the tall, old-fashioned chair opposite the bony hands fell apart, the dusty robes shifted; the Dame de Doubtance's face under the coarse yellow plaits changed and glittered and finally held back between aged cross-curtains the ghost of a lost, true delight. 'Come, child,' she said; and as Philippa, stony-faced, rose and went over, she leaned to lift the girl's own right hand. It lay, rather dirty, on the waxy sunk palm: a young brown hand, with almond nails pink with health, and a white seam where the knife slipped, when she was making a cage for the weasel.

A large tear, from nowhere, ran down the back of Philippa's nose, and she coughed. And at the same moment, as if caught reading some illicit book, the Dame de Doubtance abruptly covered that palm with its fingers and, returning the folded hand to its owner, said harshly, 'You will go to Algiers. You understand? Then, if you still wish to trace the child by yourself, you and the man Abernethy will go to the isle of Zakynthos, to the House of the Palm Tree, and you will present there a ring which my cousin will give you. After that, all will depend on her goodwill.'

Behind them, the velvet robes stirred lazily, in an aroma of *qahveh* and musk. 'Not on my goodwill,' said the musical voice of Kiaya Khátún. 'On my whim.'

It was over. Five minutes after that, a dirty white with post-tension nausea, Philippa Somerville had rejoined maid and servant in the street. On her right hand, its stone turned inwards for safety, was an old black ring stuck with gummy dark jewels. In her head was an improbable address on the isle of Zakynthos. And carved in her heart was the promise she had just made that never, until she arrived at that improbable address, would she reveal to Jerott, Lymond or Onophrion Zitwitz what had happened that morning. Between her teeth: '*I do not like melodrama,*' said Philippa Somerville to the air.

*

It was her last adventure in Lyons. How Lymond had spent the previous night no one knew: least of all Jerott, whom he had seen drunk under the table at the Ours and promptly abandoned to Onophrion's skilled ministrations. But the following morning, the extreme pressure began: to finish preparing at speed, and to move south as quickly as possible to take ship for Turkey. The name of Oonagh O'Dwyer was not mentioned, except by Jerott to Philippa.

That it took them so long, in the event, to embark was the fault largely of Maître Georges Gaultier. Part of the spinet was found faulty, and had to be mended. The painter who had undertaken to complete the inscription fell ill, and then the work had to dry. The joiners made three attempts to create a packing to Gaultier's satisfaction, and then it had to be done a fourth time because they had forgotten to use waterproofed cloths.

Meantime Archie Abernethy, travelling from Lymond's French home at Sevigny to escort Philippa back home to England, was also unaccountably held up. The full story in fact was never related because Lymond, by then extremely short-tempered, informed him that he had better save his breath for the return journey, which might begin as soon as Philippa was ready: that morning, for instance. Gaultier had promised that the spinet would be ready to travel south that day or the next.

Archie Abernethy, a small battered Scot with a skin like old hide, made no complaint, but Philippa, who had always been fond of him, found that her arrangements to leave would take at least twenty-four hours. These she spent, as she had spent the last three weeks, in endless, bitter, detailed and exhaustive argument aimed at persuading either Jerott or Lymond to take her with them to Algiers. Finally Lymond, already riled by Gaultier's non-appearance that morning, took her by the shoulders, forced her into a seat and said, '*Ecco il flagello de'i Principi*. I believe one of the most trying circumstances of this entire oppressive trip has been your craving to haunt me in a little burden like a tinker's budget. As I have said before, and am now saying for the last time, I cannot tell you with what awe my family and friends, not to mention yours, would receive the idea that I should ship a twelve-year-old girl along the Barbary coast——'

'*Fifteen-year-old*,' said Philippa, furiously, for the third time.

'Or fifty-year-old: what's the difference?' said Lymond. 'The coast's a jungle of Moors, Turks, Jews, renegades from all over Europe, sitting in palaces built from the sale of Christian slaves. There are twenty thousand men, women and children in the bagnios of Algiers alone. I am not going to make it twenty thousand and one because your mother didn't allow you to keep rabbits, or whatever is at the root of your unshakable fixation.'

'I had weasels, instead,' said Philippa shortly.

'Good God,' said Lymond, looking at her. 'That explains a lot. However. The fact remains. I am not taking a woman.'

'Dear me: but aren't you?' said Georges Gaultier, arriving at that precise moment and standing, wet cloak in his hands. 'But I did tell you, didn't I, that my assistant's a woman?'

There was a moment's complete silence. 'No,' said Lymond.

'Well, she is,' said Maître Gaultier finally; and, discarding the cloak, sat down unasked in a near-by chair and warmed his hands at the fire. 'And I'm not going without her.'

Which was how Philippa Somerville came to sail on the royal galley *Dauphiné* out of Marseilles, bound for Constantinople via Algiers in Barbary, and accompanied by His Most Christian Majesty of France's Special Envoy, Jerott Blyth, Onophrion Zitwitz, Archibald Abernethy, Georges Gaultier, a woman called Marthe and a spinet.

3

MARTHE

It is doubtful if, at the time, even Lymond realized how little of all this was coincidence. And how very far from chance, for example, was the plan which led to the spinet with its maker and all its attendants, with Jerott and a strong bodyguard to protect it, making the journey from Lyons to Marseilles smoothly by water, while the rest of the party, including Philippa and Zitwitz and himself, travelled by road. Then, a safe and steady trip on the Rhône seemed unequivocably best for that remarkable packing-case, while leaving the rest of the party mobile to make their last arrangements on land. It meant also that by the time they all met at Marseilles, and boarded their galley, only Jerott had met Gaultier's woman assistant.

Philippa, it was true, already had the strongest suspicions. Her conscience tender with the memory of her unconfessed *qahveh*-supping with soothsayers, she would have laid a heavy wager, if she had had anyone to wager with and if her mother had not always found gambling ridiculous, that the unwanted helper would be Kiaya Khátún. One of the family, Georges Gaultier had implied when Lymond, his phrasing bell-like with anger, had marshalled, yet again, the arguments against carrying women.

But to Gaultier, it appeared, the embassy was of no special moment, nor was he worried at the prospect of losing his fees. Only one person besides himself could maintain this instrument properly, and without her, he would not go at all. 'As for propriety,' he had ended, 'if the shoe wrings in that quarter, there's the English girl there who wants to go also. Let the women travel together. It'll keep them out of our way.' And, staring bright-eyed at the Special Envoy, he had ended, 'If *I'm* willing to risk it, and *she's* willing to risk it, I don't see how you can stop us.'

'If she adds one hairsbreadth to the peril of this ship and the people she carries, I can and will stop her now,' Lymond had said. 'She is one of the family, you say. You'll have to tell me much more.'

'Will I?' said Gaultier. 'Well, maybe you're right. She's an orphan —name of Marthe—brought up in a convent. We paid for that. And since she finished her learning she's been in the business helping me. She's no schoolgirl. She's been to Anatolia with me and back; and she goes to Venice on her own when it's necessary, to buy and to sell. There's not much she doesn't know about clocks, or about jewels . . . or about men.'

'I want to meet her,' said Lymond.

'You'll see her,' had said Georges Gaultier comfortably. 'If not here, then at Marseilles. You'll take her, too.'

So Philippa got her leave to bring Archie Abernethy with her and sail on the *Dauphiné*. But they had not seen the woman Marthe before they left Lyons. And permission to sail from Marseilles depended still, Philippa was grimly aware, on whether or not the woman Marthe was found to be eligible. Kiaya Khátún, she imagined, would pass like a shot.

But Jerott's manner, greeting them all when they arrived in Marseilles, was unusually difficult to define. Yes, they had had an uneventful journey. Yes, the crate had arrived in good order and was now waiting in the King's Marseilles lodging, where they would be permitted to stay until the *Dauphiné* sailed. And yes, Maître Gaultier and his assistant were also safely installed with it, awaiting Lymond's instructions.

'Jerott?' said Lymond. 'What are you not saying?' His eyes, as the orderly cavalcade paced through the muddy streets, had not left that forceful aquiline face since they met. And Jerott, Philippa saw with disbelief, flushed.

For a moment longer, the strict blue eyes studied him; and then Lymond laughed. 'She's an eighteen-year-old blonde of doubtful virginity? Or more frightful still, an eighteen-year-old blonde of unstained innocence? I shall control my impulses, Jerott, I promise you. I'm only going to throw her out if she looks like a trouble-maker, or else so bloody helpless that we'll lose lives looking after her. Not everyone,' he said, in a wheeling turn which caught Philippa straining cravenly to hear, 'is one of Nature's Marco Polos like the Somerville offspring.'

Pink with irritation, Philippa fell back into line with one of Jerott's men, but not before she heard Jerott Blyth murmur, 'Leave it. Leave it till we get in;' and saw Lymond's sharp turn of the head.

It was then that Philippa, dropping back still farther, said cheerfully to her neighbour, in an undertone, 'They're talking about Marthe, Maître Gaultier's assistant. What's she like? Pretty?'

'She's pretty,' said the man.

Philippa studied the taciturn face. 'Oh, I see,' she said. 'Mr Blyth wants her all to himself?'

For a moment, she thought it hadn't worked. Then the man gave a snort. 'Mr Blyth want her? He held us up at Avignon for two days refusing to go on until she was sent back home, but Gaultier wouldn't do it, and he had to give in. Mr Blyth and Gaultier haven't spoken since. Aye,' said Jerott's man morosely. 'It's going to be a grand, sociable trip.'

Arrived at the house, Philippa didn't even wait for her luggage. Followed, panting, by Fogge, she raced to the bedroom allotted her; flung off her cloak, changed into a pair of unsuitable slippers from her maid's carpet bag, splashed her face and hands with water, curry-combed the end of the hank of hair that hung down from under her cap and galloped, muddy skirts and all, downstairs towards the sound of Francis Crawford's light voice.

The principal chamber in the King of France's lodging, Marseilles, was small and neatly proportioned and figured with rich colour from the fruitfully painted ceiling to the allegorical and expensive tapestries all over the walls. A scented wood fire, already warm and red with several hours' burning, tinged with flickering, rosy light the gloom of the wintry afternoon and pooled with flame the smooth marquetry of the floor. Grey light, through three small lattices, touched on the crimson velvet of the window-seats and expired at the edge of the fringed stools and the few high-backed chairs. Darkness, warmth and firelight in turn owned the rest of the room. Philippa entered, following that pleasant, discouraging voice.

At first, she saw no one. Then, as a flame jumped, it revealed two people standing at the far end of the room behind the service screen, and the light glimmered, for a moment, on the pleated cambric at the neck of a man's doublet. Lymond's voice, continuing lightly, said in French, 'It seems very clear that there is some objection. I should be obliged to know what it is.'

She could not see whom he was addressing, but in any case the problem was instantly solved for her. Georges Gaultier's voice said, 'The young man is temperamental, merely. There is no possible objection that I can think of. Once afloat, believe me, there will be no time for childishness. You are more than capable of taking care of that.'

'That is hardly the issue,' said the other, cool voice. 'The point is rather that I have no desire to be exposed to it in the first place. I think perhaps you should bring your friend in. Obviously we are going to get nowhere until we have this meeting you have all been so eager to avoid. . . .'

They were going to emerge from the screen. Perfectly prepared to be an eavesdropper but unwilling to look like one, Philippa backed quickly towards the door and collided, hard, with an unseen person striding forward equally fast into the room. There was a hiss, more than echoed by herself as the breath was struck from her body. Then two cool, friendly hands held and steadied her, one on her shoulder and one on her flat waist, and a low voice said, 'Admirable Philippa. I always enter my battlefields in reverse, too. But my own battlefields, my little friend. Not other people's.'

It was the same voice. *But it couldn't be.* It was the same felicitous, dispassionate voice that she had just heard speaking from behind the screen at the far end of the room. There, a shadow emerging from the screen, was the speaker. And here behind her, as she spun round and he dropped his impersonal grasp, was Lymond himself.

A sense of danger, instant and unreasoning, overwhelmed Philippa. She saw Lymond look at her with sudden attention, and in the same moment there was a flood of light outside the door behind him and Jerott arrived, breathless, with a servant bearing candelabra behind him. He had no time to speak. As the branched candlesticks were borne in and the room filled with flickering gold, the two whom Philippa had overheard moved from behind the screen and walked slowly towards them.

One of them, as Philippa had guessed, was the usurer and clock-maker Georges Gaultier. The other, whose voice Philippa had thought so unmistakably familiar, was not a man at all, but a girl. A girl far younger than Kiaya Khátún, with high cheekbones and open blue eyes, set far apart; with a patrician nose, its profile scooped just less than straight. The face of a Della Robbia angel, set in gleaming hair, golden as Jupiter's shower. 'This,' said Maître Georges Gaultier gently, 'is Marthe.'

'Hell,' said Francis Crawford so softly that only Philippa heard him, 'and damnation. And God damn you, Lady.' Then, his face wiped clean of all real expression, he moved forward smoothly and sociably to greet Maître Gaultier's assistant, while Jerott and Philippa stood side by side helplessly behind.

An eighteen-year-old blonde of doubtful virginity, had been Lymond's first ironical guess. But, Philippa thought, Jerott had tried to send this girl home for other reasons entirely. In acute discomfort, sitting, she saw the girl Marthe address Francis Crawford for the first time. 'I have heard of you, of course,' she said. 'Objections have been raised, I believe, to my travelling. What, precisely, do you find so alarming? My character, or my looks?'

If Lymond was unprepared for her voice, he showed no sign of it. After a short, placid interval during which he surveyed her as she sat, from the shining fall of her hair to the pale blue folds of her gown, he said, 'That was only Jerott, wishing to preserve both from the barbarian.'

'Meaning you?' said the girl Marthe's light voice.

'Meaning me,' agreed Lymond.

'I think,' said the girl pleasantly, 'that you may quite safely leave that aspect to me. If it also concerns you, I have sailed the Middle Sea a great many times without either giving birth or fainting in battle. If I am captured, it is no concern but my own.'

'How disciplined of you,' said Lymond. '*Et tu ne vois au pied de ton rempart . . .*'

'*. . . Pour m'enlever mille barques descendre.* Of course not. No man would. So why should I look to be rescued?'

'Is that why you wish to come?' said Francis Crawford. Flippant though his tone was, his eyes, Philippa noticed, had never dropped from the girl's. 'To prove your masculinity?'

There was a little pause. Looking into that angelic, fair face Philippa saw the authority she had missed before: the small lines round the mouth; the winged curve of spirit on either side of the fine planes of the nose: the faint, single line between the arched brows. 'I came because I was told to come,' said the girl Marthe. 'My wishes have very little to do with it.'

It was coolly said; and she added nothing. But Philippa, sensitive to every shade of the exchange, suddenly caught the controlled anger behind it. This girl, whom Gaultier had refused to allow home, had no desire to sail on the *Dauphiné* with Francis Crawford of Lymond. And at the same moment, Lymond, no less perceptive, spoke with a coolness fully equal to hers. 'On the contrary. Your wishes are paramount. If you prefer it, I shall send you back to Lyons with an escort today.'

Sitting straight-backed, her hands modestly in her lap, the girl answered, sweetly. 'Thank you. I fear in this case inclination must give way to duty. If you have no other valid objection, I intend to sail with my uncle.'

'Your uncle?' said Jerott, startled into speech.

'A courtesy title,' explained Georges Gaultier placidly. 'In fact, she is more of a collector's piece, are you not, Marthe? In exquisite taste. Given the choice, I make no doubt that Sultan Suleiman would prefer her to the spinet. How happy,' he added, in the inimical silence, 'that you have taken to one another. I was certain that we should have your permission to sail. What an enchanting voyage, with two such ladies, in prospect.'

Slumped stricken in her mud-encased frieze, Philippa suddenly realized what he had said. She applied to Jerott, in an undertone. '*Has* he given permission? Am I going?'

Lymond had heard. Rising, in one practised movement, he gave one hand to Marthe and the other to Philippa and, raising them so that they stood before him, frieze to satin to velvet, he lifted each girl's hand in turn to his lips and holding them lightly, smiled speculatively into the blue eyes and the brown. 'You are going,' he said. 'Like an Ethiopian grasshopper plague, we're all going. And we shall know each other better than this when we come back. . . .

'If we come back, that is to say.'

*

Many weeks later, long after the *Dauphiné* had sailed, cannon firing and pennants streaming, from Marseilles harbour and when Lymond and Marthe and Philippa indeed knew each other better, two letters reached Philippa's mother at her home in Flaw Valleys, near Hexham in England: one written by Lymond, and one by Philippa herself.

My dear Kate, Lymond had written. *She is with me, and safe. You know what she feels her mission to be: and I cannot bring myself to flatten that Somerville pride. We are sailing tomorrow from Mar-*

*seilles and very soon her own common sense is going to tell her that,
unique as she is and competent as she is, she cannot be of real use to
me here.*

*Meanwhile she has a maid, a bodyguard and the company of another,
older girl whose professional expertise we require. Not the kind of
help, sweet Kate, which, tongue in cheek, you envisage. Constantinople
beckons, and we must cherish the palate. Who could refuse a royal
envoy, bearing gifts to the Turk?*

*Be kind to her when she comes back. Her love is not only for children
but for humanity. She will be a good-hearted and magnificent zealot
one day. As her mother is now.*

Goodbye, Kate. And below he had signed as he rarely did, with
his Christian name.

Philippa's letter, from an afflicted conscience, was not very much
longer.

*. . . if I don't look for him, no one else will. You know I'm sorry.
But I couldn't leave that little thing to wither away by itself. Don't
be sad. We're all going to come back. And you can teach him Two
Legs and I Wot a Tree, and save him the top of the milk for his black-
berry pie. He'll never know, if we're quick, that nobody wanted
him. . . .*

Which had, Kate considered as she scrubbed off her tears, a ring
of unlikely confidence about it, as well as rather a shaky understanding of the diet of one-year-old babies.

*

Neither of Kate Somerville's correspondents had said much about
Marthe, and a reticence about Marthe was the main feature, apart
from the foul weather, of the *Dauphiné*'s crossing from Marseilles
to Algiers.

Winter in the Mediterranean was seldom cold, but produced rain,
and wind, and current, and the small, gusty storm which could make
travel impossible for a shallow-draught boat like a galley. Corsairs
and fighting craft stayed in harbour during the winter except for the
most urgent travel or the most tempting prize: a Spanish galleasse
putting into Cádiz, full of Mexican bullion, or another coming out
of Seville with converted Spanish ryals in stamped cases for the
Low Countries. There might be a shipload of troops and munitions
being rushed to a rising: there would certainly be the sporadic
journeys of the merchants, the pilgrims, the spies, who could not
put off their duties till summer. There was always the fishing.

For the *Dauphiné*'s task, the urgency was relative. A journey to
Constantinople would not take less than four months at that time
of year, and might well take a good deal longer. Again, once arrived
there might be a wait of several weeks at least if Sultan Suleiman
were absent, say on a summer Persian campaign. If the King of

France's prodigious clock-spinet failed to arrive in the Sultan's hands before the next winter, no one would be surprised.

On the other hand, according to the Dame de Doubtance, Oonagh O'Dwyer was in Algiers. However fleeting Lymond's association with her, thought Philippa, he *had* tried to free her last year, when Dragut found and took her to Tripoli. To do her justice, according to Jerott, Oonagh O'Dwyer had not wished to be freed. She had not intended to burden Lymond or to inform him of his impending offspring. It was Gabriel who had done that. And it was Gabriel who was drawing Lymond now to Algiers, with Oonagh O'Dwyer as the bait. So, concluded Philippa, clarifying the thick fogs of quixotry, there was no immediate rush indicated to free Mistress Oonagh O'Dwyer, as the said Mistress Oonagh O'Dwyer, if alive, would certainly be kept alive until Lymond reached her; and if dead, was unlikely to alter that attitude even if the *Dauphiné* went down with all hands.

'You do grant,' said Jerott, approached with this view, 'that there might be a certain naïve interest in proving *whether* she's dead or alive?'

'Yes,' said Philippa. 'But there's no *hurry*. That's the point.'

'I'm not arguing,' said Jerott. 'I like living, too. But try convincing M. le Comte de Sevigny, that's all.'

In fact, the weather was the final arbiter. No master was going to keep a galley at sea overnight in the Mediterranean in winter in any case, and the port-hopping wind which took them bowling stormily across the Gulf of Lions to the Spanish coast and thence to the Balearic Islands changed the next day to a southerly wind with a fine cross-swell which suited the journey to Algiers not at all, and the insides of the *Dauphiné*'s passengers even less.

Philippa, with hitherto no more than cross-Channel experience, was thankful to find that the iron stomach of the Somervilles had apparently been granted her. She could have put up with being sick before Lymond, but not before Marthe, with whom she shared the chambre de poupe next to the Master's own cabin.

Marthe, it was obvious, was not the motherly type. Nor was she the sisterly type. Possessed of perfect English.when it was required of her, she displayed also perfect self-command, perfect courtesy, an exceedingly well-equipped mind and a cultivated and unalterable coolness towards Francis Crawford and all his lesser companions. During most of the journey she read: occasionally she spent an hour with the captain, who welcomed her as an experienced traveller and a beautiful young woman; occasionally she and Gaultier would sit on a hatch-lid and talk.

Lymond she had hardly exchanged a dozen words with since they met: at their daily formal meal with the Master she sat, her cool, sardonic blue gaze resting on him as he spoke, and contributing herself almost nothing at all. She made no inquiry about the purpose of their proposed halt at Algiers, and none about Philippa's presence on board. Philippa had a feeling that she was completely informed on both counts. It did not do to forget that the Dame de Doubtance stayed in Georges Gaultier's house.

For friendly company, Philippa had Fogge to fall back on—a broken reed, as Fogge was not a Somerville and took to her bed straight away. That left Jerott Blyth and Lymond himself, who, watchful during the rough weather, rescued her from Fogge's side and took her up into the raw grey daylight to see the ship in full operation.

He knew a great deal about it. As she walked the high gangway between stem and stern, looking down at the two long ranks of oars with their chained rowers—nearly three hundred of them, unwashed, unshaven, naked to the waist; as she was shown the sakers and demi-culverins arming the bows, the chains to prevent main and mizzenmast falling inboard during battle, and below, the divided rooms of the hold, for stores of food and barrels of wine, for munitions and sick men, for the captain's coals and the officers' baggage, for the livestock which a seaman, bucket in hand, was feeding as she passed—Philippa began to realize how much.

Coming back, he showed her the cordage of the two lateen sails, now tight to the wind, and explained, as the bos'n's silver whistle blew, that they were rowing *à quartier*, using a third of the oarsmen at a time, in order to help the galley to hold a few points nearer the wind without exhausting the rowers. 'One depends on them and them alone during battle, so one cherishes them, as you can see,' Lymond said. His face, when she glanced at it, was as totally unimpassioned as his voice. 'These benches, and these, need the most powerful oarsmen. It's usual to stock them with Turks, but we've avoided that this voyage, for obvious reasons. These are mostly Flemish and Spaniards, or criminals culled from French prisons.' But she knew that already, as they jerked back and forth on the smooth pinewood benches, by the letters burned in their backs.

Later, struggling with tangled hair and soaked skirts in her cabin, Philippa spoke of that tour, and Marthe listened, impeccable as always, her bright hair tucked inside a close cap and her quilted skirts still without blemish. The long mouth tilted a little, as Philippa finished. 'It is a sobering thing, one's first close view of a galley. Were you impressed by the *vogue avants du banc des espalles*?'

'Where they used to have Turks?'

'Where for two years they had M. Francis Crawford,' said Marthe. 'Did you not know?'

'He knew I didn't,' said Philippa.

'But he could be sure that, sooner or later, someone would tell you. He has to perfection, M. le Comte, the art of living his private

life with as much public attention as possible. You don't agree?'
She was smiling. She had an enchanting smile.

'I really don't know him well enough,' said Philippa, 'to pass an opinion.'

It was the last time she was able to walk about the ship. After Formentera, the southerly wind freshened, and the silver whistle shrilled in their ears through the uproar of the seas and the creak and whine of the manœuvring galley as the sheets were pulled in and released on each tack. The brown backs of slaves and seamen glistened with light rain under a chalky grey sky, and spray fell rattling on the gangways as the hoarse voice of the Master shouted to helmsman and *comite*: '*Notre homme, avertissez qu'on va mettre à la trinque . . . Forté! Forté! . . .*'

The striped sails bucked and flapped and swelled again as the galley's beak swung round, and Philippa thought, clinging to the prow rail with Jerott balancing beside her, 'Tonight we shall be in Algiers, and perhaps we'll wish ourselves back, and in a worse storm than this.'

Then Lymond, arriving noiselessly from the direction of the helm, touched her arm. '*Magna pars libertatis est bene moratus venter.* Otherwise meaning, the girl with the well-mannered stomach gets the most fun at sea. Would you mind, my formidable Philippa, if I asked you to retire to the captain's cabin for a spell, along with Marthe and the melancholy Fogge? There is a galley advancing towards us in a profoundly single-minded way. You know what to do?'

Philippa smiled back, her hands cold. What to do when attacked at sea, lessons one to ten. They had spent their first morning at sea being trained, remorselessly, by Francis Crawford for this precise event. 'I know what to do,' said Philippa. 'Offer them the raspberry wine and keep them talking till Mother comes in.'

'They're not allowed raspberry wine,' said Lymond. 'But you'll think of an alternative, I'm sure.' He hesitated.

'You told me so,' supplied Philippa.

'I told you so, quite mistakenly. You are a perfect asset to any ship. This is only a precaution: I shouldn't worry yet,' said Lymond cheerfully. 'He's probably only coming to ask for a try of the spinet.'

*

He wasn't coming to ask for a try of the spinet. Sitting on the Master's well-worn mattress between Marthe, calmly expectant, and a whimpering Fogge, Philippa knew by the sudden hail of commands, the thud of bare feet on deck and the abrupt veer of the boat that the menace was real. What *was* she, the oncoming galley? A robber, manned by murdering renegades; a fighting ship of the Spanish

Mediterranean fleet, hoping to capture or sink the lilies of France; an Algerine corsair, hating French and Spaniards alike, and bent on money and slaves?

The swinging lamp gleamed on the swords lying beside them; on the bare racks where the officers' arms had been stored; on the ladder leading up from this one tiny room to the hatchway above. They were here, the three women, because the captain's *gavon* lay under the poop, where stoving-in was unlikely, and because they had there an escape route on deck, but no door to the rest of the hold. Whatever the outcome, at least they were free of chance injury. And if pure robbery were the motive, the ship might be boarded and ransacked without their being discovered. There was enough in the chests in the main hold to satisfy most passing raiders. And the clock-spinet, of course.

Marthe said, 'Listen.' It was a low, rumbling thud, rolling the length of the deck above them. 'They're lifting the footrests to row *à toucher le banc*. He's going to try and outsail them.'

Philippa had seen them row like that, leaving harbour, chained feet on the *pédagues*, arms and bodies leaning towards the loom of the oars. She remembered the oars entering the water, fifty-two blades as one; the surge as the slaves, second foot thrusting the bench, crashed back on their seats, arms outstretched, red-capped heads turned to the prow while the loom performed its semi-circle, touching the bench in front as it passed. It was the magnificent ceremonial stroke, too hard and fast to keep up for long; the *tout avant* measure of war. They felt the pull of it now, as the ship shuddered and drove through the water; the hesitation as Lymond's voice suddenly spoke, followed by the Master's. The beat changed. They felt the walnut walls of the little cabin press against them and tilt; a sudden outbreak of running in bare and shod feet, and a new, low-pitched rumble which seemed to come from the bows.

'They've run out the cannon,' said Marthe. 'He is turning to fight.'

Then, above the shouting on deck, they heard Lymond's voice take over.

The commands were in the peculiar Levantine French used in the Mediterranean fleet. Philippa could make nothing of them, but Marthe, listening, said in the same cool, academic voice she had used all along, 'Are you interested in technique? This is a classic defence being carried out, with one or two variations. If we lift the hatch-cover a little, I shall show you.'

It was against orders, but it was better than staying in gloom and ignorance below. Leaving Fogge sitting with her eyes shut on the mattress, Marthe climbed the ladder and in a moment had the cover expertly open no more than six inches, for Philippa to see. There was a moment's silence. Then over her shoulder, she heard the other girl laugh, under her breath. 'Now indeed, now indeed we shall see,' said Marthe. 'Whether our friend shines *velut inter stellas luna minores*, or not.'

'You don't like him,' said Philippa. It was a crazy conversation. The sky was dark orange to begin with: how could it be, in the middle of the day? Between the two masts hung the sun, like a strange, pale blue sequin: the sails were down, and the odd light ran like amber over jacks of mail and shields and vizorless helms, over wrought cannon and ranked arquebuses on their crutches; on pikes and swords and halberds, and sank dying into the wadded textures of piled fenders and cables and heaped mattresses and awnings which had been structured with lashed oars and canvas into protection for the oarsmen and entrenchments within the galley itself.

On the long passages, in the prow and the poop, and in front of her, by the sloop and the iron-bound box of the ovens, the ship's seamen and officers and her own company were spaced: the Master, in a well-greased jack of mail, was standing just in front of her, Jerott beside him, watching the bos'n amidships, the silver pipe round his neck, accepting and transmitting a series of orders from Lymond, unseen on the tabernacle. As the mosaic above her shifted and changed and changed swiftly again, Philippa saw Onophrion, vast in a leather jack, standing in the *fougon*, a two-handed sword reversed in his fists, and Gaultier, a borrowed helmet framing his narrow, seamed face, kneeling beside another of the six hatches. The slave gang, no longer rowing *à outrance*, but holding the *Dauphiné* steadily, head into the wind, were unarmed. But each oarsman, Philippa observed, quite outside the usual custom, had been released from his fetters.

She saw all that, and then the deck above her cleared momentarily of men and she was able at last to catch a glimpse of the sea. Under the queer lurid sky, the water moved, heaving unbroken in a dark and metal-bloomed blue. And shearing through it towards them, sails full, oars flashing, were two attackers, not one: on the port side, a galley like their own, but with twice their cannon and three times their number of armed seamen. And from the starboard side a capital ship, Spanish-built, and armed on all sides with what looked like its full complement of four hundred soldiers. Watching them streaking towards her, Philippa glimpsed the slaves at the oar benches, their ranked faces dark olive and black. Unlike theirs, these galleys were being propelled by Moors, or Arabs or Turks. Small wonder Lymond had realized so quickly that the *Dauphiné*'s top speed was not nearly enough. There had been no choice but to surrender or fight. But how on earth could he fight?

'... No,' said Marthe, in her ear, startlingly continuing a forgotten conversation. 'I have no great love for him. It is a consolation. Think, if he were able to deliver us from this engagement, how very trying that unassailable self-esteem would become.'

Philippa gripped the ladder, hard, with her shaky hands. 'I think I could struggle along with it,' she said. 'Are they Spanish, or corsairs? I want to be able to say "no" in the right language.' Rowing against the freakish, southerly wind, the galley was almost stationary, rising and falling on the greasy dark swell, while from ahead, on either side, the two attacking ships streamed converging towards them. The big capital ship, black-painted, flew no national flag.

Marthe was listening. 'That's the challenge,' she said. 'In French; but then they could see we are a French ship. I can't tell who they are.' A line of thought showed, fleetingly, between the fair brows: otherwise she looked quite undisturbed. Philippa, envying either her acting or her stolidity, asked what they had said.

'The usual. Heave to, or we'll ram you to the bottom,' said Marthe. 'A matter of form, if you like. We're hove to already.'

It seemed to Philippa that one might as well die naïve as die ignorant, so she kept on inquiring. 'Why? Why did we turn round to face them, and stop? And *what's wrong with the sky*?'

'We turned round because we can't outrun them, and all our cannon is at and around the bows: look at it. And we're waiting because the bombardiers won't have time to load twice before the ships close; so we hold fire till well within range. When you see the volume of smoke from the first shot, you'll realize anyway that there are no second chances. It may not come to that, of course. He may parley, or offer them some of our cargo, for instance. It depends what they want.'

'And the sky?'

'Oh, that's our other stroke of bad luck,' said Marthe. 'It's just a sandstorm over North Africa, but the sirocco's blowing it over our way. Turks and Moors, of course, know it's a sandstorm. French convicts are much more liable to think the Wrath of God is upon them, however M. Crawford may explain briskly otherwise. A change of wind would be nice.'

'But you don't expect one?'

'I never expect anything,' said Marthe. 'It provides a level, low-pitched existence with no disappointments.'

'I'm all for a level, low-pitched existence,' said Philippa. 'And when you see your way back to one, for heaven's sake don't forget to tell me.' At which Marthe, surprisingly, laughed aloud.

Then, suddenly, they saw the faces at the bows turn, bluish-pale in the orange-brown dusk, and Lymond's voice, secure and carrying, began to initiate the first stages of action. For a long moment, Marthe watched, then she laid a hand on Philippa's arm. 'They're pirate ships, demanding complete surrender of cargo and crew. He's going to fight,' she said. 'Come down. We must close the hatch now.' And in silence, Philippa followed her into the dark of the cabin.

On deck, nothing moved but for the idling oars, rowing by thirds to keep the boat still. Timbers creaked. The sea slapped and hissed up and down the low freeboard, and on deck sprays of fire bloomed from gunplace to gunplace, sizzling in the burnt-orange haze. The sun had gone, and although it was afternoon still, falling chiffons of light brown and russet concealed the light from the sky and enclosed the three ships and the glittering, indigo water in a strange saffron dusk. Within it, the shining wood of the masts, the white sails of the enemy, the blanched ranks of slaves and fighting men gleamed not ruddy but a cold aquamarine; a ghostly blue-white that peopled the three ships, as they converged silently, faster, with a crew of dead men. A growling: a low-throated mutter of fear started and could be heard, travelling from bench to bench. Jerott looked round, sharply, at the tabernacle where Lymond stood; and Lymond, at the same moment, gave the word of command.

They were just within range. Under other circumstances, Jerott guessed, Lymond would have delayed a few seconds longer. But the *chiourme* needed action. The whistle shrilled, loud and clear, and was repeated twice along the slim ship. Then, instantly, the living pieces shattered and jumped; the ranks of scarlet flame jerked forward as one; the teams for each machine and each gun flashed in their drill like warp and weft of some pattern of steel. There was, simultaneously, the multiple crash of the cannon, and the coughing rattle of arquebus fire. Lead balls, bullets, stones and blasts of cutting projectiles streamed over the water from the *Dauphiné* and exploded into the ships approaching her flanks. Philippa, had she still been watching from her raised hatch-lid, would have seen something else. Hurtling through the air towards the smaller enemy galley was a strange missile: a pair of flying black balls, joined by a looping streamer of chain.

It was this that Jerott watched, and the Master, and Lymond, he knew, from his higher viewpoint behind. The captain of the red galley saw it too, but could do nothing about it. With a whine the projectile arrived, bursting through the taut folds of the sail, and with a triple crack like a whip embraced the sixty-foot mainmast, snapped it, and plunging down with mast, sail and yardarm to the deck brought the mizzenmast crashing down likewise.

Through the choking grey smoke which enveloped him, Jerott saw chaos break out on the red galley. The guns, primed to fire, remained silent; the oars driving her on to ram the *Dauphiné*'s side remained stuck like toothpicks, askew from her flanks as the slaves struggled beneath the weight of fallen canvas and timber. Jerott looked quickly to starboard.

Nothing that their guns had been able to do had checked the capital galley. With her sides bruised and her bulwarks here and there splintered she came on instead twice as fast, the bos'n's pipe shrilling, and the shouting of enraged men came from her decks.

They looked into the black throats of her cannon and saw the luminous blue of her sails tower against the dark tawny sky, and Lymond, his voice cutting through the uproar of men and ships and the compressed and walloping seas, called, '*La scie!*'

Jerott saw the beak of the capital galley, rushing towards them, suddenly hesitate; saw the bombardiers pause, their orders unfinished, the touch-flame unused in their hands. Flattening back under a stutter of arquebus fire, he took time at last to look to port.

The dismasted galley, out of hand, was driving unchecked towards them, pushed by the wind and the running speed she already had gained. Not only was she directly in her own *capitane*'s line of fire, but in a moment she would collide at full tilt with the *Daupine*'s port flank, while the capital galley performed a more orthodox ramming attack on the right. By the attack on the right, the *Dauphiné* would be held for grappling and boarding. But the beak coming at them from the left, Jerott knew, would stave them right through.

If Lymond had not already given that order. The words '*La scie!*' and the bos'n's pipe rang through the galley. There was a jolt which nearly flung Jerott, prepared and braced as he was, off his feet; and then the *Dauphiné* began, in great leaping thrusts, to drive by the poop, backwards. Trained to a hairsbreadth, the three master slaves on every bench changed hands and feet, and faces turned to prow, sent the solid fifty-foot oars pitching reversed through the water; and their wake hissed unreeling before them.

In vain, the seamen in the black galley fled to the sheets. In vain the slaves, obeying the whistle, stopped rowing and began to backwater. The corsair capital galley, proceeding briskly against the flank of the *Dauphiné*, faced the red corsair galley, proceeding unmanned on the identical, opposite course, and as the *Dauphiné* absented herself swiftly backwards, collided the one with the other with a satisfying and ungodly bang.

'Jésu!' said Marthe, who five minutes previously, uncontrollably, had again lifted the hatch. On deck, the steady stream of orders continuing, the sail was being broken out, swiftly, and while the bow-oars knelt on the gangway, bearing the loom of the oar, the blade free of the water, the first and fifth men in each bench were running the benches to their back-rowing stations. The third man fixed the footrest. The fourth man fixed the *contre-pédague*. Then the oars dipped, the foam turquoise in the gloom. In permanent back-rowing stations, the *Dauphiné* shot north towards the Isles Baléares and safety, while the two corsair ships swung locked and screaming behind.

Half an hour later, sand had begun to fall on the ship and visibility dropped to a mile. Half an hour after that, it was perfectly dark and a thick and ochreous mud, borne on a light, tepid rain, fell on crew and galley alike. Reversing her stroke and her benches and travelling on compass bearings and in life-preserving discomfort, the *Dauphiné* turned and made her way, direct under oars, to the North African port of Algiers.

At supper-time Marthe and Philippa were allowed to emerge, picking their way over a mysterious silt, to come and dine with the captain. Lymond, arriving undisturbed from a talk with Onophrion, was sociable in a perfunctory way. 'How was it below? Rather tedious, I'm afraid.'

'Not at all,' said Philippa. 'We were laying wagers over whether we'd rather be raped, or resigned to a smug little victory.'

The lazy blue eyes opened, gratifyingly, in extravagant calculation. 'Why not have both? We can arrange it.'

Marthe said dryly, 'Philippa wishes only to say thank you, and so also do I. They say in Italy, don't they, that the boat will sink that carries neither monk, nor student, nor whore. . . . How good that we have Mr Blyth.

'How good that we have Mlle Marthe,' Lymond replied. His clothes, freshly changed, were impeccable and his brushed yellow hair, free of sand, was lit guinea-gold by the gleam of the lamps. 'Of her fellow men so charming a student.'

And before the spark of blue eyes meeting blue, Philippa's undistinguished gaze dropped.

4

OONAGH

The woman, of course, is in Algiers, the Dame de Doubtance had said. And what had the nun said, in the steaming water of Baden? *I was a slave in Dragut the corsair's own palace . . . I was at the branding of all his poor children . . . She might have been queen of Ireland, she told me: that black-haired Irishwoman with the golden child on her knee.*

. . . Piffle, Jerott Blyth was thinking to himself as, dressed overall, they lay overnight in the outer harbour at Algiers, awaiting permission to enter. Drooling, dangerous piffle. A trap framed by Gabriel on the premise that no man in Lymond's position could afford to neglect the obvious gesture. A trap which, whether from amour-propre, nostalgia or a sense of personal responsibility, Lymond was intending to spring.

Last year in Scotland, the bond between Jerott and Francis Crawford had been forged, and it had seemed to Jerott then that he understood for a little the kind of man Lymond was. Then they had separated, Lymond to cross to the Continent in pursuit, it was believed, of Graham Malett, and Jerott to carry out orders and convey their company of foot and light horse into France.

He had known, when Philippa appeared and insisted on travelling with him, that he would receive no welcome from Lymond. A personal vendetta—if it were no more than that—between Lymond and Gabriel was a common thing, understood and respected. The kind of maudlin susceptibility which could wring its hands all over Europe in the wake of an indifferent mistress and an unknown and unwanted infant was something other entirely. Jerott did not know, even yet, whether Lymond had had intentions of setting afoot any inquiries, during this curious embassy, about Oonagh and the child. He had gone to Baden, he was beginning to believe, as he had drifted through other notorious centres of gossip, in order to find out what he could of Graham Reid Malett. But Philippa's coming, and the subsequent news of both woman and child, had forced Lymond into an irritating and preposterous role.

He had responded by prohibiting them all from his confidence. After that first, unchecked outburst of anger, Lymond had confined his exchanges with Jerott, as with everyone else, to the ordering, in efficiency and comfort, of their journey; and to the small-talk, albeit witty, immodest and allusive small-talk, of everyday usage. One exception to that had been their experience with the Lyons astrologer. The other was in the thin cutting-edge, so fine as to be almost invisible, in the rare exchanges between himself and the girl

Marthe. For Francis Crawford and Marthe were alike. Sometimes the physical resemblance between them was striking enough to be uncomfortable.

Such things were not unknown, or even all that uncommon. For centuries Scotsmen had travelled and trained and settled in France. Lymond and his brother had both been to university in Paris, and his father and grandfather both had lived and fought all over France. Of course, somewhere, perhaps generations ago, they shared the same blood. They shared too, obviously, the same over-bearing pride of blood. It struck Jerott as ironical that after all they had suffered in the past over Lymond's relations with women, there should be something quite as disturbing about this instant, mutual antipathy between himself and the girl.

It was with uneasiness that he saw her materialize, a dim shadow in the damp, lukewarm dark, beside Lymond and himself as they let slip the anchor that night outside the famous mole with its octagonal lighthouse, and under the low black hills where the thirteen thousand houses of the capital of Barbary, this Hell-mouth, the centre of Earthly Darkness, glimmered block upon block, a white triangle climbing the slopes. The anchor-chain rattled, and: '*Hâte le vif! Recouvre le mort!*' said Marthe's light, pricking voice, repeating the *comite's* command. A Levantine idiom, concerned with paying out cable. But Jerott, favouring her with his magnificent black stare, turned and walked across to the rail.

He heard Lymond say placidly, 'Don't be too witty. All Hassan Pasha's fleet is in there: probably about ten galleys and another fifty ships of war. Apart from the free Moors, the Spanish Moors, the Arabs, the Turks, the Jews, the merchants, the renegade Christians, the corsairs and the Viceroy's own fighting men, there are also about six thousand Janissaries and five hundred families of Turkish-trained Spahis.

'As far as they are concerned, this is an alien ship full of alien heretics. Because it suits Turkey to remain friendly with France, the Viceroy and senior officials will probably contrive an appearance of friendliness. Don't be deceived. We are one big happy party and we must continue to look like one big happy party, or a sugar-cane to an onion it'll be *hâter le mort* for the lot of us.'

'You advise prudence?' said Marthe. 'They say, be an old man quickly, who desires to be an old man long.' Standing straight and arrogant, her bright head tilted, the binnacle candles lighting the thick lashes and delicate profile, she drew attention, with force to both her youth and her looks.

Once before, Marthe had inquired blandly how old Lymond was. Jerott, who knew, had not thought fit to tell her. And Lymond, now, the indifferent blue gaze sweeping hers, merely threw her a couplet. '*Chi asini caccia e donne mena, Non è mai senza guai e pena.* I suggest you cease driving the ass, and the ass may then continue to escort the lady.'

Philippa, newly arrived, tugged Jerott's sleeve. 'Was that as rude as it sounded?'

Jerott turned. 'No,' he said mildly. 'From where I was standing, it was more in the way of a warning.'

Philippa, who had just been forbidden, with Marthe, to set foot on shore, was in no amenable mood. 'Huh! Discipline!' she muttered.

'Yes, discipline,' said Lymond, turning also. 'And I'll give you some foreign wisdom on that score as well. *'L'absence de discipline est la source de tout mal: quiconque n'obéira pas, l'amiral devra l'éventrer.'* If I find any woman has moved from this ship tomorrow I shan't eviscerate you, but I'll land at the next Christian port and put you all in a convent. Good night.' After a moment Philippa realized that it was she and not he who was about to retire; and descended the hatch stairway huffily, Marthe stepping calmly behind her.

Down below: 'What happens,' demanded Philippa, 'if they all go ashore tomorrow, and they never come back?'

Marthe was brushing her hair. It fell like pale yellow silk over her fine shift and sprang sparkling like frost from her finger-ends as she stopped and swung it back from her face. Gathering it back in its ribbon, 'I imagine,' she said dryly, 'that that has been thought of; and that the *sous-patron* and M. Zitwitz and M. Abernethy have received their competent orders. I do admire efficiency,' said Marthe. 'But how *tedious* it can be in excess.'

The sloop from shore arrived at daybreak next day, with a gift of two sheep and a bullock, and an invitation from the Viceroy to the King of France's good Envoy to enter the harbour of Algiers and present himself at the Palace. And just before noon, watched discreetly by Marthe, Philippa, Fogge, Abernethy and Onophrion and the deputy master and crew, Lymond disembarked with a company of twenty-five men directly on to the historic jetty and there, together with Jerott Blyth, Georges Gaultier and the senior servants and officers of his company, mounted the dozen dark-faced Turkish horses, like Spanish gennets, awaiting him.

Their gold-tasselled trappings were of silk embroidered with jewels, but hardly outglittered, Master Onophrion noted with pleasure, the doublets, cloaks and plumed caps of M. le Comte de Sevigny and his train as designed by himself. In black and vermilion velvet, spooled and corded with gold and lined and cuffed with white coney, the entourage of the unconcerned Mr Crawford passed under the chalk and grey Algerine skies between the iron ranks of his welcoming Janissaries and with a squadron before and behind, pennants flying in escort, passed through the gate and uphill between the white flat-roofed houses towards the Kasbah and the Viceroy's own palace.

Disdainful of fur and fretful, privately, about the cost of his buttons, Jerott Blyth sat like the born horseman he was, and watched discreetly for trouble.

The whip of the Christian world, they had named this city once. The Wall of the Barbarian; the Bridle of both the Hesperias, the Scourge of the Islands, the Sanctuary of Iniquity and the Theatre of All Cruelty. He had never been here before. More than ten years ago, when he was still in Scotland, a boy, the Knights of St John had lost eight thousand men failing to capture Algiers, and the Emperor Charles flung his crown into a sea covered with men and timber and horses. There, outside the city, his exhausted army had sunk their pikes in the mud and slept upright, like ghosts, their hands clasped on the grips.

Where the Knights of St John had never subsequently set foot Lymond, in a French ship, had more than once visited. Lymond knew Algiers and had described it minutely, before this expedition. Then, in more detail still, they had been briefed by Salablanca, the Moor Lymond had befriended from one of the thousand families of Modajares expelled from the Kingdom of Granada who had settled in strange hybrid Andalusian suburbs and villages close to Algiers. Salablanca had been freed by Francis Crawford from a second slavery in Tripoli. Last night, as Jerott happened to know, he had received his final freedom from Lymond and, slipping overboard with all his possessions bound on his head, had swum ashore without waiting for morning, to be reunited with his parents at last.

The steep, rutted street was a runnel of mud. Pressed against the blank walls with their small iron grilles were men of every alien facial contour and colour. In turban and fez, in robes white, black and brown, in striped cotton and bare brown skin girt with a loin-cloth, they flattened back to the crack of the stave as the company agha cleared the way, heron plume streaming. Here was a mosque, and another, and another. Here the square domed shape of one of the sixty-odd baths, some for bathing, some a prison for slaves.

There, in an open space, pack-camels were kneeling, with their ineffable sneers, and donkeys with panniers stuffed with green beans going down to the markets. And there in that side street was a market. . . . Quails in baskets, copper, pelts for floormats, terracotta; piles of roots and odd vegetables, half shovelled under covering rags because of the rain. Another mosque. A long blank wall broken suddenly by a deep, shadowed arch. Beyond it, squatting still as young olive-trees set in a plain, a class of small boys in red caps and dun-coloured shirts, chanting, in treble. The lustrous dark eyes in smooth olive skins turned as they passed, chanting still, and Jerott looked at Lymond and quickly away.

A water-carrier . . . a slave, and most likely a Christian. Lucky, if this were his métier, to walk bowed through the filthy paths ignoring blows and the running mucus of spittle. Some were not so fortunate. Sold to country Arabs or Numidians and greased with fat they might draw a plough with the asses and carry dung to the fields. Chained to the galleys they were open to any barbarity to appease the wind, should it fail. Ganching, flaying, crucifying were the punishments a Christian might suffer, and torture by fire and truncheon and rope. But then, thought Jerott, what nation gentled its conquered? Not the Christian world. Not the Knights of St John.

There were orange-trees in leaf in the square before the Viceregal palace, and a herd of goats sent prancing and pattering by whip and stave. The palace guards in red fez and white burnous, knives in belts, stood silent while the cortège dismounted and Jerott, turning as his mare was taken away, realized they were on a plateau perhaps five hundred feet above sea level, and saw for the first time, stalking down the hillside by block and dome and garden and cypress and minaret, the city through which he had ascended, and the harbour, the tower, the shoal of galley, brigantine, caique and galleasse lying on the grey water, with the *Dauphiné* and her flags and her blue and white awning resting among them, a lotus in a crocodile swamp.

Their men-at-arms, he saw, were to remain in the lower court, while Lymond and he and those who had been mounted passed up through the innermost gate. Jerott gazed at his own lieutenant, raised a reassuring eyebrow, and walked past all that comforting armour and up into the palace. He crossed a courtyard, skirted a small marble pond and entered an arcade lined with armed men, from which a high wooden staircase ascended to a pillared gallery above.

There, beside an elaborate fountain, they were held up for a while and Jerott began to suspect, for the first time, that something had gone wrong. Then they were admitted up the stairs and into the Viceregal gallery, and he knew it.

'You must regard Algiers,' Lymond had said, 'as a colony of the Sublime Porte, Constantinople. It has three masters. The Viceroy or Governor, to whom we owe our official respects, is Hassan, a Sardinian eunuch and renegade, who succeeded Barbarossa. He rules Algiers for the Sultan, and we kiss his hand and give him the two-and-threepenny things. The second is the chief of the Janissaries, the Agha of the moment. They, of course, are the cream of the Turkish-trained fighting troops, living in barracks or colleges throughout Suleiman's empire to watch and fight for him. The Viceroy is Suleiman's tool, but the Agha is his eye and his arm. The one-and-sixpenny things are for him. Lastly, there are the corsair chiefs who sail for ransom, booty and labour on their own account, and are prepared, at a price, to sail and fight for the Sultan if he requires it. Their head is Dragut, whom you know . . . and I know. He has many lairs—Prevesa, Adrianople, Djerba—but he has a palace in Algiers as well.'

'And you think Oonagh O'Dwyer may be there?' Jerott had asked. And as Lymond did not reply, had added, 'And what does he get in that case?'

'A free pass,' had said Lymond, 'into Paradise.'

On this, their primary state call, Jerott Blyth remembered all that as he looked past the carpet-hung pillars, and the low fountain and the marble floor and the brazier, whose satiny heat roused a host of red scimitars, and turned into moiré the transparent air through which he saw the high dais.

Seated on the piled cushions, his Capi-agha in crimson velvet beside him, was no Sardinian eunuch. The dark, heavy-jowled face with its black brows and spare-contoured beard, and the white turban binding its brow above the jewelled egret's feather, was an Egyptian face, the face of Salah Rais, one of the conquerors of Tripoli, whom Jerott had last seen with Sinan Pasha and Dragut when he and all the Knights of St John lay conquered and trussed on the sand at their feet. And Lymond—Lymond who had fought with the Knights in that action, had been a prisoner in the Turkish camp under Salah Rais's eye.

That they had been recognized was certain, or the change of Viceroy would not have been concealed from them until now. That they would be treated with even an appearance of friendliness was debatable. For while Algiers, prompted by the Agha, might tolerate France, neither Salah Rais nor the Janissaries would suffer a Knight of St John to escape them. The circled, black eyes surveyed them. 'Greetings,' said Salah Rais, briefly, in Arabic.

Arab-style, hand on heart, Lymond also bowed, and, walking forward, bent to kiss the Governor's hand. Jerott had no fear of his Arabic: it was a tongue they both knew. But to his surprise, Lymond answered in French. 'From His Most Christian Majesty of France, greetings to Salah Rais, and felicitations on his new dignity. In token of which, and in recognition of the close friendship which lies between your Kingdom and that of France, my lord begs Salah Rais to accept some poor marks of fraternal regard. . . .' The two-and-threepenny things, thought Jerott, despite himself entertained, and watched the box being opened.

The haul made an impression; as well it might, Jerott considered, watching the jewelled boxes, the chains, the belts and the bales of fine cloth begin to stack on the floor. So far so good. 'And this?' Lymond was saying, proffering something heavy, in metal.

'Ah? What is this?' said Salah Rais sharply; and as Jerott moved discreetly sideways to see, the Viceroy waved his hand to his chamberlain and, unfolding, moved down from the dais to take the object from Lymond himself.

It was a wheel-lock carbine, an exceptionally fine one, of a design Jerott had never before seen, and obviously quite new to Salah Rais. Experimental still in medium-range fighting in Europe, wheel-locks had hardly reached the western basin of the Mediterranean though the Sublime Porte, Jerott knew, had some matchlock weapons captured in Hungary. His lips tight, he watched Lymond hand the thing over, bright and beautifully made, saying, 'It is loaded. If you will have matches brought, it may please you to fire it.'

Under the turban, the black eyes flickered. 'Be it so,' said Salah Rais and, clapping his hands, gave an order. A moment later, the carbine primed in his hands, he turned towards the French mission. 'It comes from thy master, the friend of Algiers, so that the enemies of Algiers may be sent to perdition, as the lion stamps on its prey. He will rejoice with me when their sides fall down upon the ground and their souls depart from their bodies.'

He raised the short, heavy butt to his cheek and, smiling, took aim; and smiling, Lymond looked into the muzzle and bowed. 'It is for that reason,' he said, 'that on my return to the harbour four more cases of carbines will be unloaded and presented to you with His Grace's continuing esteem, together with ammunition to suit. Then may your enemies and his lie low indeed.'

There was a little pause. Lymond's gaze met and held the black Egyptian eyes. 'Even those carrion, the Knights of St John?' said the Viceroy.

'The Grand Master of the Knights of St John is not a Frenchman—yet,' said Lymond. 'The Most Christian King and the present Grand Master have severed relations. My esteemed companion, Mr Blyth, stands before you because he has retracted his vows, and I as an emissary of France to the Sultan Suleiman and a person favoured with Dragut Rais's friendship. You may use these weapons where and upon whom you choose.'

Above the tracing of beard, the full lips puckered. 'Thou art generous,' said Salah Rais gravely, and fired.

Thundering back and forth in the bare, high-vaulted room, the sound crashed on the eardrums, drowning the sharp voices of shock and fear and surprise; and the smoke hung blue in the air, the wrung-out, acid smell of it coating the tongue. At Lymond's feet, in a litter of smashed tiles and plaster, the King of France's gemmed coffer lay, a tangled wreckage of gold foil, splinters and wire. 'Now Allâh be my friend,' said Salah Rais in surprise. 'My brother the King of France has destroyed his own excellent gift, and it must now, alas, be replaced!'

In the deep, vermilion folds of Lymond's cloak fragments of tile glittered, and a powder of gold dusted one thin kidskin shoe. Throughout, he had not moved. 'The King of France presents his apologies for the inconvenient properties of his poor gift and will

53

feel himself honoured to replace the casket,' said Lymond. And, looking down at his cloak, 'I fear I present myself before Your Highness with an appearance of unseemly neglect. If you will permit me'—and drawing off his cloak, he dropped it, red and gold, among the unhinged jewels of the trophy—"I should let it lie here, with the rubbish.'

'Fortune,' said Salah Rais, 'abounds with evil accidents. It would ill become a man of the true Faith to be less generous. One will replace the cloak with a better. Thou wilt dine with me. Then I shall give myself the honour of accompanying thee to the harbour.'

A new cloak had indeed been brought: Jerott wondered by what means its degree of relative magnificence had been signified. It fell weightily from Lymond's shoulders: white tissue and ermine, the edge sewn with gold wire and emeralds. The sharp green clashed, nastily, with the red velvet doublet beneath. Dropping his hands from the clasp, Lymond said, 'It pains me, but this is a pleasure I must defer until tomorrow. If the Viceroy will descend to the harbour at noon and accept the paltry hospitality of the *Dauphiné*, I shall be proud to break bread with him. Then, on his departure, the cases of arms may suitably be disembarked with his party. We are anxious to leave with the afternoon light.'

The Viceroy of Algiers, standing, made no obvious signal; but behind him, like a breath on the small hairs of his neck, Jerott felt the cold of drawn steel. 'I regret,' said that unbroken, suave Arabic. 'Tomorrow is Friday, and among my people, no work may be done on that day. We must then beg to accept thy delightful bounty today.'

His breath held, Jerott looked at Lymond. Francis Crawford said gently, 'But today I have set aside, from the most weighty necessity, for paying homage to your two respected associates. I must call on His Excellency the Agha of Janissaries, and on my lord Dragut Rais.'

It was then, for the first time, that Jerott realized that Salah Rais understood French. With one upraised palm he stopped his interpreter with the first words of this speech in his mouth, and said himself, smoothly, in Arabic, 'Both these gentlemen, it is regretted, are absent from home. How desolate they will be. How afflicted, particularly my lord Dragut, who was extolling only last month the generosity of thyself to my people.'

Standing rigid with all his sweating companions at Lymond's still back, Jerott was aware of a crashing headache and a mounting desire to cut loose and do something silly. They were supposed to be thoroughly briefed before they left on this expedition. Lymond had said nothing, damn him, about offering cases of guns to the heathen. Nor was it clear why Salah Rais, who a moment before had clearly held the whip hand, was suddenly apparently bargaining. And without a translator. Unless . . .

Unless, thought Jerott, suddenly, Salah Rais was in fact saying: I want those carbines. I want them now, and I don't want the Agha to find out until it's all over. And if you don't tell the Agha I'll offer you . . .

'It so happens,' said Salah Rais, 'that I may be able to do thee some service. Thou hast offered a fortune, all Africa knows it, for the return of a certain woman and a certain one-year-old child. Many will come to thee with false tales in hopes of the money. Some of my own people have come to my gates with news, they claim, of the boy or the mother. While the cases are being un-loaded, it may please thee to meet these people here, in a private room in my palace? Keep by thy side whom you wish. If thou hast need of any official of mine, however senior, to attend at the harbour, I shall arrange it.'

'Indeed,' said Lymond gently, 'thou art a man born to great occasions. It shall be according to thy desires.' He picked, Jerott noticed, the fat vizier for his personal hostage. To stay with him in the palace, he kept no one but Jerott himself.

They had to wait a few moments while their companions joined the men-at-arms in the yard and, mounted again, rode down to the harbour with Salah Rais's escort to proffer Lymond's written note to the *sous-patron* and have the carbines unloaded from the *Dauphiné*'s hold. Until that was complete, Jerott supposed, they would be under courteous guard. Salah Rais wanted those weapons. A man governed by a distant and powerful nation and at the mercy of its colonial army wanted all the surprises he could achieve, up his sleeve.

Of the ethics of that, this was not the place to inquire. Instead, Jerott said in English to the man waiting silently at his side, 'I see. A policy of strict laissez-faire. When did you make it known you'd pay for news of Oonagh O'Dwyer and the child?'

'A long time ago.' Lymond was listening, his eyes fixed on the door.

'Before we met you at Baden?'

'Oh, God, yes.' And seeing, perhaps, Jerott's face, Lymond said, 'I'm sorry. But it was, after all, my own business. And my own money.'

'How much?' And as Lymond did not reply, Jerott persisted. 'How much? My God, it was my neck you were risking today.'

Lymond looked at him. 'Did I ask you to come on this voyage? I can't say I recall it.'

Jerott's colour was high. 'No, you didn't, you bloody high-handed bastard. You might at least have cut your friends in for a share of the prize-money. How much is it?'

'On the day I am brought face to face with the living child, or the living woman,' said Lymond carefully, 'my bankers at Lyons

will pay five hundred thousand ducats, in gold, to those who contrived that I found them. . . . You will wait here, please, for me.'
A robed figure, silently arrived in the doorway, bowed and beckoned.

Lymond was turning to go when Jerott, abruptly, put out a hand. 'Did you say what I think you said? You have a fortune this size? And you have offered it all?'

'It is all I do have,' said Lymond. 'And pride is expensive to buy. As Gabriel knows.'

*

Francis Crawford was away for two hours. He interviewed fifteen human beings in the small room where Salah Rais, with Egyptian irony, had summoned all who claimed Lymond's reward, in the hope of placing the Special Envoy of France conveniently in Salah Rais's debt.

The Viceroy's requital, come so patly to hand, was the speedy delivery of the carbines, even now loading on the quay under the no doubt amazed eyes of the women, and Onophrion and Archie. In exchange for it Francis Crawford received nothing; for none of the fifteen he interviewed possessed the information which he sought.

To Jerott, on his return, Lymond said simply, 'None of them. Shall we go?'

'Are you sure?' It was a stupid question. Lymond merely said, 'They didn't go away empty-handed. I have sent my respectful leave-takings to the Governor: let not a whelp go unsaluted. . . . Let's go back to the ship.'

'You're leaving Algiers?'

'What else? Dragut Rais isn't here. We'll give the Viceroy his feast early tomorrow, and sail.'

'Will he come?' said Jerott. 'Now he has his beautiful carbines?'

'He'll come,' said Lymond briefly. 'When he notices I haven't included the bullets.'

*

And that smart and equivocal transaction and its useless corollary might have been the end of the incident at Algiers.

Except that before Jerott, with Lymond, left the palace, a man found them: a thickset man whose coarse shirt hung on powerful shoulders, and who wore a round felt cap on his forceful black curls. He spoke in Arabic. 'The Envoy from the French ship?'

Lymond stopped. 'I lead the gentlemen on the French ship *Dauphiné*, yes. Your name?'

The felt cap moved, once. 'It is of no matter. But thou, thou art the prince who offers gold to find a child and a woman?'

'Yes. You have information?' said Lymond.

56

'I have more,' said the man. Beyond an avenue of slim pillars they had lit the lamps in the courtyard: against the chevrons of flickering light his face was impassive and blank. 'I have written word from the woman herself. What dost thou pay?'

'This,' said Lymond, and held out the ruby he slipped from his finger. 'And all I promise if I meet her or the child, alive, as a result.'

A moment later, he held the note in his hands.

Once, long ago in Graham Malett's white house on Malta, Lymond had received from Jerott's contemptuous hands a letter written by Oonagh O'Dwyer. *Do not come*, had said the black, vigorous script. *I do not wish to see you.*

The writing, unchanged, was still irrefutably hers. But the message this time was different. Addressed to Lymond in his full and correct name and dated the previous day—the day, thought Jerott, when, lying outwith the harbour, they had sent news of their coming to the Viceroy—it said: *The day set for our meeting is coming. I am glad, for I have been very tired. . . . These are poor people to whom gold is small use: do not overwhelm them. . . . Forget the child ever lived. It has been sold, they told me; but it may be a lie: it failed a lot, they said, after the branding. I do not want you to have him. Your life has been wasted enough. . . .* And, after a space, and written differently, as if on an impulse: *I regret nothing save for that fool of a man. And anyway, what good do regrets do?*

Below, she signed her name. There was no word of fondness or of recrimination. . . . She must, thought Jerott, looking out of the side of his eye, have been a strange and powerful woman, this mistress of Lymond's.

No . . . not mistress. She had been that to Cormac O'Connor, who wished to be King of all Ireland, and whose dream she had lived until, spoiled and gross, Cormac had lost all his vision and lost her, finally, too. Then Lymond and she had been on opposite sides, Archie Abernethy had told him. What had brought them together was one move, coolly plotted, in some far more vital intrigue. What it had led to was this.

She had no regrets. That was probably true. With the death of her lifelong struggle for Ireland, it must seem that little else mattered. And of the child she spoke with complete unconcern. Jerott wondered if she were a woman indifferent to children. Or one who, weighing Lymond's life and the child's, had made a hard choice.

Then Lymond, looking up, said, 'Where is she?' and the messenger, smiling and bowing, said, 'Dragut's house. Dragut Rais is with the fleet; he is away. The woman waits for the Hâkim there.' He paused. 'The Hâkim will not wish an escort. If he will follow, there is a side door which will take us out of the palace.'

'Wait a bit.' Jerott, catching a handful of white tissue and emeralds, held Lymond back. 'Didn't the note say something about poor people? It doesn't sound right. And in any case you can't walk about the back streets like that.'

'It had occurred to me,' Lymond said, and Jerott let his hand fall. It crossed his mind to wonder why he had not been dispatched back to the harbour, and then he realized that his appearance in the courtyard, alone, would only set inquiries afoot. Also, Lymond would need his help with the woman. It further crossed his mind to wonder why he had thought it important to come in the first place.

He kept his mouth shut while, sent off with silver, the felt-capped man returned promptly with two white, hooded burnouses, smelling strongly of goat, which he and Lymond put on. Then, stepping into the dark, noisome air, Lymond said softly, 'She is in Dragut's house? I know the place very well. Suppose you and Mr Blyth follow, and I choose the way. . . . Mr Blyth, I should warn you, has a nervous disposition and a very sharp dagger.' And as they set off, twisting and turning through the dark, precipitous streets, Jerott thought, acidly, that a slip of that dagger, if it happened, would save Francis Crawford a large sum of money. That the thought was unworthy did not make him any less peevish.

Dragut Rais's Algerian palace was of marble, and set within gardens whose walls traced, in stucco, the benign injunctions of the Prophet Mohammed. Behind the blank walls no lights could be seen, and the double-leafed doors, gilded and inlaid with woods, were decisively closed. Skirting the wall for a weak place, Lymond found, somewhere, an invisible foothold and, in spite of the hampering cloth, was neatly up and over: Jerott, left below with the silent messenger, wondered sardonically how many ducats' worth of vermilion velvet had lost its spruceness in going. From the top of the wall, Lymond's voice said quietly, 'There's a light on at the back somewhere, and voices—he probably keeps a few servants, or they move in with their families, more likely, when he goes away. The main rooms seem to be empty, and the courtyards aren't lit. Ask him where she's supposed to be.'

Jerott turned. It was as well that he did, for the doubled fists of the messenger, striking hard for his neck, met his shoulder instead. Jerott grunted, twisted, and grabbed.

He was a second too late. Ducking, the felt-capped man, muscles hard, dragged himself out of that grasp and, flinging off to one side, got his balance, glanced once at Jerott, and then darted off into the darkness. After the first step, breathing hard, Jerott stayed where he was, swearing. But he could hardly leave Lymond. He looked up.

'Bravo,' said Francis Crawford, sitting crosslegged on top of the wall, his hood shaken free on his shoulders. 'You're a credit to the bloody Order, aren't you? You *know* you've got a knife in your hand?'

There was no excuse, which didn't make it any better. Jerott said, 'I apologize. I'll go after him now.'

There was a furious pause. Then Lymond's voice, the chill gone, said, 'Don't be an ass, Jerott? You know I can't do without you.'

It was an obvious answer. But it was also something Jerott had never had from Lymond before: an apology and an appeal both at once.

He found he had nothing to say. Instead, he pushed back his hood and, giving Lymond his hand, pulled himself up to the wall-top beside him. Then, side by side, they dropped silently into the unlit garden of Dragut Rais's house, and methodically set about entering and searching its rooms.

It took half an hour. Familiar with Arab houses and their lack of all but movable furnishings, Jerott was not surprised that breaking in should be simple: there was literally nothing to steal. Possessions, packed into coffers, moved from house to house with their owner: Dragut's would be at Djerba or Prevesa or Constantinople by now. For the Viceroy had clearly been truthful, if in this respect only: Dragut Rais was not there.

Walking through chamber after bare chamber, and skirting the dark courtyards with their rustling trees and dried and derelict fountains, Jerott tried to imagine it as it must have been in the summer, when the corsair princes sailed through their rich, sunny playground and made sport with their luxurious spoils.

Oonagh O'Dwyer had been one of those captives: had lain perhaps by that marble basin and watched the fish play and tended her child . . . perhaps. Jerott had never seen Oonagh O'Dwyer, and could imagine no child of Lymond's here.

In the end, they did hear children's voices, but the screeching voices of Algerine children, black-haired, filthy and raucous, swarming in one room far at the back with half a dozen half-bred Moorish women . . . the servants, or the families of the servants left to safeguard the property. Of menfolk there was no sign: at that hour they would have business in the lower town common to their kind, Jerott knew. Dropping softly from his viewpoint through a high, half-shuttered window, he rejoined Lymond saying, 'Now what?'

Just that, for there was no use in saying, *What did I tell you? At the royal palace your rank had royal protection. In the streets, perhaps, you were able to escape notice. But you are here because you were sent here . . . by a woman in Baden; by another woman in Lyons; by a man you have never seen before who brought you this far and then ran away. It is a trap—you and I know it's a trap, of Gabriel's devising; and we have no protection at all. . . .*

'That leaves the gardens,' said Lymond. 'Not very likely, but we'll search them to make sure. What puzzles me is why they didn't attack in the house, if they're going to. They can hardly surround

59

the whole house and garden, unless they've got a squadron of troops, and they're not going to find it very easy to catch us out here in the dark. If this is all Gabriel's doing, then it's for some other purpose, surely, other than a simple ambush and killing.'

Leaving the path, they moved over the soft winter grass and through a dark maze of small, hanging trees. More paths, a fountain, a paved square lined with dark tubs. Jerott barked his shin and bit back an exclamation. Lymond's voice, even and quiet, said, 'Unless there has been a mistake, a fault in his plans. But I can't believe that, though I'd like to. . . .'

Before them the rest of the gardens stretched into darkness, unknown and quiet. From the house, muffled by bushes and trees, women's voices scratched the silence, raised in anger or argument. A cat mewed, and far off, the constant, irritating barking of a dog was taken up by another, still more distant. Of the crammed, multilingual, vociferous life that lay outside this expensive, deserted oasis there was no other sound, and they could hear the wet, lukewarm wind moving the tops of the trees and blowing a dead leaf, like tinfoil, along the brick path. Jerott said, 'There's nothing here. If it's a trick, it's just the malicious one of leading us up a blind alley. That brute who ran away wouldn't have turned his back on a fortune.'

'Unless . . .' said Lymond, '. . . Oh, bloody hell, let's get it over with. You take that wall and I'll take this. We'll walk the length of the garden and compare notes at the bottom. There's no point in sticking together anyway: if anyone attacks you in this place, you don't fight; you run, and get back to the ship as you can. If anything strikes you as mysterious, whistle.'

'Right.'

'. . . Jerott?'

Two steps away, Jerott stood perfectly still. 'I hear you.'

'You sound like a schoolmaster,' said Lymond's voice at his ear, with a trace of its usual lightness. 'It doesn't matter. Go on.'

Jerott did not move. 'What were you going to say?'

'Something regrettable. I'll say it; and then we can both forget it,' said Lymond. 'You put up with a lot, you know. More than you should. More than other people can be expected to do. . . . I find I need a sheet anchor against Gabriel. However much I try—don't let me turn you against me.'

Jerott said slowly, 'You command your own will. Otherwise I shouldn't be here.'

'You mean I swallowed my pride. But then, there are some things I don't think I could stomach. . . . And Gabriel knows them too well.'

'Gabriel,' said Jerott firmly, 'is now at Birgu, Malta, engaged in a life-and-death struggle for the Grand Mastership of the Order of

St John. He is unlikely to spend a large part of his time arranging esoteric disasters for his adversaries. He is far more likely to arrange to kill them stone dead.'

'All right. You go and get killed stone dead on that side of the garden, and I'll stick to this,' said Lymond. '*Calamitosus est animus futuri anxius,* or why worry about tomorrow, when your funeral is today. Goodbye.'

'Au revoir,' said Jerott Blyth, in stout contradiction of his own theory; and, striding off to the right, contacted the wall rather suddenly and proceeded to follow it, in cloud-muffled starlight; surveying his half of the ground as he went.

And so he was the first, in the end, to encounter Oonagh O'Dwyer . . . far down the garden and out of range of their whispering voices. So far off that Jerott was drawn to the place by a sound which had been inaudible where Lymond and he had stood before parting. In that disused and derelict garden, the sound of light, wind-blown fountains, playing in a large pool. Listening, Jerott turned and walked slowly towards it.

There were cypresses in the way; formal gardens sealed from the stars by wall and creeper and a hedging of palms. It was from this absolute dark that he turned a corner and saw stretching before him a study in milk-quartz and silver; a fantasy lit by the moon and the stars and a single lamp hung in the distance, an ox-eye on velvet.

It was a flower-garden, the green growing scents stirring already in the mild African winter. The pond sunk in its centre was a long one, edged by a vista of twinned silver sprays: from end to end, the spray rose like a mist and obscured the kiosk at the far end, a lacy thing hung with leaves, where the oil lamp burned quietly still.

And under the lamp, Jerott saw, a woman was sitting.

He stopped. From the rest of the garden there came no untoward sound; no voice, no footfall; no stir but the wind shaking the tree-tops and the kissing patter of water on water, nearer at hand. If Lymond was near, there was no sign of him. If this were Gabriel's trap, it was delicately baited indeed.

His sword drawn, moving from shadow to shadow along the tall cypresses, his footfalls lost in the waterplay, Jerott advanced to the kiosk until, reaching the last of his cover, he was able to stop and study as much as the lamp showed him inside.

The little building was of great elegance: a marriage of Fez and Granada, with flowered tiles and fine marquetry and, above, a honeycomb of rose-coloured stucco like a flower-form sheathing the chamber. Inside, there was a single divan, draped and set with fine cushions, and a rug on the floor. *She is not one,* Archie Abernethy had once said, *who has ever looked young, nor would she ever look less than beautiful. Black hair she has, you would say like a barrel of pitch; and queer, light eyes that look through you, and a neck you could put your one hand around. That is Oonagh O'Dwyer.*

The woman sitting there, straight and still on the bright velvet cushions, was not young; nor was she less than beautiful. The black hair, loose and shining, and deep, fell back over her shoulder and forward down to her waist; her chin was high above the pure line of her neck, which you could have held in one hand. Her eyebrows were black, and arched in pride, or surprise, or over some deep, long-held thought; and below the black, silky lashes, the wide eyes were packed full of straw.

5

ALGIERS

Fighting for the Order in Malta, *sub suave jugo Christi,* Jerott
Blyth had seen many things. He knew what man could do to man;
he knew, given primitive nature and primitive provocation, what
of suffering and what of brutalization and what, sometimes, of
nobility could ensue.

So he turned his back on that elegant kiosk and, closing his eyes,
leaned against the smooth birch-tree bark until the sickness cleared
from his brain and the blackness from his sight and until the turmoil
was locked hard within him.

He did not look again, after that, at that cold, lighted arbour. He
sheathed his sword and whistled; and at an answering whistle,
strode through the dark garden, heedless of noise, to find Francis
Crawford.

Lymond stood, a taut shadow on some dim, arcaded path, and
said, 'What?' sharply as Jerott appeared. Then as Jerott, breathing
hard, suddenly found himself speechless, the other man soundlessly
joined him. In the dark, he could not read Jerott's face. But he said,
as if he had, 'Lead on. I'll follow you.'

The pond this time was not a vista but a panorama, laid out before
them, with the kiosk in profile on their left. Faced with the sparkling
garden; the pool, the plash of live water against the shadowy trees
and the mellow, innocent light from the tiny kiosk, Lymond stopped
and Jerott stood with him.

Lymond said, 'It's all right: you don't have to tell me. She is in
the kiosk. And dead.' His face in the strange silver light was neither
full of pain nor distraught. He had expected it, Jerott realized. He
had braced himself hard against death; and for the reality, he was
quite unprepared. Jerott spoke, his voice steady. 'She is more than
dead, Francis. If I thought you would do it, I would beg you to go
without seeing her.'

Lymond said, *'What has he done?'* but under his breath: he did
not want or wait for an answer. Nor did he hurry. Rooted, by a
kind of desperate courtesy, to the grass where he was standing,
Jerott watched the other man walk down alone, fair hair ghostly
against the ctesiphon pattern of water, towards the softly lit room
at the end.

Lymond had unclipped and dropped the dark cloak, and on his
shoulders the Viceroy's tissue fell straight and flat, the emeralds
distantly sparkling. Jerott saw him check, violently, at what must
have been his first glimpse of the woman within. Then he recovered,
and walked steadily on to stand, nearer than Jerott had done, full

in the light of the lamp. But, like Jerott, a moment's glance was all he could bear; and then he closed his hands over his face.

For a long time he stood there, the yellow hair laced over his taut fingers; as still as the queenly, naked simulacrum of the lovely woman who had been Oonagh O'Dwyer. Then Lymond moved; and suddenly, with all his force, swung round a fist in a gesture which even at that distance conveyed a fury of abomination. The lamp, swept from its perch, crashed to the floor of the kiosk, and darkness fell on the grove.

The fountains hissed. Moving forward a step, Jerott could see nothing now in that chill pleasure-house, nor could he detect any movement to hint what Francis Crawford might do. His voice quiet, Jerott called. 'Francis . . . if you want something done, let me do it.'

'I have done it,' said Lymond. And came towards and past Jerott with the swift, easy walk which was one of his attributes; tailored shoulders outlined against a new, orange light, freshly born, which flickered, gained strength, pounced and weaved its way up from the floor of the kiosk and finally fastened, sparkling and avid, on its food.

Jerott could not follow at first. Instead, numb and unmoving, he stood and watched the fire of the other man's making: watched it seize on the wood and the fabric, on the black hair and on the stuff of the couch. The feet flared, and the hands buckled like gloves in her lap. But before leaving Francis had cast about Oonagh O'Dwyer's shoulders, in the darkness his white and miniver cloak. All the rest of her it concealed, as the emeralds, blackening, cracked and fell and the white fur, smoking, turned yellow and brown.

Jerott turned away then. Only once, as the whole pavilion caught and blazed like a jewel in the night, he looked back and saw the fur gone and the woman's body translucent as a beautiful lamp; eyes and mouth circles of fire in the hollow rind of the face. Then Jerott choked aloud and, wheeling, launched himself with all the power in his legs after the man in whose living arms she had once lain.

Later, Jerott Blyth was to realize that Lymond for a short time forgot he existed: that, leaving the fire he had kindled with that hideous lamp, he had walked straight back through the garden and up to the house, had hammered on the door and had burst without pausing into the occupied room among the women and children. At the time, racing anxiously through the garden, whistling and calling, Jerott heard the screams and, avoiding the house, found and climbed one of the perimeter walls and walked along it, scanning the street. He sensed, more than saw, the dark movement far along the same wall when Lymond, at its extremity, came to scale and drop over it and then, moving fast, vanished into a mesh of black alleys in the opposite direction. Balancing in his turn, Jerott jumped; and then, running lightly and fast, set himself grimly to follow.

Once before, under the bright sun of Malta, this merciless race had been run. Then Jerott, overtaking the man he disliked and mistrusted, had prevented Lymond from making the journey which might have kept Oonagh O'Dwyer out of Dragut Rais's hands. Running now; following those faint, echoing footsteps through tunnel and archway, round courtyard and market, Jerott wondered whether, coming fresh from her pyre, he was offering Francis Crawford yet another disservice, or not.

The night had cleared. Within the white walls of the wealthy came voices, and the muted sounds of a pipe: courtyard trees above the flat roofs glimmered, lamplit, and children chattered and cried. In the souks, men sat on the beaten earth, half naked, or coarsely shirted, or robed, and talked, moving their hands, or slept, or played endless games, traced in the mud. Tethered mules, waiting patiently, turned over the nameless rubbish heaped in the dirt; goats, jostling through with their herdboy, blocked him for two precious minutes as, slowed to a walk to avoid raised voices and stares, Jerott followed the swift figure ahead.

Coming into the crowded ways of the lower town, Lymond had been slowed, too. There was no way of knowing whether he knew where he was, or where he was going: but Jerott saw that, forcing his way through the alleys, he made some effort at least not to invite trouble: the dark cloak, retrieved from the garden, hid his hair and his clothes and protected him from a degree of attention.

It also made it harder, coming into the darker souks where the thatched and wood-strutted houses, leaning over the lane, met in a black vault above, for Jerott to see and keep him in sight. By the same token, cloaked and concealed, both he and Jerott had lost their rank and their international immunity. As an envoy of France, in a country friendly to France, Lymond was nearly untouchable. Tonight, alone in these streets, his death would be a regrettable accident convenient to many, and a triumph to some, with no blame attached. Thinking, meantime, only of that, and of the need to be at the other man's side, Jerott quickened his pace. Behind him, someone else did the same.

Now the alleys were less crowded and darker. Ahead, a lantern hung from a fig tree gleamed momentarily on Lymond's face as he swung round a corner: hurrying after, Jerott saw the lamp lit the court of a mosque and above, oddly confiding and close, the mellow voice of the muezzin gave sudden utterance, calling the faithful to prayer, and was taken up, like a bird-call, near and far through the minarets of the city. Stumbling up the next precipitous alley, Jerott did not look back, and the man behind him did not look up at all.

It was just beyond that, where the long, blank wall of a mosque or a college skirted the souk, that Jerott first realized that not one but several pairs of bare feet moved behind in the darkness. On his left a closed door clicked, for no reason, and then yawned open, emptily. And ahead and above there were other sounds; common sounds at uncommon levels.

Imperceptibly, Jerott's right hand found the hilt of his sword and eased it, ready to draw from its scabbard. He had time to do that, and to see that Lymond, lost nearly to view, was pursuing his road apparently free and quite unmolested, when, in a sudden scamper, his assailants were on him.

In the dark, there seemed a great many. Prepared, he hurled himself sideways to miss some of the cudgels: the rest took him on his shoulders and back, but left his sword-arm undamaged: the blade, as he brought it up, flinging back the hampering cloth, glittered under the moon.

They had not expected cold steel. As he cut, blindly, and felt the blade bite, the staves continued to strike him, but not at close quarters: there had been a recoil he could feel, checked by a man's hissing command in Arabic.

The voice seemed familiar. For a moment, fending off breathlessly with knee and dagger and elbow, twisting, wrenching, and dragging free to swing and slash with the two-sided blade, Jerott could make no chance to turn. When he did, it was to look into the black swarthy face of the man who had brought Oonagh O'Dwyer's letter.

Then, for the first time, retreating quickly; stumbling back uphill, his head ringing, his arms aching, bearing with him a swarm of silent attackers, Jerott Blyth took breath and called Lymond's name. Then, back to the wall, he prayed briefly, from habit; and from habit fought, as years in the Order had taught him to fight, against the Saracen; against impossible odds.

It seemed unlikely that Lymond would hear him, and if he did, in the violent pendulum of that night's events, that he would understand, or even care. That he did come was perhaps as much an automatic response as Jerott's. He came in the only way possible, running unseen along the white wall and dropping hard on the mêlée, his sword already driving through the dark press of bodies; his left arm, furled in his burnous, up and taking their blows.

He felled two men with the impact and killed the third who came at him, brushing his side with his club. Then, as Jerott deflected the blow of a fourth, Lymond used the second's respite to drive his blade, twice, through the scrambling men at his feet. Jerott, his own hands more than full, saw him offer his bared head to the sweep of a cudgel as he tugged, freeing his sword; but the blow when it came flung the striker on his side in the alley, impaled on that hungry blade. Then Lymond, at Jerott's side, faced his two remaining assailants.

One of them, with a muttered exclamation, broke away and,

turning, ran into the darkness. The other, ignoring his prayers, Lymond also ran through.

On a sobbing breath, Jerott started to talk, pointing after the running dark figure. Lymond said, 'I know. I saw him,' and smiled. Then he had gone, leaving behind him the smell of fresh blood from his clothes.

In the alley it was very quiet. Whoever had noticed the incident, lights remained out and shutters were closed. On the ground in the dim starlight the fallen shapes might have been those of ewes resting, their jaws moving softly, thought Jerott with sudden stupid incongruity, after nightfall in a green Scottish field. Only in the silence a man's voice suddenly began to pray as he had prayed, but in Arabic; and was as suddenly cut off. Jerott could not see whose it was.

It had not occurred to him to go after Lymond and the running man who had been their felt-capped messenger of Dragut Rais's house. He was very sore, for one thing; and breathless; and the man who had carried out this piece of butchery, single-handed and scatheless, was a stranger to him. So he waited; but not very long; for presently Lymond returned, with two mules; their hooves clicking up the stony mud of the souk. The felt-capped man sat on one of them. He was not bound, which didn't matter, as he could not, Jerott noticed, have walked. Lymond said, 'Are you hurt?'

It was an inquiry aimed merely at resolving how he, Jerott, was to be placed on the mule. Jerott said, 'I'm all right,' and watched Lymond mount behind the dark, thickset man. The man said nothing but Jerott, mounting slowly himself, saw his face twitch as the mule moved into motion. Jerott said, 'Where are we going?'

He did not expect a reply: it had been like addressing the thousand-year stones of a broch, a longhouse, a settlement laid suddenly bare by cold, sea-sucked sand and having, edgily, the form of house, hearth and dear human practices in its long-decayed stones. Then Lymond said, succinctly, 'There's a postern up there, and a path leading up to the hills. When Dragut left, the unwanted slaves were sold off, with most of the babies. The promising ones go in part-tribute to the Sublime Porte. The young in the next échelon are farmed out to learn hardship and Turkish and grow up to be good little Moslems. And the sick and the feeble go to whoever thinks he can flog a day's work out of them. I found out at Dragut's house where . . .'

His voice died of its own accord on the unspoken name. The little mule's feet, trampling steadily onwards, pocked the brief silence. Jerott said, 'Where she'd been taken when Dragut left? Oh, I see. And where she wrote that letter from, of course. She was . . . she was brought back to Dragut's garden after that. I imagine Dragut himself would be told nothing of what happened then. Have you found out . . . was it Gabriel's doing?'

Ahead, clear in the moonlight, was the double town wall, with the postern. A little gold, Jerott knew, would see them easily through it. Reined in for a moment the two mules stood quietly, side by side, and one of them tossed, irritably, the frayed rope which stood it as reins. 'Yes,' said Lymond.

There was only his voice to go on: the resumed burnous covered other men's blood on his clothes and also shadowed his face. Jerott said, 'Before we go . . . if you mean to go through with this, Francis; for Christ's sake, there's no stopping. You'd better make up your mind now whether you can sustain it or not.'

'No,' said Lymond. 'Let's just try it and see.'

He sounded not unfriendly and perfectly rational. Except that Jerott knew that he could not trust from one second to the next what he would do.

The house to which Oonagh O'Dwyer had been sold, with her baby, was little more than a huddle of sheds, the holes pegged over with hides and stuffed with plasterings of straw. Hens ran, squawking, as the two mules came upon it in the dark, climbing a rocky path between short, wind-twisted trees; and skirting the broken mud walls of a plantation of corn or barley or anonymous vegetables. The green leaves which made the drug *kif* were also grown in those hills, Jerott knew. He had smelt the sickly tang of the hashish in the souks as they walked, and he smelt it again now, clinging to the sour hides of the building, and mixed with the smoke of a cow-dung fire.

A cur, whose hysterical barking had attended all the last of their journey, came headlong towards them, and hurtled, teeth bared, at the throat of one of the mules. It died, on Lymond's sword, before Jerott had his own half pulled out. Then Lymond, dismounting, walked across to the ramshackle building, sword in hand, and ripped the hide door-curtain off.

If it had occurred to him that here was another trap, and with a deadlier welcome awaiting him, he took no precautions. Jerott, his sword out, his hand holding Lymond's mule and his own, saw him stand barring the threshold, the stink of cow-fat and ordure and human neglect surging out with the smoke-clouds.

Inside there was only an old man, his head sunk on his knees, and two women, perhaps mother and daughter, their hands knotted; their faces grained with dirt and malnutrition; poverty and long overwork. In the fitful light of their fire their features showed, resigned to command and brutality; answering with beaten silence Lymond's string of staccato questions in Arabic. Beside Jerott, the felt-capped man on the mule bit his lip.

Then Lymond, turning, addressed Jerott curtly in English. The next moment, driven by the flat of Jerott's sword, the mule with the felt-capped man on its back jerked and, blundering forward, plunged through the doorway of the shack and shook off its burden. The mule, backing, stood shivering in the doorway beside Jerott while the felt-capped man lay writhing on the dirt floor at the feet of the women.

There was no need to ask whether they knew him. As they knelt beside him, wailing and muttering, Lymond lifted his sword, and placing it point down on the prone man's bare, bloodstained chest, said in Arabic again, 'Now I will have my questions answered, or he dies in his place.'

Looking from the lined faces of the women to the man on the floor, his sweating face grey under the brown, his oiled black hair covered with filth, Jerott knew that whether he was a son, a brother, a husband, loved or hated, he was the breadwinner in that house and they could not afford to let him die. And indeed, it was the old man, lifting eyes glazed with drugs, who said, 'She was cheap, he said; and there was no one to carry water after the last child died. But she could not carry water, and that smooth face was no use to my handsome son, and she was dear; dear.'

'But thou hadst gold for the woman's own child?' said Lymond. His voice was both clear and impersonal.

The old man said, 'A little, long since gone. One came to buy the child, that is true. But what of the money for the woman? My son hears that some Hâkim offers a fortune for the woman alive, and the woman writes some words for my son to bear to this Hâkim when he comes, to tell him she is safe and well. Next day, they say, he will come. . . .' The cracked voice hesitated.

'Well?' said Lymond.

'When we returned from the fields, the woman was dead. Killed by her own hand. What are we to do?'

The passionless voice continued. 'What did you do?'

'He came again. He who had arranged for us to sell the child. He offered a sum—a paltry sum, but what could we do? The woman was dead—for my son to deliver the message to the Hâkim as if nothing had happened; and he took the woman away.'

'Who was this man?' said Lymond.

Then, for the first time, the man on the floor raised his head; and Jerott saw in his eyes the kind of snarling courage he had seen a moment before in the eyes of the cur outside. 'His name was Shakib, Efendi,' he said. 'The Efendi killed him this evening, in the streets of the town.'

In that bloodbath by the wall. My God, thought Jerott. He's killed the only man who can tell him about the child, if that's true. *If* it was true.

Lymond's voice was gentle. The sword, pressing a little, had driven a beaded runnel of blood over the man's breastbone. 'But is that truly so?' he said. 'How may I tell?'

69

'It is true!' The younger of the two women suddenly screamed. 'It is so! When the camel-trader last came, Shakib bought the boy-child from us—the robber! The thief!—And sold him again, for much gold, to the other. Then last night he comes, and says, "Give me the white woman's body." . . .'

Her voice died, but Lymond's voice, addressing her, remained cold and soft. 'Why should he do that? Was someone in turn paying him?'

They looked at one another. Then the man on the floor, his lips twisted, said, 'The same who paid Dragut Rais. It was a jest. The instructions came from him who spoke with the Prophet Mohammed. The Archangel Gabriel.'

There was a little pause. Then: 'Tell me this last thing,' said Lymond carefully. 'The name of the camel-trader who bought the child, and how I may find him?'

But the old man simply stared at him, and the two women shook their heads; and the man on the floor, looking up at the sword and the still face above it, bared his teeth and said, 'For that you must needs ask Shakib, Efendi, and Shakib, alas, cannot reply.'

He had no hope, Jerott saw, as he grinned into Lymond's shadowy face. Only the same guts as the dog. He died, the rictus still on his face, as Lymond drove the sword home with a jerk and then, wrenching it out, turned on his heel. The screaming of the women followed him into the night as he rammed the stained blade into its sheath and, putting his foot into the stirrup, swung into the mule's saddle, stained and sticky as well with the blood of the man who had bought Oonagh O'Dwyer to share his straw like a goat in a hut, and who had helped to bring her, in the end, to sit in that kiosk in Dragut Rais's garden.

The women Lymond had not touched. These coarse, dirt-patterned hands, Jerott thought, had handled and fed that small child, who had crawled in that dirt and lain breathing that foul, drug-laden air. Beyond his whereabouts, Lymond had asked nothing about him; and Jerott thought he understood why. Tonight, he found it too easy to kill.

Outside, it had started to rain. Far to the right, glimpsed inter-mittently through rocks and trees as they picked their way through the stones and the mud, glimmered the lights of the Kasbah, and the occasional pricking of light from the upper streets of Algiers, on the slopes of its hill. Otherwise the night was quite black, and the uneven paths scoring the hillside, twisting downhill to the invisible sea and joining village to village between the scattered gardens and castles and mosques, had to be traced by sound in the dark, and by the aid of those few distant lights.

The two men rode without speaking. God knew, Jerott thought, Francis Crawford had cause to be silent. And it was obvious that, on this open hillside in a land full of enemies, silence and darkness were their only defence. He listened, straining, against the rustle of the wind and the creak of the saddles and the mules' tapping feet. There was nothing. But bare feet made no sound; and men who were desperate for food and who knew every pitch of the hills would soon overthrow two strangers, however well armed.

And now Gabriel had had his revenge. Gabriel, not Fate, had seen to their safety as far as that wintry garden of Dragut Rais's and Gabriel had made sure that Lymond would reach the shack they had just left. From the fastnesses of Malta, through heaven knew what agent, Gabriel had planned for his enemy this gross humiliation: this ultimate hurt. In the darkness beside him, Lymond suddenly spoke, so à propos that it startled him.

'If you are interested, I think we shall be allowed to reach the ship safely, normal hazards apart.'

For a moment Jerott rode in silence, the rain running in beads round his hood. Then he said bluntly, 'I only hope that you're wrong.'

'How perspicacious of you, Jerott.' Lymond, following his own thoughts, reacted merely from habit. 'No. We are on the hook; and now we are going to be played. This is only the beginning.'

For a long time Jerott tried to say nothing. But in the end, as without event they again approached the postern and Lymond poured the coins ready from his pouch, Jerott said, 'But try and remember . . . it is Gabriel's doing. All these men are only tools.'

The money chinked. They were through, and into the dark, unlit souks. As they began to pick their way down to the harbour: 'But without such tools, none of this would have happened,' Lymond remarked.

And still the years with the Order would not be denied. 'But, Francis . . . you take these killings on your soul.'

His answer was sharp and immediate. 'I shall act as I please,' said Lymond, 'until I am . . . satisfied. Meanwhile . . . I wonder if you were right—— *Look out!*'

It was the sound of the rain, Jerott discovered afterwards, which had warned him: the infinitesimal changes in impact as it hit upon wool and felt and leather and steel somewhere close: somewhere round the next dark bend of the souk, where the overhanging wooden storeys raised crooked arms. Even so, it was too late. Reining hard, Jerott looked over his shoulder: the footsteps behind them were now plain to hear, advancing the way they had come; cutting off their retreat. Nor were there cross-lanes up which they might escape. Glancing at either wall, Jerott realized the ambushers had picked their site well. Solid wall, broken only by barred grilles or impassable doors, ran on either side of the souk. He looked at Lymond, and Lymond, insanely, had lashed his mule to a trot and, robe thrown off, was standing on its rump like an acrobat, arms

71

steady; head tilted back. Then, as it passed under the overhanging buildings, he jumped.

As far as Jerott could see, he jumped blind. But among the cross-beams and ledges of the wooden arch he must somewhere have found a finger-hold, for Jerott saw him swing free for only an instant, and then he had pulled himself up, flattened against the timber, and had turned, hand outstretched.

By then Jerott was already on his way. Broader than Lymond and strongly made, he too had developed a physical sixth sense in tackling the unknown. He balanced perfectly on his mule's back because he had to; and jumped; and, with Lymond's hand to help him, scrambled upwards and then across the arch of the bridge where they flung themselves flat on the skyline, the rain beating down on their bare heads and unprotected shoulders, as the streets below filled with the steel maces, the lances, the axes and crossbows of a detachment of Janissaries. In a gesture of stupefaction, Lymond dropped his face on the wet plaster and then raised it wryly to Jerott.

From this, Gabriel could be absolved. It was the Agha of the Janissaries, tardily returned and mad as a scolding piper on the subject of muskets, who was responsible for this sortie.

Lying on the flat-roofed building, whatever it was, beyond the bridge, Jerott surveyed the adjoining roof levels, and conjectured on their chances of escape. No body of Janissaries, however provoked, would publicly injure an emissary of France and a guest of the Viceroy's. They could, however, with the greatest propriety kill by accident two bloodstained foreigners in disguise who chose to greet them by streaking up walls. It was too late now to climb down side by side discussing the weather. They would receive a virtuous arrow between the shoulderblades before they set foot in the street. Jerott flinched as a sudden rush of ruddy light and a stream of black smoke told that someone had brought torches. Inching back after Lymond out of sight of the street, he rose to his feet when Lymond did, and when Lymond set off, running noiselessly, over the maze of uneven rooftops, Jerott followed.

It might have worked. It should have worked, even in the pitch dark, with the rain beating on their heads and shoulders and backs, if one single householder hadn't quarrelled with his wives or his mother; or hadn't wanted somewhere to die, or to sleep off his *kif*. Lymond, running first, landed on a roof which should at that season and in that weather have been empty, but wasn't. The man on whose back he landed screamed like a pig and went on screaming while Lymond rolled over and picked himself up. By the time Jerott landed as well, the alleys on each side echoed with the pad of leather buskins in the mud, and they were surrounded. In a moment, the challenge. And then the shooting would start.

Lymond measured with his eye the distance over the street. There were no bridges here. 'D'you think you can?'

'I'll have to, won't I?' said Jerott; and before Lymond could stop him, he backed, ran, and jumped.

He didn't think, himself, that he would reach it, but surprisingly he did. He had a glimpse of movement below him but he could not be sure whether in the dark they had seen him: there were no torches there yet. His landing posture was a trifle ungainly and hurt, to be truthful, more than a bit, but he picked himself up very quickly and paused to wave brazenly to Lymond, who had already started his run. Then, turning, Jerott walked back to give the other the room he needed to land.

At the back of the roof, where they had been sitting with the utmost patience awaiting him, a group of four men rose to their feet. Jerott opened his mouth to warn Lymond, but didn't manage it before one of them hit him on the head, and he knew nothing more.

*

The first face Jerott Blyth saw after that was a black one, which worried him a little, until his sight cleared and he saw that it was human, smiling, and turbaned. The next, beside him, was Lymond's. He was dressed in a clean white burnous, and apart from the intangible difference which remained in his eyes, he looked both calm and unharmed. Behind his head, a lamp indicated that it must be night still, and a heavenly smell of food reminded Jerott that it must be over twelve hours since he had last eaten. He moved, and the fancy faded a little.

'And how doth *your* gate?' said Lymond. 'Lie a little longer. As was said of the philosopher Chrysippus: you are only drunk in your legs. I was meant to jump over first.'

'Was it the Janissaries?' said Jerott. He had never been inside either the Kasbah or a college of Janisserotz, but this didn't look like either. He glanced down at the mattress on which he was lying, under a light woollen blanket, and then at the fine glazed tiles in green and apricot and blue which covered the floor of the room. A brazier, placed close to him, gave out a comforting warmth, and in its light he could trace, high on the white walls, an edging of fine stucco carving, and a phrase from the Qur'ân, repeated over and over in light blue and gold. Then he brought his gaze down again, and past Lymond, and back to the smiling dark face which had bent over him in the first place. This time, he knew it.

'. . . Salablanca,' said Lymond. 'They had seen the Janissaries waiting for us at all the posterns and portes. He and his friends were trying to reach us first, to warn us. They were all ready to slip us down the roof stairs and smuggle us here to the house of his father, if you hadn't started to yell.'

73

'He could have covered my mouth,' said Jerott indignantly, sitting up with great success and giving Salablanca his hand.

'He didn't want blood-poisoning,' said Lymond callously. 'Also he didn't know you're so damned slow with a knife. . . . If you're as sprightly as all that, hell, you can get up and eat.' And after he had, it was true, he felt almost better, given twenty-four hours' unbroken sleep.

It was a courtly household, ruled with quiet ceremony by the tall, grizzled Moor who was Salablanca's father; who remembered the white marble and the peacocks and the fountains of Granada, before Spain seized them again. He spoke Spanish, as did all the household Jerott saw, although the women who slipped in and out with the plates of rice and vegetables and meats were veiled except for the eyes, and said nothing.

In Malta, Jerott had learned a little of several languages, as was common in that high-bred, mixed society. He knew enough, now, to share with Lymond the courtesies of the table, and to listen later, eyelids drooping, when, seated deep in soft cushions, they talked of the fate of Algiers, and its rich trade and its violent, self-seeking factions, and of the nations which sought to devour it. Salablanca's father told of the tribes of the desert; of the nomads, of the trading Arabs; of the small towns along the coast which had been seized and exploited by corsairs; of Tunis, another Algiers but bigger than Rome, and torn too by warring interests and races. He spoke too of Salah Rais's rule: of his journey six hundred miles over the Nubian desert to exact tribute from the subject states under Turkey. He had come back with fifteen camel-loads of gold, so they said.

They were talking still: Lymond questioning and the men, sitting gravely crosslegged in their virginal robes, drinking small cups of hot liquid, and answering him quietly with their hands and their voices, when Jerott, beaten with sleep, was persuaded to return to his mattress.

When he woke, there was grey light in the room and the talk was ending: the men, rising, shook out the folds of their robes and Salablanca, offering scented water to Lymond, was saying as he waited, towel on arm, 'I am known. Forgive me, but if you follow me to the harbour, thus hooded and robed, none will stop you. Once more clothed in your fashion, you will be safe from the Agha. This night, it was spleen.'

He hesitated. Jerott, pausing behind in the doorway, remembered that it was through Lymond that the big Moor was here at all, and not bastinadoed to death in the castle at Tripoli. He imagined with what delicacy the old patriarch had made his thanks. No wonder they had done their best to rescue them from the Janissaries. What bitter luck, thought Jerott, that Salablanca had swum over too early to know about Oonagh. And by the time Francis had landed, her life and the honourable reserves of the grave had then both been wrenched from her grasp.

Then Salablanca looked at Lymond and said, 'We have heard of the wound done to your honour. May God make woe to attend such a man as your enemy. My father asks, as brother of brother, if he may aid you against him who wrongs you, or may avenge what is evilly done.'

'He is a great and generous man,' said Lymond. 'But I wish no help, and need no revenge. Except in one thing. . . . The woman, I am told, sold her child to the man Shakib for a camel-trader when the trader was last in Algiers. If I wished to trace this child, how might it be done?'

'Wait, señor.' Salablanca was gone only a moment; long enough for Jerott to realize that this conversation was taking place between Lymond and Salablanca so that as few as possible might be involved in it; and that Lymond for the same reason had denied all claims of revenge. Somewhere, thought Jerott, there was the man who conveyed the instructions from Gabriel, and who had seen that they were carried out. But Salablanca lived in Algiers. Lymond would not ask him to meddle with what might destroy him. On the other hand: 'Your camel-trader is a man named Ali-Rashid,' said Salablanca, returning. 'He comes often: his route is well known. We have written it for you.'

Carefully, Lymond took the paper Salablanca held out to him. 'How do you know this is the man?'

'There is only one such, between Dragut Rais's departure and now. More, the man Shakib has been seen with him.' He paused, and then said, 'The señor will forgive me, but his clothes have been burned. The chain and jewels we placed in this purse.'

'They are for your Imám,' said Lymond. 'If he will pray for a heretic?'

Salablanca was quicker than Jerott. 'For la señora?' he asked. 'She is with God. One has said: There is not any soul born, but its place in Paradise or Hell has been written.'

'What we choose to do then is nothing?' said Lymond, and his face was not pleasant. 'I have taken far too long as it is to face the consequences of my actions. You must not unlearn me my lesson. I have several other tests, still more acid, to pass.'

It was a quick, bitter memory, which Jerott better than Salablanca understood. Of a dark room, and a lit candle, and Lymond's voice asking, 'Shall we meet?'

And: '*You will see her*,' was what the Dame de Doubtance had said.

*

The journey to the harbour in Salablanca's company through that humid, grey dawn was without accident. Under the bright canopy of the *Dauphiné*, soaked with night rains, lights glimmered, and someone came soft-footed to the rail to lower a plank. Lymond, stopping, turned to Salablanca, his face blanched under the white hood. 'We owe you no less than our lives. Remember us. Serve your family well. And live with your own sons' sons, full of years.'

The black eyes smiled, but Salablanca, bowing, was grave. 'It shall be done; but presently. Now, I come to serve you.'

Lymond had not expected it. His brow creased, and he said, 'I am honoured; but you are free. Your father needs you and has welcomed you home. I cannot thus repay his care of us.'

'It was he,' said Salablanca gently, 'who, when I broached such a subject, enjoined me to come. I have brothers. I have no wish to stay here, other than for the term of your visit. I wish to make my fortune with you.'

'Well, you can forget about that, for a start,' said Francis Crawford. 'And if your place in Paradise has been written, then for God's sake hang on to it. Because we're going in the opposite direction.'

But he gave him his hand, as did Jerott; and without lingering they walked up the gangplank, gave the password and boarded the *Dauphiné*.

Philippa, who had sat up worrying half the night, did not in the end hear them come, having dropped into heavy sleep just before dawn.

It had been a day she did not particularly want to repeat; with the leaderless return of Lymond's escort, with orders to unload arms and deliver them to the Viceroy, and the further news that Mr Crawford and Jerott were still at the palace and were not to be sought out, however late they might be. It was Jerott's lieutenant, reassuring her, who told her that by this means Lymond had bought time and opportunity to search for Oonagh O'Dwyer. As the day wore on, the thought comforted her less and less.

Nor did the climate on board the *Dauphiné* help. These shining caseloads of carbines being transferred so promptly into infidel hands had started a rustle of unease among soldiers and seamen. Archie Abernethy, who had pursued his strange career in the royal menageries of Moslem and Christian throughout Europe and Asia before serving with Lymond, could not entirely keep his mind on his chosen mission to torment Onophrion Zitwitz; and Onophrion himself, each time he returned from market with his train of small naked boys bearing food-laden baskets, became gloomier and gloomier still. Although that, Philippa conceded, was due rather more to the strain of providing a royal banquet at short notice and with inadequate supplies for a Moslem dignitary with numerous religious restraints on his diet, and an uncountable force of attendants.

It rained. Marthe, undisturbed, sat on her bed reading, and emerged only for the formal intake of food. Even when Maître Gaultier, with an unusual flush under his dark skin, slipped on board after dark, greeted them, and then proceeded to stroll restlessly up and down the quayside and round Onophrion's prized line of ovens, she did not trouble to join him, but read until the lamp failed, and then undressed and slept. Philippa, enviously, wished she could do the same, and then decided she would rather be interesting and sensitive. She gave up combing her hair, which the salt air had reduced to a kind of scrim of brown hessian, and, lying down, proceeded to keep her fingernails short in the way Kate admired least. Then she overslept.

It was Marthe's voice from the ladder which woke her. A watery sun, filtered through canvas, shone through the hatchway on to the crossed arms and yellow satiny coils of the other girl's hair, and Philippa, staring glumly at that finely sculptured profile, saw there was a smile on it. 'They're back,' Marthe was saying. 'They've just come on deck after changing, and the ship's complement are being mobilized like cattle. They say Salablanca came on board with them, but not the well-favoured Oonagh.'

Sitting up, Philippa was dragging on clothes. 'What happened?'

'I don't know.' The cornflower-blue eyes narrowed, following some unseen movement on deck. 'But our Envoy is not quite himself.'

'Let me see.' Shoving past, Philippa got to the hatchway, and leaned an elbow on the cover. The deck was swarming with feet and at first she could see no one belonging to them. Then, farther down the long gangway, she saw Lymond talking to Jerott. Dismissed, Jerott turned away, dressed, she saw, in a sensational russet that clashed with the awning, leaving Lymond in full critical view.

Marthe had been right. From polished head to fingertips, his grooming was faultless. But once or twice on this journey, and once or twice at his home back in Scotland, Philippa had seen him loose his tongue and his temper like this; his face contemptuous, his manner insufferable. He had not, she judged, had any sleep. He gave orders, as she watched him, to three other men, and each in turn jumped to obey him. Then he moved off with the bos'n swiftly out of sight to the prow.

Jerott, approaching, blocked her view and would have passed if Marthe had not called him. 'Dare you pause and tell us what's happening?'

He glanced down at her, but failed to smile. 'The Viceroy is embarking at noon. After we have eaten and he has gone, we set sail.'

'The woman is dead?' Marthe put the question, sitting on the

77

hatch-covering hugging her knees, while Philippa peered up at knee level, holding her undone hooks and eyes with one hand.

Jerott hesitated. Then, surprisingly, he sank down on his heels at their level, russet velvet and all, and said, 'Yes. We found her, but she was dead. The circumstances were ... I can't tell you. But, for God's sake, put up with anything he says or does today. He has reason.'

'They like to mutilate their dead,' said Marthe. 'He must have been prepared for that, surely.'

'For what Gabriel did to Oonagh O'Dwyer,' said Jerott with precision; 'nothing on God's earth could have prepared him. Do I have to go into details?'

'And the baby?' intervened Philippa quickly.

Get rid of the women, Lymond had said. Just that: one laconic order among many. It could not be done here, but at the first opportunity, Jerott knew, they were being sent off. This was no voyage for them. So he touched Philippa's thin, bitten hand with one of his own, and said, 'I'm sorry. But it seems the child died.'

'Seems? You don't know?'

'When Dragut Rais left for the winter, they were mostly sold off. Oonagh's baby was going overseas, but it died on the way. So they say, and I believe them,' said Jerott Blyth glibly. 'You know he offered a lot of money for the return of the child? So I don't think they were lying.'

He saw Philippa's eyes become perfectly round and thought, 'Hell. Now she knows he was interested.' But she suddenly stopped asking questions and it was Marthe who said disingenuously, 'Did he? How much?'

Jerott's black eyebrows disappeared into his hair. 'It's none of your bloody business,' he said, and stood up. 'And a word of warning, besides. You don't discuss this with Lymond.'

'It would overturn him. He is distraught,' said Marthe readily, and with that cynical, brittle blue gaze smiled at Jerott Blyth's dark face. 'To pass over grief, they say, the Italian sleeps; the Frenchman sings; the German drinks; the Spaniard laments, and the Englishman goes to plays. What then does the Scot?'

To Jerott's mind sprang, unbidden, a picture of the sword Archie Abernethy was trying to clean at this moment below. 'This one,' he said, 'kills.'

*

At noon, Salah Rais along with eighty attendants presented himself on the quay beside the *Dauphiné* to break bread with his host. Resplendent in silks, velvets and jewels, with the slaves capped and shirted and the ship dressed with streamers and tassels and hangings of blue silk brocade, the Special Envoy and his entourage

welcomed him, and under the awning dispensed talk, food, music
and non-alcoholic refreshments.

No shadow of significance was allowed to dim the flowing periods
or interfere with the interminable courtesies. No reference was made
to the Knights of St John, to the inconvenient return of the Agha,
to the Special Envoy's interest in certain inhabitants of the city, or
to various incidents and inconveniences which had come to light
during the night. There were, perhaps owing to the fact that a princely
gift at the King of France's expense had been dispatched that
morning to the Agha, no hitches at all. Only immediately before
retiring and after presenting Lymond with a copy of the Qur'ân,
tastefully enclosed in a solid gold and pearl box, did Salah Rais,
through his interpreter, murmur something about bullets.

The query died on his lips. Before him on deck, already borne by
his escort, there passed crate after crate, already opened, and revealing the shining balls cradled within. As the procession creaked over
the gangplank and began its journey on shore up to the palace, the
Viceroy rose to bestow his blessing and thanks for the open heart
and generous Christian hand of royal France.

He left; and so did the eighty. On shore, Onophrion and his
minions, aided by the improvident of the town, began to clear off
the feast. Like a well-oiled machine, already rehearsed and well used
to submission, the ship prepared to take rowing stations and leave.
Jerott, standing by the poop rail with Gaultier and Archie, watched
the awnings drawn back, and the pilot depart for the outer harbour
to survey the weather.

In an hour, the ship was clear for departure. Under a cloudy
sky, in a light, lukewarm air, Marthe and Philippa joined the little
band at the poop, and finally Lymond came himself with the captain.
'*Notre homme, avertissez que nous allons partir: que le canon soit
leste pour tirer le coup de partance*. . . .

'*Boute-feu!*' The bark of the cannon. '*Leva lengue!*' Silence. '*Tout le
monde fore du coursier et tout le monde à sa poste!*'

Like puppets, they jumped, thought Philippa. Seamen to the
rambade; pilot to the poop; the *comite* to the coursier, the helmsman to the tiller, the gunners to the prow. Only the slaves, being
chained, had no need to run. At a blast of the whistle, they had
already stripped off their shirts: at another blast, naked to the
waist, they bent forward, the calloused hands repeating their pattern
along the great looms of the oars. The whistle blasted again and
again, and the *Dauphiné* started to move.

Philippa stood on the tabernacle a long time, watching the glittering
white-robed assemblage on the quay blur and dwindle, and the per-
spective of house and college and minaret, of trees and gardens, of the
corsairs' palaces, and the Viceregal Palace and the Kasbah, crowning
it all, become a flat white triangle on the hilly African slopes.

Perhaps because there was, in the end, nowhere else he could go, Lymond stood with them also, without speaking, and watched it pale and recede. Georges Gaultier, standing at his niece Marthe's side, suddenly turned and addressed him. 'You are a hard man, sir, to give firearms to folk such as these. I trust you never have cause to regret it.'

'Your sentiments also, Jerott?' said Lymond. The light voice mocked.

For a moment, Jerott was silent. Then he said, 'There's a saying. *Dio da i panni secondo i freddi.*'

Lymond turned his back on the coast of Algiers. He put his hands on the rail and returned Jerott's stare and said, 'Yes. It was cold. And God gave of his comfort accordingly, but with modifications from outlying quarters. The wheel spindles on those carbines are faulty, and all the key-spanners are missing. . . . Let us,' quoted Francis Crawford largely, with a sudden scathing theatricality, 'let us imitate the swallows, the storks and the cranes, which fetch their circuits yearly, like nomads, and follow the sun.'

And as if he had so commanded it, the light above their heads burst its watery films and drove warmingly on the ridged backs of the rowers, on the seamen and courtiers and officers and on the heads of the two girls standing, brown-headed and fair, on the poop, as the *Dauphiné* turned east, and away from the cold.

6

LEONE

Having worked extremely hard at his job, having fought for his life, and having undergone considerable strain with the briefest of rests in the previous thirty-six hours, Jerott passed that afternoon on board the *Dauphiné* in something of a dream, and at dusk, having seen her safely anchored for the night just off the Barbary coast about thirty miles east of Algiers, he checked that he was no longer wanted, and stumbled below to sink into sleep.

Philippa, watching him go, noticed that Lymond had not yet succumbed. There was, of course, a great deal to do at the outset of a voyage of this length. They had unloaded some of their cargo and taken on fresh stores of fruit and water and livestock, which had to be properly stored. The dirt of the harbour had to be cleaned away, and all the temporary dispositions made for staying in port. They had found two stowaways: Christian slaves who had slipped on board unseen, and these had given rise to concern because recent wholesale defections to visiting French ships had made the Viceroy unduly sensitive to such happenings.

But all these, thought Philippa, were properly the business of the ship's master and of Onophrion. She eyed Lymond as he moved about; wishing she were older; wishing she were a man, and battling, too, with a weight on her conscience. Oonagh was dead. Believing the child too to be dead, Lymond would now make his way direct to the Sublime Porte. But what if the child were alive? What if it had crossed the sea safely, and could be traced through the address the Dame de Doubtance had given her, on the island of Zakynthos?

Go alone with Abernethy, the old woman had said; and she had promised. And what if, after raising false hopes, the child proved after all to have died? She carried her problem into supper, found Lymond was not there, and carried it out again.

Because of the warmth of the night, the tents had not been put up. After the long stint of rowing, the slaves were already half asleep, curled in their chains, although there were lights round the *fougon*, and the smell of food hung on the air. Subdued talk came from the rambade and the benches flanking the galley, where the *chiourme* sat or lay, and she could hear voices below, where the hatch-covers had been opened to let air into the holds. Lymond she found, elbows crossed on the rail beside the unguarded tiller, in complete darkness, staring down at the invisible water. Changing her mind, Philippa turned and began to beat a retreat.

'Philippa?'

He had seen her. She said, 'It's all right. I thought I'd dropped something.'

Lymond said, 'Come here. I want to speak to you. I don't mind company: it's only food I don't want.' He waited until she came slowly up beside him, and then spoke gently. 'You know, Philippa, we can't take you with us: not now. Kate would never forgive me.'

Philippa took a long, shaky breath, and kept her voice steady. 'You mean, now the baby's dead, you don't need me?' she said.

There was a little pause. Then he said, 'Jerott told you?' And as she nodded her head in the dark, 'I see. Yes, that's partly the reason. The other is that the . . . issue between Gabriel and myself has changed in character a little. I'm going to put you on shore at Messina with Fogge and Archie and two of my men, and you'll find your way to Sevigny and home by a route which I'll give you: there are friends of mine all the way.'

'And Marthe?' said Philippa jealously.

'Marthe also, I hope.'

But Philippa, struggling with the implications of all that, was suddenly pierced by another sickening thought. 'You're going to try and kill Gabriel? Now it won't harm the baby?'

There was another little pause. Then Lymond said carefully, 'He must die, Philippa. You must understand that.'

'But he's on Malta. If you touch him, you'll lose your own life.'

'So long as he dies, what does that matter?' said Lymond with sudden impatience. 'In any case, I'm not discussing Malta at present. Even if we don't get a good wind in the morning, we can be in Sicily in two or three days. Make quite sure you're ready, that's all.'

Thinking wildly, Philippa Somerville stared at him, his face no more than a high-lighting of the dark. She was free. She could go to Zakynthos with Archie. But——

But if the child was alive, she would have to trace it before anything happened to Gabriel. Or by the terms of the pact, on Gabriel's death, the child also would die.

Restlessly, Lymond had moved back to the rail. Her first instinct had been right, Philippa thought. Tired probably beyond sleep, he had no prospect of being alone except here, for the short space during which the master was at supper with the rest. She opened her mouth to talk about Zakynthos, and instead turned on her heel, thumped down several ladders, extracted a powder from Archie and a cup of wine from Onophrion, and proceeded to try to turn Jerott out of his cabin.

Jerott, three-quarters asleep, stared at Philippa, glanced at the empty bunk bed beside him and said, 'Well, for God's sake, that's his affair. If he wants to come below, *I* shan't disturb him; I've had enough of him today. Leave him alone.'

Marthe, who had come to watch, stood amused in the doorway

and said, 'She wants to nurse him. It's an interesting experiment. But he has lost his temper so often today, perhaps he has no more to lose.'

His eyes shut, Jerott added his last word. 'Look, Philippa: don't. You can't expect him to behave as he should. You'll regret it, and so will he, afterwards.'

At fifteen, Philippa was immune to that kind of adult abjuration. Stalking out of the cabin, potion in one hand and skirts in the other, she climbed all the ladders up to the poop and marched across to her victim.

He was still there at the rail. She saw the dark sheen of his doublet; and his folded arms, on which his bent head was resting. She said, 'Mr Crawford?' stoutly, and this time there was a pause before he lifted his head, turned and saw her.

He had perhaps been asleep. Certainly, his face was bemused; and at first he didn't seem quite to recognize her. Then he said, '*Oh Christ. The bloody wet-nurse again*,' and, with a vicious blow of the hand that jarred her arm to the shoulder, jerked the heavy cup from her grasp and sent it flying into the sea.

'They said you'd do that,' said Philippa.

He had been going, she thought, to lay hands on her; but at the sound of her voice his arm dropped, and he brushed past instead, without speaking, and left the small deck. She watched him swing along the high gangway going nowhere: to the crowded castle; to the crowded planks at the side, when he suddenly stopped, his hand on the mainmast. A second later, his voice rang out; then the *comite's* whistle shrilled, urgently, again and again and again.

The ship leaped into life. Rattling steps plunged up from the cabins; the master jumped to the tabernacle and somewhere there was the rumble she had come to recognize: the rumble of guns being run out. The ship went suddenly dark, and Archie Abernethy, who had appeared out of nowhere beside her, said, 'He says you're to get down and stay down, until you're tellt to come up.'

Philippa didn't stay to be told twice. She ran, and as she ran, passing Jerott kneeling by the gunroom hatch-cover, she looked quickly over her shoulder.

There, where in the cloud-torn sky the faintest new radiance told of the uprising moon, loomed the dark shape of a ship. A ship painted black. The corsair capital ship Lymond had fooled on the way to Algiers.

*

Jerott had had two hours' sleep when it happened, and he felt like a man half-clubbed to death. He knew, as he effected, at top speed, his share of their practised defence, that if the pirate ship chose to close in, firing, the *Dauphiné* would sink where she lay.

Sails up, oars manned, guns primed and aimed, the corsair had all the searoom and the initiative. She could sink or board as she chose. Jerott wondered, heaving up arquebuses, what Lymond would do to the look-out. But it was hardly the fault of the seaman. Lightless on a black, starless night, the enemy ship might have come nearer yet, unseen but for that late-rising moon.

Still no guns. They were barely in cannon range. Give us another two minutes, thought Jerott, and we'll have our firing-power ready, at least. That was the anchor coming up. The oars were dipping, waiting for orders. Pouring like animals over the gangway, the seamen were taking up positions. Jerott, sprinting round checking crutches, glanced up again, measuring the speed of the adversary.

She hadn't moved. Standing off, just out of firing-range, she had turned to lie head to wind, and, as he watched, the mainsail slid down. Finding Lymond unexpectedly beside him, Jerott said with disbelief, 'She hasn't seen us?'

'The hell she hasn't,' said Lymond shortly; and added, 'Be quiet!' as Jerott opened his mouth to say something. In the darkness Jerott could just make out that he had a spyglass trained on the unmoving ship. Still looking through it, he raised his voice. '*Notre homme!*' and used three well-chosen words when the *comite* came.

Silence invested the *Dauphiné* from tabernacle to prow.

Jerott looked at the Master over Lymond's head, and then back to the pirate. Something was happening. Across the water they could hear voices, thin in the calm of the night, and the echo of another, familiar sound, which was just in the process of stopping. Lymond lowered the spyglass and straightened. 'Well, what's your theory? They've anchored,' he said.

'It *is* the same ship that attacked us?' Jerott got the glass, verified in silence that it was, and added, 'They're doing something aft. That's odd. They've got three-quarters of their complement on the tribord rail. Look at the tilt of her. Unless . . . Christ, is she foundering?' said Jerott, who still very badly needed his sleep.

'Don't be a bloody fool,' said Lymond. 'She's launching her caique, the same as we did a few moments ago.' And, sure enough, a moment later they saw the boat leave the corsair ship's deck, a long black shuttle sliding down the silver loom of the oars and surging broadside into the moon-dazzled waters in a bouquet of spray. Dark figures swarmed down the galley's flank as it settled, and the last aboard the caique turned and shouted.

As the skiff swerved and, in a flashing fishbone of oars, began to drive away from the parent ship, every lamp on the big corsair galley suddenly and miraculously glinted alive. Outlined from poop to rambade, she lay to her anchor at the mouth of the bay, oars shipped, guns silent, crew and officers thronging her rails. And high on the rigging, unrolling in the tremulous wind and burning scarlet and ivory like some heavenly conflagration in the newly lit lamp at the masthead, flew the eight-pointed white cross of Malta, the flag of the Knights of St John.

No one spoke. Beside him, with sharpened perception, Jerott could feel every nerve in Lymond's strained senses tightening. Jerott said, 'It can't be. Francis: Gabriel would never come to meet you like this.'

'Who, then?' said Lymond. And immediately, 'All right. Don't let's dwell on it. Master, we want the women embarked in the caique together with the escort and foodstuffs. Then let the canot down on the port side with an armed welcoming-party. Our guests can transfer into that a safe distance away, and leave their weapons behind. I don't want Greek fire at close range while the capital ship meets one or two friends, and picks us over at leisure.'

'That's all right,' said Jerott. 'Provided I go in the canot.'

It was one of the few arguments he won; and not only, Jerott thought, because he, as a former Knight Hospitaller of St John of Jerusalem, could best verify the claims of another. Lymond had not been prepared for this. A physical contingency he could easily handle: Jerott thought he had almost welcomed the chance for action just now. But for the other kind of crisis he needed time. He had not yet come to terms with what had happened yesterday. Philippa's method had not been the right one. But something was becoming necessary, thought Jerott, to mark the end, once and for all, of that interminable day.

Jerott glanced back, once, at the shadowy spars of the *Dauphiné*, lying still without lights, and gave all his attention henceforth to the long caique swiftly approaching, fully manned and brilliantly lit, with its scarlet pennant fluttering behind. He could see no weapons, nor did the rowers wear armour. The stern lantern shone on the only passenger; a man of middle height; unarmed and richly cloaked, with a dark, bearded face and a jewelled cap on his black hair.

Jerott lowered the spyglass. It was not Gabriel. It was a friend, but a dangerous friend. An exiled Florentine from a brilliant household; a soldier; a seaman; a fanatic; the man who had commanded the French Mediterranean fleet until a year ago when he had to fly for his life, so he claimed, from his rivals at court. This was Leone Strozzi, Prior of Capua, on whom the Grand Master had threatened to fire if he came back to Malta, and who had since been roving the seas, every refuge in Christendom denied him; and preying on infidel and Christian alike.

The boats drew near. Standing up, the exiled Prior in his turn was studying the oncoming canot. The next moment, his voice rang out, in insouciant and horrible English. 'Meestair Blyte! 'Ow are you? We give you a fright?'

'Not as bad, I hope, as the one we gave you, the last time we met,' said Jerott. 'Jump in, and I'll take you to Francis Crawford. Do you know him? We've an embassy to the Sublime Porte.'

The boats met. Without hesitation the Prior stepped from his own into Jerott's, sat down, and switched, with some slight improvement, to French. 'I know him: my brother, better,' he said. 'A year or two ago, I am told, he devastated the flower of France. A drunken *amateur*, who makes music and love *comme un ange*?'

In spite of himself, Jerott grinned. 'No: you've got the wrong man,' he said. 'This is a dedicated Scot with a company of foot and light horse. No drinking, no love and no music. There he is.'

The ladder was down, and Lymond stood at the top, watching them. From the moment the two boats had met, all the *Dauphiné*'s lamps had been lit: they showed Lymond's face quite clearly, as his gaze, faintly derisory, met Jerott's.

'But that is the one!' said Leone Strozzi, Prior of Capua, transferring nimbly from skiff up to galley. 'You hide him from me? It is jealousy, yes? Now I see, my dear Blyte,' said the Prior ebulliently, 'why you have abandoned the Order.' And laughing under his breath, he embraced Lymond on both cheeks, and followed him down below.

A city, an island, a nation had proved too small to contain Leone Strozzi: in the Master's cabin on the *Dauphiné* the walnut panels shivered with his broken Italian–French, his laughter, and the impact of his brutal high spirits.

He had come, it appeared, to apologize. All the world knew now, of course, that the *Dauphiné* was carrying the emissary of France, M. Crawford, whom he had had the happiness to meet once before, at Châteaubriant. But of these things he, Leone Strozzi, had been ignorant: he, the friend of God alone, whom the Constable of France had wished to assassinate; whose family the Emperor Charles wished to see humbled to dust; whom the Order in Malta had pusillanimously turned from its doors. Driven, in his exile, to seek a paltry living in these seas, he would still have removed his tongue at the roots rather than interfere with an emissary of His Grace the Most Christian King of France, or a friend—he trusted he might call M. Crawford a friend?—of the family Strozzi.

'I really must see that our flags are better lit,' said Lymond, smiling. He had not asked either the master or M. Gaultier to be present, and Onophrion had taken it on himself to serve the three men, half filling their glasses with malmsey, to allow for the shallow swing of the boat, and refilling attentively. Jerott, with admiration, watched M. Strozzi drain his second considerable offering before Lymond added, still smiling, 'But how surprising that, knowing your inestimable value, the Emperor should not have tried to entice you under his banner, despite your past unpleasant estrangements. . . .'

The dark, round-eyed face, with its sleek beard and its two Cellini gold earrings, shone with innocent joy. 'But you are perspicacious! The Commander de Martines brought me such an offer: a safe-conduct from the Emperor; permission to land in all Sicilian ports; an income of twelve thousand crowns every year with command of twelve galleys, and the position of Admiral when Andrea Doria shall die.'

'You refused?' said Lymond.

'Hah!' The gold earrings swung. 'This summer, I take prizes of one hundred thousand crowns at sea for myself.' He paused. 'In any case, how could I accept? I who had sworn never to attack my beloved France, however she may have treated me; and whose first duty lies with my Order? . . . I took my Order's advice. In fact, I presented my Order with a gift, an ornament for the altar of St Mary at Philermo, Mr Blyte. I had it made in Messina, and I could ill afford it.' (Jerott saw Lymond's eyebrows lift high and stared solemnly at his wine.) 'It bore,' said Leone Strozzi with reverence, 'the words of St John. You recall? *He came unto his own, and his own received him not.*'

'*Ut ameris Amabilis esto*. . . . And this had an instant effect?'

'The Grand Master refused to see me,' said Strozzi. 'At the time. But today—today I have received a message. I have powerful friends on Malta. I am told that if I land without warning none will prevent me, and my friends will see that I have the honour due to me. I shall return in triumph. I shall bring the Order power and riches; I shall restore it to its former position in the sight of men, and I shall so arm its defences that no Turk will dare sail within sight of Gozo or Malta. . . .'

'Grand Master de Homedes is an old man,' said Lymond. 'The Order owes itself a vigorous hand at the helm.'

He spoke calmly, as always, and Leone Strozzi's darkly animated face showed no dramatic change of expression. But Jerott Blyth, listening, suddenly caught the drift of this conversation and, after staring blankly for a moment at Lymond, abruptly drank off all his wine.

Soft-footed, Onophrion refilled his glass and the Prior's, and paused beside Lymond. Francis Crawford put the flat of his hand over his untouched glass and added, 'There cannot be a great deal of competition?'

The Prior put both his strong, short-fingered hands round his goblet and said, 'Jean de la Valette. Romegas perhaps. De la Sengle; but he is abroad. No. These are gallant Knights all, but the Grand Mastership does not mean a great deal to them. To be head of the Order is a terrible and a lonely position to which not many aspire. It troubles me that sometimes a man may aspire, and prevail, for unworthy reasons.'

'Surely not,' said Jerott, and took a long drink.

There was a little silence. 'I hear,' said Leone Strozzi, Prior of Capua, at length, 'that you have certain papers . . .'

Lymond's blue gaze did not leave him. 'I carry some papers concerning the Order, that is true. I am unhappily discredited myself on Malta at present, and have no means of delivering them to the right quarter.'

'Let us be plain,' said Leone Strozzi. 'These papers concern Graham Reid Malett?'

'By all means, let us be plain,' said Lymond. 'They contain a fully attested indictment against Graham Reid Malett's conduct in Malta and Scotland, supported by M. de Villegagnon and the French Ambassador to the Queen's Grace in Scotland, among others. Under the present régime in the Order, as you know, any accusation against Gabriel is quite useless.'

'But if the present régime were to end? M. Crawford, would you entrust me with these papers?' said Leone Strozzi.

Palpably, the crux of this whole encounter had been reached. Lymond's fingers, which had been caressing his glass, became still, and Jerott, watching the swirling wine, under his breath said, '*Drink it, Francis!*' with muted exasperation. Lymond said, 'I don't entirely see what purpose it would serve. The present Grand Master would ignore or destroy them and your own life would be at considerable risk, I imagine, from Sir Graham.'

The laughing black eyes were cold. Strozzi shrugged. 'The old man is dying. Until he goes, who is to know I have these papers? Then, when the new Grand Master is to be chosen . . .'

'Don't deceive yourself.' With slow deliberation, Lymond pushed his heavy glass away with one finger, and looked up. 'Graham Malett will know in a very short time indeed that this meeting has taken place, and that you are in possession of facts which could harm him. He didn't waste the years he spent on Malta; nor has he wasted his time since he came back this year. There are disciples or paid agents of Graham Malett in a surprising number of places— even aboard my ship, or yours, I expect. I take it that he is a serious contender for the Grand Mastership?'

His lips pursed, Leone Strozzi held out his glass to be refilled, groaned, and said, 'On that island, he is God. They tell me that he spares himself nothing: he works like a madman; he scourges himself with vigils and fastings. Is it right that this hypocrite, this self-seeking tyrant, should so gull a Christian people unopposed?'

'Whom would you put in his place?' said Lymond. In spite of himself, Jerott glanced at him.

Leone Strozzi gave another, extravagant shrug. 'I care not,' he said. 'Any believing man of good faith, however humble, could not but honour Juan de Homedes's shoes. With the help of God I shall expose Graham Malett for what he is. The rest my brother Knights must decide.'

He stopped speaking, and Lymond, studying his hands on the table, did not immediately reply. Jerott, weary and supperless and a little light-headed with wine, wondered if the two long days and nights without sleep had confused Lymond's intelligence. Jerott said, 'Give him the papers. The Order can't harm the Prior of Capua, Francis. And if he does nothing with them until the Grand Master is dead, it gives you time to do all you have to do . . . elsewhere.' Time to find the child, alive or dead, he meant to convey.

But Lymond, ignoring him, spoke to Strozzi. 'In your modesty, sir, you refrain from mentioning your own very strong candidature. As a rival for the Grand Mastership, might not your own interest offset the weight which people might attach to any papers purporting to discredit Gabriel?'

Oh God, thought Jerott. Why not accept the offer, hand over the papers and be glad of it? Why go into all this? But he knew why, and against his reason he knew that this was the quality in Lymond which, through all the ruthlessness and the mockery, fastened him to his side.

Leone Strozzi rose to his feet with a smooth deliberation, a little flush of wine on either dark cheek. 'I believe you insult me? I believe you imply that there is, in Malta or out of it, a living soul who could accuse a member of the House of Strozzi, a cousin of Queens, a nephew of Pontiffs, of falsifying documents for his own ends? Is that what you say?'

'Yes, that is what I say,' said Lymond evenly. 'Is that not exactly what Graham Malett will do?'

Leone Strozzi remained standing. 'And your solution?'

Francis Crawford leaned his colourless head back against the glossy panelling, and lifted his eyes to the Prior's. 'I have no solution,' he said. 'But if I were Leone Strozzi, and I wished to make certain beyond all misadventure that Gabriel never gained control of the Order, I should withdraw my own candidature as a condition of making these papers public.'

The colour increased in the dark, Florentine face, engorging the narrow brow and muscular cheeks and high, vulpine nose. 'And is this,' said Leone Strozzi, 'your condition for delivering them to me?'

'Yes,' said Lymond.

This time the silence was a long one, broken by the angry, uneven breathing of the man standing at Jerott's side. Jerott said nothing. No one needed to stress the perils in the game Lymond was playing. It balanced on a knife-edge, the quick-tempered violent pride of Leone Strozzi, brought face to face with the ultimatum in Lymond's words. Then the Prior of Capua, releasing his breath, pulled out his chair again and sitting down, said, 'And if I were to be elected against my will? A man may make his desires plain, M. Crawford, and Fate may still take a hand.'

It was capitulation. Jerott didn't know if it was what Lymond wanted, but he didn't now care. As Lymond drew breath to reply, Jerott said, 'As a former Knight I can pledge that we understand that. On that basis, I am sure, there can be no reason for withholding these papers.'

Lymond sat up, an edge on his voice. 'On what basis? That M. Strozzi announces that he has no desire to stand as a future Grand Master of the Knights Hospitallers of St John, and then reluctantly allows himself in the event to be over-persuaded?'

Jerott, his cheeks flushed, outstared him. 'Yes,' he said. 'What better chance have you got?'

'None, now,' said Lymond; and rising sharply to his feet, walked round the table. 'M. Strozzi, on these terms the papers are yours. I shall bring them. I have also a favour to ask. I understood you to say that you have been offered safe harbour in Sicilian anchorages, and the Emperor's favour in Sicily?'

'That is true.' Savouring his wine, the Prior of Capua leaned back and smiled.

Lymond said, 'I have some women on board whom I wish conveyed back to France. If I understand you aright, you are now on your way back to Malta with your . . . activities at sea now at an end. Might I beg that you take these women on board, with a suitable escort, and land them at Messina for me, with whatever safe-conduct the Governor can provide for their journey? As an Ambassador of France, you will understand, my approaches to the Governor might be less successful.'

Leone Strozzi did not ask if this were another condition. Expansively: 'But of course! This will be my especial care,' said the Prior. 'As if they were your mother, your sister, they shall be treated.'

Lymond stared at him. Then: 'Forgive me. I shall get the papers,' he said; and swung out.

Leone Strozzi was smiling at Jerott. 'A formidable master. He has turned very grim, *si*? You did not know him when he sowed his wild oats? My brother Piero tells a story of a wedding—was it a boy called Will Scott?—and a flock of sheep who routed an army.'

'Will Scott is dead,' said Jerott. 'I've been with Lymond for the last eighteen months.'

'And it is true?' said the Prior. 'No laughter? No drinking? No love?'

Onophrion, on Lymond's orders, had gone below to prepare Philippa and Marthe and the rest for their journey: Strozzi and he were alone. Jerott had no desire to discuss Lymond's affairs. But it was no undue distortion, he thought, as he smiled and shrugged, of Lymond's life in the last eighteen months. Only once in all that time had he, Jerott, seen him affected by drink; and then his reasons had been strictly professional. What happened afterwards, Jerott preferred to forget. And as for women, apart from that one brief episode in Baden, he knew of only two. One had been a child at fifteen: Gabriel's sister. The other, by hearsay only, had been Oonagh O'Dwyer. And each, in its way, had been a single, cold-blooded act of expediency. Aloud, Jerott said, 'It isn't as monotonous as it sounds.'

'On the other hand,' said Leone Strozzi, playing with his glass, 'one does not beget a bastard out of thin air. I hear he is offering incredible rewards for the return of some child—a pawn of prestige, I assume, in his feud with Gabriel. Tell me, Blyte—in what does this quarrel lie; this enmity between M. Crawford and Sir Graham?'

The night air coming through the open doorway was cold. Jerott shivered a little and rose to pour more wine for the Prior and himself. He said, 'It is more than personal enmity, M. Strozzi. Graham Malett is an intelligent, unstable man who is desperate for power. He has to be stopped.'

'Oh, of course,' said Leone Strozzi. 'But why by the gloomily reformed M. Crawford in particular? Were they rivals for power? Is it revenge, or jealousy, or envy, or slighted love even? M. d'Enghien's pursuit of your friend was notorious, I am told. . . .' He raised his eyebrows at Jerott's darkened, magnificent face. 'Such a severe *masculine* aura about the *Dauphiné*. Even the women, one discovers, are to be put off.'

Jerott Blyth looked at the table, took a very deep breath and, in a voice only a little thickened by malmsey and the desire to kick M. Leone Strozzi into the sea, said, 'As you will see when the papers come, there is proof that Graham Malett had been betraying the Order for some time to the Turks while on Malta. He then went to Scotland and made an attempt to take control of the very efficient fighting arm we—Mr Crawford had built up; and finally of the nation itself. It was through Mr Crawford that these threats came to nothing. In the process, Graham Malett's own sister died, and a great many of our own friends. Once, perhaps, Graham Malett hoped to make of Lymond more than a friend. He knows better now.'

'And the child?'

'It is, as you say, a pawn. If Graham Malett dies, the child dies. It was by this threat that he was able to escape unhurt from Scotland.'

Leone Strozzi's cynical black eyes, smiling, narrowed. 'One might set such store upon the heir to a land or a title. But a nameless bastard . . . ? Perhaps your Mr Crawford is not so stable as we judge, after all.'

'It is a matter of opinion,' Jerott Blyth said quietly. Through a crashing headache, he listened to the Prior of Capua talking until Lymond arrived, impeccably civil, with the papers, followed closely by Onophrion.

Mr Zitwitz was discomfited. To Lymond's brief question, he replied in a low voice. 'Miss Somerville is preparing, sir, and will be ready almost immediately, with her maid and the others. I regret exceedingly that a slight awkwardness has ensued with the other young lady.'

'Mlle Marthe? What?'

'She will not go, sir,' said Onophrion, his voice even more muted. 'I can by no means persuade her to leave this ship for the Prior's. She insists on continuing her journey with M. Gaultier and the gift for the Sultan. You will require to speak to her, sir.'

'Yes. Well,' said Lymond, turning to Leone Strozzi, 'it seems that we should be able to send you the ladies within the next hour. If meantime you feel you must return to your ship, we shall not detain you.'

'I must indeed leave,' said the Prior, smiling again. He finished placing the precious papers in his purse—the papers which, in due course, were to blacken Gabriel's name with the Order—and rising, took his filled glass for the last time in his hand. 'Mr Crawford, in circles less trustworthy than these, it is considered an insult, if not a sign of possible danger, when one's host refuses to join his guests in their cups. You are a man, perhaps, with whom stronger wines fail to agree. But you will not refuse to drain that glass of yours, I trust, once at least, to mark our present transaction?'

Under the swaying, overhead lamp, Lymond's face was civilly sceptical. 'I am really past the age,' he said pleasantly, 'when I have to prove myself a man, by drinking or any other means. But I should not like to be lacking in courtesy. Your health, Signor Strozzi.' And throwing back his head, he did in fact drain his glass.

Jerott poured him another, filled and running crazily over, when they returned after seeing the Prior back to his ship, and for the second time that night Lymond knocked it spinning out of his way to crash on the smooth deck between them, the pieces flicking brokenly to and fro in the rolling tide of the wine. Lymond said, 'I rather think *one* of us drunk is sufficient.'

'If I hadn't been drunk,' said Jerott, annoyed, 'Leone Strozzi wouldn't have gone off with those papers.'

Slowly, Lymond rested a hand on the table and found his way round to his seat. 'Do you believe he will make a good Grand Master?'

'He's a brilliant soldier and seaman, and a fine defence engineer. He's ambitious, but he's also an active leader, and that they desperately need.'

Lymond said, 'He has a feud with Cosimo de Medici to which he

and his brother have dedicated their lives. You know that as well
as I do. He will wield the Order of St John like an assassin's knife
for his own private purposes. He has not the stature to resist it.'

Jerott propped his head on his two hands, and surveyed Lymond
with his tired eyes. 'He thinks your quarrel with Gabriel is of the
same order.'

'Perhaps it is,' said Lymond. He said, without looking up, 'I am
going to follow Strozzi to Malta. That is why I must have the
women out of the way.'

Jerott's hands crashed on the table. 'But that is insane! You said
as much yourself, before we set out! You are stepping on Gabriel's
own territory, in the reign of a Grand Master who hates everything
French, and on the heels of the indictment Strozzi is carrying. It's a
folly that satisfies nothing but your own need for action. . . .
Look . . .' With an unsteady hand and a great deal of stubborn
determination, Jerott Blyth found another fresh glass, uplifted the
great flask of malmsey, poured, with uncertain success, a quantity
of the one into the other, and pushed it for the second time between
the open, unmoving hands of the man sitting opposite. 'Drink,
Francis. You must: believe me. Let go, and drink; and give yourself
a few hours of peace.'

An hour later, Philippa, with all her baggage, with Fogge, with
Archie Abernethy and four stout men-at-arms, crossed the tabernacle on her way down to the caique. She was being sent home.
Onophrion had told her; and had told her too, doubtfully, what she
had wanted to know about Leone Strozzi's inexplicable visit. Into
his hands, Lymond had confided the proof of Gabriel's villainy.
Gabriel's exposure was imminent, but not his death at Lymond's
hands. She was free of that dread; free to take what time she needed
to follow this frail and unlikely clue; to go to Zakynthos, if she
could prevail on Archie to take her; and to seek the child of whom
the Dame de Doubtance had spoken.

She was glad to go. Glad, in spite of herself, to be spared the
society of Marthe, and achingly glad to be plucked from the unhappy
muddle between herself and her mother's strange friend, Mr Crawford. *Never again*, she had said to herself over and over, as she sat
shivering in the longboat beside Marthe, with the sea lapping round
them, waiting for the corsair's guns to start firing, and the signal
which would mean their boat would be set rowing, escaping in the
dark night to the Tunisian shore while the *Dauphiné* lay dwindling
behind them. Never again, if she lived to escape from all this, would
she force sympathy or arch female attentions on a man, whatever
his seniority.

Steeling herself to meet Lymond again, for the formal farewells,
she was surprised and also shamefully relieved when Onophrion
hesitated, and then shook his head. 'Mademoiselle, if you will

permit, I think it better to send your leave-taking messages through me.'

'Why?' said Philippa. She liked Onophrion.

Onophrion coughed. 'It is merely that . . . gentlemen under stress are sometimes under the necessity of taking certain steps . . . incompatible with the usages of polite female society.'

Philippa's brown eyes shone with dawning intelligence. 'Mr Crawford is drunk?'

'I trust so, mademoiselle,' said Onophrion.

The lamp had burned low in the captain's cabin when Philippa passed, a moment or two later, and she did not care to stop and look in. Only she had an impression of broken glass, and a foetid aroma of malmsey, and of two hands, clasped outflung on the table, with a still head resting between them. It was the last memory of the *Dauphiné* she carried away with her: of that, and of a blow which numbed her arm to the shoulder. *Oh, Christ*, he had said. *It's the bloody wet-nurse again.*

Philippa climbed down their rotten ladder and sat in their rotten caique and swallowed her tears all the way across to the ship of M. Leone Strozzi, Prior of Capua and Knight Hospitaller of the Order of St John.

Coming on deck a little time later, Marthe had none of Philippa's compunction. She stopped in the captain's doorway, and studied, smiling a little, the ruined table within, and the man lying stupefied in the shadows. In his turn, watching her from where he leaned, arms folded, against the dark panelling, Lymond spoke. 'You wanted to see me?'

She covered her mistake like a veteran. For a moment the blue eyes widened and the clear brow ridged in something like a genuine alarm. Then, irony in her voice, Marthe said, 'My congratulations. Rumour has lied.'

Following her gaze to the table: 'Keep your congratulations, perhaps, for Mr Blyth,' said Lymond dryly. 'I am told you would prefer to remain on the *Dauphiné* and I regret that this is not possible. If you will kindly pack, the caique is leaving at midnight.'

'The caique has left,' said Marthe.

'By whose orders?'

'By mine. I told the Master,' said Marthe, 'that you had decided to send Miss Philippa and her entourage only. She's half-way there now.'

'M. Viénot!' Soft though the call was, the captain answered immediately. 'M. le Comte?'

'From this moment, you accept no indirect orders from me without verifying them, and no orders at all from Mlle Marthe. Signal the Prior's galley, and when the caique returns, see that Mlle Marthe and her luggage are placed in it. You might also ask Salablanca to remove M. Blyth to his cabin.'

'You are proposing to use force?' said Marthe. Her hair, combed out over her shoulders, lay on her bedgown outlined in silver from the deck lamps behind her: her voice expressed nothing but a kind of wary contempt.

'I see no need. I mean to make landing on Malta,' said Lymond. 'It is a private matter, and as far as you and M. Gaultier are concerned the official embassy ends here. Your responsibility for the spinet is also therefore at an end, and since there is an element of danger, I see no point in exposing you needlessly. You will have, I hope, a safe and comfortable journey home.'

'And my uncle?' said Marthe.

'Has expressed a preference to continue on board meanwhile. As far as he is concerned, you are your own mistress. As far as I am concerned, you are not.'

'And if the spinet sinks to a watery grave,' said Marthe, 'who will recompense the King and the Sultan? Or have you providently amassed a second fortune for that?'

'I am hoping it won't immediately concern me,' said Lymond. He gathered the door-curtain in his hand. 'You have perhaps twenty minutes to pack.' Then, as she stood unmoving, the mocking smile still on her lips, he said with the same weary courtesy, 'Mademoiselle. There is nothing personal in this. If I could take you, believe me, I should. Since I have decided against it, you have really no rational alternative. I can have you tied and carried on board; you can threaten and even carry out suicide; you could possibly damage me or my men. These would be the petty exchanges of juveniles; and we are not juveniles. . . . Please pack quietly, and go.'

'And your oath, on Gabriel's altar in the Cathedral of St Giles?' Marthe said in her pleasant, identical voice. 'Was that a juvenile foolishness too?'

There was a long silence. The woollen door-curtain, released from Lymond's hand, swung to across the cold doorway and he smoothed its folds, unseeing, with gentle fingers. Without turning, he said, 'Very few people know of that.'

'I am one of them,' she said; and, watching his back, continued softly to speak. 'Nor am I fool enough to believe that child is dead, whatever Mr Blyth tried to pretend. I know the truth now. Up to yesterday, your first duty was to the woman and boy. Now it is to the boy. If you reach any other decision, it is due to Gabriel's strength and your own moral vapidity.' And as he wheeled round, unamused, she spoke again, with deliberation, in the tongue so like his own.

'What have you learned from life, that you cannot face facts? What happened in Algiers that is so paralysing that your mind cannot work through it? Shall I tell you?' Between the strands of pale hair, the pale, clever face blazed into the blank face of the man.

'Shall I tell you? By Gabriel's orders, they took your lover, living or dead, and they flayed her. So that there might be none of her essence to bury, they flung what was left to the dogs. The skin they kept; and painted, and stuffed with wool, hair and straw, and set as in life, where you would be certain to find it. . . .

'There is your picture. Acknowledge it. Acknowledge, too, that she was not the first to suffer it, and will not be the last. That she was ill, and did not want to survive. And that, from what you were told, it seems likely that she either died by her own hand or was killed before the flaying.

'The moment of her death was *that* moment, cleaner than the death of old age. What happened later was nothing to Oonagh. Where would you have found her a grave? What dignity did she have that was not of the spirit? What happened later was aimed not at her, but at you. And you are now doing precisely what Gabriel meant you to do.'

She paused. 'There is a saying. '*O Bhikshu! empty this boat! If emptied, it will go quickly. Having cut off passion and hatred, thou wilt go to Nirvâna.*' It is not a time for emotion. You are facing east, and you cannot fight the East with emotion; only with your brain and your soul.'

The lamp flickered. Motionless in the gathering darkness, his head pressed against the doorpost, his face turned fully away, he gave no sign whether her words had reached him. Whether he did not choose to speak, or found speech physically impossible, no one could have told. The silence dragged on. Breaking it, eventually, herself, Marthe said quietly, 'Your other problem, of course, is myself. You won't solve that either, by dismissing me as if I had never existed. You may consider that you are sending me ashore in my own interests, but I put it to you that you are not. I am prepared to risk my life by staying. You must find the manhood to allow me to stay.'

Lymond straightened. Turning his head until the bruised, heavy blue eyes looked into the blue eyes of Marthe, he said, 'Who are you?' His voice was exhausted.

Marthe's, cool and articulate, did not alter at all. 'My name is Marthe.'

'What is your other name?'

'The name of my father.'

'And who is your father?'

The slender, strongly made shoulders sketched a shrug. 'Who knows? He had no ship and no money; or if he had, he found better employment for both than in looking for me. Like your son, I am a bastard.'

'No, my dear,' said Lymond. 'Forgive me. . . . But I think you are a bastard like nobody else.' And brushing past her, he walked up into the solitary deck of the poop.

When the longboat came from Strozzi requesting his passenger, he sent it back empty.

He stayed alone on the poop for a long time, and it was nearly dawn when, moving carefully, he walked down to his cabin. It was no surprise to find Salablanca there. Lymond said, 'Tell the master in the morning we are not going to Malta. He is to make straight for Djerba instead.' And walking past the slumbering Jerott, rolled on to his own neatly made bunk, and was still.

7

BÔNE AND MONASTIR

In these tart waters, there came to the *Dauphiné* a spring Jerott Blyth was never to forget.

They were no longer travelling direct to Constantinople, but instead following the track of an unknown child in a journey which might take them anywhere. And now they knew that, step by step, they had to expect direct opposition on Gabriel's behalf.

Summoning them all to the tabernacle on the day after that encounter with Leone Strozzi, Francis Crawford had made sure there was no misunderstanding about that, and had given them all, once more, a chance to withdraw from the voyage.

None had taken it. Marthe and Gaultier, Jerott supposed, had business interests they could pursue in the Levant, whatever the fate of the spinet. Onophrion perhaps had not yet given up hope of seeing his new master disembark, groomed and painted at the Golden Horn in the tournure so carefully furnished. And he, Jerott, remained for some reasons he knew, and some he would not admit to himself.

Lymond did not make it easy. His dry voice during that meeting still rang, on occasion, in Jerott's head. 'I suggest, if you come with me, that you remove from your minds the image of a live human child. We are going to be brought literally hundreds of these, now the size of the reward is known. We are going, if I know Gabriel, to be shown disease and poverty and young children in distress unimaginable. If you are coming, Jerott, you must recognize that *nothing can be done for these*. They can't eat money. We can supply them with food for one meal and medicine for one day and it will do nothing but spin out their misery by those few hours longer. . . .

'We are looking for one object, which happens to be the key to Graham Malett's destruction. That is all.'

'If that is all,' had said Jerott, 'why look for it at all?'

'Now that,' Lymond had said, 'is a very good point. I seem to remember making it myself, in fact, last night. Mlle Marthe persuaded me differently. That is why I am now warning you all, Mlle Marthe included, against sentimentality. We are looking for a pawn. And if we succeed in taking it, Gabriel's pride will be pledged, wherever he is, in attempting to recover it. That attempt, I trust, he will not survive.'

Silent so far, Onophrion Zitwitz had raised his sonorous voice. 'On what,' he had asked, 'does a child of one year endeavour to feed?'

'Does it matter?' Jerott Blyth had said bitterly.

The days that followed, Jerott passed in the routine concerns of the voyage, in perfecting with Lymond and Salablanca what he already had of Arabic and of Turkish; and in drinking.

To Lymond's single disparaging comment on this last, he had answered without civility. 'I've had enough of obedience, chastity, sobriety and poverty. Other men are not frigid, Francis.'

'I'm sure you're right,' said Lymond. 'If you find this whole project unbearably irritating, there is not the slightest reason why you should stay. What else do you find so inflaming? Marthe?'

In spite of himself, Jerott grinned. 'There's a girl who hates the sight of you.'

'She hates, if you notice, anything masculine. I can only recommend that you don't allow yourself to be drawn to her. And that you either stop drinking, or leave.'

Jerott said nothing until the indifferent gaze, returning, rested on him. Then he said, 'Do you mean that?'

'Yes,' said Lymond pleasantly. 'I mean it. And you can disregard any other conversations we have had on this subject. If you're desperate for women, you can disembark and buy a Berber slut with a ring through her nose, to the spoil of kissing, tomorrow. No doubt you'll find it easy to buy a quick passage home.'

High on his cheekbones, the blood stained Jerott's skin. But he said caustically, 'I think I might succeed in controlling my ravening hunger. But if I want to drink, I'll drink, Francis; whether it pleases you or not. If you want me off, put me off. Otherwise, you'll just have to put up with it, won't you?' And he walked out.

Their first official stop was at Bône, although they put off a skiff at Cape Tedele and at Gigeri. The peculiar difficulty of this search was so obvious that it needed no stressing. Apart from Algiers and Bône and one or two others, the rest of the harbours on this coast were closed to them, because they had been taken back by the Emperor in the fighting of the last two or three years, and now came under the Crown of Castile. And the Emperor, of course, was the sworn enemy of France. So Susa, Monastir, Mehedia, the fort of Calibia and most of Tunis itself were out of bounds to the *Dauphiné*. The only harbours she could frequent were those which paid tribute to Algiers. And from there, undetected if possible, the investigation would have to be prosecuted inland to the forbidden towns under Spain.

They had one clue: the camel-trader Ali-Rashid. That he had gone through Bône all these weeks ago Salablanca had discovered on these quiet shore-going visits, along the dunes and sandy cliffs east of Algiers. One moonlit evening off Tigzirt, Jerott had gone part of the way with him, drawn by the silvered Roman pillars standing above the sand, and had found himself wading ashore through the streets of the drowned city of Iomnium, with weeded carving pricking his fingers, and phosphorescent life rolling in clouds of green fire under sculptured black arches. It was there, in the lee of the mountains, that Salablanca heard that the trader had passed through, after Dragut had gone, in the autumn. It was a cold trail they were following.

It was there, too, that Jerott, in vinous and melancholy solitude on the aft deck at night, saw Marthe slipping in from the sea, her robe incandescent in the moon, and her hair fronding her shoulders like the dark weeds of Iomnium. 'Salablanca told me. I had to see it,' she said. 'Look.' And she opened her hands.

Blurred by the abrasive seas and disfigured with molluscs, a grey, once-marble cupid lay in her palms, its wings honeycombed, its eyes hollow and vacant. Her own, staring at it, had lost all remembrance of herself: her breathless young eagerness was something Jerott remembered once in Francis Crawford, before the years of disenchantment ground it away. 'So the sea, at least, will yield you its delights,' Jerott said. 'I thought you were perhaps like the Sarmates, who might not lie with a man till they had first killed one in battle.'

Like a rippling conch in the moonlight, her fingers closed fast on their prize. 'Must you spoil it? Must you spoil everything?' she said. And turning abruptly in her dark runnels of wet, was instantly gone.

Jerott stayed, with the explicit intention of finding a new flask of wine and emptying it, before he went down below.

The Cadi at Bône was a renegade Christian, who sent them bread, roast mutton and the regrettable speciality of the area, *macolique*, or platters of paste, meal, onions and bony pullets in sauce. Onophrion, receiving them, shrank a little and disappeared while Lymond was effusively thanking the Cadi's emissary: they never saw the platter again.

Next day, while Lymond made his ceremonial call at the Cadi's house, Jerott and Salablanca interviewed two hundred children between them.

Bône, standing lop-sided on high, ragged rocks, had in its time been a great corsair port, and had still a good fortress and harbour, a fine mosque to which the Cadi's house was attached, and the broken ruins on the foreshore of the great city of Hippo. In two sackings, the town itself had shrunk to three hundred poor houses, but there were good wells on the lower, southern side of the town and fertile ground just outside it. No one in Bône was starving though none, as they stood in their robes, black and white, brown and striped; in the thick, carpet-like textures of the desert, and the muslin of the Cadi's officials, showed the untroubled bloom of high-spirited health.

The people of Tedele had been gay, Salablanca had told them. The people who thronged the quayside at Bône as Salablanca began to shepherd them to the site he and Jerott had chosen were anxious, vociferous, sarcastic, aggressive, derisive, beseeching and, some of them, silent. Among the last were the women who accompanied their menfolk, heads folded in cotton, eyes downcast above the *yaşmak*. Jerott, grim-faced, found he had no words for the women. It was Salablanca, walking firmly among them, who was saying gently over and over, 'There will be money; it is so. The Efendi is just. Bring your children over here. The children will be examined over here. . . .'

All along the coast from Algiers, Salablanca had spread the word. And long before that, carried by the fishing-boats and the raiders, Lymond's message had reached the Barbary coast. A yellow-haired, blue-eyed child named Khaireddin, born in Djerba the previous ·spring to a black-haired *giáur* taken prisoner from Gozo by Dragut Rais, and bearing his brand, was sought, said the message, by a Christian Efendi who would pay gold for delivery of the unquestioned child to him, alive.

And to that, since, had been added the scraps of knowledge they had. That in Djerba the child had been nursed by a negress called Kedi in the harem ruled by Dragut Rais's mistress Güzel. That from Djerba, child and mother had been taken to Algiers, where both had been sold on Dragut's departure for Prevesa in the autumn. And that before the mother's death, the child had been sold, through one Shakib, to Ali-Rashid the camel-trader.

But that last, Jerott knew, had not been made public. And, looking around him in the open space they had chosen, far from where the *Dauphiné* lay berthed, he wondered how much of the original message had been understood. Children abounded. Piccolo to the bass stridencies of protest and acclaim by their sires, children cried and laughed, screamed and whimpered. Under the mild, grey sky scraps of bare flesh rolled and crawled and staggered among the swathed and sheeted adults: flesh coloured from grey-white to coffee; flesh supine in bundles and baskets or across sheeted knees; flesh ragged-shirted and mobile. Lured by the incense of silver, families had crossed the mountains, by mule or donkey or camel, to deliver their offering. Others, infected by the disease of excitement, had snatched up a child that morning from tent or hut or the bare sand itself, and brought it boldly to show. The two hundred children now being brought to Jerott and Salablanca, one by one, ranged from the shadowy head and curved plastic limbs of the infant to the firm walking toddler, shouting in Arabic the dark hair curling over his infested dark skin.

Jerott had been afraid it would be impossible. It was not. All but eighteen of these children had dark hair. And of the three fair-haired boys with blue eyes, only one was remotely near the right age.

It was wrapped in rags in a woman's arms, and lay staring un-seeing, its blond skin flaccid and its breathing shallow and harsh.

101

Jerott said, 'This child is sick. What is its name, and where was it born?'

'It was born in Djerba, Efendi. I have nursed him for Dragut Rais himself, and the great lord had him branded. See!' And bending, the woman turned back the rags.

His guts rising within him, Jerott looked at the raw and glistening flesh thus revealed. '*When was that done?*'

'In October, Efendi. Before Dragut Rais left.' Her brows, drawing together as she closed the child's covering over its wound, were as fair as the baby's.

Jerott said gently, 'If the Imám here allows it, wilt thou unveil?'

She was frightened. The blue eyes flickered from Jerott to Salablanca and back. 'Wherefore, unveil?'

'It is for the child,' said Jerott. Without looking at it, he could hear the sawing tick of its breath.

'It is for the money? The child will have money if I unveil?'

Forgetful of all Lymond had said, Jerott opened his lips. It was Salablanca who spoke, with stern compassion. 'He can have none if thou wilt not.'

She would have needed little persuasion anyway, Jerott supposed. It was already unseemly that alone she had come and spoken with men, and infidels moreover. But there were no tears on her face, which was fair and heavy and comely, and the exact print of the child's. Again, Salablanca said what had to be said. 'Alas! It is the son of a black-haired *giáur* woman we seek. Thou hast a fine boy: see to him.' And, bending, he assisted Jerott to rise, with an iron hand round his arm, and with that same grip, murmuring apology in Spanish under his breath, he drew Jerott from the place.

The crowd, disappointed, ran alongside them as they returned to the ship, and but for the Imám, sent for at first light that morning, they might have had more trouble than they did. The fair-haired woman and the baby, lost in the swirl, Jerott did not catch sight of again.

It was not Salablanca's fault. His rush of urgent apologies Jerott brushed aside when they were installed once more aboard; but he could not discuss it with Onophrion or the Gaultiers except for conveying, curtly, that he had been unsuccessful. Jerott sat stiff-necked in his cabin and was unaware of time passing until he looked up and saw Lymond, returned, before him, his jewels dimly sparkling in the seeping of late afternoon light; and heard him say dryly, 'My apologies, Jerott. Next time I shall do it myself.' And walking forward, as he flung his cap on the bed and began to untie his pale doublet, Lymond added, 'You're sober. Was it so bad?'

Jerott spoke with the raw gristle of his throat. 'They are mutilating the children.'

'They mutilated one child. Now they know it is unacceptable, they won't do it again. You understand, Jerott, that if we pay these people anything, there will be a thousand children at the next station, and half of them wilfully injured?'

'I understand it all,' said Jerott. 'Since you won't fight face to face, you and Gabriel are using children as weapons. Or is that sentimental?'

'It is sweeping, certainly,' said Lymond. 'I suggest you either try to forget it, or apply your mind to it properly.' He pulled another, plain tunic over his head, picked up his belt and said, 'I have traced Ali-Rashid to a village just south of Monastir. The quickest way from here is to ride. The *Dauphiné* will sail on to Pantelleria to-morrow and hover off Monastir, and then Djerba, waiting. You can go with her. Salablanca and I shall of course be ostensibly on board, but in fact we shall go ashore here before dawn. There are horses bought ready: we are joining a group of pilgrims and traders.'

Jerott said, 'There is no need for another summons of children if Ali-Rashid has the baby?'

His weariness barely disguised, Lymond answered him. 'Jerott. We are the puppets, and we are being encouraged to dance. If Ali-Rashid possesses that child, it will be under circumstances of distress and humiliation every bit as deliberate as today's. There is no room on this journey for the sensitive flower. I have said this before. The boy is a pawn. The piece we must take is Gabriel.'

*

It was not a large caravan which left Bône at dawn the next day going east: perhaps a hundred in all, of all nationalities, mounted on mules, on small Arab horses, on camels, with sumpter-animals following, and a small escort of Janissaries. Their business and their destinations were diverse: they travelled together for one purpose only: safety. You did not travel in ones and twos on the Barbary coast.

Despite all he had said, Jerott joined it. In plain dark frieze, like Lymond's, and accompanied by Salablanca, with some food, a goat-skin flask and essential clothes in their saddlebags, he mounted the horses Salablanca had bought for them and in the semi-dark, with none to challenge their identity, they rode out of Bône and through the melon-patches, the date palms and the fig trees that grew darkly around it.

'You speak Italian. We are a Venetian botanical party,' was all Lymond had said. And when a dark-skinned figure reined in beside him and began asking questions, Jerott did speak Italian, and sig-nalled, elaborately, for Salablanca to translate. Himself, he had no need to wait for a translation. 'The signor's brother rides at the head of the column,' was what the stranger was saying. 'Does the signor not wish to join him?'

'*My brother?*' Jerott said.

Noiselessly, Lymond materialized beside him. 'No. My young brother, is it not? Indeed, it is my wish to speak to him, and we thank you for your courtesy. We shall ride forward and join him.'

And as the horseman grinned, saluted and rode back to his place, Lymond added, undisturbed, 'Why so inconceivably perplexed? It's not a hard riddle. Consider. Who, stretching the imagination of course to its most grotesque outer limits, might be taken for my younger brother, if dressed in boy's clothing?'

'*Marthe?*' said Jerott.

'The nubile Marthe,' Lymond agreed. 'Than whom there is not in this hundred mile a feater bawd. Let's surprise her. Let's take her with us.'

In boots, doublet and cloak, with her yellow hair bundled under a cap like a callow schoolgirl defying her tutor, she should have looked mildly ridiculous; in fact, thought Jerott, it was probably Lymond's concern to make her so. But there was nothing childish about the cold hostility in her face as she waited for them, riding up to evict her, or her lack of concern as soon as she realized Lymond would make no effort to send her back to the ship.

Lymond did not let her off easily. Riding beside her: 'It's a very *pretty* costume,' he said. 'What are you hoping will happen?'

'I have some work to do for my uncle. With some races it is impossible to do business if you are a woman. With such people, or with the more foolish or excitable man, I find it simpler dressed like this.'

'Simpler for what?' said Lymond. 'In these parts, you're more apt to find the excitable men waiting lined up in queues.'

'I stand corrected,' said Marthe. 'But then, *sua quique voluptas.* You know so much more of all that than I do.'

'*Incidi in Scyllam, cupiens vitare Charibdim.* Who are *you* running from?' said Lymond. 'Your father?'

'You are welcome to think so. If you will accept the corollary,' said Marthe; and Francis Crawford, smiling in the brightening dawn, his hands closed on his reins, said, 'Pax. We can bring each other too quickly, perhaps, below the cuticle. Let us advance, as the man said, and praise the Almighty, who infused unspeakable jollity into all this our camp.'

Thereafter, in wary silence, they rode all four side by side.

Afterwards, Jerott had little clear recollection of that ride. Fields planted with corn and grazings of pale cattle and sheep gave way to light sandy plains and marshes and rocky, scrub-covered hills. Primitive villages, melting one into the other, left an impression only of filth, and smell, and a scattering of chickens and goats, and naked children, smeared grey with mud. Sometimes there was cultivation: a melon patch, a windmill.

Sometimes, outside a small town, they came across a group of young slaves, their smooth dark skins naked to the waist, washing linen in a thick stream, chattering as they pounded. They stood to watch as the column rode past, their white teeth smiling, their necks and wrists and ankles enclosed in great circles of latten, studded with glass gems. And sometimes, among the plodding groups of robed figures with their slow, laden asses, there would be a string of Moors on their saddleless Barbary horses with only rope for a bit. They came and went quickly, naked too but for their white aprons and linen cloth rolled round their dark heads and under their chins, in a glitter of long javelins, and knives.

At night, Salablanca, riding ahead, would find them a cabin to stay in, and would have the room filled with fresh straw and their mats laid, and a wood fire burning when the rest of the caravan came up, while the family squatted outside in the dark, under threadbare blankets, through the chilly spring night. Twice, Marthe left them; both times during daylight to call on some usurer friend of Gaultier's in one of the walled towns they visited. And Salablanca, prompted by Lymond, was everywhere; talking, smiling, asking questions.

They were following, without doubt, Jerott knew, in the footsteps of Ali-Rashid. And it seemed that, as Lymond dispassionately remarked, they were being allowed to catch up with him. In time, Jerott was to come to believe, it was this feeling of predestination, of having their course unalterably laid out for them, leading them inescapably to whatever doom Gabriel might plan, that was their greatest affliction.

'Of course. The carrot before the donkey,' Lymond replied at once to this surmise. 'But as long as we are following, at least the carrot is there. And one day, if we are audacious and forceful, we might capture the stick.'

They caught up with Ali-Rashid, as had been predicted, just outside Monastir, on the great western road, the Roman highway which still ran between Tunis and Tripoli.

It was dusk, and they had almost reached their stopping-place for the night, when they saw the encampment. It looked at first like one of the several they had met already, of traders bound for Guinea to buy slaves, and pepper and gold, set out in the familiar pattern: the tents of the women and children in the middle, with the flocks and the cattle next, and the camels, the horses and the dogs last, with a ring of bonfires outside. Since passing La Calle they had been in lion country, and the hunters with the caravan had ceased riding out at dawn to bring back antelope and gazelle for the pot.

Now, as they approached warily, Jerott saw that there was something quite different about the design of the camp ahead. The tents were few but the number of fires seemed immense. Then he saw that the dark patches within the fires, which he had taken for the familiar *kermes*, the scrub-oak, were in fact animals; and as the mild wind shifted, and the sudden stench came unmistakably to his senses, he identified them beyond doubt. Camels, in extremely large numbers, and with only a small number of riders. Ali-Rashid, who else?

They stopped that night within sight of the other camp, and, leaving Marthe with Salablanca, Lymond rode over immediately to the camel-trader, Jerott beside him. Others were there before them, examining the animals and holding spasmodic conversation with the traders: there were no more than six of these last, Jerott saw; and the senior, Ali-Rashid himself, a gross, bearded man wearing a skull-cap wrapped about, Turkish-style, with some blue striped cotton, and a red, frogged coat under his blanket-like cloak. Jerott, used to the subdued tones preferred by the Moors, wondered what nationality the man was. But when he spoke, sitting crosslegged with a dish of stewed mutton resting under his great belly, the dialect was Arabic. He ate noisily, without offering to share with his visitors, and when the last of these moved away, Lymond crossed to the stained Cairo matting and, saluting quietly, dropped down beside him.

Jerott did not see the sum of money which changed hands at the end of that conversation, but from the camel-trader's sudden excess of affability and the manner in which, at the end, he heaved himself to his feet, clapping his hands for his boys and attempting to press on them couscous and spirits and, finally, the services of one of his drovers, he understood that Lymond had not been niggardly.

Lymond himself, refusing briefly, stood up and said to Jerott, 'He was paid to seek out the child and to buy it. He was then told to get rid of it any way he cared after three weeks. Just about the end of that time a family of Bedouin caught up with him and bought the child from him in return for some *kif*. He didn't know why, but later realized they must have heard of the reward money. Since then, they've disappeared into the interior, but he thinks they send someone to the coast now and then to find out if the promised reward is in sight.'

The sickening smell of crude spirits mingled with the stench of the camels. Despite their refusals, Ali-Rashid had disappeared into his tent, and the sound of dispute floated out as he attempted to explain, no doubt, the extreme desirability of pleasing his visitors. Jerott said, 'That's a snake, if you like. I'm surprised he didn't creep after those bloody Bedouin and snatch the child back from them, once he learned of the money.'

'He couldn't find them,' said Lymond. 'He admits that he tried. A member of the troop that bought the child turned up yesterday with money to buy a new camel, and he would have followed him then, but he got a very clear warning that if he did he wouldn't reach there alive. He's changed his mind now. For money. You and half of the men will stay here with the camels, and at daybreak tomorrow Ali-Rashid and I with the remainder will try to trace that Bedouin and his friends back to his family.'

'And how,' said Jerott, 'do you propose to follow a handful of men and a camel on a trail already a day and a half old?'

'Haven't you noticed?' said Lymond. 'Every camel-trader notches the feet of his beasts with his own particular trade-mark. The Bedouin's was the only single camel Ali-Rashid sold yesterday. All we have to do is follow its track in the sand.'

'What sand?' said Jerott.

'Don't be pessimistic,' said Lymond. 'Ali-Rashid wants that extra money. There'll be sand and prints and maze-toothed Labyrinthodontia if need be. And to save you further effort, I'll repeat, you are not coming with me.'

'And Marthe?' said Jerott with animosity. In three days their caravan would have left Monastir.

'Yes. Marthe. Won't it be interesting,' said Lymond thoughtfully, 'to see whether Marthe elects to move on without us, or whether she stays here with you? Especially as Salablanca has sewn all the rest of the money into her saddle.'

*

She elected to stay. When, after three days, their caravan did move on, Salablanca found lodgings for Marthe and Jerott and himself in a village near by, and they settled down, in the highest discomfort, to wait.

Not that Marthe was idle. Against Jerott's advice, she rode almost daily, in her boy's clothes, in and out of the small towns of the shoreline and came back, brisk and calm, with a string of sardonic anecdotes concerning her day's observations, and no account at all of her own employment, whatever it was.

In some ways, Lymond's absence seemed to have brought to her a sense of release. Though still self-possessed, she lost a little the disdainful detachment which so incensed Jerott, and as neither he nor Salablanca showed any interest in the femininity within the doublet and hose, she began, with a characteristic dry intelligence, to take her share of the exchanges, social, speculative, essential, between the two men whose lives, wittingly or not, she had elected to share.

On the fourth or fifth day after Lymond's departure, Marthe spent several hours behind the walls of Monastir. Like most of the coastal strip at this point, the city was in Spanish hands, and if it were known that any members of a French embassy, however loosely attached, were living disguised in the neighbourhood, they would all, Jerott know, receive short shrift. He was relieved therefore when she came back, undisturbed and even complacent, in the late afternoon, in the company of the men and women from the village who supplied Monastir daily with fowl, meat, vegetables and eggs, and whom she used as her protection.

Jerott had no reason to challenge her wit. For a woman, it seemed to him at times excessive to tiresomeness. Now, almost before Salablanca could take her horse, she said, 'There is a dervish hermit just outside the village, and I am told they are great bringers of news. Might a woman talk to him without offence, Salablanca?'

'If he is a Bektashi Baba,' said Salablanca. 'That is an Order which admits women to its worship. But not otherwise. Why, wouldst thou reveal thyself to such a one?'

'It is best to be honest . . . sometimes,' said Marthe. 'Will you come with me?'

It was the first time she had even remotely indicated that she found their company necessary. 'We'll both come,' said Jerott. 'But I'm not sure what you expect. Stray children are rather beneath their level of interest.'

'I was concerned rather with stray adults,' said Marthe briefly. 'For if you are prepared to wear the year through with your needlework, awaiting our dear Mr Crawford, I must confess I am not. If he has had his throat cut, it would be a convenience to know it.'

'I see. Have you ever seen a Bedouin camp?' Jerott said, his voice deceptively gentle. 'Their tents are black, or brown, with a huddle of chickens and goats, and their women are nearly naked, with a brass or silver ring in one nostril, and beads, and blue tattooing on their lips and their cheeks and their arms. The children have lice and pot bellies and open starvation sores on their faces, and their eyes are half blind and overgrown like a black and blue lichen with flies. That is where this child is being brought up.'

'Calm yourself,' said Marthe wearily. 'I am sure the unfortunate creature, if not happily dead, will be snatched from these horrors forthwith by its sire. I want only to know when I can hope to get away from the chickpeas and couscous and back to Onophrion's cooking.'

'If you wish to leave, there is nothing, to my knowledge, to stop you,' said Jerott.

'Well, that's good news,' said Marthe, with final and unanswerable malice. 'I thought you needed the gold in my saddle.'

Deferentially, Salablanca's voice broached Jerott's silence. 'La señorita has known that the gold has been concealed in that place?'

'La señorita,' said Marthe coldly, 'in the absence of offers, has been saddling and unsaddling that damned horse like a coal-heaver for three days since you sewed the coins in the lining. It was hardly likely the weight would fail to attract my attention.'

Which left Jerott wondering, gloomily, which it was Lymond had miscalculated so severely: Marthe's native intelligence, or the chivalry of her masculine escort: himself.

*

The dervish was Bektashi: wearing a loincloth only on his skeletal brown body; his black hair matted and long; his fingernails yellow and clawed like a sick hunting beast's. He was asleep, a little distance from the village, on a bed of warm ash left by the fire of a herdboy, and the grey powder patched his face like decay as he twitched and stretched, when they called him. He sneezed, a great many times with a soprano and desperate violence, drank the water Salablanca silently offered him, and with a benign gesture, hand on heart, offered them the courtesy of the beaten earth lying before him, like a prince holding Divan.

You had to admit, thought Jerott, sitting crosslegged, listening to Salablanca's quiet introduction of Marthe, that her instinct had been right. The dervish betrayed no surprise on learning that the fair-skinned, compact boy before him was French, and a woman; or that she longed for his wisdom. It seemed likely, as she had said, that in his travels a great deal was known to him already. Speaking gently, he welcomed them and discoursed with simplicity on the subjects she raised. Jerott wondered if she was the stranger she seemed to Bektashiism, or if she knew its theme, so apposite to her own temperament: its insistence on Oneness, the enemy of all multiplicity. From the dervish, at least, she should have the truth. *The law is my words*, had said Mohammed, quoted by Haji Bektash Veli. *The way is my actions. Knowledge is my chief of all things. Truth or reality is my spiritual state.*

When at length she broached her question: 'Of such a man knowledge hides itself from me, as the ostrich lies upon its breast,' said the dervish. 'But I see that the rope thou seekest hath two colours, twisted with a black strand and a white strand. Dost thou not seek also a child?'

It was Jerott who answered before Marthe. 'They say there is among the Bedouin a yellow-haired boy-child, a year old, with an Ethiopian nurse.'

The black eyes of the dervish rested on him. His was a big-boned face, refined by asceticism; the beard sprang from a heavy jaw; and the nose, arched and fleshy, structured the groined eyebrows and unfleshed malar ridges like the prow of a ship. He said, 'Thou meanest well by this child?' and Marthe's cool voice answered modestly, 'He is the son of the Efendi about whom we spoke.' It struck Jerott how much Lymond would dislike this cursory interference in his affairs; and further that Marthe, whatever her ostensible motives, fully realized this.

'Allâh is wise,' said the dervish. 'I have breathed on such a one;

the most delicate in complexion of children, but sick with travelling. The Bedouin are a people distempered and of evil habit: the child placed with them had not prospered, and was removed in secret, they say, by his nurse.'

'She ran away?' said Jerott. 'Didst thou meet them? The child's name they say was Khaireddin, and the nurse's Kedi.'

'Kedi indeed was the name spoken,' said the dervish with compassion. 'I did not meet them, but had the story from him who found nurse and child wandering in the olive trees and took pity on them. The child bore the brand of Dragut.'

'Where are they now?' Marthe's collected voice put the question.

The dervish hesitated. 'To conceal a slave is an offence. And a slave the property of my lord Dragut a great offence.'

'He had sold her,' said Jerott. 'None need fear the wrath of Dragut; and the one who sheltered this woman and child we would make great.'

'But I know not his name,' said the dervish with gentle regret. 'Only that Mehedia was near to his village, and that for alms he was moved to offer me this.' And with long, irregular fingers, he touched the strip of rawhide round his neck. Attached to it, Jerott had already observed, was a small bag made of soft white cotton, whiskered with wood ash. It contained, he supposed, the dervish's fortune; and he wondered if perhaps the nature of the coins would hint at the donor. Marthe, watching his eloquent face, smiled. 'You don't come from Lyons, or you would know what you are looking at,' she said. 'Two ounces of oriental insect called bombykia, Mr Blyth. As useful a clue as any we might possess.'

'Bombykia?' said Jerott, whose mind was not at that moment in perfect alignment with Aristotle.

'Silkworms, Mr Blyth,' said the girl Marthe. 'The horned worm of India at whose mating men rejoice as at a wedding; from whose bowels came the robes Cleopatra wore, spun from the wind. Go look, Mr Blyth, for a mulberry bush.'

8

MEHEDIA

Go look, Mr Blyth, for a mulberry bush, Marthe had said. And Jerott Blyth went, because he thought she was right. Ali-Rashid, they knew, had sold the slave-nurse and the infant to the Bedouin. It was entirely possible that the nurse, taking the child, had contrived to escape, and had been given asylum by some family breeding silk near Mehedia . . . which was in Spanish hands.

If it was true, they might have broken Gabriel's prearranged train of progress, provided they got to the child quickly enough. If it wasn't true, they were abandoning Francis, along with the waiting-post, and walking straight into an ambush.

Faced with this logic, Marthe had merely raised her slim shoulders indifferently. 'You must, of course, do as you please,' she had remarked. 'But I really think, through all these years, that Mr Crawford has learned to take care of himself. I am sure his unique sense of domestic responsibility will impel him, unswerving, to trace us wherever we go.'

Which was precisely the kind of bitchy remark, thought Jerott furiously, that Lymond himself would have made.

In the end, Jerott chose the moderate course. He travelled alone because he would not allow their waiting-post to be abandoned. Salablanca and Marthe remained there: Marthe wild with impatience and Salablanca smiling, unmoved. The bulk of the money, well hidden, stayed with them while Jerott, carrying only enough for his needs, mounted his horse and rode east, into high spring and the enemy-held territory of Mehedia.

Soon, these flat plains would lie exhausted again under the dusk-drinking lions of summer. Now Jerott rode past green hedges and plane and pomegranate trees and date palms, through olive groves and by fields sprouting with barley and wheat. Wild mignonette sprang among the thistles between the cracked marble stones of some forgotten Roman-built path and the blue of cornflowers and wild lupin and hyacinth hazed the long grass. In the villages there was milk to be had from the pale, full-bellied cows, and honey like muslin, eaten beneath the blossoming orange trees in an orchard where the scent fed the senses like the threshold pleasures of love. And Jerott, who had wished to be alone for his own sake as well as for Lymond's, closed his eyes as he sat under the orange trees, and prayed for Francis Crawford, who did not recognize love, and for himself, who did.

Presently through the olive trees, said to bear the name of God on every leaf, he saw as he rode the rocky peninsula with the walled town of Mehedia on his left. Then the olives gave way to low green bushes, fat and glossy, rich with rotten fish and oil cake and lascivious feeding as Marthe had described them. Jerott rode through the grove of white mulberries, and past the rows of thatched rearing-houses, and began to pursue an altogether spurious line of inquiry, gently, from farmhouse to farm, about the purchase of soufflons for inexpensive, waste silk.

The silk-farmer who had presented the unhatched eggs to the Bektashi dervish was a Syrian, turbaned, round-faced and brown-haired—an amiable man, with several robed wives and a cheerful parcel of brown-skinned slaves who gathered round, white teeth smiling, until he cuffed them away.

It was Jerott's fourth farm, and it had cost him half an hour of careful talk over dried figs and raisins and a dish of little eggs cooked in saffron to identify it as the one he was seeking. Standing in the warm sheds, looking at the tiered wicker trays of black worms rustling, rustling as they ate their way through the young green mulberry shoots, he shaped the conversation with infinite patience. To take and conceal another man's possessions, even if these were only a black woman and a child too young to work, was something for which the Syrian might pay bitterly in money and in the crudest physical maltreatment. It was not an admission to be made lightly to strangers.

The insects fed. Unremittingly, day and night, from the forty meals of their first day of life, they would feed, these grubs little more than an aphid in size. Soon their first skin would be cast, feet, skull, jaws and teeth discarded in husk, and the revealed worm, wrinkled and pale, would fall to eating again. As the farmer talked, children, dark-haired and quiet, moved in and out between the piled ranks of trays with reeded baskets of leaves, gently sprinkling each shelf, or, sheltering a little wisp of dry, burning straw, coaxed the lethargic to appetite in its warmth. 'They be light witted and shy, and noise doth offend them,' said the farmer. 'Therefore it is becoming to live softly among them. They see nothing, and move little, yet for twenty centuries, it is said, from the time of the Flowery Kingdom, they have lived to serve man.'

'Your children are quiet,' Jerott said.

'They are tired,' said the farmer. 'Each day the leaves must be gathered and the grub must be satisfied day and night, and kept warm, and rats and mice frightened away. Then when it has entered its hammock, its florette, and, after reposing, has spun, the vigil begins. There is little sleep at such times. Without children it could not be done.'

'Grown slaves sleep less than children,' said Jerott.

'They cost more.' Emerging from the dusk of the huts, Jerott found the clear air of the desert above the darkening mulberry trees already tinged with the carmine of sunset. Pausing in his walk, just outside the white walls of the farmhouse, he said, 'I have a kindness to beg. I would pay thee the price of six adult slaves for one child of thine, with his nurse.'

The farmer stopped. 'Thou sayest?'

Jerott met the honey-brown eyes.' I speak not as merchant, but as brother to brother. There is a Christian bereft of his heart, a fair son taken from him in mischief and left with the Bedouin. To any caring for the boy and his nurse, my friend would give gold, and would exchange honest silence.'

The farmer glanced round. In the deepening twilight, the awakened scents of leaf and blossom stirred like the promise of food in the nostrils and the white acid of jasmine struck the lungs. There was no one near. The farmer said, 'Thou art no merchant?'

'I am from France. From the *Dauphiné*, bound for Stamboul,' said Jerott quietly. A life for a life. To place himself in this man's power was the only way he possessed to purchase his confidence. 'The child is a year old or more, and is branded. The nurse, Kedi, is black.'

There was a long pause. 'And this child,' said the farmer at length. 'This child, if he were found: what would his destiny be?'

'A painted roof over his head; a silk carpet under his foot; a rich man's clothes on his back and a rich man's food in his belly,' said Jerott. 'For your children, when I have him, there would be the same.'

A smile, reluctant and wry in the dark, overspread the silk-breeder's face. 'You speak of my jewel; soft, tender, delicate, the brother of angels and lustrous in beauty as the golden-skinned moon. The child is mine, and his slave: she spins in Mehedia, in my sister's house, and has care of the child until he may be taken to train. . . . In what way, Efendi, didst thou say thy friend, receiving his son, would remember his servant?'

'In five hundred ducats of gold,' said Jerott. 'And in his unsurpassed gratitude.'

'Come,' said the farmer. He opened the door of his house and, in the golden light of the threshold, called for a lantern and for a boy to saddle Jerott's horse and his own. 'The gates of Mehedia will be closing. Come with me, and I will take you to them tonight.'

He talked, pleasantly, on all the short journey to the high, sand-coloured walls of Mehedia. In his sister's house the white cocoons of raw silk came to be finally stored: all the cocoons save those whose life-cycle was allowed to perfect itself on the farm. On the farm, in careful small numbers, the creamy silk moth was allowed to break through to life after all its endeavours, destroying the floss of its capsule. On one spot it was born—the great awakening, the psyche of the Greeks. On the same spot, unmoving, it mated. On the same spot, two days later, it died.

'You kill them?' asked Jerott. Above, the battlements were printed black against the great stars of the sky and, faintly, he could hear the small, familiar sounds of well-jointed armour, and the voices of the watch, conversing quickly in Spanish. 'Poor servants of man.'

'Would a Believer kill?' said the farmer; and Jerott, reminded by the reproof in his voice, cursed himself for forgetting. '*We are the garden*, say the Bektashi. *The rose is in us*. Every live thing, once given in birth, is deserving of life. The silk moth is born. It has no organs of nutrition. In two days, therefore, it dies. . . . Here are the gates of Mehedia. Enter, and claim thy friend's son.'

*

At precisely that moment, Francis Crawford came slowly through the olive trees to the village where he had left Jerott, Marthe and Salablanca, and drew rein outside the headman's house.

Before the little horse stopped moving, Salablanca was at his side. Taking her time, Marthe noted, with interest, that the management was sun-blistered and saddle-stiff but evidently quite unmolested, although his clothes were stained and grimy with dust. Leaning against the doorpost, 'Return of the migrant. You could do with oiling and anting,' she said.

'I could do, in fact, with sanding and scouring,' Lymond said. 'If you care to lay a tub of any known liquid within one hundred yards, I'll absorb it by suction. Where's Jerott?'

Salablanca, unsaddling, called a horse-boy to look after the footsore little mare and entering the house began, with his magical softness, to fulfil all Lymond's needs. Marthe, coming in too, shook down her hair from her cap and perched on a stool, watching. 'He has gone to catch butterflies. You reached the Bedouin?'

'Yes. Eventually.' Standing in his hose and soaked shirt, he drank, acrobatically, from the water-jug as from a porrón and upended what was left, with majesty, over his head. Marthe said, 'No child?'

'Oh, yes,' said Lymond. Crosslegged on the floor, his tangled hair dripping over one eye, he broke up a small cake of bread and drew towards him the bowl of rice and lamb Salablanca had brought him. 'Plenty of children. But rather short of the right number of features and limbs. He had chosen a family with the pox.'

'*Leprosy?*' Salablanca, stopping, said it in Spanish.

'No, the pox. But the effects look much the same. I saw every one before they told me the nurse had run away with the boy. . . . It's all right. I was careful. I won't infect you,' he added, to Marthe.

'I do not worry. I rely on your heroism,' said Marthe. 'You remind me of Surya. In two of his hands he held waterlilies; the third blessed, and with the fourth he encouraged his worshippers.'

'As a leaf is swept away by a torrent, so you will be conquered by my omnipotent goodness. . . . Where *is* Jerott?' Irritatingly, he would not respond to her jibes. From his face she could learn nothing, except that he was a little fine drawn with sleeplessness and lack of regular food. She said, 'Where's Ali-Rashid?'

'Ali-Rashid is dead,' said Lymond sharply; and Salablanca spoke quickly. 'Señor Blyth went to try and trace the little one at a silk-farm. A dervish directed us to a village outside Mehedia.'

Lymond had stopped crumbling bread. 'He went alone? When?'

'Alone, yes. This afternoon, señor.'

'It's quite close, and perfectly safe,' said Marthe. 'And unlike Christians, Bektashis do tell the truth.'

'Some of it,' said Lymond. 'It was a Bektashi dervish who stopped me outside the Bedouin camp and told me the same. It's still Gabriel's circuit. Jerott's just cut across two of the stages, that's all.'

He stopped only to change before setting off again, on a fresh horse, with both Marthe and Salablanca this time beside him. It took them a good part of the evening to find the right farm, and then to learn that the stranger who had called that afternoon had gone to visit the silk-farmer's sister in Mehedia. 'There was a boy the gentleman wanted to buy,' said the old man who received them. 'A young boy with his nurse. He offered much money.'

'Rightly so. Your family will be rich,' Lymond said. 'How would we reach this house of your daughter?'

'Thus you will reach it,' said the old man, and described the place: as he finished he put out, unhurried, one arm to restrain their departure. '. . . But not until tomorrow, Efendi. Now none may enter Mehedia. Now the gates are closed for the night.'

*

Experienced in battle, and owning many masters, the city of Mehedia occupied a narrow neck of land washed on three sides by the sea, and contained a citadel within its high walls, whose ramparts, towers and battlements held a great arsenal of cannon. Beside the harbour, large and sheltered, was a smaller railed basin where galleys might lie.

Once dominated by Spanish-controlled Tunis, the Moors and Mohammedans who lived there had revolted against Turks and Christians alike, and set up a commonwealth which Dragut Rais had destroyed, installing his own nephew as Governor instead.

It was a double insult which the old Emperor could not afford to sustain. Three years ago Jerott had sailed for Mehedia in his en-graved armour with the eight-pointed cross of Malta on his cloak. Three years ago the Emperor's admiral Andrea Doria with his own fleet, with the Pope's galleys, with the Viceroy of Sicily and galleys and troop ships from Naples, and with the fleet of the Knights

Hospitallers of St John of Malta under Bailiff Claude de la Sengle had attacked Mehedia in blazing midsummer, and had taken it.

It had not been done without cost. One hundred and forty Knights and four hundred troops from the Order had left Birgu with Jerott, but not all had returned. There had been lavish plunder, in the end: gold, silver and jewels; and over seven thousand slaves had been taken from here by the Christians; and the son of the Viceroy, Don John de Vega, installed as Governor. The Viceroy, Jerott had no trouble in recalling, had claimed the honour of victory. To Jerott's mind that belonged to Claude de la Sengle, who had made a hospital of his tents and called on his Knights to leave the fighting in turn and attend to the sick.

So it was now held, but with difficulty. Behind the slow rising ground through which he had just ridden, with its orchards and vineyards, lay the mountains, and behind them the vast plains where the Arabs pastured their animals. So large and hostile a territory, so far from the succour of Europe, was a burden on the Emperor which he would gladly, it was rumoured, have passed to the Knights of St John. Until now, the Knights of St John had been wise enough to ignore it. Riding through the studded gates of Mehedia in the dark, Jerott bent his dark face within the fall of his head-cloth, and did not look at the torches. This soil belonged to Spain and the Emperor, who was France's bitterest enemy. And he was no longer a Knight, but Scottish-French, and on a French embassy. One mistake, and Gabriel's revenge would be part-way complete.

The house of the silk-farmer's sister lay in a crooked lane hardly wide enough for a horse, but the arched doorway was brilliantly lit, and the courtyard, although its pillars were wood, held a small fountain in a floor patterned with coloured pebbles in mortar, with bright plants, well-watered, placed about in earthenware pots. Vine-leaves, lacing the open gallery which ran round the enclosure, sea-washed the patio in shivering blackness and light as they revealed and obscured the lit rooms lying behind. From there, evenly humming, Jerott heard the sound of a spinning-wheel; and somewhere, someone was playing a flute.

Tying Jerott's horse and his own, the farmer crossed the yard and tapped on a double-leafed door, smiling at Blyth as he followed. A dog barked. The spinning-wheel faltered, and then went rhythmically on, nor did the flute-player hesitate. In the darkness, Jerott thought he heard the gates into the street quietly close. A child squeaked, and up in the gallery a man laughed, and then a door shut, muffling the sound. Behind the farmer, the house doors suddenly opened, and sound and light tumbled into the courtyard, surrounding the stocky form of a woman. When she saw the Syrian, she smiled, with blackened teeth, and welcomed him in.

The silk-farmer's sister was not young, and because of that perhaps

116

was unveiled, her eyes circled with kohl and her dark hair reddened with hènnah. She listened to her brother's brief tale as they sat, on unexpectedly fine brocade cushions, in a small room thick with dusty hangings and rugs, to which clung the stale smell of storax and spikenard and the pungent benzoin often favoured by Africans. There might have been *kif*, but if so, the stronger smells smothered it.

Jerott watched, as she talked, the bracelets jangle and clash on the woman's thick arms. They were of gold, and heavy. Silk-farming, obviously, was a lucrative trade. They clattered again as she clapped her hands and a slave, barefooted, slid in to lay fuel on the brazier which smoked dully, half-extinguished, in a corner. It reminded Jerott of the sweet sound of swordplay, in the days when his life had been a fighting man's, not a nomad's. He wondered how long it took a human being to kipper in scent. Then he realized that the Syrian had risen, and taking his arm, was saying, 'Here is Kedi. My sister says you may gladly remove her. She is finding the boy.' Jerott stood up, and a negress came in.

Once, she had been a free citizen of a proud Ethiopian court. Once, too, prized for her milk, she had been fed and cared for and although a slave, had lived in vague happiness, Jerott supposed, wet-nursing the white, the brown, the olive-skinned children of corsairs.

Now, the padded muscle and the soft, meat-fed flesh had melted from under the supple black skin, and the wide-eyed woman who now stood upright before him in her stained robe and headcloth had big-knuckled hands twisted with hardship. Her collar and cheek-bones rested in hollows, and where the swollen milch-breasts once pressed against the soaked cotton, the stuff now lay folded and flat. Jerott said, 'Dost thou speak English?' and the woman, no surprise in her eyes, said, 'I learn in Dragut's household, Efendi.'

'And did you learn Irish?' Jerott said.

This time, there was a little life in the stare. This time she hesitated, and Jerott said gently, 'It is all right. The child's father has come. We are going to take you both where you will be happy and safe.'

'The child's father?' Again uncertain, she paused. 'Who is he?'

'His name does not matter. He is a Christian, and Khaireddin must be brought up a Christian as well. He is rich. You will be happy.'

'He would take me with Khaireddin?' The slow brain thought. 'But then, what of my mistress?'

Jerott hesitated. 'How was she when you left her?'

'She was sick, Efendi. In that terrible house with the goats on the floor. She could not carry water: she said, "*Fawg may le Dia*",' Leave me to God. The attempt at Gaelic was quite recognizable. She went on, 'Then Shakib came to buy us, the child and myself, for Ali-Rashid. But the lady he left.'

There was a silence. Only when he saw the fright return to her eyes did Jerott realize he had been staring at her, with God knew what in his own face. For it was now clear, beyond iota of doubt, that this was indeed Kedi, the woman who had nursed Oonagh's son. And somewhere in this house must be the pawn itself.

'Remove from your minds,' Lymond had said, 'the image of a live human child.' For Francis Crawford, meticulously fulfilling his responsibilities, such advice would appear simple. But he was not here in this room; only Jerott, who had forgotten his own safety and whose heart throbbed with strange pulses as he looked at this withered black woman and said, 'And where is the little boy? The little fair boy? After all that, how is he?'

The Syrian, rising, smiled and forestalled her answer. 'Come and see him. He is with the cocoons, which must be turned to avoid mould. Those soft, small fingers; that delicate skin. Such beauty! Come, come and see. Kedi will await you by the brazier.'

Moving to the door after the silk-farmer, with the dizzying perfumes, stirred by the heat, confusing his senses, Jerott heard again, from the warren of little rooms and the unseen gallery above, the subdued sounds of laughter, and music, and children's voices calling, complaining, giggling. As they walked along the little dark passage curtains twitched; he caught a glimpse of a man's dishevelled white robe, and once he was stopped by a child, as he hurried after the Syrian: a lovely boy of six or seven years old, with long lashes and glistening black curls, who caught his hand, saying laughing, '*Yalla ma'y . . . hall liyâ . . . sharr biyâ. . . .*' Then the Syrian, turning back, hissed at him, and the boy, still laughing, disappeared with a flick of embroidered slipper below his expensive short gown. The smell of myrrh went with him—my God, are they all drenched in perfume? thought Jerott; and stumbled on after the farmer.

The little building to which he was taken stood at the end of a walled garden; a paved enclosure behind the house strewn with half-dried washing, dim in the dark; and a carpenter's bench and a cistern of marble, the water swimming dark and greasily in the moonlight. There was no light but the oblong lying behind them from the lit door of the house; and ahead, the traces of candlelight from the low stucco building they were approaching, leaking through ill-fitting shutters. The windows, he noticed, were barred, and there were iron rods rammed into sockets on either side of the door.

It did not seem right. Contrary to his hopes, the night air only made his muddled head worse. Leaning against the cold, substantial wall, Jerott watched the Syrian unbar and unlock the door, and tried to listen to what he was saying. 'Forgive me. Like the pressing of thirsty camels on their watering-troughs, the thieves of Mehedia would come to purloin my silk, and but for this, all my labours and those of my family are empty as water. Come in, Efendi, and rest.

It is warm, and the child shall keep you company while we gather his clothes.' And opening the door, he bowed Jerott in.

Inside, he thought, it was like a threshing-floor. Half of the brightly lit room was empty, with a lit brazier like the one he had left smoking gently by an Egyptian mat in the middle. The rest was lined with tier upon tier of wide racks clouded like an aviary with azure blue down. But these little beings, thought Jerott with melancholy, did not sing, or move, or breathe. They were, in their hundreds, winding-sheets of indigo-fed silk, each enclosing the shrivelled corpse of its host. Two thousand to make one single pound of raw silk for an emperor's robes . . . and they must be turned, and turned, to prevent mould. Fighting his lethargy, Jerott scanned the bare room.

'He has fallen asleep,' said the farmer. 'Khaireddin! Remember your lesson!' And from a drift of blue floss on one of the low shelves there came a small sound and a child's fair head lifted instantly, its face still closed and shadowed with sleep. There was a moment's pause while the child sat, its dazed blue eyes opening and closing. Then the Syrian said, chidingly, 'Khaireddin!' and, with obedient care, the little boy stepped, as unsteady as a new lamb, from the low shelf to the floor and came, with the flat-footed gait of the very little, towards Jerott Blyth.

He had waited, paralysed with nervous reluctance to see before him, distressingly, Francis Crawford again as a child. What he saw was a small European boy who was himself only; who with a baby-hood behind him of dirt and terror and darkness had been left solitary at night in a locked warehouse, and had wakened sharply to a command and a stranger; but who stood now before him, bare-foot in his crumpled striped shirt, and contrived a smile, round-eyed, with his soft kitten's mouth. On the high brow, the saffron silk hair was an irregular nimbus to which one or two soft cocoons drunkenly hung, shadowing his round cheeks; and in the baby face, curve melted into curve, reflecting each into the other, growing like fruit on the bones they would conceal until, in one year or two, there would return the structure; the marks of race with which he was born.

Returning the stare of that devouring blue gaze, Jerott could see nothing of Lymond but his colouring, and perhaps the sweep of the fine, thick lashes fringing his eyes. The spaced features, the curled nose, the faint brows and the blue veins running through the thin white skin of his temples were his own, and neither Lymond's nor Oonagh's. Jerott, a bachelor and still to all purposes a monk, none the less felt the pull: the painful desire to enfold this unwanted child with peace, security and warmth, and to set him in his grand-mother's arms, within orderly days, in the land of his heritage.

Jerott knelt, his hood fallen back from his black hair, as the child advanced; and without moving, like a man watching a nestling, said,

'Khaireddin? My name is Jerott. Kedi wants a ride on my horse. Do you want to ride on my horse with Kedi?'

He spoke, deliberately, in English; and he thought for a moment that the child understood. He hesitated in his effortful walk and, turning his head, gazed at the Syrian, his eyes widening; his brows angled, for a second, with worry. Then, as the Syrian nodded and smiled, the child stepped forward to Jerott's shoulder, and putting one arm round his neck, curled round to kiss the hollow neck of his shirt. And Jerott, caught utterly unawares by the practised, sensuous gesture, smelt at last the reeking perfume on the little boy's shirt, and saw the paint on his lips and, as he flung the child off with a reflex of unbearable, unthinking revulsion, the sneer on the face of the Syrian.

Jerott had his sword half out from under his robe when the door crashed open on a throng of armed men. He ran backwards pulling it free. The light dazzled his eyes: at the back of his mind he saw that the child whom he had hurled to the floor had even then given only one sharp croak of fright and had been silent: the blue eyes, black with terror and anxiety, were turned on the Syrian. Then he had no time to see more, for his attackers were on him, and the lights were flashing even more confusingly in his eyes, and his sword, as he bore its full weight, was like a rooted tree in his hand.

He fought, slowly, before they overwhelmed him, and realized slowly, as he fought, that it had all been a trick; that from the moment Marthe had found the dervish he had been guided here, for this moment, when it would be driven home, for ever, that the pawn between Lymond and Gabriel was a living boy-child, and that they had both failed him. Stupefied by the drug in the brazier Jerott hardly felt the blow which at length felled him; did not know when they replaced his sword in its scabbard and, leaving him prone on the bare, plastered floor, began swiftly to work on the shelves.

It did not take long. In twenty minutes the soft blue cocoons, so carefully tended, were piled on the empty half of the floor, heaped and drifting like summer clouds round the flushed fire of the brazier. Efficiently, all that was inflammable was moved well out of reach, and Jerott himself pulled to the wall, as far away as possible from the ghostly cumulus of worms in their silk biers. Then heavy carpets were pinned over shutters and door and Kedi, drugged and senseless also, was brought in and laid at his side.

Only then did the Syrian, turning, give a last order. One of the men, dagger stuck in his sash and hairy arms pilled with itching wisps of blue fleece, walked over to where the child sat silently hunched, its thumb in its mouth. It made no sound as the man scooped it up, one-handed, under the arms and walked with it to the door. The little boy only came to life on the threshold, as they passed the stout form of the silk-farmer. Gasping a little from the spreadeagled hand gripping his chest, the child ducked his head and, his eyes seeking the Syrian, pressed a conciliatory kiss on his captor's muscular arm.

It was one hour before midnight when the last man out of the warehouse upset the brazier, with care. Because of their forethought, nothing burned but the silk, and the smouldering flicker as worms and cocoons dissolved into vapour and ash was hidden from all Mehedia's high towers by the sealed windows and door. By the same token and with the same foresight, the sealed windows and door kept in the ash and the vapour.

The ash was harmless. The vapour was concentrated hydrocyanic gas.

*

At one hour after midnight the guards on the landward gate of Mehedia, who were Spanish and thoroughly schooled in their jobs, distinguished a camel-train, surprisingly making its way down towards them. Although the caravan made no secret of its progress and was well lit, the walls were immediately manned, and a dozen cannon and twenty crossbows and arquebuses were trained on it from that moment until it finally came to a halt, and three riders rode from its van and stopped just under the gates. At a sign from the captain the watch, not impolitely, called down the information, in Arabic, that the gates were closed until dawn.

There was a pause. The captain, a susceptible bachelor from Valladolid who disliked night duty for a number of reasons, saw that the first of the three riders, a turbaned Moor who was presumably the dragoman, was interpreting to the second, whom he now saw was in European clothes, and well-cut European clothes at that. He caught a glimpse of a chain which he would have priced at three thousand écus in Madrid and something very nice indeed sparkling in the gentleman's hat. Making a diplomatic guess, the captain cleared his throat, stepped to the ramparts, and repeated the same information, more politely, in Italian.

The fellow in the chain rode forward, looked up, and let off a salvo of acidulated Spanish that all but fried the guard in its armour. The captain quelled his first instinct to recoil, and instead snapped at his lieutenant. 'You have heard no commands from the Governor to admit special persons tonight?'

The lieutenant hadn't. Reinforced, the captain turned to the battlements and said as much, in frigid Spanish, to the gentleman below. The gentleman below, in highly idiomatic Spanish, responded by repeating his demands, together with various related promises of an unbenign nature. The jewels in his enseigne were as big as marrowfat peas.

'¿ Cómo ?' said the lieutenant anxiously. 'He says,' said the captain, 'that this is the train of the Donna Maria Mascarenhas, an eminent lady esteemed by the Vatican, on her way to the Holy City on pilgrimage. The Governor of Tunis commends her to the care of the Governor of Mehedia and since she has a falling sickness, which makes her journeys protracted, had sent a messenger to our Governor earlier today requesting the privilege of entry if they arrived after dark. So this fellow says.'

'Who's he?' said the lieutenant, who was a married man. 'And if there's a lady, where is she? I see nothing but camels.'

'He's steward of her household, he says. . . .' The captain could see nothing but camels either, and he knew what camels cost, and was able to calculate, quickly, the amount of baggage they must be carrying. He could distinguish a number of drivers, but no one else of consequence. Then the third rider, for the first time, moved forward into the torchlight.

'*¡Jesús!*' said the captain.

Down below, sitting on horseback beside Salablanca before all Ali-Rashid's camels, Lymond felt Marthe ride up between them. He did not need to turn to know how she looked. Mantled in the satin of her gilt unbound hair, with the wide severe brow, the white skin, the borrowed skirts and the pearls she had, unaccountably, produced, each one as big as a hazelnut, she was a vision to make all the arquebuses droop and the crossbowmen slacken and sweat. 'Perhaps,' said Lymond with virulence, 'the captain might risk his reputation to the extent of admitting the lady, her servant and myself while he sends to inform the Governor that his guests have arrived. You may assure yourself, sir, that the Moor and I carry no weapons. Unless you suppose the lady carries a culverin I cannot conceive what harm we may do you.'

Hopelessly, the captain grasped at a last straw. 'You say the lady suffers some sickness?'

'Nothing infectious,' said Lymond with cold reserve. He still had not glanced towards Marthe. 'Donna Maria suffers from fits.'

'*¡Qué lástima!*' said the captain politely. He found it hard, it was clear, to take his eyes from her. 'And what form do these take?'

'Really, I hardly think——' Lymond began acidly, but the captain interrupted him. 'Your pardon, sir. But with the safety of my troops to consider . . .'

'Really, it will hardly affect your troops,' said Lymond. 'The lady unhappily suffers fits of extreme violence, during which she struggles, screams and attempts to throw off all her clothes. Now, will you kindly arrange for us to enter?'

Five minutes later, they were all three inside.

They had twenty minutes, Lymond calculated, before the lieutenant came back from the castle with a troop of fully armed soldiers and the news that the Governor of Mehedia had never heard of the Donna de Mascarenhas but was very much aware there was a French Envoy loose in the land. With Salablanca sitting in the background, he sipped some very sweet Candian wine, along with Marthe, in one of the upper rooms in the guardhouse tower in company with the captain and one of his subordinates: in between making conversation he was calculating, if the truth were known, what kind of head the girl would have for strong liquor. The captain, who was drunk on pure sensation, said, 'You will forgive me, Señor Maldonado; but had you not told me, I should have taken the lady and yourself for sister and brother.'

'My father,' said Marthe, 'unhappily, was not a fastidious man. I have several of Señor Maldonado's brothers as well in the household. They also suffer from fits.'

'Of the same kind?' said the captain, gazing.

'Approximately,' said Marthe coolly. 'They scream, struggle, and try to throw off all my clothes.'

'But Donna Maria forgets,' said Lymond. 'Poor Horatio, poor Vincenzo, poor Nicolò, poor Giovanni: by persevering in time they all discovered total relief.' He studied Marthe. 'You look pale.'

'Lack of my usual exercise. I shall, I think,' said Marthe, 'take the air on the battlements, if the captain will allow me?'

The captain had no objections: there was a guard at the foot of the stairs. He was only regretful, bowing her out, that for the time being he was losing her company. For a moment, standing beside her on the open guardwalk in the soft night, he looked around at the small occasional lights and the dark murmuring trees and said, 'Shall I come with you?' But she refused sweetly, smiling, and he let himself in again to the room with Señor Maldonado and the Moor, whose door, with apology, he had locked.

'Señor, more wine? I am amazed,' said the captain, 'that so lovely a lady has not married.'

'But indeed she has married,' said Lymond. 'Five times. And not one husband, poor fellow, survived matrimony by more than a year. She is too good for them. The last one, dying, compared her to a nugget of gold. Do you melt it or do you rub it or do you beat it, said he, it shineth still more orient.'

'Sayest thou?' said the captain, glancing towards the half-open door. And at that exact moment, out on the battlements, the Donna Mascarenhas emitted a scream. The captain jumped to his feet.

Another scream. 'The fit!' said Lymond.

The captain strode to the door. Another scream. And another.

The captain flung the door open. Anxiously, Lymond called. 'If she undresses, I pray you do not restrain her! It can cause untold injury!'

The captain ran out but did not forget, in going, to close and lock the guardroom door on the two men behind him. Then he fairly raced round the guardwalk.

123

It was empty. But over one wall there trailed a fragment of what was once a woman's gauze veil. And on the paved path below, as, pallid, he leaned over and sought it, was a crumpled heap which had once been a woman's bright dress, with the marvellous string of baroque pearls still entwined in its folds. Silently, the captain turned and made with speed for the stairs.

Marthe watched him go, from where she lay flat on the roof in her tunic and hose, the blonde hair again bundled into its cap. When he was quite out of sight, she dropped to the walk and turning the key of the guardroom with both her small, strong-boned hands, opened it for Lymond and Salablanca to walk through. '*Ad unum mollis opus*,' said Marthe. 'Make the most of it, Mr Crawford. This is my single dissolute act for tonight.'

And soft-footed beside them, she slipped down the unguarded stairs and past the knot of excited men searching the path, and into the dark narrow ways of Mehedia.

Soberly hooded, and without chain and cap, Lymond led them direct to the house of the silk-farmer's sister. It was easy to find, for desultory fires burned here and there, although the looting had now almost stopped, since there was nothing left to take away. They stepped into the courtyard through which the stout silk-farmer had led Jerott that evening, the door hanging burst and splintered behind them, and through another smashed hole found their way into the house.

There was no one there; but what had been there was not hard to tell. Working swiftly from room to room, they were silent. The looters had taken the silk cushions, the carpets and the braziers. They had taken the fine sheets and the mats and the copper dishes for meat. But they had left, permeating everywhere, the sickening smell of the perfume; the odour of drugs; the peculiar reek of sensual abomination. And they had left the small mats, the low, dirty hand-marks and the worn toys of children.

It did not take long. Salablanca found the courtyard at the back, with the carpenter's litter of shavings still burning, and the charred hut beyond. It had remained fairly intact although its roof and door-way had gone, and the walls were blackened inside where some kind of fittings had burned. There was a great heap of black powder also at one point on the floor, which gave off throat-catching fumes when Lymond stirred it. Marthe said, 'That's silk.'

'What? in the cocoon, you mean?' They were the first words Lymond had spoken.

'I've smelt that in Lyons, when there's been a fire at the mills. The fumes are deadly, if they're enclosed in a small space.'

'This was a small, enclosed space,' Lymond said. 'This was perhaps where the fire started. Sparks would carry to the woodpile outside, and from there to the house.'

'It's not only that,' said Marthe. 'It's been deserted. You don't find a place like this picked clean by looters if the family stood by.'

Lymond said, 'If he was in there, with the gas: would he have a chance?'

'I don't know,' said Marthe. 'But if he did survive, he'd be in no state to evade murderous silk-farmers. He's probably dead. If he isn't dead, there's only one safe place he can be.'

'The castle,' Lymond agreed.

Marthe sighed. Pulling off the cap, she shook out her long hair and with careful fingers undid the points of her tunic and pulled that off too. Released from its waistband, her shift fell, in modest if slatternly folds, to the ground. 'Resurrection,' she said, 'of Donna Maria Mascarenhas, undressed, refitted and safely recovered by her steward. I flung off my skirt, screaming and climbed on the roof. . . . You and Salablanca climbed after me, and then chased me out of the building while the captain and the others were searching below. . . . How did you get out of the locked room?'

'The captain forgot to lock it as he ran out. Or didn't turn the key fully home.'

'Yes. So you followed me here . . . gave me your cloak for decency's sake . . . if you please . . . and then took me straight to the castle. You'd better take me straight to the castle. We want to be seen very obviously going there.'

Lymond slung her his cloak, resumed his own finery and for a moment stood still, looking at Marthe. 'You enjoy this,' he said.

And Marthe, surprise and contempt in her face, said, 'Of course.'

9

GABÈS

Unlike Francis Crawford, whose game with life was a strange and rootless affair played with the intellect, Jerott had a passionate instinct to live. It was a happy circumstance also that his nervous and bronchial systems were roughly as frail as a bison's.

His first impression, as the effects of the blow wore off and the effects of the drug uneasily lingered, was that someone had opened his jaws and poured a ladle of boiling lead straight down his throat. His next, as he opened his eyelids with difficulty, was that, like the unchaste virgins of the Campus Sceleratus, he had been sealed alive with a light in a cave. There were caves he had heard of where a dog would die in a day because of the seeping of sulphur . . . except that this wasn't sulphur so, thought Jerott prosaically, it couldn't be hell either, thank God. He sat up, and started to cough.

He was on the cold floor of the warehouse. It was pitch black, except for a small, volatile patch of dull red in the centre of his circle of vision. Dimly pulsing, almost lightless, it revealed that the darkness was crowded with banks and pillars and avalanches of throttling grey smoke. It revealed also the dead body of Kedi, the child Khaireddin's nurse, lying beside him. Retching and choking, Jerott flung himself on his hands and knees, and face to the ground, felt his way to the door.

He thought his head would explode before he finally found it, eyes and nose streaming, his throat raw. The door was sealed and immovable, the bars dropped outside. He tore the carpets from both that and the windows and found that these, too, were shuttered outside. Pressing his face hard against the rough frames he tried, savagely, to wrench into his lungs some thread of wandering air which would stave off the poison a minute, two minutes longer.

There was a trace, but only a trace: for every half-breath of life he was taking several of death. But it gave him the second he needed to think: to realize that the light represented something burning, which must be the cocoons, and that the fumes, not the fire, were intended to kill him.

Jerott drew a last, difficult breath. Then, stumbling to where he remembered the shelves to be, he laid hands on the wood and, with a strength which drove the splinters unheeded into his hands, wrenched off two boards and, fighting straight through the smoke, thrust their ends deep into the dully burning, venomous heap.

They wouldn't light. He had to leave them, to reel to the window and lie there, gasping: it was one of the most appalling acts of will he had ever had to perform, to leave that window and stagger back to the fire.

126

When he got there, it was to find that both planks had caught and one was almost consumed. He grasped them, careless of burns, and got them to the door. One of them, dying, went out. Jerott watched it from where he lay on the floor, nursing the other against the smooth wood of the door-leaf. It was a matter of lessening interest whether this one survived. He knew he couldn't do it again. He felt as if the gas had somehow invaded his flesh, congesting every passage and vein in his body: his head felt expanded and solid, like that of a malformed infant; his legs were useless. It was very warm.

His hand dropped, and his eyes closed.

A burning fragment of wood, falling on his wrist, stung him awake. Remotely irritated, Jerott looked up. A sheet of brilliant gold towered above him. His clothes were singed, his arm blistered, as the door roared into nothingness and, above his head, the roof began to crackle and spit. And flinching back from the fire, wincing, backing, recoiling, the fumes from the silk were retreating before the seeping, the stirring, the rushing of incoming sweet air.

He was caught very quickly, once he got out, by the regular patrol from the castle. Jerott himself did not care whose prisoner he was: he must, somehow, have managed to accuse the silk-farmer for when he woke up, momentarily, as they were entering the castle, he heard the Syrian's voice, protesting volubly, beside him. Then he fainted again.

He woke in prison. At first, shivering with cold and the pain of his burns, Jerott could distinguish nothing in the reeking darkness but a dim square, which seemed to be a small barred window giving on to the night. He lay on wet earth, and the walls, as he rolled over and touched them, were unplastered and damp. This was near the sea then; probably a room under the Governor's castle. . . . They had found out, then, that he was from the *Dauphiné* and therefore an enemy. Then he remembered that of course they had found out: it was the first thing the Syrian would tell them. It was why his death was to have been arranged, recognizable and intact, by asphyxiation. In Mehedia, a Frenchman was an enemy. The manner of his dying could be published, as Gabriel would want it published, with no danger to the Syrian's safety at all.

It was as far as Jerott reached with his thinking. His teeth chattering, his throat half closed, his eyes shut against the blinding pain in his head, he slipped back almost immediately into unconsciousness and lay unmoving once more.

The next time, he had no wish to wake. When the inconsiderate agency vibrating his shoulder and the persistent soft voice failed to stop, he tried to turn over, mumbling. The voice, mellowed for a moment with laughter, said, 'I don't know where in God's name you picked up such language, Jerott. Wake up, will you? You're going to be all right, but you've got to listen to me.'

127

It was Francis Crawford. Opening his eyes, frowning, Jerott looked into that cool, friendly face in the half-light of dawn, and said, whispering, 'How . . .?'

'Bribery,' said Lymond cheerfully. He was richly dressed, with no attempt at disguise. Releasing the prostrate man's shoulder he laid his hand, for a moment, on Jerott's hot brow and then without touching him further, sat back on his heels. 'You know. If one grunts, all the herd comes to help him. But your jailer would only allow me ten minutes in here. Can you understand what I'm saying?'

'Yes,' said Jerott.

'Right. In a moment, you will be taken before the Governor. *Admit everything*. You're from the *Dauphiné*, and you're here because you heard a European child was being held under duress for money. But this is the point. You're not one of the embassy: you're a Scottish Knight of St John whom we are escorting to Malta on our way farther east. You can prove that without any trouble, and if you need any help, Marthe will back you. She's masquerading as a Florentine called Donna Maria Mascarenhas, and you've met her in Rome. Do you see, Jerott? Gabriel's planning has broken down. *I* was meant to come to Mehedia; and if I escaped the gas, I certainly shouldn't have eluded the soldiers. But *you* have a chance.'

Desperately ill as he felt, Jerott's brain began to work again too. He struggled to sit. 'Yes . . . I understand. Francis, you must go to the house. The sister's house where the fire was.'

'I've been,' said Lymond. 'It was empty. Your fire went out of control.' After a moment, he added, 'I know what it was.'

Jerott said, 'The boy was there.'

'You saw him?' said Lymond. Then, because he had spoken too sharply and Jerott was only half conscious, he added, 'Never mind. Tell me after. At least . . . tell me now if he is living.'

Jerott said, 'I've seen him. I've talked to his nurse. She's dead. I found her when I woke in the fire. But there was no sign of the child.' His headache, for one agonizing moment, threatened to overcome him completely. He added, 'He must have gone with the Syrian's sister.'

His eyes on Jerott, Francis Crawford was silent. And Jerott, making one last, dragging effort, said, 'He is beautiful, and whole, and has learned to offer the world a humble and desperate obedience. You called him a pawn. He has begun to follow his trade.'

Lymond studied his hands. In the strengthening light Jerott saw his brows lifted, creasing, as if in habitual boredom; and his lashes flicked, once. Then with soft derision, he quoted, '*They caught thee on the mountain and bred thee like a human being. As the water-wheel turns round and round irrigating the garden, even so do thou turn and dance.*' He looked up. 'The Governor is a liverish gentleman, but easily impressed. You'll be all right. Marthe and I will make an excuse to take you off with us. Can you brace yourself, Jerott, for an hour?'

Jerott nodded. Lymond rose and surveyed him. 'I have a thought for you. The Countess of Henneberge, when aged forty-two, gave birth to three hundred and sixty-five children on a single occasion. Thank God neither you nor I ever happened to meet her.' And walking to the door, he called the jailer, smiled, and a moment later, unobtrusively, had gone.

In going, obviously, he had made further provisions with the warder. Between that time and his appearance two hours later before the Governor, Jerott was given a candle, and then some warm water and linen with which, painfully, he managed both to improve his appearance and to bind up the worst of his burns. When, finally, they brought him a dish of rank heated milk and a cake of coarse bread, he had stopped shivering, and although his stomach nearly rejected it, he managed to finish it all, and felt in the end almost ready to face what lay ahead.

It was as well. The Governor, as Lymond had promised, was an irascible military gentleman with a town house in Barcelona and a hunting-lodge, which he was missing, just outside Madrid. He disliked Syrians, despised the trade of the Syrian's sister, but had obviously in the past received too many secrets through both channels to be fastidious about either now. Jerott, walking past rows of helmeted henchmen in polished breastplates and Spanish stuffed breeches, looked at the quilted satin and perfumed black beard of the Governor behind his fine, Gothic desk, and thought of all the Knights of St John he had disrelished most. Ignoring the Syrian completely, he came to a halt and, looking down his splendid nose, addressed the Governor, coldly, in Spanish.

'Is it for *this*,' said Jerott Blyth contemptuously, 'that I fought and my brothers died on your ramparts three years ago, to save you this city? I hardly think, sir, that you carried a sword in that action, or you would scarcely throw one of my Order unheard into a dungeon. I hope, sir, that you will have an explanation that will satisfy the Grand Master and your master the Emperor, for none will satisfy me.'

The Governor glanced at Jerott and spoke to his secretary, hovering over his shoulder. 'The rogue speaks Spanish. I have no time for all this. Translate to the Syrian.' And, twitching the black silken moustache: 'The fellow reeks of the prison.' To Jerott, he said, 'Step back three paces. You offend us.'

'I am glad to hear it,' said Jerott. 'I intend to be still more offensive before this interview is over. And I have still to receive your answer. Is this how you treat a Knight of the Order of St John?'

'Bey Efendi!' said a round, placatory voice. 'Bey Efendi, I beg thee!' It was the Syrian, addressing the Governor. 'Himself, this

129

man has told me. He is of the French party on board the *Dauphiné*, the French Envoy's ship. He is a spy, Lord, who entered Mehedia to deceive thee, concealed in my poor sister's warehouse. How can such a one be of this illustrious Order? He seeketh to trick thee. . . . Is this a Lord, upon whose head the he-fox makes water?' And shrivelling suddenly at a warning glare from the secretary, the silk-farmer stopped and wrung his soft hands.

Red in the face, the Governor was staring at Jerott, and although he ignored the Syrian totally, Jerott knew that in a moment something or someone would require to pay the price for that affront to his dignity. 'You say that you are a Knight of St John and not the Comte de Sevigny, the Special Envoy of France. It is simple. Prove it,' said the Governor.

'Of course. If you insist,' Jerott said. 'It might have been better, you understand, if you had insisted before casting me into prison. . . .'

It was not hard. The vows, in Latin and Spanish, of the Knights Hospitallers came even now pat to his tongue. *I vow to God, to St Mary, ever a virgin, Mother of God, to St John the Baptist to render henceforth and for ever, by the grace of God . . .*

They came pat, the vows he had rejected. They came pat, too, the names of his colleagues, the account he could make of every house and Langue of Birgu, the history he could tell of the battle three years before by which the Knights with their friends had taken Mehedia for Charles. Sly as the recidivist; false as the recusant at the stake, he had invoked the Order he had forsaken, to save his own skin. . . .

Blocking all such thoughts from the mind, he ended. 'My name is Jerott Blyth. Check any scroll and you will find it. And be sure, when I am landed on Malta, I shall report all that has happened, omitting nothing.'

He had the Governor's attention now. The Governor, a little pale under the fashionable cap and the brushed beard, was saying, 'This sounds . . . It is true, what you say cannot be fabricated. . . . But I still cannot understand . . . Is there,' said the Governor, reaching a final, awful decision, 'any soul in this city whom we might call before us to identify you?'

It was the one question Jerott had feared. There was, he was tolerably sure, more than one soul in this city who would recognize him all right—as a former Knight of St John who had obtained release from his vows. There remained only, he realized, the alternative that Lymond in his damnable efficiency had already suggested. Jerott said, 'I imagine the city is fairly full of friends or acquaintances. The only one I can mention for certain—and I trust you will not dream of disturbing her—is the Lady Maria Mascarenhas, whom I was in hopes of encountering as she passed through. Her parents are old friends of my family's. But of course——'

'Señor Blyth,' said the Governor. 'La señora is here. If you will give yourself the trouble of sitting, I shall call her. Señor, I begin to see . . . I begin to fear . . . You will take a little wine?'

'It might help the situation,' said Jerott. 'A trifle.'

It was perhaps a mistake, for when the door opened on Marthe, he somehow expected the Marthe of the caravan, in boy's tunic and breeches, with her hair pushed out of sight in her cap. So stupidly, through the haze of weakness and wine, he did not at first recognize the tall girl whose glittering hair was banded with pearls, and whose borrowed bodice and farthingale in tight-sleeved black velvet and gauzes of white silk and spangles recalled the few untroubled days of his life when, neither praying nor fighting, he had feasted and danced slow dances at court, and had met and vowed to spend his life with Elizabeth. 'Signor Blyth!' said Marthe; and, drifting smiling towards him, gave him her hand and a lift of her fair brows that was the very echo of someone else. '*Caro mio*, but how you smell! Where are your chains? I was told you had been deservedly imprisoned . . . *tantum religio potuit suadere malorum*, my dear. I always distrusted so much religion.' And reaching up, the deep blue eyes sparkling, she kissed him, English fashion, on the cheek.

Through the hammer-strokes of his heart, which appeared to him to be visible, Jerott said calmly, 'Maria, I require your testimony, so don't, I pray you, consider my faith as a handicap. Merely confirm to His Excellency that in fact it exists. He doubts my identity.'

She made a face, floating deliciously into a chair. 'I doubt it too, when you smell in this fashion. What do you wish me to say?'

'The truth,' said Jerott patiently. 'If it please you, Maria. Tell the Governor who I am.'

She made a pretence of considering. 'What was the name now? I have such a memory. Smeet? Gonzales?'

'*Maria!*'

The Governor laughed merrily, his face a light shade of green. 'I fear the Duquesa knows only too well. Señor, how can I begin . . . ?'

'No, no!' said Marthe. 'You must not tell me! What could it have been! Tay-lor? Killi-grew? Robert-son?' The distinguished, wide-browed face laughed, and then was swept clean of laughter. 'You are hurt!'

'A little,' said Jerott. 'It doesn't matter. Just——'

'He is hurt!' Springing to her feet, Marthe swung to confront the Governor, her face hard and bright as her sharp little teeth. 'How is this? What have you done to Mr Blyth? I warn you, the Grand Master of his Order . . .'

His jaws sawing the air like a starling on the edge of a puddle, the Governor finally emitted a croak. 'You!' to the Syrian. 'Explain!'

With the only unalloyed satisfaction of that hideous night, Jerott heard the Syrian try, in five hand-wringing minutes, to explain. It sounded exceedingly lame. He had been told that, under guise of seeking a child, the perfidious French Special Envoy might try to gain access to Mehedia. And when one such had come, he had assumed . . . The man had been overpowered and left to await the Governor's pleasure . . . and then the unfortunate fire, of which he knew nothing, nothing . . .

Jerott took a deep breath. 'Your Excellency . . . fool though this man may be, I begin to see that folly and not ill-will may have been at work. Much of what he says is indeed truth. I sought a young Christian soul in Mehedia, a boy enslaved by mischance, for whose safety his father was prepared to pay many thousand ducats in gold. Believing this a mere spying device, our Syrian friend may well have deceived himself. Learn now that the boy I sought was indeed in the care of the Syrian's sister. As an earnest of his goodwill and yours, let him be found, and no more need be said of this matter.'

Almost parallel with his own voice, the secretary's low translation came to an end. The Syrian's face, like a weeping child's, puckered. 'Many thousand ducats of gold?'

'For the return of the boy, alive and well. Some of this of course,' said Jerott smoothly, 'would be the rightful property of the city.'

Sitting up, the Governor addressed the Syrian sharply. 'Where is the child?'

'Bey Efendi . . .'

'Speak! Does he live? Where have you taken him?'

'Bey Efendi . . . with her livelihood destroyed in the fire, my sister lost heart. . . . She took ship today, with the children, to find a new home elsewhere. . . . I do not know where she is bound!'

Jerott's voice was even sharper than the Governor's. 'What was the ship called?'

'I do not know! Yes, yes! I remember, Efendi. It is an English ship called the *Peppercorn*.'

'What was her cargo?' said Jerott. 'The name of her master, her pilot, her officers?'

'I do not know! But she will write, Efendi! She will write to tell where she is; and then shall I seek out the Lord and inform him. Thousands of ducats in gold! And all my silk vanished!'

Jerott stared at the Governor. 'A sad mess, Your Excellency. I wonder how far I may rely on this information finally reaching me? I fear I must ask you to make yourself responsible.'

'I shall. News of this ship will be brought to me: I shall see to that, as soon as this woman writes to her brother. Regardless of cost, I shall dispatch it to you, Mr Blyth, at Malta.'

Hell. Jerott, flogging a sick brain, looked solemnly at the uneasy Spaniard. 'Not to me, señor. This information is for one more exalted by far. Address it to Signor Leone Strozzi, Prior of Capua. That is the man whose path you have so carelessly crossed.'

'*Madre mia* . . .' said the Governor. 'And your own plans, Mr Blyth?'

'To rejoin my ship somewhere off Djerba, as soon as I may arrive there,' said Jerott austerely. 'I imagine a horse might be forthcoming? An escort . . .?'

Donna Maria sprang to her feet. 'But Mr Blyth will of course come with us. We go to Jerusalem, Jerott. Why not come with us first? Does Malta need you so badly?'

Jerott smiled. 'I must go. But I shall come part of the way gladly. Tomorrow, if the Governor permits?'

The Governor permitted. The Governor gave him a feather bed to repose on, and wine and chicken for breakfast, and an Arab mare and two sumpter-mules on to which he could load his priestly possessions from outside Mehedia. The Governor also would in no way be dissuaded from allotting him an escort of twenty armed men to see him part-way to Djerba, and to attach Donna Maria and her party to a suitable caravan, since her camels and most of her luggage, as she explained with aplomb, would be awaiting her a good deal ahead. They were about to leave, Marthe sitting sidesaddle in a magnificent cloak, with Lymond and Salablanca discreetly behind her, when the news came that the Syrian had been found dead by poison in bed.

'How, then, shall we manage?' said the Governor. 'When the sister writes to say where she and the child will have landed?'

Jerott's eyes and those of Francis Crawford met and parted. 'She will not write,' said Jerott. 'Now. If she does not know of it already, she will know of her brother's death soon.'

'But . . .' said the Governor. 'If she hears of this generous reward . . .'

'If she makes inquiries,' said Jerott, 'I am sure you will hear of it and send the news, from your courtesy, to the Prior in Malta. But I fancy she values her life more.'

The sun was shining as they rode out through the gates of Mehedia, the twenty horsemen behind them; and, after collecting Jerott's possessions, and many others under that pretext from the village, turned their horses' heads east towards Djerba.

They rode silently; Jerott with a high temperature that showed itself about noon, and enforced a rest during which Marthe scientifically rewashed and rebound his injuries, fed him orange-juice, and watched the dispassionate face of her steward. When, presently, Lymond came over, she spoke to him quietly. 'Mr Blyth needs rest. Is it quite beyond your ingenuity to get rid of these men?'

'Not at all, if you fancy a slit throat or a spectacularly close view of a lion,' said Lymond. 'Otherwise you must suffer them, I'm afraid, until we catch up with some other protection. Once we're near Djerba, it's simple. . . . Jerott?'

Jerott stared up through his headache. 'I can manage,' he said.

'Yes. I think you'll manage better tied to your horse,' said Lymond. 'Salablanca will do it. Mademoiselle, you look hot.'

Adjusting her girth, Marthe paused, exasperated, as he came over. 'It is difficult, on the whole, to look anything else in eleven God damned ells of Lucca velvet. Mr Crawford, do you know the English ship *Peppercorn*?'

Pausing, his hands cupped to give her a lift, Lymond looked sharply up. 'No. Do you?'

'Yes. She has a regular run. When I do work for Georges I meet her at the same time always in all her various ports. If she left Mehedia yesterday, I know where she's bound.'

'Then so did the Governor?' suggested Lymond, his eyes on the clever, impatient face.

'Of course. He wanted the money. But if you board the *Dauphiné* now, you'll get there before him. The *Peppercorn* goes from Mehedia to Scanderoon.'

'Scanderoon. The port for Aleppo?'

'Aleppo, Persia, and all points east and south. I imagine you were going to use the *Dauphiné* anyway to track the other ship down?'

'Yes . . .' He gave her a lift, neatly, and, as she settled herself in the saddle, gazed speculatively up at her. She said, on a spurt of unusual temper, 'If you say I look hot once again, I shall die of boredom, I think.'

'Don't die,' said Lymond pleasantly; and swinging into his own saddle, gathered the reins. 'Have a fit.' And the procession moved off.

*

The sun that day, for the first time, showed its real strength. Out of the shade of the olive trees, it struck, ringing as bronze, on the flat plains outside Sfax; on the grey flinty plains of the desert that stretched beyond, interrupted by the oasis at Gabès. The Spanish soldiers, surcoats over the burning shell of their armour, rode in bitter discomfort, silent except for the occasional command: even the open longing with which they stared sideways at Marthe gave way, in time, to gloomy endurance. Jerott, with Salablanca's dark hand on his reins, was hardly conscious at all.

He did not see Lymond, watching him, suddenly make up his mind and move over, quietly, to speak to the Spanish commander, or the change of direction which took the whole company across the gritty sand-flats to Gabès. He was aware, first, of an occasional relief as they passed the more and more frequent handfuls of palm trees, and then of the skyline of greenery and tall, interlaced trees that spoke of the presence of water. Sitting up a little, his inflamed eyes tightened against the glare, he saw the first white mud walls of

134

Gabès come into sight, and the sharp moving shadows of horsemen, breaking out through the trees. The sun, sinking golden into unsophisticated textures, suddenly struck off tinder sparks of hard light among the palm trees and these, Jerott saw, came from the riders who thronged out with their shadows from the huddle of buildings.

They poured out, a great many of them, their turbans like bog cotton above sallow faces and wide-sleeved jackets and trousers; and in their grasp the lances and bows and wide-bladed swords of Damascus flashed and glittered and the sound of their voices, shouting, fell thin and crowded on the wide desert air. Jerott felt Salablanca's grip on his reins tighten, and saw that Lymond was already on his other side, his drawn sword in his hand.

'A hundred . . . two hundred, at least,' said Francis Crawford's even voice. 'And they're behind us as well. I'm sorry, Mademoiselle Marthe . . . Jerott. It's a perfect trap, I'm afraid. Stay in the trees, and don't try to escape. We'll have to surrender.'

Jerott's disused voice was barely audible. 'The Spaniards won't. It would cost them their lives. That's the standard of the Aga Morat, the Governor of Tripoli. He'll kill every Spaniard he can reach.'

Lymond, his head bent, had already knotted a large white scarf to the point of his cane. 'Then let's hope,' he said, 'that they feel rather differently about a Special Envoy of France.' And leaving the girl and Jerott still mounted, waiting under the palms, he spurred forward, with Salablanca, to the head of the troop.

Marthe and Jerott watched them go: watched the white-robed circle of horsemen closing inwards on the knot of armed Spaniards, the light arrows already beginning to fly. 'They're poisoned,' said Jerott, and shut his lips hard. A poisoned arrow might be the kindest death an Arab army could offer a woman under the protection of Spain.

Then they saw, within that trapped band of horsemen, the snatched words between Lymond and the Spanish commander apparently come to an end. Among the polished steel something fluttered—the white scarf Lymond had tied to his whip. Holding it high, Lymond rode out from among the circling group of frantic horsemen, straight out among the falling arrows and towards the Aga Morat's blue standard.

Jerott did not look at the still face beside him, but he drew a long, shaking breath, and spoke. 'Do you see?'

And with her eyes also on the solitary horseman: 'What else could he do?' Marthe replied.

It was a long ride. Presently, the arrows stopped falling while the Arab horses stood still in their wide circle and the rearguard, at Gabès and within fifty yards of Jerott's back to the west, made sure that none breaking through should escape. They saw Lymond, swordless, reach the standard, and brown hands close on his stirrups and reins before the robed figures hid him completely. 'The Aga Morat . . .' said Marthe suddenly. 'He is Turkish, is he not?'

'Yes,' said Jerott; and forced himself into coherence. 'He commands an army which used to be based on Tagiura. He was the lieutenant of Barbarossa, the corsair, when Algiers was taken, and he helped two years ago to fling the Knights of St John out of Tripoli. He's not inimical to France, but Francis will have to persuade him that he *is* a French envoy . . .' Jerott fell silent. Two years before, Francis Crawford had fought for the Knights of St John at Tripoli, as Jerott had done. And even if he were not remembered from that, how could he explain, how in God's name could he explain how twenty armed Spanish soldiers came to be escorting them?

'If he is wise,' said Marthe smoothly, with the uncanny aptness which he found so disconcerting, 'our friend will represent himself and us to be prisoners and the Spaniards our captors. The Spanish are killed; we are free, and the Aga Morat escorts us to Djerba. How Mr Crawford will take pleasure in moving his pieces. Meredoch, son of Hea, with his holy hands severs the knots.'

'That's . . . less than generous,' said Jerott. 'I should trust him to try to save the Spaniards' lives as much as our own.'

'Would you?' said Marthe. 'Then, Mr Blyth, sit up and look.'

There was no sign, this time, of the white flag. If Lymond was there, he was unseen, among the rearguard of the Arabs. But the Aga Morat's standard was moving. Slowly taking the forefront, it was moving inwards, towards the small band of Spaniards, and at the same time, all the horsemen in that wide circle put their mounts to the trot. Slowly at first, then faster and faster, with the grey dust rising high above their white turbaned heads and obscuring the the deep blue of the sky, the Aga Morat's trained army, swords flashing, arrows flying, galloped in towards that tight knot of soldiers and, arriving with a crash and a shout that shook the choked air, they raised their blades and started to kill.

True to their training, the Spaniards held together. Back to back, with sword and dagger and the hooves of their horses as weapons, they fought and killed in their turn, were wounded, and died. Without looking round, Jerott knew that as the sound lessened, as the blinding fragments of armour showed less and less among the twisting robes of the horsemen, the line of men at his back had drawn nearer; had encircled the small grove in which he and Marthe sat their horses, and that at a sign from the standard their fate, also, would be decided.

Beside him, Marthe, perfectly white, had not moved. Jerott said, 'You saved my life at Mehedia. There has been no time to thank you.'

She did not look at him. 'I enjoy acting,' said Marthe in her clear, intolerant voice. 'As . . . he does. The human scene is well rid of us both.'

Very soon after that, the carnage was complete, and the signal they expected came clearly from the blotched and littered sand of the battlefield, where the Arab horsemen, little reduced, had already dismounted to pillage the dead. There were no Spaniards living. Some, their horses cut down beneath them, had attempted in the end, blindly, to run, and had been hewn down, delicately limb by limb and feature by feature, while begging for death. Two, released from their armour, had had the flesh of their backs slit for spread-eagling.

Jerott saw the signal pass, and the Arabs waiting outside the palm trees begin to filter towards Marthe and himself. His head swimming, he none the less pulled himself straight in the saddle and began, slowly, to pull out his sword. In Marthe's hands a little dagger winked in the sun. Jerott said, 'Though I can't help you, I shall still pray for you. Who are you, Marthe?'

She had moved to face their assailants, but at the question she turned, and he winced at the irony in the brilliant blue gaze. '*Qui nescit orare, discat navigare*. . . . Why ask now? Do you expect to live to gratify Mr Crawford's curiosity?' said Marthe.

'. . . No. You said,' continued Jerott, weakly dogged, 'that the world was well rid of you both. I cannot believe it.' The Arabs were very close now: he could see the high saddles and the tasselled housings on each little horse.

'Oonagh O'Dwyer would believe it,' said Marthe. 'And the branded baby at Bône. And the woman Kedi and these twenty soldiers, and the infant catamite, wherever he may be going. Don't you think they would all have been happier if Francis Crawford had never existed?'

'It's easy to blame. What can you know of him?' Jerott said.

'All I know of myself. Too much. And nothing,' said Marthe.

She cut a man to the bone before she was overpowered, and the knife wrenched from her as she tried to turn it on herself. Jerott saw it, and in a fury of pity and anger pulled his sword up with both hands and brought it, weakly, again and again across the thrusting mass of his assailants before they overwhelmed him. Aga Morat's men did not kill either Jerott or the girl there and then. They took them, cruelly lashed on horseback, across that strewn and bloody arena under the hot sun to Gabès, where in a clearing between the deserted white walls the Aga Morat, sitting under an awning of reeds, studied the smooth umber flesh of a young Moorish girl he had just accepted as tribute.

On the edge of consciousness, Jerott saw the scene as he was cut from his horse: the silken thighs and underfed ribs of the girl as she swayed round and round, smiling vaguely, under the prod of her handler; the intent black eyes of the Turk, as he sat crosslegged on the latticed shade of his carpet, the jewel-handled knives glinting dimly in the silk of his sash, and in his turban the Pasha's feather in gold.

In the shadows behind him, Francis Crawford, resting at ease, stirred, and murmured in Arabic, '. . . No. I favour the other. Sweet to be taken up, as medicine is by the lip; sweet as the swelling out of the new moons, and full. Take the other.'

'It shall be,' said the Aga Morat comfortably, and snapping his fingers, followed the girl with his eyes as she was forced away, running. Then he turned. 'Ah. Mr Blyth. I have been sharp with thy friends. Thou wilt in thy heart forgive me, for as a stone with which perfume is bruised, I release thereby the truth. It is long since I entertained a Knight Hospitaller of your Order.'

Swaying, Jerott stood in the sun, hanging on to his saddle. In Lymond's averted blue gaze he found no advice and no help. He said, 'As Mr Crawford I am sure will have told you, Lord, I am no longer of the Order.' The brute was not only gross: he was scented. Competing with the reek of sweat, of spiced food, of blood Jerott inhaled unspeakable emanations of sweet basil and spikenard.

'It is strange,' said the Aga agreeably. 'Doubly strange, when so short a time past thou exerted thyself at Tripoli so mightily. Triply strange, when at Mehedia, I am told, thou wast vehement in proclaiming the attachment. He who now calls himself Crawford was in Mehedia no more than the steward of this lady. And this lady, whom I am asked to believe is a Frenchwoman, there called herself a noblewoman of Italy. How may one poor in understanding as myself resolve such a tangle?'

Lymond's voice, speaking from under the canopy, was bored. 'By taking us, as I have said, to Dragut Rais, who will make all things clear.'

'But verily,' said the Aga Morat, 'when the prince is absent or niggardly with his permission, I am able to take permission of myself when I will. The lady is fair.'

'The lady,' said Lymond, 'is the special care and interest of Henri of France. To thy intelligence it must be clear that this thing must be hidden from the fools at Mehedia. Further, it is she who is to present to the Grand Signor himself the gift we convey to Stamboul from France. Should she fail from weakness or excess of the sun, the Sultan cannot be pleased.'

'She may sit,' said the Aga Morat. 'And Mr Blyth also, while we exert ourselves in this affair. It is suggested I take you all three in custody to Dragut Rais's castle, there to await his pleasure when he returns?'

'We are your servants,' said Lymond. Huddled in some haphazard patch of shade, where Marthe's strong hand had led him, Jerott distinguished a note in that level voice he had not heard before. Looking up, straining, however, he could detect no bodily signs of fatigue or unendurable stress. Lymond, on the contrary, sat with picturesque grace, his head bare, his doublet dusty but untouched, his shapely hands lying loose.

Then Jerott observed something further. As he was studying him, so the Aga Morat's eyes rested on Francis Crawford also with a curious and vivid attention. And unlike Lymond's, the Aga Morat's plump hands were locked hard together: clean and sweating and pink.

'It is said,' said the Aga Morat, 'that blindness of the eyes is a lighter thing than blindness of the perceptive faculties of the mind. The sun is high: the perception is dazzled. One has made divers chambers available to us in these poor houses for an hour. Let us retire and, by giving ease to the flesh, bring new light also to the proper functions of the mind. There, for the Hâkim's servant Mr Blyth, and the lady. In this chamber, Crawford Efendi and I shall have much to discuss. . . . Sweet to be taken up, you say, as medicine is by the lip. Such a creature I enjoy, thin-skinned, tender and delicate, light of flesh and goodly in make, impulsive in walk and beautiful in the justness of stature. Communing thus, shall not our dreaming souls melt?'

For a moment, Lymond did not reply. Then he said, in the same level voice, 'It is written before God, that after this hour we depart all four, in good health to Djerba?'

The Aga Morat had risen. Looking down, his heavy face creased in a smile. 'It is written,' he said.

Slowly, Lymond rose also. He looked neither at Jerott nor at Marthe, but stepped straight out from under the awning and confronted the Aga. In the blinding white light, the fine lines of his skin were all suddenly visible, and his eyes by contrast quite dark. But his hair, uncut since Marseilles, shone mint-gold in the sun. 'If it is so agreed,' Lymond said, 'I am solicitous for thee, as thou art for me.' And without pausing, he followed the Aga Morat into the house.

It was all Jerott waited to see. Before they pulled him into the room he was to share with Marthe and Salablanca he had fallen into an uneasy sleep; and, muttering, was hardly aware when, the hour ended, they were brought out and mounted again. Carried, finally, by Salablanca's wide pommel he knew little of the brief journey to Djerba when, leaving the wilderness behind, they flew to the shore and across the crumbling causeway to where the island stood on the hot blue horizon: a single line of silvery sand and the fronded green of uniform palms.

Forced awake, briefly, by the splashing as eight hundred hooves sought the square, sunken stones Jerott confirmed again that his companions were there: Salablanca beside him, unchanging; Marthe beyond, her lips tight and blue circles printing the white skin under her eyes. Then he looked for Lymond, and found him after a while, riding alone, among Arabs, his gaze directed ahead. Jerott closed his eyes, and relaxed.

*

He opened them in the prison they were to inhabit until Dragut Rais returned to his home; a prison of fountains and palm trees and the music of soft-feathered song-birds weaving slight winds like the flyers of the spinning-wheel from perch to perch of their cage. Roses grew by his pillow and petted carp swam to his hand in raised channels of marble veined in pink and in blue. He lay on silk and fed from black hands on new bread and nectarines and sea food seethed in fresh milk.

The negresses could not answer his questions. It was three days before, in the light warmth of new morning, they took his carpet and cushions out to the patio and, lying there, he saw the robed girl sitting near him was Marthe. 'So. Correct in faith, and the adversary of death. You survived,' said the girl.

'So it seems. Francis and Salablanca?'

'They survived also. The Aga Morat has gone. We are here to await Dragut Rais's pleasure.'

Jerott glanced round. Beyond the low walls that enclosed them he could see hedges of cypress and myrtle, and the soft hide of ripe oranges showed among the gloss of ranked trees behind them. It seemed less a castle than a loose pattern of kiosk and courtyard, joined by steps and archways and low colonnaded ways hung with vines. He said, 'The problem of escape isn't an agonizing one, is it? I'm sorry I moulted my flight feathers. What are Francis's plans?'

Marthe turned on him her wide, deliberate blue stare. She had lost flesh, Jerott thought. Although her extreme pallor had gone, there was about her an odd hint of tension and violence, which was not to be wondered at. Alone with strangers for weeks in an alien country and exposed to danger, fatigue and pitiless brutality, what man of her age would be unaltered, far less a solitary, intelligent girl? But her voice, as she answered, was the neutral vessel he knew. 'Mr Crawford is singularly planless. The problem of escape is no problem: escape doesn't exist. Djerba is an island joined to the mainland by a single well-guarded causeway. This is an open prison, that's all.'

'Then the *Dauphiné*? The ship should be here,' Jerott said reasonably. 'Why don't they get your uncle and Onophrion over to vouch for us, if they're so bloody suspicious? I thought that was Francis's whole object in forcing the Aga Morat to take us to Djerba.'

'It was,' said Marthe. 'He underestimated the local growth of suspicion. The *Dauphiné* has been impounded. She's in the pool next to the causeway and my uncle and Mr Zitwitz are on shore. Didn't you recognize Onophrion's cooking?'

Jerott sat up. 'You mean there's a French captain and a French pilot and a French bos'n and a French ship and a French bloody embassy living on board her, and the Aga Morat still won't concede we belong to it?'

'The Aga Morat,' said Marthe, 'has nothing to do with it. We are in Dragut Rais's house now. And Dragut Rais is away. And Dragut Rais's household don't feel like taking any risks. *Permitte divis caetera*, and Deus Dragut isn't at home.'

From sitting posture, with great skill, Jerott got to his feet. 'And precisely whom in Dragut Rais's household,' he said, 'are we dealing with?'

The ironic blue gaze studied him. 'You think you can improve on Mr Crawford's performance? I applaud you. Go straight through that archway,' said Marthe, 'and you will find the whole meeting in conference.'

He was not too bad on his feet, Jerott found. Leaving Marthe smiling her damned smile behind him, he skirted the pool and, picking his way over the thin coloured paving, found the arch and walked slowly through it.

It led, he discovered, to another courtyard, wider than the one he had left, and sheltered by an awning of tasselled white silk. This time there was no pool, but fine rugs lay here and there on the smooth polished paving, and at one end, a shallow flight of steps led to a low, carpeted dais piled high with cushions.

If there was a meeting, it had now broken up. The steps were crowded. Jerott saw Onophrion's bulk, his back towards him, offering something, it seemed, at the dais: around him slaves chattered, dressed in bright silks with bangles rippling on ankle and arm and a blackamoor, crosslegged, played on a whistle. In the main courtyard Georges Gaultier sat, his placid face brown and unchanged, mending a clock in his old smock of natural flax. Under the diffuse light of the awning the thin wheels glimmered under his flickering fingers and in a small cloth there sparkled the gold cogs and pins: the minute litter lay cherished, like the yellow eggs of the bombyx, thought Jerott, which is not killed but is born with no means to survive. Seeking further, at last he found Lymond, hitched alone on the marble edge of a tub, the clock mask with its two ebony hands held between idle fingers. Jerott made his way towards him, and Lymond looked up.

'Jerott. How are you feeling?'

It was what Jerott expected him to say, and yet the inflexions today and those of his awakening in the Governor's prison in Mehedia, still sharp in his mind, were totally different. Then Jerott realized he

141

was comparing two sides of a difficult illness and pushed the thing from his mind. He said, 'What've you done to your hair?'

Lymond's eyebrows shot up. 'Cut it,' he said. 'If you don't mind. I've also shaved, washed behind my ears and trimmed my nails, if you want to inspect them. Personalities aside, what can I do for you?'

Today, Jerott decided suddenly, he did not feel well enough to be mocked. 'It doesn't matter,' he said briefly, and turned on his heel.

He had not heard, amid the rush of light voices and the tinkling of bells, someone rise and come down the steps: he did not realize as he spun round that someone was approaching to greet him until she was so close that turning, he had to fling out his arms to avoid a collision.

He was holding, he found, the straight shoulders and folded-back veil of a beautiful woman. She was small, hardly over his heart, but of a classical perfection: her eyes, looking up at him, were deep brown and momentarily serious. He released her, looking still. He saw a clear, olive face with black brows and heavy coils of black hair, strung on her brow with looped pearls. Her nose was Greek, long and straight, and her lips soft and full. But her voice, when she spoke, was a full contralto, commanding its English with a mingling of accents he was unable to place. 'Mr Blyth? You are well, and have come to discover why you may not proceed forthwith to Aleppo? I am afraid I am the one you must blame. You see, I have explicit instructions from my dear lord.' She smiled, the black brows arched. 'We shall try to make your enforced sojourn as pleasant as possible.'

Jerott opened his mouth and shut it again. Then he said, 'You are . . .'

'I am Güzel, Dragut Rais's principal mistress,' said the woman agreeably. 'But I should like you, if you will, to address me as Kiaya Khátún.'

10

ZAKYNTHOS

On the Venetian island of Zakynthos, in better times known as the Flower of the Orient, off the west coast of Greece, and with the full width of the Mediterranean Sea between herself and the occurrence at Gabès, Philippa Somerville sat in the local Lazaretto in her fifth week of quarantine, playing a cut-throat game of cards for olives, with Archie Abernethy, her escort. Looking on, in varying stages of convalescence, were their three fellow sufferers from Venetian hygiene: a Sicilian currant-importer, a freelance interpreter and another dervish, one of which, said Archie gloomily, seemed to turn up, free, in every two pokes of pepper.

Determined to look on the bright side of things, Philippa collected her winnings, and ate them. 'I don't know,' she said. 'We're a nice, *representative* group. I can do card-tricks, and you can train animals and Haji Ishak can lie on nails and Sheemy Wurmit can do a comic turn with his parrot and Signor Manoli can swear in ten different dialects of Sicilian. We only need a good bass-baritone and a tenor rebec, and we could work out a tour.'

Nobody grinned. Sighing, Philippa took up the cards, gazed sorrowfully at Archie Abernethy, and began dealing again. 'I'm sorry,' she said. 'How was I to know I was a chicken-pox carrier?'

To Archie Abernethy, as well, it seemed a long time since he had left Lymond's ship just outside Algiers and sailed with Leone Strozzi to Sicily in the simple belief that he was about to escort Philippa, her maid Fogge and four men-at-arms safely home.

They had reached Syracuse safely enough. They had taken leave of Strozzi and returned to the inn he had found for them while Archie arranged the next stage of their journey. At that point, Philippa had broken the news that, far from going home, she was on her way to Zakynthos, and why. 'Um,' said Archie Abernethy, staring at her so intently that his two eyes seemed to meet over the broken bridge of his nose. 'So the Dame de Doubtance tellt ye the bairn might be there? And ye've a ring?'

He studied the ring. 'And this wasny from the old lady, but another one. D'ye mind the young woman's name?'

'It was Kiaya Khátún,' said Philippa. 'She gave me the address in Zakynthos I was to call at. And it's no use looking like that, Archibald Abernethy, because I'm going.'

'I doubt Fogge isna going,' said Archie artfully. Fogge, prone ever since Pantelleria, was prepared to set sail again, she had conveyed, in her coffin. 'And if you take the men-at-arms, who's to protect her?'

'I don't want the men-at-arms,' said Philippa. 'It's none of their business. If you're not interested in saving a Christian child from the hands of the Turk, Archie Abernethy, I'll just go on my own.'

'Oh, Christ!' intoned Archie Abernethy through his broken-backed nose, and looked at her sideways, considering.

It had been a matter for concern, of course, and even, he deduced, of unacknowledged jealousy that Marthe had not after all left the *Dauphiné*; and Philippa had displayed a certain nervous irritation during the voyage to Sicily which Archie knew was unusual. Last year in Scotland, as one of Lymond's master-company of officers, he had met Philippa Somerville and knew her for a lassie of good sense and courage. On the other hand, he was not sure how much she knew of his own doubtful history. Once, long ago, his brother had been Lymond's right-hand man in the days of his outlawry. Once, too, he himself had fought with Lymond in Europe. But all the rest of his life, Archie Abernethy had been something else: he had been a keeper of menageries. Two years before, he had kept the elephants of the Royal House in France.

And before that—a good deal before that—he had been in Constantinople. Except that as menagerie keeper to the Sultan Suleiman the Magnificent he was known as Abernaci the Indian, and not as Archibald Abernethy of Partick-head, Glasgow, Scotland. A matter of tactics not so far removed from the truth. India was only one of the countries with which Archie had become familiar in the course of his life. In his professional capacity, he was perfectly capable of conducting Philippa wherever in Europe or Asia she might find reason to go. But what he knew and she didn't was that, on the other side of the Mediterranean, Francis Crawford was already following the only authentic trace they possessed of a child born to the Irishwoman and sold first to a hovel in Algiers and then, it appeared, to a camel-dealer. Jerott Blyth had told Philippa the child had died on being dispatched overseas as a piece of pure fiction to drive her away.

That the child was dead, Philippa would not believe. That it had been sent to Zakynthos seemed very likely indeed, Archie could see, to one exposed to the Dame de Doubtance's mystic pronouncements. Unfortunately, although always meticulous to the letter, the Dame de Doubtance's statements, Archie from past experience was aware, were sometimes a wheen irregular in the spirit of that which they seemed to convey.

So she was a capricious old besom. There was no child at Zakynthos, because the child was known to be still in North Africa. If he, Archie, mentioned that the child was in North Africa, the benighted lassie would turn straight about and sail back to Lymond. If he didn't, she would go to Zakynthos, draw a blank, and return quietly home. Zakynthos, although it paid yearly tribute to Turkey, was

Venetian-governed and safe. So, thought Archie, grinning his crooked, disingenuous grin; let's go to Zakynthos together.

He had begun, in the last few weeks, to grow his black beard again. He knew his languages: he could at a pinch take the turban and blend into his old, familiar identity. The girl was young and plain enough to avoid notice, and in cheap clothing even more unremarkable, passing for a tall twelve. Sewn into Archie's cloak, his baggage, his undershirt was a small fortune in gold which Lymond had supplied for their journey, and part of this Archie used to launch the frail Fogge and her four men-at-arms on their slow journey home. Then, with Philippa, he boarded the English ship *Mary*, laden with tin, pewter, lead, rabbitskins and kerseys from Newbury and bound for Odysseus' kingdom.

Unhappily, since Odysseus' time, the Flower of the Orient had drawn up a few rules. If you wished to enter Zakynthos you had to *far la quarantana*, and stay ten days at least in the Lazaretto outside Zakynthos to obtain your *sede* for the three signors of health.

It was a pleasant enough place, consisting of single stone cells built round a patio and low-roofed, of necessity because of the earthquakes. And although the windows to the outside were small and stoutly latticed in fir, they were allowed to walk in the courtyard and sit in the shade of the fig tree, and the guardian, who lived with his wife over the entrance vault, supplied them with bedding and bought all their needs, as they required, in the town.

Philippa, with a room to herself and the services of the guardian's wife, was full alternately of impatience and a kind of weak-minded alarm over her own rashness. She ought to be at home in Flaw Valleys, doing her morning exercise on the lute, at which, said her teacher, she would have had a distinguished future, had she not been born English.

Instead she had sailed over the blue sea from Sicily to this narrow white town lying at the foot of its green hill with the Proveditore's castle on top; the stony earth studded with olive trees, with sheep and goats grazing; the wide harbour with its piled barrels of oil and its packed ships of every country on earth. Nations at war found in Zakynthos discreet haven for merchant ships, and the banners of the Lion, the Lily and the Crescent flew there together. What happened outside, in the turmoiling dangers of the intricated Isles of the Ionian and Adriaticall Seas, was none of Zakynthos's business.

Faced with ten days in the Lazaretto, Philippa longed to march outside and grapple with the strangeness of it all, exercising whatever sophistication she had acquired in these months of untoward travelling and the despised talent which was the only one she had ever been credited with: a gift for plain common sense.

Not that life in quarantine was humdrum. Sitting in the courtyard between Archie Abernethy and the wee man with the parrot, she was able to watch the Aïssqoua dervish in meditation, interrupted by brief performances of frenzy twice daily, when he rolled on sword-edges, kissed snakes, chewed glass and clutched red-hot iron bars. Philippa heated them for him, when the guardian's wife refused to come in because of the snakes, and inspected his blister-free palms admiringly afterwards while he and Archie held a long foreign conversation which had to do, Archie said, with transcendental meditation. The little man with the parrot, who had come off a ship just in from Syria, sat for a while allowing the Arabic to flow over his head, and then leaning towards Philippa said, 'Are youse English?'

In public, Archie was an Indian animal-trainer and Philippa was, as the fancy took her, niece, wife, daughter or assistant, of nameless origin. Since they always ended up speaking English to one another, it was not a deception they were able to keep up for very long, and in the Lazaretto, Philippa supposed, it hardly mattered. In any case, she was all too familiar with the cadences of that inquiry. 'I'm English,' said Philippa. 'And my friend is Scots, but he prefers to use his Indian name for his menagerie work. And you don't need to tell me what you are.'

The man with the parrot, who was a very little man with a triangular grin and a black bonnet with two dangling earflaps, said frothily, 'No, I ken. I'm Sheemy Wurmit frae Paisley. Trader. And that's Netta. She's no weel.'

Philippa gazed at the parrot, and the parrot rasped Sheemy Wurmit's arm with one gnarled grey claw and stared blearily back. It was moulting. 'I can see that,' she said. 'Archie, this is Sheemy Wurmit, and his parrot's no weel.'

Philippa, who had never before had the experience of introducing two Scotsmen to each other, found to her relief that they got on rather well. Sheemy, indeed, viewed Abernethy's dark, turbaned face with a certain reverent awe. 'Ye'll hae seen a Rhynocerots then,' he said. 'Oo: a right gruesome beast, yon. And yon great humphy-backit deils wi' the long grisselly snouts hanging down twixt their teeth. That's an awful sicht, yon.'

'Elephants,' said Archie.

'Whatever ye call them. And Ziraphs. Hae ye seen a ziraph? All speckly reid and white neck, wi' a camel-heid on the tap that could lick the roof off a ten-storey tenement. Yon's a disgrace against Nature. I seen one cut up back there outside Cairo, for why I'd not care to guess, gin ye needed a speckly stair-runner.'

'Cut up?' said Archie quickly. 'D'you mean dissected?'

'I mean cut up,' said Sheemy Wurmit. 'By a fellow called Giles.'

'Peter Giles?'

'I dunno. Giles. He was on his way to Aleppo to get another beast there. He makes drawings of their insides. He'd done it before, with one o' yon humphy-backit . . .'

Philippa, watching Archie's reminiscent black eyes, remembered suddenly who this must be. Archie's hero, Pierre Gilles of Albi, scholar and zoologist, who for years had toured the Levant on commission from the monarchs of France, finding and buying precious manuscripts for the French royal libraries, and sending home unique animals for the French royal menageries. Archie knew and revered Pierre Gilles of old; and for a moment Philippa wondered if the pull was strong enough to divert him to Aleppo, and away from his search for the child. But although he asked one or two questions, Abernethy soon dropped the subject when it became clear that the other man had no other information; and taking Netta instead, began to examine the parrot.

Later, as the parrot's treatment progressed and they met, day after day, in the courtyard in company with the dervish lying peacefully on his swords and the Sicilian merchant muttering over his papers, Philippa learned that few people knew their Europe better than Sheemy. As *terdji-man*, or interpreter to traders, and dabbling in the barter line sometimes himself, he crossed and recrossed the seas. Just now, he had stepped off a boat bound for Venice with a cargo of Tripoli ash for glass-making: 'Man, that'd gie ye a hoast,' said Sheemy. 'Rubric from Aden: that's another hell o' a cargo. Ae spatter o' rain, and your hinter end's reid as twa cherries.'

'What's the cargo you like best to carry?' said Philippa.

'Wine,' said Sheemy fondly. 'Now there's good living for you. A wee hole through the bung and a good stout reed in your jaws, and ye can sook like a lord till you're paralysed. I've had it that far down the barrel I've had to join three reeds together and I took a week to get over the crick in my neck.' He rubbed it, remembering, and scratched. 'I dinna ken if it's the ash or the lice, but I could fairly caper with itches.'

'You've got spots,' said Philippa, viewing him critically. 'I expect it's the garlic.'

The triangular mouth funnelled like an exhaling cod. 'Christ,' said Sheemy Wurmit, and after a quick squint down his shirt, to her surprise, he shot into his chamber, undoing his strings as he went. A moment later the Sicilian, who had been listening unashamedly, followed him, his face white where it wasn't powdered lightly with pimples. A great deal of shouting followed, in which the guardian and his wife took a full share; and a small crowd began to gather, like magic, outside the walls. The dervish, scratching abstractedly, looked up from the board full of nails he was lying on, and spoke to Archie Abernethy, who was pitching dice all to himself in the dust. Archie said, 'I expect they think it's the pox.'

'That's nonsense,' said Philippa firmly. 'My goodness, as if I hadn't seen spots just like that all over the stable-boy just before I came away. It's chicken-pox; that's what it is; and I've had it, and we're due out on Thursday.'

'It's chicken-pox,' agreed Archie. 'And you've had it, but we're not due out on Thursday. Instead, we've just got ourselves another forty days' quarantine.'

The dervish proved a very bad patient and they had to tie mittens on him to stop him from scratching the scabs. 'You'll be marked for life, Haji Ishak,' said Philippa sharply. Her Arabic was becoming much better under Archie's tuition, and Sheemy gave her two hours of Turkish a day. It was at the end of one of these that he showed her his pearls.

Philippa had wondered, but had not asked, why the little drago-man had left ship at Zakynthos. Now, looking at the lustre and size of the heaped pearls in paper-thin kid which he untied and set down before her, she didn't ask if they were bought or smuggled or stolen, but smiled and admired them until he put one in her hand and told her to keep it. 'Another o' Nature's marvels,' said Sheemy, brushing aside her alarmed thanks. 'A fellow told me. On the twenty-fourth of the month this dew comes down on the water and it's collected, wrapped, and flung into the sea; and then at the right time these other fellows get let down on ropes to the sea-bed and bring it all up.'

'The dew?' said Philippa. 'In bags or boxes?'

'In buckets,' said Sheemy, oblivious. 'Or nets. Y'see, it's all changed into these wee creepy worms in hard jeckets.'

'Oh,' said Philippa. 'And then what do they do?'

'Take their jeckets off,' explained Sheemy. 'And there's the stones in their pooches.'

'What stones?'

'They stones. The pearls. These. That's where they come from.'

'It *is* one of Nature's marvels, isn't it?' said Philippa. 'And now what will you do with them?'

'Sell them,' said Sheemy, smiling a fond, triangular smile. 'There's a Venetian laddie here that Signor Manoli buys his currants from: ye'll have seen him, maybe, passing in bills of lading and chatting outside the window. He's no let in, and I canna pass the stones out, but he's crazy to have them. Come the end o' this damned quarantine and I'll be up to the House o' the Palm Tree like the wind.'

'The what?' said Philippa.

'The House of the Palm Tree. Where this merchant Donati does business.'

'Donati,' repeated Philippa. She didn't look at Archie. She didn't, in fact, focus on anybody but bent all her powers of mental digestion on this pair of facts. The House of the Palm Tree, Zakynthos, was where she had been sent by the Dame de Doubtance in Lyons to find the lost child Khaireddin. And Donati, *Evangelista* Donati, was the name of the Venetian woman whom Sir Graham Malett had chosen to chaperone his sister in Scotland in the last months of her life.

It might have been coincidence, but it was unlikely, thought Philippa shakily. The Donatis were creatures of Gabriel. In the end, blaming Gabriel for the death of his sister, Evangelista had turned against her employer, and after Gabriel's flight Madame Donati had also left Scotland to return home, one took it, to Venice.

But Evangelista Donati was a woman, and had been attached to the girl. The rest of the family—this merchant Sheemy spoke of (a brother? a cousin?) who exported currants in Zakynthos—might have no cause to quarrel with Gabriel. Philippa knew how strong and how lucrative was the spell Graham Reid Malett could cast. She said, without giving herself time to regret it, 'Sheemy. I've a story to tell you.'

Afterwards, Archie said she was soft in the head, and she knew she had taken a risk. But there was something about Sheemy Wurmit she was ready to trust; and in any case, she was revealing no secrets. She told him about Sir Graham Reid Malett, Knight of Grace of the Order of St John who had returned to Malta after failing in his plans to control Scotland. And she told how he was taking his revenge on the man responsible for that failure by concealing a child; and how, by threatening the child's life, he was also preserving his own.

Sheemy's eyes became unglazed. 'Here, I heard of that!' he said. 'The coast's fairly agog over some Frenchman offering a ransom in gold for a wean. But he's not a Frenchman?'

'No,' said Philippa patiently. 'His name's Francis Crawford of Lymond. The family come from Midculter.'

'Oh, *them*,' said the Paisley man slowly. 'I kent the grandfather, the first o' the barons. So this is the heir?'

'No, it's the third baron's brother,' said Philippa, who since her several visits to Scotland had become notably brisk at genealogy. 'Richard, the present Lord Culter, has a little son of his own who'll succeed him.'

'Oh, I mind fine,' said Sheemy. 'He married late, did he not? And until he got the boy, this brother Francis you speak of was the heir? And wait you a bitty: wasn't that younger brother outlawed? Now I see it. A wild one, and out for the title. If I were your baron Richard I'd watch out for my son. Men've been known to kill their nephews before now, and put their sons in their shoes. Nae wonder he wants his own laddie found.'

'I don't know *what* you've been reading,' said Philippa. 'But you'll never go through life with your head stuffed full of nonsense like that. They may go on like that in Tripoli, but you can take it from me that Mr Crawford would never dream of harming his brother or nephew even if he could put his own son in their place, which he couldn't, as the poor thing isn't even legitimate. No one,' said Philippa, blotched unbecomingly with temper, 'seems to be able to credit that a father should care what becomes of his son.'

A breath of embarrassment, in passing, kissed the gummy, triangular grin. 'Oh, I wouldna say if they came to your notice you wouldna gie them a dandle,' said Sheemy. 'But after all, who's tae ken where they are, or which is yours or another's? A wean's a wean: wet at baith ends and no very smert in the middle. . . . All right,' he said hastily, as Philippa opened her mouth. 'All right. Your friend's a right big-hearted Da. But are ye sure he doesn't just want the bairn so that he can kill Sir Graham Reid Malett?'

'Does it matter?' said Philippa. 'So long as someone gets that poor child out of Gabriel's control and back to where he belongs?'

There was a short silence. 'It was awful wet in Paisley,' said Sheemy. 'But maybe you're right. Anyway, ye can aye count on Sheemy. Sheemy's the one for a rammy. We'll go to the House of the Palm Tree together.'

It was a while before they got there, as Sheemy's parrot died in the morning, and three days after that Haji Ishak went down with the mumps. His suffering, reported Philippa, was terrible to see, and she cuffed Archie, who was sitting in the yard among the glass and the cold iron bars, laughing hysterically. Forty days later, they were given their signed *sedes* and let out of quarantine, their clothes stinking of brimstone. The dervish disappeared. The Sicilian went off to the harbour. And Sheemy Wurmit, Abernethy and Philippa made for the House of the Palm Tree, Zakynthos, at last.

*

The long, narrow street between the west side of the harbour and the foot of the hill was unpaved, and the House of the Palm Tree nearly a mile along its length. Trotting, in her down-at-heel shoes, to keep up with the two men, Philippa fell over her feet, clutching her cloak as her eyes spun in her head, registering the throng of pushing humans and animals, the figures robed, furred, brocaded, naked, the heads bare, turbaned, veiled and capped in every size and colour of headgear, the skins of every mutation from umber to russet. Donkeys tripped past, pregnant with impossible loads; caparisoned mules with a Greek woman, earringed and décolletée, sitting astride,.or a Venetian, sidesaddle, with a high silk collar and cloak, her chains jangling.

Down towards the harbour, where she counted the masts of twenty ships and the banners of eight nations, crawled the heavier traffic: the hand-drawn barrows, the bullock-carts, the hogsheads of oil and wine labouring in procession on sweating dark backs. Children danced in and out; dogs, in a rolling of bristle, pressed against her creased skirts; there was a strong smell of goat.

There was a smell of incense: from a low, plastered building came a dim gleam of candlesticks and the familiar harping of Latin: it was an Italian church, with a Greek chapel next door. Every seventh or eighth house, she thought, had been a warehouse or a Greek Orthodox church: Mammon and God, as usual, went hand in hand. Archie said, 'What will you say to him?'

'What?' said Philippa; and then, shaking herself, gave Abernethy her full attention. For weeks, she had considered this whole interview, bearing in mind the singularly few confirmed facts which had brought her. When Dragut Rais left Algiers for the winter, Jerott had said, the children were mostly sold off. The baby Khaireddin had been going overseas, but had died on the way.

It might be true. It might be false, but Jerott might believe it to be true. And, Philippa had already concluded, with an unsentimental logic which would have shattered the Chevalier Blyth, it might be false and Jerott might jolly well know it. Two chances out of three said that the little boy was alive. And reinforcing these two was the Dame de Doubtance's firm belief that she, Philippa, would have news of the child here in Zakynthos.

There had been authority in that prediction. There was also, for Philippa's money, a strong suggestion of mischief. If this Venetian merchant of the House of the Palm Tree was indeed related to Evangelista Donati who had cared for Gabriel's young sister, then the child had been sent there for hiding by Gabriel and she, Philippa, had only to mention Lymond's name to be splat like a pike.

On the other hand, Signorina Donati had ended by turning against Gabriel, and might be willing to help, even if her relative were not. Philippa had not been able to find out whether there were any womenfolk in Marino Donati's household, but she was going to. She said to Archie, 'I don't think we should mention Mr Crawford at all. We've come to sell Sheemy's pearls, and I'm there to persuade the Donati ladies to buy them. Leave the rest all to me. You know. O boo de la thing.'

'What?' said Archie, in his turn.

'You know. The thing they say about camels. At the end of the trail . . .'

'You mean the thing Mr Crawford says,' said Archie with ungenerous malice. '*Au bout de la trace on trouve toujours ou le chameau ou le propriétaire du chameau.*'

'That's it!' said Philippa. 'That's it exactly. Only of course,' she said cheerfully, 'Mr Crawford says it in French.'

*

The first thing that was immediately plain about Marino Donati was that he was unmarried, and that this was not in any way a surprise. A big, stocky man with indigo jowls and a soapy brown

151

dome blotched with pigment, he wore an embroidered silk robe, certainly not for comfort, over his sweaty, creased tunic, and an intaglio-cut ruby fastened his belt.

He showed no interest in the black pearl Sheemy offered him: rolled it irritably to and fro on his thick palm while referring, trenchantly, to the bad state of trade; and when Archie, unruffled, in passable Italian pointed out the ladies' pleasure in trinkets, Signor Donati answered, shortly, that there were no women in his house but kitchenmaids, and he wouldn't have those if the footmen could be induced to stay on without. Sheemy, genteel but casual, held out his hand for the black pearl, received it, and, untying a quantity of thin chamois, laid it prosaically among the three or four score perfect pearls thus revealed and began carefully to retie them.

Marino Donati let him actually put them away in his pouch before he said, with equal detachment, 'I wouldn't touch them myself, with the demand for coloured jewels this year. But if you have a few top quality matched pearls, I might know of a buyer. He would expect some concessions on price.'

'Would he?' said Sheemy. 'Ah, he's a man after my own heart. But what's to be done; and the worms that proud that it takes a shower of golden zecchinis to open one little sneck? An oyster's a hard man to cross.'

'A Venetian,' said Signor Donati bluntly, 'is also strongly resistant to force. I am conversant with current prices.'

'No more ye should be,' said Sheemy with equal treachery. 'But the latest prices of pearls, you'll allow, is something I'm more likely to know. For example'—he flipped open the chamois—'there is a pearl that a Queen could put in her ring. In Florence it would fetch forty ducats, and I'd take more than that at Anet.'

Lying on the table, the pearl shone sulkily and then, unaided, began to trundle slowly down the polished wood. The chamois shivered. Somewhere in the house something fell with a crash, and a child cried. As if at a signal, all the pearls in the chamois stirred, eyed one another and, jumping a little, ran out on to the wood and filled the table with a small and myriad droning.

They began to drop off. Sheemy, his hands all-embracing, his eyeballs glimmering white, began to sweep them towards him: Archie, fists cupped, tried to salve those that fell; Donati, ignoring them both, had half risen to his feet and, holding on to his chair, started to speak.

A chest slid past him. Another crash, lightly porous, told of fallen pottery, and was followed by other sounds of heavy objects falling, both indoors and out. Shouting started, and the barking of dogs, both drowned out almost immediately by the loud and irregular clanging of a number of bells. Philippa, rising, slipped out of the room. The floor, vibrating under her, reminded her very much of the *Dauphiné*.

152

The merchant's house, built low on two storeys, was no more than half a dozen small chambers erected round the main stockrooms. The smell of fruit followed Philippa through two bedrooms and along a small gallery: once she opened a door and closed it hastily against a warm hail of small fleshy objects running into her shoes.

Of all the rooms Philippa discovered, the signor's study was perhaps the most interesting. She stayed there briefly until, impelled by the waves of vibration, she fled to the kitchen below. It was empty. She moved quickly through it, and out into the courtyard, which held two running menservants, a maid having hysterics, and a young man seated peacefully on the edge of a well. Somewhere a child was still crying. She had located the sound in the stables and was making towards them when the young man called out in Italian. 'It is Jacomo, who is frightened of earthquakes. He is not hurt, signorina.'

Philippa, who spoke dreadful Italian and was not impressed by beautiful young men, said over her shoulder, 'It is sometimes worse to be frightened than to be hurt, as you may find out,' and ran on.

The stables were empty of horses. Prone on the straw, screeching, was a negro child of about four. His cut velvet eyes staring at Philippa, he continued to scream, in regular staccato pattern, while she gathered him up in her arms, tut-tutting in calm reproof of his conduct. He stopped screaming. 'O marvellous one,' said the young man, still seated behind her. 'Made breathless by the garden of thy grace. Instead of tears, but dew; amorously biting the lip of the tulip. Jacomo and I crave leave to worship thee.'

'Why?' said Philippa. She grinned at Jacomo, who grinned liberally back. 'That's just common sense. If you comfort children, they think there's something to be frightened about. If you scold them, they know it's all right.'

'This, I see, is thy philosophy for earthquakes,' said the young man. 'And for fire, holocaust and plague: what is thy remedy?'

Sitting down on the well's edge with Jacomo held firm on one knee, Philippa thought. 'I'm awfully afraid I should just go on scolding. I don't like the steamy emotions.'

'Why, what could befall thee?' said the young man. 'These are the sweet passions; the frangible arts. Lacking them, thou wilt become as Signor Marino Donati.'

'Bald?' said Philippa tartly; and the young man, who was evidently far from simple, at this simple reply dissolved into a cascade of silvery mirth. Philippa gazed at him with reproof, which developed into a stare of frank interest.

He was a Geomaler, she realized. His sleeveless tunic was of royal purple linen, and his bare arms and legs in their thonged sandals were brown with the flawless tan of the nomad; his smooth cheeks rose-brown, his shining dark hair resting combed and clean on his shoulders. No possessions lay on the soft dust beside him. The richest object about him was a long girdle of silk, thickly embroidered with bullion, which he wore wound round and round his slim waist. At each end was a small silver cymbal; and small bells, sewn to tunic and sandals, made a sudden lyrical sound as, now, he stretched and rose to his feet. Perhaps Greek, probably rich, certainly well-born, he was a Pilgrim of Love; one of the queer dilettante sect of whom Archie had told her, travelling Asia from patron to patron, giving of poetry, music and love in exchange for a livelihood. 'You disapprove,' he said.

Philippa set Jacomo down, but he clung to her, and she kept an arm round him. The bells had stopped ringing and the loudest noises had ceased, but the earth still stirred itself in tremors under her feet, and in the street people called. But for themselves, the courtyard was empty. 'Disapprove? No,' she said. 'Provided that Signor Donati is not your patron.'

He had dark grey eyes, with which he held hers in thought. He said, 'From today, he is not.'

Philippa grinned. 'A convert?'

His eyes did not change. 'My preacher saith: "I esteem not Mohammed to be more excellent than Jesus—on the twain be peace." As for Signor Donati, my wish is that he shall obtain always precisely that which he desires. I can imagine no worse evil for his end. I shall take boat for Lesbos.'

'Why Lesbos?' said Philippa.

'Why not? The child would offer thee something.'

Entranced by the self-sufficiency that took as natural her interest, while evincing no curiosity at all about herself, Philippa had forgotten the boy. It was true. Rummaging inside the cut-down shirt he wore, the child had hauled over his black wool a piece of grease-polished string and, attacking it with his teeth, was attempting to free the blackened token through which it was strung. Putting her hands over his, Philippa said, 'No, no. My goodness, what would your mother say? You can give me a kiss; that's all I . . .'

After a long space, she added, absent-mindedly, '. . . want.'

'The ring troubles thee?' asked the Geomaler. 'Why?'

She said it in her head twice, and then said it aloud. 'Because I have its twin.'

'How?'

Splat like a pike. Philippa, desperately following her mythical fortune, said simply, 'I'm looking for a European child, a white child about eighteen months old called Khaireddin, who was brought up by Dragut. The ring was supposed to help me find him. . . . How did Jacomo get the twin ring?'

'Jacomo? Jacomo was brought from Algiers as a slave with his mother along with one or two other children, some white. When the other children left, Jacomo was given the ring.'

'It belonged to one of the other children? Whom did it belong to? Where did they go?'

With a shiver of bells, the Pilgrim seated himself again, without answering, on the rim of the well. 'But I do not understand. He is thy child?'

'*Use* your common sense!' said Philippa. And then looking down, her face red, she said, 'Heavens. Steamy emotions.'

'So thou hast learned one thing about thyself today,' said the young man thoughtfully. 'I think I may teach thee much.'

'Manners, for a start,' said Philippa, still blushing. 'I'm sorry. I feel strongly because . . . because of the injustice of it all, not because it's mine. Its father and my mother are old friends, and then the baby fell into bad hands and is being used as a kind of hostage against its father——'

'By Signor Donati?' asked the young man sharply. 'No. That is unlikely. But by him for whom he works? That, perhaps.'

Philippa did not answer. There was no need. For good or ill the truth was out. 'I am right, I see,' said the Geomaler. 'The child was confided to Marino Donati by this same Knight of St John who conspires with the Turks?'

'Who *what*? What do you know about Gabriel?' said Philippa, sitting bolt upright. 'Oh, *bother*, here's Archie.'

The Geomaler smiled. 'By the harbour,' he said, 'there is a house painted blue, owned by one Ziadat. I shall be there. My name is Míkál.'

'Mine's Philippa,' said Philippa. She hesitated.

Míkál smiled again, and still smiling, drew the child Jacomo from her side to his. 'No living thing has ever suffered through me. Assure thyself of this,' he observed.

'I know,' said Philippa. 'I'm sure,' she added, more convincingly. 'It's just that I was hoping you'd make an exception for Graham Reid Malett.'

*

Sheemy had sold his pearls, for a sum with which he seemed guardedly pleased. Philippa heard all about the transaction, in boring detail, all the way back to the harbour, where they bought some pies in a cook shop and sat on the harbour wall, eating them. Half-way through these, Archie had time to address her. 'Yon was damned dangerous, running about in an earthquake. Where did you go?'

'I didn't like it,' owned Philippa. 'But it seemed such a good excuse to explore. And I found out . . .' She stopped. Then fumbling under her cloak, she brought out, laid flat on her palm, the two gemmel rings, from the Dame de Doubtance and from the child Jacomo's neck. 'I found out Oonagh's baby was there.'

155

In absorbed silence, they heard her tell of Míkál. Pilgrims of Love were not outside Archie's experience. He had, she had found, a wide tolerance of the crankier aspects of the human dilemma, although Sheemy's indulgent contempt was more commonplace. 'Ye think he knows where the wean's gone?' he said. 'That's why ye want to go to this house?'

'I don't know. But he does have something more to tell me. And I've found out something else. Gabriel is selling information to the Turks, probably through Marino Donati.'

'Sir Graham Malett? From Malta?' said Archie. 'How?'

'He didn't say,' said Philippa, her brown eyes shining. 'But I think I can guess. Sheemy, where's the Sicilian merchant?'

'On board his ship, I expect,' said Sheemy, surprised. 'D'you want him?'

'No. But I want his bill of lading,' said Philippa.

The dragoman, unsurprised, nodded his head. 'Secret writing? Consider it done.'

He brought it to them that evening, in the blue house by the harbour, which turned out to be a lodging-house, of which Ziadat was the owner. Míkál, on inquiry, was out. Philippa, heavily aware that, sooner or later, she would have to get used to communal sleeping arrangements, dumped her mattress, newly bought in the market, along with Archie's, Sheemy's and two others in one of the small rooms. Then, before any others came in, she bespoke a candle and, with the two men peering behind her, held the bill of lading close to the flame.

Between the lines of the clerk's black irregular script a brown tracery began to appear, deepening in the heat to form even lines of palimpsest writing in an educated hand. The language was Italian; the writer was clearly Marino Donati.

The code was an easy one too. They broke it in ten minutes, Sheemy dictating while Philippa wrote it down with her tongue out. When it was finished, they read it in silence.

Your news coming Strozzi attack Zuara received and passed on. Aga Morat will counter. Distinguish yourself blue panache. . . . There followed an inquiry about the new defence at St Elmo. The last line ran: *The Subject is at Djerba, to be held till after Zuara. The Object goes to Stamboul.*

'The bloody traitor,' said Archie. He stood up, his broken-nosed face like the bark of an olive tree. 'Graham Malett. He's going to stand there and let Leone Strozzi lead the Knights of St John straight into the arms of Morat. . . . Blue panache, ye bastard!' said Archie, his black eyes half closed in his cracked face. 'I'll be there watching out for the blue panache all right. And I ken someone else who will, too.'

'*The Subject is at Djerba.*' Philippa hadn't even heard what

Archie had said. Instead, trying the final phrases over on her tongue, she repeated them. '*The Subject is at Djerba. The Object . . .*' What did that mean? A routine report, using a code inside the code. Philippa said slowly, 'Archie . . .' and broke off as, just within the rim of her hearing, a brush of high, tinkling sound passed over the noise from outside. 'Míkál?' said Philippa, just as the curtain over their doorway was raised with great gentleness to one side.

'Surely,' said the dark-haired young man in the violet tunic, and, susurrating silvery music, he walked smoothly in. 'And these are thy friends?'

Performing the introductions, Philippa was all too conscious of the Geomaler's dark grey eyes resting on the bill of lading dropped on the table, the interlaced foreign writing plain in the candlelight. Míkál, smiling, bowed. 'I see thou hast lit on the secret. I have witnessed the signor, often, shading a little paper over a candle. He does not expect simple minds to understand.'

'I was lucky,' said Philippa. 'I'm afraid I opened Signor Donati's desk on my way through his rooms. There were several packets of bills already treated, but until you talked about Gabriel, I didn't realize what it meant.'

'Did I mention Gabriel?' said Míkál.

'No. I did. Your purity remains undefiled,' said Philippa tartly. 'Whatever happens to Gabriel, if there's justice, will be my pleasure. We only wanted you to tell us, if you will, about the child.'

She wasn't feeling casual. It had taken a great deal of nervous energy to defy Archie's outspoken disbelief and drag him to Zakynthos. His lack of reproaches over the delay in the Lazaretto had been a burden itself; and now she had embroiled Sheemy Wurmit mercilessly in her single-minded affairs. Her friend of the religion of love said in his musical voice, 'Thou wouldst learn of the child from Algiers, the white child whose ring was given to Jacomo?'

'Yes. What is his name?' said Philippa. 'And what is he like?'

The candle shivered, starring his earrings with silver, but without lighting his eyes. 'His nurse, the mother of Jacomo, called him Lambkin, Kuzucuyum,' said Míkál. 'I know no other name.'

'He's healthy, is he?' said Archie; and in the dim light Míkál's mouth sketched a quick smile.

'Like a bullock. Hewn from sparstone, like satin, containing its light. Masked like a Schwatzen horse with yellow silk hair, chopped along the bridge of his nose. A nose; two eyes, and a mouth. He speaks English.'

'From Jacomo's mother?' asked Philippa briskly. Her voice, ratting on her, split in the middle.

'From the nurse he had left in Algiers. He is between one year and two. He walks, eats, shouts, laughs, sings, and is a proper boy-child. That is why the Commissars took him away.'

'The Commissars!' said Sheemy Wurmit sharply.

'Thou knowest, then,' said Míkál, turning. 'The Commissars for the Levy of Children. They came here a month ago for their tribute and took him, with the rest of the levy.'

'Why . . . *where* has he gone?' said Philippa without any breath left at all.

'East, to be sure: they make the Devshirmé only every four years, and children have to be gathered from Albania, Servia, Bosnia, Trebizond, Mingrelia—from every part of the Empire as well as in Greece. One in three male children, at the choice of the Deputy. That is the custom. Then . . .' Míkál shrugged. 'The least comely will till the fields in Natolia, learn Turkish and how to endure hardship: they are circumcised and become followers of Islam. Presently, they are brought to Constantinople, to the Aga of Ajémoghláns, and are taught crafts, or the art of war. The best of these may become Janissaries. The worst carry water and wood, clean the Seraglio, care for the gardens or the horses or the barges, or serve the Spahis and Janissaries themselves. He will not be one of these.'

'What then?' It was Archie, as Philippa's voice failed her.

'The good corn; the beautiful; the bright, are the Grand Sultan's own. With three thousand hand-picked children the boy is on his way to the Topkapi Seraglio at Stamboul. For four years he will live in the harem, serving and learning, under the wisest men of the Empire. He will be taught Turkish, Persian and Arabic and the Sheriát of Islam. He will learn to run like a gazelle, to ride, to shoot, to cast the javelin, and the arts of wrestling and falconry. He will be taught music and poetry and the exercise of his senses. If he is chosen as a page, he will be adorned with delicate tints, dressed in sweet scents and in clothes of scarlet and white. In time, he may fill one of the highest offices of the land. He may become a judge, a jurist, a court official, a governor of a province. He may become Agha of the finest of troops, the Janissaries, the Bostanjis, the Spahis. He may, if he is brilliant and wise, become Grand Vizier, or supreme head of the civil and military empire under the Sultan. For thus does the Sultan rule. Through former Christians, without parents, without money, without brothers, without power, who owe all to him; and in dying, will leave it to him once again. . . . This child: the child of thy quest has gone to all this. . . . Wilt thou bring him back?' said Míkál.

'Yes,' said Philippa.

'To what?'

There was a silence. Frightened, Philippa looked at Archie, and then at Sheemy Wurmit and, instead of an answer, saw the same question reflected in two pairs of eyes. To what?

To his heritage? He was a bastard. To the world of Gabriel? But that meant hurt, deprivation, and ultimate death.

In Constantinople, or Stamboul as she must learn to call it, he would be rich, cared for, and safe. He would learn the graces his mother would never teach him, and the arts his father would never take the time to bestow. With every talent trained and cherished, he might grow to position and power incomparable. But . . .

Her face red, Philippa said, 'I'm not bringing him back to anything. I'm taking him away from something.' And again, Míkál said only, 'From what?'

'From the life you've described. From being a scholar, and also a page to the Sultan. From dying rich, and dying without kinsmen. From distorting in Islam a temperament shaped for Western philosophies. From wielding a power that may bring him face to face on a battle-plain with his own flesh and blood. . . . Míkál, will they allow me to buy him?'

'If thou hast money enough, go to the Commissaries who accompany the levy and make thy wish known. If they are already in Stamboul, then——' He broke off as Philippa jumped to her feet.

'The *Subject*! Of course. Archie, that's what the message meant. *The Subject is at Djerba.* Who else is Gabriel tracking so carefully but Mr Crawford! So the *Object*——'

'. . . is the baby,' said Archie.

'*The Object goes to Stamboul*,' quoted Philippa exultantly. 'It fits!' She frowned. 'But if Gabriel is already intriguing with Turkey, he'll make sure that they don't sell the baby to Lymond. We ought to get it back now, before it gets to Stamboul; before Gabriel even knows that we've found it. With Mr Crawford chasing false clues all over North Africa, of course Gabriel's suspicions will be lulled. Think of it,' said Philippa gloatingly. 'We let Signor Donati, without suspecting anything, supply another bill of lading in place of the missing one, secret writing and all. Mr Wurmit—you *will*, won't you?—travels on the same ship to Malta, sees the Grand Master and exposes Gabriel's collusion with Turkey. Gabriel is finished, and Leone Strozzi's expedition to Zuara is a howling success. Meanwhile,' said Philippa dreamily, 'Archie and I follow the children, find and pay for our yellow-haired bullock and bear him home to his father on elephants. Paeans, circuses.'

There was silence. Then Archie Abernethy cleared his throat briefly. 'You've overlooked a wee something,' he observed. 'If Mr Crawford's a prisoner on Djerba, it's on Gabriel's orders. If anything happens to Graham Malett, Mr Crawford'll no live long after it. Man, they'll fill him with stuffing and bread him. He's got to get out of Djerba beforehand. Moreover——'

'Moreover, I'm no blate about going to Malta,' said Sheemy Wurmit comfortably, 'but the way winds are, I might well get there two weeks too late. There's no date set for this attack on Zuara. It might be over, for all you and I ken.'

Philippa's bony jaw squared. 'I see,' said the heir to the Somer-villes. 'It's the good old freemasonry of gentlemen squires. You want to go straight to Djerba, get Lymond out, and sprint off to Zuara to save the Knights and make leched beef of Blue Panache in person. You've forgotten one thing. If Gabriel dies, the child dies. If you go, how do I get to that party of children?'

'I take you,' said the Pilgrim of Love. Reclined with grace on a mattress beside them, he had faded from their attention, occupied with planning and argument. Now, as he stirred, the lamplight fell on his graceful limbs and his angular, open-eyed face, and the little bells whispered. 'In a place known as Usküb, in north-west Mace-donia, the children are gathered. They will not have reached Stam-boul yet. I shall take you to them, I and my friends. You will be safe. But it means you entrust yourself and your money to me. You are not prepared to do that.'

Philippa considered him. A plain child, her thin face weathered to the colour of good oxblood hide; her hair reduced to mud-coloured thatch by the sun and her hard-worn, voluminous skirts not only grimy but distinctly frayed round the hemlines, she was unequivoc-ably nobody's moppet. She said, 'I think I trust you. But Mr Abernethy has more experience of the world than I have. Archie?'

Archie Abernethy drew a deep breath and, from the bottom of what was indeed a profound experience of men and animals, drew of his knowledge of both. 'Your name is Míkál,' he said. 'And you're one of the Pilgrims of Love. I've kent others. They're not all pure, not holy, nor indeed very strong in the heid. But one and all, they've been well-meaning bairns. What I must ask you now is not whether you mean well; I think ye do. But have ye the wits to safeguard and cherish a lassie?'

'It is said, "Every soul is held in pledge for what it earns,"' said Míkál. 'I vow to you, by my soul, that I shall protect her.'

'You are vowed to love,' said Archie. 'If she is threatened, or the gold she carries, what will protect her?'

'They are the slaves of violence, whose master I am,' said Míkál. 'Can there be doubt who will prevail?'

'I spoke of a man,' said Archie. 'A man at present in Djerba. The gold is his gold, and the boy is his son. If the girl is harmed, or the son, or the gold, God will dance for him.'

'I hear thee,' said Míkál blandly. 'God send thee no more rest than a Christian's hat: but thou art a good man.'

'I understand lions,' said Archie.

*

They took their leave of her, Archie and Sheemy Wurmit, next morning: Sheemy to travel to Malta, blithely, to meddle in Sir Graham Malett's affairs, not without hopes of reward; and Archie

160

to take passage on a south-bound trading-ship which would, expensively, land him by skiff outside Djerba. He was dressed in his turban, his speech accented in Urdu.

It was Philippa's last link with home—the very last. The last link with Scotland. The last link with Kate. The last link, perhaps, with Francis Crawford, on whom, through the years, she had spent so much unhappy dislike.

There had been no hint, in that cheerful, self-confident upbringing on the North Tyne, that one day she would find herself alone in the Ionian Sea, on the verge of a journey into the unknown with a stranger of one day's acquaintance, seeking a child of that same Francis Crawford's.

She had been happy at home. Gideon, the most gentle of fathers, had in his life been her hero; Kate had been and was her beloved. What the grown-up future might hold she had always mistrusted. She feared and disliked the sophistication of courts; she treasured the freedom of childhood; she shied from the bore and the prig, the sentimental and the smart, the intense and the humourless. She had been cynical, as was Kate, about senseless adventure. A different thing, she and Kate had told each other, from the slaking of a well-formulated cultural hunger. . . .

'Oh, *Kate*,' said Philippa, with a lemony smile; and, drying her one cowardly eye, blew her nose and went off briskly to place her honour, her quest, and her hopes of minimal daily nourishment without overmuch garlic at the feet of her Pilgrim of Love.

11

DJERBA

On Djerba, the August sun, burning, had set fire to the whole white-hot arc of the sky; blazing down on white sands and white walls; on the painted green and black of the palms and their shadows; on the idle nets, the sun-dried shallops drawn up on the beaches; and the lustreless spars of the *Dauphiné* as she lay idle at anchor in the inner pool.

In the villages; in the little market town near the palace, the curs slept in the shade; the camels rested, chewing, their liquid eyes almost closed; mules stood motionless, drooping in the silent courtyards. And in Dragut's palace also, in this the worst heat of the day, people and animals slept, those that could; and those who could not amused themselves in their various fashions.

The mistress of Dragut's palace, who called herself Güzel, or Kiaya Khátún, had taken her lute to the picture-maker's, a cabin in a little-used courtyard behind the stables; and was playing and singing, absently, in her thickly golden contralto, while she watched the old man who, in spite of the heat, was working with spidery delicacy among his papers inside. She didn't turn as Marthe came through the open door, but continued what she was singing, her eyes downcast, her brow clear under the little band-box hat with its short, pristine veil.

> *Le temps a laissié son manteau*
> *De vent, de froidure et de pluye*
> *Et s'est vestu de broderie*
> *De souleil luyant, cler et beau. . . .*

Marthe, her airy sarsenet breathing over the marble floors; her unbound hair caught behind each ear with an ivory comb, bent over the pans of still water and said, 'If, as I assume, you wished to dispatch Mr Crawford out of earshot, you may rest assured: you have.'

Kiaya Khátún's eyes, amused, studied the girl for a moment; but Kiaya Khátún's voice, undisturbed, concluded her song.

> *Il n'y a beste ne oyseau*
> *Qu'en son jargon ne chante ou crie*
> *Le temps a laissié son manteau*
> *De vent, de froidure et d'ennui . . .*

'I know,' said Güzel cheerfully, laying down her lute. 'He was here earlier, watching Youssef. Extraordinary, is it not, how he cannot bear music? Here, in the land of the Lotophagi, where we should make love and live of the dew, and the juice of flowers and roses. . . . And you, as well as Odysseus, are discontented.'

Youssef, laying his papers aside, had risen slowly from his low stool, and bending over the nearest water-tray, was preparing his pots of pigment. As the girl watched, he stirred the water with his finger, and set swimming upon it, drop by drop, the oily colours: cerulean and indigo, maize, russet, umber and aubergine; spot by spot merging, blending, coalescing and shoaling, in forms elliptic and cycloid; into whorl and veining under the soft, titillating finger. 'Can he hear your music?' said Marthe.

'Youssef has no tongue. He cannot speak; but he can hear,' said Kiaya Khátún. 'Does it not please you, to live in the company of such men? Your young, dark-haired friend is learning to recognize that he is in love with you. You should consider him.'

'Should I?' said Marthe. Beside her, the old man had shaken drops of sage and vermilion on his water-mosaic. She watched him shape them. 'Poppies,' she said. 'Güzel, they are beautiful. This and your music . . . you have happiness. Why cannot I find it?'

'Because you do not look in the right places,' said Kiaya. 'But why consult me? I only give you advice which you do not take. Look, he is placing the paper now on the water.'

Marthe did not look. In a voice which she could not quite prevent from shaking, 'Jerott Blyth is *nothing*,' she said. 'I would choose a cur, a cat, a house goose for company sooner.'

'He is a man,' said Güzel quietly.

Silence fell. His arms bare, his movements smooth with the skill that defeats age, Youssef lifted the sheet of paper floating on the colour-skeined water and, turning it dyed side uppermost, laid it flat.

On a groundwork of delicate veining, a handful of poppies glowed, their vermilion petals and green leaves spiralling in an echoing mosaic of colour. Her eyes full of tears, looking at it, Marthe repeated, 'It is beautiful. Is there nothing for me?'

Her fine eyes watching the girl, 'What about Odysseus?' said Kiaya Khátún.

Marthe turned away, and moved to the door. 'He is not a man,' she said. 'He is Chaos, a mythical bird with a name, but no body; agreeable only to the eye of the mind. . . . The Aga Morat's tents have come back.'

'He finds the plains here suit his cavalry trainers. . . . Recognize him, then, with your mind. Why not? Two cold temperaments may consort well together.'

Marthe looked round. 'There is a saying: When two hungry people lie together, a beggar is born. He will get what he will get; and so shall I. . . . Shall I play for you?' And taking the lute Kiaya quietly held out, the girl Marthe sat, her face pale with the heat, and added crisply, 'If I serenade Mr Crawford, perhaps it will make my regard for him plainer.'

She had a high voice; not trained as was Güzel's, but tuneful and pure. Through the still heat of Djerba the words floated with an almost professional clarity:

> *Je prie à Dieu qu'il vous doint pauvreté*
> *Hiver sans feu, veillesse sans maison*
> *Grenier sans blé en l'arrière-saison*
> *Cave sans vin tout le long d'été.*
>
> *Je prie à Dieu, le roi de paradis,*
> *Que mendiant votre pain alliez querre*
> *Seul, inconnu, et en étrange terre*
> *Non entendu par signes ni par dits . . .*

At the end, 'It is a way of life you defend,' said Kiaya Khátún, unmoved. 'But not necessarily a good one.'

She said no more, although the old man Youssef, limping forward as Marthe left, laid in her hands, still shining, the chambletted picture of poppies. Marthe thanked him, and moved out of sight through the courtyard before, with trembling fingers, she tore it across and across.

*

Presently, for the mistress of Dragut's palace was nothing if not purposeful, there arrived the hour Kiaya Khátún had determined to devote to her principal prisoner. This time she took some trouble, as she had not done with Marthe, to ensure that there should be no witnesses.

In the past weeks the woman whose name was Güzel had had several exchanges with Francis Crawford, about whom she knew something from a great many sources.

She was also well aware that this prolonged captivity, with heat, boredom and frustration, was undermining the nerves of some of her prisoners. For their own reasons, Marthe and Jerott Blyth quite evidently were finding it hardest to bear. Onophrion Zitwitz, who within two days had deferentially taken over her kitchens and marketing, clearly found in these activities some relief from his anxieties. Gaultier, with a placidity she found a little irritating, drifted quite unworried into a pleasant routine which took him from room to room, admiring the lavish fruits of Dragut's plunder: aligning an ivory here; correcting a timepiece there; replacing, with loving care, a fallen jewel in its setting. Time to Georges Gaultier alone, it seemed, was of no moment: first of all the company he had eaten the lotus.

To the casual eye, the same seemed at first true of Lymond.

Certainly, in none of their exchanges so far had any intemperate word passed between prisoner and captor. She found him outrageously charming, and cleverer by far than she had expected. She discovered that she was being sounded, with great skill, on a number of subjects, and it was early established, without discomfort on either side, that she was not amenable to bribes nor to any equivalent service he might offer her. He was to remain under duress, without concessions, for precisely as long as Dragut might choose.

After that discussion, she saw him less. The first key had failed. With skill and adroitness, he proceeded to try all the rest. But her servants, as she well knew, could not be suborned. Dragut's hand fell too heavily for that. The guard on the galley was impregnable, and so was the watch on the causeway. In any case, he had no money—she had seen to that: the saddles taken carefully to pieces, the quilting unpicked. He had been carrying a sum which would outfit Dragut's fleet next winter.

What he did next, in fact, was nearly to escape her. Blyth was not yet recovered. Knowing, she supposed, that she would not touch a sick man, and that Gaultier and his niece from an old friendship were safe from her, he had laid his plans with precision, informing nobody, and after half killing a guard one moonless night had swum out to the fishing fleet, one of whose members, at market one day, had not been immune to promises. Mr Francis Crawford had been three miles out of the bay when they had caught him: she had allowed them some latitude in subduing him. Dragut had said only that he should not, if possible, be killed. The fisherman had been ganched.

That had been four days ago, and she had not sent for him until now. Dragut had had made for her, Turkish-style, a kiosk in one of the gardens, its walls set with mother-of-pearl and pierced to admit the faintest airs from rose and hyacinth, mint and lemon and thyme.

Inside, around three of the walls ran a low silk-covered divan, full of cushions: in the centre, the floor was made of glass, below which a channel of fresh water ran. In hot weather the voice of the brooklet was cooling. In winter it flooded the kiosk, and the divan grew grey mould. You cannot, thought Kiaya Khátún with regret, have everything. She sat down among the cushions, her bracelets tinkling, and listened for Francis Crawford, her painted feet crossed.

His footfall was light, but Güzel heard it coming; even heard the hesitation, at one point, between step and step. She said, raising her voice, 'Don't, I pray you, give way to nostalgia. This is not Algiers.' As she finished, he appeared in the doorway.

'Of course it isn't Algiers,' said Lymond, his voice brittle with hard-controlled temper. 'Algiers is full of fat Turks.'

They stared at one another. Heavy bruising was evident on one side of his face, and there were cuts on his eyebrow and lip. He didn't limp, but a stiffness suggested itself under the light Arab clothes he wore; the white cotton, loosely tied at the waist, fell clear to the ground.

'You wish me to respect your sensibilities?' said Güzel. 'You behaved ill-advisedly, and your ally has been punished. You are fortunate that Dragut Rais is not here, or someone's life would equally be forfeited for the guard whom you attacked. I make it clear now that if there is any repetition your steward Zitwitz will be bastinadoed to death. Not one of your colleagues, Mr Crawford, but your servant.' She paused. 'I wonder where you obtained the ring you gave to the fisherman?'

Standing still in the doorway, his eyes veiled: 'You know, surely,' said Lymond. 'It came from my newly betrothed. Now let's go and ganch *him*, liver, lungs, tripes and trillibubs, and add a last of seal's fat to the commonweil?'

'Sit,' said Kiaya Khátún. 'I find rhetoric tiresome.'

Lymond crossed the glass floor, paused by the shot-silk upholstery opposite her, and sank down, with some care, among the cushions. 'But the situation breeds rhetoric,' he said. 'Like fleas in a bucket of pigswill. . . . *Make thou fast, Gabriel, the gates of hell.* For example.'

'Thank you,' said Güzel.

'Not at all. The food, however,' said Lymond, dispassionately, 'is excellent. They shall not hear therein vain or sinful discourse, except the word Peace, Peace. Continue. I have been extinguished red-hot in vinegar and am tempered to talk. It's a nice day.'

'The King of England is dying,' said Güzel. 'If Mary Tudor is Queen and dies childless, Margaret Lennox will succeed her.'

Unblinking, Lymond spoke softly. 'Who says so?'

'The court. Of all women, she is Queen Mary's favourite, and Elizabeth is a bastard. Then Lennox rules Scotland.'

'He may,' said Lymond. 'Until I have killed Gabriel.'

'There is more,' said Kaiya Khátún, blandly. 'The French army is in confusion; the French fallen back from Thérouanne, and Seigneur d'Essé slaughtered. The King, they say, speaks only to Mistress Diane and St André, and not at all to the Constable. The fate of your company is not so far known.'

'I shall find them,' said Lymond. 'When I have killed Gabriel.'

'There is more. . . . Hugh Willoughby is sailing for the Frozen Sea by the palace of Ivan Vasilovich, Emperor of Russia, to find the courts of the Great Cham of China. Sir Thomas Wyndham goes with two royal ships to the Gold Coast, hoping to capture Portuguese trade with the Orient. Cabot tries still to sell his secret routes to the Emperor. De Villegagnon goes to begin a new life in Brazil. . . . And if Gabriel kills you first?'

'It will all go on,' said Lymond. 'With someone else. The waters

166

recede, leaving a fruitful mud behind them. And I shall be immediately reborn as the son of a Brahman. Your last steady position, I take it, was with Gabriel?'

Kiaya Khátún lifted shapely black eyebrows. 'My advice is disinterested. The price of Gabriel's death seems a little inflated.'

'And what of the boy?' said Lymond lazily. 'Three empires and a fortune in our grasp but for him! He will never appreciate it.'

Güzel said, 'You do not even know if he is whole.'

'He does not even know that I exist,' said Lymond.

She rose. 'That seems important?'

'To me,' said Lymond, 'that seems equal to the sorrows of Job. I've enjoyed this so much. You must visit *my* kiosk.' He rose, straightening his shoulders. 'Give your masters my compliments. How did you come to look for me with the fleet?'

Kiaya Khátúm smiled. 'Every camp has its traitor,' she said. 'Yours is no exception. Goodbye.'

*

Nursed by slaves and fed by Onophrion Zitwitz on fish wafers and coloured jellies, egg custards and stamped oranges with honey and cypress root, Jerott Blyth had made swift convalescence. During this, he had seen little of Lymond, who clearly did not want his company; and the news of Lymond's attempted escape had left Jerott speechless. The next morning he passed the doomed fisherman, a sickening carcass on the walls, on his way to answer a summons from the Aga Morat, whose pavilions dotted the sandy plain: his escorting soldiers hurried him past with the points of their lances.

All their guards had been changed and increased in number, and two armed men now followed each of them whenever they stepped outside the palace: Lymond's doing assuredly. Rumour had it that Dragut's woman had proclaimed that any further escapes would be paid for by the torture and death of Onophrion: Onophrion, shrugging, had said, without any great originality but with characteristic fortitude, 'To make an omelette, eggs must be broken. My death is no loss compared with Mr Crawford's, when one considers the garments one has prepared for him; chest after chest; all of them unused.'

Walking across the sand between the Aga Morat's soldiers, it struck Jerott that only a short time ago it would have seemed inconceivable even to ask himself whether or not Lymond intended to put Onophrion's life thus to risk. Insulated in his own island of trouble, he had failed to notice the extent of the breach—the empty bed, the unspoken counsel—which now lay between them.

Entering the Aga Morat's tent, blinding scarlet and gold under the morning sun, the first voice he heard was Francis Crawford's, speaking softly as he did in extreme anger, and in Arabic. Then, as his eyes grew accustomed to the shade, Jerott saw that the Aga, his lips scarlet against the black mass of his beard, was inflated with rage also, sitting outglaring the speaker, his small fists like gourds fastened on to his horse-wand.

Jerott's feet moved on the carpet. Lymond swung round, his face disfigured with bruises and anger, and said, 'You are not needed here. You have the Aga's permission to go.' There were deep weals on his arms. Puzzled and angry in turn, Jerott said, 'What's wrong? The Aga's just sent for me.'

'And you came. That was obliging,' said Lymond. 'Now the Aga wants you to turn and go back. Will you pack up all your cold-boiled emotions, and do what the hell you are told?'

The Aga Morat, gasping with fury, said to Lymond, 'You will pay. . . . You will pay. And for nothing.' Then Jerott, meeting Lymond's blazing blue stare, turned and strode out. Behind him, he heard Lymond fling back at the Aga, *What else do you have?*

For the rest of that day, if he came back at all, Lymond eluded him; nor did he use his bed that night. By the second night, too stiff-necked to go about asking and too uneasy to sleep, Jerott left his mattress and wandered out into the dark, his loose burnous brushing the little hedges and potted trees, the tiled steps and chalices of un-sleeping fountains winking under the moon. Scents marbled the night, streamed and skeined in the air, as tangible as the dyes in Youssef's exquisite picture: lemon and orange, mint, marjoram, rose and the thick, warm perfume of peaches . . . *My beloved is unto me as a cluster of camphire in the vineyards of Engedi.*

His beloved was dead. He could not remember her face; he could only remember what she was not: that her wit did not lance nor her indifference wound; that her eyes were not blue nor her hair long and heavy and fair.

It was Marthe; Marthe who filled his mind tonight; when an invisible key opened the door he had tried so hard to keep shut. He did not know, even now, why it had seemed so imperative to form no relationship with Marthe; he did know that his instincts had been all against trespassing on the no-man's land which lay between Marthe and Lymond.

But both Marthe and Francis Crawford had shown that, far from bringing them irresistibly together, the terrible similarity between them had driven them apart as surely as the opposite poles of the magnet. She was no one's property, thought Jerott, his heart pumping deeply. Since they were so alike, then . . . might he not hope that whatever had once prompted Lymond to befriend him might also please Marthe?

He stopped. The last flight of steps he had climbed had brought him out on the corner bulwark of the Palace: below him, faint in the starlight, rolled the sandy plain, feathered with palms, and the silvered arena where lay the Arab encampment. Behind him, a light voice spoke, known to him in every timbre and cadence and damnable mockery. 'Moping, Mr Blyth?' said Marthe herself.

Very slowly, he turned. Once before she had stood thus with the moonlight behind her on the deck of the *Dauphiné*, and his heart, against his will, had hesitated and caught. Tonight, she had bound her hair in a plait which fell to her waist, and the gown which robed her from neck to foot smelt of myrrh. Waiting; studying him, she saw all the colour leave his face, and heard the sharp breath he took to relieve the constriction over his heart. Walking forward, she laid her arms on the wall, and drew breath in her turn.

'Moping, on such a night for happiness? African roses in the moonlight, and a lover, sleepless, roaming the garden . . . I saw you from my window,' said Marthe's silver voice thoughtfully. 'I saw you, dark and beautiful and restless, walk by the fountain, and I thought . . . to reach the nadir of tasteless and vulgar fatuity, I ought to plait my hair and walk out to meet you. Have you lost him again?' said Marthe with interest. 'He does get mislaid easily.'

But this time she had been too cruel, and too clever. Drawn so wantonly close to the pinnacle, Jerott could do nothing but fall. Quick as she was, she could not escape his two hands, trained soldier's hands, dropping with the weight of the pillory over her shoulders and arms, or his voice confronting her, insistent, striving to be understood, '*Marthe. I love you.*'

He said it again, under his breath; driven suddenly into shock by the feel of her. Marthe studied his face. After the first second she made no effort to move or to escape: her face showed neither apprehension nor any of the actual pain he was causing her.

Instead, she said, 'It seems we are sparing no cliché. You impertinent oaf of a schoolboy. . . . It's because you can't have Francis Crawford that you want me. That's all.'

His hands did not fall: as the cock is snapped back by the trigger, so his unlocking grip sprang apart, and she was free. Jerott drew breath twice and let it out without speaking; and then stood still, breathing raggedly while the seconds passed, his face haggard with shock.

If Marthe felt any shred of sympathy she showed nothing of it. Bland and austere in the moonlight, she merely stared at him, curious, as he searched for something to say or to do. How long he stared back at her neither of them knew; until, all the lines of his striking face blurred with revulsion, 'No,' he said. 'Oh, no. You're wrong.'

'You didn't know?' said Marthe. 'Then it's quite time someone told you, isn't it? . . . Don't apologize. I am not easily outraged. As you know, they are very broad-minded about these matters in Islam. . . . Or if you don't know it, Francis Crawford certainly does.'

Jerott said, 'He has made no . . . Marthe, this is madness! What are you talking about? I tell you I love you. You. Not anyone else.'

She was picking a spray of orange-blossom to pieces. Leaning on the smooth wall, the fat golden plait shining beside her, she let the white petals fall, one by one, down into the abyss below, the crushed scent filling the air. 'I am quite wrong about Lymond? Tell me, why did you come out tonight?'

After the slightest pause he answered, 'Because I couldn't sleep.'

Her fingers working, she spoke without looking at him. 'Because you were worried, perhaps; as a good captain should be, when his commander is missing without explanation? How many nights has he spent away recently?'

'One or two. Several,' said Jerott.

'And would you like to know where he is?' inquired Marthe. 'I would take you to see him, except that he will be very comfortable and possibly sleeping by now. Also we might have some trouble leaving the palace.'

Jerott Blyth moved with sudden impatience. 'Look,' he said. 'This is nonsense. They wouldn't let Francis out of the palace at night.'

'He goes under guard,' she said. 'But like the camel who cannot govern his appetite and will perish in clover, still always he goes.'

'And comes back,' said Lymond agreeably, just behind her.

She turned. Jerott heard a single, sharp intake of breath; but her impassive face gave nothing away. Lymond, equally still, with the faint light touching his hair and the disordered white shirt and European breech-hose he was wearing, stared her full in the face, wide-eyed and unblinking, for a long moment; and then, stretching one negligent arm, let fall through his fingers a small sprinkling of white, shabby petals. 'Don't throw them away,' he said, in the same pleasant voice. 'You may need them.'

'You *were* outside the walls?' said Jerott. He wondered how much Lymond had heard. He found also he actually wanted to be sick. Without answering, Lymond said briefly to Marthe, 'Let him go.'

'That was my intention,' said Marthe. She added, her voice clear as a diamond, 'But first he is anxious to know where you have been.'

'In that case he will, I am afraid, remain anxious,' said Lymond. '*Assai sa, chi nulla sa, se tacer'* sa, so to speak. Furthermore, if we are to have enlightenment, I propose that we have general enlightenment. Will you call Kiaya Khátún, or shall I?'

A little silence fell. The heavy gold plait, loosened by some light humidity of her skin, had begun to unfurl over Marthe's shoulder: the sheen of it, pulled slanting over her brow, gave to her eyes underneath a shadowed, fey quality, disturbing and troubled. She said, 'Do what you wish. I don't care.'

'But I do,' said Lymond. 'I know you are bitter. I won't believe you are jealous.'

170

Marthe broke into laughter. Flinging back her head she laughed, open-throated: genuine laughter, with a thread of hysteria somewhere behind it. The little petals, unregarded, tumbled down the folds of her robe to the ground. When she could speak: 'I don't want Jerott Blyth!' she exclaimed.

'Be quiet!' For the first time, Lymond's soft voice bit. 'I know that. I spoke of something quite different.'

Jerott was trying to get away, blindly, like a man stumbled on devils. It was Marthe, he realized, who, changing place swiftly, had blocked his exit, and Lymond who, now stepping back, said quickly, 'Go to bed. Forget what you've heard.'

Jerott stopped. Marthe said, in the identical soft voice, 'Yes, go to bed, Jerott. But first embrace your master goodnight. Or take his hand. Or lay your head, if you can, on his shoulder. Why do you think he is careful tonight to stand off from you? Because, my dear Blyth, if you go near him, you will know where he has been.'

Jerott paused. In front of him, Lymond had not moved. To pass him, there was no need to approach closely. If he so wished, in his turn, Lymond had only to move backwards to avoid any contact at all. But he stood still and continued to stand still as, drawn by the girl's hatred, and his own hurt and resentment, Jerott walked along the flower-strewn wall, slowly, closer and closer until, with a flash of his hand, he was able to grip Lymond hard by the arm.

There was no need to speak. Lymond's blue eyes, narrowed and filled with a kind of weary distaste, stared back into Jerott's, and Jerott, his fingers and thumb closing on skin and bone, blood and muscle and vein like a tourniquet, harder and harder, admitted to his understanding at last what his heart had already guessed.

Plain in the perfumed night; strident over the soft odours of trees and flowers and cirtons, the scents of sweet basil and spikenard rose from Lymond's moist skin.

Braced though he was, the violence with which Jerott, turning, flung him off forced Lymond to step back to steady himself. Watching the other man stride down the steps and into the garden: 'I am no longer Superintendent of the Five Cereals,' murmured Lymond. He turned, the cold mockery back in his eyes, and stared into Marthe's impassive face.

'I love you not. . . . Oh, I love you not,' he said. 'Engrave it on the rinds of the cypress trees, and swear thy ring-doves to witness. You are a night-hunting sable, my Marthe, and your fur is soft, and your teeth are sharpened and wounding; but so are mine; so are mine. . . .'

He was very close to her: the hair identical to hers ruffled over his brow; the eyes open and inimical, of an identical blue. She could smell, sickeningly, the scent of him and sense, greater than her own, his physical power.

'We are in the mud. Let us wallow,' said Lymond bitterly. And

171

grasping her with fingers as pitiless as Jerott Blyth a moment before had used on himself, he bent his head and forced on her, with extreme and deliberate violence, the longest and the most savage kiss of which he was capable.

Bruised; stifled; contaminated, she could not quite weather it. Half weeping with hatred and with nausea, she gripped the wall as it ended and but for that could not have remained upright when he opened his hands.

Facing her in the moonlight, Francis Crawford too was none too steady: in his heavy-lidded eyes there was a queer lack of focus; a masking almost like blindness. But, after a moment, he spoke his farewell to her in something near his normal, light voice. 'And whether that approached incest or not, I suppose only you know,' he observed; and turning, walked down into the night.

*

The next day, perhaps because it was all too obvious that, with the exception of Georges Gaultier and Onophrion, no two members of the imprisoned party were speaking to one another, Kiaya Khátún allowed them all out under guard, with the rest of the population of Djerba, to watch the Aga Morat's men at equestrian exercise.

Jerott, who had gone to sleep at dawn, to waken with a crashing headache, had avoided Marthe's quarters and anywhere Lymond might be encountered. Without thinking at all deeply about anything, he was chiefly aware of the need to be back in a company of men, fighting something. The recollection that the best company of men he had ever known was Francis Crawford's simply made him feel sick again. He sat down beside Georges Gaultier, who was talking about Aleppo, and ascertained that from its port he could find a ship to take him virtually anywhere he pleased. 'You can get anything in Aleppo,' said the little usurer mildly. One of Kiaya Khátún's doves, stalking forward, hopped on to his hand and he fed it, idly, from a screw of loose grain. 'You've never been there?'

Jerott Blyth shook his head.

'I suppose it's the Sultan's third city now. The main market, anyway, for Baghdad and the whole of the East . . . Goa, Cambaietta. Sugar, cotton, opium, Chinese silk, dried ginger, elephants' teeth, porcelain, pepper and diamonds . . . you can get anything in Aleppo. There's a French station, too. They would look after you, if you have to wait for a ship: and plenty of merchants who have English or French.'

'Pierre Gilles,' said Jerott suddenly. 'Doesn't Pierre Gilles spend a lot of time there now?'

'Now let me see,' said Gaultier. He flicked out the last of the grain, screwed the paper into a ball, and shied it, absently, at the waddling audience of birds. 'The scholar; the man who used to collect animals for the King of France's menagerie? I thought he lived in Rome, but you may be right. . . . Master Zitwitz, our friend here tells me he is leaving for Aleppo.'

Onophrion Zitwitz, treading past from market with a caravan of small boys and donkeys, all equally laden, paused and surveyed Jerott. 'You have cause to believe, sir, that we are conceivably in the first instance about to leave Djerba?'

'None at all,' said Jerott. 'Except that Mr Crawford wishes to go to Aleppo, and by some means I am perfectly sure he will contrive to get what he wants.'

Onophrion's train was blocking the courtyard. He waved it on, then requesting permission, seated himself deferentially a little away from the two men. 'I am troubled,' he said, 'about this projected tour to Aleppo. I say nothing of our imprisonment here, or whether the corsair, when he returns, will or will not decree that we shall all be put to death: that is a matter for Mr Crawford to deal with. But should we be freed, what grounds are there for thinking the child we seek is at Aleppo? Forgive me, but they seem slender.'

'You know what they are,' said Jerott. 'He was taken by ship from Monastir by the silk-farmer's sister in an English bottom bound for Scanderoon. Whether they landed there we don't know. We can only follow and try to find out. If they are found in Aleppo, no doubt Mr Crawford will ship the child home immediately. If they are not, he is perfectly capable of pursuing them both without me. I'm afraid my own affairs are beginning to require my attention.'

However much I try, don't let me turn you against me. But since Marthe had joined them at Bône, Jerott thought, the man who had spoken those words had not been the same person. Or perhaps it was he himself who had changed.

*

The *Peppercorn*, sailing east with a good deal of cargo to unload, ran into unpleasant weather after two weeks between Malta and Candia, and had to lower her sails.

The silk-farmer's sister, who was an old friend of the captain's, was largely unaware of it: she had moved into his cabin a long time ago and was cementing the friendship with hashish. The cook, shredding salt meat and biscuit for the officers, took a bowl below now and then for the child Khaireddin, whom the woman had put in the gun-room. There was no light, but room enough for his pallet, and at night he shared the room with the *comite* and one or two others who ignored but did not ill-treat him. Only, alone during the first day of the storm, he could not keep his feet, being so young, and, rolling and sliding, was tossed for a while between the stores and the walls until, wedged in a corner, he fell abruptly asleep.

When he awoke he was still alone, and one of the crates, shaken loose, was knocking about in the dark. He had learned not to cry, and made no sound in fact until, the ship tilting still further, the security of his corner suddenly dissolved, and he found himself again sliding to and fro in the dark, the loose cases beside him.

When the *comite* unlocked the door the child had screeched himself into hysteria and the silk-farmer's sister, irritated, gave him a thrashing. Then relenting, she lifted him on to his mattress, which the carpenter had nailed to the floor, fastened him to it safely with a lashing under his arms, and checked that the crates had been safely re-corded. He smiled at her hugely as she finished, and attempted, with distraught eyes, to press a kiss on her hand. When he screamed again, through the night, the *comite* got up, cursing, and tilted the ale-jug against the child's mouth.

It worked like a miracle. Finding his night's sleep assured, the *comite*, as time went on, felt better disposed to the child. He cut the dirty fair hair which tangled over his eyes; picked off his lice; and, since he was always wet, found the boy a box full of straw to sleep in, tossing the soaked mat overboard. Then, having made the gun-room habitable, the *comite* largely forgot about him, except to observe to the silk-farmer's sister, in case she had not already noticed, that the brat could hold his drink like a man.

12

DJERBA

The prisoners on Djerba were taken out of the palace in the afternoon when the sun, low in the blue sky, had lost the worst of its heat, and led to the arena where, flanked by the Aga Morat's open-fronted pavilions, they sat under awnings on Turkey carpets covered with cushions, and prepared to watch his Arabs perform.

Emerging from the depths of the palace in his own clothes, his hair still damp from the baths, unscented, unsmiling, Lymond did not speak to Jerott, although he answered Kiaya Khátún's greeting with formal correctness. Marthe, her eyebrows lifted, said, 'Good morning, Mr Blyth. Smile! You look like a toad in a creel full of flowers,' and walking past him, still smiling, put her hand on her uncle's arm. Onophrion followed. Güzel, watching them, her face thoughtful, left the palace a little later, with her attendants, to take place of honour beside the Aga Morat himself in the big, three-sided pavilion. That, later, she was to regret.

The heat was stifling; and the noise, thought Jerott out of his permanent nausea, high-pitched and ululating, might have come from a pack of hysterical hounds. The arena was nothing more than a vast rectangle of plain, neither roped nor in any way circumscribed for the safety of the riders or of the robed and half-naked throng of spectators greeting, arguing, jostling in fez, turban and cap. Sellers of water, of sherbet and sesame bread pushed their way calling through the crowds; a patch of turbulence, marked by bleating, showed where someone had brought a kid and some hens maybe for barter.

Desert Arabs watched in small clusters, silent under striped goat- and camel-hair, their wives veiled in blue cotton smocks, their glass rings glittering no less than their eyes. There were ragged Zinganges, thieves and idlers, selling stolen muscadines and waiting with ready fingers for unguarded purses: a Greek merchant, blue and white turban wrapped round his toque, clapping hands to have sherbet brought to himself and his secretary; women veiled and silent but for the silver chime of the earrings inside their long hair.

Today, Kiaya Khátún was also veiled. Greek-fashion, the white silk fell back from her brow over her long blue-black hair, knotted with gold buttons and pearls and twined with coloured silk ribbons. Her charsháf, falling from the bridge of her nose, covered a fine shift, with wrought silk work at neck and borders and wrists, and she wore a silken coat over it, embroidered with jewels at its edge and dully shining, its leaf patterns damasked in white satin. Under the veil her earrings were tassels of seed pearls, the knots studded with rubies, but her fingers were ringless. From her head to her pale gilded buskins, she spoke of power and wealth.

Beside her, in the Turkish collarless coat, buttoned with acorns, the Aga Morat was attempting, with smiling deference, to disguise the fact that they were quarrelling. His teeth shining white through his beard, he said, 'My lord Dragut said nothing to the contrary.'

'My lord Dragut,' said Kiaya Khátún tartly, 'could not have foreseen that the prisoners would be driven into such a position that they would be ready at any cost to attempt an escape. They are to be kept here, by whatever means, until the Knights of St John have made their attack on Zuara and have failed. If I cannot keep them under lock and key, I will keep them with drink and with drugs. Once they are comatose, you are welcome to visit whichever you choose.'

'I find it difficult to understand,' said the Aga, smiling harder still through his black beard, 'why then they are here and not locked in the palace.'

'Because, such is the wonder of your horsemen, my lord Aga, that my palace this day would empty itself, leaving the prisoners to Allâh knows what mischief. Here, under your omnipotent eye, at least they are safe.'

And the Aga Morat, longing in his eyes and rage in his heart, said, 'I bow to thy wisdom. What is undone may be spun again . . . after Zuara.'

Which was why Jerott Blyth, having allowed the sour milk to pass him, and the water-carrier with his sewn bearskin over his shoulder and his brass staff and cup, suddenly saw weaving through the crowds standing beside him something he did want, carried strapped over his shoulders by a crooked, grey-bearded pedlar in a frieze cloak and goatskin boots.

From over a hundred heads Kiaya Khátún also saw him, recognized the shape of the bladder he carried and said to the Aga Morat, 'There is the seller of *harech*. If they do not buy from him now, I shall see that he is sent to them later. By this evening we shall have some in the palace.' It amused her to think that Dragut, the dreaded killer of the Levantines, was also a true son of Islam, and in his palace permitted no drinking of wine. None the less, she well knew, he would approve any order of hers which kept Francis Crawford and his adherents idle on Djerba while Islam overthrew the attacking Knights of St John.

She looked over all the intervening heads to where Lymond sat on his cushions. He was very still, in a soft almond silk Onophrion must have had brought from the ship; his freshly cut hair burnished; his shirt-pleating white against his lightly browned skin. Then Jerott moved, and Lymond, turning, saw the pedlar of *harech*, summoned, begin to push his way over.

176

Kiaya Khátún saw Lymond say something sharply and, putting out a hand, grip Jerott's arm. And everyone there saw the white anger on Jerott Blyth's face as, turning, he chopped his arm free with the edge of his hand and stood, awaiting the pedlar. Then the horsemen galloped on to the arena, and the little scene dissolved, as men knelt and stood to see better. Satisfied, Kiaya Khátún sank back and watched.

Two hundred yards wide, the exercise-ground stretched on either side of her awning, and receded before her for much farther than that. In the middle distance before her they had aligned three markers of sand, a spear as mark stuck in each, with sufficient space between for six horses to gallop abreast. And in lines of six, level as beading, the riders dashed along the sand now, one line to each course, straight-backed on the small, high-saddled horses, bow at pommel, quiver at shoulder and lance, streaming its long scarlet gold-lettered pennant, held straight as the wires of a cage in each horseman's grip.

For display, Güzel saw, the Aga Morat had given them identical clothing in Dragut Rais's colours. Each rider, besides his white turban, wore a scarlet knee-length coat with wide gathered sleeves over white shirt and striped girdle and long, loose trousers of blue. Flashing past the three heaps of sand to the far end of the arena they had dismounted as one, and each throwing off his coat and quiver, unbuckled and flung down his saddle, remounted, and seizing a handful of darts, set off bareback at full tilt on the return journey, strung out along the four courses, mane, tail and girdle fringe streaming. One after the other the darts arched and tocked into the targets as each man, his horse gripped in his thighs, fled past, turned, flung and, whooping, galloped on up to the awnings and bending, scooped up the staves waiting there. For a second they were all beside her, jostling, shouting, steaming; then, assembled like mercury, they were lined up once more and dashing back to the mark, staves in hand, had struck it and, turning, had flung down the staves and taken up quivers and arrows.

The horses were beautiful: chestnut, golden bays, piebald and dappled, with the small tapering head and arched neck of the Arab, and the swift, free-shouldered gallop. And the speed, whether one cared for horses or not, was entrancing. Smiling her appreciation, Güzel glanced away for a moment to the other awning on her right, found what she was looking for, and watched, her brow creasing. Then, making up her mind, she turned and spoke to the Aga Morat. On the arena the bowmen, galloping from both ends, were passing and repassing in pattern, shooting at the mark as they went. 'I should say,' said Georges Gaultier with a connoisseur's interest, 'that that's dangerous.'

He was, perhaps, the only interested party in the immediate vicinity who was not watching Jerott Blyth and Lymond. After the blow which had loosened the other man's grip, Jerott had wrenched himself free of the crowd and, pulling out the few coins which were all Güzel had left him, offered them all to the *harech*-seller. Those whose view he was blocking shouted, and the guards, standing along the open back of their dais, murmured insults and watched with contempt. The *harech*-seller, unhooking his cup, filled it with raw spirit and leaned to give it to Jerott. Lymond took it, and quite calmly emptied it out on the sand.

It splashed a little over them both. The smell of it, reeking from his clothes, turned Jerott's head: he had drunk nothing, after all, since his illness. As the pedlar scrambled for the fallen cup among the wet cushions, he turned on Francis Crawford, his face hollow, and brought up his hands.

Lymond said, very softly, in English, 'This is part of a plan to escape. Pretend to strike me, and listen.'

'You stinking catamite,' said Jerott; and with all his considerable strength launched a blow at Lymond's face which was very genuine indeed. It was parried with an abruptness that rattled his teeth.

'All right, Jerott,' said Lymond levelly. Without pausing, he closed in, gripped Jerott's arm, and against the wildest resistance managed, in two apparently smooth steps, to engineer a full wrestler's lock on the other man. In humiliation and acute physical anguish, Jerott drew a deep breath and prepared, at the cost of a fracture, to shove. Lymond said, 'The Maltese fleet under Strozzi is attacking Zuara. They'll step into a trap: Gabriel has warned the Aga Morat.'

Jerott frowned. His face scarlet, his shirt soaked, his muscles corded with effort, he did not think of giving in. But he had stopped pushing while, breathing quickly, he said, 'How do you know?'

'Archie Abernethy.'

Jerott looked up. 'How? Where is he?'

'Break my grip and say something aloud. . . . He was in camp, peddling liquor, last night.' He pulled his hand free, swearing, and Jerott, who perhaps had not meant to bite so deeply, staggered back and said, 'Who's going to stop me?' for the benefit of the English-speaking spectators. Onophrion, worried, got to his feet. Jerott added, breathlessly, 'Philippa?'

'All I know is, she's safe. . . . If you're coming with me, listen,' said Lymond. He ducked, and then swung a punch that did not quite go wide. 'And then knock me out cold.'

'With pleasure,' said Jerott. His dark eyes were bleak. 'And if I succeed?'

'You won't,' Lymond said.

But all the same, when Jerott hit him a few seconds later he hurtled back through cushions and shoulders and struck a tent-pole like a shellfish cracked by a seagull. Onophrion, too late to stop it, caught

178

him as he slithered down to the ground and, tut-tutting, propped cushions about him. Sitting down, neatly and quietly, Jerott Blyth drank off three cups of *harech*, and handed the bowl back for more.

In the arena, they had saddled the horses, and, stringing off down the courses full pelt, began one after the other to alight and resume saddle over and over; feet racing beside the galloping horse, wrists jerking, spine, thighs and calves in the blue pantaloons soaring; seat in saddle again until, approaching the mark, they snatched their bows, strung and shot. They did the same, bending and unbending their bows three times between setting-off point and mark; the same alighting and jumping up on both sides of the horse; the same jumping right way and reversed; the same standing, hallooing, on their mounts' heaving rumps.

The arrows whickered into the marks. The horses' hooves, neat and small, flashed pounding from position to position, slithering to a halt in front of Güzel in a shallow veil of white grit. Teeth flashed. Bodies hurtled, lissom and sinewy, and in a triumph of shouts, at the end of each violent, brilliant course, the scimitars flashed, pulled with a cry from the sheaths and glittering, a dozen half-eclipsed suns in the bright cobalt sky.

Georges Gaultier said, 'Even if you have bought the whole cask, Mr Blyth, I should desist. That stuff can blind.'

Jerott Blyth pulled himself upright on his cushion, lifted the cup at his feet after two misses, and held it out. 'Have some.'

'No, thank you,' said Maître Gaultier. 'For spirits one requires a strong head or else a weak brain, and I fear I possess neither.'

Jerott grunted. The boy had gone. Beside him, bought outright with money borrowed from anyone who would lend it, was the *harech*-vendor's cask, half empty: a dark dribble from his less than accurate pouring contoured the crimson silk cushions with their velvet raised pattern. A little way off Salablanca, warned off already, sat watching him crosslegged. Jerott said, 'Bloody Muslem: y'r old man had the idea, hadn't he? No wine. A d'vil in ev'ry grape. Didn' say a word about spirits, did he? Cunning old devil.' He poured himself another cup, belligerently, his eyes half shut, and viewed the field. 'Cur-tailed, skin-clipping heathens.'

The riders, with graceful accuracy, were shooting now with saddles girthed and ungirthed, buckled time about with crackling speed. Jerott turned his head from bleary contemplation of that, and viewed Lymond over several intervening heads. Lymond, dizzily sitting up, was at least sober, with Onophrion bending fussily over him. As Jerott watched, one of the Aga Morat's men also approached and, leaning down, spoke.

It appeared to be a summons of sorts. Jerott saw Lymond look up, holding the back of his head; and then Onophrion, bending, began to help him to his feet. He looked vaguely taken aback and as if, thought Jerott with satisfaction, he had a hell of a headache. Escorted by the messenger and two guards Lymond, walking, disappeared into the Aga Morat's draped dais. 'Stinking catamite,' Jerott repeated.

The rider nearest to Kiaya Khátún alighted, flipped a somersault and, vaulting back into the saddle, shot three times, accurately, into the mark. The next, calling a roar from the crowd, lay on his face prone in the saddle, the little mare's tail in his mouth, and shot, grinning. The next, riding bareback and without bridle, stood on his hands until close to the mark; somersaulted, took aim and shot. Güzel said, 'A drink, Mr Crawford. It will help to remove the effects of your young friend's bad manners.'

Sitting very still, with the Aga Morat's plump hand on his shoulder, Lymond said, 'I thank you; no.'

'Abstinence, like the cock sparrow, cannot be long lived,' said Güzel blandly. 'They say, *si peccas, pecca fortiter*.' The cup she held out, unlike Jerott's, was made of jasper and ringed with Corinthian letters, gilded and damascened. But the drink was the same.

'Indeed, some Stoics uphold you,' said Lymond, wide-eyed, his gaze on the arena. 'Liberty to drink and to debauch are said to recreate and refresh the soul.'

'Then——' said Kiaya Khátún.

'I have no soul,' said Lymond. 'Forgive me.'

'But your servants have,' said Kiaya Khátún. 'Or at least flesh which may suffer. Drink, Mr Crawford.'

And as the Aga Morat's hand slid from his shoulder, he took the cup slowly from her and drank; and when she refilled it, meeting his eyes, he drained it again; and a third time.

Soon after that, Jerott rose undulating to his feet and, mouthing a long and explicit, if slurred, insult in Arabic, lobbed a cushion into the arena. It fell in front of a bareback rider at a crucial moment of balance: the horse shied, and the rider, saving himself in a snap of white and scarlet and blue, fell rolling like tumbleweed in the path of the next, and was kicked. From the three sides of the arena and the two stands at its head a communal moaning arose, and Georges Gaultier, seated just behind Jerott, reached up and, with force, drew him down to his seat and held him there, addressing conciliatory Arabic to the guards. The injured man was dragged off.

'God grant sweet rest to the Knights of St John.' It was Marthe's bitter-sweet voice. 'The other great cavalier, too, bids fair to be crapulous, I observe. O Kama, Kama: with thy bow made of sugar-cane strung of bees, and thy five flower-tipped arrows?'

Jerott, sweat trickling down his dark face, didn't look round. He paid no attention to Marthe or to Gaultier: he was beyond caring about Onophrion's hovering bulk or Salablanca's sober, lingering stare. He had ceased too to glance at the pavilion where Lymond was sitting, totally relaxed with gentle abandon, the weight of his brow on his knuckles.

Jerott stood up.

There were some insults lightly bandied in Islam, and a few more lying between those and matters answerable only by death. Taking the offensive, middle course, Jerott Blyth called to the riders, and as they pursued their concentrated courses, ignoring him, he bent and, again picking up cushion after cushion, hurled them into the arena with the very evident object of causing what mischief he could.

Misconduct of that order was not likely to be overlooked a second time. Jerott looked over his shoulder, saw the guards converging on him and, heaving a last unforgivable missile, walked out weaving into the arena himself. Lymond looked up.

Jerott could hardly have chosen a more exquisite moment. The horses were racing in couples, a single rider erect with one foot on each. Before the mark, bow in hand, each had to let fly three arrows into the wand: past the mark, each had to turn, keeping his balance on the two lumbering horses, and shoot, with accuracy, three arrows more.

Two did so and, finding Jerott straying noisily at their feet, swerved and passed him. The third, with more time to consider, threw away his bow and snapped his fingers, glancing behind him. The rider behind drew abreast. For a matter of seconds, the four horses thundered side by side. Then, releasing one of his horses, the second rider balanced on the remaining bare back, and then lightly jumped the intervening space between it and the next. For a moment the two riders stood, and then sat side by side. The next moment they had swept up to Jerott. He felt a hard hand under each armpit; a jerk that almost displaced his shoulder-blades, and then he was hurtling backwards through the air between the galloping horses, his heels jarring and bumping, and hazily aware that if either of the two riders holding him chose a course which diverged from his fellow, then there were really no working alternatives. He would split.

In the Aga Morat's pavilion, Francis Crawford, with some trouble, stood up. 'Christ,' he said vaguely. 'It's Jerott.'

'It is, indeed,' said Kiaya Khátún. And as the Aga, black-faced, turned to his guards: 'No—leave it, my lord Aga. If you will. Let us see what sport they make of poor Mr Blyth.'

As a spectacle, the chastisement of poor Mr Blyth already looked promising. He had had the sense, largely because he was stone cold sober, to lift his feet from the ground so that he hung, a dead weight, from the arms of his captors as he was swept backwards between them. Then, finding this wearing, as he had hoped, one of them called out aloud.

There was an answering shout from behind him. He had just time to realize that the riders on either side of him were about to overtake, between them, a third horse, when the powerful arms holding him began swiftly to lift him, higher and higher. They released him; and with a thud that drove the breath from his body he dropped, reversed, into a third person's saddle.

The horse he was now on was racing like hell. Checking his first impulse to somersault over its tail, he got on with the job of turning right way round in the saddle. It was a hilarious business, according to the shouting and laughter around him, and he slipped a couple of times for good measure. The bearded figure of his rider, grinning, paid no attention whatever to the scrambling behind him but reaching the mark, shot coolly three times, then, leaning down, ungirthed his saddle.

It was a dirty trick. With horses occupied and riderless thundering around him, Jerott felt the saddle beginning to slide: as the leathers came in sight he flung himself, knees working, on his stomach across the horse's spine and crooked his arms over its flank. The rider, posed on the slipping saddle, had his eyes on a riderless horse just approaching: as it drew level, he smiled at Jerott in a derisory flash of white teeth and, abandoning the sinking ship, jumped.

Jerott, whose vanity was suffering, got one arm free and snatched. He was too late to stop him. With accuracy and ease the rider alighted, smiling, on the back of the next galloping horse, balanced a moment, and then sat in the saddle, an expression of distrust on his face. Between himself and Jerott Blyth, careering bareback on the neighbouring horse, flew, unreeling, twenty yards of white muslin, as, like an old wife at her spindle, Jerott unwound his turban.

Havoc ensued. Whooping, kicking his heels, he brought down four horses, darting off at an angle with the tightening streamer before the turbanless Arab finally shot off his horse in a tangle of cane frame and felt cap, exposing to Mohammed, untimely, his single-lock handgrip to heaven.

Jerott looked round. It had not perhaps been wise. For a Moslem to bare his head was shame; to have it done for him by a Christian was serious injury. He reduced his horse's speed for a moment, thinking, as the other riders, in numbers, began to ride hard towards him. He still had the end of the turban, wrapped several times round his hand.

With the rest of it lying coiled on the grass, it was now useless. He was beginning to unwind it when it tightened. 'Well done, Brother Blyth,' said Lymond's voice, clear and carefree as he had heard it so many times, in action, at home with his company. 'First round to God and St Andrew. May I play?'

Bare-headed and coatless, he stood on the sand, laughing at

Jerott. Then, the other end of the muslin wound round his wrist, he turned and, running hard, laid his hand on a loose horse and vaulted into the saddle. With the reins in his hand: 'All right,' said Lymond. 'Let's go.'

'He's drunk. He'll kill himself,' said the Aga Morat, grumbling.

'Let him go,' said Kiaya Khátún, for the second time. 'Horsemanship to these men is second nature. They will provide a spectacle and no doubt will receive a suitable drubbing. Humility is a virtue Scotsmen require to be taught.'

Jerott, well fed, well rested, fully recovered from his fever, was a natural horseman, with the horseman's broad shoulders and strong, capable hands. The beautiful little Arabian mare between his knees answered him like a polo pony: horse and man might have been one as, his eyes on Lymond, he swerved and galloped as he sensed Lymond intended. They used the twisted turban between them as a trip-rope until it parted, slashed by a scimitar. Jerott, escaping from that, was knocked flying by a usurping body landing on the rump of his horse: twisting, he landed hard on the ground on his shoulder and, rolling over, staggered unhurt to his feet. In the middle of the next course a performer, standing elegantly on his head, saw Jerott racing towards him and tried, too late, to recover. As Jerott's hard body hit him he heeled over with grace into the mark, and Jerott settled, happily, into his place.

That horse had a bow at the pommel. 'An advance, my boy,' said Jerott. 'Now for some arrows.'

It was Lymond, with six men on his tail, who leaned down from his stirrups like an acrobat and scooped two from the piled heap of quivers. He threw one to Jerott, nocked, and raced belly to ground for the mark, sending a stream of arrows into the target: as he reached it a man with a staff rode straight at him, and struck. Before he got there, Lymond was out of the saddle. The pole struck empty air, pulling its owner out of the stirrups, and Lymond, dropped under the girth like a spider, swung himself in the same movement into the saddle again, laughing, his hair tangled and soaking with exertion.

It had been a boy's trick, Jerott remembered. Standing bareback on your father's horses; somersaulting, chariot-riding. Francis, buried in books, had never publicly attempted it. What private practice, Jerott wondered fleetingly, had gone into that? Then he was under attack himself, a racing horse on either side, and a hand grasping his reins.

Kicking his stirrups free, cautiously, Jerott got to his feet. A hand flashed to his ankles. In the same second, jumping sideways, he landed first on the back of the third horse, and then, neatly, on the back of its rider. He dug his hands and feet in.

It is remarkably difficult to dislodge a man sitting astride your shoulders when riding full out. Provided he clings, if he falls he cannot fail to fall with you too. Faced with that dilemma, the horseman between Jerott's legs gritted his teeth and tried to feel for his scimitar. Jerott kicked it out of his reach and, closing his hands, gave him a friendly squeeze in the windpipe. Out of the corner of his eye he saw Lymond's horse, too, was racing up.

In a moment's dazzling revelation he saw, as well, what he intended to do. 'You bloody fool!' shrieked Jerott, and then hung on for grim death as Lymond, galloping neck and neck, loosed his reins, calculated and, standing, jumped first on to Jerott's horse and then, with the same momentum, on to Jerott's own back. For a fearful moment, the pyramid swayed; and then, settling, held firm as the horse, trained to a regular pace, settled again into its stride. Three men high, the assemblage swept down the course, and among the shouting they had been too busy to hear came, without question, a scattering of applause. Below him, Jerott felt the Arab look up. 'Thou wouldst make sport, Efendi?'

Looking down, breathless, from above Jerott, Lymond answered. 'We only make sport.'

'Thou wilt try the swords, Efendi?'

'Hell——' began Jerott, and was cut off by Lymond. 'We'll try anything. Call the others off, will you? Jerott, you take one horse and I'll have the other.' He dismounted with credit while they were still moving, with two neat somersaults, from the horse to the ground, and Jerott, with success, did the same. The other riders, pattering up, dismounted: there was an air of less than kindly expectancy. Jerott said to Lymond in English, 'My God: do you know what you're . . .' and broke off as two horses were led up. They were saddled, and fixed to the saddle on each side, erect and cutting-side inwards, were three razor-sharp swords.

'What better?' said Lymond. 'We have the field to ourselves. They will be at this end, and we shall be at the other, escaping.'

'Through the guards?' inquired Jerott sarcastically.

'I thought,' said Lymond reflectively, 'through the back wall of the Aga Morat's pavilion. Keep your elbows in, Brother.' And with extreme care, he mounted, and took bow and quiver.

Jerott looked at his horse. He had to mount, sit between those six vertical blades and, riding at full gallop, shoot at the mark, three times on approaching and three times turning, after he had gone by. He visualized that turn, flexing his shoulders. All right; it put them in possession of swords. They even had a bow each and a quiver of arrows. They had, as Lymond said, the field to themselves with no other horseman ready to shoot or to strike.

But they were also making straight for the Aga Morat's pavilion, on either side of which his turbaned guard stood, hedging all the back of the crowd, knife and scimitar ready. Escape on any other

184

side of the square was impossible, the crowd was too thick. Escape of any kind, to the Aga Morat's mind, was presumably unthinkable, as long as they did what they were assumed to be doing: putting up a performance. That meant that, swords or not, he had to shoot, or do his damned best to shoot, until the last moment. He became aware that from the glittering cage of his saddle, Lymond was watching him. Jerott said, matter-of-factly, 'I think you're out of your mind,' and, lifting himself into the saddle, took up his bow.

They rode side by side on the disembowelled sand, among the discarded arrowheads and the splintered litter of display: a fragment of turban-cotton, pinned by a dart, trembled in the late afternoon breeze from the sea. In the west, against the rubicund sun, the green valance of palm trees was turning to fretwork and a pitch torch, lit somewhere high in the palace, caught Jerott's eye with its flame. Marthe, her long-sighted eyes on the two men, spoke, murmuring to her uncle. 'They are not drunk.'

Georges Gaultier, his eyes fixed on the arena, replied without turning round. 'It is not possible. You saw what Blyth drank here alone.'

'It wasn't *harech*,' said Marthe.

Gaultier turned. 'He was stinking of it. I tasted some on my hand when the cup spilt.'

'The first cup,' said Marthe. 'The container held only water.'

Georges Gaultier continued to look at her. 'Then?'

'Then they plan to escape. It is none of our business,' said Marthe. 'He will go to Aleppo.'

'And we?'

'We shall go to Aleppo too. Why should they keep the *Dauphiné* when its patron has gone?'

'You are right. She will not hurt you,' said Gaultier. 'Zitwitz and the Moor must take their chance.'

Jerott was nocking his arrow. Onophrion, he thought. What happens to Onophrion and Salablanca if Francis walks out? Or whatever happens, perhaps it's worth it, to save the fleet from Malta. . . . He had calculated the only angle at which he could draw his bow safely between the blades of the swords. Once he began to shoot, he had to repeat it exactly, twice, changing his aim. Then he had to turn in his saddle. He would face that when he came to it. . . .

Jerott drew back his arm. His horse was tired. He kicked it on and got the mark in his eye, his fingers tightening, just as it came to him why this escape was necessary . . . why nothing and no one would be allowed to stand now between Francis Crawford and whatever was about to happen at Zuara. . . .

It was because Gabriel would be there.

In the Aga Morat's pavilion, no one spoke. Side by side, the two horsemen approached the heap of sand with the mark, now a little askew, and not so plain in the low-slanting sun. Lymond shot first, his arm in its white sleeve brushing back into the steely interstice once, twice and a third time; before he stopped, Jerott had begun. Watching, Kiaya Khátún thought she saw the point of a blade stir as he shot; but it was true; as true as Lymond's, and, without pausing, he shot twice more and then smoothly twisted and let fly again, backwards, passing the mark. Kiaya Khátún heard the shout which told that Lymond had completed his six shots, and then, under her gaze, Jerott also released his sixth and last arrow and the shout rose again. He was smiling.

Lymond, glancing across at him briefly, did not smile. Slackening speed, he had slung his bow and one by one, deftly, had disengaged the swords from his saddle. They flashed and fell, clapping, dancing, pirouetting, until there was only one left in his hand. Then, assuming that Jerott was doing the same, Lymond gathered his reins and set his horse straight at the centre of the Aga Morat's tent.

Güzel saw him coming. Before the Aga, she was on her feet, stumbling on the cushions: she had hardly moved a yard before the horse was among them, and Lymond, slithering down from the saddle, had gripped her and flung her on the mare's back. She curled like an eel, sliding over and down to escape on the other side when Jerott, still mounted, grasped and bodily held her. Then Lymond in the saddle again thrust her before him and, slitting with the point of his sword through the screen of silk backing the tent, lowered his head and burst through, Jerott following.

Crushed side-saddle in front of him, her head under his chin, her fists gripping his waist, Güzel heard the uproar about them; the Aga Morat's scream; the pounding of feet and the shouts of the guards. Arrows flicked into the sand, but not too close: they had realized, she thought, that to shoot might mean killing Dragut Rais's mistress. And no one within two hundred yards had a mount. . . . She said, 'You will never get over the causeway.'

'We are not going to the causeway,' said Lymond. And indeed, he was driving his horse north, past the palace, leaving the dusky sky on their left. North, to the sands and the sea.

'You have a ship?'

'We have a ship,' agreed Lymond. 'You will not sail on her. You will remain in a safe place until the Aga Morat agrees to our terms: to release the *Dauphiné* and allow her to sail with all our company, our money and our furnishings quite unharmed. He will do it. He has no desire to offend Dragut Rais.' He twisted round then speaking quickly to Jerott; changed direction and moved on to grass.

We are out of sight, she said to herself. *And he is throwing them off the trail.* Against her cheek he was breathing deeply and regularly: she could have counted the beats of his heart; quicker than hers, after all his exertion; but perfectly steady. She said, shifting a little, 'I have no desire to offend Dragut Rais either. Turn back.' And with the little knife from her sleeve she slit the silk over his heart, and the linen beneath it, and held it there, point down. She could see her veiled face in the blade.

His heart-beat did not alter. 'Jerott would shoot you.'

'But not before the knife has gone home. Turn back.'

'To allow the Aga Morat to knife me?'

'He will not touch you,' said Kiaya Khátún. 'We have orders only to keep you for a limited time.'

'Until after Zuara,' said Lymond.

For a moment Güzel was silent. Then: 'You know?' she said. With her free hand, sitting erect, she dropped the veil from her face: her grip on the knife did not waver. Then she looked up and saw the mockery plain in his eyes. 'Wasn't I meant to know?' he said. 'I thought that was the whole intention.'

Her brown eyes narrowed. 'Nothing must jeopardize the Aga Morat's counter-attack.'

'Of course,' said Lymond. 'The Knights' attack on Zuara must fail. But equally, they must realize the cause of their failure. Islam has perceived, has it not, that Graham Reid Malett cannot be of use to it much longer as a Knight of St John. Once his treachery is exposed to his fellow Knights he has no alternative. Spain, France, Scotland, England are all closed to him. Only the Ottoman world is left open. And there he will go.'

'So it is hoped,' said Güzel. 'Turn and ride back.'

Francis Crawford reined in. Under her knife she saw his shirt reddened where the blade had fretted, a little, with the movement of riding. He said, 'Kiaya Khátún, the peaches of immortality ripen only once every three thousand years. Sooner or later we die. If it happens to me here and now, nothing will alter. Only Mr Blyth will do what has to be done.'

For a long moment she faced him. Behind, she heard Jerott rein and begin to trot back. The shadows were long. 'Yes. You have courage,' she said; and twisting, her arm raised like a butcher's, she plunged her blade deep in the neck of his horse.

She felt him take a breath then. He kicked his stirrups free as the blood spurted and, grasping her, pulled them both clear as the beast fell. She sat up as Jerott, after a look, dismounted and dispatched it with his sword. 'You will leave me here,' said Kiaya Khátún, with composure. 'I believe with one horse you will still reach your ship, and I in turn know my way to find help. The *Dauphiné* will be set free as you ask, with no harm to your friends.'

Jerott, looking from Lymond's stained shirt to the horse's carcase, was brief. 'Take her up in the saddle. I'll run beside you.'

'No. I believe her,' said Lymond. Rising, he gave her his hand,

and as she stood, studied her, from the Greek nose to the luminous, clever brown eyes. 'I think we are too late. Are we?'

'The pitch-pine torch from the castle was the signal,' said Güzel. 'And the equestrian display was meant to deceive. The fleet of the Knights of St John is within a day's sail of Zuara, and the Aga Morat's men under their captain left before dawn to take up their stance.'

Standing still, he had not freed her hand. 'You do not like Gabriel,' he said; and Kiaya Khátún, smiling a little, examined him coolly in turn.

'I like whom Dragut Rais likes,' said Güzel. 'Where it does not displease Dragut—may Allâh protect you.' And, unsmiling, she stood on the sand and watched Lymond move off, with Jerott riding pillion behind.

Minutes later, they stopped at the shore. The skiff they found awaiting them had two pairs of oars and took them, at Lymond's killing pace, over darkening waters to the little hired brigantine. Archie Abernethy was on board. As they pulled the shallop in, Lymond walked to the poop giving orders interwoven with English for Archie or Jerott. They were to make straight for Zuara.

Within minutes the anchor was up, and then the striped mainsail filled and she moved off, silently, without lights or ensign under a bravery of stars. Then Lymond, crossing to where Abernethy sat on a hatch, dropped beside him and remained there, head bent, elbows on knees; his knuckled hands sealing his mouth.

Archie said nothing. Jerott, seated with his back to the mast, felt his head roll to one side, opened his eyes and sat up. His back ached. Lymond said, still without moving, 'Tell me about Philippa.'

Archie Abernethy had been waiting for it. He had been dreading it all the way from Zakynthos, from ship to ship and mule to mule and mile to mile of that hurried, frustrating journey. He said, 'She's all right. I'll tell you later. Why not go below? I'll call you. You'll fight all the better.'

Lymond did not move, but there was an edge Jerott knew in the soft voice. 'Tell me now.'

'Well . . .' said Archie Abernethy, and told him.

After the first three words, Lymond dropped his hands and sat up: by the end he was on his feet, staring at the stolid face of the mahout. '*You left her alone in Zakynthos!*'

'Yes. Well. I had to warn ye,' said Archie. 'Man, ye'd be there yet if I hadna got it all fixed. And the lassie is fine. I wouldna have left her if I wasna sure she'd be safe.'

'You were under orders,' said Lymond, speaking with fearful precision, 'to escort Philippa Somerville to her home in England. You tell me now that you have left her among total strangers in a country quite unknown to her, and about to attempt a journey, by herself, into the wilds of Macedonia in order to buy . . . My God, I think you must be insane,' said Francis Crawford; and for a second his voice split, lacerated by his nerves. 'A child of twelve, let loose among Turks . . . what bloody daisy-field at the back of your mind persuades you she'll be safe? The whole thing is a trap. It must be. You know as well as I do that the child wasn't sent from Algiers to Zakynthos in October. It was passed from hand to hand along the whole North African coast until it ended up at Mehedia where Jerott here saw it. Christ, didn't you tell her?'

Archie Abernethy got up. He had resumed his turban: under it, his weathered skin was very dark, but composed, although his eyes were uneasy. 'It seemed to be the right bairn,' he said. 'It was in the care of Evangelista Donati's own brother. It was the right size and colouring; it was branded; it came from Algiers; it spoke English. And,' said Archie, rushing it a little for his own good as well as Lymond's, 'it was the wean the Dame de Doubtance had told Mistress Somerville to go off and find.'

He told Philippa's story to a silent audience. Jerott, biting his lip, was thinking too hard still to comment. And Lymond, retreated again to the hatch, became very quiet indeed. Archie Abernethy ended, paused, and said, 'I'd back the wean to be genuine, sir. She's a fey woman, the Dame de Doubtance, and the bairn had her ring.'

'The Lady of Doubtance is a fraying-post for bloody neurotics. We are dealing with facts.' Lymond stopped. 'Jerott. Which child do you think sounds genuine?'

'We *know*,' said Jerott. 'My God, I know anyway. . . . I've held him in my arms, Francis. Only one is called Khaireddin, and only one had a nurse called Kedi who spoke Irish Gaelic like a native. The other's either a trap, or some damned funny idea of the old woman's.' He couldn't see Lymond's face in the dark, but risked it. He said, 'You seemed to believe her, anyway.'

There was a pause. Lymond's voice, when it came, was normal but tired. 'Oh, I suppose I believe her. Whether I can interpret her correctly or not is another matter entirely. . . .' Then, after a longer pause: '. . . *Christ*,' he said. 'There *can't* be a doubt. There can't be two boys so alike. . . .' He stopped again, his lips pressed together.

'And tomorrow?' said Jerott. 'I gather Gabriel will be there?'

'With the Knights of St John,' said Archie, relieved. 'And distinguished by a blue panache, so's his circumcised friends ken not to scratch him. He'll be there, and so shall we. He's ours for the taking.'

In the dark, Jerott spoke only to Lymond. 'And you will kill him, notwithstanding,' he said.

Curtly, Lymond replied, 'I shall kill him.'

'Then all you have to do afterwards,' said Jerott, his voice equally weary, 'is to watch and see which child will die.'

189

13

THESSALONIKA

'There are eighteen varieties of verse-form in Ottoman poetry,' wrote Philippa in the diary she began that autumn on leaving Zakynthos. 'All Ottoman poetry is about love.' After some thought, she added, 'Geomalers have very long memories.'

The beginning of the diary was one of several formidable steps she took, with Míkál's help, after Archie Abernethy and Sheemy had departed. She bought a mule. Her clothes were in rags, and moreover foreign: she invested in cheap new ones: brown linen for bodycloth, and a long gown of rough frieze with a coarse over-robe.

She bought also two linen squares, which she wore, breathing heavily, over her face and head. Into her pouch she put the handful of little squared aspers they gave her as change: the rest of the money Archie had left her was sewn into her smock, or else wrapped round with thread in the mending-things she packed, with a spare set of clothes, in her saddlebags. Behind her saddle went a little wool mattress, a quilt, and two light, long-haired rugs, bound in a roll.

She had no stockings, but Míkál obtained for her a pair of red leather shoes with pointed toes and thongs, classical style. He also brought for her several very beautiful handkerchiefs, for which he would take no payment, saying she was to receive them as a gift. She wondered, in her waxing sophistication, in what kind of coin he had paid for them.

There were a dozen, finally, in the party which accompanied her out of Zakynthos. Five of them were Geomalers like Míkál, dressed for travel in purple smocks more or less like his, with whole unsewn skins on their shoulders as cloaks, tied in front by a knot in the forelegs. They had no baggage, other than their cymbals and bells, and sometimes a little book of Persian love sonnets, or a staff, or a garland of flowers. They all had long hair, some of it loose and shining like Míkál's, and sometimes thick and sticky with dressing. The other six included two boys, a weaver, a bow-maker and two merchants going to Petrasso.

Only the merchants were mounted. The others ran at her side as she rode docilely down to the harbour, on Míkál's instructions: the tops of their heads smelt of turpentine, and the rain of bell-sounds mingled with greetings, chanting, laughter and snatches of song reminded her of a children's party Kate had once arranged at Flaw Valleys, when the cook's illegitimate niece had been sick.

There was a frigate there, bound for Morea. No money changed hands that Philippa saw. The little party, chanting and jingling still, swept on board with the merchants, and in a matter of minutes she was sailing out of Zakynthos, bound east for the coast of Morea. With some trouble, Philippa stifled her questions. She was to follow the four-yearly course of the Children of Tribute, which was always the same. From village to village and city to city of occupied Greece she was to travel east and north in their footsteps towards Usküb in north Macedonia, where they gathered, Míkál said, before entering Stamboul itself. He would take her. He would protect her. And once she had found and bought the baby Khaireddin, he would set them both on board ship for home.

The Pilgrim with anchusa wound in his hair had a mad scourge of a bell in F sharp. In her lighter moments, Philippa wondered if Míkál's friends would allow her to cull them, say to two major chords and a diminished seventh in G.

They arrived at Petrasso. It was a city, rich with the currant trade, but Philippa saw none of it. The children had gone the easy way, along the Gulf of Corinth to Athens: three days' soft travel alongside the water, and then a climb through bare rock to the ruins of Corinth, the Isthmus; Megara.

Míkál spoke of Old Athens: 'It interests you? The walls are there; nearly six miles of them round, but there are few houses within them now, though a great many ruins. But ruins one can see anywhere.... *Aşk olsun!*' He smiled, his voice caressing, and the man he had addressed returned the greeting: '*Aşkin cemal olsun!*' and stopped to speak. Philippa was getting used to this exchange, hour after hour. 'Let there be love!' and 'May thy love be beautiful!'

She looked at the chipped marble horse-trough in the crown of the street, which had once been a classic sarcophagus; deep-fleeced lambs were still incised on its flanks. The vagaries to which the terms 'love' and 'beauty' were subject never failed to surprise her. Then Míkál came away from his friend with his hands full of radishes, and the matter seemed of minor importance.

She was not allowed to see Athens. However slowly the tribute was sought, picked and packed, it seemed that the commissioners had long since left Athens and had begun to make their way, so report said, through Thebes and Lamia north. 'We shall take boat,' said Míkál, 'to Naupactus.'

They took boat to Naupactus. It was merely a ferry, crossing the Gulf of Patras to the mouth of the Mornos, whose valley north they would follow. Of Naupactus she had a brief impression of Venetian ramparts, water-mills, a citadel with some rather old-fashioned guns, and a sheep's head a notary gave them, opened and warmed, with the inside minced up and cooked in oil and fat mixed with salt and some sumac seeds. She bought some bread to go with it, much against Míkál's wishes, and they had a feast, after which he sang her twenty-four verses in Persian from Ummídí, pausing from time to time to translate.

191

They had lost the merchants bound for Petrasso, but had kept and added to the boys, and had found a vineyard-owner, taking his family up to the terraces. Philippa travelled for a while with the women and children in a small wicker cart with low wheels and round front, pulled by two oxen, while three of the boys rode her mule. They left the family at the vineyard, among the rows of small stiff shrubs, unstaked; but she had a big wooden pot full of grapes at her saddle-bow when she mounted once more. The discord of the bells, she noticed, had almost ceased to concern her.

It was very hot. Through the worst of the day, she curled up and slept on her mattress, the bells sleeping and still all around her; then they would walk and run and dance far into the night, whirling torches and singing, until they found a cottage, or simply a herdsman with a fire and an olive-wood crook, his goats all about him, and would eat whatever they had been given—fruit and pumpkins, un-pressed cheese carried crumbling in goatskins, unleavened cakes baked in cinders and mixed up with sesame seeds. Then they would drink from running water, talk, sing and at length, sharing the fire, would sleep until dawn.

During the four days from Naupactus to Lamia they crossed a mountain range as well as seven miles of plain; and Philippa listened to six hundred couplets in mesnevi verse and a diwan of four hundred gházels, in Turkish metre with internal sub-rhymes. Míkál translated.

At Lamia, having cut off by this device the whole way through Attica, they learned that the children had passed by already, still travelling north on the road to Thessalonika. They were given three wild duck, lost a boy who decided to linger, and joined a wedding party going towards Volos. They were asked to the wedding.

It was a three-day journey along a shore track to Volos, and they sang all the way. The village at which the wedding was held came in sight on the second day, and Philippa, stopping the mule, dis-appeared into the scrub and reappeared washed all over, in a fresh change of clothes. While she had been away, Míkál had woven her a garland of ivy and poppies. She exclaimed with pleasure. 'There is that which melts the soul,' said Míkál, 'in a young deer walking impulsively, in trust, in grace and in courage. I have opened the book of love . . . I read and write in it. Thou, too, shalt read.'

Philippa, who had no illusions about her style on a mule, felt her nose become glossy. She said, 'I don't know about love; but I know all about kindness. I just wish to goodness you'd all get a good job teaching somewhere.'

But Míkál merely fluttered his beautiful eyelashes and laughed at her. 'I have it now, Philippa Khátún,' he said.

They admire, confided Philippa to her diary that night, *the Beloved with a chin like an orange, tulip-cheeks and an eye shaped like an egg.*

Also, what is a four-eyebrowed beauty? Whatever it is, Kate darling, I don't think it applies to the Somervilles. And so, although it is the very first compliment I have ever received, I don't suppose it will go to my head.

The Pilgrims danced at the wedding. It was a poor village, but the church was full of flowers and candlelight; the altar swimming with silver; the nimbused heads of the saints watching her, under thin, painted eyebrows, from the gold- and enamel-wrought ikons.

They swept into the sunlight in clouds of incense and garlands to the music of lyre, zampouna and meskale, the bride and bridegroom handlocked with silver and flowers, gilded crowns of worked paper on their dark heads. With the veils thrown back, and the long shreds of gold tinsel like fountain water sparkling and tinkling behind, Philippa saw how young they were, girl and boy. They would spend all their lives here, she to bear children and work in the fields, to cook and draw water and spin, and to bruise wheat and rice there, in that Corinthian capital, upturned for a mortar.

He would fish, on windless nights, as they had done under the Caesars, with his four brothers in one boat, with a lamp and a trident; he would plough the painted shards in the fields with his unwheeled plough behind his two oxen: he would take his stick and his axe, when he had to, to fight off Bulgar nomads; Turkish brigands; he would sow his crop, and, when the time came, he would hand over, if he must, his most beautiful child to the Commissars of Tribute.

Seated on a splendid new carpet, her embroidered tunic carefully spread, her hair wound with ribbons and beads, the bride giggled beside her new husband; their parents, stout, toothless, gleeful, stood behind calling. It was the time for presents: each villager, walking up, bent and, kissing the girl, laid a small gift on her lap, hardly ceasing to talk, while she, searching behind her, found and offered to each a small sheaf of flowers in return. They were roses, Philippa saw, tied and plaited with care in fine spangles.

She had a pair of buckles from her old shoes. Kate had bought them in Newcastle because they looked like two snakes in silver, and therefore very seemly, said Gideon, for Somervilles. Philippa brought them out before her worse nature could catch up with her better and, kneeling, put them quickly on the little bride's lap.

It was clear that the girl had no idea whatever what they were for, and Philippa, whose Turkish and Arabic were prodigious, had, except for esoteric pronouncements of love, no suitable phrases in Greek. Smiling broadly and firmly, she got her roses and backed, until she was within reasonable distance of the spit with the wild boar on it, and then sat swallowing nobly until the feasting began.

When the Pilgrims left, they set off in moonlight, with the villagers for their escort until they had reached the main track. They had danced the Romeika and the Candiote, the Wallachian and the Arnaoute; they had sung, they had told stories and long poems; there had been laughter and drinking. Between Greek Christians and the Pilgrims of Love there was no barrier, Philippa found. The Pilgrims, their philosophy Arabian, their arts Persian and Turkish, embraced love and merriment as the Greeks did; and the Greek nature responded.

The Pilgrims played. The lyrist walked ahead of them, showing the way, his rough three-stringed lyre like an old rebec, held and plucked at arm's length: behind, torches flickered and laughter sparked around the little mule as Philippa rode along, talking to the villagers who thronged on foot around her with Míkál as her interpreter. 'They ask what years thou hast, and from where thou comest, and where is thy husband?'

'Tell them I'm sixteen, and I come from the Border between England and Scotland, and I'm not married,' said Philippa. She had spent her birthday in the Lazaretto at Zakynthos, and they had taught Sheemy Wurmit's moulting parrot to sing 'Happy Birthday to You' as a surprise, and she had been so pleased she cried. . . . 'Why hast thou no husband?' added Míkál.

The inquiry, it seemed, was on his own account. Philippa stared down at him, astonished. He said, 'In thy country girls marry, do they not, at fourteen; at fifteen? Thou hast nothing? No lover, no sweetheart at home?'

Philippa choked, and covered it up as well as she could, dismissing the image of some stiff-necked young Tynesider, cap in hand, knocking at Flaw Valleys' front door. 'I'm Philippa's intended, ma'am. May I come in?' And her mother's expression.

She said, 'I can't think why, Míkál; but when I was at home we didn't think of it; and of course I've been travelling since.'

'Sometimes,' said Míkál, 'one must travel to find what is love.'

'Sometimes,' said Philippa stoutly, 'one must travel to find what is kindness. I know what is—— I know what love is.'

'Thou knowest the love of old women,' said Míkál. He sounded cross. The youngsters who had been running at her side had moved away, tired of the foreign speech. He said, 'I read thee Anvari, Jelál and thou dost not tremble. The fountains make thee thy bride's veil; the lyre spins thee thy ribbons; the mallow under thy foot is the hand of thy bridegroom.' In the torchlight, the deep, dark eyes opened on hers. 'Khátún, what is his face?'

'A lemon?' said Philippa.

Much later that night, when they had spread their mattresses at a farm which had made them all welcome, and all was silent at last, Philippa wrote up her diary. *We are close now, I think. The Children passed through quite recently. They took the bride's little brother Philocles, but no one spoke of it except to extol the brave new life he*

*would have. I have had two poems addressed to my liver. I have solved
a mystery. Do you remember the boy in the buttery who grew a hairline
moustache when he was courting, and lost a sock in the milk? That,
my dear, is a four-eyebrowed beauty.*

*You didn't ever happen to mention, Kate dear, whether you wished
to start curing a son-in-law ready to lay in, so I take it you don't.
I very much don't, rather. I want to grow old and sour all by myself,
at Flaw Valleys, modelled on my old and sour mother. Anyway, who
could be sure of a husband in this country? Sneaking off, for all one
knew, to some four-eyebrowed lout in the buttery. . . .*

They caught up with the Children of Devshirmé on the outskirts
of Thessalonika. Since the night of the wedding Míkál had been less
adhesive, though he spent a little time eliciting precisely her interest
and indeed her irritating single-mindedness on the subject of this
unknown child Khaireddin.

He received no satisfaction, since Philippa had no satisfaction to
give. Kate approved of the child's father, and so did she. Kate all
her life had championed the under-dog, and so therefore did she.
And what more oppressed puppy in all the world was she likely to
find than this one?

'It is a crusade,' said Míkál at last. 'O Soul Sensible, when wilt
thou waken?'

Philippa knew that one. *There are three degrees of souls: Soul
Vegetable, Soul Animal and Soul Sensible. Common Sense is a pond
into which the five streams of the outer senses flow. Soul Sensible has
two faculties: Virtue Motive and Virtue Apprehensive.* Virtue Apprehensive. 'He'll have grown. They change a lot. You maybe won't
know him,' said Philippa.

'He may be dead,' said Míkál, hopefully. 'If he is dead, where
shall we go?'

*

They were testing the tribute-money by the Arch of Galerius. As
each person brought forward his tax, the *gümüsh-arayân*, or silver-
searchers, weighed the coins, and then poured them into the little
oven within the big iron charcoal-burner. The metal was red-hot,
but in spite of the fumes and the blistering air the people of Thessalonika pressed round, watching uneasily. No one would expect all
the coins to be true. But over a certain proportion of base metal and
double the fee must be paid in these little horned aspers, with their
message drawn in the silver: KING OF KINGS, RULING OVER KINGS.

Philippa reined in her mule. She had passed, at Míkál's insistence,
the tented city ringed with Janissaries which lay on the brown grass
outside the walls. She must speak, said Míkal, to the Chief Commissar of Devshirmé, or to an Odabassy of Janissaries, at least. In
this, the richest city of Thessaly, taking tribute would be a long

affair, conducted in the city itself by the Commissars and their clerks, with the Janissaries to keep discipline and the strong arm of the Sanchiach who, with his Spahis, governed Thessalonika for the Beglierbey, the Lieutenant-General who ruled over all Greece on behalf of the Sultan. So to the town, said Míkál, she must go in her turn to pay tribute and buy back the child.

She had seen his point; but was prepared to argue. How could he expect her to buy something she had not even seen? What if she could not find him; if he were not there; if they took her money and then denied his existence?

Last night Míkál had burnished his leopardskin and combed out his long, fine, dark hair. He had sung to himself, she thought, as if he were very happy, swaying his body so that the little bells of his sash and his dress accented the verses. Now, smiling and calling to those who greeted him in the press, he said, looking up in surprise, 'Thou readest, Khátún. In the Commissars' books each boy's name is written, and his birth, and his price. He will be brought to you.' And as the crowd opened out before them, and she found herself in the Via Egnatia, with the crowded figures of Galerius's great arch alive in the sun, Míkál said, 'Give me your money.'

And taking from her the gold which last night she had unpicked from all the hidden corners of her clothes and her baggage, he moved with his magnificent walk past the stinking heat of the brazier, and flung it, chiming, on the deal table where the Commissars sat. 'The lady pays,' said Míkál. Philippa, dismounting, followed him in a hurry and stood, panting, beside him.

'For what does she pay?' asked the Chief Commissar. He had black moustaches and wore a very white cottage loaf on his head. He had a long jewelled knife in his sash. Philippa opened her mouth and said in squeaky but impeccable Turkish, 'I wish to buy back the boy-child bought of the merchant Marino Donati, Zakynthos.'

The Commissar's small black-rimmed eyes studied her. 'I see. The name of this child?'

'His name is Khaireddin, or . . . I am told his nurse calls him Kuzucuyum. He is between one and two years old, with yellow hair,' said Philippa. 'If you will have the money counted, I am sure you will do us the honour to agree.' There were twenty Venetian zecchinos in Míkál's handkerchief lying there on the bench. Two thousand five hundred aspers. And a five-year-old girl had been bought the other day for five ducats.

The Commissar did not lift the handkerchief. He did not call for his registers or turn to his clerks. He said, 'Take thy bounty. Alas, the child you mention cannot be resold.'

Philippa's heart began to beat very heavily. She drew a long breath. 'Thy pardon, lord; but I cannot think you know the child of whom I speak. He is of no account, base-born of Christian parents, and too young as yet to train. I assure thee, if he is sold to me, there will result nothing but goodwill for the Sultan.'

The black eyes, narrowed against the sun, were not even derisory. 'Through a base-born son of a Christian?'

Philippa took another enormous breath, which promptly evaporated, invisibly, through her pores. 'His father,' she said threadily, 'is at this moment bearing to Stamboul for the Sultan a gift of some price from his master, the Most Christian King of France. To reunite son and father would be an act of which surely the Grand Seigneur would approve.'

The Commissar raised a finger. Released by the signál, the clerks opened their books; the slow procession of tax-payers began to move forward; the little weights clinked in the scales as the aspers were poured out for weighing. 'The child you mention,' said the Commissar briefly, 'came from the harem of Dragut Rais at Algiers. I fear thou hast mistaken his origins. He is not for sale. You may have the aid of my Odabassy to find your way without harm out of the city. Allâh be with thee.'

The gold thrust into her hand, she was dismissed. Philippa looked round wildly. Míkál had gone. The other pilgrims, intoxicated by the crowd, had already started to disperse: she could hear the bells and the cymbals and the laughter, in trickles and spurts, through all the noise of the throng. Her mule, unattended, had drifted to a stall selling mish-mish and was licking a bowl.

Philippa looked again at the table of Commissars. The chief, his back to her, was transacting some brisk matter of business; the rest, writing or questioning, had resumed the wearisome routine which had already occupied them, week after week. She realized that even if her voice were operating properly, making a scene was unlikely to do any good. To begin with, they held a low opinion, she knew, of women who conducted their own affairs. And to change one's mind in public before one's fellows was a thing no man would countenance.

Philippa shoved the gold under her veil, hoping her sash would prevent it from falling promptly straight down to her feet, and fought her way to her mule.

The saddlebags weren't rifled. The stall-holder hadn't even complained over the mish-mish. A Janissary, in his tall, white felt bonnet sat on horseback holding the reins of her mule. He wore a long knife tucked into his coat; a scimitar on his thigh, and a straight sword and a little axe on the side of his pommel, with a bow laid across the saddle-front and a quiver strung on his back. He carried a steel *gurj*, and as the wide sleeves slid back, she saw the mark of his *oda*, slit into the skin of his forearms with gunpowder. He had a silver quill driven straight through a pinch of skin above his left eyebrow and left there, like a one-eyed eagle owl, and his gaze bore an icy disfavour, like the gaze of a sergeant inspecting a constant

197

deserter. He said, 'If it please thee to mount. We are in haste.'

Philippa took a last quick look round. No Míkál. Well: his business was love, not argument and the rough ways of the military. At the gates, when they freed her, she would no doubt discover the Pilgrims. And between them, surely, they would hit on a way of tracing the child in that seething city of tents. If she could have him no other way, she was quite ready to steal him, Janissaries or nothing. What was a Janissary, said Philippa (to herself) stoutly, when one had made the acquaintance in Scotland of the Crawfords, the Scotts and the Kerrs? She mounted; and, the corps falling in quickly behind, she and the Odabassy rode in silence out of the city.

Outside the gates, she was irritated and also uneasy to see, there was no Míkál either, and the other Pilgrims of Love were conspicuous by their absence. Her thin lips tight, Philippa looked up at the Odabassy, whose ambling pace had not changed, and said, 'I fear sir, my friends are not here; but if thou wilt set me by some honest house, I shall remain there till they find me.'

The silver quill turned in her direction. 'Presently,' said the Odabassy; and rode speechlessly on.

'For example, that house?' said Philippa, risking it, after five minutes more.

'Presently,' said the Odabassy; and continued to ride.

'I think,' said Philippa, 'I should like to stop *now*.' And she pulled, hard, on the reins.

A strong hand, coming from beside her right elbow, reached up and taking the reins clean out of her grip, flicked the little mule on. Blazing scarlet under her veil, Philippa swung round on the Odabassy. 'The orders of thy Commissar were to set me outside the gates of Thessalonika!'

The quill turned and inspected her, with lofty indifference. 'My orders, Khátún, are to bring thee immediately for questioning to the presence of my lord the Beglierbey of all Greece.'

*

The Viceroy of Greece had been hunting. That indeed was the purpose of this modest lodging in Thessaly; and to preserve his vigour for primary demands, he had brought only two or three of his seraglio with him. The courtyard of the viceregal house, when Philippa entered it, perforce with her Janissaries, was full of dogs: not the flop-eared mongrels, shaggy as Cretans, which she had seen in every village since Petrasso, but white greyhounds, large and slender, their legs and tails stained red with kinàh. She saw some hawks, hooded, being taken indoors, and the small horses, mixed Tartar and Arab, whom she saw being led away by the saisies, had drums hung on the pommels.

The grooms were Berberine. The servants she saw moving in and out of the stables and service buildings which lined three sides of the yard, were of aggressively mixed stock, a great many of them coloured, and some of them walking in chains. She was prepared to be angry when she saw that all the faces which turned towards her in the bustle of the courtyard were perfectly cheerful and instead of angry she became frightened, at the kind of servitude which could bring resignation and active acceptance so easily in its train. She dismounted, and led by the Odabassy, walked up to the tall timbered building, overhung with galleries and enlaced with admonishing texts, which occupied the fourth side of the courtyard.

In the doorway, an Ethiopian awaited her; quite different from the Moors she had seen carrying saddles outside: a big man, his glossy black skin sheathed in lawn and a pale figured weave. As he dismissed her escort and turned, signing her to follow him, Philippa saw the rings on his plump fingers and thought, suddenly, he is a eunuch. Then he opened the door of the selamlìk, and stood aside as she walked in.

The room was vacant. It was bigger than any she had yet seen. In the centre of the floor was an elaborate brazier, now empty, set in a pattern of tiles. All the rest of the room was a dais covered in carpets, on which thick mattresses, two or three deep, had been piled at intervals round the far wall, and heaped invitingly with coloured silk cushions in each window embrasure. The walls were white, with a calligraphic frieze of phrases from the Qur'ân picked out in blue and gilt: *Hasten to forgiveness from your Lord: and to a garden.*

Philippa smiled, her wrestling hands stopped for a moment; then, folding her arms solidly over her stomach, she stumped up the three little steps to the dais and marched to one of the windows. All right: they liked flowers. They liked music. They liked animals and birds. You never saw a badly used dog; and the granaries in Cairo, so they said, were never closed from the sky, so that the pigeons might feed when they chose. But they killed by ganching and slicing and cautery, and by doing what they had done to the woman Oonagh O'Dwyer.

Philippa gazed down on the kitchen courtyard. There were serving-women there; one or two; and a big marble bath full of water, and some cloths laid out bleaching on the sparse grass by the wall. Underneath her some shallow trays were also spread in the sun, filled with a golden mess she did not at once recognize. Then the open lattice under her fingers stirred against a warm breath of air, and the perfume of peaches pressed into the room.

She had tasted that in Larissa . . . peach jam, confected by sun-heat alone cooking the trays of ripe peaches and sugar and syrup as they lay, day after day. . . . If they would not sell her the child it meant, of course, that Gabriel had found out and warned them.

Perhaps the merchant Donati, writing another of his bills of lading, had described his strange visitors too well. Perhaps Sheemy Wurmit, arrived in Malta to discredit Graham Malett, had told too much too soon, and Gabriel had been able to send his instructions. . . .

She was English, and allied to Spain, Turkey's most implacable enemy. Turkey had nothing to lose, materially or politically, by her death. She had wondered, working it out, why the Beglierbey's sanction was necessary, until she recalled mentioning that a French embassy to the Sultan was involved. Just at present, Turkey did not wish to fall out with France. There was a chance, then; a slim one; if she could persuade the Viceroy that this child was indeed the son of the King of France's Special Envoy. Or were Gabriel's services so valuable that, in spite of that, he could persuade the Turks to do anything that he asked?

A child had come into the yard, jostled by three lambs on a string. It held them with difficulty, its fat bare feet braced in the dirt, and shrieked with delight, its shirt of striped Joseph silk smeared with their muzzles. Inside the kitchen a woman spoke sharply.

The child heard, too. Philippa saw its capped head turn, rocking its balance; as it tried to recover, the lambs tugged, ears flopping, pink tongues out, baa-ing, and pulled the string from its fists. It sat down, its back straight, its hat tipped over its eyes, its mouth an enormous O of astonishment. While Philippa watched, the O became a chinless and ecstatic grin. In three difficult stages it got to its feet, knocked its hat off, stared round and located the vaulting tails of its charges and directed itself after them, making up in noise and enthusiasm what it lacked in technique.

It looked down, Philippa noticed, as it stepped into the first tray of jam, hesitated, and for a moment was even in danger of sitting. Then, with admirable devotion to duty, it stepped into the other four trays without pausing and pursuing the clear imprint of twelve jammy hooves over the bleaching cloths, heeled precariously round the gate into the garden and disappeared, followed by a growing number of adults. The last Philippa saw of it was a flash of wary blue eyes, a hamster grin, and a cone of thick yellow hair, resting levelly on its belligerent eyebrows. Under her veil, Philippa's larynx shrank to a pin-head and her eyes swam with unwanted water. She snorted.

'I speak,' said a voice behind her in English, 'to Mees Somerville?'

You cannot whirl round in a floor-length robe and two veils. Achieving the change of direction with dignity, Philippa found herself opposite an elderly Imám quite unknown to her: a soft-skinned Turk in the turban of the Haji who has made the sacred journey to Mecca, his grey beard brushing white woollen robes, his prayer beads hanging in his sash. He smiled. 'Forgive me: I frighten you,' he said. 'I am Bektashi Baba, an elder follower of Haji Bektash Veli, of whom you may have heard. The Beglierbey, who prays to be excused, has asked me to see you. You will do me the honour to seat yourself and take *qahveh*?'

Now where, thought Philippa, seating herself warily on a pile of fat cushions, have I heard that before? And then she remembered: the house of the Dame de Doubtance in Lyons, and the harsh voice saying, 'My cousin will bring you some *qahveh*, which you will dislike until your taste is formed.' Philippa sat very straight, remembering not to pull on her veil, until the tray was brought with two cups by a Greek slave in a snowy tunic and laid on a small stool before her; and the Bektashi Baba, slipping out of his soft shoes, climbed the three shallow steps and, after seeking permission, seated himself at a discreet distance on the same divan. The slave poured the hot coffee, and waiting as Míkál had taught her until he had left, she unhooked her veil and lifted the cup.

It was the same aromatic burnt mud. Nostalgia poured in on her. She set her jaw and drank, as the Bektashi Baba smiled again and gently spoke. 'Now, my child, you will tell me everything and I shall help you. Why you, an English girl, should travel alone with the Pilgrims, inquiring after a base-born child you have never met. . . . This is true, is it not?

'Everyone keeps asking me that,' said Philippa, peevishly. 'It can't be so very rare to find a child sent for tribute by mistake. I'm trying to buy it back before anyone gets into trouble, that's all.' She put down her cup. 'You didn't frighten me, but I just wondered how you knew my name.' *Attack, little flower*, Kate had said calmly to a tear-stained Philippa once, after an inquisitorial visit from a much-hated aunt. *Answer rude questions with naïve questions as near to the bone as you can get them.*

On Bektashi Babas, the technique had no effect. Her companion merely raised bushy grey eyebrows and said, 'From Míkál, naturally, I learn it. The matter interests the Beglierbey, for his information from the merchant Donati led us to believe that the child was a godson of a Knight of St John. You have told the Commissars this is not so. It is possible therefore that the child you seek is not the one brought from the merchant Donati.'

'The child I seek,' said Philippa with brittle clarity, 'is between one and two years old, is called Khaireddin, and is branded with the mark of Dragut Rais, in whose harem he was placed when he was born. He was sent from Algiers to Mario Donati in Zakynthos when Dragut left Algiers to sail east in the autumn. He is the son of M. le Comte de Sevigny, the Special Envoy of France now in process of conveying a valuable gift from His Most Christian Majesty to the Grand Seigneur at the Sublime Porte. The boy is a love-child, but one by whom the Envoy sets great store. If anything were to prevent his purchasing the child, I am sure he would feel bound to mention it at court on his return.'

The Bektashi Baba smoothed his beard but his eyes, Philippa was furious to see, were indulgent. 'I see. And the child you seek: did this boy have a nurse? Or was he in the care of his mother?'

Careful. Philippa said, 'His mother's dead now, but I don't think she took much to do with him after he was born. He was looked after by a negress called Kedi.'

'I see,' said the Bektashi Baba again. He rose, and walking barefooted over the thick carpets, paced to the tall window and gazed out. Then, his frail fingers on the lattice, he turned and looked thoughtfully at Philippa. 'Daughter, forgive me, but I must tell you that this is not the same child. The boy sent us by the merchant Donati was born in Zakynthos, and spent only some months in the household of Dragut Rais in Algiers before being sent back to the House of the Palm Tree. He bears the brand of Dragut, it is true, and his age could be as much or as little as you say. But he had no nurse with him when he arrived; and his present guardian calls him by the child-name he has always borne: Kuzucuyum. Also, all these arrangements I have spoken of, and all the instructions concerning his placing in the harem at the Sublime Porte, have come to the merchant Donati from Malta. Of a Comte de Sevigny there has been no mention till now.'

Philippa went scarlet. 'Of course there hasn't!' she said; and scrambling up, to an unregarded rending of cotton, marched to where the Baba stood at the window. 'Because Graham Reid Malett doesn't want his father to have him! Don't you *see*?' said Miss Somerville, shoving the second veil back from her perspiring forehead, and glaring at the amused, bearded face. 'They hate each other, Sir Graham and the child's father. Sir Graham is only trying to hide the boy so that Mr Crawford won't get him; and Signor Donati is helping. . . . It remains to be seen,' said Philippa with sudden and awful dignity, 'whether the Grand Seigneur considers the friendship of a Knight of St John or that of the kingdom of France better worth having.'

'It is a grave dilemma,' the Bektashi Baba agreed. 'Too grave indeed to be quickly dismissed. . . . You say the putative father is to be in Stamboul directly. The merchant Donati should not find it impossible to convey the problem also to the putative godfather. Thus it may be legally settled at the end of our journey, and not hastily out of hand and insufficiently informed as at present. . . . You know where M. le Comte de Sevigny, for example, is at present?'

'I think I can find him,' she said. Like mice whipping cheese from a trap, thoughts flashed through her head.

'With Míkál's help, and perhaps the services of a Janissary, you will then be able to place the difficulty before the French Envoy too. An excellent solution, is it not?' said the Baba. 'And meanwhile we shall carry the child to Stamboul, where all will be settled.'

They were going to let her go. No, they probably wanted her to go, under guard, in case she tried to make off with the child. In any case, they were prepared to let her free into the Christian world with the information that a Knight of St John was in friendly communication with the Turks.

Which meant . . . which meant, thought Philippa quickly, that they either knew Graham Malett's reign in Malta was reaching an end, or wished it to reach an end soon. They had found out perhaps that Gabriel's spying had been discovered by Archie and Sheemy? Or perhaps he was simply outgrowing his uses in Malta, and they wished to have his interest in Constantinople? In any case, she wasn't getting the child. They would take it to Stamboul . . . a journey of weeks at this rate. And meantime, unless Archie stopped him, Lymond would meet and kill Gabriel at this place called Zuara.

With Gabriel gone, the Turks had no reason to harm a child who might or might not be an Ambassador's son. But Gabriel's agents, whoever or whatever they might be, had their money to earn. If he died, the child was to die. And who would prevent it, if she were not there?

Philippa turned, her gaze falling past the Bektashi Baba on the little courtyard below. It was empty. 'I understand it all,' she said. 'I have one favour to ask. Could I see the child?'

The black eyes did not move from her, but she could sense the faintest hesitation before the Baba spoke. 'But of course, daughter,' he said. 'His guardian, alas, is ill; and he is with her here until her fate will be known.'

'She is dying?' said Philippa.

'As the hand puts the candle to rest. Our Order says, She becometh the secret, she will become Real with the Real One. She is in here. The child is with her.' And moving gently from the window, the Baba stepped down to the lower part of the room, slid his feet softly into his slippers, and led the way from the chamber.

The room where Kuzucuyum's guardian lay ill was a small one: the carved lattice was shut, and only the display plates on their high cornice shelf reflected the sunshine filling the chistlik's gardens outside. There was a niche in the wall, in which sat some books, and a small cupboard on top of which bedding-rolls lay, and a blanket. Otherwise there was nothing at all but a tapestry mattress laid on the carpeted floor, and a still form, its head neatly wound with brushed black and grey hair, lying sheeted upon it. The Baba smiled and withdrew, closing the door, and as he did so, the head on the mattress stirred weakly and turned. It was Evangelista Donati.

If Philippa was astounded, the sick woman herself was at first paralysed by the shock of the encounter. Her black eyes, shining like agates, stared at Philippa; her cheeks, loose and yellow with illness, gathered in folds about the tight mouth; then with violence thrusting herself on one elbow she spoke, in the tones of the governess: the hard, precise timbre, inflected with Italian, which Philippa had heard her use, over and over, to Gabriel's sister Joleta. '*What are you doing here? Who sent you?*'

Back in Scotland, as the duenna and confidante of the child-sister Joleta, Evangelista Donati had been a woman of power and maturity, though no longer young. The years spent with Gabriel and his sister had not been innocent ones; but they had filled her life with vitality; and with Joleta's death at the hands of Graham Malett, her brother, more than a wicked, wayward, beloved creature had died. All Evangelista Donati's purpose in living had gone.

And after she had denounced Graham Malett; had told the world the truth about this great and gallant knight who was great only in vice, she had fled from the world, and from his vindictiveness, until, hiding in the house of her brother Marino Donati at Zakynthos, she must have met the child; and learned who he was, and have appointed herself, flouting Gabriel, the guardian of the boy whom he had sworn to degrade and had threatened to have killed.

So Philippa calculated. And so, looking at that anxious, malevolent face, she interpreted the cause of her distress and, walking forward, dropped on her knees by the mattress and answered immediately. 'It's all right. I'm from Mr Crawford. I've come to buy back his son.'

The sick woman sank back. The Baba had been right: Madame Donati had about her, like twilight, the climate of death. The handsome woman who had fascinated Peter Cranston, who had so irritated Sybilla, had gone, and here were only the material elements of her: the beaked nose; the thin, ringed hands. Madame Donati said, thinly, 'They are afraid of Graham. They will not sell him. . . . Is Mr Crawford here also? How . . . how did you find the child?'

Philippa said, 'Someone in France suggested I go to your brother's house at Zakynthos. Mr Crawford didn't know: he's in Djerba, I think. . . . Look, *you* can tell them who Khaireddin is, can't you? They won't believe me. They pretend to think he's Gab—— Sir Graham's godson or something; and they're trying to send me away.'

The black eyes were contemptuous. 'You are young, are you not? They do not care who he is, this child. They wish only to placate Graham. Give them what proof you will: it will make no difference to the Viceroy.'

'But . . .' said Philippa uneasily; and then decided to say it. 'If Lymond kills Sir Graham, Khaireddin will die.'

The clever eyes in the dead face had noticed the hesitation. 'Unless I, who am dying, was to have been his assassin? A natural thought from a Somerville. Unfortunately, you can dismiss it,' said

Evangelista Donati harshly. 'I am here—I *was* here without Sir Graham Reid Malett's knowledge.'

Philippa, her voice sharp, pounced on it. 'He knows you are here now?'

'He knows,' said Evangelista Donati with irony. 'And *you* know now, for certain, that the assassin is indeed with us in camp. I die of poison, Philippa Somerville; and after my death and your departure, the child is theirs to do with as they please.'

'Unless,' said Philippa, 'I go in your place?'

There was a long silence. The sick woman said, finally, 'I have been punished, Mistress Somerville, for my betrayal. I have also been killed because Sir Graham has no desire to see Khaireddin fall into friendly hands. You would have to guard yourself, as well as the child.'

'I could try,' said Philippa. And added, obstinately, 'I'll *have* to try.'

'Or . . .' said Evangelista Donati slowly.

'What?' said Philippa. She wished her heart would be quiet.

'Unless you made yourself sacrosanct against even Graham's designs. Then the child could be your full concern. And as soon as you reach Stamboul, you could give him proper protection. . . . Do not imagine,' said Madame Donati bluntly, 'that you will ever be permitted to hand the boy to his parent while Graham Malett is alive. While Sir Graham lives, he will be your charge and you cannot be free of him. Your life will be in Constantinople during that time; and although the boy may one day be free, you, Philippa Somerville, may end your days there.'

'How?' said Philippa; and folded her arms tight across her flat chest, crushing veil, robe and shift into final annihilation. 'What would I do?'

'You would go to the black eunuch who controls the girls among the Children of Tribute,' said Evangelista Donati deliberately. 'And you would place yourself under his care as a prize for the Grand Seigneur's Seraglio.'

'*What?*' Philippa yelped.

It was one of her shriller sounds. Being rhetorical, it drew no further response from Madame Donati. But on top of the cupboard, where the bedding-roll lay beside the blanket, a certain movement made itself heard; a stirring and scuffling and some heavy breathing under stress, which resolved itself into the blanket rising into a caterpillar-like vertical, threshing briefly, and then unwinding to drop to the floor. On top of the cupboard there was revealed, peering over, a yellow satin oval of hair, topping the round sleepy face of a very young child, rudely awakened, but glad on the whole to be with everyone once again. 'Hullo,' said the child of the peach jam, in English, to Philippa.

'Kuzucuyum?' said Madame Donati. And at the sound, even

Philippa dragged her eyes from the cupboard top and looked at the woman beside her; a woman soft-eyed and gentle in voice; putting into one single word the love and yearning stored in all these starved months since the death of Joleta. 'My lambkin: this is Philippa. You must say Philippa Khátún. It is polite. She is going to give you dinner and put you to bed when . . . when I have to go away. Lift him down, Mistress Somerville.'

Slowly, Philippa rose, and walked over, and held out her arms.

He was square-built, and solid. There were dimples all over him: on every well-fed joint and pivot and haunch; but he was as firm as a hard peach; and on each calf the new walking-muscle had already started to swell. The face close to hers, laughing, was nothing but monstrous blue eyes, and a briefly nodal arrangement of gum and small rectangular teeth. 'He has been called Kuzucuyum for so long . . .' said Madame Donati. 'It might be as well to continue.'

Philippa had forgotten her. She turned round, the child in her arms, and saw the yellow face on the mattress had gone grey, and the thin hands were wrestling together. Bending, she put the child on its feet. 'Run,' she said. 'And kiss your . . .'

'Aunt,' said the little boy; and laughed, and scampered across the floor to throw himself on the sick woman's chest. Philippa saw her gasp; and then draw the round head tight to her breast. Over it, Evangelista Donati's black eyes made their only appeal and Philippa read it. 'You meant,' she said slowly, 'that in the harem, or going to it, no one dare touch me? And that once there, no one could touch Khaireddin either?'

Evangelista Donati said, her voice only a whisper, 'It is a terrible thing to do for a man . . . or a child. It is a school which will never end; a company you may never discard. More than that I can promise you. The Sultan is old: you will not suffer. You may choose to die in the Seraglio, or be married to the best blood in the land, for only these are given wives from the harem. But once committed, you will never escape.'

'You risked death,' said Philippa. Her throat was dry.

'I have met death, and I am thankful,' said Madame Donati. 'And if *you*, you are to care for the child, I am glad. Because to Graham it will be a mortification I would die more than once to inflict.'

And upon the sight of the sick woman's eyes, wildly glittering, and the sleepy roll of the bright yellow head, and the knowledge that hatred for Gabriel, more even than love for the boy, was the fuel which had powered this sick will and forced Evangelista Donati to the point of decision, Philippa heard herself saying, 'Then I shall go. I shall take care of Khaireddin after you. I shall enter Topkapi with him, and look after him until he is able to leave. But,' said Philippa, and an odd tear, infuriatingly, made its way down one sun-hardened cheek, 'I don't know *what* Kate will say when she hears.'

14

ZUARA

It was hot, that August; and the wind blew from the desert, south-west; so the fleet of the Knights Hospitallers of St John of Jerusalem under Leone Strozzi, Prior of Capua, took a week, under oars, to travel from Malta to the African coast between Djerba and Tripoli, where lay the rich little town of Zuara.

Leone Strozzi was impatient. It was so near, this great prize for which he had laboured all winter. Under his guidance, Malta was fortified. Using Sicilian peasants and knights for his workmen, he and his friends had built two forts to shield the Knights from the continued assaults from the Turks. Built and paid for by the melted gold plate sent to him, with the chains from their shoulders, by the Order's Knights in Malta and overseas, they were the first commissioned since that domineering, avaricious old man de Homedes became Grand Master seventeen long years before.

But now Grand Master de Homedes was dying. Over eighty, warped and all-powerful still, there were signs that at last the strong heart was faltering, and the current of intrigue in that closed community of four hundred celibate Knights, vowed to poverty and chastity and obedience, was running faster and thicker as each day went by.

All that summer Leone Strozzi had worked at the fortifications, and had sailed the Mediterranean with his own two galleys, taking prize after prize. His had been the voice loudest in the Sacro Consiglio; his had been the Langue with the best table, the finest entertainment, the liveliest talk. And he had only two rivals. Jean de la Valette, Grand Prior of St Gilles, was twenty years older than Leone Strozzi, and for all his brilliance and his dedication lacked the final, self-centred violence of purpose which could drive a Florentine forward. And for the other, Sir Graham Reid Malett, Leone had plans of his own.

All summer, Gabriel had been the one constant threat to Strozzi's ambition. Gabriel the saintly, Gabriel the magnificent leader and strategist, Gabriel the seaman, Gabriel the priest. And it was sham. He knew it was sham, but none would listen to him. He had handed the proofs of it to the Council: the papers written by de Villegagnon accusing Graham Malett of betrayal and worse, and they had disappeared without a trace, into the hands of the Grand Master's powerful Spanish circle of sycophants and then, he supposed, into the fire.

He had been hasty, he realized it. And the Scotsman he had got them from had been right. When he complained; when he took his story to the reputable Knights who would listen, they had shrugged their shoulders in disbelief. His reasons for discrediting Gabriel were too plain. And even de la Valette, approached in the end, had said gravely, 'It demands investigation: you are right. While the Grand Master lives this is impossible. You must possess patience; and watch; and so shall I. Under the eyes of us both, he can surely do no great harm meantime; if you are right.'

So he had watched. And of the several mishaps which had occurred during that season, none so far as he could see were attributable to Gabriel. The Carrack, sailing to Sicily, had been unexpectedly way-laid by a considerable force of corsairs and but for pure accident might have been lost; but how could Gabriel be responsible for that? Twice, ships bringing them supplies had been sunk without warning, despite absolute secrecy as to their schedule, and for a while their wheat supplies had run short; but again, this could be nothing but mischance. In fact, their supplies from the East, which were under Gabriel's direct control, had come in with smooth regularity, and they had lacked neither wine nor fruit; which was a pity, Leone considered, as on the whole the Knights regarded the possession of bread as a matter of slightly lesser importance.

The only untoward happening since he had arrived, in fact, was the unexpected death of the little Scots dragoman in Gabriel's house the other week. He had come on a cargo vessel from Zakynthos, and had been for a long time in the Lazaretto before that, so it was plainly a matter of foreign disease, and for a while there had been a minor panic in case it was an outbreak of plague, and the poor man had been given a hasty burial at sea. But after that, Strozzi thought, Graham Malett had been a shade abstracted through his pretentious posturings during the weeks of planning this raid; and although he was here now, behind Strozzi's Admiral ship, sailing with de Guimeran in one of the Order's four galleys, *La Catarinetta*, he had been, thought Strozzi, remarkably subdued.

It was as well. Now, with the Grand Master's death surely imminent, Leone Strozzi was about to achieve a small but dazzling coup for the Order. Thirteen miles east of Djerba on the North African coast, Zuara was not a great city. But because of a good harbour it had become rich in commerce and also a profitable lair for all the Barbary corsairs east of Algiers.

He was going to reduce it. He was going to give the Moors inside the town such a fright that they would think long before they allowed Turkish or renegade ships to shelter again; and he was going to teach the corsairs that they had their own depots and harbours and ships to defend before they could freely rove the seas plundering others.

Slaves in Malta had described the fortifications to him. They were all on the north. The land side of Zuara, they said, was both unguarded and unfortified. They had only to advance to the ditch unseen through the palm trees, and Zuara was theirs.

So the Moorish slaves said. He had no reason to disbelieve them: they had too much to lose. He was taking several of them with him as guides; and the Order's galleys, and his own brigantines fully armed. And aboard he was carrying twelve hundred men, including the three hundred best Knights of the Convent. Three-quarters of all the Knights on Malta were sailing with and under Leone Strozzi: de la Valette was under his command; Graham Malett must look to him for orders.

They had already made their dispositions: his own nephew was to lead the advance scouting party; the Commander de Guimeran was to lead the advance guard proper, and the Chevalier de la Valette the main body of troops following. He himself, Leone Strozzi, would bring up the rearguard with the reserve infantry, throwing them in where required; directing the order of battle. It would succeed. He would cover himself with glory. And the youngster of his own name, Piero's son, his charming young nephew, would make a name in his first big engagement.

Flushed with triumph; buoyant with expectations; illumined with shadowless vanity, Leone Strozzi stood under the fluttering red silk of his banners and watched the pale coasts of Africa come nearer and nearer.

The *Catarinetta* had her accident on the morning of the 14th of August, their last day at sea. How it happened, no one afterwards was exactly able to say. One moment, the little fishing-smack with the striped sail was skimming towards them, set on a parallel course; and the next, with a crunch of broken timber that shook the *Catarinetta*, she was under their flank, and the few men who had been aboard her, hurt, dead or dying, were spilled in the sea.

The slaves, shouting, had shipped oars automatically, but by the time de Guimeran recovered his balance and ran up on deck, the *Catarinetta*'s impetus, despite the jar, was enough to have driven her some distance onward. He satisfied himself that no irreparable damage had been done to her sides and, leaving Gabriel to initiate emergency repairs, de Guimeran replaced him at the tiller and gave orders to turn.

Afterwards, he remembered that Gabriel, working like a slave himself, his face lined with remorse, had still turned and demurred, hesitantly. There were no survivors by now. And they had the lives of twelve hundred men in their hands. Already the other galleys had forged far ahead. They must keep up, or endanger the coup. De Guimeran didn't listen. He had seen one dark head in the water which was not floating helplessly, and one arm alternately upraised and thrust forward swimming. He completed his orders and *La*

Catarinetta swung round, her sails filling, and flew back the way she had come.

By the time she reached the wreckage, the swimmer was the only man living. Standing amidships, boarding tackle in his hands, de Guimeran nursed the galley along, order by order, until it lay as close as was possible to the swimming man. There was blood on the face under the black, streaming hair, and he was swimming, de Guimeran saw, one-handed, but doggedly for all that. He was not dressed like a fisherman. . . .

Gabriel, standing beside him, his work abandoned, said suddenly, 'He will need help; his wrist is broken. Let me support him up the ladder . . .' and, without waiting for permission, vaulted lightly over the rail and into the surging water beside the wounded man. The swimmer looked up.

'It's . . .' said the Chevalier de Guimeran. 'My God, it's Jerott Blyth.'

To that, Jerott knew later, he owed his life. Half conscious from a blow on the head and the pain of his wrist; clouding the water with the blood from the shallow cuts which covered his body, he looked up as someone jumped into the water beside him, but he did not hear de Guimeran's shout. He was looking instead at the man treading water beside him: the smiling, big-featured face; the guinea-gold hair, regardlessly cropped; the magnificent shoulders under the soaked doublet, with the Cross of St John white on its breast. 'My dear Mr Blyth,' said Sir Graham Reid Malett, tenderly reaching out one muscular arm and placing it, relentlessly, on Jerott's tired shoulders. 'It is no use. I'm afraid you must drown.' Then the water closed over his head.

He came up once, as another body splashed into the water beside him. For a moment he saw Gabriel's face quite clearly: saw his eyes narrow, and heard his voice say, 'De Guimeran . . . really, I can manage this by myself, I am sure.' Then he realized that the firm hand under his other arm was de Guimeran's, and that despite anything Gabriel might wish to do, he was being propelled surely and swiftly to safety.

Graham Malett caught up with him again, just before he dragged himself, with de Guimeran's help, up the rope net they had let down over *La Catarinetta*'s low sides. Jerott felt the powerful body behind him, and the ungentle grasp on his loose arm just as he reached the top of the rail. Then, with a sudden quick movement, entirely invisible to any of the craning heads watching above, his broken wrist was seized without mercy and twisted.

Like summer lightning, the pain fled through his nerves. Jerott's heart thundered once; he heard the tearing gasp as the breath left his lungs; and then he pitched forward on the deck of the *Catarinetta* at de Guimeran's feet, quite unconscious.

He was alone when he woke; lying on a bed in the gunroom, in darkness. Sitting up slowly, he found that someone had doctored his cuts, although his head still ached and he had a dull and constant throb from his wrist, bandaged tightly and strapped lightly in place across the front of his shirt. De Guimeran, he supposed, would carry a surgeon. He wondered why unexplained death had not overtaken him while he was unconscious, and deduced that Gabriel had failed to find the opportunity.

Or perhaps . . . It was extraordinarily quiet. With care, Jerott got to his feet, and picking his way between bedding-rolls and packing-cases and assorted litter, found the door and then, in the next hold, a ladder leading up to the deck. His head swimming a little, he climbed it and looked round about him.

It was night. Even if he had not seen them, black against the indigo sky, the smell of the palm trees would have told him they were anchored close off the coast, lightless, with the other ships of the fleet lying silent around them. But for slaves and seamen; perhaps a knight as second officer deputizing for captain, and one or two caravanisti, they were empty of men. The expedition had arrived, and had landed. But not at Zuara.

Jerott turned. An unknown voice, speaking diffidently in the darkness, said, 'Chevalier Blyth? I was to pay you M. de Guimeran's compliments, and say he hoped not to be long delayed. I trust you find yourself better?'

It was not the time to point out that he was no longer a Knight; that he had abandoned the Order. Jerott said, 'Are you in charge? Do you know where you are?'

He heard and groaned at the slight hauteur in the reply. 'My name is St Sulpice: I am in charge, sir, and at your service. And we are at Zuara. The landings were completed while you were unconscious, some hours ago.'

Jerott said, 'Have you ever been here before?'

'At Zuara? No. It is new to all of us. Therefore, the pilot.'

'Who was the pilot?' said Jerott, but he knew the answer already.

'An excellent man, I believe. A Genoese,' said St Sulpice defensively, 'taken on by Sir Graham Reid Malett. You do not consider him at fault?'

'I know he's at fault,' said Jerott Blyth dryly. 'He's brought you to a place at least twelve miles too far east.'

They wouldn't believe him. Hurried consultations with the skeleton crew on the Admiral galley and then the others merely brought the same conclusion: if Jerott was right, then why had the Prior not sent a skiff back to warn them when he and his men discovered the error? It might not, of course, have been immediately noticeable. They might even have landed the army before it became obvious. And by then it would, Jerott thought, be rather easier to march twelve miles by the coast than to face embarking twelve hundred men all over again and sailing farther along.

Easier, that is . . . if you did not know that the mistake was intentional; that the district was warned; that the Aga Morat and his troops were only waiting somewhere to spring the whole trap. He said, persuasively, 'Let's settle it, then. Send a skiff ashore and see what information it can pick up. We may even have found the Prior left a message for the fleet which has somehow gone astray. . . .'

They sent a skiff. He didn't go with it. It was too late, anyway. They had left hours ago: they would be nearly at Zuara by now, or would have met whatever fate was planned for them en route. As a messenger of warning he had utterly failed, and through no fault of his own. What danger had Gabriel scented on seeing that fishing-vessel, which had made him take such instant steps to annihilate it? Somehow, he must have learned, in the messages from Zakynthos, that his secrets had been penetrated—even that Archie had escaped with the knowledge, bound for Djerba.

This, for Gabriel, might be the last disservice he ever planned to perform for the Knights. With exposure now almost certain, he had used the last of his authority to lead his fellow Knights into disaster. He had no intention of going back to Malta, Jerott suddenly realized. That was why, having failed in the water, he merely ensured that Jerott would remain silent for long enough for the expedition to leave. Nothing must discredit Gabriel before he had achieved this night's work. Afterwards, it did not matter. The great landing, planned once probably to throw Leone Strozzi for ever out of the running as a possible Grand Master, was being used instead to raise even higher Graham Malett's stock with his master the Turk.

The skiff came back, with consternation aboard. It was true. This was not Zuara. The army had gone; marching on foot. They had found the pilot, his neck broken; and a shallop floating loose on the shore, with a dead man in the bottom. 'It is a trap,' said Jerott. 'A trap I came to warn you about. We can do very little now to set it right. But if you trust me, I will tell you what I think we should do. . . .'

He divided the fleet into two parts. The smaller he left, fully lit, under a junior commander at a spot within six miles of Zuara. The rest he took himself, with St Sulpice assisting, to lie off Zuara itself.

They rowed there *à outrance*, against the wind; and the wind brought them ashes, and the stink of charred flesh and gunpowder, and the thud of cannon and the crackle of small shot, and the shrieking, ululating roar of a town in sack.

Somewhere in that conflagration was Lymond. And somewhere, Graham Reid Malett.

*

The decision had been Lymond's, as every decision had been Lymond's on that unpleasant little trip out of Djerba on the fishing-vessel Archie Abernethy had procured them. Jerott, who was known to the Knights, would intercept the fleet and warn them by sea. Lymond and Abernethy would meet them, for double safety, as they landed, and would by then be able to give Strozzi, with some luck and some very hard work, an idea of the dispositions of the Aga Morat's two forces, and of the true fortifications of Zuara.

If the odds were overwhelmingly against them, the Knights could withdraw. If, turning the ambush to their advantage, they had some hope of success, then they might well go ahead. Whichever way it turned out, Graham Reid Malett, Jerott knew, would never leave that beach-head alive.

Now all that had gone for nothing. Because of Gabriel, the fleet had not been warned by himself. And again because of Gabriel, the landing had not been made near Zuara, but far down the coast, where Lymond could not possibly have met them. He might hope, thought Jerott, to take the coast road east from Zuara himself and intercept Strozzi, if he had seen, in the dark, the direction the fleet from Malta was taking, and was able to guess roughly the land route they might choose. But was that even possible, at night? And if he found them, might he not be shot down on sight? Invading at night through enemy country, no one would think of asking questions before they let fly. . . .

Or he might wait near Zuara for the advance scouts, and find both Strozzi to warn and Graham Malett to kill by that method, if the Knights had not already been ambushed by the Aga Morat's force from Tripoli before they ever got to Zuara.

Whichever he had done, the Knights had entered Zuara: so much from the seafront was plain. Perhaps, with no fleet to succour them, they had had no alternative. Perhaps, seeing the galleys there waiting, they would now attempt to withdraw. Giving his orders; seeing the boats lowered ready, Jerott hesitated still.

Never till now had he fully realized how widely Francis Crawford and he were now separated; how much damage Lymond had himself wilfully caused, in the last weeks, to the relationship existing between them. On board the fishing-vessel, waiting to be slipped ashore with Archie just outside Zuara, Lymond had seemed to him as hard and self-contained as the culverin on the rambade, uttering no words that were not orders; his intelligence shut against all life and all humanity that did not concern his one purpose.

Once before, Jerott had seen him like that, in Algiers. He had seen him as he was now, with every skill of mind and body tuned to the ultimate pitch in pursuit of one object. Francis Crawford like that was uncontrollable and very close to invincible. But not invincible. And not impervious to the reckoning afterwards.

213

Walking to the side of the *Catarinetta*, Jerott thought of many things. Of the nuns at Baden; of Shakib and the others who died in Algiers. Of Ali-Rashid the camel-trader, and the branded infant at Bône. Of Kedi the nurse, and the Syrian silk-merchant, and himself close to death at Mehedia. Of a child's arm round his neck, and a child's kiss in the hollow of his shirt. Of the Spaniards who died at Gabès, of Philippa's danger; of this, the betrayal of a whole Order of Knighthood.

He heard his own voice saying, *She is more than dead, Francis. If I thought you would do it, I would beg you to go without seeing her.* And Lymond's own voice, long ago in Scotland, before the child Philippa snatched the knife from his hand and allowed Gabriel to make the escape which had led to all this; Lymond's own voice in the Cathedral in Edinburgh, saying, *For Will Scott, for Wat Scott his father . . . for the pain you occasioned the Somervilles and the corruption and death of your sister, for what, above all, you hoped to do to this realm of Scotland, I call your life forfeit.*

Jerott Blyth set his lips tight; checked the sword and the dagger Archie Abernethy had given him, and the brigantine jacket he had begged from St Sulpice; and letting himself down into the shallop, with St Sulpice, the Serving Brothers and all the men he thought could be spared, had himself rowed to Zuara at speed.

*

The gates of Zuara had been open, with no guards on duty. Strung-up after that nervous, twelve-mile march with his troops, Leone Strozzi found that puzzling. And yet there was no reason to be over-wary. They had walked through twelve miles of palm groves and beach; past walled gardens and mud houses and high banks of Indian fig; along sandy tracks between patches of melon and peppers and apricot and orange and pomegranate trees, without meeting so much as a dog.

If anything was strange, that was strange. But then, God's will was in the work to their hand. God's will ordained that instead of scrambling through a ditch at the back, they should walk through the city gates in the front. He made certain dispositions, and laid down certain rules: each company had its work to do. They were to meet in the central square without scattering or plundering until all posts of danger had been seized. And to secure their exit, he left several companies guarding the gateway outside. Then they marched in.

The key positions were not hard to occupy, because there were hardly any men to be found in the city, which was a pity, as he had offered two crowns for every Moor's head brought to him afterwards. And resistance, once they had occupied them and roused the citizenry to their predicament with drums and trumpets in the main square, turned out to be of a token kind only, for the city was filled largely with old men, women and children.

It was when they discovered this that the army of Malta, regrettably, ran amok. It was not, of course, the fault of the Magistral Knights and the Knights of Grace, the Chaplains of Obedience, the Serving Brothers, the Piliers, the Priors, the Bailiffs or the Knights Grand Cross of the Order. But officered by the Knights were nine hundred soldiers of mixed nationality and a uniform appetite for money and women.

They fired the buildings as they ran through, looking for prisoners and plunder with tree branches dipped in pitch for their torchlight. They fought one another over the silver bracelets on a child's ankle, or the earrings from an old woman's lobes, or the coins round a girl's canvas cap. They stuffed embroidered silks into their shirtfronts, and rings and aspers and ducats into their pouches. They found opium, and finely chased seals, and hoards of coral and gold and pearl buttons, and spilled open chest and cupboard and market stall to find more. Girdle cakes of barley and millet bounced upset in the flickering dark with the ringing wares of the brassworker, and a basket of wild artichokes rolled with its soft leafy fists among the spilled salt, fat and cheese of the suqi dealer along the warrens of small vaulted passages, with dead men underfoot.

Two crowns for a Moor's head; and as slaves, the women and children might be worth even more. La Valette, with great trouble, had gathered over a thousand prisoners in the dark square, ready to march them out to the ships which were so mysteriously tardy in coming, when the Moor Ali Benjiora found him: a man he knew well, who had served under him once at Tripoli.

Conspicuous by his height, and his curling white cropped hair and beard, de la Valette bent to hear the man's words; made him repeat them; and then, raising his voice in the uproar, found and summoned Leone Strozzi. 'There is an ambush. The Aga Morat's army, he says, is surrounding us from two sides, half from Tripoli and the rest under the Aga from Djerba: four thousand horsemen in all, with arquebuses and bows. We are to be trapped in the city.'

Strozzi's eyes, brilliant with excitement, glowered at the Moor. 'How is this true?'

'It is true,' said de la Valette. 'I know this man and I trust him. More than that, he was shown the troops and told where to find us by someone known to both of us: the French Envoy, Crawford of Lymond.'

'Then it is true,' said Strozzi slowly. He looked round. The pillage was almost over, the city was blazing; the worst had been done. More, he saw, looking beyond the smoke and the flames out to sea, his ships had at last come. It was time to cut losses. 'Retreat! The drums will beat retreat!' he said with energy; and flung back his

215

bright helmeted head shouting. 'To the shore! Retreat to the shore! All captives to the shore, and make ready to embark! The Chevalier Justiani, make your signal to the Admiral galley. All boats to the shore . . .'

He thrust through the uproar, shouting. A moment later the drums started, but even where de la Valette stood, in the square itself, they were hardly audible. The Knights of St John were being called on to retreat, and none of them yet knew it. The Chevalier Parisot de la Valette, opening his purse to reward the Moor Ali Benjiora, was struck by a thought. 'You came into the city: how did you come in?'

'Through the gates,' said the Moor. He slipped the gold into his robe.

'Through the gates? The commander of the companies guarding the walls let you enter?'

'What companies?' said the Moor. 'There is no one, Hâkim, outside the gates. They all came in, it is said, long since to plunder.'

So for the second time that night, the gates of Zuara stood open to an invader, but this time to a succouring force; a brutal friend who was prepared to let a city die in order to trap its assailants.

Jerott landed on the shore, the other skiffs hard behind him as the Aga Morat with four thousand armed cavalry thundered into the burning city. Facing him, every gate to the sea was flung open, a yawning red mouth in the night, and the black shapes of people poured through; Moorish women and children, wailing and screaming, soldiers cursing, Knights carrying wounded. Shouldering against the tide, sword in hand, Jerott pushed through into the town, seeking for a face he knew in the dashing smoke and the distorting glare of the flames. Then he saw that pillage had stopped; and carnage had begun.

The horses, these brilliantly ridden horses of the Aga Morat's, were the chief terror, Jerott found. Grazed by the encircling fires, they reared and plunged and kicked, ripping the smoke and pounding flesh and bone in their path. Scimitars flashed, and the blade of long, double-edged daggers, used again and again; and the steely face of small axes, attacking their food. Here and there, and then suddenly everywhere at once, the echoing thud of arquebus fire could be heard. He saw one man's face, rearing over him, spear ready to lunge, and recognized it as he parried, burying his sword in the man's unprotected thigh. It was one of the men he had ridden with, on the display-ground at Djerba.

The Knights, on foot, fought back grimly. Their heads shielded by close-helm or salade, armed with breastplate and backplate under the short surcoat, they defended themselves as they could with their great oval shields, their axes, their two-handed swords, staggering to the rush of the horses; driving against the white-turbaned figures. The soldiers, in leather jerkins or brigantines like his own, were running; retreating to the sea gates in haste, their prisoners dashing free as they went.

Parrying, defending himself, assisting whom he could where he could, Jerott fought his way across the square to where the battle was thickest: round the tall flag with the white cross which was the standard of the Order. The sacred standard, his duty to which, in all the years of his training, had become ingrained in his soul: never to fall into enemy hands; never to touch the ground; never to be defiled; never to be abandoned. And beside it, taller than the rest, was a Knight in full armour with his visor lowered, a Knight unrecognizable by anything except the blue panache on his helm.

Fighting towards that, Jerott passed by and ignored the familiar faces which surged thick about him now: Tolon de St Jaille, de Guimeran, le Plessis Richlieu, Justiniani, Sforza, young Strozzi, Piero's son, the Chevalier Poglieze . . . Knights of every country, the best of their kind; and brave men. Then the Knight with the blue panache turned towards him, his sword drooping; his gloved hand pushing back his vizor, and Jerott's sword was already half-way towards the naked face within when it was struck up, sharply, by another blade from below. 'No, you fool,' said a hard, emotionless voice he barely recognized as Lymond's. 'The man you are killing is Leone Strozzi.'

Continuing to fight, automatically; his eyes on the banner, his ears alert for Strozzi's commands as, retreating, the Knights began to turn back towards the gates and the sea, Jerott saw that, apart from that one stroke, Lymond was not fighting. Instead, concealed by the darkness and the smoke, he had found a place from which he could watch: and there he stood still, wearing only the arms Abernethy had brought him; a shirt of chain mail over the almond silk trunk-hose he had been wearing at Djerba, now stained and scuffed; a sword-belt; a dagger; a purse. His hair, Jerott saw, was uncovered, although he had been given a morion, and his eyes, ceaselessly roving over the dark receding mainstream of the struggle, were narrowed like those of a marksman waiting for the partridge to rise at the tock of a drum.

So he had not yet found Graham Malett; or Graham Malett had not yet found him.

Soldiers, Knights and Serving Brothers now, fighting for their lives against horses and men, were clear of all the souks of the town. The desperate knots of resistance where the great officers, bound by their vows, preferred death to surrender to the heathen were one by one scattered and hewn down. The square underfoot, roughly paved with brick and small pebbles set in mortar, was thick and viscous with blood, and trammelled with foot-catching lumber: of hacked bodies and strewn clothes and loose armour plate and ownerless weapons. Outside, along the harbour pool and the shoaling sands of the shore, those who were already free of the town would be streaming, fighting in their heavy armour as they went, making for the boats, which but for Jerott would not have been there.

Because of that, Jerott saw, fighting one-handed shoulder to shoulder with his former brothers across the square beside the standard, unaware of the agony of his unslung wrist, there was at each of the sea gates a jammed mass of their fellows unable to get through; fighting back to the gates under shock after shock of arquebus fire and scimitar and striking hooves as the Aga Morat sent line after line of cavalry bursting through them until soon the gates, fleetingly blocked by the living, would be closed to them for all time by the dead.

Jerott left the standard. Running to the gates, he found Strozzi's nephew beside him, bound on the same errand: to free by any means humanly possible the block at the gates. For the next few moments, shouting orders, hurling men from him, using his sword where necessary to force their own men into the open on the other side, there was no time to do anything but what he had been trained, by the Order and by Lymond, to do. Then, as the gates began to clear and the last of Leone Strozzi's conquering army, dragging its wounded, began to stream through on to the dark sands, Jerott spoke gaspingly to the boy still at his side. 'Where is Gabriel?'

The black eyes, so like his father's and his uncle's, shining with dread and excitement, glanced round, briefly, at Jerott. 'Dead. . . . He fell on the way to the city. They say even his body had gone.'

The pain in Jerott's arm, breaking through his consciousness, suddenly made his head swim. Killed . . . killed, after all. And not by Francis. Francis who, for the first time in his life, had stood aside from a battle, running no risks, and hazarding no injury which would flaw his efficiency in the one thing he had set himself to do: to kill Graham Malett. Turning, without a word, Jerott abandoned the boy and the crowds fighting out seawards into the boats, and struggled up through the sands, against the reeling mass coming towards him; the last of the rearguard under Strozzi, the blue panache, worn so fortuitously by Leone and not by Gabriel, lit by the flames.

With them came an onrush of Turks; a fresh party of cavalry, thrown into the town and racing over the square to pursue the Knights into the sea. Jerott saw them coming towards him, and knew he was isolated, and they were too many; and he would have no chance. The leader was pale-skinned, not olive like the Turk or tawny like the Moors of the coast. His robe, backlit by the fire, was white and almost transparent, and round his magnificent head he wore a black and gold foulard, wrapped over fold upon fold with a fall of fringe to his breast. He was smiling.

He was smiling still as he galloped past Jerott and reined, just beyond, where the boy Strozzi stood. Jerott, turning, saw the lad's sword-point fall, and the grim purpose on his young face change, suddenly, to a look of amazed welcome. Then the Turk, with a little flourish of his own damascened blade, leaned forward amiably and plunged it through the boy's heart.

It was Gabriel.

The boy dropped. Jerott, standing stock still, saw Leone Strozzi turn from the surf of the shore and, sword in hand, begin at a lumbering run to hurry towards them. He saw Graham Malett, still smiling, withdraw his long, smoking sword and turning, broad-shouldered and golden in burnous and turban, look into his eyes. And he felt a hand on his shoulder and a voice which was Lymond's again; low, level and friendly, say, 'The standard needs you. This is my affair. Go.'

As Jerott drew breath, the choice was made for him. Struggling over the sand, laden with armour and weapons, Leone Strozzi on foot was no match for the mounted Turks dashing over the beaches towards him. As Jerott, light in his brigantine, threw himself forward; and others of his entourage, running behind, strove to surround and protect him, matches flared in the dark and half a dozen arquebuses spoke. Flinging up his arms, Strozzi fell. Behind him, Jerott saw Tolon de St Jaille falter and then drop, and another behind him cry out. Then he was at Strozzi's side, kneeling, and saw the blood pouring dark over the sand from the ball in his thigh.

There was a Majorca Knight, one of the most powerful in his Langue, just behind. Between them, Jerott and he lifted the Prior, and with Toreillas carrying him in his arms and Jerott at his side, the other Knights shoulder to shoulder about them, they plunged out into the surf. With the din of the sea in his ears, drowning the musket shot and the cries, the clash of weapons and the pounding of hooves far behind him, Jerott forced his way through the water, using his sword as he went.

It was shallow. The smallest shallops had already come in as far as they dared and had taken off again, laden with soldiers: except for the Knights, most of the fighting men now surviving must be on board. For the bigger skiffs, deep water was needed. Straining his eyes, he could see far out, black against the lit galleys behind, a shape which must be the longboat of the Admiral galley, waiting for them. It seemed to him that he ran alongside the stumbling Toreillas with his burden for an eternity before the water deepened and, pursuit falling off, they forced their way through the current until the sea was waist high.

How many, Jerott wondered, could swim? Very few. Wearing a hundred pounds of plate armour, none at all. Some, with soaked fingers, he saw attempting to unbuckle back- or breast-plate: some succeeded, and at the next, careful burst of arquebus fire fell, sagging, into the sea.

Jerott sheathed his sword. With his good hand under Toreillas's elbow he guided him from rock to rock and ledge to ledge under the water until finally they were on the last spit of the long underwater shelf, and the longboat was bobbing there at their sides. Jerott waited to see Leone Strozzi and the Majorcan Knight safely aboard, and then, turning, made his way grimly back to the shore.

For a second, as he raced to help Strozzi, Jerott might have seen relief and another, unguarded expression on Lymond's face. Then, moving faster even than Gabriel's horse, surging through sand dunes towards him, Lymond turned, ducked as a scimitar skimmed him, and, seizing the man's stirrups as he fled past, drove his knife into his attacker. He left it there. Then, running hard, Lymond vaulted into the saddle as the other man tumbled out and, gathering the reins, pulled the little horse round on its haunches as a sword flashed red in the air where he had been.

Opposite him, reined in also after that single, opportunist cut of his blade, Graham Malett sat still in the saddle, the fire striking sparks from the gold of his turban, his big-boned classical face as calm as his voice. 'Francis Crawford, who was once a slight inconvenience . . . does your life please you at present?'

The blue eyes were wide. 'It has brought me here,' Lymond said. He could sense horses behind him. The little mare sidled, under his knees; and Gabriel's horse edged round also in front of him, keeping his distance. He added, paraphrasing the Qur'ân, *'Let not pity for me detain you in the matter of obedience to Allâh.'* The sea, where every movement was magnified, was not very far off. He continued edging towards it.

'You know the Qur'ân,' said Gabriel. His pace, following, was entirely leisurely. 'It is a dramatic work. *And those of the left hand: how wretched are those of the left hand,'* he quoted, the deep voice enriching the phrases. *'In hot wind and boiling water and the shade of black smoke, neither cool nor honourable.* I am afraid,' said Sir Graham Reid Malett gently, 'that you, my dear Francis, are of the left hand.' He thought, seeking the words, and then added to it, mournfully: *'And if they cry for water, they shall be given water like molten brass which will scald their faces . . . Evil the drink; and ill the resting-place . . .* Sour-gutted devils, the Ottomans. A lesson in Western civilization is going to do them no harm.'

They were in the sea. The counter-attack, which had followed the attack on the Prior, had spent itself, although for a while the Knights still on the shore had made the Aga Morat prudently order his men to withdraw and, dismounting, rake the beaches with fire. Anger on both sides had made the last skirmish a bitter one, and the beaches were black with the fallen. Far off, on a long spit running

220

out to sea, the standard fluttered, with fierce fighting going on about it. The shallops had come in, and about them the sands were emptying as the remaining men ran, under fire, for the sea. Around the two men, there was no sound but the rush of the waves and the splashing hooves of their circling horses. For the moment, they were alone. 'A lesson in *what*?' Lymond said. 'What a pity your uncivilized cross-kissing colleagues chose another Grand Master.'

'Grand Master to those old women? Who wants that?' said Gabriel. He laughed. 'After this, my dear, Charles will foreclose on Malta, and the Knights will be flung out on their gallant white crosses. I don't mind sharpening my knife on a dunghill like Scotland or a sandcastle like Malta, for when the time is ripe, I shall rule over an empire. Stop sidling, my swan. I am going to hurt you, but I am not going to kill you, just yet. You are going to provide me with a deal of merriment still. I do not like being inconvenienced. I wish my friends to note what the consequences are. . . .'

The fires were dying. In the east, a hairline of light over the sea told that dawn was not now far off, but now it was dark, and in spite of the heat of the day the little chill wind of pre-dawning had risen to stir Gabriel's turban and ruffle Francis Crawford's damp hair. He had picked one of the trained horses. Used to the trick, it gave no sign as, still moving gently out through the water, Lymond slid his hand low and began to unbuckle the girth. 'Incidentally,' said Gabriel softly, 'there is a marksman on the beach with orders to do nothing at all but keep his weapon trained strictly on you. Tell me: have you burned any straw lately?'

For the space of a breath Lymond's fingers unloosing the buckle stopped in their work; and then went on smoothly and steadily to finish it. He said, 'The worst of fires may be drowned in the sea.' His horse was still.

'But we have no fires here, have we?' said Gabriel. 'No sparks? No recrimination? No temper? When I think of the floggings some poor, half-demented fools at St Mary's used to receive, I feel I must reprove this docility. Your mistress flayed? Your son scarred and degraded? Your person made a laughing-stock over the whole Middle Sea? And platitudes are all you can give me.'

'They cost me least trouble,' said Lymond. 'What words could insult you?'

For a moment the smile lost its perfume. Then Gabriel said, 'What do you propose then? A bedevilment by needles? What must I do to provoke you? You do not, by the way, use my title. I am not yet degraded by the poor Order, you know. In fact, I may say, you may no more unknight me than I may unlady your mother. Tell me,' said Gabriel, 'about the beautiful Marthe?'

'Who can tell about the beautiful Marthe?' said Lymond levelly. 'Since she is not signed in the genitive?'

221

And Gabriel throwing back his head laughed, and laughing gave a mock groan, and said, smiling, 'My God: my God: why alone are you not my slave? Why do you not adore me, who care for nothing and are distressed by nothing in this world, except what touches your vanity? You wish to wrest your son from my power. . . . Have you even discovered that there is not one child, but two? Do you care which is yours? Does it matter to you if one is taken from me and one is left to suffer and rot?'

His hands still, his work abandoned, Francis Crawford stared at the other in silence. Then: 'Who is the other child?' said Lymond at last.

In the growing light, Graham Malett's glorious face was filled with indulgence and joy; he was in power and at peace, with the world on a string at his girdle. 'Does it matter?' he said. 'Never on this earth will you distinguish them, nor is there any person now living who knows one child from the other. To be sure of finding your boy you must now find and take possession of both; to be sure of nurturing your boy, you must nurture and cherish not one but both. Of the two children you have found—you are right—one is your son. The other,' said Graham Malett joyously, in his rich singing voice, *'the other is mine and Joleta's.'*

However strong the self-discipline, for every man there is a point beyond which the impulse to kill will not be denied. Gabriel knew Francis Crawford. He attacked, when Gabriel was expecting him to attack, but not quite as he expected it. The freed saddle, pulled from the mare's back, hurtled through the air and struck Gabriel's raised sword from his hand as Lymond, light and most punishingly practised, launched himself from his own horse on to Gabriel's shoulders and bore him, dragging and with a final walloping splash into the dark, running sea. On shore, fire flashed and an arquebus spoke, and then another, but it was too tardy, too far away, and too dangerous, in the indistinguishable dark.

It was deep. He had made sure it was deep, for Turks do not swim; and Moors do not care to risk their lives for a renegade knight. Gabriel could swim. Gabriel had the advantage of weight and height; of friends who would rescue him wounded; of constant, practised training in battle over all these last months which Francis Crawford was aware that he lacked. So the killing had to be done now, in this first moment; as they both fell choking into the waves. There was no time to unsheathe his sword. But Lymond's right hand, with the long dagger ready, drove with all his force straight at Gabriel's heart.

It hit not flesh but metal. It slid from some object laid like a carapace over Gabriel's heart and, dragging bloody across the skin of his chest, lost its force harmlessly in the sea till Lymond pulled his hand back and, flinging himself off, trod water in a sudden deep channel, and then, finding his footing, braced himself against Gabriel's counter-attack. As it carried him under the water, he knew suddenly what it was he had hit. It was the crucifix; the great silver crucifix of the Knights of St John, which Gabriel wore still, undiscarded in haste, below the folds of his burnous. And through all that followed, Lymond carried the irony of it, wry as aloes, at the back of his mind.

Insensibly, the sky was lightening. To the successful defenders of Zuara left on the shore; to the Turks rounding up captives, to the Moors picking over their booty; to the men appointed with their arrows and arquebuses, straining their eyes over the dark water, the attack was at first merely a dimly lucent explosion of spray, followed by the slow, surging shapes of two horses, half swimming for shore. Then as the sky paled from second to second from indigo to jade it was possible to make out the two heads, darkened with water; and on the beach the Aga Morat suddenly ejaculated, 'Allâh! Allâh preserve him!' while from the sea, Jerott Blyth, having seen the standard on board and the last of the shallops filling, swam towards the fight that he knew he would never reach until it had ended, one way or the other.

Gabriel, of the magnificent shoulders and the thick, corded arms, was content merely to find his grip, and to hold his man down. Slender, twisting, Lymond eluded him . . . not always, but so far for long enough to rise retching to the surface for a starving portion of air before he could coil down, knife in hand, and avoid the drowning weight on his hips and his shoulders, the strangling arm under his chin, the knife Gabriel held prepared in his bear hug, to slit into belly or chest. *I am going to hurt you, but I am not going to kill you just yet.* So Gabriel had said, when his own life was not yet in question. It did not apply now; not any longer, since he discovered, as he would not admit he had discovered, how close a match he had found in one other man.

In his anger, his physical power seemed to increase. Once, knife in teeth, he caught Lymond on an upsurge and, gripping his body, flung him as a cormorant disgorges a fish, helter-skelter, crashing into the water, exposed to the lunge Gabriel then made, knife in hand. The blade scored the length of Lymond's body as he rolled, choking, to avoid it; but the plates of the brigantine saved him and he dived, dragging down Gabriel in his turn; refusing to be kicked off; holding until his lungs as well as Gabriel's were bursting and then rising with a backward kick between the other man's legs and behind him, ready to swallow his air, and seize the leonine head as it rose, and plunge it down, drowning again, the knife in his hand edging his throat.

That time, Gabriel let his knife drop. As it swayed glinting down into the depths he instead put up his hands and, seizing Lymond's two wrists held the knife from his throat and in a wrestler's grip, increasing the pressure, began to force the other man, in a kind of iron slow motion, over his head, turning Lymond's wrist as he did so that he must drop the knife, or allow it to break. And that time, they did not surface.

To Jerott, striking out blind to everything else, it seemed impossible, as from moment to moment the water swirled without breaking, that either man could stay below and alive for so long. To the horsemen gathered on the beach and wading reluctantly into the water, it seemed that both men were lost and it was consequently safe to venture outwards and plunder the bodies. It was to the credit of Jerott's heart, if not of his good sense, that in spite of the oncoming horsemen he swam on, doggedly, through the opaline sea until, with the outer thread of the whirlpool of movement touching his fingers, he saw something rise in the centre, and lie in its ringed silver chalice, passive as seaweed, with the dark blood swaying like fronds at its sides. It was Gabriel: his eyes closed, his face suffused, with the arteries of both wrists deeply and raggedly slit, and his life's blood pouring out. Of Lymond, there was no sign at all.

Jerott took a deep breath; and dived.

Francis Crawford was there, not far below, his eyes closed; his hair moving pale in the water. Perhaps he had been trying to surface: perhaps, holding the bleeding man down, minute after minute, he had left it too late. He made no resistance as Jerott gripped him and pulled him above, nor was there any time for elaborate revivication with the Aga Morat's horsemen trampling the waters. Jerott thumped him once on the back; saw, grimly, no change on the closed and motionless face and, consigning the outcome to fortune, seized Lymond in a less than classic one-handed grasp and kicked out with him backwards, away from the mêlée, to where he knew the last skiff was waiting.

It was a forlorn hope, exposed as they were. Taking his heaving breaths, he saw, indeed, the muskets lift and the arrows aiming, and braced himself somehow to turn over and dive. Then the Aga Morat's voice, just out of hearing, snapped an order, and repeated it peevishly; and reluctantly, the weapons dropped and the riders, Gabriel's body supported among them, turned splashing away.

The wages of sin. The wages of sin, thought Jerott, is life. An irony. In his grasp Lymond stirred, and choked, and Jerott, changing his grip, trod water and supported him until, suffocatingly, his lungs were empty of water and his eyes opened after the pain of the first rasping breaths. Empty of thought, the blue eyes for an interval looked into his; and then Jerott saw them change. Jerott said, 'He is dead.'

The sky was damask and rose: every nuance of rose from pale madder to the raw golden vermilion of the rising sun's edge. Around them the sea swayed and lapped them like a rose-tinted counterpane. Against the light, the town, sullenly smoking, raised smudged fingers of ruin and protest. By contrast, the horsemen could hardly be seen in the black shade of the walls except as a thin flash of steel, and as the source of a distant faint calling. The voice of a muezzin, faithful, undaunted, rolled across the roseate water.

'O God, Most High. I attest that there is no other God but God. I declare that Mohammed is the Prophet of God. Come to prayer; come to the temple of salvation. God is great; and there is no other.'

The children, said Francis Crawford. '*O mill . . . what hast thou ground?*'

15

ZAKYNTHOS AND ALEPPO

'Consider their wines. Their wines, mademoiselle, are exquisite.'
The voice of Onophrion Zitwitz, singing his favourite litany, hung
in the sultry air under the *Dauphiné*'s poop awning. 'The lagrime de
Christo, now: so beautiful that a Dutchman, they say, tasting it,
lamented that Christ had not wept in his country.'

'It's a spirit,' said Marthe, without charity. 'Almighty God: what
are the fools doing?'

'Fighting a battle,' said Georges Gaultier mildly. 'It takes time.
The Knights sailed for Zuara only ten days ago, and the wind was
against them.'

Marthe turned with angry impatience from the poop rail. 'They
may be dead,' she said. 'How long will you wait before we sail to
Aleppo?'

Turning his head, her self-styled uncle glanced at where Salablanca
sat, silent and unregarded in a corner. 'Not at all,' he said. 'That is,
once our good patron arrives back on board. Or we have news of
his death.'

Freed from Djerba on Güzel's instructions after the escape of
Jerott and Lymond, the *Dauphiné* with her crew and all her remaining passengers had sailed, as directed by Lymond through Salablanca, straight for the island of Malta. There they now lay, in the
great harbour under the guns of Fort St Angelo on one side and
Leone Strozzi's fine new fortifications on the other. The creek leading
to Birgu, the Knights' city, was barred to them, and they had made
no effort to enter; but had dipped their flag in salute to the white
cross flying from every battlement, and had satisfied the skiff which
put off to ask them their business.

They had no business, they said, other than to await the return
of the Knights of St John from their attack on Zuara, and to take
on board their patron and two others whom they had reason to
believe might be with them. His patron, M. Zitwitz had said,
entrusted with this reception, was a dear friend of the Chevalier
Leone Strozzi, who would respond favourably, he was sure, to any
kindness shown the *Dauphiné* during her enforced stay.

That the kindnesses, materializing, should take edible form was
not therefore altogether surprising, though Marthe, in her impatience, could be heard to say that she wished Fate would take
M. Onophrion and hang him to cool in a brook, like a jar of his
own preserved Leipzig cherries.

The fleet came back from Zuara next morning; and watching them
come, sails full and banners streaming in a following wind, those on

226

the ramparts of Mount Scibberas and St Angelo, no less than on the decks of the *Dauphiné*, soon realized that something was wrong. The galleys were intact. No staved wood or torn sail spoke of disaster: only a silence which lay on the water like the white haze of humidity which made the sweat check and run like a thief over spine, loins and ribs.

Men could be seen: pale punctuation of flesh among the timber and metal and cloth. But no trumpets blew, carrying far over the water; no voices cheered; no hackbuts sparked off with joy. Instead, as the galleys came nearer and nearer, all those watching saw that the ships themselves were half empty: that the walks and platforms which had left crowded with soldiers and knights showed shining wood to the sky except where, under an awning, a few lay recumbent. The only sound in Leone Strozzi's fleet came from the open hatches, and it was the sound of his wounded. The chain was raised, and the leaderless fleet passed in to its anchorage, and its dead to their tombs.

Salablanca alone was still on deck when at dusk a boat put off from Birgu and brought the French Special Envoy and his escort at last back to his ship. Jerott, climbing aboard one-handed after Francis Crawford, saw Salablanca smile and say, 'Allâh is beneficent,' but did not hear what Lymond answered, if anything. By the time he in turn landed on deck Lymond had already made his way aft, where the voices of Marthe and Gaultier could be heard.

Salablanca was looking at him. Jerott said, 'Gabriel is dead. He betrayed the Knights into the Aga Morat's hands, and the cream of the Order has gone. . . . Strozzi's badly hurt, but he'll live. They kept us, to answer for what had happened . . . but it is clear beyond question now, to them all, that Gabriel was and had been a traitor.'

Salablanca spoke softly. 'Mr Crawford himself killed him?'

'Yes,' said Jerott.

'I am glad,' said Salablanca. 'But the child . . .?'

O mill, what hast thou ground? Lymond had said. And since then, had hardly spoken at all.

'There are two children,' said Jerott. 'I don't know what is to be done. But you'd better come with me so that we can both receive our orders.'

By then, Lymond was already standing with his back to the carved rail of the poop, the blue awning dyeing his lightly tanned skin and borrowed clothes, addressing Gaultier, reclining watchfully in the captain's great chair, and Marthe, sitting perched on the table with her hair tied to fall down her back; and Onophrion, standing varnished with sweat in his stiff clothes, deferentially listening.

'I regret,' Lymond was saying pleasantly, 'that Sir Graham's death brings with it certain complications. Unless I forestall the news, the lives of two children become forfeit. We have also the safety of Miss Somerville to consider. I propose therefore that we split forces. The only information we have about the ship which took the first child from Mehedia is that it calls at Aleppo. On my instructions, Salablanca has found and chartered here in Malta a vessel which is willing to take two of you to Aleppo. Jerott and Marthe will sail on her. M. Gaultier, M. Zitwitz and Salablanca will come with me to Zakynthos on the *Dauphiné*, and thence follow the Children of Devshirmé to Constantinople.'

'Unchaperoned?' said M. Gaultier. He had sat up. 'Marthe, travelling alone with Mr Blyth? I am afraid, Mr Crawford, that as an uncle——'

'As an uncle, you permitted her to go ashore by herself at Bône dressed in boy's clothing without an avuncular qualm,' Lymond said. 'I have nothing against her being attired in boy's clothing in perpetuity if you feel it will protect her from an unsanctified bed.'

Jerott said, his face flushed, 'In any case, I'm afraid I don't care, Francis, to take the responsibility——'

'*L'amor' è cieco y rede niente*,' said Marthe. '*Ma non son' cieche l'altre gente*. He wants to stay with Mr Crawford.'

Jerott's voice was stony. 'I am prepared to go wherever I can be of most help. I meant only that I expect to be too occupied to give the attention I ought to Mlle Marthe's safety. I think M. Gaultier should come with us.'

'Then who,' said Lymond agreeably, 'do you suggest looks after the spinet?'

'Onophrion?'

'Jerott,' said Lymond, with the thinnest edge beginning to show in his voice. 'I am taking the *Dauphiné* and all the appurtenances of a royal bloody envoy because I am proposing if need be to mortgage the King of France down to the last bow on his mistress's nightcap in order to get the Somerville child out of this safely, with the baby if possible. For that I need Onophrion. No one in the presence of Onophrion could take this embassy lightly. We shall proceed in state, carrying our riches upon the shoulders of young asses, and our treasures upon the bunches of camels. I require you, if you mean what you say about helping, to be a young ass in Aleppo, not Zakynthos.'

'Excuse me,' said Onophrion Zitwitz respectfully, and they all turned. 'But there is always Mr Abernethy, I believe.'

'Not this time,' said Lymond shortly. 'He left for Aleppo even before Gabriel died. Philippa knows the danger and may be able to protect the Zakynthos child, if she has found him when the news of Gabriel's death reaches those parts. The other child, if possible, will have to be found before the news reaches his keepers.'

'This child . . . the other child . . . do we understand,' said Marthe, untying the ribbon in her bundled fair hair and letting it fall, smooth and swaying, over the thin, severely laced stuff of her dress, 'that your late unhappy mistress had twins?'

228

Malevolent, Jerott opened his mouth; but Lymond was quicker. 'You are not asked,' he said briefly, 'to understand either me or my late mistress. You are requested only to go to Aleppo. Do you wish to, or not?'

'Are our wishes being consulted?' said Marthe. 'Yes, I shall take your disciple Jerott, *manco passioni humane*, and he shall be returned to you weaned. Shall I go in disguise? A wild beast's skin on my horse's buttocks, and a hammer at my girth like a Pole?'

'I feel,' said Lymond, 'you would fail to convince as a Pole. Go as yourself. Unless M. Gaultier still has objections? In which case Marthe will of course come with us, and we shall leave Aleppo to Jerott and Archie?'

'No . . . no,' said Georges Gaultier. 'Though I shall need her to help with the spinet at Constantinople.'

'She will be there,' Lymond said.

*

They waited until he had gone, with Salablanca, to view the brigantine *San Marce*, which had been hired for the trip to Aleppo. But although it was leaving, they had been told, in the hour, Marthe made no immediate movement to pack. She said instead, to Jerott, 'Are there no balloons, no bunting, no dancing round bonfires? Does the machine not make festival when the great Gabriel is dead? Or is the whole programme a farce, clicking from item to item, and none of it real? *Is* there such a person as Gabriel? Did he live? Is he dead? And after him we have Child One; and then another to seek; and who knows, yet another and another: this man will traverse Europe, a crazy Pied Piper drawing waifs, flotsam, lagan and deodands in his train. Is Philippa Somerville lost? Or safe at home in England with Fogge . . .? Tell us, Mr Blyth. If he is mad, I can agree with him.'

'He isn't mad,' said Jerott.

Onophrion Zitwitz stirred. 'Your pardon, Chevalier. But there would be no urgency, surely, in finding these children if Sir Graham Malett were not dead.'

'He is dead,' Jerott said. 'And by Lymond's hand. So either child or both will perish. You don't hold festival, Mlle Marthe, with that hanging over your head.'

'It was an assassination, then?' said Marthe, sweet contempt in her voice. 'I thought it remarkable our friend should be so finely unblemished. What a pity he could not risk asking a question or two. About the identity of the children, for example.'

'It . . . was a fair fight,' said Jerott. A body, floating mindlessly in the sea, blood waving like weed from its half-severed wrists. And another, swaying below, who had held on too long; beyond the last thread of air and the last spark of consciousness, with all the strength of his considerable will. 'And the identity of the children was a device of Gabriel's own caprice. Both are branded; both were in Dragut's harem. No one knows one from the other. Both, it is to be assumed, will suffer now Gabriel is dead, for Gabriel didn't care for either, except as a means of revenge. One is Lymond's son. And the other is Gabriel's. And no one living now knows which is which.'

'Then,' said Georges Gaultier, rising from his fine chair, 'rather than perpetuate the one or the other, I must say I should prefer to let them both die.'

*

Of the two ships which parted company that night, the *Dauphiné* had the more uncomfortable journey. To begin with, it was hard work. After months of desultory sailing and captivity, she was required to fulfil her royal function once more: her slaves and her sails had to be redressed, her decks varnished, her colours freshened, her officers dressed in their creased and mildewed best clothing.

The stores under Onophrion's care had suffered no harm. Long before the landing at Zakynthos, Lymond's clothes were in exquisite order; the food stores inventoried; the silver and menus made ready. In Lymond's efficient hands the running of the ship likewise became invigorated and orderly. To Salablanca, the spectacle was familiar. To Onophrion, it was what he expected in any man he distinguished by serving. And to Gaultier, it was another manifestation of the loutish physical world, which so often insulted the sensitive man and his art. The world to which, with pleasure, he lent money at exorbitant interest.

They arrived at Zakynthos, guns firing and French flag fluttering high on the masthead, and lay still in the pink evening light, the rigging outlined in the firefly light of twelve hundred candles. The Proveditore came to supper, and spoke of Venice with maudlin nostalgia; her four hundred bridges; her thousand gondolas; the shops under the Arches; the sound of La Trottiera, ringing at noon.

And her women, *grande de legni, grosse di straci, rosse di bettito, bianche di calcina* . . . While Onophrion filled the guest's goblet and placed before him in turn the roast Ambracian kid, the palm hearts, the Tartessian lampreys, the fried figs and clove rissoles, the pies of capon and marrow, the cold broth of almonds and cinnamon, the fried bread done in sugary batter and the leched pears in malmsey, Lymond spoke about those.

Gently, and by devious ways, the House of the Palm Tree and the merchant Marino Donati entered the talk. It was a pity, said the Proveditore, that the Envoy had not called sooner, for Signor Donati was a man of great sympathy, with some treasures to show. But alas, against all the commands of Mother Church (the Proveditore unsteadily crossed himself), the poor man, a mere two weeks since, had seen fit to take his own life.

He was able, however, before he was escorted with care to his castle, to outline in contentious detail the route taken to Usküb each year by the children of Devshirmé. And Salablanca, visiting the House of the Palm Tree in all innocence next day seeking a friend, was able to verify that the death of the merchant Donati was all too true.

He did more. He spoke to a woman of his own race, once the cook, and now living in a corner of the shock-splintered building, awaiting the notice of the new occupant, or of the officers of the town, or whoever would shelter and feed her and her children once more. From her, he heard of Míkál and the Pilgrims, and of Philippa's departure, as Archie had described, to follow the Children of Tribute to the north. From her also he heard of the twinning ring, which had hung round the neck of the white child.

'Kuzucuyum—Lambkin, they called it,' she said. 'A faint spirit half-slipped betwixt the skin and the flesh, till they sent him to Prince Dragut's to recover. Then in October came back this same Kuzucuyum; beautiful and bright in the colour of his body, and energetic and firm in his soul.'

'This child was born in Zakynthos?' had asked Salablanca. 'Of what parentage?'

'Ah, base, base,' said the woman. 'Of a girl unwed and a father unknown. She came for the birth, and left after, and only the master's sister and I were there when the time came. The master's sister held her wrists when she shrieked, but it was I who severed the child.'

'The master's sister . . . who was this?' Salablanca had asked. 'And when?'

'Her name? Signora Donati: that was all I ever knew. And when? Two years ago, or three: I do not know. She was duenna, they said, to the child: the child who was brought to bed of the boy. A poor duenna, thou sayest, who permits her jewel to be ravished so young. A child, the mother was; with hair the colour of apricots, sunning in June.'

'Who was the mother?' he had asked gently, and the cook had grinned, her black eyes wrinkling above the black veil. 'To ask this was forbidden. But they said—and I think it is true—that the child was well born in her own land, and of good blood. They say her brother was even a Knight of St John of Jerusalem, vowed to chastity, eh? How dost thou think he would look on his sister, were he to discover the truth?'

'He knew it,' said Salablanca, and paid her, not in aspers or crowns, but in zecchinos of gold.

Retold quietly to Lymond, with all the formality Spanish could lend it, the story had still an implication which nothing could soften. Before Salablanca, Francis Crawford did not always school his expression. Now, standing head bent in his cabin, gazing heavy-eyed and unseeing at his own interlaced hands, he did not try. One child born of Oonagh at Djerba. One child born of Joleta here at Zakynthos. Both in Dragut's harem. One had come back to Zakynthos and joined the Children of Tribute. One had gone with Oonagh to be sold to Ali-Rashid the camel-trader, and finally to the silk-farmer of Mehedia and his sister's terrible house. Which?

One was his son. And one was Gabriel's.

Let them both die. Gaultier had said that, or so Jerott had told him, in his voice meant to be overheard. *But what of the child?* Marthe had said that; and Philippa too; but only Philippa, he thought, had meant it. And Philippa had made no vow at St Giles....

Think of it, not as a child but as a pawn. He had said that himself once, to Jerott. Because he knew . . . God, he knew! Jerott's terrible romanticism, which would taste death so readily; so splendidly offer the blood of his fellows, in defence of the weak and the puny.

This child; this unknown son of his blood, was worth one life: his own. From its unmindful genesis, its heritage from birth had been suffering; an evil not to be tolerated: an evil outweighed only by the greater evil of Gabriel's survival.

But Gabriel was dead. As a man, this child would be one's offering to the future races of men. The burden of his upbringing, wherever it fell: however tiresome or onerous, was of no importance compared with his living grasp of the future. This, one felt of one's son. Was it not also true of Gabriel's?

From that monstrous connection, a child had been born as blameless as his. Neither child, from reports, was malformed or mentally maimed. Gabriel's son had escaped the physical risks of his heritage; other taints, it might be, had escaped him as well. What was original sin? Was it more than an arbitrary pattern set in the loom, of talents and weaknesses, picked out from the warp of one's forebears? Who could say then that, more than his own, Gabriel's house might not hold the potential of genius?

It was a theory that cut across every natural instinct . . . Oh, Christ: of course it was. If you were Gaultier, you said, kill them both. If you were Jerott, you would fret cut your soul to distinguish the one from the other, and then crush Gabriel's son like a leech beneath the sole of your foot. If you were . . . who you were . . .

'Señor?' said Salablanca, and touched him.

'It's all right,' said Lymond. 'An unaccustomed course of straight thinking. Like the drinking water of Porretta: it either cleans you or bursts you.'

There was a little pause. Then, 'You have read in the Qur'ân,' said Salablanca softly.

Lymond looked up. 'I have read. It is wise.'

'It is wise. It says, *You have the appointment of a day from which you cannot hold back any while; nor can you bring it on before it is time.*'

'Blessed be all the Prophets, and praise be to God the Lord of Both Worlds,' said Lymond, with sudden sharp irritability. 'But I sometimes think an arthritic moorhen could beat them for speed.... Tell the Master we sail before noon.'

'We sail? Where, señor?'

'To Thessalonika,' said Lymond. 'To call on the Viceroy.'

*

As the swiftness of the Danube, they say, could be gauged at Belgrade by the clack of the boat mills, so might the nervous hostility between Jerott Blyth and the exquisite Marthe be judged by the increasing venom between them as the *San Marce* took her laborious way eastwards from Malta. In the middle of September, she landed them, brawling like butter-wives, at Scandaroon, the port for Aleppo.

A trained fighting man, accustomed to hard words and hard blows and the company of men like himself, for years ruled by the self-discipline required by the world's greatest order of chivalry, Jerott had come to terms now with the fact that one man could make him feel and act like a rhinoceros in a cloud of mosquitoes.

Marthe had not perhaps quite the purely detached ability to hurt which Lymond exercised with such care. But with Marthe in every other way it was far, far worse. The eyes, the mouth, the brain, the body through which she expressed her indifference and her contempt were those of a woman he wanted. A woman high, cool, remote as a cloud forest, trailing mosses and bright birds and orchids; a woman with a body like moonlight seen through a pearl curtain. A woman whom he had not touched since, her sardonic blue eyes studying him, she had said, 'You only want me because...'

For the thousandth time, Jerott shut his mind to that episode. He had work to do. He was looking for a woman and a child who had left Mehedia in July on a ship called the *Peppercorn*. At Alexandria, he asked. At Candia. At Cyprus. At every port the *San Marce* touched, Egyptian, Syrian, Venetian. At all he received the same answer. The *Peppercorn* had not called this year.

They loaded and unloaded cargo. The heat; the flies; the bothering wind, always in the wrong direction, began to affect Marthe as Jerott had seen Lymond react under stress; as a slate under a little axe cleaves into sheets thin and hard and more brittle. At Cyprus, she said, 'There go the pilgrims. Two days in a longboat to Joppa, and then a mere thirty miles overland to Jerusalem. The Holy City your Order fought for and whose keys they still possess, don't they, Mr Blyth? Although the keyhole has gone. Doesn't it stir your

233

Christian soul: although the Turks have taken over the Tomb of David and the Centacle, and the Franciscans of Mount Zion shake at their prayers? Have you no yearning, after your years of self-denial and prayer, for a garter which has touched a weed in the Garden of Gethsemane?'

Standing spaced apart from her, his hands brown on the rail, his skin darkened to chestnut by the sun under his thickly clinging black hair, Jerott watched the pilgrims and their boxes disembark and set off across the dazzling sea. 'If you have faith, you don't need the trappings,' he said.

'You mean you have faith, and they do not? So help you, God and holidome? Oh, come, Mr Blyth,' said Marthe. 'After worshipping at the feet of the late Graham Malett and lying down under the feet of the ever-present Mr Crawford, you are still the unshaken shrine of the ancient faith of the Knights that uplifts but does not blind?'

'I claim nothing at all. It's your choice of subject, not mine,' said Jerott.

'Certainly, you are not defending your beliefs,' said Marthe, looking at him speculatively. 'You disappoint me. But then, you have abandoned your Order. Perhaps you have found another more to your taste? God appears in multifarious guises. Why not the Mussulman's God, that is good and gracious, and exacts not of him what is harsh and burdensome, but permits him the nightly company of women; well knowing that abstinency of that kind is both grievous and impossible? It might make this journey more comfortable for us both.'

Looking into that cold and beautiful face: 'You mean,' said Jerott curtly, 'to fulfil the role of the nightly houri made of musk?'

Marthe smiled. 'I mean,' she said, 'that although I despise the hanging jaw of hunger, I do not intend that the needy should look to me for their banquet.'

'To Kiaya Khátún, then?' said Jerott. And caught his breath at the look on her face.

Then it changed; and her lashes covered her eyes. She said, 'Francis Crawford has much to answer for, hasn't he? *I break what is thine, because thou corruptest what is mine?* You are wrong. Kiaya Khátún makes her own Paradise.'

'Who is she?'

The arched brows rose. 'Who knows? In Stamboul she is a powerful woman: a friend of Roxelana, the wife of the Sultan; the beloved of Dragut whose palaces she controls. Before that, in Venice. They say she is a Gritti, by an exiled Doge and a Greek slave. No one knows.'

The straight nose; the dark eyes; the handsome, olive face; the black hair strung with jewels; the small, plump hands holding the

234

knife steadily at Lymond's heart, precisely, to sever the skin. Jerott said, 'She has lived with many?'

Marthe laughed at him. '*C'est Vertu, la nymphe éternelle.* She has chosen her field of power and has lived with the master of it as long as it pleased her. You have met her. Try to tell me you haven't felt the tug of the magnet.'

Her hair gleamed on her shoulders, amber and silver and Indian yellow, coiled like heavy syrups enfolding the sunlight; and her white, polished skin was coloured with sun. 'No,' said Jerott. 'I felt no attraction.'

The smile remained in her eyes. 'That was because, perhaps, the magnet was turned in another direction.'

Jerott's dark gaze was suddenly alert. 'You think . . .?'

'I think that when Kiaya Khátún tires of the mysteries of the polygone étoile, Mr Crawford has need to look out, for she will choose and brittle her deer if it pleases her; and undo him most woodmanly and cleanly that she might.'

'He has no field of power,' said Jerott, and watched her turn to the rail slowly, still smiling, her eyes seeing nothing.

'Have you heard of the *sheb-chiragh*, the night lamp?' said Marthe. 'On a certain night, the Arab says, when the water-bull cometh up to land to graze, he bringeth this jewel with him in his mouth, and setteth it down on the place where he would graze, and by the light of it doth he graze. . . . She is the lamp, and should she come to him, he may graze where he pleases.'

It was then, in bewildered understanding and pity, that Jerott made the error of touching her. She turned on him, alight with malice, supple as a ribbon of steel, and said, 'I am tired of the game. Go to the classroom and glut yourself on penny tales whose language you understand; for you misread mine to a tedium. . . .'

He took his dignity and left her; and because he was vulnerable to her as he had been vulnerable to Francis Crawford he found the same solitary and belligerent salve for his troubles: he drowned them.

*

According to the French factor at Scanderoon, where they landed two days later, it was no mean advantage to view the pleasures of Scanderoon through a thin veil of alcohol. Jerott, supervising a little unsteadily the disembarking of his and Marthe's boxes, and replying in kind, wherever necessary, to her descant of bright, acidulous comment, was inclined to agree.

To begin with, it was so foully unhealthy, between marshes and mountain, that they had not been permitted to land until two hours after sunrise, when heat had cleared all the poisonous mists from the bogs. Scanderoon itself, huddled between the ruins of a waterlogged castle and a scattering of lizard-infested shells, amounted to no more than forty reed-thatched board houses, most of them occupied by a diverse coterie of quarrelling merchants, unified only in their physical miseries. Agents in Scanderoon seldom lived to retire home on their wealth.

In a limited way, the French factor was helpful. Jerott and the lady were placed in a khan, a hollow square surrounded by two tiers of arcaded buildings, built from charity and offered for the accommodation of the passing tourist or trader. In the Grand Seigneur's empire, there were no inns. Here, the stores and the stables and the commonality were served on the ground floor, Marthe and Jerott in separate rooms on the upper floor, with the two servants he had acquired on the way, for their style.

Once settled, he wasted no time. Already he had verified from the factor that no ship called the *Peppercorn* had made landfall this year, to his knowledge; but that sometimes, of course, such a ship, if she were English, would unload her cargo, say, in Cyprus and send her passengers by small boat to the coast. English ships did not call at Scanderoon. There was no agent. Only the ships of the Seigneury, or of France, or of the Great Turk's own domains.

Jerott's head ached. Marthe had disappeared, with her slave, allegedly to consult the Syrian merchants on the same business. The French agent's damp timbered house, in which he sat, smelt of goat grease and *bukhur-jauri*, the strong Javanese incense beloved of Negroes. He caught sight of the woman, a veil half over her woolly hair, round the edge of the door. He didn't blame the man: not here. He said, 'If such a small boat landed persons, say of Syrian nationality, or even Western Europeans, what record of such people might I find to exist? My superior seeks particularly a dark-haired woman, a Syrian from Mehedia, and a fair two-year-old child.'

For that, said the agent, he would require to study the records of the Cadi, whom he would find at Aleppo. There also were the merchants who traded with such second-hand cargo, and the priests and the Patriarchs who looked after the spiritual welfare of newcomers. He would ask in Scanderoon if such a pair were remembered, and where they had gone. Sometimes, men came and took boat for Tarsus, only eight miles off over the bay, especially those engaged in the silk-rearing business. Did M. Blyth wish to make inquiries at Tarsus?

Through a haze of wine, which affected his efficiency very little, Jerott initiated inquiries at Tarsus. He had all the merchants of Scanderoon narrowly questioned. He examined the records. He collected Marthe, who was standing, absently covered in Baghdad pigeons, in the Syrian merchant's courtyard, discussing the uses of turpentine. And when all these activities had drawn a blank, he bespoke the services of baggage-mules, horses, a Janissary and two

Ajémoghláns the following day, to convoy Marthe and himself in safety to Aleppo. Then he returned to the khan, ate a leaden meal of mutton and rice, quarrelled with Marthe and, retiring to his mattress, drank himself into a nightmarish sleep, punctuated by the howling of jackals.

The journey from Scanderoon to Aleppo, which occupied slightly more than three days, was marked by no roguish departure from the general atmosphere of exasperation and gloom. At Belan, they slept on the ground. At Antioch, between high Biblical rocks, they lodged in a house, also on bare ground, with a pillow, a mattress and a quilt. They crossed the plain of Antioch, and hired a boat over the Orontes, which was low. They left the wildfowl and the water-buffaloes of the coast and met instead the tented villages of the Bedouins, with flocks of dangle-eared goats and the thick-tailed Syrian sheep, dragging thirty pounds of fat and wool at its back.

They had no provisioning to do. The Janissary visited the villages and called at the low goat-hair tents to buy bread-cake and water, and brought them goat's milk and yoghourt and dates to add to the meat and sour butter they carried. On the last evening, approaching Hanadan, a village eight miles from Aleppo, there occurred the only incident in which Janissary and Ajémoghláns were required to act in their protective capacity.

The raid in fact came from nowhere just before the sudden extinguishing of night. Two of the horses had gone lame, and their reduced pace had made them late in arriving within the safety of Hanadan. Torches had been lit, to scare off brute dog and jackal as much as to frighten off thieves. But even so, the raiders perhaps believed that the little caravan was very much more numerous and heavily laden than in fact it was. They came whirling out of the darkness, on small Arab horses: a blur of white headgear, coarse cloaks and striped kaftáns, with the burning pitch shining red on their swords. Then the Janissary, scimitar at his side, fired off a hackbut, and throwing it down, charged steel flashing with the Ajémoghláns at his heels; and the raiders, seeing the economy of the luggage and the scarcity of well-plenished merchants, weighed risk against risk and, bringing their horses round, rearing, made off in the dark.

The Janissary, remarkable so far for his silence, returned pleased and loquacious. The man with one eye—had they noted?—the leader was Shadli, the dog, the son of a drunkard, who forced money from every caravan of note from Scandaroon to Aleppo, and some-times from Aleppo as far as the Grand Sophy's frontier. Demanded money, and if the caravans did not pay, then the tribes descended and lives and money, all were lost.

'I have heard,' said Marthe, 'there are Kurds in these mountains who worship the Devil.'

'It is true,' said the Janissary. 'God is good, they say; and will harm nobody; but the Devil is bad, and must be pleased, lest he hurt them. But these are not Kurds, Khátún. These are Bedouin, who call themselves the Saracens of Savah and, living in their tents, earn their livelihood thus. But they are spendthrifts. The money goes: always they want more. When the army is here, you will see: then they raid the opium caravans and sell direct to our soldiers. When our army goes to war,' said the Janissary, 'all the opium-bearing fields are despoiled for their comfort and courage.'

Jerott found, stiffening, that Marthe was looking at him. 'Did you know that?' she said. 'Fifty camels a year loaded with opium come in from Paphlagonia, Cappadocia, Galatia and Cilicia. The Janissaries take it daily—half a drachma and you wouldn't notice it. A whole drachma might perhaps bring a man to a state no more objectionable than your own. But of course, before they resell, the tribes will adulterate. What began as four-ounce cakes in India might finish as slabs of half a pound or even a pound, and this can cause trouble.'

'If it is pure,' said the Janissary harshly, 'there is no insult.'

'Have you ever seen a man starve in order to buy himself a hundred grains daily, and then be deprived of his source? That isn't an insult,' said Marthe. 'That is the root of the tree that grows in the bottom of Hell.'

It was no news that Turks lived on opium. 'You said something about "when the army is here",' said Jerott.

'It is so. Rustem Pasha, the Grand Vizier, has left Stamboul,' said the Janissary. 'From Scutari he brings an army to Aleppo, where it will be joined by the armies of Damascus and Tripoli and Aman. Didst thou not see the soldiers at Antioch? Together they winter here. Then in the spring, my lord marches on Persia.'

'Another Persian campaign?' said Jerott. He was thinking. Men, money, munitions, poured into the dry fields of Persia. And none for France, facing not only the Emperor, but the Emperor's niece newly crowned Queen of England. What of the French invasion of Corsica now? What of his friends, the trained company Lymond had created, which he had abandoned to go on this self-destructive, harrowing search? Paid off for lack of funds? Decimated for want of good weapons? Hell, thought Jerott, staring at the bloodshot roof-tops of Hanadan. I've had enough. If the brat's not at Aleppo it's dead, or it's going to cost more than our blood to redeem it. If the trail ends here, it ends and I go back to France. My God, I'm a soldier, not a wet-nurse to somebody's bastard.

'I prefer you, I think, drunk to sulking,' said Marthe. 'Consider. An angel descends with every drop of water and lays it in its appointed place. If it rains, you will be dry, or you will be wet. Why then flinch or rebel?'

'Because,' said Jerott with emphasis. 'I'm not a bloody Saracen.'
'What a pity,' said Marthe. 'Another difference, I fear, to divide
us. Because I, of course, am.'

*

As always, Jerott rose to the bait. That her remark was a simple
statement of truth took a long time to penetrate; but in the end he
was brought to admit, in his heart, that given the person she was, it
was not beyond understanding. Thinking back, he even remembered
how, outside Mehedia, the thought had once crossed his mind when
she overplayed, by a fraction, her ignorance of Bektashi dervishes.
She had travelled in Moslem countries: she had seen, as Jerott, his
voice raised, reminded her, that they treated their women as servants
and playthings. It did not trouble her.

She did not say, look at Roxelana. She did not say, look at Kiaya
Khátún. But she did say, coldly sardonic, 'What better hopes have
I in Europe? I have no birth, no money, no inheritance, no future.
I live from Georges Gaultier's charity, and the caprice of the Dame.
No man of ambition will marry a bastard. To marry beneath me is
to become a servant: to accept anything other than marriage is to
become a plaything. I have little choice wherever I go. I prefer a
society which accepts that I have no choice, and does not pretend
that I have. I prefer a God who does what he wills, and rules as he
desires, and enjoins on me not to prevent anything against its
destiny. I prefer a religion which can say:

> *Yiğit Olanlar anilir*
> *Filan oğlu filan diye*
> *Ne anan var, ne baban var*
> *Benzersin sen piçe tanri.*

Jerott did not need a translation.

> Those who are heroes are known,
> Such as this man, who is the son of that other . . .
> Thou hast no mother and no father:
> Thou resemblest a bastard child, God.

'You think it blasphemy, no doubt,' she said. 'It isn't. It is divine
simplicity, I believe.'

He made one last attempt. 'You are leaving a civilization which
rules by the intellect for a civilization which rules by the senses,' said
Jerott.

'And *you* would dissuade me?' said Marthe.

16

ALEPPO

'. . . The Sultan of Cambaia has moustaches so long, he ties them up with a fillet like a woman, and he has a beard white to the navel.'

The glories of the Orient. 'Indeed,' said Jerott Blyth flatly; and wished for the hundredth time that supper were over; that the French Consul were not away on affairs, and that the attaché who was their host in his place was with the Sultan of Cambaia, with his moustaches tied tight round his larynx.

Outside those high stone walls were the streets of Aleppo, third city of Suleiman's Empire; built on its four hills with its mosques and its minarets and its khans and its high garrisoned castle; its souks and its low arcaded houses and its fountains from the underground flow of the Singa; its great suburbs; its four miles of gardens and vineyards, its fields of cotton and rice, figs and melons and cucumbers, cabbages, lettuces, beets, plums and pears stretching to the walls of the Old City, wrecked by the Tartars; and everywhere the patient bullock treading its blindfolded circle as the wheels turned and the river-water trickled into the light stony ground, and brought it fertility.

Riding today to the French Consul's house, Jerott had recalled that most of the population of Scotland could be fitted into this Egyptian city, still the greatest market in Asia, after forty years of Suleiman's rule. *Qui vero in Indiam, Persiam, aliasque Orientis regiones profisci cupiunt, semper istic negociatores reperiunt, qui ultro citroque commeant,* Bellon had written. And still the camel-trains poured in from Taurus; the great Persian boxes streamed up the Euphrates, the treasures of India were carried in by boat and camel and packhorse from the Red Sea and the Gulf: turtle-shells in barrels from Bombay, and wax and seahorse teeth, and negroes and gum.

Here Venice bought her drugs, her indigo and her spices, her mohair, cotton and wool, and in return unloaded these shining bales of satin and damask, of scarlet and violet wool, these boxes of gold and of silver: three hundred and fifty thousand ducats' worth of trade every year. In all, to Venice; to France; to the merchants of Egypt and Cairo, Aleppo sent annually one hundred thousand ducats' worth of her own silk cloths alone; and five hundred thousand ducats' worth of other things.

For this kind of business you must have great khans for your traders to dwell in, and many agents, both diplomatic and spiritual. You must have food and water in plenty, and shops where strangers can buy food, and ovens where it may be cooked for them. You have your warehouses for the non-perishing goods: the gems, the amber, the lignum, the aloes, the musk. You have your interpreters and your hirer of camels; your covered bazaars, your mosques with thronging stone cupolas, lined with gilt and mosaic inside. Within the tall towered walls with their eleven gates you have a Cadi and a Beglierbey, dispensing justice; customars to deal with trade taxes; pensioned horsemen—the Timarriots—to keep order.

Within the castle walls lived two thousand people, a garrison of five hundred Janissaries and their Agha. And these men jostling in the streets were the permanent residents they controlled—Turks, Moors, Arabs, Jews, Greeks and Armenians; Maronites, Georgians, Chelfalines, Nostranes; the spendthrift Bedouin with his tent on a dungheap; the poor Greek who earned his asper a month swabbing his boothkeeper's path-frontage daily. The dumb and the mad. The naked fool led by dervishes, eating flies and the eyes of dogs raw. The call of the muezzin, floating many-threaded from tower to tower, which canopied the roaring voice of the streets, speaking all the tongues common to man: Italian and Arabic, Turkish, Armenian and Persian, Hebrew and Greek, and the alien incomers' tongue of the Chaldee, the Tartar, the Indian.

A shifting, bright alien population, numbering hundreds of thousands. In which a woman and child would be, as the Janissary who brought them had pointed out pityingly, 'small, Efendi: small as the white point on the back of a date-stone'.

The French attaché, with whatever cause, was more bracing. 'A woman without friends, in Aleppo? She would need help. The priest. The Patriarch. The services of a consul to procure her the shelter of a khan, to change her money, to obtain a carrier, an interpreter, a Janissary, a guide. Whoever has helped her, one can discover him.'

'And if she had friends waiting?' said Jerott.

'Ships come as the wind blows. How could they wait?' said the attaché. 'Wherever they are, she must seek them. Yellow hair is not common. Somewhere is the horse, the camel she used. . . . In a week I may have news for you.'

'It must be sooner than that. Wherever he is, he is in danger,' said Jerott.

But the attaché shrugged. 'In the East, God knows, time is different. To achieve any desired end: it is slow. But dangers hasten slowly, as well.'

He was out in both reckonings. Before the end of a week, he had concluded his inquiries and doom, the brisk doom of the Christians, had arrived.

It began with the culminating explosion in a series of skirmishes to do with Marthe's desire to explore Aleppo, in Arab clothes, accompanied by the Ethiopian woman he had bought for her, and no one else.

241

Jerott had complained, before coming on this trip, that he could not in good faith be accountable for Marthe's safety. It did not prevent him, when he found her slipping out of a side door that first morning, from seizing and berating her before the absent French Consul's interested household, until she stopped him by stalking back into the house.

When, in her own room, she confronted him, it was like facing the worst of Francis Crawford; with the difference that Lymond was usually right, and therefore cut deeper still.

It was unpleasant enough. Marthe stood, robed from head to foot in the coarse undyed robes of the Arab, her veil crushed in her hand, and demanded, softly, to know by what conceivable right her safety, spiritual, moral or physical, was any business of his. 'Do you imagine,' said Marthe, 'that I cannot conceive of the risks? Or that I have not the intelligence to weigh them? Or that perhaps I may not be able to judge better than you the course I must take in my own affairs?'

'My God,' said Jerott. He slammed the door and, walking across, flung his cap on her table. 'Perhaps for one second you would sit on the lid of your irreducible ego and listen to me. I regard you, masculine or feminine, as the greatest genius the world has ever produced. I agree you have a superior knowledge of your own affairs and are far more capable than the Consulate, for example, of weighing up the risks. Suppose even, for the sake of conjecture, that I don't give a brass bagcheek whether the first Tartar you meet doesn't drag you back to his tents and elect you Broody Mother to the whole bloody tribe. All I am saying is that, first, if anything happens to you, I've got to face Francis Crawford and also your uncle. And second, if you must face risks with good reason—and there had damned well better be a good reason—then there'll be a good few less risks if I come along with you.'

'No,' said Marthe simply.

That was the first time. Flinging out furiously ten minutes later, having achieved precisely nothing, Jerott retired cursing to his room and stayed there until his servant warned him, as he had been instructed, that the mademoiselle had left her room once again.

That time, Jerott thought he had never seen her look so angry. The blue eyes were open pits of cold hatred when she saw him; but this time, she did not turn back or argue. Slipping the black veil into place over her face, she brushed past him and continued on her way out of doors.

'Very well,' said Jerott. 'Only I am afraid you will not remain very anonymous. I am coming with you, and, as I hope you have noticed, I am wearing one of Onophrion's more vernal creations in pale green watered silk. Always mindful of my master's dignity. We shall be a pretty pair.'

Then she turned back, and slammed the door in his face.

The key was on the outside. Jerott turned it, withdrew it and, taking it with him, found the two Janissaries the attaché had allotted him and went out, followed by the sound of furious hammering.

It was dusk when he returned. To get out now, she would have to pass the Consulate guards; and in any case, as Jerott well knew, she was no fool. No woman who knew her Middle East would venture unescorted now. He unlocked Marthe's door, tapped on it, and turned back into his room without waiting to speak with her.

Next morning, awakened from light sleep by his servant's touch, Jerott thought, without pleasure, that it was the same rotten business again. He had a headache, and no prospect of remaining anything but distressingly sober if he was to keep his self-willed companion in sight.

But the news was not of Marthe's imminent departure alone into the stews of Aleppo. Marthe, it seemed, had come to her senses. She wished, for her uncle's sake, to view the merchandise in the covered bazaar and also to help with any inquiries which Mr Blyth might be making in pursuit of the child. If Mr Blyth felt he could dispense with his Janissaries, she, Marthe, would dispense with her Arab clothing and confide herself to his protection dressed a la Christianesca for the day.

It was a stilted surrender, and the pricking of his senses should have warned him. As it was, he sent off a cordial message of agreement, while reserving the right, childishly, as a bonus for trouble taken, to retain one Janissary if he jolly well wanted.

With their Janissary, scimitared and white-capped behind them, Jerott and Marthe explored Aleppo. He had some officials to visit whom the attaché had suggested, but all the detailed investigation was already under way, he knew, through the tortuous channels known best to the Consulate. To be walking from alley to alley, and meeting people, and asking the same stupid questions was only a method of keeping busy, of stifling one's restlessness; of persuading oneself that one was here for some good; that a life might be saved if one worked hard enough.

And at his side throughout, there was Marthe . . . quick-witted and intuitive, articulate and thoughtful. He had loved her for her beauty and for an excellence with which he was already familiar. That day, engrossed together in the fate of the child, he met her mind to mind and fell in love with her, with every grain of his spirit and cell of his body; with the essential finality of death.

If Marthe knew of it, she gave no sign. It was she who found the tekke, the house of the dervishes; and, standing under the gateway, said, 'Of course Islam is anathema to you. But in some things, my faith and yours are not far apart. The Bektashi think that the fervent practice of worship engenders in the soul graces; and that in the

243

science of hearts the soul may procure wisdom. . . . I have a favour to ask.'

'Ask it,' said Jerott.

'This is a Bektashi tekke: a place where the dervishes gather for worship and instruction. They do not mind the presence of infidels, nor do they forbid women. Will you allow me to take you inside?'

'The Janissary——' Jerott began.

'The Janissary cannot enter. Mr Blyth, these are holy men sworn to contemplative and utter humility; dedicated to tolerance and devoted to love. The Way is one, they say: the Form is many. There is nothing to fear in a tekke of the Bektashi Order.'

'It sounds,' said Jerott, 'as if they have some of the right ideas. All right. Let's go in.'

*

Inside, as they stood shoes in hand, stockinged feet deep in soft carpets and the leather curtain whispering shut just behind them, the darkness was almost complete. The place seemed large. Motion-less, his hand on Marthe's arm beside him, Jerott became aware of the echoing murmur of many voices, muted by hangings, from each side and before him: the air was filled with spice and frankincense, and the sweet, snuffed odour of new, deep-piled carpets, and the churchly smell of warm wax.

They stood, he then saw, in a little vestibule, its walls tiled with glimmering tablets of ultramarine and white and a strong Venetian red. A text, in gold, sprang to life in a flicker of candlelight: *God saith: I was a hidden treasure and I desired to be known; so I took a handful of my light and said unto it, 'Be thou my beloved Mohammed.'*

The candle went out. Beyond Marthe, there was a movement. Smoothly, she began to walk forward. Under his hand, her arm was quite cool and relaxed. He moved forward with her. A candle flickered.

The law is my words. The way is my actions. Knowledge is my chief of all things. Truth or reality is my spiritual state. . . .

I am he who has the keys of the unknown. No one after Mohammed knows them except me. And I know all things. I am the first and second blasts of the trumpet at the resurrection.

I have put five things into five things. Having all, I have put knowledge and wisdom in hunger; do not search for them in satiety. I have put riches in contentment with little: do not search for them in avarice. I have put happiness in knowledge. Do not search for it in ignorance.

Before the last text, a great candle had been lit, as tall as Marthe, gilding the calligrapher's beautiful whorls.

On my head is the Crown of High Estate. In my eyebrow is the Pen of Power; in my eye is the light of saintship; in my ear is the call to prayer of Mohammed; in my nose is the fragrance of Paradise; in

244

my mouth is the confession of faith; in my breast is the Qur'ân of wisdom; in my hand is the hand of the Ever-Living God; around my waist is the girdle of the right guidance; on my tongue is the confession; in my feet is service; at my back is the appointed time of death; before me is my lot in life.

In the radiance of the candle Jerott turned. They were, he saw, in what seemed to be an antechamber to the main hall of the tekke: before them hung another curtain, not this time of leather, but of dark blue and green velvet, with gold and coloured Kufic inscriptions wrought in silks at the foot. Beside him stood Marthe, her hair veiled, her long Western gown covered by a loose white linen robe. Before him, turbaned and immaculate in white, stood a Bektashi dervish, proffering a similar robe, folded, over his arms. 'May thy light be exalted light, Efendi,' said the dervish. 'Though thou dost not serve Him whom I serve, nor do I serve that which you serve, yet doth the Baba bid thee enter the meydan, for the sake of the believer who comes with thee. Robe thyself. Robe thyself, and thank not me, but Him who is the Opener of Doors.'

Jerott stared at the dark, smiling face. He knew it. He had seen this man before. Where? When?

And then he had it. A beggar sitting crosslegged in the sand, his hair hung matted and black round his shoulders; his naked body covered with ash. It was the Bektashi dervish who had directed them to Mehedia.

Jerott glanced once at Marthe's composed, unreadable face; and then followed her, tight-lipped, into the meydan.

The hall was large and oblong in shape, its outer confines hidden in darkness; and the ceremony, some kind of ritual of worship and initiation, had already begun. Taking his place as directed to sit crosslegged against the wall beside Marthe Jerott saw that the place appeared to be lined with robed and turbaned men and not a few women, watching like himself the centre of the meydan where, spaced out on sheepskins over the carpeted floor, the Baba and dervishes sat. At the far end of the room, lit by symbolic candles of odd moulds, stood an empty throne on a high, four-stepped dais, with ritual objects of brass and silver placed on each stair, and behind it, written in gold: *There is no God but Allâh; Mohammed is the Prophet of God; Ali is the Saint of God.* There was a smell of rose-geranium and jasmine, mixed with the metal odour of freshly spilled blood.

A sacrifice? Perhaps. Jerott's hand, under his robe, moved to the place where his sword should have been, and then reassured itself that the knife he had hidden was there still, strapped inside his sleeve. Franks were not permitted to wear weapons abroad in towns under Suleiman's rule. Suleiman, they said, was a Bektashi, and a Bektashi Baba stood at the right hand of the Agha of Janissaries at

Constantinople. Jerott did not look again at Marthe. Unclasping his cramped fists he sat, as loosely as he could, and watched, in the darkness, for danger.

The initiates, it seemed, came in barefoot, and singly, each kneeling first with his two hands on the sacred threshold, and kissing each hand in turn. This one was a middle-aged man. He approached the chief Baba, the Mürşit on his sheepskin on the left of the throne and performed the full *niyaz*; the prostration, kissing the floor and then the right and left knee of the Baba and over his heart, thus forming a cross. Then came the ablution, seen before at every street corner, at every mosque fountain. The feet: It is an obligation required by the Merciful, the Compassionate, to be cleansed of every instance of having walked in rebellious and mistaken paths. The face: Wipe thy face clean of the acts of disobedience which thou hast committed until now, and of the impure water of ungodliness with which thou hast been polluted.

Jerott said to Marthe, 'Do you pray? Do you turn to Mecca when the muezzin calls? I have never seen you.'

Around them, as the ablution went on, a kind of ragged chorus had developed; a single phrase, repeated with vehemence over and over, punctuating the ritual: *Allâh Eyvallah; Allâh Eyvallah; Allâh Eyvallah.* God, yes by God. 'You may take it I pray,' said Marthe softly, 'as often as I have seen you at your devotions.'

'Brother, arise.' The cleansing was over. 'In accordance with the rites of Mohammed, Ali awaken the candle of this soul.'

The man getting to his feet before the Baba looked ill with nerves, Jerott thought. To a man of his faith, of course, it was probably the most important moment of his life. The Baba, settling round his waist some kind of woollen rope belt, did not smile, but he touched the man's cheek, in passing, and the initiate, flushing, snatched and kissed the hem of his robe as he knelt. Jerott shifted uncomfortably. 'May good things conquer: may evil things be repelled; may unbelievers be defeated; may evil speakers be ruined. . . . When we cry out for help, may they respond to our call. . . . In the name of the King; call upon Ali, the manifester of marvels. . . . O best of those who help . . . O overturner of hearts and minds . . . the rites of our Lord, our Patron Saint, Sovereign Haji Bektash Veli . . .

'God: there is no God but He. Everything shall perish except His face! Judgement is His, and to Him ye shall return.'

They were chanting. The initiate was trembling: his nasal voice, following the Mürşit's, hurried, stumbling on the words. 'From the soul and by the tongue with love, I have become the servant of the Family of the Mantle . . . I have awakened from the sleep of indifference; I have opened the eye of my soul . . . The East and the West is God's, therefore whichever way ye turn, there is the face of God.'

Someone got up and, lifting the big engraved copper bowl from the steps of the throne, removed the lid, together with a small oval stone which had lain on it. It appeared to be full of something . . . blood? Jerott could not see, and Marthe, obviously, was not going to be informative. It was passed round the dervishes, beginning with the Baba, and ending with the cupbearer himself, the picturesque chords of speech broken by sips until the text and the circle were complete. There was soft movement in the darkness to each side of the throne and turbaned servants, moving noiselessly on the carpets, began to make their way among the dervishes and into the outer confines of the room. The smell of warm, seasoned food, and another familiar whiff, which Jerott could have sworn came from some form of alcohol, began to seep into the air.

The big bowl had been refilled. The Cupbearer, making full *niyaz* to the Baba again, kissed his two knees and offered him the cup, his thumb laid along its edge. The Baba took it in the same way, the cupbearer kissing the thumb of the Baba and being at the same time himself kissed by the Baba, who then closed his eyes and for a moment held the bowl to the fine white linen of his breast, his lips moving in prayer before drinking.

The bowl was removed. Another dervish, kneeling, unfolded before the Baba and set up a small stool, placing in the slung straps of its top a large shallow brass bowl of food, in which he laid a spoon, its face down. The Baba ate, and taking from a third man a folded napkin of white silk, embroidered in violet silk calligraphy, he wiped his lips. A murmur ran through the hall. The Baba put the spoon to his mouth, and a second time wiped his lips; then a third time repeated the ritual. '*Allâh Eyvallah!*' said the man on Jerott's left, and the cry was taken up from group to group of the spectators. '*Allâh Eyvallah! Allâh Eyvallah!*'

Moving heads extinguished Jerott's view. All around him people were shifting, talking; groups were changing and re-forming; servants, pressing in among the mats and cushions, had trouble setting up tables and ferrying vessels in and out of the darkness which was no longer quite so dark, as candle after candle was lit round the walls and from the great hooped holders he now saw swaying in the hot scented currents over his head. Although the dervishes were still there, all the activity in the centre of the arena seemed to be unimportant and forgotten. The ceremony was over.

Marthe's face was flushed. She said, 'There is a special food, the *aşure*, they will bring first. You will not dislike it—it is made of raisins and almonds and dates and hazelnuts and such things. Then they will bring pilaf and other dishes.'

'What were they drinking?' said Jerott.

She said, 'The bowl is the holy vessel, the *Meydan Tasi*; and the stone he took from it was the *Kanaat Tasi*, the stone of contentment. The big candle with the twelve pleats, for the twelve Imáms, is the

Kanun Ciragi, with the three wicks representing God, Mohammed and Ali. The throne, of course, is the Throne of Mohammed. The Haji Bektash Veli was a very great man, born over three hundred years ago.'

'He didn't lack for imagination,' said Jerott. 'What were they drinking?'

'In the name of Allâh, the Beneficent, the Merciful. Lord, quench thy thirst.' It was the dervish, the dervish of Mehedia, a drinking-bowl in his hands.

'Mademoiselle?' said Jerott. It looked like thickish, uncoloured water. She shook her head.

'I am not thirsty. Taste it.'

'What is it?' said Jerott.

'It is what the Baba drank. It is safe, Lord,' said the dervish gravely, irony in his black eye, and lifting the bowl: 'If the Efendi will permit, I shall sip from it.'

And he drank too, while Jerott watched him, stonily showing no trace of humiliation or resentment, or of the gloom which enveloped him. The drink was almost certainly safe. He would probably get pleurisy, quinsy and pox from the cup. He took it back and sipped from the other side, holding the stuff in his mouth. The dervish moved on and spoke, bending, to Marthe before stepping away. In Jerott's mouth, the liquid was sweetish and thick, and rather savourless. Harmless, anyway.

He swallowed. 'What did he say?' And as he spoke the words the stuff roared down his throat, drawing a chariot and six horses and taking the lining of his soft palate with it. He broke off, his mouth shut, staring open-eyed at Marthe, and then said, thickly, 'My God. What was that?'

'*Al yazil.* Raki. You might call it a brandy,' said Marthe. Her face was grave, as the dervish's had been.

'Brandy!' said Jerott, his voice louder than it should have been both for safety and propriety. 'I thought . . . Does no one read the Qur'ân here? What's all the talk about Wine the Red Insane One? I thought every Moslem who drank went to hell?'

'Wine,' said Marthe softly. 'We are forbidden wine. The Prophet said nothing of spirits. In any case, it is symbolic in the Bektashi Order. You have heard of the Bektashi breathings? The breath which they believe cures the flesh, and instils the spirit of God? The word for breath is also the word for wine, or raki: *dem.* The other name for the tekke is *humhane,* or wineshop. *Bade* is the word for wine made from fresh grapes. It also stands for divine love—the longing to know God and the joy of experiencing Him. We say, *Askin dolusnu tutar destinde*: he holds the wine of love in his hand. Drink it.'

Jerott looked down at the cup. 'That stuff? I want my senses 'about me.' But all the same, in his stomach, a small, comfortable fire had started to burn, and was flickering, wistfully; hoping for fuel.

'Eat, then,' said Marthe. 'They are meant to go together. When you have eaten, you need have no fear of the raki.'

It might have been true, had they not refilled his goblet so often. Marthe did not stop them, and after a while, since he remained so exquisitely clear-headed, he saw no point in confusing the cupbearers. By then they could hardly have heard him refuse, in any case, for the music had begun, from some source he could not quite make out; sinuous wind music, loosely serpentine like the golden verses sewn on the curtains and woven into the carpets: reedy flute music, with the tinsel patter and throb of a corymb of drums. A man and a woman rose, prostrated themselves in front of the Baba, and started to dance. The arena cleared.

The sheepskins had gone; the dervishes, seated crosslegged beside the Baba, cups in hand, swayed with the music and someone began to sing to it; a kind of chant which the others took up. 'These are *Nefes'es*; the intonations,' said Marthe. 'The sound of them, with the special properties of the raki, leads to a state of spiritual ecstasy, and the desire to express this in dance. Others will follow.'

There were a dozen figures already on the floor, dancing in pairs; man with woman, man with man. The figures were formal, and performed in deliberate sequence: a swaying of the body to right and to left, slowly with the surge of the music, then quickening fraction by fraction till, breathless, each dancer stopped.

They stopped with their robes touching, their breasts heaving still with the effort. Then each put his or her left hand on the breast, bowed, and still bent, their heads close, they swung their arms rhythmically, hypnotically, to right and to left, again and again as the music wavered and pulsed.

Jerott watched their faces. Of the dancers nearest him, the woman's face, half hidden by the fall of her hair, was white and glazed with the heat. Her brows, raised with the effort, had creased her white skin into a thousand fine lines: Jerott could see water run down her temples, and the pulse there beginning to throb, as her skin darkened with the uprush of blood. Full of raki, full of exaltation, her head down, she swayed to and fro, her arms swinging like white silken chains.

When the figure ended she staggered, and her partner, smiling, his eyes fixed, caught and steadied her: somewhere someone had fallen. More and more men had pressed in with the dancers. The music changed and, swaying, they began encircling the room. The music got quicker, and louder, and moving round, in a swirl of warmly fumed, linen-swathed bodies, of sweating skin and sinuous hands, close together couple by couple, each dancer began to revolve.

Jerott found he had a full bowl of raki in his hands. He drank it and got up. 'No,' said Marthe.

He was stronger than she was, and he could prove it. He closed his hand on her wrist and pulled; and although she resisted at first, she suddenly came quite easily, so that he nearly cannoned back into the other dancers. There were tears in her eyes. He stretched open his own, to see more clearly.

They were tears of rage, or of pain. She was rubbing her wrist. Her arm, under the loose sleeve of the robe, was milky white on the underside, and toasted very pale gold on the outside, like a chicken half done on the spit. He thought that picturesque, and was going to tell her so, when his gaze fell on her throat, just above the high linen neckline, and he wondered what colour her skin was, just under it. They had somehow got into the press of the dancers, swaying and crowding thick against them, and the drums throbbed like a headache and the flutes sobbed and ached as, underneath all the raki, something within him was aching, searching, demanding.

Marthe had made herself very flat and was leaving him, disappeared almost to nothing between two walls of dancers. Jerott stretched out an arm, and closing the hand again on her wrist, pulled her through back to him, although he saw she was in pain, and was sorry that it was the same wrist. He took the neck of the white robe and the neck of her dress together, between his two fingers and thumbs and tore them carefully down perhaps six inches. Her skin part of the way was the golden brown of a half-roasted chicken, but the rest was pure white.

Her eyes were huge. He had never seen such a blue. Not anywhere. He would hold to that against anybody. She looked round, her yellow hair stuck to her cheek, as though searching for somebody, but she didn't speak or call, Jerott was happy to find; although with the chants and the drums, no one would hear her. It struck him that they had privacy, in a sense, and he held her wrist hard, and said, 'I love you. D'you love me? I love you. I don't love anyone else, do I? You have all I want. I don't need anyone else. I love you.'

'And I love you,' said Marthe. She relaxed suddenly, one hand holding the slit edge of her robe; her cheek laid on his shoulder. They turned; revolving, nested in the curves of the music; sleepily; the drums throbbing soft and then loud. The floor was not quite so crowded. 'There is another room,' said Marthe.

Her light bones lying against him were part of him: the voice was the voice of his heart. Jerott threaded his hand down the silken fall of her hair and down her warm spine and stroked her as they moved until she stirred and looked at him, and he realized that a long time ago she had spoken. Her face was different.

Speech was difficult. He nodded, and held her as she steered him through a curtain of changing sequins which sometimes became

250

people; and into a place where there were no sequins but a cool darkness where he was able, with a little difficulty, for she was strong, to set her down somewhere while he slit the overrobe carefully down to the bottom.

She had to prick him with it more than once before he saw that the shimmering thing in front of his eyes was his own knife, unstrapped from inside his sleeve, and that she was holding it ready to stab. His hands dropped, and Marthe rose to her feet, in her nearly immaculate Western gown, and looked down on him as he swayed where he knelt.

'Take your sops, Mr Blyth, and go back to the schoolroom,' said the light, weary voice. 'For every disingenuous small boy there is a disingenuous small girl, I suppose, somewhere.' She spoke to someone, and surprisingly, before him, there was another bowl of that damned fire-water.

He drank it off and, smiling, fell asleep at her feet on the carpet without seeing how long she stood there surveying him; a frown in the unique cornflower eyes.

He woke twice, after that: once lying in the open by a reeking dung fire, which had brought on the coughing which roused him. Between paroxysms he was aware of the night sky, and a dark circling of tents, and of Marthe's voice, speaking in Arabic to someone. It sounded peremptory.

The other voice, a man's, he did not know, though when the fire suddenly flared he saw the black and white stripes of a Bedouin cloak, and a turn of jaw which looked somehow familiar. Then someone moved, and he saw the man Marthe was addressing. He was Shadli, the leader of the Saracens of Savah whom they had driven off on the way to Aleppo.

His stomach heaved. By the time he was less occupied with his own ills, the conversation, whatever it was, was over, and there was no one there but Marthe and some Bedouin women, their cheeks tattooed in blue circles. He shut his eyes, but took the liquid someone forced through his teeth and was at once thickly asleep. But that, until much later, he thought was a dream.

The next time he woke, it was daylight; and he was in his own bed.

*

To dissect a fully grown giraffe with any success, in the open, in Aleppo, in September, demands an esoteric assortment of talents, such as, for example, a smart turn of speed.

At sixty-three, Pierre Gilles was a few years past his best, but he was going to have a damned good attempt. A day after he came across the beast, on its last legs on the road in from Cairo, he had bought it, had it brought to the French Consul's house in Aleppo, and ignoring the cries of the attaché, who was a fool, had got the men scurrying to fill the courtyard with straw, set up the tables and basins and a stool for his secretary, Pichon, and fix the awning from wall to wall, ready for day. He had started work then and there, by torchlight; and by dawn, when he stood back for the first time, sweating, and drank off the Candian wine that they brought him, the beast was already half flayed, and Pichon had ten pages of notes.

That was when he went indoors, devil take it, to exonerate nature and to snatch, while he was there, a quick bite of food; and this damned girl caught him.

When he came out of that argument half an hour later, he was red in the face, from the old cap on his head to the uncurled white beard which straggled over his blotched working-smock. He seized his apron and jerked it over his head with an imprecation in Latin which made his secretary sit up; and even when he had his knife in his hand again, he found it hard for quite ten minutes to concentrate.

By noon, when all the bins were full and the flies were proving a problem, he went indoors again, for the sun staring through the awning was fairly unpleasant, although it had taken a fool like Pichon to faint from it. In his room he stripped, upended a jug of water over his great hulk and put on the smock again without resuming his clothes.

Pichon's notes, so far as they went, were on the table. Stripping off a chicken wing they had left for him, he chewed and wrote, his fist making faint red smears over the Latin, swearing under his breath. Then he drank some grape-juice, which was better than wine when you wanted your hand to be steady, and strode out of the room, the battered notes in his hand, just as a young man, with a face as livid as Pichon's, came out of another door and collided with him. The young man apologized.

The voice was educated. Looking at him with attention, Pierre Gilles thought the boy looked reasonably intelligent. From the suntan under all the picturesque black hair, he had obviously been here or travelling all summer, although the accent, he thought, had been Franco-Scots. Gilles made up his mind, and snapped, 'D'you write Latin?'

Sometimes Jerott forgot that the blazon of chivalry, with all the status it once had carried, was no longer his. In any case, he had an incredible headache. He stared at this enormous, round-shouldered old man in the filthy nightgown and buskins, and snapped back. 'Of course.'

Pierre Gilles was relieved. 'Good. Excellent.' Placing one bony hand on Jerott's left shoulder, he pivoted him forward and, propelling him amiably before him, walked him out of the house, talking as he went. Herpestes, who had also had some chicken, was waiting ahead of him and jumped on his shoulder as he passed: Gilles paused to stroke him, and Jerott, walking on, arrived at the steps down to the courtyard and stopped as if poleaxed.

Instead of swept tiles and potted orange trees, blood-drenched straw packed the yard, in the midst of which reared the ruins of some red enamelled object almost wholly covered with flies. There was an arrangement of tables and buckets and basins and an array of shining objects like knives, of which he was not immediately sensible, as the effect of the white awning with which the courtyard apparently had been roofed was to produce a concentration of heat and stench quite unimaginable.

Jerott stared in front of him, trying not to breathe, and aware of the blood draining from his own skin in sympathy with the abused organs within. Then a word reached him of all the old man had been saying. *Giraffe*. The old monster was cutting up . . . *dissecting* a giraffe. And—Jerott looked suddenly at the blood-smeared notes which had been pushed in his hand—he was recording the details. In Latin.

No one who had been long in Archie Abernethy's company could fail to know who this was. Jerott felt sick. His head ached; and the thinking he had done since he came to his senses that morning had not helped to make him feel better. *If the brat's not at Aleppo, it's dead*, he had convinced himself somehow. *Or likely to cost more than our blood.*

He had meant to go back to France. He had no intention of wet-nursing anyone's bastard, then or now. But now he meant to find that child, alive, whether anyone wanted it or not.

Jerott swallowed. When it had to be done, it could be done. That, at least, you learned in the Order; and he had relearned it, to some purpose, under Lymond. He took a deep breath and, turning, spoke to the old man as he joined him, the grey, cat-like creature on his shoulder. 'I believe, sir, you must be M. Pierre Gilles d'Albi?'

'Yes. Naturally,' said the anatomist. Several sick-looking men, obviously hired as menial assistants, had appeared and were waiting for him: he ignored them, peering, frowning, at the carcass and then up at the sun as he tied the leather apron-strings over his smock. 'The stool's over there.' Without warning, he shot a glance at Jerott under drooping white brows. 'But it's too much for you, is it?'

'No. I'll do it,' said Jerott. 'If I may introduce myself? My name is Jerott Blyth. I'm a Scotsman from Nantes, and I have a very good friend who is a lifelong admirer of yours. Archie Abernethy.'

'Good,' said Pierre Gilles. He strode forward, Jerott following, and knife in hand, slit something disgusting and peered inside, his right hand continuing to work. 'Take this down. *De Gyraffa, Bellon dicet, quam Arabes Zurnapa, Graeci et Latini Camelopardalin nominant . . .*'

Five nerve-racking sentences later, he paused. 'Do I have to translate?'

253

There was pen and ink on the table. Scribbling furiously, Jerott shook his head. 'No.'

'Thanks to God.' Something flew past into a bin. 'Did you say Abernethy?'

'That's right. Archie Abernethy. He looked after the menagerie at Tarnassery, and I think he was in Constantinople too. He also had the care recently of the King of France's elephants. By the name Abernaci.'

'Oh. Now, what have we here?' said M. Gilles. 'Ah. Take this down . . .'

There followed five minutes' furious dictation, followed by the flight through the air of another section of giraffe. 'There's a bit here I want to draw later. If it lasts. Abernaci? Oh, I remember him well. A small fellow, with a broken nose? So he is still alive, is he?'

'I expected to meet him here, in Aleppo,' said Jerott. 'We're both with Francis Crawford. It's a special embassy with a gift from the King to the Sultan.'

Pierre Gilles stopped working. He straightened, his hands bent at the wrists like a begging dog's, and said, 'You are in the same party as the girl?'

'What girl?' said Jerott, a little bemused in spite of himself with the stench and the Latin and the heat and the effect of the raki.

'The girl who calls herself Marthe, I think it is? You are a friend of Marthe?' said the anatomist.

It required a moment's reflection, but Jerott decided on the truth. 'No. We are in the same party, but the rest of us know very little of Mlle Marthe. She is assistant to the antiquarian-craftsman who manufactured the gift,' said Jerott.

'Georges Gaultier, I understand. A rogue and a usurer. Take my advice and do not meddle with either of them. Hold that, will you?' said Pierre Gilles.

Jerott took it, hurriedly laying down his pen. 'Why? Do you know them, sir?' he said.

The anatomist, screwing up his eyes, was taking measurements. He reeled them off, noting them down himself with bloody fingers, before he said, 'I simply advise, do not meddle with them. Now pass me the hacksaw.'

It was all Jerott was able to get out of him on that subject, and almost his total pronouncement on any other. To Jerott it had seemed suddenly likely that if anyone had seen and heard of a white child landed with a Syrian woman somewhere along the coast, or even here in Aleppo, Pierre Gilles might have done so.

In an age of eccentric scholars, he had a reputation all his own: this shrewd old man with the powerful frame and flamboyant stride and extravagant temper. Fluent in the classical languages and at home in half a dozen others, he had always gone his own way, loosely armed with someone's commission: travelling with the French Ambassador d'Aramon in the wake of the Sultan; resting at Rome to write up his notes and publish his books, loosely under the patronage of some Cardinal. And always with Herpestes on his shoulder.

As the afternoon wore on, and the anatomist, up to his elbows and over in a frenzy of work, either did not hear what he was saying or barely took time to answer, Jerott stopped talking and confined himself to his notes. Only once, as Gilles's pet slipped softly from the bench where he had been sitting and streaked, long and grey and deadly, to pounce on something at the edge of the courtyard, Jerott glanced round at the bright eyes, and the sharp black muzzle and the feline whiskers, and said, 'What do you call him?'

'Herpestes,' said Gilles. He worked for a moment, then straightening, stretched and wiped a hand over his streaming brow. He looked at Jerott. 'Does that mean anything to you?'

Jerott grinned. 'Only because I knew about him. *Herpestes ichneumon*, a genus of digitigrade carnivorous quadrupeds of the family Viverridae. They have them in Egypt, as house pets for rat-catching.'

'You have had a good tutor. I see no reason,' said Gilles, still inspecting him, 'why you should not come to Constantinople with me and help that fool Pichon. Your Latin is rather poorer but you have at least a strong stomach.'

'I am honoured,' said Jerott, amusement struggling through the stone ballast occupying the place of his guts. 'But I was trying to explain, I am staying here because I am looking——'

'For some child the Turk is amusing himself with. I recall. But did you not also say that in a day or two you would know from the attaché whether or not the boy has been in Aleppo? If the attaché finds the child for you, you may send him home and come to Constantinople with me. If not, you said, did you not, that the child would probably in any case now be dead?'

'If he's alive, he'll still be in danger,' said Jerott. It sounded limp. 'I shall have to go back home with him. And if he isn't here, I'll have to go on trying to find him.'

Pierre Gilles had just made a plan, and he did not wish it disturbed. 'What?' he said. 'What is this you fear for the child? He is ill, or delicate? We shall initiate inquiries from Constantinople, and it will be found. The Grand Turk is more powerful than a little consular attaché.'

It was a long time since Jerott had taken orders from a stranger. He said curtly, 'I am afraid it would be too late. The child was a hostage for the life of Sir Graham Reid Malett, one of the Knights of the Order on Malta. Sir Graham was killed in the battle of Zuara last month by the child's father. As soon as the news reaches its keeper, it will be dead.'

'One moment,' said Pierre Gilles. He lifted his beard and stood,

255

arms akimbo, screwing up his face against the mellowing light falling
through the stretched linen over his head. 'The light is going. What
mysteries my friend here has left, I think he must keep. And the
Consul, if he comes back tomorrow, will wish the use of his courtyard
perhaps. Yes, I think we may consider that we have done. Herpestes!'

The ichneumon ran towards him and leaped on his shoulder. The
sweating labourers, summoned also by signal, came and received
their instructions. The anatomist turned back to Jerott, untying the
strings of the apron and peeling it off, to Herpestes's annoyance.
'You say, Blyth, the urgency comes from the death of this knight
Graham Malett?'

'Yes,' said Jerott.

'Then,' said Pierre Gilles heartily, 'there is no urgency. The knight
Graham Malett is alive, though no longer a knight. It is a joke, I fear,
against Malta the length of the Coast. Have you not heard of the
great new Pasha just installed in Zuara? He is your dead man: your
Graham Reid Malett himself.'

*

There was no urgency. As the sky darkened and evening fell,
Jerott sat in his room, staring with unseeing eyes at the wall, thinking.
When someone knocked on his door and asked him to go to the
attaché's chamber, he was already prepared for what he would hear.

The child was not in Aleppo, and was highly unlikely ever to have
been in Aleppo. 'It is strange,' said the attaché, doing his best under
bothering circumstances, 'that M. le Comte thought it necessary to
send to Aleppo in the first place. The ship *Peppercorn* you speak of
is an English bottom, and does not call at Ottoman ports.'

'They said something of the sort at Scanderoon,' said Jerott. 'We
thought there was an English agent here perhaps.'

'There are negotiations, but so far no one,' said the attaché.
'Meanwhile, English ships, you understand, may call only at those
ports under the control of the Seigneury, such as Crete and Candia,
where you have already been. Sometimes, depending on the weather,
the *Peppercorn* calls at these places, but she has only one regular port
of call at this season, and that is to load mastic on the island of
Chios.'

'Chios. In the Aegean?' asked Jerott.

'Between Samos and Lesbos, yes. It is ruled by Venice but pays
tribute to Turkey. You do not know it? It is a garden, Mr Blyth,'
said the attaché. 'Flowers, and trees, and great red partridges, tame
as chickens. And the handsomest women in Europe, to be had for a
song. They understand these matters better than in Aleppo,' said the
attaché, who had become vaguely aware of a certain undercurrent of
atmosphere in the Consulate, and in any case wished to be free of

visitors before the Consul came home. 'Each girl pays a ducat a day to the Captain of the Night, and she may do as she pleases. You will go to Chios?'

'I want to reach M. le Comte before he arrives at Constantinople,' said Jerott. Gabriel and Francis, he had been thinking all evening. Gabriel was alive, and Francis did not know. Francis travelling; believing he was safe at least from that quarter. Francis arriving in Constantinople, and Gabriel's men there, awaiting him.

The attaché was shaking his head. 'If M. le Comte left Malta when you did, M. Blyth, he will be in Constantinople by now. Or long before you might reach him. It is October soon, M. Blyth, when the winds are strong and the galleys are laid up, and even trading vessels spend weeks in harbour. You would never reach him in time. . . . But to go to Chios, this would take you part of the way, and maybe discover the child for you en route?'

'Yes,' said Jerott. 'Could I get a ship at Scanderoon for Chios now? Or how long would I wait?'

The attaché looked doubtful. 'There is none there today, and it is now late in the season. You would do better, Mr Blyth, to go over-land. You might join a caravan; or M. Gilles would be happy, I am sure, to go with you, with a suitable escort of Janissaries: the way is very familiar to him. . . .'

Jerott wasn't listening. He interrupted. 'You said that there was no ship in Scanderoon today bound for Chios. . . . May I ask how you can possibly know?'

The attaché smiled. 'You do not know of our magic channels for news? I know by pigeon post, M. Blyth. Between all the main trading-centres along the coast, and between Scanderoon and here, they fly daily with the message tied by a thread to the leg. They take four hours to travel the eighty miles which probably took you three or four days, and we have all the news of shipping as it arrives, and they likewise learn in Scanderoon when the big caravans from Persia come in. It is a charming method. They have names, even, the little ones,' said the attaché fondly.

Marthe, standing among the Baghdad pigeons in the factor's courtyard at Scanderoon . . . Gaultier, fondling Kiaya Khátún's doves in the palace at Djerba . . .

Jerott stood up.

The attaché got quickly to his feet. 'You wish me to arrange this then? To travel by land to Chios, yourself, Mademoiselle, M. Gilles and M. Pichon? There will be many good men to escort you: the Sultan's army is already travelling south to Aleppo and many are riding to join them. You will have a swift passage to Chios, and thence to Constantinople to meet M. le Comte. . . .'

'Yes. Arrange it,' said Jerott. He had enough instinctive courtesy left to thank the foul little man as he ought before he got out, and strode to the suite used by Marthe, and hammered on the door with the butt of his knife till it cracked.

She was singing. He had never heard any expression of happiness from her before, much less this joyous uplifting of voice, light and free. He drowned it with his hammering, and when he stopped, it had halted, too.

The servant opened the door. Jerott looked past her and saw Marthe standing looking at him, dressed for supper, with a string of beryls in her pleated hair, and one of her few fine dresses with funnelled bodice and wide taffeta farthingale in a blue which echoed her eyes.

He wondered, his heart sick, what had happened to the over-dress he had torn, in the crazed half-dark of the tekke, where they had filled his cup over and over, because otherwise she could not shake him free. 'I love you,' she had said, before she had led him from the room. And then, dull contempt in her voice, *Take your sops, Mr Blyth, and go back to the schoolroom.* . . . 'Send the woman away,' said Jerott.

The servant looked round. 'No,' said Marthe. She was not singing now. 'I prefer her to stay.'

'Get out,' said Jerott quite pleasantly to the negress, and with a quick flash of her eyes, she drew her dress together and, ducking under his arm, scuttled out of the door. Jerott walked in, and slamming the door shut, locked it. Finding he still had his knife in his hand, he put that away and looked up. 'I take it,' he said evenly, 'that you are working for Gabriel?'

'Ah,' said Marthe. She was a little pale, but otherwise quite composed. 'You have found that Mr Crawford's little assassination was ineffective after all.' She sat down, where she was, on a low stool, folded her hands and, looking at him, fetched a sigh. 'No,' she said. 'I am not working for Gabriel. I have told you. I am nobody's servant. You may believe it or not, as you wish.'

Jerott, still standing, did not stir. 'But you will agree that you knew before we left Mehedia that the *Peppercorn* was an English ship, and therefore would never be found at Aleppo?'

'Yes. I knew that,' said Marthe. 'I am sorry. But there was no question of killing Gabriel first at that time; and as it happens, he is still alive; so the child has been in no danger. No harm has been done.'

'*No harm . . .!*' said Jerott; and then, controlling his voice, went on. 'But it would have made no difference if Gabriel *had* been killed, would it? After all, you must have believed for quite some time, as we did, that he was dead. But you and your uncle had business at Aleppo, and you made sure you would get there, whatever happened . . . whatever misery anyone else . . . whatever prolonged misery a child of two might still have to suffer.'

258

'Every element in life has its due importance,' said Marthe. 'Some greater, some less. As it happens, no time has been lost. I can tell you precisely where the child is. You will find him at the House of the Nightingales in Constantinople.'

Jerott laughed. 'There is a widespread and sudden compulsion to set out for Constantinople: are the clouds raining Lancashire egg-pies and peacocks?' he said. 'Pierre Gilles begs me to accompany him; the Attaché cannot wait to get me on my way, at least as far as Chios. I wonder who is waiting at Constantinople, apart from the other victims of this farcical pilgrimage?'

'I cannot help it,' said Marthe. 'The child is there. I received the information here in Aleppo, and I know it is true.'

'Not at Chios?' said Jerott. 'Be careful. The *Peppercorn* calls at Chios, you know: not at the Sublime Porte.'

'I know. He and the Syrian woman landed at Chios and then . . . Look,' said Marthe. 'There is presumably no reason why you should believe me, but equally there is no reason why you shouldn't at least go to Chios and inquire for yourself. Any number of independent witnesses, I am sure, will have seen them both.'

'What do you have to do with the Saracens of Savah?' said Jerott abruptly; and Marthe looked up, her eyes wide.

'I wakened . . . once,' he said. 'Were you buying, or selling? *Who pays you, Marthe?*'

'You don't understand,' she said. In her lap, the loose hands had ground together: between the fair brows a single line showed, of anger and disgust and a kind of futile perplexity. 'You don't understand: how can you? You were born into a household, with parents and wealth; you knew your friends and your enemies; you knew your position in life; whom you were fighting for: whom you were against. I am alone. *Every man is my enemy.*'

Jerott stared at her. She said, loosing her hands and standing up, 'You wish to travel on your own to Chios and then to the Sublime Porte. It is of no importance. I shall make my own dispositions.'

'No,' said Jerott. 'On the contrary. I want you where I can see you. I want you with me every step of the way. I want you where I can see you when you meet Francis Crawford.'

'He knows,' said Marthe. And then, as Jerott took a quick breath, 'He knows at least that the child is not at Aleppo,' she added. 'He has known since Djerba, I think.'

'Then why. . . ?'

'Why let us come? Why send us, in fact? Don't you know, Mr Blyth? Oh, he made sure that the hunt for this child wouldn't stop: he has sent Archie, I am sure, to scour every Venetian port in the whole Middle Seas in an effort to find where the *Peppercorn* landed . . . why do you think that Archie failed to come here? This was the one place he was told to leave strictly alone.'

Why let us come? Jerott's mind, trying to read that other, more subtle mind, thought of many things: of the strange woman Kiaya Khátún; of the agony of that dark night at Djerba, when Lymond and Marthe had spoken over his head; of Lymond's unaccustomed voice, saying on the edge of that tragic garden in Algiers, *I can't do without you.* And Marthe's, saying, *Yes, I shall take your disciple Jerott*, manco passioni humane, *and he shall be returned to you weaned.*

'God damn you both,' Jerott said through his teeth, and, flinging away from her, stood, breathing hard, at the one unshuttered window, unseeing, his hands fists on the sill. 'You summon and you throw away. You treat love like a bird for the table . . . Like a pawn, now in frankincense, now discarded and thrown in the dirt. You don't know what love is, either of you. And God help us and you, if you ever find out.'

Sitting very still in her chair, Marthe had not moved. 'You speak of me,' she said. 'I am happy to exercise your imagination. Who is the other?'

'You know who I mean,' said Jerott. 'Only one other person can hurt as you do. And that is Francis Crawford of Lymond.'

'Of course,' said Marthe. 'He is my brother.'

17

THESSALONIKA

In one thing, the French Consular Attaché at Aleppo was right. His Most Christian Majesty of France's good galley *Dauphiné*, sailed hard and effectively, entered the harbour of Thessalonika under perfect control and dropped anchor, after an eventful voyage, before the month of August was out. And before even Onophrion, soft-footed and deft, had spread his dishes for dinner, His Most Christian Majesty's Special Envoy, whose acid tongue the ship's complement, from master to slave, respected and feared, had written and sealed a note for the Beglierbey of all Greece, requesting an audience.

It was taken ashore while Lymond and Gaultier sat down to their meal.

Until now, for reasons of his own, Georges Gaultier had taken little to do with the Comte de Sevigny under any of his various titles. Twice before, against his will, he had played a part in Mr Francis Crawford's affairs, at the behest of the old woman whose word was his will. A third time, he had done so when he had compelled Marthe to come on this voyage with him. But that was the end. In his own line of business, Georges Gaultier liked to control all the odds. The Dame de Doubtance was in Lyons, not here. What he did here was nobody's concern but his own.

He had not enjoyed the journey. For one thing, the speed had been excessive: in wind, the galley had been made to carry sail after sail until her masts groaned with the strain: in calm, the slaves had rowed in shifts, à outrance, until both he and the master had forecast a revolt.

It had not come, he realized, because Lymond's judgement of what men could or could not bear was seldom at fault. At intervals also, they had stopped to put ashore or pick up Salablanca or Onophrion or one of the officers to make inquiries. They knew the route the Children of Devshirmé had followed, but the route Philippa had taken with her group of young men was different. Here and there, on the coast, they had picked up traces of her and once, outside Volos, Onophrion had returned with the skiff full of villagers, their arms full of bread and baskets of honey and fruit, whom Lymond had asked on board.

They had brought lute and viols with them and danced on the poop till the sun sank in the sea, and Onophrion set a feast for them under a still, starry sky, with candles burning overhead in the sheets. There had been a little girl, a bride of no more than thirteen, with great silver shoe-buckles hung in her ears, who had caught Lymond's attention, Gaultier saw; and the royal Envoy crossed over to admire them and speak to her.

He had not been the only man watching Lymond. As the girl smiled and Lymond got up to leave her, a slender figure walked out of the shadows: a young man with long, wet hair and a remarkable face, slanting-browed and hollow-cheeked with the narrow jaw and wide, sensual mouth of the Slav. He wore a loose purple tunic, streaming with sea-water, and no adornment but his grace: Georges Gaultier, who loved beautiful things, watched him enchanted. Now, face to face with Francis Crawford, he had chosen a moment when the other man was not surrounded: was in fact out of earshot of everyone but Georges Gaultier, still sitting forgotten near by. They confronted each other in the moonlight, the fair-haired and the dark; and the young man drew a long breath and smiled, his white teeth gleaming, his long lashes veiling his eyes. 'O Áshiq Pasha . . . they had not told me thou wert . . .'

'. . . eligible? I am not,' said Lymond without heat. 'You are Míkál?'

The teeth flashed. 'Thou hast heard of me? And yet I am without the bells.'

'There are other forms of identification,' said Lymond. 'Where is Philippa Somerville?'

'I come to tell thee,' said the boy Míkál in his musical voice. 'We sit, yes? Philippa Khátún spoke much of thee. And the child of thine she must find. She says the mother is dead, and thou hast no lady now.'

'A reasonably accurate assessment of my plight,' said Lymond agreeably.

'Then thou hast need of a friend. I am thy friend,' said Míkál. He looked through his lashes and must have seen, as Gaultier saw, the quickly suppressed flash of laughter in Lymond's eyes, for he suddenly laughed himself, in his clear voice, and added, 'Within limits?'

'Within limits,' Lymond agreed; and, moving for the first time, dropped lightly to sit on the other side of the hatch-cover against which Míkál was reclining. 'And especially if you will tell me where Philippa Khátún is.'

'I cannot tell thee where she is, but I know where she goes. She found the little child, which was taken from Marino Donati's house in Zakynthos—thou knowest Marino Donati is dead?'

'Yes,' said Lymond.

'Good riddance,' said Míkál cheerfully; and blew an extravagant kiss. 'And the sister too: dead at Thessalonika just after Philippa Khátún had met her. So they gave Philippa Khátún the care of the child.'

From his light-gilded hair to the rings on his clasped hands, Lymond had become very still. 'Donati's sister? Do you by any chance mean Evangelista Donati?'

'It is right,' said Míkál. 'She was taking the child, so they said, to Stamboul with the Children. Now Philippa Khátúm will take it instead.'

'But . . . did she not try to buy it ?' asked Lymond. 'Did she not ask your help ?'

Míkál shrugged his elegant shoulders. 'They would not sell. And as for helping her—this a man of war might have done. Thyself, hadst thou been here. But we, Crawford Efendi, are Children of Love. We do not hurt or take life. I am asked to see that she is safe, and she is safe. She will come to no harm.'

'I am not yet quite clear about this,' said Lymond; and Gaultier, listening, recognized without difficulty the tone of his voice. 'Philippa Khátúm failed to purchase the child, and was unable, without your help, to take it away. She therefore stayed with it and, no doubt, the rest of the Children when they left Thessalonika ? Then where is she now ?'

'At Stamboul, perhaps,' said Míkál. 'Or Constantinople, as many still call it. . . . It does not take long. Perhaps three weeks, if they make many stops. Or they may have sent her ahead with the child. Yes, in Stamboul assuredly, I should think.'

'I see. Then, if they refused to sell the child, it presumably is now in the Seraglio. And Philippa Khátúm, I should hope, is in the French Ambassador's house, awaiting me. Do you think this is so ?'

'No,' said Míkál. 'How could she protect the child from an Ambassador's house ? There are assassins, she says, who will kill the child when the man for whom he is hostage dies by thy hand. . . . Is that true ?'

'It is true,' said Lymond. 'And he is dead.'

'So. How could she take him to Stamboul and still not protect him ? Not so. It is arranged instead that she will go with him, where no assassin or any harm can touch either. Is it not well done ?'

'I'll tell you that in a moment,' said Lymond. '*Where is she going ?*'

'To the Sultan's Seraglio,' said Míkál simply.

'Oh, Christ,' Lymond said.

There was a long silence. 'Thou art distressed, Efendi ?' asked Míkál at length, soothingly. 'She will live like a queen. In her own country she has no husband, no riches, no palace ?'

'You are perfectly correct,' said Lymond. 'It would also be hard to find three possessions she would find more ridiculous. Was this by any chance the woman Donati's idea ?'

'I think it likely,' said Míkál peacefully; and Gaultier, glimpsing Lymond's face in the moonlight, swore under his breath. Tomorrow, more ruthless sailing; more of this total indifference towards the rights and requirements of his fellow-passengers. Salablanca was a nigger and used to it; Onophrion was a servile old woman by nature. Gaultier was finding it more and more hard to put up with it. He got

263

up and already was moving away as Onophrion came forward to tell Lymond that their guests were now disembarking.

Míkál stayed where he was; but Lymond rose to give the villagers his last greetings and watch them climb down into the two boats: their own, and the *Dauphiné*'s caique, with Onophrion officiously in the bows, which was to take back those who had swum, like Míkál, to the galley.

Gaultier noticed that Míkál was still not among them. He saw the two boats cast off, with Onophrion's high-pitched voice floating over the water, and turned back, enjoying the quiet now that the flutes and lyres and tambourines had stopped, and there were only the quiet sounds of the ship settling down for the night. After a while, he made his way to the ladder which led down to his room and was about to descend when he saw Lymond, who had been speaking to the patron, walk back to the hatch where he had been sitting with Míkál. Gaultier paused. He heard Lymond say, in his clear speaking-voice, 'I am sailing to Thessalonika, to obtain a licence from the Viceroy to buy back Philippa Khátún and the child, if I can. If they are not yet in Constantinople, it might work. If they are already in the Sublime Porte, then I shall make submissions to Suleiman.'

Míkál's voice was gentle. 'You will use the name of France to redeem your son and the maiden?'

'To redeem these two children,' said Lymond concisely, 'I would use the names of Prester John and Antiochus Tibertus and even that of Güzel Kiaya Khátún.'

'Who is she?' said Míkál.

'You must ask her, next time you meet her,' said Lymond, and lifted his eyebrows as Míkál got to his feet. The candles flared. For a moment, both men facing each other were illuminated in brilliant light: Gaultier could see the flat, fluted back of Lymond's fine doublet, and Míkál, his hair a soft nimbus about the high cheekbones, the long limbs brown and bare as a girl's. Then, with the burst of light, came one small, tell-tale sound.

A second before Míkál, Lymond looked up. Gaultier heard him shout, and saw him in the same moment thrust the young geomaler spinning and, flinging himself back on the rebound, cannon into and drive back with his shoulder the seaman lingering nearest him. As he did so, the yardarm of the mainmast, thirty-three solid metres of smouldering wood, crashed where he had been, followed by flakes of still-flaring hemp from the burning sheets which had severed it.

Someone screamed. Then Lymond, Míkál and the splintered mess where the yardarms had fallen were all hidden by the rush of seamen and officers to the wreckage, followed by swift deployments to put out the fires flying like pennants from the standing rigging and sheets and now endangering the masts. Someone, groaning, was carried past Gaultier and taken below—an oarsman, he thought. No one else appeared to be hurt.

On any ship but Lymond's, Gaultier thought, a thousand metres of sailcanvas would have fallen, burning, with that yardarm. But the *Dauphiné* was not permitted to ride at anchor with her mainsail still bent. The circumstance that, on a windless night, the candles of such a ship should become so oddly disarrayed was not, as he said later to Onophrion, a matter on which he had any views.

Master Zitwitz, instead of being flattered by this ironical offering, had been insufferable. 'Your pardon, M. Gaultier,' he had said, his round eyes severe in his round, boneless face. 'But only Mr Crawford's presence of mind averted what might have been a very great tragedy. I do not regard it as a matter of levity.'

On the subsequent voyage, which was quite as unpleasant as he expected, Maître Gaultier did not mention Onophrion's insolence, although he took occasion to complain on the two instances, in a temperature near the nineties, when the meat was not perfectly fresh. Whose carelessness was responsible for the fire, it seemed, was never discovered, although Lymond's inquiry was of the kind which turned the ship silent with its repercussions for twenty-four hours. Then they were in Thessalonika, and one of the ship's trumpeters with two soldiers and Míkál as guide had gone ashore to hire horses and ask the Beglierbey of Greece on Mr Crawford's behalf for the honour of an audience.

'I wonder,' said Georges Gaultier to Lymond as they sat at dinner that noon, 'whether that delicious impromptu party on deck outside Volos was as innocent as it seemed. Could, for example, someone have been jealous of Míkál?'

'No doubt the world is full of individuals of either sex jealous of Míkál,' Lymond answered. Sitting there in the sunlight, in one of Onophrion's exquisite doublets, peeling one of Onophrion's peaches, he looked like any rich man at leisure; who would cultivate his sensibilities like a man with a garden of coffee trees. 'But if you are referring to the descent of the yardarm, I doubt if Míkál was intended to suffer. There had already been two similar and ineffective accidents before Míkál set foot on the galley.'

Gaultier sat up. 'Have there? When?'

'On the way to Zakynthos. A barrel of pitch, left on the gangway which rolled . . . where it might have caused considerable harm. And four days after that, when landing Salablanca, the caique nearly sank.'

'You were in it?'

'I was in it,' agreed Lymond. 'But you were not.'

For a little they stared at one another. Then Gaultier said, 'Are you making an accusation?'

'No,' said Lymond. 'Only an inquiry.'

For a long moment, Georges Gaultier gazed at the other man;

then he grinned. 'I would draw your attention to two facts,' he said. 'Apart from myself, a remarkable number of other people, Mr Crawford, were not on that caique. And ask yourself: if I wished you harm, why should I have taken such pains to preserve you, as I did, when you were injured at Blois?'

It was an incident long past: an incident which would remind the Special Envoy of the royal galley *Dauphiné* that he had not always been a Special Envoy, or the favoured of France. Lymond said, gently, 'Because you were under orders. I merely ask myself under whose orders you may be functioning now.'

Then Georges Gaultier stood up, the blood mantling the mottled skin, and said, 'I obey no one's orders. I please no one, Mr Crawford, but myself. I had no hand in any of these so-called accidents. But were another to happen tomorrow I, dear sir, would do nothing to stop it.'

Very soon after that, the trumpeter and his party returned to the ship from the Beglierbey's house, bearing apology and invitation at once. His Excellency the Viceroy was at present travelling to Constantinople to accompany the Grand Seigneur on his forthcoming journey. But in his absence, the Controller of his household begged Monseigneur the Ambassador of France to take supper that evening in the Viceregal house, and to repose himself that night in one of the Viceregal beds.

Lymond read it through in silence, and then said to the trumpeter, 'Who gave you this?'

The trumpeter was afraid of Lymond. He flushed and said, 'An Imám, M. le Comte. One of their holy men with the big turbans. Or a Bektashi, it might have been.'

Lymond said, 'This is addressed to His Most Christian King's Ambassador to the Sublime Porte, which I am not. It also mentions a journey on which the Beglierbey is accompanying the Sultan. Did you gather what this journey was?'

The trumpeter shook his head. 'Only that the Sultan was about to leave Constantinople, and the Beglierbey and his army were joining him.

'*And his army?*' said Lymond. 'Míkál, have you heard anything of this? No? Onophrion, you will make inquiries, if you please, when you do your marketing. Then it behoves us to depart in style for supper at the Beglierbey's residence. Whether we stay the night is another matter.'

'Forgive me.' It was Onophrion. 'But M. Viénot tells me that unless M. le Comte permits him to remain here overnight, it will be difficult to continue to sail with such speed. There are some repairs which he has been deferring since Zakynthos. And the *chiourme* are . . .'

'The *chiourme* are men, not a paddling of ducks, who had an excellent rest outside Volos,' said Lymond. 'I shall see the Master about the other matter. In the meantime, I advise you to get your water and stores on board as quickly as possible, then be ready to come with me to the Beglierbey's. Salablanca has a list of whom else I require. . . . Míkál, will you be kind enough to guide us once more?'

The Pilgrim of Love smiled; his slow Tartar, mischievous smile. 'Of course,' he said. 'Áshiq Pasha . . . you are hard on your children. The Qur'ân says, "Nay, obey him not, but adore and draw nigh".'

'Fortunately, perhaps, the Qur'ân is not the ultimate authority on board the *Dauphiné*,' said Lymond. 'Does that disturb you, Míkál? How do you reconcile your present service and your religious scruples, or don't you have any? *Est-il permis à un musulman de favoriser les Francs? Est-il licite, en outre, qu'ils fassent entendre en ce lieu leurs chants impies, et que le son de la cloche couvre la voix des musulmans?*'

Míkál was smiling still. 'It is an old quotation,' he said. 'When I hear thy voice raised among the impious chants and the heretic call of the bell, I shall tell thee my answer.'

Thoughtfully, Lymond studied the smiling face, and in his own face was a trace of answering amusement. 'I think,' he said, 'that some time I must introduce you to a gentleman called Jerott Blyth.'

*

This time no one had been hunting in the Beglierbey of Greece's Thessaly lodge. Instead, a guard of honour in scarlet and gold filled the courtyard, through which Lymond and his followers rode between the file of their escorting Janissaries. A black eunuch, in emeralds and silk, welcomed them on the threshold, bowing and smiling, and led Lymond to the selamlìk, while Salablanca and Onophrion followed to stand discreetly just inside the door. Characteristically, Míkál had vanished.

Within the selamlìk, on the low, cushion-filled dais which occupied the window half of the room, a grey-bearded Bektashi Baba rose and came forward smiling, the prayer-beads brushing his long calico robes, and said, 'Your Excellency. I am honoured. There is a saying, Whoso is absent suffereth loss. My Lord Viceroy assuredly endureth loss this night.'

Already, his hand on Salablanca's shoulder, Lymond had stepped out of his shoes and, cap in hand, was walking up to the dais. From the door Onophrion, approving the hang of the one-shouldered cloak and the line of the dark silken hose, which it met at mid-thigh, saw the dervish's eyes flutter. To Eastern eyes, used to the modesty of an ankle-length robe, the costume was strange. Then Lymond swung off his cloak at a gesture of the Bektashi Baba's, and giving it with his cap and gloves to the smiling eunuch behind him, said politely, 'The honour is mine. I fear however you have been misled. I come merely as a Special Envoy to the great prince Sultan Suleiman. M. de Luetz, Baron d'Aramon, holds with unequalled distinction the post of French Ambassador to the Sublime Porte.'

'Thou wilt be seated? Verily,' said the Bektashi dervish with placid regret, 'I am shamed that thou speakest my language when thine should have fled from my tongue, as a garment becomes dissundered and worn out by being long folded. Thou wilt eat? My servants put our poor fare before thee. I bear news then, which I trust will rejoice thee. The Baron d'Aramon, may he be blessed, being faint in his condition of health, is about to leave his office for France, and since winter is nearly upon us, none may now be sent before next spring to succeed him. Therefore, when you reach Stamboul, you will find there letters from France now awaiting you, accrediting you as full Ambassador to the Sublime Porte. My felicitations.'

'Thank you. It is an unsought but magnificent honour,' said Lymond dryly. They had brought low tables, and a burden of great steaming bowls in copper, silver and bronze: Onophrion, his nose twitching, craned to identify them. His gaze on the bowl; his fingers picking here and there among the heaped rice and meat: 'Truly, as ducks are drawn by the decoyman into his pipes, the wind bringest thee news,' Lymond added.

The Baba smiled. 'You have heard perhaps of M. Chesnau, who accompanied M. d'Aramon on the Sultan's Asiatic campaign five years since? He has just passed through here, returning to Stamboul with a secretary of M. d'Aramon's in order to deputize at the Embassy until you should arrive. From him I have these tidings.'

'Surely then it is a misfortune,' said Lymond, 'that I shall not bow before the lion face of the King of Kings, the Sultan Suleiman. I hear he marches.'

'It is true,' said the Baba. He drew from his sash a piece of ivory silk whose border, six inches wide, was filled with the interlaced titles of Allâh, and wiped his grey beard. 'After next summer, the Grand Sophy will try our patience no longer. The Sultan marches from Stamboul by the end of the autumn to rest in his pavilions at Aleppo until the spring, when like the lion you call him, he will spring on the jackal of Persia and tear out its throat. . . . It is possible,' said the Baba blandly, 'that you might reach Stamboul before the Sultan leaves. Should this felicity be withheld from you, surely Achmet Pasha would welcome the emissary of France as he would greet the august friend of his household, and would listen, assuredly, to any representation he might make.'

Achmet Pasha. A man of little account. The second Vizier. Onophrion Zitwitz's eyes fleetingly met Salablanca's, and then dropped. The Sultan, then, was leaving his capital, and the Grand Vizier Rustem Pasha was also in the field. Lymond did not even raise his head, although his smile deepened. 'Indeed, I see thou art a man of discretion. There is indeed a matter on which I had hoped to speak to the Beglierbey tonight. Thou knowest perhaps of the Western child born into Dragut Rais's harem which we are endeavouring to recover, and which was mistakenly included among the Children of Devshirmé? Also of the young English girl who has attached herself to the child in an apparent attempt to protect it?'

Lymond looked up. His voice was unhurried; his brown face under the sun-bleached neat hair entirely calm. 'It is a matter of concern to us that both the child and the girl should be returned to France unharmed, and the French King would not be niggardly in his rewards. Does it seem likely to the Baba that before they reach Constantinople, these two might be overtaken and stopped?'

'They are in Stamboul,' said the Baba. The Smyrna grapes in their celadon platter had been taken away, and he clapped his hands for the ceremonial cups of khusháf and sherbet, while scented water and towels were brought. 'The older one, Donati Khátún, believed there to be some risk to the boy-child in camp, so the child and the English girl were given places on a ship leaving directly for the Sublime Porte. I trust,' said the Bektashi Baba mildly, 'that I speak of the two which are in thy mind also? The elder one, who has since joined the blessed of thy faith, believed the child to be a son of shame, born to one of the Knights Grand Cross of Malta.'

The rosewater ran from its silver spout over Lymond's two uplifted hands and drained between the fine fingers. He said, watching his hands being dried, 'There is some confusion over the child's birth which is of little importance. The child has French protection.'

'Whatever its birth, I believe it is happy in its heritage,' said the Bektashi Baba indulgently. 'The Knights, I hear, have chosen a new Grand Master.'

Imperceptibly Lymond's voice sharpened. 'Juan de Homedes is dead?'

'He is dead, and a French Knight, they say, has been elected.'

'A Frenchman? Or belonging to a French Langue?'

'A Frenchman, I believe,' said the Baba, ruminating. 'Claude de la Sengle was the name.' He paused. 'Thou knowest this man? He is of little esteem?'

Relaxed once more on his cushions, Lymond's voice was no more than thoughtful. 'He is worthy: he will trouble neither thee nor the Order unduly, which could be said of few others. . . . It seems then that if I desire to present myself to the Sultan, I should sail to Stamboul with the greatest possible speed?'

'Tomorrow,' said the Baba peaceably; and laying down his cap, again clapped his hands. 'Thy ship sails tomorrow. Tonight there is music and dancing for thy delight. Dismiss thy servants. Rashid will be thy other self.' And the eunuch, kneeling by Lymond and offering, smiling, a bowl of something which was neither khusháf or sherbet, was the last thing Onophrion and Salablanca saw before they were politely dismissed.

269

On the surface, nothing was wrong. On the surface, two clever and subtle intelligences had dealt, fencing, with a number of forbidden subjects and had made themselves, on the whole, remarkably well understood. But Onophrion was uneasy. Fed, though not to his satisfaction, he roamed the kitchens, peering into the ovens and prodding the carcasses. He opened a box of sugar, newly in from Alexandria, and pouring a little into his plump, shining pink palm, tasted it and expressed satisfaction. The ship it had come from was in the berth next to the *Dauphiné*, and the ship's clerk, waiting for his bills to be signed, was anxious to keep him in talk.

By the time he got away the music in the selamlîk had stopped, though there was much ringing of small bells and occasional laughter. The senior office-holders of the Beglierbey's government, one would gather, had joined the Ambassador and his mentor in their evening of pleasure. Onophrion found Salablanca sitting alone in silence, as close as he could get to the door of the selamlîk, and said, 'I am unhappy. I have spoken to some who have just brought in some goods from the harbour. There are men lingering outside the garden.'

Salablanca did not get up, but his black eyes did not move from Onophrion's face. 'They wait to rob?'

'Had they been ordinary thieves, they would have stolen the spices. They wait, I believe, to ambush and kill.'

'Then?' said Salablanca. 'He sleeps here tonight. They cannot ambush Janissaries in daylight tomorrow.'

'They might break in tonight,' said Onophrion. 'Who knows, in this heathen land; they may be in league with the household. In my view, he ought to be guarded. After all, we brought quite a few of our own men with us.'

'Overtly, it cannot be done,' said Salablanca.

'Discreetly, it can,' said Onophrion. 'If one of us remains in his room and can call out at the first sign of trouble.'

'This I shall do,' said Salablanca softly.

An expression of lofty distaste crossed M. Zitwitz's fleshy pink face, and was gone. 'I'm sure you will. Customs being what they are, I don't suppose he'll be expected to warm his own bed either. Mumsconduren, they call these dervishes. Practitioners of incest. A gentleman all the world over is entitled to his amusements, but I consider it puts an unwarranted strain on good manners to press him with these kinds of attentions.'

Salablanca's dark face and soft voice both kept their gravity. 'Do not fear. Monseigneur's integrity is, I am certain, inviolate.'

For a moment M. Zitwitz, who never gossiped with his inferiors, looked at him. Then holding his counsel, he turned and plodded away.

*

In the event, the sheets were warm when finally Lymond was

allowed to retire to his room in the small hours of the morning. He closed the door gently behind him. Then, pulling his way down the jewelled ties of his doublet, he walked lazily up to the bed and stood looking down on the beautiful body which lay there, brown and lithe as a cat.

Lymond slipped off his doublet. 'No, Míkál,' he said. And swinging the dark green silk for a moment from one idle finger, he allowed it to fall, spreading lightly over the breathing bronze flesh. 'With or without bells. I dare not have you catch cold. You would be a walking tintinabulation of clangers.'

There was a blur of movement. The green silk was on the floor and the boy's sweet warmth, enveloping, was where Lymond had been. But Lymond had moved quite as swiftly and was there no longer, but at the window, which looked out, he saw briefly, on a little courtyard, with flat trays of something dark and aromatic laid out on the bricks, and a garden beyond. Míkál, arrested with dignity and grace in the place of his failure, stood breathing lightly a little way off, and said, 'Hâkim?'

His back to the window, Lymond took a quick breath, and held it for a moment, his eyes searching Míkál's. Then he said gently, 'Thou art faultless: delicate as a flower. May thy love be beautiful. May thy beauty be light. May thy light be exalted light. But with another, Míkál.'

The dark brows in the faun-face were straight. 'I have played to you,' said Míkál.

'I know,' said Lymond. He hesitated and then, clearly against his will, he said, 'It isn't that music doesn't matter: the reverse, as it happens. So my defences against it are very strong. Can you understand that?'

The reasoning was plain enough, evidently, to Míkál. He dropped on the mattress, stretching on his two slender elbows, and looking up at Francis Crawford with a kind of hurt anger, mixed with a queer bravura challenge, he said, 'Will the tongue of Ummídé speak for me?' And went on in his soft and desperate voice:

Thou art a half-drunk Turk; I am a half-slain bird.
Thy affair with me is easy; my desire of thee is difficult. . . .
Thou settest thy foot in the field. I wash my hands of life.
Thou causest sweat to drip from thy cheek. I pour blood from
  my heart. . . .
When shall the luck be mine to lift thee drunken from the
  saddle,
While that crystal-clear arm embraces my neck like a sword-
  belt?

Lymond had not moved, although his heavy gaze this time was downbent; and there was no levity for once in his face. He said, 'I am sorry. It is a hurt for me, too. There is no apology enough for him who holds the wine of love in his hand.'

'I ask for no apology,' said Míkál. 'I ask nothing but kindness.'

'I have learned,' said Lymond, 'that kindness without love is no kindness.'

Pushing himself slowly backwards, Míkál stood slowly up. 'Thy love then is given to women?'

'To no one,' said Lymond; but the boy's intent ear caught the breath of delay. 'To whom, then?' said Míkál. 'To one of your friends?'

This time, no trace of hesitation was visible. 'My love is given to no one,' said Lymond. 'To neither man, woman or child. Duty, friendship, compassion I do owe to many. But love I offer to none.'

Míkál did not say anything. For a long time he stood still; then, moving slowly, he walked round the mattress and up to the window, to come to rest, without attempting this time to touch him, in the space before Lymond. Then he spoke to him gently. 'How many years hast thou, Hâkim?'

Francis Crawford's real age. Something the Dame de Doubtance had known and the girl Marthe had not. Something which, building up mastery over a strong and heterogeneous company of battle-tough men, he had never revealed. *Timeless as Enoch . . .*

'I am twenty-six,' Lymond said. And flinched as Míkál, his eyes dark with pity, leaned forward dry-lipped and kissed him once, on the cheek, before turning lightly and swiftly to walk through the door.

*

Salablanca watched him go. He waited until he thought all sounds inside the chamber had ceased, and easing the door, slipped inside to find some corner where he could rest on guard until day. It was not his fault that Lymond, wide awake and sensitive that night to every change in the air, had lain on the brocade mattress, and had watched him beneath half-closed eyes from the moment the door-handle stirred.

He saw that it was Salablanca, and half smiled, unseen in the dark, and lay still thereafter, part-dressed under the single thin quilt, his sword by his hand. Purgatory, said the Qur'ân, was a beautiful meadow peopled by the spirits of the feeble-minded, illegitimate children and those neither good enough for heaven nor bad enough for hell. There was no privacy there either. But at least there was no need to talk.

An hour after that, the intruder arrived. The fir-wood lattice was beautifully hung. First there was a mere shadow between it and the moonlight; then it swung open quite without noise, and a man, naked but for a cloth round his waist, dropped without sound into the room.

The knife in his hand was curved, a foot and a half long; and even Salablanca's shout didn't stop him as he flung himself towards the Ambassador's bed. Lymond, lying quite still, watching him through his lashes, let his assassin reach the bed and lift up his arm before he threw himself rolling off the mattress and on to his feet, sword in hand.

The knife had descended. The man hesitated, pulling back his steel in a drift of light moonlit feathers as Salablanca reached him behind, and the intruder turned, teeth bared, to deal with him.

Lymond's sword got there first. It drove through the naked body, hard and slanting to avoid Salablanca just beyond and the man screamed, dropping the knife, and then holding his side, bent low and ran, swift as a rat for the window.

Lymond got there on his heels as the would-be murderer, blood streaming dark over his waist-cloth, hung on to the balcony and dropped. There was a clatter, and Lymond, jumping wide after him, laughed breathlessly, and Salablanca, following, heard him say, 'Mind the jam. . . .' Mother-naked; streaming with peaches and gore, the wounded assassin somersaulted, groaned, picked himself up, and staggering, set off through the yard to the garden, Lymond and Salablanca almost upon him.

It was then, in the moment of success, that a sword flashed in the darkness ahead of them; and another and another. Wild and unkempt, half-naked like the wounded intruder or covered in animal skins and rags, a pack of men ran out into the courtyard, blocking Lymond's path and surrounding Salablanca behind him, while the injured man, scurrying past, made good his escape.

It was well organized. Easy to find a gypsy, a delly, and pay him to break in and kill. Rarer to instruct such a man, if he failed, to draw his victim, escaping, into a trap such as this. Lymond, fighting quite simply for his life, parried one blade with a shower of sparks in the darkness, flung himself under the arc of another, undercut at a dark body and backing, called to Salablanca, ducking and cutting as he went. Somewhere behind him was a door. He thudded against it, heeling to one side as a sword drove past him to splinter the wood and felt, parrying with one hand, for the handle.

It was locked. A flash of white and a clot of black moving figures, like a night swarm of wasps, told where Salablanca must be. Bending, twisting, striking, Francis Crawford fought in silence until, catching someone's blade in the steel of his crossguard, he used the second's advantage to drive the man plunging before him, straight-armed through the throng to where Salablanca had been. His side touched the marble edge of a water cistern just as a second and third man, closing in, turned their swords on him and he dropped like a stone, cutting as he went at the bare flesh of their thighs. To the clash of metal on metal, the panting of men under stress, the clatter of trays and the scuffle of naked feet on the brick, there was added a scream and a splash, which gave him an instant's satisfaction. Then there came the rush he had feared.

He parried some of it, but there were too many this time. He had time to think that Salablanca must be dead: to admire in a detached way the speed of it, so that although now doors were opening and voices calling, it was now much too late. A blade seeking his throat seared hot against the side of his neck; another took his sword arm, and as they kicked the useless blade from him and closed in he went down at last, unconscious of the thrusts he had taken; using all the tricks in his experience to hurt, to maim, to stay merely alive.

The noise was increasing. Light, flickering and jumping, had entered the courtyard and was sending monstrous shadows up the walls of the outbuildings and house: there was a tread of many feet and a shouting and a clatter of steel. Above him, a gross bearded figure, grinning, had risen from the mass of his assailants, sword in hand. . . . His executioner. For the last time, using all his considerable strength, Francis Crawford tried to throw off the men pressing upon him, but there were too many: he was locked, hands, arms, legs, thighs, lying there in the dust with the sword over his heart. Then the delly astride him, still grinning, put his fists one above the other on the pommel of Lymond's own blade, and holding it upright, prepared to drive it straight down like a man piercing a well. And since there was no hope, Lymond laughed, looking up at him, and said, in English, '*And so . . . it was all for nothing at all. And who is to care?*'

The body which cannoned into the swordsman at that second was a big one, and solid, or it could not have thrown the assassin off his balance as it did, and collapsed the group of men intent on their victim. It hit the delly as if a block of the marble cistern had fallen on him, and as he staggered and half-fell over Lymond's body and the kneeling forms of his fellows, the newcomer produced, without fuss, a short, broad-bladed sword, and sank it into the assassin's heart up to the hilt.

It was Onophrion Zitwitz. And as Lymond, wordless for once, lay and stared up at him, the Janissaries on his heels poured over the courtyard, sweeping men like rubbish before them. The men holding Lymond rose and scattered until, scimitars falling, shoulder to shoulder, the white caps engulfed them as well, and nothing living was left in the courtyard of those who had taken part in that excellent ambush but the dying. No one escaped.

Lymond saw it as a shifting embroidery round the dark bulk of Onophrion Zitwitz, bending over him, anxiety on his sweating pink face. 'Your Excellency . . .' said Onophrion; and Lymond, who had borne the title for less than half a day, began to laugh and stopped because it hurt so much, and said, 'My dear Onophrion . . . *Tes mains*

274

sont des nuages. Another moment and the pie would have burned.'

'You are wounded. Your Excellency . . .' The high-stranded voice faded. 'I saw, but I could not help. I had to leave you to summon the Janissaries.'

'One man could do nothing. You did right. You expected this, then?' The laughter of relief and reaction had gone. *Salablanca . . . Salablanca . . . Salablanca . . .* But give this man his due first.

'I was uneasy, Your Excellency. It fell to me to keep watch outside. Salablanca watched in your chamber. We did not bring it to Your Excellency's notice.'

But it had come to His Excellency's notice. And His Excellency, ruffled more than he would admit by a trying episode with an importunate boy, had ignored Salablanca's presence and given him neither instructions nor thanks. If he had, that first would-be assailant would never have left his bedroom alive. 'Salablanca?' said Lymond.

'Is dead, Your Excellency. They have carried him inside. . . . You cannot rise. I will find you a litter.'

'No. There is no need,' Lymond said.

It was possible to sit, and to stand, and to walk. It was possible to see Salablanca where he lay, his eyes open and sightless in his blood-sodden clothes, and to close his lids and take from his neck the prayer-beads he wore, to send to his household in Algiers where there were, comfortingly, so many brothers. It was possible next day, with no humiliating swathe of bandage revealed beneath one's high shirt and tight cuffs and impeccable doublet, to stand in the graveyard among the stony forest of turbans and hear the Bektashi Baba's calm voice addressing his Maker.

'O God, be merciful to the living and to the dead, to the present and to the absent, to the small and to the great who are among us. . . . Distinguish him who is now dead by the possession of repose and tranquillity, by favour of Thy mercy and divine forgiveness. O God! increase his goodness, if he be amongst the number of the good; and pardon his sins, if he be ranked among the transgressors. Grant him peace and salvation, O God. Convert his tomb into a delicious abode equal to that of paradise and not into a cavern, like that of hell. Be merciful to him, Thou most merciful of all Beings.

'Lord, great and true, Thou buriest day in night and night in day. Thou leadest forth the living from the dead and the dead from the living. All things come from Thee and return to Thee again. Forgive the sins of mankind for Thy glory's sake. And lead us to the Light, for Thou art the Light of Light.'

And it was possible to sail then, in all one's wealth and magnificence for Constantinople, with the words of Míkál at the graveside, buried deep as the tomb in one's memory:

'Duty; friendship; compassion. Which moved him to die for you?'

275

18

CONSTANTINOPLE

Dear Kate. As you will see from the address, I am staying as a concubine in the harem of Sultan Suleiman the Magnificent, son of Sultan Selim Khan, son of Sultan Bayezid Khan, King of Kings, Sovereign of Sovereigns; Commander of All that can be Commanded, Sultan of Babylon, Lord of the White Sea and the Black Sea, most high Emperor of Byzantium and Trebizond, most mighty King of Persia and Arabia, Syria and Egypt, Supreme Lord of Europe and Asia, Prince of Mecca and Aleppo, Possessor of Jerusalem and Lord of the Universal Sea.

You will be glad to know I am keeping well, thanks to a lot of exercise and a good loosening sherbet the first day. The food would not be very acceptable in Hexham, but I am appending a very good recipe for Turkish Delight, for which you will need the pulp of white grapes, semolina flour, honey, rose-water and apricot kernels. Perhaps Charles can get them in Newcastle.

There are two hundred and ninety-nine other girls here: but no one else from Northumberland. Tell Betty I have the dearest little black page. She will laugh when she hears that he answers to Tulip. . . .

'Fippy!'

Philippa, who could recognize that cry over two courtyards, also recognized that some people answered to funnier names than Tulip, and grinned, lifting her pen from her diary. She lowered it again to write, in her black script, a large adolescent *Ha-ha!* under the foregoing, and shutting the book, went off at speed indoors to locate the calling Kuzúm.

He was standing at the top of the stairs to her sleeping-quarters, the cone of yellow hair fanned out with exertion; a wary expression in the round cornflower eyes. 'Hullo?' he said.

That ingratiating tone was all too hideously familiar. 'Hallo,' said Philippa to the light of her life. 'What have you done?'

The child she had brought all the way from Thessalonika: the child whom Evangelista Donati had called Kuzucuyum bent on her a gaze of reproach. 'I'm a very wet boy,' said Kuzúm.

He waited blandly while, detonating mildly, she thudded up the stairs to his side, and continued to gaze up at her blandly as she skidded to a halt and, staring down, said, 'What's that on your head?'

'That's my little hat,' said Kuzúm.

'That's a wooden spoon,' said Philippa. She disentangled it from the thick, silky hair. 'It's sticky. . . . *Why are you a wet boy?*'

'I sat in my dinner,' said Kuzúm. 'Just like Tulip. What did you said?'

'I said Tulip fell in by mistake, and I wish you had a better grasp of the English language. . . . It's not funny.'

'Laugh again,' said Kuzúm, his eyes beaming.

One of the negresses, smiling, had come to clear up the mess on the tiling. 'I'm not laughing. You won't be, either, in a minute,' said Philippa with relish. 'You'll have to have a clean shirt and a bath.'

The head nurse bathed him, and the noise reached even the room where she was unrolling his mattress. But when he came round the door, he was fresh and pink and filled with a universal and boundless goodwill. 'Here's me again!' he said. 'Hullo, Fippy darling!'

'Hullo!' said Philippa the stalwart, who in between matters which were not funny at all had set herself, with grim humour, to frame a coy letter to Kate.

'Hullo, darling!' she added; and dried her wet eyes, as he hugged her, on the bright yellow head.

Ragna, the mother of Worm, she thought later, gazing out of her window. You made a heroic entrance, in a long plait and leggings and a cloud of Teutonic brimstone, and found yourself instead, child on knee, examining the spots on its bottom and trying to correct, irritably, an inadequate siphoning system and a low-pressure nose-blow.

Because of Kuzucuyum, she could recall almost nothing of that hurried voyage from Thessalonika to record in her diary. To Evangelista Donati she owed the arrangement which had brought them to Stamboul safely by sea. No matter what happened to Gabriel now, they were away from the Children of Devshirmé and that shadowy, unknown figure by whose hand Madame Donati had already died.

Here, they were safe. Here in Topkapi, the Sultan Suleiman's Seraglio, luxury being the steward and the treasure inexhaustible.

Mr Crawford had said that. That besides being a professional mercenary he was highly educated had become plain by degrees to Philippa. He knew for example that Constantinople, which the Turks called Stamboul, had become after the fall of Rome the capital of the whole Roman Empire and the richest city on earth: *It hath none equal with it in the world except Bagdat, that mighty Citie of the Ismaelites.*

Fragments of what he had told her, briefly, on the rare occasions when he would talk of their destination, came now to her mind. '*. . . Pillars and walls he hath overlaid with beaten gold, whereon he hath engraven all the wars made by him and his ancestors . . . and he hath prepared a throne for himself of gold and precious stones, and hath adorned it with a golden crown hanging on high by golden chains, beset with precious stones and pearls the price whereof no man is able to value. . . . Furthermore,*' Mr Crawford had quoted, staring out over the water, '*the Grecians themselves are exceedingly rich in gold and precious stones, their garments being made of crimson intermingled* *with gold and embroidered and are all carried upon horses much like unto the Children of Kings.* .... Justinian rode into his new Church of St Sophia, the most beautiful and most costly in the world, and said, *Solomon, I have surpassed thee.* Christians held it and the city of Byzas before it for nearly twelve hundred years, Philippa. Then the Turks took it all from them.'

'When?' she had said. (Kate would have known.)

'A hundred years ago,' he had answered. 'Exactly. They took twelve kingdoms and two hundred cities from the Christian world, and made a stable of St Sophia under ceilings covered with gold. The ceilings are still there, though they have picked out the eyes of the saints and broken the statues. St Sophia is a mosque, and Topkapi, the official home of the Sultan and the centre of the Ottoman Empire, was built on the ruins of the sacred palace of the Byzantine emperors, on a tongue of land surrounded by sea. The city was renamed Stamboul, or Dâr-es-Sâada, the Abode of Felicity. The seat of government of the richest country in Europe; the most cosmopolitan race since the Romans. It is referred to all over the world as the Sublime Porte. And over the Imperial Gate is written *May God make the Glory of its Master Eternal.*'

Its Master the Sultan. Her master. And the master of this, Lymond's son.

Embarking at Thessalonika, Kuzúm had been interested in the ship; and had gone with her confidingly, and had allowed himself to be rolled in a real rug in a real hammock for his afternoon sleep. Only when he awoke and neither his nurse nor Madame Donati was there, and he was still on the ship, and his meal was late, and different, and in different bowls, did his chin tremble; and when Philippa told him, slowly and clearly, that Madame Donati had had to go away but that he was going with her for a little holiday to a big house to find some new toys he bent his head so low that only by kneeling could Philippa see the tears run slowly off his round cheeks and catch the one whispered word: '*Home.*' It was when she had to deny this that the real crying started, developing into a fragmented screaming that could be heard all over the ship, with the same word gasped over and over. She left him after a while, when he would not let her touch him and her every word seemed to make matters worse, and sat listening in the next chamber, the tears making unnoticed furrows in her own dirty face; powerless to help.

What was home? Djerba? Algiers? He had been too small to recall that: probably too small to recollect his first nurse or even his mother. Home was probably that formal, unfriendly house at Zakynthos, where he must have stayed with the Donatis for the better part of a year before being taken away on his travels with the Children of Tribute.

But Madame Donati had gone with him. And however unaccustomed to small children she was; however unbending and acid, she had loved him. With astonishment still, Philippa remembered the yearning in the sick woman's eyes as the child came to her; and the look on her face when she embraced him for what she knew would be the last time.

From her, Kuzucuyum had had love, and a grounding in English which someone else had also obviously begun, long ago. He had become used to travelling because, whatever the change in surroundings, his routine, Philippa guessed, had been kept uniform, a feat which must have required something approaching fanaticism. And that was the root of the difficulty now. Kuzucuyum had taken to her. He was quick and happy by nature, she thought; and affectionate. But all the rest was his world. It had fallen apart, and she could not put it together again.

He cried, at intervals, all through the night, and even when quiet was shaken, in sleep, with single, spasmodic sobs. He ate nothing. The sight of her, Philippa found, was enough to start an eruption for the whole of next morning: in the afternoon she sent in her new little black slave Tulip with some yoghourt and sat with her head aching, listening.

Silence. Tulip was eight. One of the Children of Tribute, he had been picked by Madame Donati to serve her because, although he had joined them from Egypt, by some freak of chance he spoke not only Arabic but English. Sitting beside him the previous night, when he also had shed a few tears, very easily assuaged, Philippa guessed that his mother had served in a renegade household, perhaps of a merchant or seaman turned Moslem corsair. At times his accent had distressing overtones of Cockney. At the moment, to Philippa, listening next door, it had the timbre of angelic choirs. He was speaking; there was silence; there was more speaking: and then Kuzucuyum repeated a word, and both little boys laughed.

Philippa cried, briefly, and then went in to take away the empty yoghourt bowl and kiss Tulip. Kuzúm, his face still a featureless mosaic in pinks and his ears full of tears, regarded her without expression and then said in an uneven whisper, 'I'm a very wet boy.'

The first and biggest obstacle was over. She felt her way; building up trust; piecing together for him a new day and a new night; a new vocabulary of word and intonation and catch-phrase to take the place of the one he had lost. The Aegean went by. She did not notice Gallipoli or the Hellespont: the Sea of Marmara might have been the duckpond at Wall.

They came to Constantinople in the morning, sailing in sunlight through the blue waters of the long harbour creek called the Golden Horn; the Bosphorus and the green shore of Asia receding behind them. Philippa took her two children by the hand and went up on deck.

Wreathed with cypress; bossed with the golden fruit of her domes and the sunlit stalks of her minarets, the Abode of Felicity girdled her seven low hills, green and white and gold in the sunlight as an enrichment of Safavid jewellery; and against the clear cobalt sky, the gilt crescents flashed on their spires like a garden of sequins. Before her, the seawall, toothed and towered, curved out of sight, the deeper blue of the Golden Horn washing the wharves and sheds at its base; and on her right the same water touched the opposite shore, where the tile-roofed white houses of Pera rose to the vine-covered top of the hill, and there were church spires among the pale minarets. Somewhere there, the lilies of France flew over the French Ambassador's house, where a Special Envoy bringing gifts for the Sultan was no doubt still awaited, in vain. . . . The Special Envoy she had last seen in Algiers, about to encompass the death of Graham Reid Malett; and perhaps himself Gabriel's victim by now. If Archie found him; if he learned of Kuzúm's existence, he would come: he might even manage to purchase the child. But one could not, of course, expect to buy one of the Sultan's own personal odalisques. . . .

In spite of herself, Philippa grinned. Then the interpreter who had been among her small escorting party of Janissaries touched her arm, and pointed to a tongue of land on her left where, bowered in plane and willow and cypress trees, glimmered a crowded chiaroscuro of marble-flanked buildings and coloured arcades; of towers and cupolas in gilt, in copper, in bronze; of the glitter of faience and coloured mosaics; the reiterated sheet gold of the crescent of Islam and the reiterated red coiling silk of the Islamic flag. 'Topkapi,' said the dragoman, and smiled. 'The Seraglio of the Sultan Suleiman. There, too, his harem.'

Then, her hand on the shoulder of either child, for a moment Philippa stopped smiling.

She had to wait some time before the Janissaries reporting her presence transmitted the order for herself and the children to land. Then, unmistakably, she saw activity round the long, low boathouses on the Seraglio shore, and soon after that, to Kuzúm's shrieks of joy, Philippa and the children and their minimal possessions were descending into a bright golden caique with the throat and head of a dragon, rowed by silent men, all alike in Phoenician-red nightshirts. 'My goodness: *look* at the cushions,' observed Philippa, settling in. 'You wouldn't need to keep cats.'

The sea gate to the Topkapi Seraglio was of iron, intricately wrought, and Philippa, bearing the dead weight of her protégé ('Kuzúm have a see!') in her arms, counted ten men guarding it; speechless also; their headdress pillows of white feathers. ('What kind is that hat?') She stepped through on to a path made of smooth, coloured marbles which, as far as the eye could reach, had been flanked on each of its sides by a continuous barrier of cloth, higher than Philippa's head. Because of it, the garden which lay on each side of her was invisible save for the tops of its trees and its tallest flowering shrubs. Walking along the strange, roofless tunnel, Philippa could hear the spray of multiple fountains and the low murmur of voices: smell the odour of wet grass and flowers and newly turned earth. Behind her, the tall gates were shut.

In her arms Kuzúm was quiet, and she felt Tulip falter beside her. She smiled and spoke to them both while at the back of her mind, sinkingly, Philippa recognized the true object of these barrier screens. They were not to prevent her from viewing the garden. They were to preserve the Sultan's new personal property from all other impious eyes.

The walk led to another wall and another gate, this time roofed and encased in elaborate porphyry. Here, when the gate swung slowly open, her interpreter spoke briefly and turned away, leaving Philippa face to face with a powerful negro in a white sugar-loaf hat and a gown of pale blue brocatelle which fell to the ground. This one bowed gravely, hand on breast, and snapped his fingers. Slaves (she supposed?), rushing from nowhere, assumed her baggage and vanished with it, while the eunuch (she supposed?), turning, led the way down a long flight of steps.

Kuzúm, who had the same dead weight as a young hippopotamus, clung to her shoulder-blades with a good handful of robe and half her hair excruciatingly in his grasp: turning her head, to the limited degree she was able, Philippa saw, towering above on her left, the colonnades and the glassy walls of the palace she had just seen from her ship with their ranks of domed roofs in leaf-gold and lead. Then, turning, she followed the eunuch.

Later, she knew that she had been taken through the maze of low courts—playgrounds, gardens and pools, exercise-ground, animal compound—which lay under the west walls of the Topkapi buildings and led in their turn to the honeycomb of ancient vaults and arcades which was all that was left of the sacred palace of the Byzantine emperors, on which they were built. At the time, she had an impression only of a procession of scents: animal, herbal, citrous. There was the smell of damp wood and old and new stone and mortar; and a stream of scent she did not recognize until, passing from wall-shade and tree-shade and the empty spaces tenanted by silent, white-hatted negroes or hurrying, black-skinned women slaves, they burst into a sunlit pleasure-garden filled with perhaps three dozen young women, playing at ball; and the scent was as strong as if the clouds had opened and sprayed them with civet and rosewater.

There was nothing like it in Hexham. Staring belligerently, Philippa saw that, with variations, they all wore calf-length trousers and pale chemises in sarsenet, or something quite as transparent, covered just by a short damask waistcoat and, sometimes, an open,

281

floating kaftán. Pinned on their heads were small, cylindrical caps, vizored with veils: they were plastered with jewellery, and their hair, Philippa noted, plaited or loose, twined with pearls or ribbons or laces, was by some curious chance either bright red or soot black without exception. Then they came running.

Until that moment, when they came jostling around her, plucking with little, stained hands at her soiled robe; dragging back her pin-scratching veil, and she heard their high, foreign voices and their laughter, it had not occurred to Philippa Somerville that these girls and no others were henceforth to be her daily companions. With them she must learn to live in a wholly enclosed society, closer than sisters. And in their company the whole of her life from this day onwards must be spent. The whole of her life, from the age of sixteen.

In that moment, as she came to a halt, they took Kuzúm from her. Her hand to her bared head, she suddenly realized it, and whirling round, saw him silent in the arms of a chattering girl, mute, his blue eyes filled with unshed tears and his chin wobbling. 'Well!' said Philippa, in English. 'I don't suppose there's another boy east of the Isle of Wight with so many good-looking aunties. They've got a ball. Do you see the ball? Do you think they would let you play with it? Tulip, ask them.'

Tulip, his black face stiff under his little yellow cap, said something in Arabic, not looking at anybody; and the girl holding Kuzúm laughed and put him down, while another girl on tall, velvet pattens bent down, not without difficulty, and smiling, rolled the silver ball towards him.

Ignoring it, Kuzúm walked forward steadily over the grass on his short legs and bending over the girl's foot, his brief robe sticking out over his rump, said in a little voice, 'Is that a meant shoe?'

The girl laughed, and poked him gently in the stomach with one toe, while Philippa, coming forward, picked him up cheerfully and said, 'They're stilts, my lambkin, for keeping her nice slippers dry. We'll come back, but the gentleman is waiting to take us into the house now. Say goodbye. . . .'

They kissed him, laughing, and someone put the silver ball in his arms as Philippa, smiling, turned and followed the eunuch again. Her veils, a little torn, lay heaped over her shoulders and her forehead felt damp. With the little gesture he always made when tired or uneasy, the little boy had released one hand from the ball and was lying limp on her shoulder, the back of one soft wrist at his mouth. Philippa, trying to keep her own hands steady, gripped him firmly and followed the eunuch up a long flight of white marble steps and into Topkapi itself.

A labyrinth of courtyards and tall, narrow corridors. Bright tiles in blue and orange and green; soft scarlet carpets; heavy hangings of Diarbekir silk and Saracenic patterns on linen; ceilings caissoned and painted; walls wainscotted in tiles and mosaic and lapidary work with jasper and marble; cedarwood lattices and inlays of glass and enamel. Little windows in stained Cairo glass, throwing sapphire, ruby, onyx lights on the walls. The murmur of light, muted voices; of fountains; the rustle of taffetas; the low, golden notes of a lute. The scent of dried roseleaves and incense and boxwood and flowers; of amber paste burning, and jasmine powder; of lemon oil and something frying in honey. A guardroom, with black faces and white turbans and a dimness cloisonné with steel. An open space, floored with mosaic, where on her left she caught sight of a big doorway, rimmed with sunlight, through which she heard birdsong and sensed the freshness of flowers. Then the eunuch opened a door.

She was in a long, open-air passage flanked on either side by the doors and windows and arcaded pillars of what seemed to be the black eunuch's living-quarters, which stretched high on either side, plunging the narrow courtyard deeply in shadow. Ahead, there was a fireplace built into the wall, turreted like a turbèh and tiled, but it was unlit. Above her, Philippa could see the windowed tower she had already observed, higher than the rest, with its four-sided spire. Then she was in darkness, following her conductor through a doorway on her right, up a staircase, and breathlessly, into a small room with a raised dais, where a man sat crosslegged, awaiting her.

Beneath the white, sugarloaf hat was a negro's face; but his robes, spread over the cushions, were of green velvet on a crimson silk ground, and the trimmings were sable. Then she knew this was the Kislar Agha; the Chief of the Black Eunuchs and supreme head of the harem. Philippa put down Kuzúm. Then, holding the child tightly by one hand, she followed, shakily enough, Kate's universal dictum. When in doubt, curtsy.

The Kislar Agha neither rose nor acknowledged her. Instead, his unwinking black gaze on her face, he spoke, in Turkish, to the interpreter who appeared silently at her side, and the interpreter, bowing, addressed her in English.

The questions were brief. Philippa, her knees shaking with nerves and resentment under her creased robes, answered them curtly. 'My lord asks, what age art thou, and hast thou heretofore known men? My lord asks, art thou whole, or unfit, or blemished? My lord asks what religion heretofore thou hast practised? My lord asks, what tongue dost thou speak?'

There was only one thing Philippa wanted to ask. She snapped the answer to the last question and said, 'May the child. . . ?' but the Kislar Agha was already speaking again in the brisk, sexless voice.

'Now thou art in the palace of thy lord. To the Mistress of the Harem thou wilt make accounting for thy body; and to the Imáms for thy soul. Thou wilt embrace henceforth the teachings of Islam: the tongue of Osmân will replace thine own, and with infidel speech and ways thou wilt lay aside the infidel name thou bearest. *Durr-i*

Bakht: Pearl of Fortune is thy name. To me and to the Mistress of the Harem and to thy teachers thou owest service, obedience, humility. To our Sovereign Lord the Sultan Suleiman and Khourrém Sultán his wife, thou art as a grain of rice beneath the foot. Conduct thyself well, and thine will be the blessings of Paradise. Ill, and thou wilt weep tears of blood.'

Philippa said, her voice cracking, 'May the child . . .?'

'The Ethiopian may serve you.'

'But the other——'

'The white child is already provided for.' It was the Kislar Agha's final pronouncement. He had lost interest in her even before the translation was complete, although she heard a command in Turkish which she did not quite catch. As the eunuch who had brought her came forward to take her, she said quickly, 'I want to take both the children with me.' Kuzúm was clutching her skirt.

The eunuch hesitated and it was the interpreter who spoke. 'The child goes to the Head Nurse, Lady; and thyself to the Mistress of the Harem. They dwell in the same courtyard.' And backing, with Kuzúm by the hand and a smiling Tulip behind her, Philippa got out.

Afterwards, Philippa remembered only a brief journey to the oblong courtyard, at the bottom of a shallow flight of white marble steps, where the Mistress's suite lay. Too brief: for soon, now, Kuzúm would be parted from her and soon she must face the woman now ruling her life: the Mistress who was also controller and head housekeeper of the harem as well as the Kislar Agha's own deputy.

However frightening and distasteful the last interview had been, at least she had suffered no physical indignity. But to the Mistress of the Harem fell the responsibility of ensuring the health and seemliness of all the girls who might be invited to receive the embraces of the King of the World. Something fairly abominable, Philippa recognized, was about to happen; and she chatted, cheerfully and continuously, to Kuzucuyum, and helped him down his stilted descent of the first few steps, and when he came to a halt, dragging behind her, lifted him in her arms and reminded herself, with his lashes brushing her cheek, that he was his mother's unwanted firstborn; born into danger and loneliness; and that he had no one else.

The suites of the Head Nurse, the Head Laundress and the Mistress all led off from the same pleasant courtyard, with the serving slaves' kitchens and dormitories tiered around the same space. The Head Nurse was black, and came out of her quarters to meet them; chuckling at Kuzúm and speaking to him in Turkish. Philippa said impulsively, and uselessly, in English, 'Oh, please. . . . He doesn't understand. He speaks English. Could I stay with him just a little, until he gets used——'

The eunuch's voice came, sharply, calling her new name. Philippa said quickly, 'Or Tulip. Tulip, stay with him. I'll come back. Kuzúm,

I'll come back.' She knelt. 'Look, Tulip is staying with you. This is your new nurse. She's your new nurse, who will take care of you. Show her your ball. I'll come back.'

The eunuch called again, and getting up, with an unregarded cracking of seams, Philippa hurried into the dark entrance of the Mistress's quarters, and was conducted along soft carpets to a little chamber behind. The eunuch, bowing, departed.

After the sunlight, it was dark inside, and scented, with a warm aroma she imperfectly remembered from a long time ago. A voice spoke, and a young, plainly dressed girl with a long-stemmed fan rose to her feet, bowed, and slipped out past Philippa. The voice spoke again in Turkish and Philippa, recognizing the command, took a long breath and went in.

The room was too small for a dais, but a deep mattress paned with bright velvets and heaped with pearl-braided cushions served as a throne for the speaker. The Mistress of the Harem was not veiled. Her hair, under a small golden cap, smelt of Cingalese tuberose, but she was dressed in brown silk, gold-brocaded from throat to knee with birds and boats and combers and hounds, beneath which heavy bracelets gleamed in the dusk, at her wrists and her ankles. The design of the silk was not Moslem, and neither was the face, which was smooth-skinned and straight-nosed, with high, painted brows.

It was a face she had seen before. A great many thoughts went through Philippa's head in the little silence that followed; but the chief one she found, despite her shaking knees, to be anger. 'You sent me to the House of the Palm Tree to find him,' said Philippa to Kiaya Khátún, whom she had last met drinking coffee, in Lyons, with the Lady of Doubtance, that strange old astrologer. 'And I did; and I'm grateful. But did you mean us both to come here in the end, all the time?'

Kiaya Khátún, friend of Dragut; friend of Khourrém Sultán; skilful administrator who might choose and relinquish her post as she pleased, for there was none other to equal her, looked at Philippa and smiled. 'Be seated, child; and take *qahveh*. None will run off with your child. If he cries, you may go and comfort him: the Head Nurse is a good woman but stupid; and remarkably amenable. Now. You were saying . . . How long ago it seems!' said Güzel, sipping gracefully. 'I really cannot remember what I hoped for the boy. But the Dame de Doubtance . . . the Dame de Doubtance, I remember, was most insistent that you should by some means enter the Seraglio. She thought, I believe, that you would benefit by the experience.'

'Did she?' said Philippa, her back stiff. 'Then since the arrangements to get me in have worked so nicely, I take it there'll be no difficulty about getting out. Today, for instance.'

'And leave the boy?' said Kiaya Khátún softly. And as Philippa did not answer she added, 'Tell me, my child: do you speak Turkish?'

'A little.' *Geomalers have very long memories.* She wondered what had happened to Míkál, who had taken her to Thessalonika, and had abandoned her. A creature of Gabriel's, surely, would have killed her prior to destroying the child. Or . . . Enlightenment broke on her. Did Míkál have not a master, but a . . .

'Since you arrived, have you spoken Turkish or shown that you understand it?'

Philippa's attention returned to the Mistress. 'No . . . I don't think so. I haven't had a chance. Why?'

'Good,' said Kiaya Khátún. 'It would prove, I think, beneficial if you continued to show ignorance. You will be taught it, of course. But it is an extremely difficult language to learn.'

Philippa, who had not found it so, opened her mouth, thought, and shut it again. Kiaya Khátún went on. 'It would be better, also, if your acquaintance with me were not known to exist. You are here at this moment in order that I may conduct an examination. You will say, if you are asked, that this has been done. . . . You are, I take it, a virgin?'

It occurred to Philippa that never in the whole of her life had she been required to give as much thought to that circumstance, happy or unhappy, as in the last half-hour. 'Yes,' she said, not very politely.

Kiaya Khátún smiled. 'Drink your *qahveh*,' she said. 'You do not consider it so, but the place you will fill is one of high honour. You have heard, I am sure, how the Sultan's wife Khourrém was no more than a Russian slave-girl in this harem when she won the Sultan's love. She is called still Roxelana, "the Russian one". She was then the second only of the Sultan's four principal ladies: the first, Bosfor Sultán, had already given him his son Mustafa. But it was Roxelana in the end whom the Sultan married: the first ruler for nearly one hundred and fifty years to take a legal wife to himself. Twelve years ago she moved from the Old Seraglio to share his apartments here in Topkapi, and the harem has grown with her and her three sons, now all grown and away. But Roxelana stays, and the Sultan, they say, makes no move without her advice.'

Philippa got to the mud at the bottom of her cup, and put it down. 'The prospects for advancement,' she said, 'seem rather limited.' Gideon's farm-manager had once said that, and Gideon had laughed.

Güzel smiled. 'Roxelana will not live for ever. Nor, for that matter, will Sultan Suleiman; and his son Prince Mustafa, though married, is not as his father is. Suleiman, as is known, has since his marriage taken no woman but Roxelana to his bed.'

Philippa felt herself, rather unpleasantly, go perfectly white, and then scarlet. Her heart was behaving like a very old blacksmith. She said, 'So he won't . . . I shan't . . .'

'The chances are,' said Kiaya Khátún blandly, 'that you will remain a virgin. Unless you cannot resist the other blandishments you will meet. But hard-headed Border common sense, I am sure, will prevail. . . . The Mistress of Baths, I am told, is awaiting you.'

The eunuch had appeared on the threshold. 'Kuzúm,' said Philippa quickly. 'What will happen to the child?'

'Ah, the child,' said Güzel. 'He is privileged. He will live here for three years in the care of the Head Nurse: you may see him as much as you wish. Then he will be given tutors and will join the older children here in the harem for schooling. At eleven, he will leave the harem, and you will not see him again. It will be your loss, not his. With such training, the highest office is open to such a man. Everything, naturally, except marriage.'

'Why?' said Philippa. 'Don't they allow——'

Kiaya Khátún rose. With small, tapered fingers stained rose, she smoothed down the stiff folds of the silk and pulled the dark hair more becomingly round her straight shoulders. 'My dear child,' she said, and signed, imperceptibly, to her servant. 'The game of posterity is not one that this Sultan chooses to play. By the time Kuzucuyum is of marriageable age, Mr Crawford's son—if he is Mr Crawford's son—will not be a man, but a eunuch.'

In the scented steam of the baths, stripped, kneaded, scoured and anointed; made smooth from her head to her feet, Philippa faced the hardest battle of her day. From the lined, painted face of the Mistress of the Baths to the half-naked women who attacked her tanned skin, giggling, with their rough cloths she was vouchsafed no mercy; and as she lay helpless on the marble, not over-clean; knot-boned and flat as a boy, with her tangled, mouse-coloured hair and unremarkable face, nothing spared her the comments of the other girls of the harem who came and went, rose and ivory, half veiled with steam, and touched and stroked and prodded her, laughing their silly cackling laughter, until the Baths Mistress pushed them away, commenting, lewdly and cruelly, in the Turkish she was not supposed to understand.

She lay prone, her wet eyes sunk deep in her sweating wet arms while they worked on her back; and sought grimly some styptic for tears. In her mind she saw her mother Kate's soft brown eyes, and heard her speaking serenely. *There are four ways to meet persecution. Ignore it, suffer it, do it better than they do. Or just make them laugh.* It had been the head cowman's son, that time. 'He hasn't got the least sense of humour,' she remembered saying despairingly. Kate had been unperturbed. 'I know, dear. You'll just have to be funny for two.'

Her ear caught Greek in two—no, three voices. And somewhere, someone said a sentence in French. She had some kind of lingua franca then. She needn't be dumb. When they turned her over, and someone said something, and there was a general laugh, Philippa said forbiddingly, in Greek, 'In case you haven't noticed, you are now viewing the side which bites. You may, if you wish, paint a cross on it.'

Someone laughed. One of the bright voices in Greek said, 'Not a cross, English One. What is thy name?'

'I don't remember,' said Philippa. 'Pearl of Fortune, I think. What's yours?'

The Greek girl was red-haired, with a retroussé nose and a mouth full of flashing white teeth. 'I am Laila,' she said. 'And my other friend here Perfume of the Desert. What other tongues hast thou?'

'Only French,' said Philippa apologetically, with a gasp as a heavy hand whacked her flanks.

'Then this is Fleur de Lis, and the others have Turkish or Italian names. You will get to know.' Fleur de Lis was short-legged, with a neck like Venus and the head of a saint. Her comments had been not only the best barbed but the most unflinchingly true. She said, '*Tu as douze ans?*'

'If you think I look like twelve, then I'm twelve,' said Philippa kindly. They were all around her now, helping the maids to pour rosewater and wrap her in towels. Her hair, washed and rubbed and pomaded, was pinned on top of her head, her blood ran in wide, silken channels and they had taken her bones out and polished them. Philippa stood up and shut her eyes in a daze of mental anguish and physical euphoria, and propelled by small soft hands, moved to the beds in the outer hall. There was a flash of white skirts, and a voice screamed '*Fippy!*'

It was Kuzúm, naked, his eyes blue as the sea in his shining pink face; his yellow hair, curled by the steam, sticking up in wet spikes and roulades. He ran into her arms.

'He wouldn't sleep until he'd seen you, Khátún,' said the under-nurse with him; and as if she didn't understand, Philippa smiled at her over the child's yellow head, and sitting down on the couch, sat him up on her knee.

'What you agoing do?' he said.

Philippa smiled and kissed the nape of his neck. 'Sleep, my cherub.'

'Kuzúm sleep aside Fippy? What's there?' said Kuzúm with interest, and pushed one fat finger under her towel.

'Me,' said Philippa cheerfully. 'And oh, Kuzúm ... look at all your lovely new aunties!'

But in her heart she was saying: 'Khaireddin Crawford ... we are two people who may never know what it is to be a man or a woman. But we shall make friends, and find happiness, and comfort each other.'

*

By the time Lymond left Thessalonika, bound for Constantinople, both Philippa and the boy had been in the harem for some weeks. He learned this himself, almost at the outset of the voyage, by the simple accident of encountering the ship which had taken Philippa, now on its way south.

To Georges Gaultier, and indeed the master and crew of the *Dauphiné*, it had seemed an excuse at last for slackening the ruinous speed at which they had been held since leaving Malta. In this they were disappointed. If the girl and the child were in the Seraglio, they were safe perhaps from any vengeance Gabriel might have wreaked from the grave. But if any petition for their freedom were to be made, it must be made to the Sultan before he left, as was rumoured, to march south with his army. And further . . .

'It is to be understood,' said Onophrion Zitwitz deprecatingly to M. Gaultier, as he ended his customary tirade a day or two later. 'The girl is young and inexperienced, and moreover plainly reared. Plunged into luxury; decadence . . . forced to witness and take part in who knows what licentious conduct . . . It is not unnatural that His Excellency wishes to make all speed possible.'

They were then within sight of the narrow straits of the Dardanelles, having been tossed backwards and forwards in extreme discomfort since leaving harbour. Autumn winds, pranking all round the compass, combined with sudden sail-drenching rainstorms, had held them up in spite of every expert device and had exhausted the oarsmen to an unfortunate degree. 'We'll be in the narrows tonight,' said Gaultier, his lean cheeks raw with the wind. 'Why the hell doesn't he get on a horse and ride for the Porte, if he's in such a hurry?'

M. Zitwitz picked up the remains of the broker's uneaten cold meal, and hesitated, as if unwilling to risk a discourtesy. Then he said, in the same tone of deference, 'Because, sir, one cannot carry this beautiful spinet on horseback. Is it not so? And to present petitions, he must call in state, with his full train and the King of France's new gift. . . . In the narrows and in the Sea of Marmara beyond we shall have shelter. It will not be long, sir.'

'It was too long,' said Georges Gaultier bitterly, 'six months ago.'

Thoughtfully, Onophrion went about his business. To a detached observer, it was obvious that not only the speed and the climate were to blame for the tension on board the *Dauphiné*. Since Thessalonika, Lymond's moods had been unpredictable. His care for a swift passage was tireless and his instructions could not be faulted; but he took less trouble, sometimes, to make them palatable to the hard-worked seamen who must fulfil them; and with the officers of the ship, with Georges Gaultier and with Onophrion himself, he was either uncommunicative or abrupt to the point of discourtesy. Onophrion continued with his task, which was to set dinner, as well as he could, on a damp cloth in the master's cabin, and then went on deck to locate Mr Crawford.

The new Ambassador was on the rambade, where he had been walking for the past hour; up and down, his yellow hair soaked and tangled, his flying cloak ruined with salt. Despite the long summer's sun and the sting of the wind, his skin above the dark cloak was as pale as a troglodyte's, and marked faintly with stresses which had not been there when, six months ago, as Gaultier said, they had started their voyage.

Salablanca's death, of course, had been a blow. There was concern for the girl. But more than that; with an effort of imagination one saw perhaps what it meant to take a year, virtually, out of one's life to perform a duty towards two young unknown children, for whom one felt responsibility, but no bond: to leave the live world; one's career, one's affairs to spend empty days on land and on shipboard, travelling, waiting; being forced to wait for an object one did not even desire, except with one's intellect. To Mr Crawford, the death of Sir Graham Reid Malett was the justification for such a waste. Now, he must feel the justification was indeed small.

Lymond had seen him. Buffeted by the wind, he came back slowly over the gangway and paused, his hand on the doorpost, his eyes on the food-laden table. 'After all your effort,' he said. 'I'm sorry.'

'Your Excellency will not dine?'

'I think not,' said Lymond. 'Will you tell the captain I have gone below for a space? Call me, if you will, in an hour.'

Onophrion Zitwitz, a man of great experience, looked at his master's strained face and was of a sudden inspired. The injuries Lymond had received at Thessalonika had been treated that night by the Beglierbey's own physician, and Lymond had not mentioned them since. But after the death of Salablanca the new Ambassador had had no personal aide to look after either his physical welfare or his grooming and both, all too obviously, had been neglected.

Onophrion Zitwitz, taking a calculated diplomatic risk, leaned forward and shut the door to the deck. 'If Your Excellency will sit down,' he said, with considerable firmness in that sedate, well-drilled voice, 'I shall pour you some aqua-vitae and ask the barber-surgeon to come.'

'What: for a blood-letting?' said his master. But he left the door and sat down, with precision, where Jerott, drunk, had once sat; and after a moment, without speaking, dropped his head on his arms. So Onophrion, waiting neither for the barber-surgeon nor the spirits, unfastened Lymond's cloak and as much as he could reach of his doublet, and slipping in his plump, soap-smelling hand, located the wad of stiff, fraying bandage which bound his right shoulder.

Without comment Onophrion withdrew his hand, and taking the sharpest of the knives which lay on the table, slit unhesitatingly through velvet and lawn and the bandage itself until he laid bare the neglected sword thrust, swollen, angry and raw.

Without moving, Lymond said, 'Would it not be better below?'

Master Zitwitz looked at him. 'If you can climb down, Your Excellency. The wound is poisoned.'

'I began to think so,' said Lymond. 'But then it pained me only at intervals. It didn't seem worth a commotion.'

With Onophrion Zitwitz there was never a commotion. In five minutes Lymond was below decks and the surgeon was on his way; and hot water; and Master Zitwitz had even, at the back of his mind, a menu for the small trayful of food he proposed bringing when the whole nasty business was over. Francis Crawford, prone on his bed, had not spoken since he arrived there.

Onophrion said, suddenly, 'Bearing pain will not bring him back.' And as Lymond twisted round, his eyes open, his face taut with angry astonishment, the steward recoiled and went on, as if no one had spoken, 'If you will forgive me, sir: between here and Constantinople it will be impossible to keep Your Excellency's shoulder dressed and your clothes as they should be without a personal servant. If Your Excellency would permit me to appoint one of my own men . . . I have trained him myself. . . .'

'Appoint anyone you like,' said Lymond; and flung himself back on his face.

Far from coming on deck in an hour, he did not appear again that day, or until half the next morning had gone. But when he did, the change was quite remarkable. With his fever dispelled; rested and groomed by his new servant Adrian and fed, at two-hourly intervals, by Onophrion's solicitous hand, Lymond had recovered all the sangfroid that Gaultier most disliked. 'Idleness: an excellent remedy, don't you find it, M. Gaultier? *Il se gratte les fesses et conte des apologues.* Especially when one is fond of fables, as you and your niece undoubtedly are. . . . But there are snakes in the Valley of Diamonds, M. Gaultier; and a wind that turns stones into wax. And although you throw your meat into the valley, and release a thousand starving eagles, they may pick up the meat, but with no diamonds adhering. . . . Where is Marthe now, do you think?'

M. Gaultier, against his inclination, humoured him. 'In Aleppo with Mr Blyth, I should suppose. Or on her way to Constantinople.'

'With Mr Blyth, I wonder? They say, *Dammi con chi tu vivi,* M. Gaultier; and *io saprò quel' che tu fai.* What do you suppose Marthe is doing?'

'Filling in time, Mr Crawford: as are we all, until this interminable embassy is at an end.'

'Patience, M. Gaultier. It is an Oriental virtue. *Empty thy head of wind, for none is born of his mother save to die. Wert thou a rampart of well-wrought iron, the rotation of the heavens would break thee none the less, and thou shouldst disappear.*' The levity returned to the pleasant voice. 'It is not, I am sure, a philosophy beloved of pawn-brokers.'

291

The weather improved. Tribute at Hellespont paid, they sailed between the two castles, and at Gallipoli they found M. Chesnau, the French Envoy to Constantinople of whom the Bektashi dervish at Thessalonika had spoken, held up by a fever of which his secretary had already died. Since he could not be moved, Lymond made what improvements he could in his housing and comforts and went on his way, his letters of credence as full Ambassador in his hands. They sailed by the Thracian coast, passing Rodesto and Perinthe and rowing all night to cross the Gulf of Selimbrie and get to the castles of Flora and St Stephano. From there, Lymond sent a horseman to warn d'Aramon, the retiring Ambassador, of his arrival.

A day later, the *Dauphiné* anchored at night below the Seven Towers, the State Prison of Stamboul; and in the morning rowed round the sea wall until, turning Seraglio Point, she entered the creek called the Golden Horn and stood off the Scarlet Apple of the World: the city of Constantinople at last.

In Topkapi, Kuzucuyum heard the guns and the trumpets, and screaming, 'Bang-cass!' in ecstasy, turned so fast he sat down. The Pearl of Fortune, hearing him, snatched him up, her shining hair flying, and flew with him to the highest viewpoint she was permitted; when cheek to cheek, they looked down together.

White and gold, the silk pennants ran, fluid as writing from the yardarms of the incoming ship, and the ensigns from her mastheads were of the same colour. Her screens were out amidships, of cloth of silver and gold, and green boughs garlanded her low flanks, below the slow sweep of the oars. Her very wake was silver, in the carmine sea of first dawning: silver clouds rose from her culverin and constellations flashed from her trumpets as she repeated over and over her salutes.

There was a spyglass Philippa, in the person of Pearl of Fortune, had cajoled from a silly lassie from Candia in exchange for a New-castle kerchief. Putting the glass to her eye, she maintained it firmly against the fat hands of Kuzúm, and peering through the joggling lens, focused over the tops of the kiosks and cypress trees, on the shining strip of water, peopled with caique and galley and galleasse, with ships of war and commerce and pleasure, of fishing and ferrying, until she found again the newcomer she had been watching.

It was a galley. It was a royal galley sliding in at the salute, oars upraised and parallel. And above it there unrolled, white and gold and dearly familiar, the lily banner of France. The glass swept from Philippa's face and she dragged it back again. '*Kuzúm!* Not now! In a moment, my lamb. In a moment. . . . Oh, *please!*'

It steadied, and she saw again what she had glimpsed. On the mainmast was the royal standard of France. On the mizzen was the coat of arms, in blue and silver and scarlet, of Crawford of Lymond and Sevigny.

With fearful suddenness, Kuzucuyum found himself in full

possession of the disputed spyglass. 'Hullo?' he said uneasily, surveying what he could see of his Fippy.

With children, you have no private life. 'Hullo,' said Philippa reassuringly. 'It's all right. I . . . banged my hand.'

The vast blue gaze turned anxious. 'Is it a little just a scratch?' said Kuzúm.

'Yes . . . it's all right,' said Philippa. 'Let's go and have breakfast.'

'Kiss it butter?' said Kuzúm, who was nothing if not thorough. He delivered the kiss, bending his brushed yellow head, and then turned the appraising gaze on her again. 'Is it all butter now, Fippy: is it?'

'It's all better, my lambkin,' said Philippa. 'It's all better; or if it isn't, it doesn't matter a docken.'

*

Later that morning, anchored off Seraglio Point, Lymond received on board the Deputy Vizier and the Chief Dragoman of the Porte, and accepted for himself and his principal staff five exquisite sets of full-length Turkish robes.

The gifts from the French King, carefully graded and labelled, had already been checked and prepared during the last days of the voyage. The Dragoman and the Vizier, expressing unqualified delight, in turn received theirs, and after drinking, with no sign of theological uneasiness, a full bottle of Onophrion's Mudanian wine, departed with formal expressions of goodwill all round.

'We are in time?' asked Onophrion, at length, coming to clear off the goblets.

'We are in time,' said Lymond, turning his eyes from the slow-moving domes; the packed houses, climbing shoulder on shoulder; the white minarets like cactus-fingers crowding the skyline; the old pink and cream sea wall and the green of the gardens and trees, seen through the empty, tiered eyes of the aqueduct of Valens. 'Sultan Suleiman will receive us on Tuesday.'

They had been given three members of the Corps of Janissaries for the length of their stay, to act as guides, interpreters, advisers and bodyguard all in one. They visited the Customhouse, briefly; then, turning her back on the gold and copper cupolas of Stamboul, the *Dauphiné* crossed the Golden Horn to Galata.

Built by the Genoese and still the foreign trading-quarter of the great city opposite, Galata sat on one ear on its hillside, locked within its tight walls and protected by the many-eyed tower which rose high in its midst. On the shore, by the wharves and the crumbling warehouses, the sheds for ship-building and artillery, the big trading-galleons lay shoulder to shoulder, their jutting rudders and flat, pear-shaped sterns staring down at the long, slender galley as she rowed smoothly past. She tied up at Artillery Gate, where the great bronze cannon from Rhodes and Tripoli and Gozo and Mohács lay unheeded in the long, weedy grass; and M. d'Aramon, Baron de Luetz, present Ambassador and longtime good servant of France in the Sublime Porte, walked forward from the quay where he and his suite had been waiting, and came aboard to greet his successor.

A man of tact, he gave no sign that he might be comparing the unconscious, half-naked prisoner of Tripoli with the man who came to receive him on deck, his short fair hair ordered and gleaming, his hands ringed, his doublet made by a master. The preliminaries, graceful as they were, did nothing to dispel the little ironies he still perceived and enjoyed, in the back of his mind. Then M. Crawford of Lymond and Sevigny, seating him where the Second Vizier had so lately sat and presenting him, through Onophrion, with an extraordinarily good cup of Muscat, began to ask questions about the status of France in the great Turkish empire; and the shade of amusement left M. d'Aramon's face.

Long ago by the post; by the interminable exchange of secretary and messenger from Stamboul to Sofia to Ragusa to Venice; across Europe to Anet or Fontainebleau, he had known of this slow, seaborne embassy, and of the elaborate gift which might reach the Sultan in time to sweeten his mind towards France; to persuade him to send Dragut and all his fleet of renegade seamen and corsairs to support France's attack on Florence and Corsica.

Now it was here; and the Sultan, accepting it, was about to march into Persia to fight a war of more moment to him than a petty investment in France's affairs was ever likely to be. The timing was bad: one had to accept it; and join in the cultivated and slightly derisory laughter, and make capital out of the pleasures or trials of the voyage.

It surprised the Baron de Luetz to be asked questions: perfectly permissable questions, courteously framed, and with no malicious intent. It surprised him still more to find his answers the subject of speculative discussion, bulwarked by a formidable massif of facts. Somewhere on the *Dauphiné*, on her dilatory journey from home, there was a tireless mind which had made it its business to observe, analyse and digest; and for whose findings the Baron began to feel considerable respect.

Whatever the aforesaid pleasures and trials of his voyage, Crawford, it was clear, had made it his business to talk to many people, from the eminent to the most casual trader and mercenary. To his observations on the struggle in Italy between France and the Emperor Charles, M. d'Aramon could add his own latest news from dispatches. To his information, political, commercial and social, on the outposts and subject countries of the great Turkish empire, M. d'Aramon found he had little to add. He said, as the unloading went on around them, and the Muscat level slowly receded, 'May I say, Mr Crawford, that I believe you have chosen a career for which you are decidedly suited?'

294

The unexcited blue gaze widened, sceptically. 'Merry Report the Vice, court-crier and squire for God's precious body? It is an appointment I can hold, I'm afraid, only briefly. . . . I am told there is some unrest in the army, and that is why the Sultan has decided to march south himself?'

'That is the rumour.' M. d'Aramon shifted a little in his chair. For the past week, on this score, the Corps Diplomatique had had to exercise considerable tact. 'The Seraglio, you will understand, is sealed from the world, and very little is heard unless the Grand Seigneur wishes it. But it seems that the army marched south in the late summer under Rustem Pasha, the Grand Vizier, less to attack than to defend the eastern borders against some inroads made by the Shah. On the way they passed through Amasiya, where Prince Mustafa, the Sultan's eldest son and his heir, rules the region. . . .'

'You speak of the son, not of Roxelana, the Sultan's present wife, but of his first concubine Gulbehar?'

D'Aramon nodded. 'He is, nevertheless, as you know, the heir. His wife and son are not in the harem but at Bursa, on the other side of the Bosphorus and he himself, until he succeeds his father as Sultan, will live elsewhere and administer the Sultan's Asian lands. He is, in my belief, a modest and able young man. But——'

'But this autumn the Sultan, here in Constantinople, found reason to believe that Prince Mustafa and the army were conspiring against him?'

The Baron de Luetz rose; and walking to the door, pulled back the hide curtain which gave them privacy from the labouring seamen on deck. There was no one within earshot. Nevertheless he left it open, and when he returned to his seat, his voice was pitched low. 'May I ask how you knew that?'

'I am naught but the lewd compilator of the labour of old astrologians. I guessed it,' said the new Ambassador mildly. 'What I don't know is, how did Suleiman hear of it?'

There was a little silence. Then, 'That is not known,' d'Aramon said quietly.

'I see,' said the younger man, tranquilly. 'But it is true, is it not, that Rustem Pasha is married to Roxelana's daughter?'

'That is so.' He had it, damn him.

'I have even heard,' pursued his host softly, 'that the Grand Vizier was Roxelana's first . . . employer?'

'It may be true,' said M. d'Aramon.

'I have a petition of my own to present to the Sultan on Tuesday,' said Mr Crawford of Lymond and Sevigny, with no change of tone. 'It will, I think, be granted and should not reflect in any way to the discredit of France. If by any chance it is refused . . . If it is refused, I shall have to use other means, and I shall resign as Ambassador. If this happens, I strongly advise that no other appointment is made until the situation with Roxelana is resolved. A chargé d'affaires should be sufficient.'

'Chesnau will be here,' said the Baron thoughtfully. 'Since I shall be there to present you . . . may I know the form your petition will take?'

The arched blue gaze, unwavering, showed no desire to avoid his. 'I wish an order to remove two persons from the Seraglio. One is a English girl who has just arrived there in error. The other is one of the Children of Tribute.'

None of his amazement revealed on his face, M. d'Aramon put, with diffidence, his last question. 'I am sorry. But I am sure there will be no difficulty, provided you are willing to be . . . generous. They are . . . family friends?'

Lymond rose. 'The girl's mother is an old and dear friend of my family.'

'And the child?'

Outside, a French voice, speaking bad Turkish, was raised in dispute: other, authoritative voices joined in and there was a trampling of feet. Lymond, moving swiftly, said, 'He is a member of my own family . . . Forgive me a moment. When I return, perhaps we should go ashore. . . .'

For a moment the Baron de Luetz sat looking at his successor's back as Crawford moved towards the scene of the trouble. The quarrelling stopped. Beside him the steward, moving soft-footed round the table, poured M. d'Aramon a last cup of wine and removed the now empty flask. But instead of going away he hesitated and M. d'Aramon, looking up, saw that the man, a Swiss, he thought, with a heavy frame and a pink, overfleshed face, was attempting to speak. 'Well?' he said.

Onophrion Zitwitz bowed, the flask clasped to his breast. 'I overheard. . . . If you will forgive me, my lord. You should know. His Excellency will not speak of it, but the child in the Seraglio is his son.'

*

If Lymond found M. d'Aramon's manner to him at all different when, returning, he disembarked and riding at the Baron's side, their joint retainers behind him, climbed the steep hill to the French Ambassador's house at the top, his own did not change from the formal.

From the big white house, with its herb and flower garden, its pebbled walks and its fountains, one could look through the vineyards of Pera and down to where the busy town of Galata descended the hill to the water. Across the creek, on the other side of the Golden Horn, lay Constantinople.

In the six days which must pass before their audience, both the retiring Ambassador and his successor spent some time among the

296

papers in M. d'Aramon's study, arranging the affairs of the French King and his humbler subjects in Turkey. As he learned to know him better, M. d'Aramon began to recognize the restlessness to which Crawford was sometimes subject; when after a morning of rapid and capable case-work he would walk up and down the low balcony, staring across at the Abode of Felicity, the famous skyline which had taken the place of the New Jerusalem, the holy city, come down from God out of heaven, prepared as a bride adorned for her husband, whose priests had cried on its completion: O Lord, guide it on the good path for infinite ages . . .

Then M. d'Aramon would suggest they assume the loose robes they wore, Turkish-fashion, over their Western dress in the street, and with Crawford at his side, and the Janissaries following, would walk down through one of the twelve gates of the century-old walls of Galata to the Tower of Christ, first built by Anastasius, or down through the narrow streets of the merchants to the ruins of the Genoese fort from which, a hundred years before, the chain had stretched over the Golden Horn to Seraglio Point.

It was a walk the Baron de Luetz himself never failed to find exhilarating. Once, walls had been built to divide the town into quarters for the true Peratins, the Greeks and the Turks. Long ago these divisions had risen like multilingual yeast and most bountifully overflowed: Franks, Jews, Moslems, Ragusans, Florentines and Sciots thronged and spilled up and down the ill-cobbled streets: sailors, joiners, caulkers; Armenian merchants in long Greek dress and blue, red and white turbans, calling the charms of their cloths and their carpets; Ragusans dressed like Venetian merchants; yellow-turbaned Jews interpreting, smooth-tongued, or hurrying between shop or broker or printing-press; Janissaries; gardeners from the vineyards and occasionally, as nowhere else in the realms of the Sultan, a drunk man, ejected from one of the town's two hundred taverns.

For this was a Christian town as well as a Moslem one, with Christian vices and virtues. As well as mosques there were churches, convents and synagogues: mingling with the voice of the muezzin, proclaiming five times a day the omnipotence and unity of God, was the two-toned chime of iron on iron, the primitive call permitted by Islam to all the Greek churches, in the absence of the infidel bell.

Indeed, to a stranger, the overwhelming force of its noise was the first impression he received of Galata. The vibration of its foundry and craft-shops; the chanting, the calling and hammering from the crowded wharves where the ranked ships up to five hundred tons could berth tied up to the houses, and during winter a thousand vessels could lie in the whole half-mile width of the Horn.

The rumbling of carts and the clatter of mules struggling up and down the steep slopes, laden with cargo, pressing aside the little asses bearing women to church or baths or burial-ground: Armenians

297

sitting sidesaddle in their high linen headdresses, speaking Slav or broken Italian; Peratine French and resident women of other races in taffeta, satin and lace, buttoned with gold and silver, their caps wound about with jewelled silks, their arms heavy with bracelets, as their escorts rode ahead, pressing aside the loud-mouthed, cheerful throng.

Snatches of laughter, and a song from a wine-booth. A shrieking block in one alley as a long chain of Armenian porters, arms interlaced, brought up from the harbour a great two-ton fat-bellied keg on a pole. The clangour, night and day, outside the gates from the new arsenal with its hundred arches or vaults for the building and dry-docking of galleys.

D'Aramon took the new Ambassador everywhere: even to the foundry and barracks at Topkhane, on the Bosphorus shore, where the viziers and Imáms sat on sofas crying *Allâh! Allâh!* as the stokers threw wood on the furnaces; and the founders, naked but for slippers and caps and the thick protective sleeves on their arms, mixed gold and silver for the True Faith with the bubbling brass in the foundry; and sheep were sacrificed, screaming, in the red glare of the furnace as its mouth was forced open with long iron hooks, and the white metal flowed to the moulds.

That day, they were too late for dinner, and M. d'Aramon took his colleague instead to a Greek tavern serving a good Ancona wine and spiced white bread and honey and Tomourra caviare, cut whole and salted. 'As you know, I dare say . . . in Stamboul you will find cookshops, but no taverns or inns as one would expect in a Christian country.' M. d'Aramon was feeling stimulated and modestly pleased with himself. It was some time since he had travelled about Galata on foot. He was a little footsore, perhaps—the streets were shocking—but otherwise for his age quite remarkably fresh.

'*Nulla apud Turcas esse diversoria* . . . Yes, I know,' said Crawford mildly. They were the first words he had spoken for some time. He had not, M. d'Aramon noted, indulged overmuch in the caviare, although he had taken a little more wine than was his usual remarkably spare habit. A trembling flicker of sapphire blue flame from the ring on the other man's hand, lying still by his goblet, drew the Baron's attention, just as Crawford added, in the same breath, 'I wonder . . . are there horses one might hire to the Embassy?'

'My dear sir!' Instant solicitude; but beneath it, an undeniably selfish shadow of pleasure. Exhausted. And he could give him . . . what? Twenty years? But it was, of course, a very steep climb back to the hilltop at Pera.

M. d'Aramon obtained the horses, and with his Janissaries walking behind, returned home with the new Ambassador who smiled, but did not again speak until, dismounting in the Embassy courtyard, they walked indoors together. There he turned, and holding out his hand to M. d'Aramon said, 'Will you forgive me? As Abraham entertained the angels with hearth-cakes, you have entertained me, and I am deeply indebted. It is to my shame that I have not your energy.'

His voice was steady and the hand he offered was cool. But from the roots of his damp yellow hair, all Crawford's skin, d'Aramon saw with surprise, was sparkling with sweat.

He said something, he remembered, and stood watching as the new Ambassador, withdrawing his hand, smiled and turned into his own private chamber. Later, d'Aramon was thinking about it again, in his own study, when the fat Swiss steward scratched on the door and then entered.

He brought the explanation for this curious behaviour, quite simply, with his apologies.

'M. le Comte has recently had an infection of the shoulder, Your Excellency, which troubles him if he does not have a sufficiency of rest. He would not himself venture to upset your programme, but if you would be so kind as to ensure that he has an opportunity to dine here at the Embassy each day, followed by an hour, no more, in which to repose . . .'

'But of course,' said M. d'Aramon, roused to a lively anxiety. 'I did not know. He did not, of course, mention it. I trust no harm . . . I hope,' said M. d'Aramon hurriedly, as another thought struck him, 'that Tuesday's ceremony will not be too much for him?'

'Thank you, sir. It is kind of you, sir. You may rest perfectly assured,' said Master Zitwitz with gentle and absolute confidence, 'that His Excellency will attend Tuesday's ceremony with no difficulty whatsoever.'

19

CHIOS AND CONSTANTINOPLE

About half-way between Aleppo and Chios, it came to Jerott Blyth, like Achillini discerning the bile duct, that he hated ichneumons.

Afterwards, with the mountains, the steppes, the gorges behind him; having lived through the sleepless days in the stifling heat of the tents and passed the labouring nights in the saddle of his small Turkish horse, which could walk or gallop but was unable to trot, or on the jolting back of one of the two hundred camels in their long caravan, Jerott was prepared to admit that for many reasons that long journey, six weeks in all, between Aleppo and Constantinople was one of the worst in his life.

Through all the misery of mosquitoes and dust-storms, of stale meat and sour milk and brackish water, through the perpetual cries of the camel-men; the plodding clank of the bells, the barking of the leashed dogs in the casals they passed; the rauccous groups of itinerant merchants forming and reforming among the riders, inquisitive, insistent; stinking, some of them, worse than their camels, there rode at his side Pierre Gilles discoursing in Latin on the glories of Constantinople (*forma illius est triangula*), and of the ancient city which battle and fire had reduced to ruins (*Adde incendia, et ruinas, quas cum alii barbari, tum postremam Turci ediderunt, qui iam centum annos non cessant funditus antiquae urbis vestigia delere*).

Listening, with the ears of suffering and boredom, Jerott recognized dimly at least that to Gilles the old city of the Byzantine emperors was more real than the city of Suleiman: as he spoke of underground cisterns, baths and palaces, of the Forum of Constantine and the purple pillar beneath which, Cedrinus had written, twelve hampers of holy writings had been buried; of the Gate of Diana showing the contests of Gygantus, the thunderbolts of Jove, the Neptune with Trident; of the triple bronze snakes from the Shrine of the Oracle at Delphi, whose three heads ran with milk, with water and wine; as he told of the golden pyramid of cupids whose flying bronze image revealed how the wind blew.

He heard of the Sacred Palace with the Halls of Pearl and of Gold; of the Throne of Solomon with its golden lions and its rose trees of gilded bronze with jewelled and enamelled birds on its branches which sang in harmony as the lions roared and music played while the Emperor spoke to his subjects. Of the mystic phial of the Sigma whose wine flowed through a golden pineapple into a silver basin filled with almonds and pistachios. Of the jewelled reliquaries and the looted statues of marble and bronze; of the great library with its works of philosophers, poets and scientists; works of horoscopy, astrology, numerology; manuscripts in Persian and Hebrew and Greek; fragments of original scriptures . . .

'You should write about it,' said Jerott one day, stemming the flood, and Gilles, jolting about on his mule, the ichneumon on his shoulder in the folds of his cloak, raised his eyebrows and shrugged. It was Pichon, the secretary, who came alongside later and whispered, 'His papers were lost, Mr Blyth, on the journey he took with the Sultan and M. d'Aramon five years ago. All his notes for just such a book, and a deal of original writings he came across in his research. All lost as the army travelled through some defile not far from Bitlis. A disaster for the world. He has never forgotten it, or been able to bring himself to start over again. It is better not to open the subject.'

With which Jerott, having succeeded better than he had hoped, most heartily agreed.

For on his other side rode Marthe, the exquisite enemy, whose presence for him was a physical anguish which did not grow less. Marthe, the cold and the treacherous, whom he wanted; and who was sister to Francis Crawford of Lymond.

He is my brother, she had said in Aleppo; and staring silently back at her, the lines of anger still on his face, he had known beyond doubt that it was true. No freak of genetics, pranking through generations, could account for two people, man and girl, endowed each with the same wayward mordacity; the same isolation; the same double-edged gifts. After a long time, Jerott had said, 'Does he know?'

Sitting as she had sat throughout, her hands loose on her lap, Marthe answered without any movement. 'He guesses, I think. Once, he came near to asking; but you may be sure he will never question too closely. He is far too afraid.'

'*Afraid?*' Afraid to acknowledge, to provide for an illegitimate half-sister? It was the oddest thing Marthe had said. If it were true, thought Jerott; no wonder she was bitter. And yet if Lymond had suspected the truth—and looking back, play by play and prick by prick, Jerott suddenly realized, with extraordinary clarity, that of course he had—why had he chosen to ignore it completely? To treat her, from the day they first met, with a hostility hardly disguised?

Pride? Hardly. The loud-mouthed brown-haired egotist who had been second Baron Crawford of Culter might have sown his wild oats over half Europe, surely, without reflecting upon the honour of his wife Sybilla or either of his two sons. If there was a byblow fallen on hard times, one did what one could. Lymond was not a poor man. Neither was Richard, the third Baron, his brother. Jerott said, aloud, 'I don't understand.'

In Marthe's blue eyes, studying him then, there was a curious look. 'He doesn't want you to understand,' she said. And added quickly, as he opened his mouth, 'Save your breath. I have nothing to tell you. I am a bastard, brought up in the charge of the Dame de

301

Doubtance, of Blois and Lyons, of father and mother unknown. All I have been told all my life is that a rich Scottish lord, Francis Crawford of Lymond, is my brother.'

'Then when you met him, you thought . . .'

The cool voice was sardonic. 'One early outgrows one's visions of being transported to luxury. I knew when he stood in that room in Marseilles that he had not known I existed.'

But Lymond had realized in the end who she was. Day by day, becoming surer and surer. And far from acknowledging it, had openly shown his distaste. Jerott said, helplessly, 'I still don't . . . some of the things he has done I . . . cannot condone. But I have never known him be less than generous.'

'Then we are different, my brother and I,' said Marthe dryly; and rose to her feet. 'Generosity is a virtue I have had no chance to study. Or it may have escaped me, perhaps, through the parent we do not have in common . . . always assuming, of course, there *is* one parent we don't have in common. . . .'

And Jerott, riding sticky and filthy in that tumultuous cavalcade, thought once again of all that these words could imply, and remembered the look in Marthe's eyes as she spoke them. And it struck him that if Francis Crawford and his sister showed little mercy towards the world and each other, it was not without cause.

They had never spoken of it again. He had no cause to trust her. He knew her dishonest. He was aware that she was travelling to Constantinople merely to rejoin Georges Gaultier and that although she had offered him, supposedly, the whereabouts of Lymond's child—the child, my God, thought Jerott distractedly, of her own blood—she felt no concern about its recovery.

And in spite of all that, he remained obsessed with her: with the long veiling lashes round the intense blue of her eyes; the high polished brow over which her hair fell, cream and ochre and lemon and chrome in the sun; and the colour of the sun on her cheekbones and the thin bridge of her nose. The slimness of her arms . . . the long, slender bones of her foot. Her voice; her wit; her laugh when she was entertained.

For whatever reason, Marthe laughed easily on all that laborious journey: even when, reaching the big khan at Ulukişla, they and all the caravan were detained, together with all those travellers already within, by a detachment of mounted Spahis from Eregli, a day's journey north. By the third day, when the tally at the door of the khan was full, and Jerott was becoming extremely uneasy, they were released and allowed to continue their journey. Eregli, when they stayed there next day, was full of activity, and there were Janissaries' tents, with the ceremonial cooking-pots of more than one company set in the plain between Eregli and their next halt at Karapinar. The rumour was that the Sultan was on his way south.

At Konya, two days farther on, Jerott and his three companions together with Marthe's woman and two guiding Janissaries left the main caravan and waited with their mules and horses and three baggage camels and driver for a party travelling west, to Izmir.

It was less warm, there on the high plateau, than it had been: the hills around the old town were dusty and bare, and the khan neglected. Using the night once more for sleeping, their rest was perpetually fractured by the voice of Herpestes, and the rats he slaughtered and brought to his master, bloody and warm from the kill. During the day Jerott listened, without enthusiasm, to the voice of Pierre Gilles describing the glories of ancient Iconium: the citadel (into which they could not penetrate) and the mosque with its ranks of stolen Byzantine capitals (which they could not visit). There was a tekke on the east of the town where the founder of the Whirling Dervishes lay in his marble sarcophagus; but Marthe merely smiled when Jerott suggested, acidly, that she should pay her respects, and the quality of the smile, and the recollections it brought, had a predictable effect: he began drinking again.

Thereafter the journey to Izmir was blurred by that circumstance. He remembered the ferry to the island of Chios because the ferryman was a thief whom he had to throw into the water, which gave him much satisfaction, even though some twenty close relatives of the Syrian arrived, none less than nine feet in height, and would have served him in the same way or worse if his Janissaries had not prevented them. He remembered a voice, presumably Marthe's, quoting with gentle amusement, 'Alas . . . if angels should sniff at his shroud?' and the old tub-thumper saying, in plain French for once, 'What happens if we can't get a ship?'

At that point, governed by a soldier's instinct which never entirely deserted him, Jerott Blyth painfully pulled himself together. Whatever Marthe and Pierre Gilles might desire, he had not come to Chios as fast as abominable travelling conditions would allow merely to take ship for Constantinople. He had come because the *Peppercorn* had called here to load mastic, and to disembark, so it was said, a Syrian woman and a two-year-old boy.

In the grip therefore of a high degree of nausea and a mind-wrecking headache, Jerott deposited the whole of his party, with ichneumon, at the house of Joseph Justinian, the French Consul at Chios, and left them drinking cherry syrup on the wooden balcony into the gardens while he went, with the help of a secretary, to find the English Consulate, and then those officers of the Seigniority, the Genoese administration, who might be able to tell him the fate of the *Peppercorn*'s passengers.

It wasn't difficult. It was extremely simple, in fact. The *Peppercorn* had sailed in, loaded with mastic, and gone. The Syrian woman had disembarked; reported as required to the Council, and had set up

303

business in Chios. For some reason, Jerott had expected to find her, like her brother, settled in one of the silk-growing colonies, or in one of the villages of the Mastichochonia, where *pistacia lentiscus* wept its gummy St Theodore's tears from August to September. It had not occurred to him that she might simply continue with the trade she had followed in Mehedia: that of running a brothel. He obtained its direction, dismissed the unwilling secretary, and set off.

Chios the island was little more than a hundred and twenty miles round all its circumference. Chios the city lay round its harbour with rocky hills at its back and a big double-walled castle to the north, sharing its hill with the colonnades of a natural hot bath, built like a temple. The flag of St George flew over a bourse as adequate, he was told, as that of Lyons or the Royal Exchange in London itself and the city, four miles from the mainland, was a trading centre for the fine mohairs of Anatolia as well as its own silk and cotton and marble and the aromatic resinous gum with which one qualified one's new wine or spirits, or drank mingled with honey and water.

Chios paid ten thousand ducats in tribute to Turkey, and could afford to. Its soil was a garden. Outside the walls Jerott had seen fig trees, almonds, apricots; date palms, orange and lemon trees; grapes, olives, pomegranates and a wealth of late summer flowers. The streets were narrow but the houses, unlike Turkish houses, were handsome, of dressed snow-white stone; and the people were richly attired: Greeks, Genoese, Jews and their beautiful wives in velvet, damask and satin, their sleeves laced with silk ribbons, their narrow aprons fringed and embroidered. Their hair was long, under tall ribbed coifs of white satin, sewn with pearls and with gold, and half veiled in yellow and white, through which their chains, their jewels and trinkets glittered and trembled. Look out, had said the attaché at Aleppo, for the partridges and the women, whose very husbands acted as panders. Nine English shillings a night, had added the attaché at Aleppo, seeing him off. And supper included.

And indeed, under his feet, all red beak and claw, waddled the partridges. And before him, swaying and graceful, the women walked to and fro, smiling. Quite insensibly, Jerott quickened his pace.

The house of the Syrian woman was tall and wreathed in vine-leaves. A discreet notice, in Greek and in Turkish, directed custom to the garden gate at the back. Jerott, reading it, was aware of a burst of laughter from the alley behind him, but was unaware until he turned and found himself surrounded that the laughter was directed against himself.

The men were all, he thought, dellies: the roving adventurers from the north who, dressed in wild-beast skins and with little else but their weapons, earned their livelihood by their strong arms, and attached themselves to anyone who would pay them.

These were dressed partly in skins and partly in folds of coarse cotton. They had good boots on their legs, and strong swords at their sides, and there were perhaps five of them, rolling together. They were drunk.

Jerott, who was alone, and on the French Consul's advice without his dress sword and dagger, cursed the mischance that had brought them. It was possible, and, from their jeers and their cackling laughter as they approached him, very probable, that they were merely after some sport. Caught where he was, he was fair game. He might also be expected to have on him at least the price of his proposed entertainment. Eyeing the happy quintet as they closed in on him, Jerott decided with resignation that this time discretion was preferable. Beside the front door at his back there was a bell-pull. He backed to it, grasped it and heaved.

The five men stopped. Opposite him and to right and to left ran a blank wall. No help there, and no help it seemed from a chance passer-by, for the alley, so far as it went before curving out of sight on each side, was completely deserted. Behind him, the bell jangled into silence without eliciting more than renewed sounds of derision from his tormentors: as he pulled again, Jerott said calmly, in Greek, 'You look as if you would know, friend. Are they the right sort in here? Whom would you recommend?'

One of them at least was sober enough or had enough Greek to understand. The man nearest to Jerott, broad-shouldered and with a fringe of red beard, grinned, showing the yellowed stumps of his teeth, and said, 'They will lay you out well, *giáur*.'

'I trust,' said Jerott unhurriedly, 'it will be the other way around.' Damn the women. It came to him that assaults from the street were perhaps not unknown at this house. No matter how long one rang or one knocked, they would probably take good care to ignore it. At the back, if he could only get there, they would have their clients' entrance, and probably one or two of a guard. Meanwhile, he did not need to turn to know that the wall in which the front door was set was both windowless and too high to scale.

Ah, well. 'They are out. A pity,' said Jerott; and ignoring the ring of men, turned, casually, as if to walk away to his left.

They jumped on him just as, at the last second, he wheeled and ducked in the opposite direction, his hand already holding the knife he always carried, inside his doublet. He cut at the sword-arm hurtling down on him; dragged himself free of one over-extended grip, broke another; half dodged a cudgel on one side of his ribs and cut a slice through the muscle of a bare, hairy thigh. Then he was off like a hare with the pack of them after him; up the side of the building and praying that the garden gate by which the Syrian lady's clients might enter was unlocked, narrow and handy.

It was handy. It was narrow. It was not only unlocked but open.

And not only open but completely blocked by a satisfied client, in the act of letting himself out.

He was a very little man, in a turban; and hardly, Jerott supposed, with regret, at the top of his strength. But he was too hard-pressed just then to pause to consider. Jerott flung himself at that half-open door with a wordless bellow of warning, and flinging the little man back with his shoulder, spun round to push the door shut against the onrush of men at his heels.

He was too late to close the door, but the sight of him waiting, knife in hand, in that narrow gap was enough to make the first two hesitate as shoulder to shoulder they threw themselves through the fast-closing entrance. Then their swords flashed, and Jerott's knife came up in a shower of sparks, and there was another, much louder clatter of steel at his elbow which was followed, almost immediately, by a squeal from one of the two dellies before him. One of the men crowding in from the street suddenly dropped back, and as another leaped into his place, Jerott snatched a second to glance hurriedly round to the source of the noise.

It came from the little man in the turban who, recovered from the thrust which had bounced him back inside the garden, had returned to the door and was standing on the balls of his feet, with eighteen inches of steel in one hand and a long-handled axe in the other. Inside the turban, the scarred, sun-darkened face was familiar. 'Well, now,' said Archibald Abernethy. 'D'ye think we should rush them; or just let them run on inside and exhaust themselves?'

Suddenly, the odds were utterly perfect. So long as they fought in the doorway, they couldn't be rushed. They had weapons. They had all Jerott's formidable experience. And they had every dirty trick a little Scots mahout had learned in a lifetime of Eastern bazaars. As the second man gasped and fell, choking, Archie pursed his lips and gave a small whistle. 'It doesna seem fair,' he said, axe whirling, dodging and stabbing at Jerott Blyth's elbow. 'But I heard the lassie call them in yesterday.'

'Who?' said Jerott, gasping. Two against three now: even better. A pity to summon help at this stage and just spoil it. Then, like a nightmare ride of some dwarvish Valkyrie, the air turned black, as prompt to their call, half a hundred unwieldy scarlet-beaked partridges laboured on urgent wings out of the firmament, and hitting turbans, weapons, arms, shoulders, chests in their haste, descended with the weighty assurance of the loved into the garden.

Inside the house, an interrogatory door opened. Outside the house, another door shut, as the men pressing upon it from the outside abruptly withdrew and fled. 'O michty,' said Archie with sorrow. 'They've flattened a partridge.'

Jerott Blyth took him by the shoulder and shook it. 'Were you inside?'

'Oh, aye,' said Archie.

'The Syrian woman is . . .'

'Oh, aye,' said Archie. 'I know. I went to see her.'

'What about it then?' With an effort, gasping, Jerott kept his voice low. 'Does she still have the baby?'

'No. She says it's in Constantinople,' said Archie. 'At the house of a nightingale-dealer. She paid the sponge-boats to take him.'

It was the same direction Marthe had given him. 'Do you think she's speaking the truth?' Jerott asked. Someone had come through the house door and was crossing the garden towards him. He opened the door and a partridge strutted in, clucking.

'I think so. She didna know why I was asking. But I was going to ask down at the rocks to make sure.'

Jerott, too, had seen the brown Egyptian divers, sliding into the water knife in hand to wrest the sponges from the sharp rocks, and the dead treasure from the bones of the ocean. They carried oil, it was said, in their mouths to spit out at the bottom, through whose magnifying gouts the smallest coin became plain. Or with sponges stopping their mouths, soaked in oil, stayed below, seventy, a hundred fathoms under the surface, until their air was exhausted. There were many tales of the divers: how they were reared on dry biscuit so that they would remain thin, how they were trained from small children, and might not marry until they had stayed half an hour under water. He had seen the small boats travelling north, laden like ill-treated asses with their ragged, billowing cargo: the sponges brought ashore every night in mountainous sackloads for drying. . . .

There was no one in the lane or the alley. Shutting the door, Jerott walked away, without looking back, from the Syrian's house. He said to Archie, 'They could hide a child in a sponge-boat.'

'It struck me,' agreed Archie, 'that it would be an easy way to get the wean into the town.'

They went, none the less, down to the harbour; and on the way Archie heard Jerott's account, edited, of how he had traced the *Peppercorn* here to Chios; and in return heard Archie's story, unexpurgated, of how he had called at every port used by the English until, by elimination, he had landed at Chios. 'You'll not have heard from Mr Crawford?' he ventured. 'If he got the other child and the Somerville lassie?'

Francis. It was Francis's money he had been using just now, out on the rocks, to smooth the path of their interrogation. It had been Lymond's money which had paid for the confirmation they had just received: that a child of two years had indeed left on one of the sponge-boats, some time previously, bound for Stamboul. Because Marthe had shown no concern for the child he, Jerott, had come determined to find it.

If he still wished to find it, he must go to Constantinople, with

307

Marthe; with Pierre Gilles and his bloody Herpestes. And worst, he had to come face to face with Francis, whose past actions he could not condone . . . whom he had promised never to leave . . . about whom he knew something which, he suspected, for his very life he must appear not to know. . . .

He had told Archie nothing of that; and only the barest account of Marthe's and Gilles's presence. 'I've heard nothing,' he said. 'He may even have the girl and the child and be on his way home.' But it was a faint hope. Lymond would never have left without sending word of it.

'No,' said Archie. With Jerott he had walked out on the low mole, scanning the small boats tied up in the harbour and the big galleons anchored outside in the channel, their lamps beginning to glow in the sinking evening light. On the other arm of the bay, the Genoese lantern, freshly lit, burned red against a sky washed with pale apple green. A flock of cranes, a black wedge against the pale light, flew across the sky and was gone on the long wintering journey south. 'It's getting late,' Jerott said.

'It's late.' Under the turban, the broken-nosed face was passive and lined. 'Pray God it's not too late.'

Jerott stopped.

'He's in Constantinople,' said Archie. 'That I've heard. He couldn't catch up with the girl or the wean before they both got there, and he hasna got them out yet. They've made him Ambassador.'

Jerott was startled out of his thoughts. 'But d'Aramon . . .?'

'M. d'Aramon's going back to France, and a loon called Jean Chesnau is going as chargé d'affaires. Mr Crawford's made accredited Ambassador, which means he's got the power of France behind any demands he may make. . . .'

Jerott let out a long breath. 'Then surely they'll give him both Philippa Somerville and the boy that she followed. The other child we only have to locate. He isn't a child of Devshirmé, poor brat.' He sobered. 'Unless a report of Gabriel's death somehow got through and was acted on.'

There was a short silence. A longboat, pulling strongly, moved out into the harbour, its wake thin as a paint-line behind it. A cloud of fireflies, like sparks from newly lit wood, fussed through the darkening air and was gone. An aroma of cooking, borne from a galleasse which had just put up her awnings, floated, seductively, over the water. 'They say . . .' said Archie. 'They say in Candia that Gabriel isna dead.'

'I know,' said Jerott. 'What have you heard?'

'They say he was nursed back to health in Zuara,' said Archie in his flattest Scots voice. 'And they say that Rustem, the Grand Vizier now with the army, has sent a new deputy north. He's been in Stamboul this week or two back. By the name of Jubrael Pasha.'

'Oh, my God. Francis . . .' said Jerott.

'If it's true . . . it's too late,' said Archie. 'It'll all be over by now.'

*

After nearly a month at Topkapi, Philippa was elected to more than Paphian honours: she was appointed to make music for Roxelana herself.

Thus were justified all the crowns Kate and Gideon had spent on her study of lyre and of spinet. It was the only field, so far, in which the Pearl of Fortune had shown any precocity, other than the feat of keeping her head, her reason and her sense of the ridiculous amid conditions of civilized lunacy.

To her fellow odalisques, she was aware, the only lunacy was hers and her protests a matter of friendly derision when, upon her third bath and her seventh hairwash of the week, she struggled against the stinging boredom of uprooting her hairline and eyebrows.

At first, sitting through extraordinary lectures on how to paint her lips red; to dye her eyebrows and lashes, to draw, with a steady hand, a black line above and under her lashes with a filthy mixture of antimony powder and oil they called *surmèh*, Philippa was too over-awed to protest. When you are living, surrounded by giant black eunuchs, in a palace where the master has power of instant and hideous death, you do not niggle at trifles. When they spent half an hour painting her finger- and toe-nails, going on to demonstrate the uses of *hènnah* against perspiration and the alternative uses of *kohl*, *kajal* and *tutia* as a cooling eyeblack which also guarded the wearer from the perils of the Evil Eye, she began, after a day or two, to suffer a terrible impulse to giggle. She acquired her own moleshair brushes and pots, and learned how to get the paint off with linen and cream. She learned how to make *kohl* with lemons and plumbago over the Bath Superintendent's brazier; and how to make face-powder with ground rice, borax and cowrie shells, mixed and dried in a melon rind with beanflour, lemons and eggs, but when they tried to put it on her face she exploded in a cloud of sneezes and laughter, and they had to give up for that day.

She grew bolder. She refused the Chinese mudpack of oil and rice-flour and would not let them shave off her eyebrows, although she submitted to the day-long hair brushing, the dressing with tonics of olive oil and maidenhair fern; the plaiting and scenting. On that point, watching her long, mouse-coloured hank gather lustre and colour, she was prepared to admit that, as Kate used to say naggingly, a little attention produced amazing results.

Under the bathing and massage, also, her skin was improving: that must be said. The fruit, too, had something to do with it: the apples and pears; the plums and raisins and figs; the grapes and peaches and melons. The red cherries of Sariyár, each yielding a hundred drops of their juice. The juice of Bokhara apricots, Mardín plums; Azerbaijân pears. Grapes from Smyrna; apples from Kojá-ili; Temesvár prunes. Water-ices made of snow flavoured with fruit-juice, pomegranates . . . Khusháf made from Stamboul peaches flavoured with amber and musk.

Kate and Gideon and she had led a life of simplicity: a loving community of amiable pursuits with which, making music, laughing and talking, they had filled the flying days of her childhood, when baths and diet and fussing about one's appearance would have been as irrelevant as engraving the Lord's Prayer on the head of a pin.

Something of grace and good grooming, no doubt, had been missed. Walking up and down rebelliously, over the deep carpet in Kiaya Khátún's room, Philippa did not enjoy having pointed out to her, in that deep, even voice, the undoubted faults of her posture and carriage. Because one cannot clown one's way quite through everything, she learned to stand and to sit so that no one sang out something rude and nothing forced her to think out a reply. Under the Mistress of the Wardrobe, she learned to execute fine embroidery, to make rose-leaf pillows; to distinguish brocatelle from brocade, velvet from Bursa from Cyprus velvet; to tell the quality and the price of a pearl.

They were allowed to use their own small kitchens for lessons and experiments. It was unlikely, to say the least of it, that she would ever find herself explaining to Betty, in the big, cosy old kitchen at Flaw Valleys, how to make crystallized violets, or mince-meat pies, or rice dressed with butter and almonds, but she found this the least boring part of the day. Because of her appearance she was spared some of the other things which came every day, in covered dishes, from the long range of harem kitchens. Such as tripe, the Prince of Dishes. She had stopped quoting that, since the Kislar Agha had spoken about it. Tripe, with pepper and cloves, had been one of the Prophet's favourite dishes. The Prophet had been fond of his food. *'The love of sweetmeats comes from the Faith. The Faithful are sweet; the wicked, sour.'*

The Prophet had said a few other things too, as she was reminded on the day when her eyebrows were plucked. It had been altogether one of the less happy days, when Kuzucuyum, who had a slight temperature, had been kept in the nursery quarters, and when, that morning, she had received with the other novices her first lesson, in Kiaya Khátún's golden, ironical voice, on how to attract, to foster and to satisfy the peculiar cravings of man.

One does not live on a farm in the Border country of England and remain unduly naïve. On the other hand, for Philippa up to that day, the world had been divided into people, some of whom, like Kate and herself, were female, and some of them male. Whatever the sex of your friend, you extended to him or to her the kindness, the courtesy, the thoughtfulness which affection prompted, and would expect to receive the same in return. Very occasionally, at Flaw Valleys, Philippa had observed someone—a servant, a neighbour—embark on some long, subtle campaign designed to prompt favours. They had received short shrift from Kate.

Between human beings, it was an indignity. Between friends, it was an insult. Between man and woman, as a means to promote love, it seemed to Philippa, there would be surely nothing more childish and degrading than a planned and detailed exercise to provoke and allure.

'Look, it doesn't hurt,' Laila had said soothingly as Philippa sat bolt upright under the tweezers. 'You'll look a different person.'

Philippa gazed at her with the eyes of despair. 'But I'm a different person *now*. All they're doing is making us all look the *same*.'

'Lie down.' The Mistress of the Baths stood no nonsense. 'There is a standard. You must conform to it.'

Fleur de Lis, amused, said, 'Your hair shines. You do not mind that? Then why object to having your features improved?'

Between finger and thumb, the tweezers nipped their implacable way over her skin. 'All right,' said Philippa. 'Let's take care of what's there already. But why spend so much time and emotion and energy upon improving on it? I'm happy with my face as it is. If it's not frightening you or the eunuchs silly, I don't see why we can't all leave it alone.'

The Mistress paused, tweezers in hand, and regarded her. 'You have good points,' she said. 'The eyes; the bones. I have little to complain of in the hands. The flesh will come. But you have not yet that which will draw your lord's eyes as you stand with the others in the Golden Road. One day—Allâh preserve her, long hence—Roxelana Sultan will enter the green fields of Paradise, or, Allâh forbid, the Lord himself will leave to walk in the paths of the Blessed. Then each night one of you will be chosen; and will be sent to me, and to Kiaya Khátún and the Wardrobe Mistress to be bathed and painted and scented and robed as you have been shown. Then, when you enter the Grand Seigneur's chamber, and the old women part the sheets at the foot, and you draw yourself up, as you have been taught, until you lie at his side . . . then you will have need of every art you have learned, to charm and to arouse; to pique and to surprise; to know when to satisfy and how to leave unsatisfied something he will not take to another.

'If you please him; if you do as you have been told, you may become First Khátún, his bedfellow, with a suite of your own, where he may visit you: where you may cook for him and entertain him by day as well as by night. If you bear him a son, you may rule, through your son, the whole Ottoman Empire. *Now* will you lie still while I pluck?'

In spite of her goose-pimples, Philippa laughed. But later, taken to task alone by Kiaya Khátún for her disobedience, Philippa indulged

311

in spite of herself with an outburst. 'The cooking lessons, the sewing, the scenting, the painting—it's nothing to do with life or culture or accomplishments or self-respect. It's a ritual aimed at provoking the senses. It's the same as scrubbing the pigs the day before market. The effect on the girls doesn't matter. We're being turned out and polished like buttons, for the Sultan's petty adornment.'

Kiaya Khátún, unsurprised, did not stir from her pile of delicate cushions. 'Of course,' she said. 'That is the function of the harem precisely. Did you believe you had joined a seminar for feminine culture? Very few of your companions, I promise you, would wish it. Do they strike you as unhappy? They have nothing to do but study how to make themselves desirable. Were they to tell you the truth, their only complaint might well be that, under this Sultan, it is put to no use.'

Philippa's straight brown gaze did not waver. 'I know. They're not unhappy,' she said. 'Any woman will run to seed like that, given the chance. You get sort of hypnotized by the mirror, and you're still painted when they lay you in your coffin. I don't want it to happen to me.'

There were some papers lying at Kiaya Khátún's side. She picked them up with her little, ringed hands, and looked up at Philippa. 'If you are summoned by the Sultan you will have to go. You know that.'

'Yes,' said Philippa. 'The boys are told the same thing. But *they* go to school.'

'Outside the bedchamber,' said Kiaya Khátún, watching her quietly, 'the boys will have men's lives to lead. Moreover, it has been ordained by Mohammed that women should not be treated as intellectual beings . . . lest they aspire to equality with men.'

'Do you agree?' said Philippa Somerville directly.

There was a little silence, during which Kiaya Khátún, her black eyebrows arched, stared at Philippa, coolly surprised. But when she spoke, she sounded less angry than thoughtful. 'You are an outspoken child, are you not?' said Güzel. 'I will answer your question with another. Are there any of your acquaintance, men or women, with whom you do not consider yourself equal?'

'Kate,' said Philippa, and flushed. 'My mother. And my father, when he was alive. And there's a woman in Scotland . . . whose name is Sybilla,' She stopped.

'You have, I see, a commendable degree of honesty,' said Güzel gravely. 'There are three people to whom you feel inferior.'

From pink, Philippa went scarlet all down her neck and the flat, transparent front of her blouse. 'Then I put it badly,' she said. 'There are three I know will always be better than I am, no matter how long I live. As for everybody else, I don't see how I can tell till I'm older. When you're sixteen you're inferior to practically everybody. I can do what I like with Kuzucuyum, for he's only two. If he were sixteen he might very well show me up as a moron.'

312

'And his father?' said Güzel.

'Shows everybody up as a moron,' said Philippa, who had learned a good many skills in a month. 'The point is, even if you were equal to him, you wouldn't feel equal to him, if you know what I mean. My mother can handle him.'

Kiaya Khátún veiled her eyes over the laughter within them. 'Your mother,' she said, 'seems to have enjoyed a large number of successes. . . . I am having you registered for a short course of tuition in the Princes' school. You will be escorted there and back every morning, and we shall see later whether the course might be developed. The report here says that you are exceptionally quick to train, if one ignores your slow progress with Turkish. Also'—as Philippa, paling with pleasure and amazement, was opening her mouth—'you are further advanced than any in the harem, I am told, in the execution of music. In the afternoons, from now on, you will have the extra duty of presenting yourself to play in the apartments of Roxelana Sultan, and to perform any other service she may require. This will take you out of the main building of the harem and is an exceptional honour. I shall accompany you.'

Which was how, as Philippa confided to her diary later that evening, the Fates took a hand in the headlong diploma course in Running to Seed.

Next day, Philippa was moved out of the little dormitory she shared with nine others, and given a room, along the same narrow corridor, to herself. It was still more of a prison than a room, with tiny windows overlooking a courtyard and a double grille in the corridor wall, locked on its inner side, through which the slaves were able to kindle her lamp. Apart from rugs and cushions and a single low folding table, the room was empty. Her bedding, neatly rolled, was kept on a wide high shelf, reached by a ladder, together with such possessions as she had.

To suit her new dignity, her wardrobe was increased, and the number and quality of her jewels. To look after them she had, in addition to Tulip, a pleasant soft-spoken negress for her own, and a small allowance of slipper-money for presents. And for the first time, that morning, she missed the interminable painting and prinking, and went instead, with her servants and eunuch, down the narrow stairs and along the network of passages until she came to the Black Eunuch's courtyard, where on her first day the Kislar Agha had seen her. There, in a series of small interlocked rooms overlooking the courtyard, the young princes of the harem were once educated.

Now, since the Sultan's heirs were grown men and none had been born since except to Khourrém his wife, the daily tutors had little to do but attend a handful of the younger well-born: a vizier's two sons, and the son of a friend of Khourrém's. Blowing under her veil, with her new high arched boots pinching, but a vast satisfaction under her flat nacré velvet, Philippa sat down crosslegged with her escort in a row at the back of her juniors, and proceeded, with an eagerness which would have paralysed her mother's entire sensory system, to imbibe the principles of logic, metaphysics, Greek, grammar and rhetoric, for a start.

The afternoon was a different matter. In the afternoon, painted, trousered, kaftáned, and perfumed to a disturbing degree (one of the Five Sensuous Offerings) Philippa followed Kiaya Khátún with reluctance through the threaded stairways and walks of the harem to a courtyard, and across the courtyard, where a fountain played and carp glinted red in a pool, to the rooms of Khourrém the Laughing One; now Roxelana Sultán.

The wife of Suleiman the Magnificent had a large chamber; bigger than any Philippa had yet seen. Its floors were of coloured mosaics, overlaid with a pattern of rugs and drenched with light from above, where the cupola, gilded within and without, was ringed with a fillet of windows. The walls were of tiles: green and orange and white, masked here and there by the velour of deep hanging rugs. Silver lamps hung on long silver laces from the ceiling carved in a fretting of stucco, and the embrasures all round the walls, where her jewelled ewer stood, and her books and her lute, were each framed in a lattice of cedarwood. A motif of tulips, half concealed by the coloured silk hangings, was inlaid, discreetly, in ivory within the dark wood of the door, and the backless throne on which Khourrém sat, wide as a bed, was padded with furs.

The small figure on the spread leopard-skins had none of the repose or the classical beauty of Güzel. Philippa saw a Roman nose, set in a pure oval face with a pursed mouth and plucked brow wreathed with shivering pendants. The jewelled silk gauze which draped her high headdress like a fragile pavilion fluttered and rolled as she turned her head, speaking in rapid Turkish to a negro page-boy behind her, and then to one of her mutes. Philippa knew how her lips were so rosy and her eyebrows so high and deliciously arched, but the round dark eyes on either side of that imperious nose were Khourrém's own native beauty, and her speech was articulate and precise. The confidence of a middle-aged woman, who twelve years ago had simply left the Old Seraglio, a thing unheard of, with her slaves, her companions, her pages, her black and white eunuchs, and had joined her lord, here.

She ceased speaking and, at a sign from one of the eunuchs, Kiaya Khátún glided forward. Philippa, her neck aching, her eyes humbly downcast, heard her new name being repeated and the fact that although she had little Turkish, she could respond to simple commands. She was aware of being looked at; then Roxelana Sultán raised her voice. 'Come!'

Obedient as one of the mutes, Philippa summoned all her hard-won training and glided too, without mishap, over the carpets. The brown eyes were shrewd; the clothes rich but neat: the three-foot train tucked into the wide jewelled sash; the slippers curled, and of a skittish red satin. Khourrém had a neat ankle, and knew it.

She was being asked to bring sherbet. Philippa bowed, hand on heart, thought strengtheningly of Kate, and turned smoothly, to catch the eye of the small page, who already had a jug in his hands. Keep at it, and head eunuch for you, thought Philippa to herself, and grinned at him, accepting the jug, while he brought her a tray and cups to go with it, trotting behind with a towel. He might have been twelve.

The cups were solid emerald. She filled one for Roxelana and one for Kiaya Khátún who had seated herself, on command, by the steps of the throne. The page brought a table and Philippa laid the sherbet tray on it, restraining herself from a mad desire to drain the whole jug. 'Now, the lute,' said Kiaya Khátún. 'Khourrém Sultán desires you to play for her.'

No shortage of helpers. The eunuch brought the lute: the page-boy arranged a pile of cushions for her to sit on.

Someone had presented the instrument: it was made western-style, with an inscription in Latin. It was quite out of tune.

No Gideon, now, to chaff her and give her an A. Get it wrong now, dearie, said Philippa to Durr-i Bakht; and they'll stitch your mouth shut and tip you into a jar. She tuned, quickly, and got her strings at least in the proper relationship before wondering what on earth she was expected to play. Kiaya Khátún saved her the trouble. 'I have told the Sultana,' she said, 'of the song "The Knight of Stevermark" I encountered on shipboard. Play this, if you know it. Even better: if you know the words, sing.'

Philippa stared at Kiaya Khátún. Then she drew a long breath. 'I know the tune. The words are not very . . . I know only one version.'

'There *is* only one version,' said Kiaya Khátún. 'If you know it, sing it. I shall translate.'

And she did, very adequately, Philippa thought, singing her way doggedly through fifteen verses and all the double-entendres.

Roxelana enjoyed it. She began to smile half-way through, and by the end had broken into open-mouthed laughter. Then, summoning Philippa, she pulled off and gave to her a jade pin from her robe. Philippa, who yearned above rubies for one swig of the sherbet, thanked her stiffly in Turkish, and drew a smile and a word of dismissal. The page came for the lute. Philippa bowed, backed and fled.

Later, Kiaya Khátún summoned her. 'You did well. Your work was acceptable: Khourrém Sultán finds you witty. Next time you will be alone. You will perform for her only classical works: you will find she has a taste for them, and is perfectly knowledgeable, so she will demand a high standard of playing. But you will notice also that she enjoys laughter. Your invention must suggest what you do.'

'Clown?' said Philippa, without further surprise. Here, lunacy flowed with the fountains.

'With grace. Always with grace,' said Kiaya Khátún warningly. 'Khourrém Sultán makes a powerful friend.'

It had been a long day. '. . . If I can go?' said Philippa pleadingly. 'I promised him bubbles if he behaved in his bath.'

'I suggest,' said Kiaya Khátún gravely, 'you restrict your use of the personal pronoun. Misunderstandings occur. And in Topkapi, the sentences are irreversible.'

20

CONSTANTINOPLE: TOPKAPI

'Let us be common,' had said His Excellency the French Ambassador, sitting at his desk in the Embassy in the days prior to his ceremonial presentation to the most high Emperor and mighty king, Sultan Suleiman Khan. 'Our clothes wrought upon goldfully, glorious as Assurbanipal with a dab of clove-gillieflower scent on the pulses. Let us be common and arch.'

On an annual income from the French Crown, supplemented from one's own estates, one might live generously but not extravagantly as Ambassador at the Sublime Porte. M. d'Aramon et Luetz, whose own presentation years ago had cost him over three thousand pounds in entertainment and gifts, was silent as Onophrion's preparations drew to a close; and he began to have an inkling of the amount of gold the Controller had been permitted to spend.

By custom, all those in the Ambassador's party must be uniformly clothed. That meant livery for, say, twenty servants and two pages; robes, or short gowns over matching doublets and breeches for the dozen chief French citizens of the city who would accompany them, and court dress of the most elaborate kind for the Ambassador and M. d'Aramon, presenting him, together with lesser suits for the half-dozen Embassy officials with them. Cloaks, tunics, caps, shoes and jewels for forty or more.

Most of the garments, M. d'Aramon knew, had come on the *Dauphiné*. The last week had been spent fitting and enriching them. Submitting, courteously, to Master Zitwitz's deft, measuring hands, the retiring Ambassador approved without comment the ice-blue velvet proposed for his doublet, and the massive blue and silver over-robe the Controller lifted like a child from its coffer and offered for his admiration. 'Cloth of silver, Monseigneur, with an ogival frame of blue velvet and raised knots and leaves in pulled loopings of silver silk. There is a matching cap in blue velvet with aigrette feathers. All the household are in blue and white satin, and I have put the merchants, with His Excellency's agreement, in black silk lined with scarlet. The shirts for yourself and His Excellency are of lace, edged with silk Florentine thread. I thought a pleated collar instead of a stiffened wing, as I gather the Turkish robes you will be required to wear may be collared and heavy. I should advise you to unclasp the over-robe and give it to me before assuming the Turkish attire.'

'And what,' said M. d'Aramon, with gentle amusement, 'will His Excellency be wearing?'

'The same as M. le Baron, if you will forgive the liberty,' said His Excellency's soft voice from the doorway. 'Onophrion couldn't face the problems of precedence and neither could I, so we had two lots made. I'm sorry about the useless blue velvet. It is supposed to indicate that you are prepared to wear it once and then throw it away. You could wear it afterwards, perhaps, at a large, vulgar banquet.'

'I gather,' said M. d'Aramon dryly, 'it is necessary to impress.'

'It is necessary,' said Lymond briefly, 'to beg. . . . I came to tell you, there was a blind and somewhat sickly descendant of Sohâib Rûmi downstairs requiring help to write a letter in French. Your secretary swore that both he and the boy with him were probably rogues, and they certainly couldn't pay an asper, but I thought it might be politic to help them. If any harm comes of it, it's not your secretary's fault.'

'My secretary is wrong. We are here to assist,' said M. d'Aramon firmly. He had watched his successor in the past week, with the merchants who came to kiss his hands; the suppliants; the formal, inquisitive calls from his fellow Ambassadors of Venice, Ragusa, Epidaurus, Chios, Transylvania, Florence and Hungary. The French Embassy had a name for generosity. Its doors were open to travellers: its purse—even his, d'Aramon's, private purse—had been ready to help the stranded visitor with clothes, money and horses: at his own expense also he had bought and freed not a few Christian slaves, whatever their country, from the hands of the Turks.

It was a tradition he would like to see followed. He hoped, not for the first time, for many reasons, that Crawford's petition would be swiftly successful.

At dawn on Tuesday, a cool autumn day, the Mehterkhané, the Sultan's musicians crossed the Golden Horn to the French Ambassador's house, and with the low roll of drum and kettledrum below every unlatticed window, commanded the household to its duty. Onophrion, his supreme moment arrived, calmly holding in his plump hands the whole tangled skein of the ceremony, roused and fed, dressed and gathered his charges, hardly aware of the thundering of trumpet and cymbal outside. The Baron de Luetz, for all the times he had experienced it before, still could not avoid the extra beat of the heart; and this time, the knowledge that it was the last time: that for him, without greater title or honour, it was quite finished.

Georges Gaultier, uncomfortable in fur-collared black, was uneasy about many things. . . . Marthe's long absence, and the performance of that damned spinet. It had gone yesterday to the Seraglio, un-crated, touched up; erected, on the special litter made for it; and he had handed it into the gateway himself.

They said it was safe. Lymond had said that if anyone nicked off an emerald pimple it would be a God's blessing. He had seen the gloves Lymond would be carrying today, and the matched sapphires set in his chain, with a diamond pendant the size of a crown. . . . He wondered again, furiously, where that fool of a girl had got to.

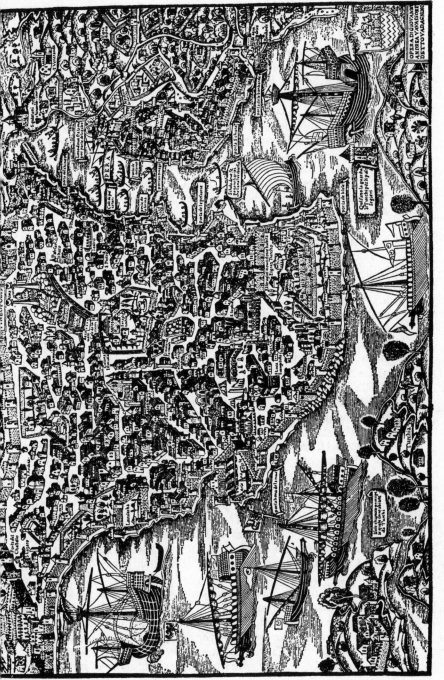

Plan of Constantinople drawn by Giovanni Vavassore about 1520.

Lymond was already awake, standing silently at the window in his trailing bed-gown, when the drumming began. In the Golden Horn, a porcelain mist rose like steam from a dish of bright liquid brass, blanching tone from the undulating skyline of the city over the water, a mosaic of olive and grey, the sun touching gold from its domes.

On the headland climbed the dark cypresses and the crowded roofs of the Seraglio; the Divan Tower, the minarets, the domes, the dentelé toothpicks of the flues. On the right, the twin minarets and the piled yellow whaleback of what had been St Sophia. The snail-domes of mosque upon mosque: Beyazit, Mohammed the Conqueror, Selim. The half-finished building of Sultan Suleiman himself. . . . For the True Believer, the ways to Paradise were legion. One built khans, mosques, hospitals, fountains. One repaired bridges, and gave bread to dogs, and bought and loosed singing birds from their cages. About caged children, the Prophet was less explicit.

The light was brightening. Francis Crawford turned away, abruptly, and began, with care, to dress.

Two hours after that, the Sultan's golden caique came for them, with its eighty red-capped oarsmen; its prow a gilded feather curled round its cable; its curtained pavilion inlaid with mother-of-pearl, gold and tortoiseshell and with rubies and turquoises edging the exquisite marquetry of its roof. They embarked smoothly, in a living pattern, this time, of silver and satin and jewels, leaving the music and crowds on the waterfront and gliding out on the bright water, where the fishermen poled over, calling, and the carved sterns of the merchantmen were crowded with faces.

The mist had gone. Half-way across, the *Dauphiné*, rowed out to midstream from the berth which was costing the French Crown twenty pounds daily, let off two volleys of small shot, and then two rounds of each of her guns, followed by an outburst of fanfares from her trumpets, her banners lifting in the first morning wind. On one of the hills someone was putting up kites: the small chequered shapes twitched and spiralled and floated, drawing the gaze to the sky. On the waterline below the seawall of the Seraglio one could also distinguish for the first time a jostling line of pale colour and dark beside the Seraglio quay. 'The welcoming party, with horses,' said d'Aramon. 'The two Pashas will have silver staffs: the Kapijilar-Kiayasi, the Grand Chamberlain, and the Chiaus Pasha, the Chief of the Ushers. The rest are a guard of honour: thirty or forty. Two gifts here.'

'And one for the helmsman,' said Lymond. French-fashion, his white cap-feather dropped rakishly over one cheekbone. His face, underlit by the sun and the silver, was perfectly cool, and his short bright hair crisp, like a cat's, in the damp. There had been an argument with the man Zitwitz about perfume, in which Lymond, acidly, had capitulated. ('Many here smell strong, but none so rank as he.')

It occurred to d'Aramon that it was a long time since he had witnessed a display of cold-blooded thoroughness to equal it.

They landed. The light Arab horses, trellised with pearl and trailing velvet and tassels, were not easy to collect and control, when oneself in the fanciest costume. But two by two, formalities finished, the procession was formed, and passing the sea gate of Topkapi, the Sultan's kiosk of marble and crystal, the Fish Gate, the Imperial mill, bakery and hospital set against the outside Seraglio walls, and the broken marble of the older civilization which had shared Seraglio Point, turned its back on the sea; and following the high turreted wall of the palace, climbed the low hill to the summit, where shone the vast golden dome of St Sophia, and the tall, white marble tunnel of the Bab-i-Humayun; the Sublime Porte itself; the Gate to the Royal Seraglio.

Like a carnival party; like a company of playactors, whose painted cloths and sparkling glass jewels were real, thought d'Aramon grimly, the two Ambassadors with their gentlemen and their escort rode between the two lines of white-feathered door guard and into the square quarter-mile of exercise-ground, green with trees and lined with strange irregular buildings, which was the first of the four courts of the Palace. 'I wish you good fortune,' said the Baron d'Aramon to his companion. 'May you return through this gate bearing your son and the child of your friends. You have travelled far for this moment.'

A brief, one-sided smile pulled at the new Ambassador's mouth. 'Thank you,' said Francis Crawford. '*Aussi Dieu aide*—perhaps—*aux fols et aux enfants*. . . . What are the buildings?'

D'Aramon told him. On the right, the long hospital, with its red tiled roofs, and the low freestone buildings of the main well and waterworks. On the left, the dome of the old Byzantine church of St Irene, once filled with the weapons and armour of Greeks and Crusaders. An arcade and horse-trough, a wood- and tool-yard; and the cupolas of the Mint and of the Pavilion of Goldsmiths and Gemsetters, where worked the shield-makers and cutlers and swordsmiths, the gold-chasers and engravers, the workers in amber and copper and silver, the glovers and upholsterers, the carvers and makers of musical instruments, whose art, like the dials of the spider, clothed and veiled the precincts of mastery.

This was the courtyard of the Janissaries, the children of Hadji Bektash, the first standing army in Europe since the days of the Romans. They stood on either side, rank upon rank of blue robes, unmoving; silent; the bird-of-paradise feathers of ceremony in the copper sockets of each high white felt bonnet, curling and falling knee-length behind. Riding from end to end of that long double column, with the doors of the Sublime Porte closing behind, the Baron de Luetz felt again the fear which never failed to grip him, after all these years, on finding himself inside these high walls: the awe forced on every stranger by the weight of the silence.

It was a court used by many outside the Seraglio: a court of business and training, a place full of affairs, the laden mules passing to and fro between the guard and the buildings, and turbaned men of many races bearing burdens or bent on swift errands. Nevertheless, there was complete silence. A cough could be heard, distantly, in the still, heavy air. The tread of their horses' feet, as they moved over the flat unpaved dirt and then crossed some broad, cobbled path, formed alternating patterns of tone, and the chime of bridle and bit and the soft tread of their escort echoed back from the buildings. In silence, they crossed the wide court, and in silence halted before the Inner Wall and the true entrance to the Seraglio: the battlemented gate-house and twin octagonal towers of the Ortokapi; the Gate of Salutation.

Across the First Court, Ambassadors and officials of the Inner Service had the privilege of riding. Within the Ortokapi, none rode but the Sovereign of Sovereigns himself. As their escort, moving silently forward, held their horses, the principals of the French Embassy and their retinue dismounted in a ripple of white and black and scarlet, pale blue and silver, and on foot entered the great marble porch; while above them the spiked heads of the Sultan's detractors and traitors knotted the white stone among the bronze shields and scimitars which hung on its surface; and these, stirred by the movement beneath them, quaked into a shimmering curtain of silver and gold. Within, a double wrought-iron door led into the Ortokapi vestibule. There, the Ambassadors' feet sank into carpet and the two pages bearing the heavy silver stuff of their trains lowered it, at a faint smile from Lymond, and stepped smartly back.

On either side, as before, stood the Janissaries, but dressed this time in silk with jewelled gold on their brows. Before them, two men waited to welcome them: the Agha of Janissaries, black moustached and hugely turbaned, his long hanging sleeves lined with fur. Then after him the most powerful civil authority in the Seraglio: the Bostanji Bashi, who under the title of Head Gardener was master of all security within the Seraglio, possessor of great estates and exe-cutioner of the great. To them, bowing hand on breast, the Baron d'Aramon presented his successor. The swarthy faces did not change, nor did the new Ambassador, speaking most formal French and awaiting, courteously, the interventions of the interpreter, show either excitement or apprehension. Then, gifts presented, they were in the big reception chamber which led off the vestibule to the right, and awaiting permission to enter the Court of the Divan.

From the Hall of the Divan, Rustem Pasha as Grand Vizier and supreme head of the civil and military hierarchy under the Sultan governed the kingdom for his master with his judges and Treasury officials, with his three lesser viziers and the Grand Mufti, head of the Islamic religion. The Grand Vizier, who ruled over six thousand salaried servants and a harem, they said, as big as the Sultan's: who had in his palace, they said, six hundred silver saddles and eight hundred sabres with jewel-covered hilts and a library of five thousand ancient manuscripts—who was worth altogether three-quarters of a million silver ducats—the Grand Vizier was leading the army against Persia. In his place Ibrahim Pasha, the second Vizier, would welcome and feast them before, at last, they were summoned to the Sultan himself.

They waited perhaps half an hour, their staff standing rigid under Master Zitwitz's forbidding eye; Gaultier shuffling uneasily among the black and crimson robes of the sweating, whispering merchants until Lymond's pleasant voice said in his ear, 'Griping, isn't it? What are you worried about? Unless they've dropped the bloody thing in the Bosphorus, it'll be the sensation of the Seraglio.'

'If it works,' said Georges Gaultier. The lines on his face, usually dirt-coloured, were orange.

'Well, if it doesn't work, there's always the jewellery,' said the new Ambassador blandly. 'And if they've picked off all the garnets, there's still the spinet. And don't have the face to tell me *that* doesn't work, even though your brilliant niece didn't arrive.'

For in those last days of panic Lymond himself had tuned the spinet, perched on a stool, his head to one side, patiently tapping, listening, adjusting while Gaultier worked on the case, against time, adjusting the weights, repairing and repainting the damage caused by friction and damp and the vagaries of temperature during the long nine-month voyage. Marthe's boxes were there, with their hanks of Nürnberg wire; the fish glue, the felt, the pins and the nails, and the kid bag of vulture feathers for plectra. It had taken two days, the tuning, in between Lymond's other affairs; and he appeared both to know what he was doing, and to enjoy it.

At the end, there had rung through the rooms of the Embassy a faint, fast cascade of sound M. d'Aramon had never heard in that air before, and seldom anywhere else. With Gaultier and, in time, a gathering group of the household, he had heard the brief recital through, from a neighbouring room, and had entered with con-gratulations and diffident questions. And Lymond, answering, had been, Gaultier thought, more communicative and relaxed than at any point in the past months when the sound of a flute, finely played, would have made him turn on his heel.

So music to this man was a weight or a counter-weight, like those working the delicate wheels of Gaultier's automata. It would be interesting to know, thought Gaultier, what change of balance had created the need for it now.

Then they were summoned to return to the vestibule, where the inner gates, the gates of the Court of the Divan, now stood fully open.

They opened on a wide-eaved canopy, upheld by ten marble columns with copper chapters and bases, and lined with a ceiling of Persian work, panelled gold upon turquoise, whose shape and colours were repeated in the tessellated ground at their feet. The arcade of which this was part surrounded the four sides of a courtyard smaller than the one they had passed: a garden filled with fountains and small, blowing willow trees, and lawns edged with box and the tall black ovals of cypresses.

The sun had come out, filling the court with sharp greens and blue shadows; striking gold from the stalked domes of the kitchens behind the long gallery which closed the right side of the garden, and from the Treasury domes on the left, and from the single cupola, far in the distance, of the gate to the third and forbidden court: the Gate of Felicity.

To the left, far ahead, stood the low, arcaded pavilion of the Council Chamber which was known as the Divan, with its four-sided tower and tall spire, crowned with the flashing gold crescent which could be seen over all Topkapi. Today, the gazelles which sometimes grazed on the sunny slope of the garden had gone. Instead, still as a Persian miniature, Kapici and Janissaries, in patterned rows of long robes and bright sashes and unstirring plumes, lined the wide path to the Divan and stood guarding each gate.

Led by the Bostanji Bashi, Lymond stepped from the blue and gold of the vestibule into the sunshine and, followed by the severe column of his suite, walked down the patterned path and between the slender pillars and under the wide gold-latticed canopy of the Divan.

There, the door of the first chamber was open, its green velvet hangings held back by a pair of negro child pages in turban, trousers and slippers. Inside, the Baron de Luetz glimpsed the stirring of jewels and bright silks of the Divan's highest officers, standing round the walls of the room to receive them. On the far wall, lit by a diffusion of sunlight, there was a gleam from the flowered Iznik tiling with which the room was set, joined and edged with wrought gold, and the deep crimson and green of the silk rugs on the floor and behind the Vizier's throne, opposite. The Bostanji Bashi, turning, bowed and waved Lymond in.

So, robed and jewelled in blue velvet and silver, and followed by his page and the person and page of M. d'Aramon, Francis Crawford entered the Hall of the Divan, and, stepping upon the deep carpet, faced the throne of the Vizier.

'*Welcome*,' Gabriel said.

*

Philippa saw it happen. Because no prayers or promises would move the black slaves or the eunuchs or even, in despair, Kiaya

Khátún to let her view, from whatever thrice-guarded vantage, the reception of the new French Ambassador, she had taken her books and her papers and marched off, changing to a graceful prowl as she remembered, to bury her hopes and excitement in a course of philology, followed by the works of Abd-ul-Baki, the Sultan and Khan of lyric verse, somewhat spoiled by being translated, for her benefit only, into the hybrid mixture of Mediterranean languages the girls all called Frankish.

By pure accident she was seen by Roxelana Sultán, who had formed a liking for her, and who required, for that moment, a feminine escort who could not speak Turkish. She talked briefly to Philippa's eunuch, and, dismissing both him and her servant, signed to the Pearl of Fortune to lay down her papers and follow her.

Once before Philippa had been beyond the Black Eunuch's court-yard, to the little paved court with the fountain from which rose the steps inside the Divan tower. Beyond that again, she had been told, was the anteroom to the Carriage Gate, where she and the other girls would enter the great covered carts in the Second Court to travel with the harem, if the Sultan ever required it.

For a moment she wondered if indeed she was about to be taken out into the open air; to ride perhaps by Roxelana Sultán's side on a visit to St Sophia. . . . But it was Tuesday, not Friday; and instead of passing through to the Carriage Gate, the Sultana signed to her to open the door into the tower. Holding it open, Philippa saw with interest that there was no living being in sight: no eunuchs; no servants. Whatever Roxelana was about to do, it was not to be wit-nessed. Then she followed her mistress up the steps of the tower.

The small, low room she presently entered held a carpet and a cloth-of-gold stool, and was lit by one narrow window, intricately gilded and grilled. It looked, Philippa saw, as her mistress seated herself, spreading her robes on the stool, directly down into what must be the Hall of the Divan. And Roxelana, she now realized, had no business there at all. For it was, if harem rumour was correct, the Sultan's personal listening-post. Unveiled; her heart thudding underneath the Tartar cloud shapes on her kaftán, Philippa dropped at a sign to the carpet, and sat crosslegged staring at the moving headgear below.

The variety of turbans seemed endless. A doughnut, closed in with pleating and a button on top. A severe square, cuffed and pleated meanly and vertically. A cone, with a headband. A cottage loaf, swathed round the brow. A circle of quilting, with dewlaps drooping above. An immaculate study in bandaging, with the pleats at right angles; the whole thing rakish and flat. And another, round as a ball of thick wool. The tall cone hat of a Bektashi dervish, and the great onion globe of the Agha of Janissaries, wound round a fez. Then he disappeared, and was replaced by the Grand Mufti, all in green. They nearly all had moustaches: *Prolixos duntax mystaces gestant.* Bellon, quoted by Mr Crawford. She now knew what it meant.

The spinet they were presenting had come. She had heard that, and knew it had gone into the Treasury, with the other big gifts: the rest they would bring with them. She wondered if Mr Crawford had found out yet—but of course, Archie would have told him . . . unless anything had happened to Archie?—if he had found out that she was here. And Kuzucuyum.

One could not, of course, whistle through the grille. Or, since Roxelana's presence was illicit, one would disappear sacked into the Bosphorus. So one must simply be prepared to look, and to listen. . . . I wish, Kate used to say, you would one day discover the sneaky and (on occasion) intoxicating uses of a little self-discipline. . . .

So Mr Crawford was expected, down below in the Divan. Philippa tried to recall what she had gleaned of the ceremony. He would come in through the door opposite her, with his chief officers and the departing Ambassador, and would talk to the Second Vizier, acting in Rustem Pasha's absence. He, she supposed, since she couldn't see him, must be seated in state opposite the door, and immediately under her window.

Then they ate—in the adjoining room, perhaps, walking through the doorless arch in the pierced screen which was all that divided the two rooms. Then they would robe to go to the Sultan, but by then, probably, Roxelana would be bored and would have required her to leave. . . . Heavens, she'd asked her something twice already. Scarlet, Philippa bent to pick up the little fan Roxelana had indicated, and when she straightened, Lymond stood in the doorway below.

Blessed with relations in London, Philippa was well versed in court costume; and her weeks in the harem had accustomed her to inordinate finery. So she paid no attention to the maligned velvet and silver and looked only at the way he stood; his hands loose on his thighs over the folds of his over-robe; and the poise of his head, dark against the green of the garden; and the fining-down of his face since she had seen him last, outside Algiers; and the absence of carelessness in the eyes and the unsmiling mouth. Then another voice below her window said, '*Welcome.*' A voice that she knew.

Coming in from the sun, for a second Lymond must have been blinded. She saw his eyes widen, and his lips part, and then close, straight and tight. He had control of himself in a heart-beat, and in another had swept off his plumed cap and, gloves on heart, executed a slow, sweeping bow. But Philippa could sense the extravagance of the shock he was covering, even when he spoke softly in English. 'Life is full,' said Francis Crawford, 'of small disappointments.'

A long time afterwards, when she knew that he had been told Gabriel was dead at Zuara, Philippa remembered that moment. At the time, she heard instead the rich, beautiful voice of Graham Reid

Malett replying: the voice which in Malta had urged his fellow Knights to disaster, and in Scotland had almost seduced a nation from the hands of its keepers. 'In the name of the Prince, Allâh, and of my lord Rustem I, Jubrael Pasha, welcome thee. May thy days in this city pass swiftly, as with a whip of light the angel driveth the clouds from the heavens. May thy sojourn here endure for ever, and thy life seem to thee long.'

He spoke in Turkish. Her heart cold, Philippa saw Roxelana's brows, puzzled, lift for a moment; then the dragoman translated, deftly restoring the compliment which had eluded Gabriel's ambiguous phrases. Then d'Aramon entered, and halting in his turn, stared at the man he had last known, in Tripoli, as a Knight of the Order of St John.

Turning, Francis Crawford smiled at his colleague; his eyes wide and blue as the stones in his chain. 'Allow me to present the new Second Vizier, Jubrael Pasha, late of St John and St Andrew. Convalescing, I understand, from *la rhume ecclésiastique*?'

His face stern, M. d'Aramon bowed and, unsmiling, set about presenting those in their train. Glancing at Roxelana beside her, Philippa saw her lips twitch with amusement. There was an intention, then, to subject the Embassy to this small humiliation: to force from them the courtesies they would under other circumstances withhold from a renegade. It occurred to Philippa that at this moment France needed Turkey, her ships and her trade probably a good deal more than the Sultan had need of France. Neither side would break off relations, but pinpricks of this kind they might regard as amusing and harmless. But surely an Ambassador's life was still sacrosanct? Any nation which engineered the death of an accredited diplomat unprovoked surely invited an open declaration of war?

The greetings and presentations on both sides were over. The lesser mortals had filed out to be fed; and on two low velvet stools, their over-robes spread like open flowers around them, the new Ambassador and the old sat and held conversation with the Vizier and his companions.

The talk was formal, and general. In the little room behind the grilled window the heat, rising from the chamber below, was becoming uncomfortable. Roxelana, her hair veiled in thick silk, sat and slowly unwound the fine cloth; then, touching Philippa on the shoulder, gave it into her hands.

It had to be folded, naturally. How could the Sultana wear a creased veil back to her apartments? Philippa rose quietly to her feet, approached the grille as near as she dared, and in a cloud of patchouli, shook and folded the silk.

Lymond had been speaking, at length, on some matter of trade. He ended, and allowed one of the Cadis to take up his point before glancing briefly upwards to the source of the scent. Philippa saw his eyes rest for a second on the grille; and then drop to the Cadi again. Very soon after that, at some signal from the Vizier, the company, still talking, rose to its feet. The stools were removed. M. d'Aramon, engaged in talk with the Mufti, moved to one side, towards the door of the inner room where their meal had been laid. And as Lymond, standing alone, waited for him, there walked for the first time into Philippa's sight the magnificent figure of Gabriel, the Angel of Revelation and the Messenger of God, robed in heavy white satin threaded with gold, and patterned with the crescents of Islam in deep golden velvet. The under-robe and the long tight sleeves were edged with jewelled embroidery, the belt fashioned of plaques of jewel-set gold, and the white folds of his turban, swathed about its hard velvet crown, were clasped with a setting of rubies.

Below the pure muslin, the fair, big-boned face was no less pure: the eyes blue, the skin tanned golden with the Mediterranean sun; the smile clear and affectionate. 'Where is the whipping-stand now?' said Gabriel gently to his one-time commander. 'Verily, thou art as the Peacock of Paradise, whose plumage shone like pearl and emerald, and whose voice being so sweet was appointed to sing daily the praises of God. . . . Thou knowest the legend?'

He spoke in Turkish, and Lymond, without the interpreter, answered in the same language. 'Is not thy version, as ever, unique?'

Gabriel's blue eyes were troubled. 'Not so. Through this Peacock, they say, Satan entered Paradise in the tooth of the serpent, in punishment whereof the lovely voice of the Peacock was ravished from him for ever. . . . It is long since the Elders received an Ambassador young, ambitious, fragrant as a parcel of musk in red silk. Even those of pure disposition and right belief may covet thee. . . . Use thy lips wisely. They are meant for laughter; not the spreading of evil. . . . The calumny against my lord Rustem Pasha has displeased the Sultan mightily.'

Blue eyes did not move from blue. Lymond's fair brows lifted. 'Is it a calumny to maintain that Rustem Pasha is truly zealous in the care of his master? Then I am guilty.'

'I have heard otherwise in Pera,' said Gabriel slowly. 'I have heard it said that there is no unrest in the army: that Rustem Pasha's solicitude is false, and aimed only at discrediting others. This is the rumour put about by the French Embassy.'

'I know nothing of it. But I have heard another rumour,' said Lymond, 'which I shall not relate to you or to any other man, and which, if I hear it repeated, I shall stamp in the dust, for I do not believe it and nothing will bring me to believe it. You would do well, instead of listening to evil, to defend the innocent against the hidden frothings of malice. Above all women, honour is due to Khourrém Sultán.'

A slow joy, forcing its way upwards like air through a porridge-pot, filled all Philippa's clean massaged chest and caused her to glance, bright-eyed, at the intent face of the woman beside her.

He had guessed. Whatever obscure political game they were playing, he had guessed that the Sultana must be there, at the listening-post; and perhaps even that she, Philippa, was there as well. And, looking at Roxelana, she saw that this was what the Sultana had come to hear and to see: that all her attention was focused on these two men, and that, of the two, she was intent chiefly on Gabriel.

Philippa recalled something else. There had been a visitor yesterday to Khourrém's apartments. A man, for she had aided her mistress to veil, holding the diamond-set mirror in pale and dark jade and placing ready the sherbet and *qahveh*. Then she had been dismissed, leaving only the mutes and Roxelana's personal eunuch. . . . Gabriel's golden voice, floating up to the grille, drew back her attention. 'Khourrém Sultán needs no defence,' said Jubrael Pasha sharply. 'The Sultana is likewise above evil and beyond criticism. It injures thine own honour to suggest otherwise.' He clapped his hands. 'We shall dine.'

Pages, their bright tunics kirtled into their sashes, their trousers of satin, their slippers embroidered and jewelled, came to draw off the stiff surcoats and sprinkle rosewater on the Ambassador's hands. Gabriel, smiling, waited while his own were moistened and dried and then clapped his hands, this time thrice.

Beside Philippa, Roxelana was stirring to go. Soon, the men were to move through the archway, where d'Aramon already waited, to dine in the inner room of the Divan; and would no longer be audible. The sharp triple clap made her turn, and Philippa, turning too, saw the Chiaus Agha had returned to the doorway, and was standing there bowing, a small child at his side. A small child in leaf-green tunic and trousers, a round embroidered green cap on his fair head.

It was Kuzucuyum. Oblivious of all but that round, stiffened face, staring terror-struck at the bright room filled with glittering strangers, Philippa stood stock still at the window, her own shock and apprehension measuring every millimetre of his. The Usher, whom he did not know, was urging the little boy forward, a hand on his flat back, but Kuzúm hung back, his face lengthening, his blue eyes dense and enormous. 'Come, child,' said Jubrael Pasha, irritation crumbling, for an instant, the patina of that beautiful voice. 'Conduct yourself as you should. Make your obeisances, quickly.'

'He doesn't know Turkish,' whispered Philippa. Khourrém Sultán, watching her curiously, had returned and was standing also, observing. The child looked round. The Usher, losing patience, said something sharply and pushed. Again the child looked round, his eyes desperate; and Philippa knew he was looking for her. The temptation to call became so strong that she put both hands, hard, over her mouth. Then he crept forward, very slowly, and kissed Gabriel's feet, and then gripped and kissed the hem of his robe. He kissed properly: solid kisses which could be heard; and then, straightening the flat, leaf-green back, looked up at Gabriel with anxiety, his eyes filled with tears he would not let himself shed.

But Gabriel's smiling blue eyes were elsewhere: on Francis Crawford, who had become quite still when he saw the small boy, and remained as timelessly still as the worn, martyred dead on the Ortokapi, his eyes fixed on the child. Then when, stubborn and obedient, the little boy made his grovelling gesture, Philippa saw Lymond's eyes come up and meet and hold Malett's.

Graham Malett smiled back, as he spoke again to the child. 'There is the Ambassador. Salute him,' he said.

Let him go, said Philippa to herself. *Oh, let him go. He's done all you can ask him. . . .*

'The Ambassador begs to be excused,' said Lymond quietly, in English. And to the child he said, in the same language, 'Tell me: what is your name?'

Kuzucuyum stared at the stranger, his lower lip straight and tight, his eyes round; his eyebrows tilting. Then in a whisper, he said, 'What did Fippy went?'

In English. In English, merciful heaven, thought Philippa, so that Lymond knew and took one step forward and stopped himself, as Gabriel rapped out, 'Do your duty!' and the Chiaus gripped Kuzúm by the arm.

He was two years old: maybe less. A woman would have known he was beyond coaxing: coercion was the last straw. Lymond stepped back instantly, but this time the child did not obey. He dragged behind, his mouth trembling, and when the Chiaus's silver rod, with an order, came down hard on his knuckles, he screamed, and continued to scream in long, whooping cries, crouched under the arm of the Usher, his eyes closed, his tears pouring over his two fat clenched hands and rolling black on the silk. Gabriel stared at the Chiaus. 'This is an insult to the Ambassador,' said the new Vizier bitingly. 'Take him away. He shall be whipped on the belly.'

'As the injured party,' said Lymond steadily, 'I am happy to overlook the offence and absolve him from punishment. He would be unlikely, at that age, to survive it. On the other hand, I should be delighted to buy him from you.'

'I thought you might. He is endearing, is he not?' said Gabriel. 'When silent. But not, I fear, at any time or any price, for sale to Your Excellency. Now'—as the screaming receded and powerful arms bore the child struggling from the Divan—'shall we eat?'

Khourrém Sultán's rose-painted fingers, closing on her bare arm, pulled Philippa up short just inside the Divan tower door. 'Wait,' said Roxelana; and gasping, Philippa slowed and halted, her face scarlet as she returned, suddenly, to her own situation. 'You know this child?' said Roxelana. 'He is in the harem, of course. Do you . . . ah,' she broke off, with a sound of impatience. 'Of course: you cannot understand. Veil yourself, girl.' And as Philippa, with care, obeyed her gesture, Roxelana covered her own head, and walking briskly, climbed down the stairs of the tower and through the silent courtyards until she came to her own quarters.

'Now,' she said to the Pearl of Fortune, having settled at last on her divan, a cup of syrup in her fingers, an interpreter at her elbow. 'I understand you see much of this child in the harem; it is good that you have a care for him, and that he will obey you. It is not seemly that you become for him what his nurse or mother should be. In a year or two, his life will be very different. The rule of the white eunuchs is not tender, and he will suffer all the more if he has been coddled in childhood. You call him Kuzucuyum, but you also know perhaps that his real name is different. You have just seen him, all unwittingly, encounter his father. The child is the son of the new Vizier, Jubrael Pasha.'

\

*

No food in all Turkey was more costly than that served at the ceremonial dinner to which a Grand Vizier entertained a new Ambassador; and none was eaten more quickly. The meal was timed to take just half an hour; and was spread in the second room of the Divan, with the two principals side by side on low thrones, gold-fringed napkin on knee, while a stream of servers and pages brought the dishes of which they partook, one after the other; served on wide silver platters edged with fresh bread, and laid on stools of red Bulgar leather.

There at last, away from that eavesdropping grille, distant from his associates and his interpreters, Graham Reid Malett spoke English, plainly and pleasurably, as roasted pigeons followed the grilled swordfish in vine-leaves, to be followed in turn by kids' flesh with dressed rice and sauces. 'Satan, they say, on arriving from Paradise, commanded garlic to spring from his left footmark, and onions from his right. Conceive,' said Gabriel, 'if he had never fallen. To taste either, we had to foregather in hell. . . . These are wild geese from Chekmeje. You must try them. You have twice laid hands on me personally. As Ambassador, your body is sacred until you are outwith these precincts. After that, however much our sovereign lord and yours may try to protect you, none can guard you for ever from the unknown assassin, however much we may deplore it. You will suffer the death I have chosen for you, here in Constantinople.'

'Then I have nothing to lose,' said Lymond gently, 'by killing you now.' Chatting quietly, their eyes on their plates, they presented a picture, thought d'Aramon, of civilized amity: two well-bred courtiers of uncommon looks and audacity; one in Western clothes and the other in the dress of the East. Yet at least, renegade and Christian, they must fear and dislike one another; and at the worst, as he now had good reason to believe, they might well be implacable enemies....

'Why make empty threats?' said Gabriel, smiling. 'You would have tried it already, but for the consequences to others. We have the boy, as you see. Whether he is mine or yours I do not know, nor does it interest me. I have no stomach for snivelling infants, but in a few years from now, I will find him of use.'

'And the other child?' said Lymond. 'One for each pillow? Both the camel and the camel-driver and the coffin being Ali?'

'The other child is in Constantinople.... Pastry is fattening, but I imagine that does not concern you? Or the roseleaf jam with white cracknels? The sweetmeats are admirable, but I cannot say I am looking forward to a lifetime of sheep's feet and yoghourt. You know the truth of the tag. The toasting of cheese in Wales and the seething of rice grains in Turkey will enable a man freely to profess to cook like a master.... I shall permit you to find the other child. You may even think he resembles you more than this one. I am no judge. Then you will die. You have had a long journey, my dear Francis; and you have put me to a certain amount of additional trouble. I have prepared for you a detailed, an exquisite death. You will not enjoy it. But in the end, what will you suffer? *Hic jacet arte Plato, Cato, Tullius ore . . . Vermes corpus alit, spiritus astra petit.* In the meanwhile, let it be perfectly clear. If the slightest accident should befall me, the extreme penalty will be paid in return by both children and the Somerville girl.'

Porcelain bowls on porcelain saucers had replaced the preserved lemon flowers, the pastes and cream and pistachios. In them were sherbets of raisin juice and rhubarb and rose-leaves; lotus, tamarind and grapes, honey, violets and melons. Sipping: 'You have the Somerville girl?' said Lymond. 'But how can you prove it?'

'You received all the proof you require at Thessalonika, my très cher Ambassador. I made sure of that. She is in the harem, but do not concern yourself. She will not share the fate of Oonagh O'Dwyer. I found her crude, so she is being trained. She is young, in mind and body. There is room for response. She will be part of the reward I request in return for my first service as Grand Vizier. On her I shall build my harem.... *Allâh, Allâh, except Allâh. This has gone; may a richer one come. May the Divine Reality give blessings. Let there be light for those who have eaten....* We must go, I fear, so that you may present your credentials and your petition. You will not be surprised, now, should the latter unhappily fail....' And he rose, the stiff white satin falling around him, and stood wiping his fingers.

The Turkish robes were being brought. Stripped also down to his doublet, M. d'Aramon allowed himself to be placed inside a collarless black damask robe, on which leaves and blossoms and nosegays of flowers rioted in red and gold silks, and the wide sleeves and twenty small buttons were knotted with rubies. Lymond stood up. 'You spoke of threats. You have indulged in a great many. . . . I prefer to make promises. I am going to take the girl and both children safely from you, whatever the outcome of my petition today. When I have done that, I shall allow nothing to stop me until you are dead. For that is the difference between us,' said Francis Crawford with simplicity. 'There is no price I will not pay after that for your death.'

For a moment Gabriel studied him, amused contempt in the bland face. 'Where is the open mind, the width of vision, the sense of history, the awareness of changing society which we used to have forced on our attention? You have chosen to walk among the minor paths, and blunt your wits on simple minds. . . . For ten years, the Sublime Porte have sued me; have sent me gifts and every sort of beguilement. Dragut is ageing; the Sultan himself is unfit now for the field. I can give them all the skills and experience they require; the special knowledge of Christian harbours and Christian ways which they seek.

'Now they have me, do you think they will risk alienating my loyalty? If I order the girl to be ganched or throttled or torn apart between horses, it will be done. If I wish it, I can have the brats drowned and trampled; their tongues uprooted, their eyes seared with hot copper. Think of Rustem Pasha: his power; his wealth. In his absence, his power is mine. In the Sultan's absence, my rule can become absolute. . . . Do you suppose that any living person in the Sublime Porte will dare do what I have forbidden? Try the strength of your credit if you wish. You will find it is limited.'

'I had an extraordinary feeling,' said Lymond, 'like a bat sitting in a cannonball tree, that I was going to be thrown on my own initiative. All this stirs one to ask why you troubled with Scotland?'

Gabriel smiled. 'It was ripe, then, for practice. This is ripe, now, for picking. . . . The Sultan, I believe, now awaits you.'

Outside, under the splendid arcade, d'Aramon and the chief officials of the Embassy were already waiting, their Turkish robes dimly glittering with the reflected greens and golds from the ceiling, the sun and the trees; drawn up in form to walk round the remaining edge of the square to the Gate of Felicity. Behind them, two ushers waited to place Lymond's robe, in turn, over his shoulders. By whatever delicate coincidence, it was of miniver, lined with a white brocaded silk flowered with castles and lions in faint gold embroidery. Turning, he waited for them to approach, and, slipping his arms through the short sleeves, allowed them to fasten it briefly. Then he turned back to Gabriel and bowed.

'It is a matter of deep regret that I cannot kill you at this moment,' said Lymond gently. 'Because there are three children at the adventure of God I cannot address you either, as I should prefer. But I promise you failure. Whatever happens, I shall take the children and free them.'

Gabriel smiled. 'Believe it if you must. You cannot alter what is in store, or avoid the long appointment with pain which awaits you. My other friends will take heed from your . . . infelicity. . . . I bid you goodbye.'

For a moment longer, encased like chrysalids in the plate-armour of ceremony, the two men faced each other in silence, and M. d'Aramon, watching apprehensively from the door, felt the tension already within the Divan tighten to a point beyond sound.

He did not know that for one man at least the room had become filled with the scents of a night garden in Algiers; choked and over-laid with the stench of a hideous burning. He did not know that, in spite of what Lymond had said, Gabriel was at that moment all but a dead man, and the lives of Philippa Somerville and two unknown children all but destroyed. But he saw Francis Crawford's hands spreadeagled suddenly, hard at his sides; and something inspired M. d'Aramon to say quickly, 'M. l'Ambassadeur! We must leave.'

Then Lymond turned abruptly from Jubrael Pasha and, without speaking, walked through the door of the Divan and joined the procession outside.

It was the last fine day of that autumn. Glaring high from a lucid blue sky, the sun struck down from the studded rows of lead domes and lanced into the eye from the gold leaf and copper enriching the courtyard, and the silver-tipped staffs and the clothes of the Janissaries, the Kapici and Chiausi in their unmoving ranks. The silence was complete.

Gold danced in the shadows of Bab-i-Sa'adet, the Gate of Felicity, as the French Ambassador's train approached it through one of the flanking colonnades of verd-antique pillars. Below the high, dazzling soffit of its canopy a deep carpet had been laid before the innermost gate: the gate through which entry was forbidden to all but Suleiman Khan the Magnificent and the chosen members of the Inner Household and those whom, as today, he might receive in private audience in the Arzodasi, the Throne Room just inside its gates. Beyond that was the unknown: the state apartments, the harem, the quarters of the eunuchs and the little, painted pages locked behind the three gates of the outer courts, and the ranks of Spahi and Janissary and all the public officialdom of the empire.

White eunuchs guarded the door: tall men of many races robed in gamboge and sable, stark and pure in their turbans as a cliff-face of gannets. Between them stood the Kapi Agha, the Chief White Eunuch and High Chamberlain, the head of the Third Court of the Seraglio. He bowed, hand on breast: once to the new Ambassador and once to the old; and then, turning, faced the high portico, wrought in panels of marble and wreathed with the golden calligraphy of the Qur'ân, which contained the Gate of Felicity: the great double-leafed doors of Bab-i-Sa'adet. He raised his hand, walking forward, his train of vermilion velvet brushing the carpet. And as Francis Crawford moved forward behind him, the doors opened slowly.

They opened on flowers and birdsong: on a dazzle of white and gilt marble set in willows and cypress and boxtrees; on galleried walls of marine and turquoise blue porcelain whose gilded Greek pillars were veiled in the spray of the fountains spaced down the long, sloping courtyard. Underfoot, the carpet continued over pale and formal mosaics, under the inner canopy of the Gate of Felicity and to the door of the Sultan's kiosk, which faced it directly, and which was bedded, as a jewel in velvet, in the caissoned files of his household.

They stood silent; slot upon slot of deep colour and quick shifting fragrance: the White Eunuchs in bright taffeta coats and loose trousers and slippers; the hundred dwarves, sullen and scimitared; grotesque in gold satin and squirrel fur. The Imáms, in crimson. The two hundred Imperial Pages, in tunics of cloth of gold to the knee, their sashes of bright coloured silk; their boots of red Spanish leather, and the long locks of hair curling, under the cloth-of-gold caps, from the shaven heads of the Sultan's own household. And the deaf mutes, their stiff elaborate hats in violet velvet, their robes of cloth of gold flashing as their hands moved: the only human beings in all that magnificent courtyard allowed, through affliction, to talk.

The kiosk of Suleiman the Magnificent was three-sided, its marble sides inlaid with jet and porphyry and jasper and arched with legends in silver; its coloured windows laced with wrought gold. Inside, over all was the deep Indian yellow of leaf gold in shadow. Hangings of silver tissue, dimly sparkling on silver gilt columns; an icy crust of carved stucco; an enamelled glint of white and emerald tiling; a ceiling deeply inlaid and gilded, supporting a crystal-paned lantern of silver, its rim set with turquoise and opal.

From the open, third side, a carpet of embroidered carnation satin led to a low dais, whose own carpet was worked in silver, turquoises and orient pearls. On it sat enthroned the master of all this magnificence: Suleiman, by the grace of God King of Kings, Sovereign of Sovereigns, most high Emperor of Byzantium and Trebizond; most mighty King of Persia, Arabia, Syria and Egypt; Prince of Mecca and Aleppo; possessor of Jerusalem: Sultan Suleiman Khan, the Shadow of God upon Earth.

He wore cloth of gold, figured with deep, crimson velvet and edged, fluting on fluting, with a white fur pinned and studded with rubies. Rubies burned from the scimitar hung at his side, and in the cluster of pigeon's-egg jewels set in gold which held the peacock plumes in his white turban and clasped the enchained jewels which lay swagged in its folds.

The face was aquiline, bearded and dark. Not the face of a happy man; but a face of authority, thinned by indifferent health. More than thirty years Emperor, Suleiman, now nearing sixty, belonged to the age of England's Henry VIII and the first King Francis of France: the age of magnificent despotism and supreme theological rule. He sat, a shadowy figure within his glorious casket, as still as the cipher; the symbol, which for this occasion was all he was expected to be.

Behind the cloth of gold and the diamonds and the blank face of ceremony was a living, powerful emperor. Following the Kapi Agha and his successor to take his place, with his fellows, under the arcade opposite the wide throne-room door, M. d'Aramon wondered what hope Francis Crawford could sustain now of disrupting that sovereign calm.

Standing still at the head of the gentlemen of his suite, Lymond's face was unreadable above the stiff magnificence of his gown, black fur upon white, each lattice pinned with an ermine tail. Breathless under the weight of his own brocade, d'Aramon could guess at the malice behind the costly gesture, and admire the self-command which could ignore it. Then there was a movement behind them, through the arch of the Gateway of Felicity, and two by two, as they waited, the Ambassador's pages filed into the court, and pacing slowly to the Sultan's kiosk, displayed to their recipient the gifts of the Most Christian Monarch of France.

To d'Aramon it was familiar. In so many countries had he stood and watched the wealth of his master lavished, like this, upon some petty king, some heretic figurehead: the bales of lawn and velvet and brocade; the vessels; the swords in their jewelled velvet sheaths; the furs and chains and belts and horse harness of silver; the hawks and greyhounds and thoroughbred stallions. Converted into luxury the produce of their fields and vineyards, the labourers' sweat; the land-owner's taxes. The Baron de Luetz watched the file of pages bear their glittering burdens to the kiosk, and pause, displaying them, and wheel pair by pair to deposit each in its warehouse. On either side of the kiosk, the Kislar Aga and the Kapi Agha, standing motionless, made no gesture, and within, straight-backed on his throne, the Sultan made no sign until, their breathing coming hard in the silence, there came forward the four liveried servants bearing the litter with the last present of all.

Within this bower of sunshine and extravagance, the horological spinet sparkled like a piece of bossed and wadded embroidery; a confection of gold leaf and sumptuous quartzes enthroning in white sapphire the bald face of time. Bending, the four sweating pages brought its litter to rest at the door of the kiosk and bowing, Georges Gaultier, choked in charcoal velvet, slid the spinet from its ivory drawer and touched the little spring above to set the automata alive. A shower of silvery chimes fell on the silence, and the casket of the spinet erupted into a blizzard of angular movement before the still ranks of its audience, like a dragonfly pinned to some page of a royal Book of Hours.

It lasted a long time. Towards the end, d'Aramon could see the mutes' hands fluttering and saw, by Gaultier's face, that the performance had been all that he had hoped. He bowed, and within the kiosk, in a dry voice which hardly penetrated outside, the Sultan spoke to his dragoman. The interpreter, moving from his side, stepped out and addressed the designer. 'My lord commends thy artefact and is pleased to bestow this sign of his pleasure. I am to ask if the spinet also makes music?'

Georges Gaultier's fingers, receiving the small leather bag, left black marks where he gripped it. 'Not by itself, Monseigneur. It requires to be played.'

There were no further questions. The Kapi Agha raised his hand and as the dragoman stepped back into his place, the four pages lifted the litter and moved, with Gaultier following, to deposit it. Beside him, d'Aramon felt Lymond move and saw, turning, that the Chiaus Agha, staff in hand, was standing before him. Then, wheeling, the Usher walked, with the new Ambassador following, his robe brushing the smooth mosaic, to the mouth of the kiosk. There, bowing, the Chiaus Agha left him, and turning, Lymond began to pace to its door, just as the Chief of the White Eunuchs and the Chief of the Black left their posts and approached him.

They fell into step beside him, one on each side. They grasped his long, hanging sleeves; and twisted their hands in the folds; and between them pinioned his arms hard and flat at his sides.

Lymond made no resistance. To d'Aramon, the steadiness with which he conducted himself through all the ceremonial was a cause for profound satisfaction. Walking behind with the six other gentlemen to be presented, he saw Lymond, in the grip of the Aghas, walk in step through the open wall of the kiosk and into the Presence.

If there remained any curiosity in Suleiman's soul, none of it showed in his eyes. He remained motionless as the new Ambassador was brought forward: his hands on the arms of his throne did not move, nor did he stir, as Lymond, kneeling between the two eunuchs, kissed first his knee and then the hanging sleeve of his robe; and then, still in the same double grip, was taken backwards to stand to one side against the kiosk's glittering wall. Then, releasing him, the Kapi Agha and the Kislar Agha returned to the door and, laying hands on d'Aramon, brought him and similarly his six other companions to make their salute. Only when all eight had made obeisance and stood silent within the kiosk did the dragoman move slowly forward and, receiving from the Capi Agha the sealed papers already entrusted him, unfold and read the terms of the Ambassador's commission.

He ended; and the sallow, fine-bearded face turned with indifference to where Lymond stood. Suleiman Khan said, 'It is to our satisfaction. May His Excellency convey to our dear friend and brother of France our delight with these his expressions of amity, and with the continuing bond thus illumined. We are pleased to welcome his Ambassador, and to bid our Treasurer increase by one-half the present allowances of meat, firewood and money accorded his household. May his acts honour his master.'

It was the moment. The translation ended, and into the silence, bowing, Lymond said in French, 'The most humble servant of the Sultan Suleiman Khan and of the Prince Henry, monarch of France, I beg leave to speak.'

So he was going to make his petition, thought d'Aramon. He had, after all, nothing to lose. It was a pity that the touchstone, the measure of Turkey's present regard for her ally of France, should be a boy-child and a girl. . . .

'Très haut, très puissant, très magnanime et invincible prince . . .' Lymond was speaking French, his manner unexceptionable; his voice even and clear. His measured phrases, echoed by the translator, spoke of the glorious alliance between France and the Ottoman Empire; of the liberal blessing of trade; of the success of Turkey's captains and generals in the western shore of the sea, despite the grasp of the Emperor Charles . . .

'Despite,' went on the even, articulate voice, 'those servants of Charles who, under whatever guise, never cease to attempt to drive asunder my lord's kingdom and yours. There is an issue now standing, an issue of no political significance but of great personal import to Henry my master. I am told, although I cannot believe it, that malicious tongues have already coloured with impropriety His Grace's modest request. From this and His Grace's natural desire for restraint, some confusion has occurred among the most innocent. I beg therefore to make my prince's mind clear and to free from misunderstanding the benign bond that unites our two countries. . . . I refer, my lord, merely to the return of two children, who find themselves by mishap within Your Grace's Seraglio, and whom I am empowered to recover for Henry my master, at whatever price you desire.'

He finished, with care; although the Kislar Agha was already at the side of the Sultan, his murmuring words too low to hear. The Sultan's black eyes, lifted to Lymond, sharpened a little. The dry voice said, 'I am told that the two children you mention are in fact an English girl of some sixteen years and a young child newly arrived from the House of Donati in Zakynthos. The Kislar Agha will recite you their names.'

The Kislar Agha did, correctly. 'Are these the persons?' asked the dry voice. And awaiting Lymond's assent in translation, went on without emotion. 'There is indeed, as you say, cause for confusion. The girl, you do not dispute, is from England and therefore of no concern to your master of France. The child, I am assured, belongs neither to France nor to England, but is the son of our Vizier Jubrael Pasha. You will do me the courtesy to say to our brother of France

338

that until his claims on our goodwill are more lucid, I fear we cannot help him. You will further say that he should provide himself, I advise, with an honest ambassador. We hear you have sought this child before, and not in the name of your master.'

He had indeed made his petition. He had abused his credentials, and he would suffer for it. Regret, in d'Aramon's mind, was mixed with dismay at his presumption. It was with something near disbelief that he heard Lymond say gently, 'My lord, it is true. For how could I make a brigand, a thief or a corsair aware that he harboured the son of Henry of France?'

The Baron de Luetz stood stiffly, his face pale with anger, listening to question and answer: frank answers, steady and circumstantial. A child born to a Scotswoman, Janet Fleming . . . acknowledged a bastard of France. Stolen in mistake for another—hence the confusion with Jubrael Pasha. If Jubrael Pasha could prove this his son, the Ambassador would waive any claim. But the King, on the other hand, possessed clearest proof that the boy was his bastard. . . .

'And the girl?' the dragoman mentioned.

'Belonged to the English Border and for long has had a relationship with the Scots court. Lady Fleming herself dispatched her to care for the infant.'

The Sultan murmured. 'You say there is proof,' said the dragoman. 'Where is your proof?'

Lymond spoke softly. 'With such a hostage of Fortune one does not carry proof, nor does one make such a quest public except between men of honour. On the child's return to his home the King will furnish ample proof, together with the concrete expression of his joy and goodwill. Between allies, a word is enough.'

There was a small silence. For a girl and a child, thought d'Aramon, a nation was going into pawn. For a girl and a child, if he stood silent before these untruths, his own career, already finished, was finished in ignominy. He could claim, perhaps, that he believed what the Ambassador said to be true. He knew it was not.

Then Suleiman spoke and d'Aramon knew that although he waited, head bent in deference, for the translation to end, Lymond had understood every word. 'Between France and Turkey,' the Sultan had said, 'as you say, one word is enough. Between thyself and Turkey, who knows?'

Lymond's voice, answering, was infinitely sober. 'My lord, none. You have seen my credentials. You may only put the matter to test. It places an incredible value on two valueless lives.' He paused. 'The enemies of the Ottoman Empire are cunning. That this circumstance might divide the Sultan from his allies did not seem to me possible. Rather was I concerned that the princess Khourrém Sultán would suffer a loss from her household which might discommode her. Whether she does so or not, and whatever Your Grace's decision, I

339

pray you to allow me to add to the gifts of King Henry my master a personal gift from myself to the princess your wife. I can envisage no other happiness than to have it accepted.'

Already, d'Aramon had noted the long, silk-bound packet in the discreet hands of the Ambassador's page. The Kislar Agha received it, and drawing off its purse of white satin, presented for the inspection of Suleiman the long filigree casket thus revealed.

The pale face did not change. But light in a shimmering band slid over the delicate cheekbones and aquiline nose and lit the dark recesses of the unwinking eyes. The negro moved, and the Baron de Luetz, catching sight for a moment of what the casket contained, drew in his breath. Then Suleiman Khan, dismissing it, said dryly, 'We thank you. Whether she will accept them is a matter for the princess my wife. Should she suffer no loss, she may desire no compensation. For my part, my reply is quite clear. What the King of France asks, instantly he shall have. Bring me this offer in your master's own seal and holograph. Prove to me that the boy in my Seraglio is the son of King Henry; or prove to me merely beyond doubt that he is not the son, as is claimed, of my Vizier Jubrael Pasha. And he is yours, without payment, to leave when you will, and the girl also.'

The shut casket shone on the dais. For a long moment, pale gold and white fur, the wilful emissary of France stood still, silenced by failure. Then he said, simply in English, 'Be it so,' and making the proper obeisance of courtier to Emperor, waited for the approach of the white and black eunuchs, and, in their grip, moved back from the audience.

It was finished. Outside the kiosk d'Aramon and his six gentlemen moved in order behind him, and in turn the servants and staff, Gaultier and Onophrion Zitwitz, until once more the cortège was complete. With a rustle of plumes, a bending and unbending of colour, a flashing of jewels, the ranks of the Household saluted them. The Gate of Felicity opened, and led by the Chiaus Pasha, in silence, the Ambassador's column filed out, the gates closing behind them.

Still in the court of the Divan, the Janissaries and Spahis stood silent; the robed officials gathered under the canopy bowed as they moved past; the shadows of the cypress trees lay like bars on the paving and the willow-fronds danced.

The Gates of the Ortokapi opened, and closed.

Outside were their horses; the bright-harnessed mares from the Sultan, held ready for mounting, and the vast horse-parade of the Janissaries with company after company drawn up, their salute like a wave of the sea. The Sublime Porte, the great doors to the Topkapi Seraglio, opened, and closed, and the Ambassador of France, his head high, his eyes seeing little, rode out into the dust and the stench and the noise of Constantinople.

21

CONSTANTINOPLE: THE MEDDÁH

Many years later, understanding it all, the Baron de Luetz, who survived, used to tell how that day they left the Sublime Porte to the measure of the Chorea Machabaeorum, the Danse Macabre, the Danza General de los Muertos. They stepped from the high throne of Suleiman the Magnificent, and under the dark aegis of Gabriel.

Lymond knew it. He acted through the whole elegant masquerade: rode to the shores of the Golden Horn and, taking his leave of his escort, crossed it and remounting climbed the packed streets to the Embassy with metallic precision: careless of the amazed and whispering tongues and the curious glances from those in his train. As they rode side by side through the shops and buildings of Pera, d'Aramon, unable further to govern his temper, burst into low speech. 'I thought you a man of honour, professing to hold me in friendship. You told me you had an honourable petition to present. I have heard you present a tissue of lies, prostituting the name of France to gain your own ends. I cannot hope that you have considered the figure I shall cut, returning home after a lifetime of service, of knotting this friendship between Turkey and France. I have stood by today and seen a rogue snap it asunder.'

Lymond's face remained schooled to a hard kind of patience. He said, 'France will disown me: you will not suffer. Give me a few days only, until I have the Sultan's final reply. Then you may repudiate me.'

The crowd pressed in. The Baron de Luetz smiled and nodded, his face livid, and a moment later went on, in the same low, sharpened tone, 'You already have his reply. He has refused.'

'I have his public reply. He is concerned to keep his new Vizier's loyalty, and less to fulfil a problematical demand from the French. I have offered him another way, if he esteems it at all worth the trouble.'

How much had those diamonds been worth, in the casket sent to Roxelana Sultán? With justice the Sultan might, if he chose, tell his Vizier that Roxelana, pleased by the jewels, had let it be known that she wished to keep them, and to return the boy and the maiden instead. He might even claim, if he wished, that his wife had ordered their release without his, Suleiman's, knowledge. The Baron de Luetz said, harshly, 'You plot well. Perhaps you will even succeed, with so many innocents dragged in to your aid.'

Lymond turned in the saddle. Light on the reins, his jewelled gloves were held low and half-curled before him. The snowy fields of his ermine, spread round him fold upon fold, were spiky with damp; and sweat misted all the spare planes of his skin. He said—and there was savagery in the soft voice—'The Devil is Graham Malett's already. Who is left, their riper age rotten in all damnations, but the innocent?'

The blood came coursing down the hill towards them just after that: smooth as rosewood in the white dust. Between the doorposts, on the Embassy's high wrought-iron gates, they found the dismembered bodies of the Ambassador's porters, carved hot like young lamb, and spitted there among the dark flowers.

It was the beginning: the first of the unholy incidents which none could explain: for which no culprit could be found, although the Sublime Porte, expressing unqualified horror, tripled the Embassy's cordon of Janissaries and agreed by return to Lymond's formal request that all his staff might henceforth carry weapons.

Weapons did not save those who died when the well water was poisoned; when a wall collapsed in the yard of the kitchen boys; when a carter going for hay was half flayed and blinded, and a sewing woman taking bread to her family was drowned in her own half-empty cistern. Food failed to come, or was rotten. Servants from outside, frightened, no longer arrived, and those within, afraid to go out, quarrelled and wept.

It was Francis Crawford, taut and careful, who pulled them together like the children of a beleaguered city and taught them the rules they must follow for their own self-defence. He forced from the Sublime Porte still more Janissaries, and a modest chain of supplies from their benignity to keep the small garrison nourished. The work of the Embassy came to a halt. By the end of a week, and the first morning without incident, hysteria was giving way to antagonism. The new Ambassador had enemies. But for the new Ambassador, none of this nightmare would have happened. M. d'Aramon was approached.

His own preparations to leave had been halted: how could he desert his seat and his flock through this horror? He listened to what his people had to say; and went to find Mr Crawford.

Lymond had been out. His cloak, marked with grime, lay where he had dropped it, and he was standing, as he did not often do now, looking out of the high windows of his room and over the wet roofs of Pera to the grey domes of Stamboul beyond. It was not the first time, d'Aramon knew, that Crawford had left the Embassy, and had succeeded in coming back quite without harm. Alone of the household, it seemed, he could go abroad with impunity or stay at home without mishap. It had been in d'Aramon's mind to point this out to the uneasy household. Instead, on reflection, he walked into the room and, closing the door, put it to Lymond himself.

'You think I am behind these outrages?' Francis Crawford had little patience, these days, with trivia: he turned, and kicking the

342

fallen cloak to one side, moved past it restlessly, to his wide desk and back. 'Why? To force Suleiman to do what I want, in case France blames him for attacking the Embassy? Not very plausible. As it happens, now untenable.'

'Why?' Sometimes one must be blunt.

'While I was out, a parcel was delivered this morning. It is there.'

M. d'Aramon followed Lymond's glance to the desk. On it was merely a long packet, wrapped in white silk. The embroidery was Persian. 'Open it,' Lymond said.

M. d'Aramon knew what it was, even before his fingers felt the filigree of the casket and his eyes were blinded by what lay within. There was also a letter, signed by Khourrém Sultán and written in a firm hand in very good English. Khourrém Sultán, overturned with the ill fortune which made it impossible for the Ambassador to receive that which was dear to his master, was likewise constrained to return that which would cause her to suffer, daily, a reminder of another's unhappiness. Close by the seal, someone had inscribed a small, six-pointed star. 'I'm sorry,' said M. d'Aramon.

'You needn't be,' said Lymond. He returned to the desk and, taking the letter, placed it back in the casket and covered it. 'Your reign of terror is over. You came just now, I take it, to ask for my resignation. You have it.'

Into M. d'Aramon's mind came a memory of a calm voice pronouncing. *If my petition is refused . . . I shall have to use other means.*

He said, 'You say our reign of terror is over. How do you know?'

'Perhaps you haven't heard the news?' said Lymond. The shape of his hand on the casket caught d'Aramon's wandering gaze. With tension and inadequate food they were all lighter, all blanched like roots in a glasshouse. Francis Crawford said, 'The vigorous and never successless Suleiman leaves for Scutari today, and thence south. It leaves Graham Malett in undisputed possession. That is why I am resigning.'

And as d'Aramon continued to look doubtful, Lymond smiled. 'You don't understand? The attacks were made in order to force me to leave. While I am Ambassador, it is difficult even for Graham Reid Malett to treat me just as he desires. As a discredited fugitive I shall have no one to avenge me.'

'Then . . .' said M. d'Aramon; and gathered firmness. 'Then you must stay.'

This time, however briefly, Lymond laughed. 'I wonder how many men, placed as you are, would have said that. I thank you. But even if I were content to see the members of the Embassy reduced one by one to the graveyard, I can no longer as Ambassador pursue my own object. I have failed to free the two children or kill Graham Malett as an envoy of France. Let us see what private enterprise will do.'

Onophrion helped him prepare. He would take nothing but the

343

plainest of dress, and a cloak in whose pockets could be carried all else he required. Onophrion gave him a waterbottle, and, overriding protests, a satchel with enough dried food to last several days.

Alone of the few who knew Lymond was leaving, Georges Gaultier did not go to him that evening to wish him Godspeed. Since the attacks began, Georges Gaultier had kept to his room, and had stared back in hostile alarm when Lymond, only four days before, had laid before him a summons with the seal of the Capi Agha, from the Seraglio. The message, in Turkish, was easy to decipher. A tuning fault had developed in the horological spinet. The presence of M. Gaultier was requested to repair it.

The usurer's eyes had tightened on reading. 'It cannot be so. The spinet was in perfect order when it left here.'

'It *is* so,' Lymond had said gently. 'I arranged it myself.'

For a long moment, Georges Gaultier stared up at him. Then: 'Excellent,' he said. 'Then you may repair it yourself.'

It was then that Lymond, sliding forward a stool, had seated himself softly, saying, 'I cannot do that, as you know. I am speaking of the safety of Philippa Somerville.'

'Oh?' said Gaultier. 'You're not asking me to stab the Grand Vizier? I am merely to come out with Mistress Somerville in one pocket, and the child in the other?'

'You are merely, at no risk and out of the goodness of your heart, to take a message to Philippa Somerville from me,' Mr Crawford of Lymond and Sevigny had said.

And Gaultier's thin mouth had twisted. 'Is she my family friend? No. This is where I make my living, Mr Crawford. We cannot all afford to be troublemakers. If you wish to meddle with the Seraglio, ask someone else.'

The Ambassador had persisted, still quietly. 'No one else can plausibly touch that spinet save yourself. Or Marthe, if she were here.'

'Then you will have to wait, won't you?' had said Georges Gaultier. 'Perhaps the girl will do it for you. You will, I'm sure, have no qualms about asking.'

'They ask for someone tomorrow. It is at the Seraglio's bidding: you will be perfectly safe. No one dare touch you.'

Georges Gaultier grinned. 'Make my excuses,' he said. 'An old wound in my shoulder . . .'

'Or a new one,' said Lymond. The blade in his hand was slender, its hilt set with cornelians: above it his eyes were cruel and cold. The dealer hardly felt the featherweight pressure as the steel slid through his tunic and shirt, and then the sting as it touched the soft flesh of his shoulder. His cheeks blanched, he stared up at his tormentor.

'You will do it,' said Francis Crawford.

And Gaultier, staring into those unyielding eyes, maintained stubbornly, *'No!'*

344

He saw the face above him harden and change. Then Lymond calmly leaned on his knife, driving it slowly through skin, flesh and sinew till Georges Gaultier, his voice piping, his fists ineffectually beating, gave a snort and fainted away.

Afterwards, the tale had lost nothing in telling, nor had it enhanced Lymond's popularity with the household. They feared him: they blamed him somehow for every catastrophe, even while granting that but for his skill and providing they would have suffered far more. Since Gaultier was in a sense a man of his own company, the Baron de Luetz had not interfered. But it did not, at bottom, make him any less relieved, in a strange emotion streaked with anxiety, to know that by the morning his self-willed successor would be gone.

Where Crawford was going, and how he proposed to cross the Golden Horn, at night, without being observed by his enemies was something M. d'Aramon took care not to ask. After dark, there was little legitimate traffic. A few fishing-boats . . . the dairy-boat drawing its hidefuls of rank butter behind it. He had heard the man Zitwitz making certain inquiries and reporting on them to his master, but he had made no effort to eavesdrop. The less he knew, the better for him and for France.

By morning, Francis Crawford had gone, and France was without an Ambassador.

*

Much later, under wintry skies dove-grey with rain, Jerott Blyth crossed the Bosphorus and landed on the mud flats of Topkhane with his baggage and horses, with six beaver-tails and the folded hide of an elephant, with the garrulous old man called Pierre Gilles and the ichneumon called Herpestes, and with the young woman called Marthe, whose brother feared and ignored her.

Archie Abernethy was no longer with him. As far back as Chios he had looked from afar at the horses, the boxes, the camels, the golden-haired Marthe and the broad-shouldered, white-bearded man with his pet on his shoulder and had shaken his head. 'If it wasna the Wooing o' Jock and Jenny, I've heard of nothing to beat ye for gear.'

'We've nothing to gain by concealment,' Jerott had replied curtly. 'We're part of the Ambassador's suite.' They had found no ship to take them to the Sublime Porte, and Pichon, faced with another overland journey, had left them. Jerott, desperately anxious to make speed to Constantinople, was saddled with Gilles, who took his own time and to whom Marthe adhered, Jerott thought suddenly, like a warder to some elderly captive. And Marthe in turn Jerott would not let out of his sight, although her nearness was misery.

'Aye,' said Archie thoughtfully. 'A kistful o' tin pennies like yon will fairly make the streets rattle. I've a mind to make a more modest entry myself.'

'Go as you please,' said Jerott. 'You'll get there quicker. I don't suppose even Gabriel recognizes you like that.'

'I was thinking as much,' said the mahout with cordiality. 'Forbye, I might lay my finger on one of the weans. Better a fowl in hand nor two flying, whichever fowl it will be.'

'Have you money?' The inexhaustible revenue from Lymond. Give a Turk money with one hand, and he will permit you to pull out his eyes with the other.

'Oh, aye,' said Archie, the scarred face composed. 'And if not, I've a trade I can ply. There's ae matter more. D'ye plan to be sober or wilsum?'

Jerott's dark face reddened with anger. 'You may look to your own practices,' he said. 'And leave me to mine.'

'Aye,' said Archie, without undue conviction. 'For if Mr Crawford is killed, we'll need all the wit we can muster between us.'

Archie vanished without the rest of the party's being aware that he was there. It took Jerott three weeks to retrace his steps to Smyrna and drag his party north, over plains fertile and barren; through streams and by hills and over mountainous roads swept bare by rain into glistening structures of agate and porphyry.

Sometimes they were fortunate to sleep in a khan, where charity provided them with a modicum: wood, meal, oil, some meat and some bread, and where all, Gilles assured them with resonance, would be accepted, *sive Idolatra, sive Turca, sive Judaeus, sive Christianus*. For the rest they slept within the mud walls of a village, set in boulders and dirt, its flat roofs terraced with wicker; or a township among dwarf oak and arbutus and chestnut trees, where boar roved wild on the hills and the low ground in summer was feathered with purple spireae.

They passed fields of cotton and buffalo dragging their rough wheelless ploughs; herds of glossy black Caramanian sheep and a flock of goats, clothing a whole living hillside as they flowed home to the fold, the low sun red and capricious with shadows. Sometimes a windmill. Sometimes an ass-driven waterwheel, its buckets sounding like camel-bells. Once a caravan crossing their path of thirty camels laden with mushrooms. But mostly a silence, broken by the chattering of their mules' feet on stone and on boulder and the chime of the harness, and the voice of the drivers, lazily: '*Gel! Gel! Gel!*' . . . Hurry, while over their heads eagles and ravens floated and vanished.

The roads were plain; and with their guides and their drivers and their Janissaries they were well protected. But this time they were thrown more on their own resources than before: their fellow travellers were evanescent and few: for audience, for entertainment, for sympathy, they had only themselves.

The most experienced traveller among them was the first to adapt. Pierre Gilles was still more than capable of the outrageous pronounce-

346

ment; the sonorous intonation, the exposition in French and bastard English and the purest of Latin on every phenomenon met by the way. But it was muted and measured, and in its way, often welcome. The hostility he could not help displaying, sometimes, to Marthe appeared no more, with an effort, than the tart impatience of the old with the young. On Jerott he enjoyed lavishing, at times, his powers to instruct and to shock.

With the half of his mind and the fraction of his heart which were free, Jerott warmed to the old fiend; while hypnotized, as the hare by the snake, with the presence of Marthe.

She too, out of necessity, had sheathed the barbs of her weapons. The brittle gaiety she had brought from Aleppo had changed into tranquil sobriety. Cool, deft and imaginative, she added to the ease and comfort of an uneasy and uncomfortable journey and if she spoke, spoke of practical things. Once, she went with Jerott to the shack of a blacksmith, and helped him choose the thin iron shoes from the unperforated shapes, big and small, hung round the booth, and watched the smith fit it cold, crouching, his shins crossed, supporting the hoof.

The coins he was given in change were small and blackened. Even before they left the booth, Jerott sensed her excitement, and when Gilles later identified them it blazed out, her eyes sparkling, her face illumined with eagerness. They were from the days of Alexander: worth something for their antiquity: worth more for the wonder of their existence. Then the flame was extinguished, and she was careful again.

Of her, Jerott asked no questions. And only once, approaching the snows of Olympus, with the city of Bursa ahead, did he ask Gilles about his precise plans.

For a moment, the old man was silent, riding along, his feet in their great leather boots dangling, shovel-stirruped, half to the ground. 'Plans. I find them unnecessary. If some papers of interest propose themselves, I shall examine them. I have an offer from the Seraglio Librarian, and another from one or two monasteries. I have in mind a leisurely stay, perhaps in the city. You will reside at the Embassy. I shall call if I need you.'

There was no object in pointing out yet again that he was not a paid employee; that he was concerned with a quest of his own; that the length of his own stay in Constantinople was problematical at the least. Jerott said, 'You mean to stay in the city? Where?'

Pierre Gilles cleared his throat. 'Anywhere not entirely unsuitable. The girl here has an uncle who is buying a workshop between the Bazaar and the Hippodrome. They can give me a bed.'

Jerott Blyth reined in and stared at him. 'Gaultier is buying a house? He and Marthe are staying in Constantinople?'

'So it appears. There will be plenty of work for him,' said Gilles roughly. 'Few other clockmakers in the city: no one who can work with Western musical instruments. No other agent for antiques. He's a Christian, but the Moslems don't care. So long as he pays up his taxes.'

But Jerott, riding on, was silent. He had been wrong. He had envisaged at worst a quick confidence trick: a swift act of treachery. But to throw in their lot with the Ottomans was something again. If Gaultier, that careful man, was uprooting his business and investing in property, it meant that whatever happened, he was sure of security. Or that the prize was so big that he could afford to lay out and lose in the process the price of a house?

Gilles said, 'If you look over there, you will see the horses bringing down the snow for Suleiman's sherbet. The ajémoghláns do the work regularly, and it's taken to the Sublime Porte and kept underground till needed. *Heu prodiga ventris hi, nives, illi glaciem potant, poenasque montium in voluptatem gulae vertunt.* Pliny. They did it in Nero's time, too. D'Aramon prefers water frozen in snow. He keeps a civilized household. I hope your friend does as much.'

Odd that until Archie put the thing into words, he, Jerott, had never even thought of the possibility of Lymond's dying before him. His own hurt, his vexed abhorrence of so much which Lymond had done and said, had blinded him to the fact that this was not an exercise in high ethics. Gabriel had gone out of his way until now to preserve his victim at all costs, tenderly, as in Nero's flakes and crystals of ice, so that he might distinguish more clearly the nauseating destruction of all those around him.

It had to end some time. Some time, the cat would trap the mouse for the last, teasing time, and his true and exquisite punishment would begin.

If it happened: if he and Marthe and Gilles got to Constantinople and found Lymond dead, what then? Jerott thought. And though his hands were cold on the reins he found the answer easily enough. If Lymond could come so far and risk so much for the sake of an idea: an idea of duty and compassion which had nothing to do with the affections; a concept of evil quite apart from the calls of revenge, then he could do no less. Up to his rescue from Mehedia, Jerott realized now, looking painfully back, he himself had done almost as much, freely and gladly, for the opposite reasons. All he had done had been done for Lymond. With the vanishing of that star from his firmament he had found nothing to take its place: nothing to drive him but pique.

He was quiet when they rode into wall-less Bursa through the plane trees and pines, and was hardly surprised, so elegiac was his mood, to find himself in a city of mourning. It was Marthe who elicited the reason, in a khan of anxious and uncommunicative travellers. On his way south to join Rustem Pasha and the army, the Sultan Suleiman had halted to make camp outside Eregli, and had summoned from his post in the provinces his son and heir, Prince Mustafa, whose command of the Janissaries Rustem Pasha had so extravagantly praised.

It seemed to Suleiman, they said, that Mustafa had alienated his people's affections. It even seemed that Mustafa had put it about that the Sultan was old, and incapable of leading his army; and that he, Mustafa, would be better ruling now in his place.

Whatever the truth, Suleiman had sent for his son, and whatever his misgivings, Mustafa had promptly come. Within the royal pavilion, he had failed to discover his father. Instead there awaited him three mutes, with a bowstring, which they knotted, and pulled round his neck. It was said that from behind the hangings, Suleiman watched his son die.

In Bursa lived Mustafa's widow, and their four-year-old child. 'Let's get out,' said Jerott briefly. And they did.

Ten days later they crossed the Bosphorus, and rode up the hill to the French Ambassador's house. Rain, the fifth blessed of God, soaked the vines of Pera and Onophrion Zitwitz, welcoming them in, spoke like a man who had forgotten the sunshine.

M. d'Aramon had gone back to France as soon as the Sultan left the city, and in his place M. Chesnau had arrived at last from Gallipoli and was acting as chargé d'affaires. M. Gaultier remained, in moderate health, anxiously awaiting Mademoiselle. M. le Comte . .

'I understood Mr Crawford had been appointed Ambassador,' said Jerott. His pulses thudding, he did not know how angry he looked.

'It was so. He was received by the Sultan,' Onophrion said. 'Unfortunately, the Sultan was unable to agree to free Mistress Somerville and the child, and M. le Comte resigned his position, to recover his freedom of action. I do not know whether you have heard that Sir Graham Malett is Chief Vizier in Rustem Pasha's present absence. . . . Mistress Somerville and the child are in the Seraglio. The whereabouts of the other child is not known. May I ask whether your own inquiries have borne better fruit?'

'We haven't got the other child, if that's what you mean,' said Jerott. 'Where is Mr Crawford?'

Onophrion flinched. 'Forgive me. I believed I had told you. On resigning, His Excellency left the Embassy quietly. We have not heard from him since.'

'I think,' said Jerott, 'it is perhaps time we did something about that. Would you kindly inform M. Chesnau that we and M. Gilles are all here, and have M. Gaultier told that his niece has arrived? He should perhaps know,' said Jerott acidly, 'that he has bought a house half-way between the Bazaar and the Hippodrome, and that M. Gilles is going to stay with him. With his ichneumon.'

*

Despite his thinness and pallor, and the dark rings which came so easily under his eyes, the child called Khaireddin grew daily more handsome; flat-backed and blue-eyed, with arched feet and small, well-made hands, and yellow hair curling like silk. His manners were pretty, because he was beaten daily, where it would not show, when he made a mistake; nor was he allowed to taste his broth, his rice, his bread and sesame oil until he had recited the words he did not understand and practised the other things he had to do.

It was better than the boat filled with sponges, for there the grown-ups had forgotten to feed him at all, and had flung him off when he tried to beg, frightened and smiling, in the only way he knew how. He seemed to remember when it was better still, on a long, long journey inside a boat, when he ate a lot, and always seemed to be sleepy, and had no lessons at all. But that was a long time ago.

Názik, the nightingale-dealer, saw that all his charges were watered and fed, and kept in good looks. Alone among the bird merchants and fowlers of Constantinople he had a house, instead of dwelling in gardens and heaths, his nets and lime-sticks spread; his falcons and gled-kites taking partridge and woodcock and duck to fill his customers' pots and to feather their arrows.

Built of timber, secure under the arched walls of the Beyazit Mosque, the house was long and narrow, with an upper storey for his own private purposes, and behind, a netted enclosure for the free-flying birds. His talking birds he kept separately, and his cages, and his children.

Of the last, Khaireddin was perhaps the most amenable: he was certainly the youngest by far, and the source of a large part of his master's income. Thinking of the future sometimes, Názik wondered if the great lord whose money he was receiving would one day die, and the child be left on his hands. Once the boy was older and more skilful, and free of the infant ways which made him so hard to keep clean, no matter how often he was shouted at, he could be trained to bring in a fortune.

There was a cage, in onyx and pearl, which Názik longed to buy for him. He had already shown him the other, the iron one which could be heated on charcoal, into which he put boys who disobeyed. In fact he had used it only once, on a young Jew who had hacked off a customer's hand. The noise had upset the nightingales.

His orders were never to let the boy out of his sight, nor far from the shop. Within those limits, he could use him as he pleased, so long as his life was not endangered. For that amount of money, no less than the threat which came with it, Názik would have kept the boy under lock and key, had he proved wild or unruly. But he was too young to be cunning, and too weakly willing to be troublesome, except out of stupidity. Názik had found him once touching the bright, fruit-laden ships in the stalls of the fruit merchants, and twice with the story-teller. In each case he had let him come home unmolested. Allow him to be seen, his instructions had said. His shop was watched, he knew, to see if they were carried out.

About the reasons for it all, Názik felt no curiosity. There was no limit, he knew already, to the whims of mankind.

*

In the Seraglio of Topkapi, the child called Kuzucuyum was divested of his leaf-green silk tunic and trousers and whipped, as Gabriel promised. It is fair perhaps to say that Roxelana Sultán had not expected it, or she would not have kept Philippa, clumsy-fingered, at her side for an hour; so that when the girl left at the end of it, and fled through the dim mesh of corridors in a rush of warm, scented air, it was already over when she came, gasping, to the head nurse's courtyard.

He was too shocked even to cry properly. He lay like a waterless flower in the cot, blood streaking his white linen wrappings, and sobbed soundlessly in a high, rushing alto; his eyes unseeing, his round fists thrust on his chest. When Philippa touched him, choking, he went rigid; when she spoke to him, he paid no attention. She had failed him, she understood. With loving reassurances she had coaxed him to live among strangers, and the strangers had turned on him, and she had not come. It had happened before, although she was not to know that, and neither did Kuzúm remember his branding.

But something of the terror of it must have remained, for although the weals were light and healed fairly quickly, he became very quiet and balky to feed: sitting in round-eyed defiance with a mouthful of food, deaf to persuasion and orders, although if they pressed him too far, he would begin to tremble, and Philippa made them stop. You could not explain, in another language, that he was summoning all his courage to test the boundaries of permitted behaviour, beyond which he now knew it to be so terrible to trespass. He had been shouted at and attacked: he did not know why. How was he to know when it might happen again?

Philippa saw his strained face looking after her each day when she had to go, and ached because he did not call her back. He loved her, but she had not saved him before. How should he look to her to save him again?

Evangelista Donati had been so confident. Once within the Seraglio, she had said, who can hurt you or the child? Yet Graham Malett, their prime enemy, was here, in power, and claiming the child as his own. And the Sultan was leaving, they said.

Philippa knew, when she saw Gabriel's golden figure from the Divan window, that whatever demands France might make, she and Kuzúm would never be freed. But it was worse still than that.

Through them, she now saw quite clearly, the final conflict with Lymond would be forced to its climax.

The ridiculous present the Embassy had brought, the horological spinet, had been wheeled into Khourrém's rooms, and no doubt she, Philippa, would be expected to play it. Fear and apprehension, daily occupying the pit of her stomach, had made her in other ways grimly determined. She took a long time to approach the Sultana's private apartments, and a long time to find her way back. She sometimes took a long time even to turn the handle of the door: particularly if the visitor was Gabriel.

After all, she understood very little Turkish, and certainly not Turkish spoken softly and fast, without an interpreter. Even if she were seen, none would concern themselves. From taciturn, Philippa turned very gay among the other girls, though to herself she was capable of long stretches of silent communing. Then came the day when she was asked to perform on the spinet, and she had her first close inspection of the ungainly thing: a chest of drawers topped by a campanile.

To her relief, the frenzy of bells and of puppetry stilled as she drew out the keyboard. It at least was fashioned properly: the naturals formed of ebony had arcaded ends; the accidentals had slips of ivory. Flowers, in leather and ivory, were set into the soundboard. Inside the drop front was pasted a small oblong card, unseen until the drawer was opened. On it, someone had written in English, *I have tuned this myself. C. de L. & S.* The script was level and small, and extraordinarily clear. She had never seen it before.

With hands which shook very slightly, Philippa ran her thin, flat-padded fingers over the keys. The quilling, she realized at once, was very light indeed; the touch of the plectra gave a soft bright tone which ran like spray under the hand—all except . . . there. Pausing, Philippa played it again, and then continued, launching into the piece she had chosen, while she thought. At the end, dismissed to busy herself with sweetmeats, she put her request in a low voice to the eunuch who understood English, who presently approached Khourrém and received the necessary permission. If the spinet required adjusting, she might stay behind when Roxelana Sultán went to the bath, and do what she could.

There was only one note out of tune: one of the lowest accidentals, seldom employed; but so glaringly off pitch that, once struck, it was bound to be noticed. With great care, alone in the silent room, Philippa drew out the drawer to its fullest extent, exposing the sound-board with its shimmering parallel strings. There she made an interesting discovery. Caught in the turns of the wire where the faulty string coiled round its wrest-pin was a small scrap of paper. And on the paper, when she carefully unwound the wire and released it, was nothing but a minute drawing in ink of a six-pointed star.

352

Philippa stared at it for a long time before she realized what it meant. She turned it upside down and reversed it: she even took it to one of the candelabra and heated it, with all too clear recollections of the house of Marino Donati. There was nothing there at all but the imprint of a star. A star with six points, not the eight of the star of St John. The star of David: the symbol of Jewry.

At that point Philippa held the paper in the candle flame and watched it burn, and then, thoughtfully, returned to the spinet. A Jew, in this haven of Moslems? No, wait. No Jew, but there *was* a Jewess. A dark, middle-aged woman with more than a hint of a moustache, who came in weekly to instruct in cosmetics and undertake small commissions: the matching of silks for their embroidery; the passing, Philippa suspected, of love-letters. . . . It had seemed more than likely, to Philippa's practical mind, that everything she was told the woman took straight to the Kislar Agha or Kiaya Khátún—it was, after all, a harmless enough outlet for their excess of romantic imaginings and could come to nothing: no man unauthorized had ever entered the harem and left it alive. Was she to gather from this that she could trust the Jewess?

Or was it all a trick of Gabriel's, to mortify her and taunt Mr Crawford still more?

She could not recognize the writing. Supposing Lymond had sent it: how could he guess she would be the first to perform on the spinet? Or was it well known at the Embassy that there was a dearth in the Seraglio of performers, and had he guessed that, at any cost, she would apply for permission to play it?

Chewing her nails thoughtfully, until she remembered, Philippa stared at the strings. Then she noticed something else. The faulty string had been slack. It had also been doctored. It had been filed, very lightly and carefully, at the point where it would require to wind round the wrest-pin in order to secure its true pitch. If she were to tune it properly now, it would break.

And someone would have to come from the Embassy to repair it. There were no spare wires: she had asked.

Again, a trap for Mr Crawford? No, hardly. The Ambassador himself could scarcely come, wire in hand, to mend the Sultana's spinet without causing unusual comment. Gaultier, then; or Marthe. Someone who could bring her a message or take one away; or at very least learn some news of her and the child. It must be so: it must be from Mr Crawford.

Looking again at the card, Philippa grinned suddenly at its very austerity. Gabriel, surely, of the deep, insalubrious mind, would have signed it *F.* or *F.C.* Only Lymond, surely, would have appended that collection of impersonal surnames. And to him, somehow she was sure, belonged that small, picturesque script.

Philippa pulled the card off and, regretfully, burned it. Then she tuned the spinet quickly and deftly, standing clear as the wire snapped.

She was still there when Khourrém Sultán came back and comandeered her services in rewriting a letter in English. The coincidence seemed so great: that it should be to Lymond, and that it should refer to herself, that Philippa, rather pale, thought at first it was a dastardly trick. Then she realized that the Sultana had probably not even connected Durr-i Bakht, the Pearl of Fortune, with Philippa Somerville: might not even know in the first place what petition the French Ambassador had made which the Sultan had rejected. She was merely refusing the present Lymond had offered her since she could offer no service in return.

So it seemed. Philippa had copied the thing out, correcting the phrases with her heart hammering. The eunuch might read English, although he could not write it: she dared not alter the sense. But she could and did mark it, when no one was looking, with a small star of David close to the seal.

It was done and she was kneeling, awaiting dismissal, when Khourrém Sultán opened the casket and ran through her hands, for the last time, the *tespi* in diamonds it had contained. Staring at it, Philippa did not hear the words of dismissal. When they were repeated, she looked up at her mistress with her face aghast, as if she had witnessed an accident; and her eyes full of shocked tears. Then she bowed herself out of the room and, stumbling through the harem, curled on her own cushions and cried.

*

As Lymond had once had cause to observe, Ishiq, the lad who guided the blind Meddáh, took good care of his master.

Holding the story-teller's purse, with its small store of aspers, he charmed the ferryman at Tapano to take them both over the Golden Horn for a canto of Yúnus the illiterate, the mirror of whose heart, as they said, was undulled by the turbidity of loopings and lines. Once over, he soon established a circuit, as he often had before, with other masters: the courtyard of Ayasofya and the market under the Hippodrome; the covered bazaar and the gardens of the Beyazit Mozque.

They did well. Despite his grey hair, the Meddáh's speaking voice was sweet and untroubled; and he told the stories people liked best to hear, such as the one of the Persian khoja who played a trick upon a Baghdad khoja and his son, as well as the heroic romances, and tales of his own, shaped to his company. They were given meat and yoghourt and sweet water to drink, and slept most nights on straw: on the third day they were bidden to perform at a wedding, and on the fourth they gave of their art at a circumcision ritual and banquet.

These Ishiq enjoyed. But they were tiring and noisy for a man in

354

ill health, and sometimes Ishiq's arm ached from guiding his master and tending him when the day's work was done. Best then he liked the days in the Beyazit garden, with the nightingale-dealer's birds singing under the walls of the Old Seraglio, even in winter; when one of the children would steal out over the waste ground and stand at the edge of the brazier, listening, until the marvellous tale ended, and Ishiq went round, collecting aspers and bread in his greasy cap, and those who did not want to disperse would gather round the Meddáh, asking for more.

He was kind to the children, perhaps knowing that the black folds round his eyes frightened them. For them he told short, strange stories in which a child always triumphed, even over the great Cham himself, and to the small one from the nightingale shop he was always gentle, talking slowly and clearly, until the boy would stand almost touching, at his knee. Then he would run away.

That day the Meddáh was very tired. It was cold. Although the coarse brown robe he wore was stiff and thick, it was worn, and the bands of fur round the hem and yoke and wide sleeves were bald and glazing with age. When a slender man, well but quietly dressed, called Ishiq over and, after commending his master, offered them both warm food and a bed for the night Ishiq did not hesitate, but listened to the directions given him; and so soon as the crowd was dispersed, he tugged the Meddáh's worn sleeve, and helping him to his feet, began to guide him as he had been instructed: up over the crown of the hill and down the twisting lanes on its slopes to the north-west, until they came to the long, double-arched line of the aqueduct of Valens, and the lane of rough-timbered houses beside it.

It was raining. Unlike the principal streets, this was nothing more than rubble and mud, so narrow that the overhung storeys almost met crooked window to window, and the wet had hardly laid the stink of turned fat and cabbage heads rotting. He stopped where he had been told.

It did not look like the house of a wealthy man. Ishiq hesitated; but his arm ached, and the Meddáh, dragging, felt the threshold with his stick and leaned on it, as on a crutch. Then the door opened and the man who had spoken to them in the garden appeared, smiling, and beckoned them in.

It was strange inside. The house was crowded with people. Two playing chess on a painted cloth looked up and smiled, and a man, naked but for a wolfskin, turned round, a sheep's leg-bone held against his ridged brow and snapped it, throwing the pieces away, before picking up an ox's chest-bone and doing the same thing, absently, on his elbow. Another man, in a corner, was stringing a bow, humming. Ishiq, lagging, turned to see his guide ahead turning and beckoning, and taking a fresh grip of his master, he pulled him doggedly on.

355

The next room was a bedchamber, the mattresses already lying unrolled, with the quiet man standing beside them. 'He is unwell, your master?' he said gently to Ishiq. 'Perhaps he should sleep. Or are you hungry? When have you eaten?'

'Not since morning,' said Ishiq. 'But the Meddáh has not eaten for more than a day. He feels no hunger.'

'He should eat,' said the stranger. 'Wait. Come with me to the kitchen. We shall let him repose while I send for some food I know will please him. Then you will both sleep.'

He was kind, and courteous. Ishiq went to the kitchen, where he was made much of by the old woman there; and when he went back to the bedchamber it seemed that the Meddáh had already eaten and was sleeping. Assured that his master was well, Ishiq curled up and slept.

He did not know, some little time later, that the kind stranger knelt down beside him and after listening a moment said, 'He is asleep. He will stay so for a while. Tell him to come in.'

He did not see the curtain move and a second man enter, clean and sweet-smelling and clothed all in silk. Or had he been awake he would have seen him move over to the other occupied rug and kneel by the still, blindfolded face of the Meddáh, upturned and silent in sleep.

For a moment the man in silk watched him. Then he stretched out a long, graceful hand, and turning back the worn fur of the collar, began to slip from the story-teller's shoulders the folds of stiff, heavy robe, pulling it little by little from under him until he lay revealed in pale, soft lawn and close-fitting breeches, his arms lying still at his sides.

The man in silk smiled, and from the other side of the bed, the quiet man who had acted as guide caught the smile and returned it. Then the comely man lifted his hands, and running them up the sleeping man's face, with one movement smoothed away the grey wig, and pulled the black scarf from over his eyes. Underneath, the sleeper's hair was not grey, but fair and shining and dark-edged with sweat. And the eyes below the bandage were not blind, but half-waking and blue.

'Sweet singer,' said the man in silk gently. 'O bird of the dawn. Learn love from the Moth, who yielded up its life in the flame without protest. The footprints of the dog are like roses. What, then, are thine, coming to me?'

The sick blue eyes closed. '*Mikál*,' said the Meddáh, his voice almost soundless.

'Yes, Efendi,' said the musical voice. 'And this is Murad, my friend. Thou hast no money?'

And the Meddáh, who was young and not old, and dressed in European shirt and trunk hose and whose name was Crawford of Lymond and Sevigny, opened his eyes and spoke, in the spent voice which was not a pretence. 'You gave me something to take, a while ago. What was it?'

Míkál gazed at him; the beautiful boy whom he had last seen long ago at Thessalonika. 'That which would ease thee. Hast thou no gold, that thou couldst not buy it thyself?'

'I have money. What was it?'

For a moment longer, Míkál looked at him. Then, taking a cup from the floor, he held it so that its contents could be seen. 'This. I did not know how much to give thee. But thou hast need of more, much more than is wise. Thou art ill, Hâkim.'

'I know that.'

'Thou dost not know why?'

'No. . . . There have been other times like it; but never lasting so long. This time . . . it was bad,' Lymond said.

'Until now? The pains have gone?' asked Míkál.

'Almost. . . . What did you give me?'

'Hâkim . . . it was opium,' said Míkál gently. 'Enough to send sweet sleep to the strongest of men for twenty-four hours. Yet after an hour thou art awake and in pain, for thy body knows this drug and will not be satisfied. In this cup is the rest of thy sleep; and thy death, if thou must continue its slave.'

You have all the afflictions of the highly-strung, Sybilla had said to him once, long ago. *All your life you will have to disguise them*. And so, as with everything else, he had set his teeth through each attack and gone on. Until he realized, with his mind darkened with fantasies and with every nerve burned stark to the quick, that this time there was something finally, fatally wrong. 'Where is Ishiq?' Lymond said quietly. He had managed, at least, to pull himself up and sit like a sane man on his rug.

'Asleep, over there. He knows merely that thou hast paid him, as I suppose, to take the place of his master. With thine eyes covered he could not guess thy need of the poppy. Nor did he break faith with thee. For five days I and my friends have sought thee in vain. Thy betrayer, beautiful as a bird, is the colour and form of thy voice.'

'My debt to Ishiq I know. My debt to you I am beginning to learn. Míkál, I do not think it possible that I could have come to rely on opium or anything else without my own knowledge. How could it be?'

'There is an old Turcoman saying, *The soul enters by the throat*. For many months, thy body has fed on it, Efendi, to make thee thus distempered without it.'

'*Without* it?'

Míkál was patient. 'This illness, lord, is suffered by those who need opium and cannot obtain it. Always before there has been one at hand to give it to thee, in whatever secret manner it is administered.

Now thou art away from thy enemies and they laugh, for without it, thou wilt be sick unto madness.'

Every camp has its traitor, Kiaya Khátún had said. And Francis Crawford knew the traitor in his. He said, 'Thank you. It is clear now. I have only one thing to ask. Is there a remedy, or must I take opium until . . .' He did not finish. He had seen this with other drugs: the mindless dervishes, led by their keepers. The mad, communing with God. Greater and greater doses, to produce less effect, until mind and flesh, besotted, fell slowly to pieces. To end, with nothing accomplished. *Know that this world's life is only sport and play and gaiety and boasting among yourselves, and a vying in the multiplication of wealth and children.* Indeed, Gabriel was great.

'There are two paths,' said Míkál. 'Thou mayest shun the drug. This is the great illness thou hast tasted, exciting in mind and body a commotion from which the reason may steal away, as the diffusion of the odour of perfume.'

'And the other?' His voice this time was under control: the Meddáh's voice, pleasant and light. He could not steady his hands, or marshal the tuned body slipped out of tone, but the soul was still there, thought Míkál. Resting his hands delicately on his crossed legs, he answered.

'The other course is to withdraw thyself day by day from the drug, disregarding thy senses and tied to thy purpose, as to the piece of wood stuck in the wheat pile, round which the bulls and cows tread and turn. It will take many weeks during which I shall stand thee in stead of thyself, for thou wilt be languid and faint, as a man with a wound which will not be staunched.'

'There is no time for that,' Lymond said. 'What I have to do must be started now; and I must be able to do it. When it is finished, I can take your first course, or your second.'

In his purple silk, the fine hair laid on his shoulders, the bells bright on his ankles, Míkál sat still as an image. 'When it is finished,' he said, 'there may be no choice. I have told thee, already thy body accepts and wears as a halter that which in another person would kill. With this drug, thou hast dispensed with the warning of pain. The soul pursues its desires and will not know when the body has failed it.'

'I have no choice now,' said Lymond; and shrugged; and lifting the cup Míkál had shown him, drank it down to the dregs.

22

CONSTANTINOPLE: THE GOLDEN ROAD

The house Georges Gaultier had bought was indeed exactly half-way between the Bazaar and the Hippodrome of Constantinople. That he bought it after and not before the arrival of his niece Marthe and her learned friend Pierre Gilles from Aleppo was something nobody stressed.

Jerott helped them take their belongings across the Golden Horn and into the City from their temporary abode with the French chargé d'affaires. No one else seemed particularly interested in aiding them: Jean Chesnau, who ran the Embassy now was not a d'Aramon. And Gaultier did nothing: hanging back green-faced and groaning, nursing the wad of bandaging round his left shoulder.

Hearing the story of that wound, from many sources, Jerott wondered what on earth had possessed Francis to inflict it. He had hoped of course to make contact with Philippa through Gaultier, but the man was craven and this was his punishment. Its crudity Jerott found troubling. It was unlike Lymond: and a number of other things he heard about the late Ambassador's behaviour were perplexing also. Jerott wished again, bitterly, that he had not left before they arrived, and that he could have shackled Marthe under the eye of the one person living with the capacity to understand and control her. For reasons of his own, if Marthe was right, Lymond had refrained so far from doing either. But the time was coming, Jerott thought, when he must.

In the meantime he had disappeared, and Jerott could hardly force his company on a strange ménage. He would continue to stay at the Embassy, but at least he could make a reason for discovering where this odd household of three—and Herpestes—was proposing to stay. Then he had Francis to find.

He knew they were watched. But he had seen no sign of Gabriel and heard nothing from him, although Chesnau had told him of the palace the new Vizier had occupied, to the south of St Sophia. As soon as Lymond had left the Embassy, the persecution they had been suffering had ceased.

The damned place was full of hills. Riding up from the waterside behind the packmules, half the time they were climbing a running gulley of mud between the high pavements and twice, without the swarm of half-naked children who ran with them, they might have got stuck. Gilles, digging in his purse, announced, '*Natura sunt Turcae avari et pecuniarum avide*,' and flung them a handful of coins. His need for a secretary, it seemed, had suddenly vanished. Staring bad-temperedly from under his spicular eyebrows, he had informed

Jerott, in plain French, that he would send to him at the Embassy when and if he required him. The anger, Jerott thought, was not directed at himself, but at Marthe and her uncle. In which case, why go and stay with them?

The New Jerusalem was not looking its best today. The gold-domed mosques and slim minarets among the wet gardens were splendid enough, and so were the baths and the carved marble fountains and the stone palaces of the aghas, with their looted Byzantine porticos from the older, buried palaces of Justinian, for which he had stripped the temples and towns of an empire. But where now were the bronze roofs and gilded tiles of Constantinople; the silver columns; the statues of Ulysses and Helen; of Homer, in talk and dispute, so alive he was thought nearly to breathe? And where the figure of a bronze Justinian, clothed like Achilles, looking east with the world in one hand and his other outstretched, forbidding the barbarian to advance?

A Barbariis et incendiis deletas esse, said Gilles. Destroyed by those barbarians; by earthquake and by fire. Less than fifty years ago thirteen thousand people had died here when the earth moved and broke the conduits from the Danube to the City, and the waters of the Golden Horn deluged Stamboul and Pera. Seven years ago the Bezestan, the round covered market to which they were now climbing, had been burnt to the ground, and all the houses beside it. Hence the rough shacks and booths which clung to the walls of the mosques, crowding the workshops already tucked into the arches of hammam and medrese. There were other streets, small and twisting and arcaded with pentises of wood, which were lined with booths: passing, one caught the smell of goat fat and uncured leather; of crushed sesame seeds or melting honey; or of new sawdust from a lathe shop making handles for hatches, with outside a stack of new wood, white and red-gold yew from Mengrelia, dripping and satiny in the wet.

The houses too, Jerott thought, looked temporary: some of white clay bricks and some wooden-framed, the timber filled with sun-dried clay brick, their latticed wooden balconies projecting over the street. They came in all sizes and shapes, but most had no more than two storeys, with a slanting roof of thick-ridged clay tiles, or flatter roofs sometimes planted with orange bushes and shrubs. And everywhere, open spaces and ruins: the arches and columns and fountains and baths, the churches and gardens of the city built to match Rome.

Gilles knew them all. Here was the Forum of the Bull: there the house of Concordia and the Temple of Thomas the Apostle. Under this plain the hot baths of Honoria and the Forum of Theodosius. There the baths of Achilles, which Justinian making the aqueduct remembered, and whose conduits he was able to use, so well in those days were the pipes and passages recorded, leading the great underground network of water to the city's cisterns and fountains and

360

baths. There, still standing, the historied column made by Arcadius, a hundred and forty feet high, with its spiral banded design celebrating the victory over the Scythians; and here the column, now pinned with iron and broken with fire, which once held the statue of Constantine Helios, whose sunny nimbus was framed by the nails which had pierced Christ on the Cross.

The rain had swept most people from the streets. Men went by barefoot, their burdens strapped to their heads, their splashed skirts kilted up to their calves: children played: a laden buffalo pressed by, and a tripe-seller's donkey. Few beggars, for the crowded almshouses of the Mehmet Mosque took care of charity, *loi, foi, nation que ce soit*. Instead, sometimes, the crumbs of a rude justice: the bones and flesh of a criminal staked outside the house of the injured; or the cry, *Yâ Fattâh!* from the pavement where a paralytic crawled for his living. They turned a corner, into a street which was little but a quarry of broken stone and mud, with houses set like playing blocks in the dirt; or sometimes huddled two or three together among a scattering of winter bushes from which broken marble glimmered, the vestiges of some Byzantine palace or church.

Outside the biggest house, a square whitewashed structure with a rough wall enclosing a yard, Gaultier stopped, and the procession of packmules behind him. '*Here?*' said Jerott, astounded.

'It is not easy,' said Georges Gaultier with asperity, 'for a foreigner to obtain premises in Constantinople. Until I can find something better: here.' Marthe did not look round, but he had the impression she was smiling. Then Gaultier opened the gate, and they moved inside and unloaded.

Such was the briskness of the whole operation, that within an hour Jerott found himself, deep in thought, on his way back to Pera again. From the little he had seen, Gaultier's house was as unprepossessing inside as out. . . . The walls were plain and plastered; the floors wooden and uneven; the ceilings timbered and cursorily painted in a particularly nasty shade of mid-green. Even with the carpets and cupboards and bedding they had brought with them, it would hardly look, Jerott thought, like the Star in Bread Street. The ichneumon had appeared quite distraught.

Marthe at least had had the grace to thank him, with characteristic irony. 'Receive the blessings of St Blasius, patron of bones in the throat. It cannot have been a congenial task. After all your admirable sheep-herding from Aleppo: what a pity you won't be able to guess, in the end, what knavery we are planning.'

'I could have you watched,' said Jerott, rashly. With her cheeks flushed and her eyes sparkling, the fine-chiselled face took the breath away.

Marthe laughed: a true laugh of mischievous pleasure. 'Do,' she said. 'Why not? You might see the ichneumon.'

She had the door half closed when he said, on a sudden impulse of despair, 'Marthe . . . what are you going to do? People die here, you know, for very little. Who will help you?'

She stood in the doorway and smiled. 'Who will help me? Myself. What am I doing. . .? Don't you remember the jingle?

Where are you going, pretty fair maid, said he,
With your white face and your yellow hair?

That was all she said, and she shut the door, laughing. It took Jerott most of the journey home to find, searching his memory, that he had no recollection at all of the rest. Francis would have known.

*

Elsewhere in the city, a number of interesting occurrences took place.

The blind Meddáh, of whom the boy Ishiq took such good care, continued to make his rounds of the city and to give pleasure to the simpler-minded of her citizens, who found the story-teller quiet, but by no means enfeebled. At night, he was given shelter at the house near the Valens Aqueduct which the Pilgrims of Love shared with their brethren and other friends of the road.

It was one of these, curled up outside the Mehmet baths preparing to spend a comfortable hour in the ashes, who accosted the Jewess Hepsabah courteously for alms as she came out pink from the apodyterium, her slave behind her with the covered brass bowl on her head holding her linen, her smock and her coverlet. It also held, as everyone knew, the embroidered chaplets and girdles and scarves Hepsabah spread out and sold wherever she went.

She gave alms, with a loud and not very delicate quip, and received in return the address of a suitable customer whose house was surprisingly near the Valens Aqueduct. There she encountered at least one face she knew; was given rather too much Greek wine and a great deal of gold, and both exchanged news and received a number of instructions. These, on her next appointment at the Seraglio, she carried out.

Archie Abernethy arrived. Unlike Jerott, he made no production of his entry, but slid in one bright frosty day and made his way to two or three people he had known, long ago, in his chosen profession. Under Suleiman the Magnificent there was no central menagerie: only a collection of beasts kept in temporary confinement in the empty rooms of the half-ruined building called Constantine's Palace, against the east city wall. The rest were maintained, for the Sultan's amusement, in the courtyards and sunken arcades of the old Royal Palace, below the walls of the harem.

Hussein, the Chief Keeper of the Royal Menageries, was an Egyptian: a lethargic man with a paunch who was pleased to see

362

Abernaci, the old Indian friend so light on his feet and so full of boundless vitality, who could spend all day shuttling tirelessly between the two collections; flying out of the city to bargain for fodder and back to arrange the profitable purvey of dung. A man full of ideas.

Archie reported to nobody: there was really no need. In a matter of days one of the Pilgrims of Love, who had been drifting aimlessly in the region of Constantine's Palace and other places frequented by animals at regular intervals, came up and slipped the Egyptian twenty aspers, as was the custom, to have a closer look at the beasts. Abernaci showed him round; and they had quite a comfortable conversation. After the visitor had gone, Archie and the Egyptian drank some of the aspers, guardedly, like the old gentleman of the city who shouted before taking wine, to warn his soul to stow itself away in some corner of his frame or leave it altogether, lest it be defiled. Then they went about their business as before.

Jerott's trouble was that he had no idea where to report. If Lymond were still in Constantinople, and alive, he was making no effort to contact the Embassy, although surely by now he must be aware that he, Jerott, had come. Of Archie's movements he was ignorant; and it did not in fact occur to him that he might also have arrived in the city. Instead he set out to apply all his hard-won experience, doggedly, to tracing his leader.

It was not the simplest of tasks. To begin with, he had to lose the Janissary with whom the Embassy despite his protests persistently saddled him. He did so after a few days, during which he walked the poor man mercilessly all through Pera and Constantinople, sightseeing; getting his bearings. It was during these excursions that the house of Názik the nightingale-dealer came to his notice, and he remembered what Archie had said. The following evening he asked the Janissary's advice on a matter of entertainment, and was led, with a certain grave camaraderie, across the Golden Horn and into a building, where he paid handsomely for the privilege of forgoing the said entertainment and left by a window, while the Janissary waited patiently below.

It did not take Jerott long to reach the waste ground outside the Beyazit Mosque, empty now of its slumbering pigeons and the unloading camels and the throngs round the letter-writers and the sellers of sherbet. Hooded and unrecognizable in the long Turkish robes they all wore outside the Embassy, Jerott sat crosslegged under the trees in the Beyazit garden as the lamps lit in the mosque, and the turbaned heads of the tombstones on their narrow white shoulders peopled the grass with queer shadows, and watched the timber house with the aviary under the walls, its lights streaming over the ground.

Unlike the other houses beside it, the house of Názik came to life in the evening. People came and went in the grey, fading light, and he could hear children's voices, and a raucous cry, often repeated, of some large corvidian bird. Once a dog howled and was silenced, sharply, with a blow.

Jerott slipped nearer as it grew darker. Far above his head, the voice of a muezzin called in its minor key from the minaret: long, slow notes broken by three or four more of a quick appoggiatura; blending into strange chords as other, distant voices took up the call. Already the space round the square had become a path for dark figures moving into the mosque. Soon, after their ablutions before the silver spouts of the fountain, they would kneel inside on the soft carpets as he had seen them, before the carved wooden minber and the candles thick as a man, in their heavy brass sticks. Pale soles in couples, shining in a carpeted gloom, filled with the fluttering movement of backs bowing and straightening; and the sound of many voices, made small by the echoing space but still sharp and attacking, like the muted arguments of men in a bazaar. The sky was Prussian blue, the trees blue-black around him.

Across in the nightingale-dealer's house, two shadows among many, a man and a small child, emerged and were lost in the darkness. Jerott got to his feet. Where? Yes. . . . There, downhill, where the ruins of some ancient building glimmered in the stray lamps, the rows of windows framing the indigo sky. A man and a child: a child from whose hair the lamplight struck sudden gold: whose walk was too slow for the man, who paused suddenly and, bending, swung the boy up on his shoulders.

He was too far away to distinguish properly their shape or their features. Suddenly the shadows closed on them utterly, and Jerott, soft-footed, started to run.

The hands which closed on his shoulders came from nowhere and were many. Silently he fought, and at first with success: his strength they had not expected, nor his profound expertise in the matter of hand-to-hand fighting. They did not call; but he felt one man go down with a gasp and another grunted and fell back as he hit him. But there were more, coming on undeterred, and although he was a courageous man and a good soldier, Jerott could not handle them all. He went down, cursing the absence of companions and weapons and even the absence of the Janissary, provided so carefully with this very contingency in mind.

Except that these did not appear either casual cut-throats or robbers. Silent as they had been from the beginning, they pulled him to his feet, holding him in spite of all the force of his body, and having tied his hands and gagged his mouth, swiftly under his hood, marched him between them into the darkness after the man and the child.

The house they took him to was downhill, and not far away: just before they dragged him inside he saw the ghostly arches of the

364

aqueduct straddling the sky. Then the door slammed behind him and he was thrust into a small room where a young man with long hair and silver bells on his ankles and sash looked at him searchingly. 'Untie him, and take his cloak off. Ali, thou hast suffered?'

Ali, with a burst nose, had suffered. Jerott said, in indignant French, 'I have suffered too. Is this Turkish hospitality: to set on a foreigner?'

The boy with the bells, he was rather worried to see, was suddenly all attention. 'A foreigner? Thy name?'

'A guest,' said Jerott awfully, 'of the Embassy of France. Whom you will be kind enough to inform of my presence. My name is Jerott Blyth.'

'Ah . . .' said the youth with the bells. And turning gracefully, waved to Jerott's captors. 'It is well. You may depart.'

'But——' said he of the burst nose.

'. . . in Love,' said the youth gently. There was a shuffling, but that was all. Jerott's attackers filed out, reluctantly, and shut the door behind them.

'Well?' said Jerott.

'I was told I should meet thee,' said the other man thoughtfully. The lustrous, long-lashed eyes surveyed the splendour before them: the black hair and flushed, high-nosed face; the muscular body. 'My name,' he added after a moment, 'is Míkál.'

Jerott, running a hand through his disordered hair, dropped it and stared back. He knew about Míkál. The Pilgrim of Love to whom Archie had entrusted Philippa, and who had abandoned her at Thessalonika, with the result, incredible though he still found it, that both she and the child were now in Topkapi. Míkál who had joined Lymond's ship, following, and had gone with Lymond to the Beglierbey's house where Salablanca had died and he had so nearly been murdered as well. . . .

Speaking of it, Onophrion had drawn no conclusions, but Jerott had plenty. He said sharply, 'What have you done with the child?'

'Ah: thou hast seen him,' said Míkál. 'He is safe. More: he will return to Názik's house shortly. We have paid only for part of the night. Thou shalt thyself watch him depart.'

'I'll see him now,' said Jerott. He had nothing with which to enforce the demand: only the power to dominate: a solder and a knight over a pilgrim of love trailing bells.

Míkál smiled. 'We have swerved from courtesy,' he said, 'in our welcome. This I regret. There is a saying: *Night is the stranger's.* Thou wilt sit and feast with me of pigs endorred and flampayne powdered with leopards, and like King Solomon's great bird the hoopoo, thou shalt tell me thy secrets.'

Jerott merely repeated it. 'I want the child now.'

'There is a saying,' said Míkál with composure, '*Chi pecora sifa, il lupo se la mangia*. Make of thyself a sheep, and the wolf will eat thee. Alas, I am no sheep. As to the child's presence, I say God will give. I offer thee meat in many dishes instead.'

Jerott said, gently, 'Did you hear what I said? I want the child here, now. Or I shall break every little, shell-like bone in your body.'

Míkál considered him. From his flesh Jerott smelt jasmine and sensed the faint shiver of bells. Míkál said, 'Threats are as froth in the mouth of the camel. Set aside thy vehemence and thy choler. The child is now in the care of his father.'

Jerott's reaction was instant. But even so, Míkál was at the door of the small room before him, hands outspread barring his exit. 'Patience! Wouldst thou uncover thy master like a plant which the wild ass digs up with its hoof?'

Jerott Blyth placed his palms on the door on either side of the Geomaler's head, and staring into the beautiful face said with clarity, 'If Mr Crawford is here, I want to see him. Immediately.'

Tilting back his head, Míkál raised his eyebrows. 'There is no barrier. I shall take thee myself. Only, one chooses the hour when one calls on an opium-eater.'

There was a moment's silence. Jerott took down his hands. He said, 'Are you speaking of Lymond?'

'I speak of Mr Crawford thy friend, the child's father,' said Míkál. 'To take the poppy in old age or in childishness is a paltry thing, not uncommon. To take it in the flower of manhood, like a she-pig with an itch in the belly—this is melancholy indeed.' And as Jerott, his brows drawn, stared at him speechless, Míkál added swiftly, 'Dost thou believe I defame him? Follow then, and observe.'

There was no one in the passage when Míkál opened the door. He took Jerott to the upper part of the house: through two darkened rooms, and came at length to a curtain which hung before a lit door-way. There he stopped and, lifting one delicate hand, drew the edge of the hanging aside so that Jerott without being seen could look into the room.

The light within, which seemed so bright after the darkness, was only the soft flicker of candlelight, and the jewel-like glow of a brazier set on the carpeted floor and from which the faint, pleasant smell of sandalwood stirred. To one side, his hair bright as the embers, a child played with a handful of shells, sitting straight-backed arranging them between his bare legs; squirming sleepily on his stomach to prod them into rows, his thin white shirt rucked up around him. Even in that light Jerott could see the bruising marks on his thighs: spreading blossoms of purple and yellow which disappeared under the cotton. The boy's eyes were sunk with fatigue and he was not clean, although he had been washed superficially, and the tunic was fresh. But the profile was quite unmistakable. It was the child Jerott had last seen in the arms of a Syrian silk-farmer in Mehedia, his saffron hair hung with blue floss, his eyes black with terror.

There was no fright on Khaireddin's face now. It was almost without expression indeed as he concentrated on his shells, moving them slowly from one design to another on the carpet beneath him. But there was something visible: something not quite a smile: a kind of secret awareness that rested in all the curves of the baby face with its dark, swollen lids. Then Jerott saw Francis was there too.

Quiet as the child, he was stretched, half-sitting, half-lying on the rim of the candlelight, his weight on one elbow; his hands loosely entwined. Jerott had the impression he had been speaking. A moment later he realized he *was* speaking at intervals, in soft, disinterested Turkish, the words drifting in and out of a leisurely silence. The boy gave no sign: bent over his play, he might have been alone in the room. Only one could sense that he was happy, and listening.

There was nothing casual about the blue eyes fixed on the downbent blue gaze of the child. Francis Crawford's face in this fleeting moment of privacy was filled with ungovernable feeling: of shock and of pain and of a desire beyond bearing: the desire of the hart which longs for the waterbrook, and does not know, until it sees the pool under the trees, for what it has thirsted.

Jerott's throat closed. He made to move backwards and was stopped by Míkál's hand on his shoulder and Míkál's soft voice in his ear. 'Now dost thou believe?' And reluctantly, Jerott looked again at that motionless, gentle-voiced speaker and saw this time something different: the eyes which were too blue, and the shadows which were too dark; a toning and tension of skin which was subtly absent. The face of a man, as the Geomaler had said, living on drugs.

Then Míkál ripped back the curtain.

Lymond sprang to his feet, his face horrifying in its change to stark fury. The child gave a whimpering gasp and crouched, shivering, where it knelt, its head tight in its arms; all the neat patterns of shells tumbled sideways. Exposed helplessly on the threshold, Jerott found his mortification swept aside in a surge of answering rage. He said. 'Poor bloody bastard: he hasn't a chance, has he? Kicked from cradle to whorehouse; his mother slaughtered by Gabriel, his father propped up by opium.'

'*Get out*,' said Lymond. His voice shook: whether with reaction or rage or opiates hardly mattered. Jerott had never seen him so uncontrollably angry. '*Get out and stay out, you blundering sheep. . . .*'

'Try and keep me,' said Jerott, his face white, and swung on his heel.

'*Wait*,' Lymond ejaculated. He took two steps forward and stopped, his eyes still wild with anger. 'What else have you done? How did you find me?'

'He followed the child,' said Míkál deprecatingly. Jerott, shouldering past him, did not reply. He was half-way across the dark room on his way out of the house when the curtain behind him was ripped off completely and his own shadow sprang up before him, black on a lit square of light. He paid no attention. He flung the second door open, his left hand on the doorpost. There was a flash, and a spark arched through the dark and stayed, quivering, between the spread-eagled fingers of his left hand.

It was Lymond's knife; thrown by Lymond, who following it noiselessly and almost as fast stood now behind Jerott and said viciously, 'Opium or not, I can still throw a knife. Next time it will be through the thick of your hand. *Turn and go back.*'

Seen close at hand, the pupils of both his eyes were like pinpricks. 'To hell with you,' said Jerott, and snatched at the knife. Lymond's long fingers, streaking past, got there just before him. Then the knife was gone, flung across the length of the room and Jerott's right hand was dangling, numbed by a blow on the wrist.

'Turn and go back,' said Lymond, his face livid still. 'That house was watched. This house will now be watched. Míkál, you are a fool. Had you waited, you would have discovered he is besotted over a woman. Go and find out, if you can, whether Mr Blyth has been followed. Jerott, get into that room.'

Míkál's immense eyes were appealing; his manner placatory. He said, 'Efendi . . . the child is due back to Názik in five minutes. . . .'

Lymond stopped dead. For a moment he stared at Míkál, then very slowly he turned and walked back to the threshold of the candlelit room, and moved a little inside. Jerott followed.

The child was crouched in a corner, as far away as he could reach. He had been weeping, but silently. When his client came in—his client who had thrown a great knife—Khaireddin rose, his nose red in his waxen white face with the great rings round the distracted blue eyes. He rose and, walking shakily over to Francis Crawford, reached up and stroked the hand which had thrown the big knife. Then holding it in trembling hands, his eye sideways, he laid it against his wet cheek. 'Beautiful Hâkim: give me thy kisses. . . .'

He stopped gasping as the man's hand was wrenched back from his small ones; and began to sob helplessly, without looking up. 'I am good,' said Khaireddin. 'Oh, I am good. I will eat. I have stopped being naughty. Give me kisses, Hâkim.'

'Oh, my God,' said Jerott; and turned his back. He knew Lymond was kneeling. He heard him take a long, soft breath and expel it; and then take another. With that he spoke to the child, his voice low but level and friendly. 'Thou art good. Men quarrel, and are friends. Thou and I are friends without quarrelling. . . .'

Jerott looked round. The child, level with the kneeling man, had moved nearer, his eyes wide, his face uplifted as if to embrace him. Before he could touch him, Lymond rose, and, looking down, smiled. 'Keep thy kisses. Thou art almost a man; and a man chooses to kiss

only the persons he loves. Then thy kiss will be a big gift indeed. . . .
It is time to go. Míkál's friends will go with thee.'

'I am good?' said the strained treble.

'Thou art good,' said Francis Crawford in a dry voice; and looking
up, watched as Míkál slipped from the doorway to take the tired
child away.

'There was no one,' said Míkál briefly. 'He has not been seen.
Come, Khaireddin. It is time to say goodnight to the dark.'

The far door with its splintered frame closed softly behind them,
and their footsteps could be heard moving through the other dark
rooms. Lymond did not move or speak. Jerott, behind him, dropped
suddenly on the worn cushions and holding his face hard in his hands,
said, 'I'm sorry.'

'You are sorry now,' said Lymond without expression. He turned,
his face stiff, and stood looking at Jerott. 'Now that you have seen
him. He has been living like this, and suffering like this since he was
born. That is why I am here. For that, and to kill Gabriel.'

Jerott dropped his hands. He said in a low voice, 'Why did you
let him go back?'

Lymond continued to look at him. 'He is watched. We are not
ready for him to disappear yet; only for him to know us and trust us.
There are others to be made safe.'

Jerott's dark face was lined. 'Philippa, in the harem? Francis, what
can you do? And who else? You can't mean Gabriel's child? That
was your son, man, who went out just now. That was the child Kedi
nursed; the one I found with the silk-farmer. What better proof do
you want? That and his looks . . . and his guts.'

'Thank you,' said Lymond. 'If that is a compliment.' He turned
round, and finding a chest by the brazier, sat on it. 'As it happens,
I've seen the other child too. There is nothing to choose between
them, for looks or anything else. The other is under Gabriel's shadow
as well.'

'But Kedi,' said Jerott, aghast. He tried again. 'It is known that
Kedi brought up your baby. Every independent scrap we know con-
firms that. And Kedi was with this child, Khaireddin, when I found
them. The babies could not have been changed before that without
Kedi knowing.'

The fire had gone from the blue eyes: only a tired irony showed
there. 'What did you promise Kedi?' said Lymond. 'What future did
you paint for her and the child, once you had rescued them? Freedom, comfort and happiness; no more whippings and misery. She
would have called the child Jesus of Nazareth if she thought that was
the infant you wanted. . . . Of course she would know, none better,
if Joleta's child had been substituted for the one she had cared for.
But she wouldn't necessarily admit it. That was why she was killed.
As for Philippa's child, there is no proof there either. Joleta's baby was

taken when young to Dragut, and returned to the House of Donati many months afterwards. Whether it was the same child or not, no one, it seems, can now say. Children alter. Joleta is dead, and Evangelista Donati and her brother. . . . Does it matter? Should it matter which child is which? What would your Grand Master say, Jerott?'

Jerott looked back, his grey gaze heavy and straight. 'I should not like to give my life for any child of Joleta and Gabriel.'

Lymond said curtly, 'No one expects it of you.' But he added, 'Would you stand back and watch that child suffer and die? No? Then I promise you, whatever its parentage, you could not do it either for the boy they call Kuzucuyum.' And surprisingly, considering the dark face of the man at whom, in cold blood, he had thrown his long dagger such a short while before, Lymond laughed. 'A sentimentalist to make troubadours flinch. You didn't answer my question. . . . It doesn't matter. Tell me your news.'

In essence the story was easy to tell, if you omitted everything of substance about your visit to a tekke of Bektashi Dervishes in Aleppo, and your subsequent suspicions of a beautiful woman called Marthe. Of the kinship between Marthe and Lymond himself, Jerott said nothing. He talked at length about Gilles and his encounter with Archie at Chios, and he gave an account finally, if a brief one, of the house Gaultier had taken south of the Bezestan to share with his niece Marthe and Gilles. Lymond chose to question him in some detail about that, and about the relationship between Gaultier and Gilles. On Marthe, he spared Jerott's feelings. Or perhaps, reading between the lines, he guessed more than he wished to put into words.

At any rate, as Jerott ceased, Lymond said, 'Laudable, Jerott. It wasn't an easy assignment. I should apologize too for what happened just now. . . . It was partly Míkál's mischief and partly anxiety. It would have caused so much damage had you been followed.'

'And partly opium?' said Jerott.

For a moment Lymond thought, studying him. Then he said, 'I think you should try to put that out of your mind. You will see me taking it quite often. So long as I do take it you will not, I think, notice much difference. I am not using it to escape my responsibilities, if that was what mainly exercised you. But I should be indebted if you would keep what you know of it meantime to yourself. It will, I suppose, be all too obvious one day, but there is work to do first. Archie is here, and will help.'

'What can I do?' Jerott said.

Lymond changed his position, with care, and clasped his hands round his knees. 'Do you mean that?' he asked.

'Of course. You don't suppose you can do it on your own?' said Jerott. 'What can I do?'

Lymond grinned. 'When the clay for thee was kneaded, as

370

they say,' he remarked, 'they forgot to put in common sense. You may sit there while they bring something to drink. Then you may listen.'

Unsuspected, Jerott left half an hour later, to join his Janissary and make his staid journey home. Back in the house by the aqueduct Lymond walked slowly through to his chamber, and opening the shutters, stood there for a long time looking at nothing, until he found Ishiq's face at his elbow.

'And in the night, give Him glory too, and at the setting of the stars,' said Francis Crawford. 'You don't understand me, but I am only, like Khaireddin, saying goodnight to the dark.'

*

Shortly before this, Philippa Somerville was debarred from the Sultana's rooms.

They had discovered, she supposed, that the Pearl of Fortune was none other than the English girl for whose return the French Ambassador had petitioned. A week or two earlier, and it might have mattered, but by then she had already begun taking lessons, in the harem, from Hepsabah the Jewess. She had learned how to dress her hair with jewels and ribbons, unaided: how to trim her nails so that they grew oval and shapely. She learned to embroider, picking up irregular threads in a weave as fine as the eye could distinguish, and marshalling them into a hazy garland of violets and peonies, each stitch even; each design impeccable inside and out. She embroidered slippers for Kuzúm, and veils whose edges were fronded with carnations and jasmine, cut out and skilfully sewn. She learned how to pick a lock with a hairpin, and how to melt off a seal.

Philippa had quite a lot of news, in those early days, to pass on through Hepsabah to Francis Crawford. There were letters, if you knew where to look for them, from Gabriel to Roxelana Sultán, and from Rustem Pasha, the Grand Vizier with the army. There were snatches of talk overheard between Gabriel and Roxelana. There was evidence, finally, incontrovertible, that the supposed sedition of the Prince Mustafa against his father and his father's Grand Vizier had been something fabricated by Rustem Pasha, by Gabriel and by Roxelana, the mother of the Sultan's next heir. And that the chain of events which led to the death of Mustafa at the hands of the Sultan was due to them also.

At home in Flaw Valleys, Philippa had seen plenty of violence: had watched Flaw Valleys overrun by its enemies, and her father ride out again and again to come back with half of his company: the rest dead men tied to their saddles. Intrigue and sudden death had been the stuff of government in her country as long as she could remember. But this was the first time Philippa herself had brushed shoulders with it: had been forced to take it by the diseased hand and use it for her own ends.

She was frightened. Dealing with Hepsabah she used a bright, matter-of-fact tone which covered her nervousness. She was shocked by the Jewess's tranquillity. She knew—probably everyone knew—that in order to make himself Sultan, Suleiman's father had strangled two brothers and five of his nephews. But at least the guilt was on his own head. The tragedy had been re-enacted by this Sultan through no fault of his own, but the machinations of Roxelana, his lover and helpmeet.

Nor to Philippa's direct mind was it clear how this information could benefit Francis Crawford. No single man, and a foreigner already suspected at that, was going to overthrow the three most powerful people in the Empire next to Suleiman himself with any ease, whatever the proofs. Likelier by far that to keep his love and his pride, the Sultan would declare the proof forged, whatever his private misgivings, and would throw their accusers instead to the lions. It was not her business, however, to say as much to Hepsabah. Since Lymond had asked for it, she passed on as much as she knew; and waited, her stomach turning, for what the rest of the winter would bring.

Of Kuzúm, she now saw much less; and in that, sickeningly, she saw Gabriel's hand. Once she heard him calling, 'Are you there, Fippy? Come out to Kuzúm?' and heard his treble explain, after a space, 'I need to waiting for Fippy to come out.' He had run out of the courtyard and up the harem steps to discover her, but when she got there he was gone. The head nurse said he was at his lessons, but she could not discover what lessons she meant. Unless the grovelling ritual whose traces she had seen, for the first time, on the day of the Ambassador's visit.

When she did see him he looked pale, but although he said little, he sat very close. He had also begun to lean more on Tulip: perhaps, thought Philippa drearily, he felt a child near his own age less likely to betray him. She heard Kuzúm scolding him sometimes, over the wall: 'That a too much mouthful, Tulip.' At least, that way, he was keeping his English. She knew the nurses had orders to talk nothing but Turkish to him now. *The shepherd clutch thee fast: the wolves are many*, said the words of Jelál, ringing all day in her head. *O my black lamb, O my black lambkin, heed me!*

Then she was summoned to the rooms of the Sultan.

It happened on a Thursday, the day Hepsabah usually came, and worried her at first as she was expecting a message from Lymond. She stared at Kiaya Khátún, her mind busy, and only slowly realized what Kiaya Khátún had in fact said. The rooms of the Sultan.

But the Sultan was now in Aleppo. She opened her mouth, but Kiaya Khátún forestalled her, the dark Greek face placid. 'You ask yourself, why the Sultan's apartments? I answer that it is a State ceremony. You are fortunate in being chosen to share it. I have told the Mistress of the Baths and the Mistress of the Wardrobe to prepare you. When they have done we shall see, I trust, the harvest of these our long labours to lead you to ripeness and beauty. When you are ready, they will lead you to the Golden Road and a eunuch will come for you.'

In the baths, although they giggled and shrieked and conjectured, the other girls had no idea what was going to happen. To some of their suggestions she closed her ears, although she made jokes, as best she could, while they sluiced and scrubbed and anointed her; a different scent for each foot of her body. She knew them all now. Only a few were spiteful. Most were cheerful before what they felt somehow must be her good fortune, and only a little envious of the stiff marten trimmed robe they slipped over her head, and the three thousand crowns' worth of pearls bound in her thick, shining hair. Her pattens were inlaid with mother of pearl and with silver, and her little cap was edged with seed pearls and topped with a worked plaque in silver. She was not given a veil. Then they took her to the Golden Road.

She waited there perhaps ten minutes, her negress smiling behind her. It was narrow and carpeted, and dark in spite of the small silver lamps on the arcaded walls and the most beautiful faience in the world: tomato red, scarlet and coral, thick-laid on a flawless white ground. . . . Dear Kate, thought Philippa as the smell of mutton reached her, sickening, from the apartments above, I am robed and waiting to be taken to the Sultan's apartment. I wish I had paid either more attention or less to my instructors. I wish I knew what was happening. I wish I were at home.

A voice in her brain, more than erratic in its grasp of adult phraseology said, *I need to waiting for Fippy.* An invisible pen in her mind, hovering over her invisible diary, reread the last entry and, stoutly, scored through the ultimate sentence. She had asked Lymond for money, through Hepsabah. So soon as she had it, she could at least ensure that, outwith Gabriel's eye, Kuzúm would be fairly well treated. What might happen to Kuzúm under Gabriel's direction was a different matter. But while she could influence his fate, her place was here, and not at Flaw Valleys. . . .

She followed the eunuch, when he came, along the Golden Road, beside the big courtyard and between the suites of the khátúns and the harem mosque and past another courtyard to the big door which gave on to the selamlìk terrace, with its fountains and pool. There the eunuch turned left, and almost immediately halted outside a bronze door, surrounded by marbles.

Inside, Philippa knew, was one of the smaller reception rooms. Outside, dressed in bright coral satin, were two of the royal tressed pages, their painted eyes oval as eggs. The eunuch bowed, and one

373

of the pages, with an answering salute, consulted briefly within and then returned and held open the door. The eunuch stepped back and Philippa, trailing amber brocale and well-massaged hauteur, drifted inside.

On one side, against marble and eyeleted wainscotting, stood the Kislar Agha, the head of the harem. On the other, broad as Zeus in plumed turban and flowering velvet, sat Graham Reid Malett. Jubrael Pasha. Gabriel, himself. The door closed behind her.

Lying back, his elbows in cloth-of-gold cushions, Gabriel inspected her. The face wearing that cursory smile hadn't changed in all the months since last she had seen him in the cathedral in Edinburgh, hardly able, even yet, to understand that all his plans had fallen in ruins; flinging that last, angry challenge at Lymond. The ruddy, fine-shaven skin was the same, and the distinguished brow, and the light blue eyes, large and level and free of all guile. Gabriel said, 'My compliments, Kislar Agha. The improvement is considerable. Now kindly disrobe her.'

Like puppets in a rather poor comedy, the eunuch and the Kislar Agha bowed and advanced. Philippa's heart gave a single loud report and began pattering like a mouse on a tow-line. She said acidly, 'The Sultan won't like it.'

Gabriel looked at her, finding the interruption mildly distasteful. He said, addressing her for the first time, 'The Sultan, through his wife Khourrém Sultán, has made me a free gift of one of his slaves. My choice has fallen on you.'

'To remind you of home?' inquired Philippa.

Gabriel looked over her head. 'Take note. Tonight the boy will have six lashes at bedtime.' The blue gaze, smiling, slid back to Kate's daughter again. 'You object to being exposed?'

Philippa's brown eyes were full of surprise. 'Only when my buttons are stiff. My goodness, who's going to care when it happens nearly every day of the week and three times on Saturdays?'

For a moment the blue eyes held hers. Then Gabriel turned and spoke to the Chief Black Eunuch. Then he addressed Philippa softly. 'The Kislar Agha tells me you are a virgin.'

'Ask the Kislar Agha how he knows,' said Philippa. 'Or perhaps you have attended one of our lecture courses?' She began philosophically, stilling the shake in her fingers, to unfasten the clasps of her outer robe. 'It's better with music,' she said.

'I think you are being impertinent,' said Gabriel. 'As it is, the child Kuzucuyum will receive tomorrow a beating of six strokes. On your conduct and compliance will depend all his future wellbeing. When I call for you, you will come. Whatever I demand of you, you will perform. Very soon, Mr Francis Crawford of Lymond will be dead and the poor boy will have none to protect him but you ... the poor boys, I should have said.'

He smiled, that forgiving, magnificent smile. The eunuchs, at a sign, had stepped back without touching Philippa, and, raising her eyebrows, she proceeded to fasten her over-robe once again, her expression stoic, her knees, unseen, like peeled wicks with relief. Gabriel said, 'You know, I take it, that there are two claimants to the proud name of Crawford?'

'The other is Tulip?' Philippa ventured.

'The other is a boy now in Constantinople, found and identified by the energetic Mr Blyth. He also answers to the name of Khaireddin, but whether it is Mr Crawford's son or another substituted for him in earlier days, no one unhappily can now say. But there is no doubt that one of the two boys is Mr Crawford's unfortunate by-blow; and one of them, as it happens, is mine.'

Philippa's mouth dropped very slightly open. She shut it. 'How awkward for you,' she said thinly. 'What does the other one look like?'

'Let me think,' said Gabriel. He pursed his lips. 'Handsome; fair-haired; blue-eyed. No clue there, is there? Attractive. Bright for his age, one suspects, except that we don't know his age, do we? One must be older than the other by several months, though not more than a year; but one has had a spoiled upbringing and the other a deprived one, so how does one measure growth? Luckily, I have no strongly patriarchal emotions. I do not intend Mr Crawford to have either child. For myself I do not care if I keep one or both or if neither survives. I shall do whatever gives me the greatest personal satisfaction. . . . It pleases you, I hope, to learn that you have been lavishing your feminine instincts perhaps on that dear child born to Joleta and myself?'

'On the other hand,' said Philippa, 'if I were impertinent again, your son might receive six other lashes?'

'On the other hand,' said Gabriel gently, 'it may not be my son, but the son of your mother's friend Lymond. You cannot depend on it. You will never be able to depend on it.'

Philippa drew a long breath. It was the longest, most adult duel she had ever faced in the whole of her short life. She did not know what to believe or what not to believe: she only knew that strategy had worked, a bit, in her favour. She hadn't been stripped. She had given nothing away. She had shown nothing, she thought, of the pain and horror he anticipated from her. She had not afforded him, in fact, the entertainment he had expected. . . . She must not become a challenge. But she might force him to tire of her. She said, 'Do I become your slave immediately, Sir Graham, or wait until supper?'

Gabriel rose. 'You will stay in the harem long enough, I hope, to mourn Mr Crawford. After that, I have the permission of the Sultana to take you then to my palace, together with whichever child I select. The other will remain in the harem as surety for your most tractable conduct. I shall make it my personal business,' said Graham Reid Malett, 'to keep you aware of the course of events. You may return to your rooms for the present.'

Philippa bowed. The Kislar Agha bowed. The eunuch who had brought her, moving past, opened and stood by the door. 'Ah,' said Gabriel.

Philippa straightened. 'That reminds me,' said the Vizier, stroking his nose. 'You may take a message on your return to Kiaya Khátún for me. Inform her that Hepsabah the Jewess will not be coming today. She has been found in the At Meydan, dead and about to be plundered of a large sum of money. Perhaps the poor woman's savings. She had no relatives and since the gold was given to me, I have presented it to the two charming children you see guarding the door. They will use it, I fear, only to slip deeper into delightful and improper vices; but what can one do? They are kind boys, as your Kuzúm will discover one day. . . . Goodbye, my dear Philippa.'

Dear Philippa bowed and got out. She was sick into a fountain on the way back, and again in the Golden Road. She thought viciously, through an evening of violent shivers, that at least her visit had cost them a new strip of carpet.

23

CONSTANTINOPLE: THE HOUSE OF GAULTIER

Very soon after that, on a bright, mild winter's morning when the birds, deceived, were singing in the plane trees and there was a little green growth in the Embassy garden, Jerott Blyth left, with his body-guard, to pay an unexpected call on the house of Gaultier, and specifically on his niece, Mlle Marthe. Leaving the Janissary to await him, discreetly, on the dusty waste ground outside, Jerott climbed the single step and banged on the door.

He had not been back to the house since the day he helped Gilles and the rest to move in. That he was here at all was unknown to Lymond. Sooner or later, Jerott well understood, the matter of Marthe was going to be forced on Lymond's attention, perhaps even by Marthe herself. Meantime, Jerott Blyth was the last person to anticipate it.

An old negress opened the door. She was not well versed in Turkish, or indeed in any other language Jerott tried her with: he reached the conclusion, correctly, that she was exceedingly slow in her wits; and for this virtue indeed had been chosen. But when, alarmingly, the dark young man on her threshold showed no signs at all of retreat and, on the contrary, was inching his way steadily into the house, the negress gave up and, bidding him wait, went off into the back of the house.

He didn't wait. He had penetrated the first room: as bare as the day they had taken possession, when the door opened and Marthe hurried in. Her long hair, hastily pinned, had allowed some strands to escape and lie in coils against her slim neck, which was dirty. Her gown was not very clean either, but she had pinned a fresh apron on top in his honour.

She had assumed at the same time no alien courtesy. 'I have a client,' said Marthe in that cool, familiar voice which brushed through the nerves. 'I am afraid you must be brief.'

'My dear lady,' said Jerott. 'I shouldn't dream of detaining you. I have all the time in the world. I shall wait until you have finished.'

He looked round for somewhere to sit, but Marthe, without moving, said in the same contemptuous voice, 'I am sorry. We are discussing with him the repair of a harpsichord. It will take a very long time; and then I have another engagement.'

'You *are* busy, aren't you?' said Jerott cheerfully. 'Uncle too? What a pity. Then I shall just have a talk with Maître Gilles.'

'I am sorry——' Marthe began; but Jerott, his black eyebrows lifted, interrupted her. 'He's busy dissecting the harpsichord?'

'He is out,' said Marthe curtly.

Jerott's eyes were on the shadows behind her. He looked back at Marthe, grinning. 'Without Herpestes?' he said.

It was bluff, but it worked. The girl who was Lymond's sister turned and, closing the door, returned and sat down, her back straight, on the big tapestried chest which was nearly all the room contained. 'What do you want?' she asked.

'A service,' said Jerott.

'Lymond has sent you?' She spoke the name with scorn. Lymond's Christian name she had never been heard to employ.

'He doesn't know I am here.'

'Ah. You have found him, then,' said Marthe. 'I imagined you would. He prefers limelight to obscurity, like the Prophet whose wives could find a lost needle by the light of his body. But how rash of you to inform me! Should I not rush to the Seraglio with the news?'

'You might,' said Jerott. 'Except that, unlike your brother, I have a feeling that you prefer obscurity to limelight just at present. And also I remember what you did at Mehedia.'

Marthe smiled. 'Donna Maria Mascarenhas? Don't rely on that, Mr Blyth. My uncle and I had to get to Aleppo. I am afraid I have no more services to perform for you or your friends.'

Standing quietly at the far side of the room, Jerott watched her, his splendid aquiline face grim. 'You are a human being,' he said. 'You know now what Graham Reid Malett is. Neither he nor Francis will rest until one or the other is killed: that is their own affair and not yours. But before that can happen, the children have to be saved. One of them is already half destroyed and the other in the harem has begun to suffer as well. Gabriel is now in complete power, and has arranged to make the Somerville girl his own. . . .'

For a moment Marthe was quiet. But when she spoke, there was still contempt in her voice. 'What do you suggest?' she said. 'That I give myself up in their place?'

'I suggest that you go and rewire the spinet,' said Jerott simply.

'And?' said Marthe.

'And give Philippa Somerville the one piece of information she needs to enable her and the child to escape.'

'To escape from *Topkapi*?' Marthe stared and then laughed. '*Juste ciel*: your minds must have rotted. No one leaves Topkapi, or enters it without permission.'

'You don't know your brother,' said Jerott.

'Nor do I wish to,' said Marthe. She stood up. 'I tell you for the third time: I do not perform services. Your ingenious master must find another emissary, that's all.'

'There is no one else now,' Jerott said. He moved forward until they stood face to face; her head only a little lower than his wide, frowning eyes. 'It isn't for Lymond, or for me. It's for Philippa and

378

the children. You have every excuse to enter Topkapi and no risk to run. In a matter of days after that we shall be all gone except Francis, and whatever the outcome of that, you'll be left in peace.'

Her dirty, imperious face was set hard; her eyes cold. 'I have only to denounce you to the Janissary outside to be left in perfect tranquillity. My answer is no.'

'*How much do you want?*' Jerott said.

The great, the insufferable anger banked behind those brief words struck no answering fury from Marthe. Instead there grew on her face a charming, lop-sided smile; a smile full of irony and small, cruel amusements. 'More than you have,' she said.

He said, 'Your brother is rich.'

'He has shown me no sign of it,' Marthe replied. She smiled again. 'Shall I tell you a small interesting fact? The banker's orders which paid for this journey, and for the bribes and rewards and gifts it entailed, are now fully withdrawn. There was enough, Master Zitwitz told me, to cover the last weeks at the Embassy, and then, but for their clothes, it was virtually finished. Lymond has no reserves. He has only a second son's property in Scotland, and an estate in Sevigny, France, and a vagrant mercenary company, whereabouts unknown. You cannot pay me with these.'

I am good! had cried the small, frantic voice. And Lymond had taken his hand away, holding back every impulse; and had answered him gently, his voice level and schooled.

Jerott thought of what one man had given, over all the past year; and without removing his gaze from Marthe's defiant blue eyes he put up one hand and unfastened and flung off his cloak. Beneath, tucked out of sight, was his dagger. He slipped it out of its sheath; tossed it once, glittering in the air, and looked again, smiling, at the pale, dirty face of his hostess. 'Then,' said Jerott, 'I shall pay you with your own coin instead. Lead me, mademoiselle, to your client with the mud-covered harpsichord.' And as she opened her mouth quickly to scream, he put one capable hand over her face, and twisting her into his powerful grip, dragged her, knife in hand, through and out of the door.

She was quick-witted and supple, and not without training. But he hurled her like a kitten through the bare rooms and deserted passages of her house, while she bit and scuffled and kicked and tried in vain to free her mouth to scream a furious warning. She fought for his knife and was cut and found in Jerott's face hard indifference to the blood streaming down her neck and her arm. They burst into the kitchens and the negress, her hand to her mouth, scuttled into a corner and crouched, her breath hissing. Jerott flung open door after door. In one was a tumble of bedding: that of Gilles and Gaultier doubtless. In another he found the neatly rolled mattress and almost clinical orderliness extended to all her possessions by Marthe. Of the two men there was no trace whatever. Nor, needless to say, was there a sign of any mythical client with harpsichord.

It was then that he let his hand slip and she bit it; and seizing her moment as he snatched it away cursing, she filled her lungs and screamed with all her power. Somewhere, a voice called in answer, greatly muffled; and there was a metallic sound, and a series of regular thumps, clearly approaching; and another sound he could not identify: a low booming, veiled and threatening as the roar of some ravenous animal.

'Thank you,' said Jerott to Marthe; and stood and waited, his hand once more covering her mouth. 'It seemed time for a short cut. I feel I can deal with friends Gaultier and Gilles without requiring the advantage of utter surprise. . . . What a pity you couldn't resist that little poem, you know. I couldn't solve it, but Francis did, without thinking. He said, if you are at all interested, "Leave her, for God's sake. She's welcome to anything she can get." . . . Where would you say they are going to come up? The next room, perhaps?'

He kept his hand over her mouth as he walked her again through the door; but she made no resistance now. Only, as the sounds became definite and close and he was able, smiling that grim smile, to free her entirely, did she say, standing beside him, 'Why don't you? Why don't you leave me then, for God's sake?'

But by then the door-handle was turning: the door to a small apartment little more than a cupboard, which Jerott had overlooked in his haste. There was a sudden sharpening of the distant, sonorous noise. Then it opened, and Georges Gaultier burst through, a spade in his hands.

Jerott had respect for a spade; but very little for Georges Gaultier. It was Marthe who nearly tripped and disarmed him on his lunge forward: with a twist, Jerott recovered his balance and handed her off with a painful grip of one hand, as with the other he sank a blow deep in the little man's stomach. Gaultier retched and collapsed, the spade clattering to the floor, while Jerott stood and looked down on him.

He was very dirty. Over his shirt, his neck-strings hanging loose and his sleeves tightly rolled up, he wore a short leather jerkin, rubbed and stained with sweat and water and earth. Below it, long coarse woollen stockings and fustian breeches were also blotched and grimed on their creases: his stub-toed shoes were scuffed and blackened with wet. 'Are those the hands,' said Jerott, 'out of which trusting young harpsichords feed? What, no ichneumon?'

Gaultier stopped sobbing for breath and said, wheezing, 'How dare you force your way into this house and assault us?'

'How dare you spring out at me with a spade?' said Jerott mildly. 'Or were you going to work in the garden?'

'Marthe. . . ?' The usurer struggled on to one elbow and looked a her, but Marthe, walking away, had dropped on to a mattress and was sitting there, her chin in her hands.

'He knows,' she said. 'You fool; can't you even hold a man off with a spade?'

'I don't want to kill anybody,' said Gaultier. 'You let him in. There must be a Janissary outside. You can't kill a man with a Janissary outside.'

'Not unless you kill the Janissary as well,' said Jerott. 'Marthe might, but I doubt if you have the stamina, Gaultier. Suppose you let me into that cupboard instead.'

Gaultier did struggle to his feet and ineffectually try to stop him, but Marthe stood back, her face frozen. His hand on the doorknob, Jerott gave her back stare for stare.

> '*Where are you going, pretty fair maid,*
> *With your white face and your yellow hair?*'

And as she did not answer, he continued himself, his voice soft against the grunts of her uncle, again laid on the floor:

> '*I am going to the well, sweet sir, she said;*
> *For strawberry leaves make maidens fair.*'

Then he opened the cupboard door and walked through.

It was a small room, once adjoining the kitchen, with the remains of some shelving on the white plastered walls, and a smoke-blackened circle where a lamp was accustomed to hang. The floor had been flagged, but some of the slabs had been lifted and piled neatly against the stained walls, leaving in the centre a square hole, perhaps three feet by two, with a caking of stone dust and slime and many wet, muddy footprints marking the edges. From the threshold Jerott looked straight down into the hole. It was very black; but far below, gently moving, there was an impression of water. Flush against the walls of the hole was a worn wooden ladder, scaled and darkened with damp. The roar was very loud now.

'Don't go any further,' said Marthe. She stood up. 'If you go down there I shall brick you in. I swear it.'

His foot on the top rung, Jerott looked up and smiled. 'Would you?' he said. 'I doubt it, you know. Pierre Gilles is down there. And I don't think somehow you want Pierre Gilles bricked up. . . . If you want to stop me,' said Jerott conversationally, 'you can always call in my Janissary.'

But Marthe had already turned her back on him and walked back into the room, without watching Jerott climb, lightly and carefully down into the hole.

I am going to the well, sweet sir, she said. It *was* a well, the sides green with glutinous mosses. Small, transparent creatures slid past his hands as he gripped the wet rungs, looking down at the darkly moving surface below him, whose pattern was contoured by the faintest glimmer of light.

He had climbed down a third of the ladder when the walls of the well stopped. He could see the edge of the brickwork rising past his feet as he descended and the ladder continuing below him, unsupported, into an expanse of rippling water, which was wider than the bottom of a well: which had no confines; which spread to right and to left of him as he moved down until at last he was standing within a foot of the surface, the mouth of the well a luminous square in the brick archway over his head, and his ears filled with the bellow of Thor and the hiss of storm-raising dragons: a mighty and echoing noise which drummed and seared through his head until he felt like a man caught in a millrace. Jerott looked about him, and was silent.

He stood in a limnophilous palace of marble whose faint columns, rank upon rank, marked the darkness like runes and upheld, with their ghostly carved capitals, the winged vaults of the ceilings which spread, mottled with moisture, far over his head.

Its carpet was water: water which ran green and icy and clear under his feet and licked and floated and sucked at the white marble pillars in their dim and motionless rows: a forest rooted in foam. A forest a thousand years old; built by Justinian as part of the vision by which his new Jerusalem would flower with springs and fountains and blossom: by which, conducted by pipe and conduit and aqueduct, the sweet waters flowed from the hills to the cisterns lying like this one, sunk under the city. Some were known and still used. Some were shattered by earthquake and lay exposed to the air; deep green basins transformed into gardens or sunken alleys for workshops. Some, like this, had remained secret and safe while the buildings overhead crumbled and wasted, and the trapdoors were forgotten where men in the upper air once drew their clear water from the great manmade cavern below. Or perhaps those who still lived there thought it merely a well, and lowered and raised their buckets in ignorance.

There was a boat moored at the foot of the ladder: the boat Gaultier must have used. Jerott had stepped into it when he heard a movement above, and the square of dim light over his head blazed with flickering yellow. Then as he watched Marthe appeared, climbing barefoot down the ladder, her skirt-tails tucked into her waistband; a wax torch in one hand, wincing and flaring in the eddying draughts. Then she was down, on the last rung of the ladder; her smeared face pale in the torchlight. She said, 'Since you are here, let me take you.'

There was no sign of Gaultier. Jerott untied the rope and slotted the torch into the ring specially made for it, while Marthe lifted the pole and slid the small punt, delicately, between the long colonnades.

There were fish in the water: pale darting shapes which swarmed close under the light, flashing their thin silver sides. The columns were thick: perhaps six feet in perimeter with a passage of twelve feet between each pair, and there must have been four or five hundred of them, vanishing into the green roaring gloom. How high they were, it was impossible to tell; although from the marks on the pillars Jerott thought the cistern now held possibly as much as it could. After a thousand years, there must be small cracks and fissures in the signinum plaster and the thin sturdy bricks. Despite the ceaseless fall of the watercourse, the smooth drums of the columns and the worked Corinthian capitals were sharp-cut and intact, the masons' marks still engraved on the stone. Marthe said, steeling her voice against the rush of the water, 'We have seen only two other well-holes in use, cut in the vaulting. You can tell by the ferns. . . . There, if you look.'

He looked where she pointed: to the damp carved acanthus leaves over his head, out of which there curled, living and green, a thin clump of fern. There was no sign of the daylight which coloured it: the trapdoor, if there was one, was fastened and dark.

Soon after that they reached one of the walls, the thinly layered pink brick rising sheer out of the water into the darkness above; and Marthe, turning the skiff, began to feel her way along the rough sur-face, counting pillars, Jerott saw, as she went. Then she stopped. Set deep in the brick to her hand was an iron ring, old and eaten with rust, to which she tied up the boat, slipping the wax light at the same time out of its holder and bringing it up to the wall. In its light Jerott could see that the uniform courses of brick were here broken; and that beside the ring was a framing of stone: a rectangular aperture which had been filled in roughly with unmortared bricks of a different colour and shape.

'An old conduit,' said Marthe. 'When the level of the water drop-ped, it fell out of use. Master Gilles found it twenty years ago when he was exploring the water-system of the Hippodrome. He found that the pipes which supplied the central spina with fountains were part of a big system which ran under the seating and below all the main offices, supplying water for drinking and ablutions, and for the pens of the animals. It links up with other systems under what used to be the main Forum, and the churches of St Irene and St Sophia. He came across this watercourse when he was investigating what was left of the Church of St Euphemia: he had just begun to explore it when the Turks got it into their heads that he was removing precious antiquities from their ruins, and forbade him to investigate further. He has been back since, but never to St Euphemia. He had thought then of doing it this way, through a house, but couldn't find anyone he could trust to help with the digging. . . . There are many fractures with earthquakes, and much of the passage is blocked. But he wrote, in code, what he had found; so that his patron might one day benefit from it. . . .'

'And these papers were lost on the Persian campaign?' There was no need now for Jerott to make his voice carry: the incoming water, far through the forest of columns, reached them as a low, booming hiss. Above his head, streamers of light danced and slid on the arches and columns, thrown back by the torchlight and the changing mould of the waves. Pichon had said the old man had lost all his papers. Where? He didn't remember. And had come back from Rome this time, hoping to find them.

And had found them. Jerott said, 'Who found them? The Bedouins? The Saracens of Savah, who came to watch you arrive safely at Hanadan, and strangely failed to attack?'

'Yes,' said Marthe. Resting in the swaying boat, the torch slack in her hand, she looked dispirited and cross and queerly perplexed; and Jerott could understand, if not sympathize. Since, with his Janissary waiting outside, she could not lose him or dispose of him, there was nothing left but confession. On his own he was bound now to discover the truth, and with an upheaval which would wreck all their privacy. What, wondered Jerott, would she ask of him now? She said, her voice level, 'The Bektashi knew that we buy papers; old manuscripts and broken fragments they consider of no value. They sent us word there was a packet of great importance, and some seals and some fragments of metal, wrapped up in a bag. They sent us a page of the manuscript, and we realized that it was Gilles's account of a great discovery he had made, but in code. . . . They put a high price on the packet.'

'But you bought it?' said Jerott.

She nodded. Her hair, slipping, had coiled in great loops round her shoulders. In the bottom of the boat a little water, drifting backwards and forwards, ran over her strong, slender feet. 'In Algiers we obtained what they wanted and wrote them by pigeon. In Aleppo I met Shadli and bought the manuscripts and the fragments. They are safe, where Maître Gilles can get them——'

'When he has traced the full extent of his discovery for you? Do you know what it is he has discovered?' said Jerott. 'What if he was wrong, and you have paid Shadli for nothing?'

Marthe stood up. 'Come and see,' she replied.

The loose bricks fell inward: a simple façade, which Marthe re-erected behind them when she and Jerott had entered the opening, leaving the boat rocking outside. 'My uncle ferries the boat back to the house, and then comes for us. Usually, that is. Just now you again hurt his shoulder.'

'When I go back, I'll probably hurt the other one,' said Jerott blandly. 'So where is Gilles? Somewhere in here?'

'Follow me,' Marthe said, and, stooping, started away from the cistern and along the lightless brick tunnel which led from it.

It smelt sour. The walls were coated with moss, and stuff which oozed and glittered in the light of the torch. Here and there the walls had cracked and falls of earth and thin bricks made their advance slow and difficult, although this, Jerott saw, had been much worse until recent hands had forced a rough clearance. In that narrow space, it must have meant days of hard, claustrophobic work for all of them; with nowhere to put the excess dirt except, labouring, the distant mouth of the cistern; and always the fear that what had fallen might fall again; that the ceiling would cave; and what lay above them come crashing on top.

It was not airless. Sometimes the passage would branch, and a draught of dead odours would make the torch flicker and smoke: then, Jerott noticed, there was always, high on the walls, a minute mark which Marthe checked, in silence, before choosing her route. Twice Jerott noticed a lamp hanging; a new lamp from an old bracket unlit. The second time, Marthe took it down and kindled it, and henceforth carried that instead of the torch, which she gave to Jerott instead. Once, struggling past a half-concealed opening, he caught a glimpse of another great cistern like the one they had left, but empty; its splendid porphyry columns sunk into mud. And once, a crypt, its stone sleepers prone and oblivious; their praying hands raised to the crazed vaulting hanging broken over their heads. Then suddenly there came a moment when the blackness ahead of them grew a thin veil of light and Jerott saw, far in the distance, that the conduit gave a sharp turn; and that beyond the turn a strong lamp was standing.

Since the last broken-backed breach in the tunnel, they had been walking steeply downhill. On his right, Jerott saw another ancient aperture, closed and heavily barred; then they reached the turn at the bottom. Something long and whiskered and lithe ran over Marthe's bare foot. It had happened before and Jerott, behind, had seen her set her teeth and go on without faltering. But this time the creature itself turned and, springing, climbed on her shoulder.

Jerott had his knife raised to kill when he recognized the ichneumon. Then a lamp blazed in his eyes, and Pierre Gilles's abrupt voice said, '*Amor ordinem nescit*. Are you not afraid, Mr Blyth, that your greedy young friend will undo you? She has worked hard on her endeavour and has no wish to share it. Unless of course you have joined forces with this unhappy pair?'

He stood bent in the lamplight surveying them: a big-boned old man with a grimed shock of white hair, whose expression was no less forbidding for being smeared with dust and with slime. Marthe spoke sharply. 'You have your papers. Or will have, in a day or two. You have said—do you not believe it?—What is wealth in comparison to knowledge?'

'You pervert logic. I have offered a fair price for my papers several times beyond what you have paid to redeem them. Instead you require me to hide in a city where I am known and respected; and to dig like a dog. . . .'

'How else,' said Marthe, 'could you have uncovered the truth of the matter you described in your notes? The Turks had forbidden you this piece of territory. We offer you a chance to finish your research: a piece of pure science unblemished by gain. And you will receive back your papers for nothing.'

'Master Gilles means,' said Jerott gently, 'that he doesn't like blackmail.' He looked at the old man. 'What did they threaten to do if you failed to comply?'

'Ha!' said Pierre Gilles. 'You are, I see, a simpleton like myself. They undertook to destroy all my papers. The whole folly is now academic. I have completed my investigation and shall leave Constantinople as soon as I am told where to recover my belongings.'

Beside him, Jerott saw that Marthe had become very still. 'You've found it?' she said.

'It was a simple exercise in logistics. And from the traces found in some of the passages, quite inevitable, as I have told you. It is there behind me. I have left a light down below.' And the old man moved to one side, with exaggerated courtesy, taking his lamp.

Behind him, Jerott saw, the passage they were pursuing travelled a short way and ended: whether in a wall or in a chance fall of earth was not easy to say. On the left, where Gilles had been standing, the floor of the conduit had sagged even more, making a space littered with tiling and straw in which a man could almost stand upright. Near the floor on the same side the brickwork had shattered and fallen, leaving a sizeable gap. A gap through which, Jerott now saw, a dim light was streaming from a small room sunk far below the level at which they were standing: a room whose floor was a picture, pebble by pebble, of a panther attacked by a trident, and a chariot-race with quadrigas: Jerott could see the horses' eyes flickering white in the terre verte and cobalt, the terracotta and gold.

In the centre was a small marble fountain, full of rubble still; and a broken bench on one side still lifted a white lion's foot, in protest at outrage. The atrium of a Byzantine nobleman's house, kept intact when fire or earthquake reduced the buildings above it; and the shock which had tilted the conduit resettled the earth at strange and different levels. A room which someone discovered when in dire need of refuge; and used; and resealed with newer bricks and mortar and plaster, which could be distinguished even now from the breach Gilles had made. 'You may go down. There is a rope,' said the dry, impatient voice. 'It is all there. I have examined it and started an inventory, so far as I can. You will be so kind, perhaps, as to make haste. It is exceedingly cold.'

Jerott turned. Marthe, lamp in hand, was looking at him with dense, cornflower eyes. 'Go down,' she said. 'And tell me what you can see.'

The room was bigger than he thought, and more beautiful. The mosaic pavement, spreading under his feet, had been swept clear of dust so that the swirl of motion and colour could clearly be seen. The walls had been painted: horses pranced and strange birds strutted in pairs, and odd and delicate persons in toga or chlamys stood and watched, or ran mysterious races. There was a small silver mirror still hung on a wall, and a silver jug with a spout, thin and blackened with age, standing still in a niche.

The ceiling had held up; but the end wall was nothing but bricks and tiles and great slabs of marble, where the rest of the house had caved in. The opposite wall was intact. Against it, Master Gilles had spread out his cloak, smoothing the folds over the tesserae. On that in turn he had placed a number of objects: nearly all rectangular and tinged a uniform blackened grey. Some still bore the shreds of silk cloth in which each had been wrapped. Against the side wall were others, stacked one on the other in varying shapes and textures and sizes; and all coated likewise with a great silting of lime dust and rubble. As Jerott stood looking, he heard Marthe descend and come to stand quietly behind him.

Neither moved; and the voice of Pierre Gilles, scholar, anatomist and historian, mouthing sonorously from the ceiling, made them both jump.

'Item. The gold chest set with rubies, containing the iron chains of St Peter. Item, a gold cross set with jewels and pearls, and three golden lamps and two score silver candelabra, with golden apples depending. Item, two golden chalices and one golden dove. Item, the headdress and belt of the Prophet Elijah, encased in a silver casket thickly covered with jewels. Item, a great leather case containing five score golden plates, each set with pearls and small jewels. Item, a casket of gold within a casket of silver, containing the robe, the girdle and the icon of Mary the Mother of God. Item——'

'*From St Sophia?*' said Jerott. His gaze, since Gilles started to speak, had been only on the old man at the top of the rope, calmly reading his stupefying list: an inventory which, if true, meant only one thing: the treasure from the altar, the sanctuary and the chapels of the church of St Sophia: the furnishings of the new tabernacle of God and the relics brought to it from all over the Christian world. The apparel of the Heavenly Bridegroom, believed ruined and thieved by the barbarian when he tore the silver from Justinian's columns and the gold from the aisles.

'. . . Most of it has gone,' said Gilles's reflective voice. 'The silver altar table and the crown of Constantine and the silver chariot of Constantine and Helena: all the large objects have gone. There were forty thousand pounds of silver in the priests' sanctuary alone. But consider what price, for example, the Virgin's casket might command among the Church Fathers? Your young friend conceives it effort well spent.'

'And do you?' Jerott said. Marthe, he could feel, was on her knees, her fingers gently probing. There was a little creak as one of the caskets opened, and he heard her take a short breath.

There was a pause. Then, 'Who would not have yearned to make this discovery?' said Gilles. 'It is one I have traced over long years and through many sources, until this one manuscript yielded the last clue I wanted: a block of distorted notes which I had no time to decipher before they were lost. I had been working in the vaults of St Sophia when I was asked to leave: they were afraid of what I might find and take, never dreaming that the real treasure was far off, under the earth.... If you had followed the tunnel uphill instead of turning here to the right you would have found where it branches. One conduit runs clear and direct to St Sophia: it was the one I was seeking and it is unblocked still: I have been there. The other branch is short and runs to the Hippodrome. Only this arm was blocked by fallen debris, perhaps when the palace of Ibrahim Pasha was built, or the summer praying-place destroyed for the Mosque of the Three—both must be near. The conduit was roofed with marble slabs from many buildings just here: when you come up you will see them, some with letters and some with low relief ... one can see even the stamps on the bricks. So near is history.'

'So you don't regret it?' said Jerott.

'I have seen them,' said Gilles. 'I shall examine and record them, perhaps, before my friends take them from me. ... I should like to have been known as the man who found Justinian's treasure. I should like to have seen the pieces studied by scholars and placed together, as they have always been, in the sanctuary of the church, not competed for and sold to covetous and ignorant collectors. Had I been able to present this to my patron, I could have commanded any position, any sum for my travels and studies. ... I regret the irresponsible and mischievous way I have been compelled to give up what is mine, and I find it hard to forgive these two stupid people for what they are doing. ...'

'But?' said Jerott. Beside him Marthe was also standing, her head flung back, watching the speaker, her blue eyes lit with cold anger.

'But there is one other consideration,' said Gilles, 'outside all tuum and meum. In this war which you as a Knight of St John have fought, between Christian and Moslem: what could be inflaming— what could turn a game of conquest into a game of implacable hatred —sooner than this, the theft from Suleiman's capital of perhaps its greatest treasure, and that proudly displayed and celebrated in Rome? Then the hordes surely would descend, and who would protect us?'

'The relics could be received privately,' said Jerott. 'It need not be made known where they were discovered, or how. No one else in the city knows they have ever been here.'

The old man, lying on the piled straw outside with the ichneumon on his shoulder, shifted a little and began to get up. 'It is cold. We must go. As you say, it might have been done secretly thus. But where then my reward and my acclaim? . . . I am philosophic. The treasures were imprisoned, and they have been freed. They will take their place again in the world, and so shall I. I have again the notes I looked on as lost, and the manuscript I grieved for: I may return now and begin on my book. It is the girl and her uncle who will suffer. I have lost only my vanity.'

'Be philosophic,' said Marthe. Her voice was shaking. 'Condescend, and forgive. It is easy when you are wealthy and learned and travelled, and have a lifetime of achievement behind you. I use my wits, because they are all I possess. If they bring me at last what everyone else has denied me, what right have you to condemn us?' She swept her arm round the silent room. 'I have spent my life as you have among beautiful things. I know how to care for them. I feel for them as you do, and so does my uncle. These must be sold, but with my share of what they will bring I can become a person. For the first time a human being with a life of my own; a home and friends and possessions, and work I may follow in peace and become namely for . . .'

Jerott said, 'You speak like an embittered old man. Where are your children?'

She looked at him, her eyes full of anger and unshed tears of self-pity. 'Where they will stay, my drunken priest,' she said harshly. 'They are not yours to speak for.'

He climbed the rope then without speaking and made his way stooping up the short arm to the main passage where Gilles already awaited them, the powerful lamp in his hand. The wall behind him, lit for the first time, was packed shoulder-high with bales and piled blocks of straw. Jerott said, 'Why is it so cold?' He was shivering.

'You wish to know?' said Gilles. Turning he strode up the slope until he came to the opening, heavily blocked, which Jerott had already noticed. 'This can be opened only from the outside here,' said Gilles. 'It led once to a cistern, now dry. Then another entrance was discovered, on the far side of the cistern and nearer the surface, and this aperture was forgotten. These underground caverns are put to many uses, as you have doubtless seen. This one is a storehouse for snow.'

'Of course,' said Jerott. 'To cool Suleiman's sherbet. . . . Hence also the straw.'

'Snow for the Seraglio, probably,' Gilles agreed. 'Or perhaps for the use of the viziers or the aghas in their great houses. In time of heat, the winter robe of Olympus is an exquisite luxury.'

The door he had been unblocking swung open as he spoke, and Jerott, moving forward, pressed his fingers into the stiff, compacted mass which filled all the opening. So tightly was it packed that his numbed fingertips could hardly drive through the surface. A cold fresh air swept through the passage.

'It is cold enough,' said Gilles; and swung the door shut.

Behind, the light in the treasure-chamber had gone out. Marthe rejoined them a moment later and without speaking they made their way slowly back to the boat. Drifting back over the green water between the silent dark columns there was a desolation in Jerott's soul such as all the shifting experiences of his life had never bred in him. Wide-eyed and tense in the darkness, he could have wept for them all; and not least for the old and beautiful things once nourished on incense and prayer and now brooding, conserving their power. *Now the spider spins his web in Caesar's palace hall, and the owl keeps watch on the Tower of Afrasiâb.* So Mohammed the Conqueror had said as he vanquished the city: a conquest which looked not to the past but to the future: a conqueror who built his own temples and palaces and formed and wisely governed an empire which bid to become as rich and wide as the Caesars'.

How small, beside that, was Marthe's smarting ambition; the old man's rightful disgruntlement: his own silent hurt. The change had come, and must be accepted. The treasure was unimportant now in its own right except in the one aspect which Gilles had detected: as a bone between dogs. There was a wider vision, he was beginning to see, which Gilles had and which Francis had: pursuing a vendetta which was universal far more than personal: a self-imposed mission to destroy a brilliant and powerful man whose vicious ambition could throw nations into the arena like the beasts of the Hippodrome. Jerott knew then, with his head if not his heart, that in trying to save the children, they had all been wrong. Nothing mattered but Gabriel's death.

Francis had known that, in St Giles, when he had chosen to kill rather than beg for the life of his son; and only Philippa's intervention had saved Graham Malett. A second time, after the horror at Algiers, Lymond had been dissuaded only by Marthe, in the long darkness of the aftermath, from seeking out Gabriel on Malta and killing him then, without regard for the child. Dissuaded by Marthe, who had no interest in Lymond or child, but wished merely to pursue her own objective, unhampered by the death of an envoy. And a third time Lymond had attempted it, at Zuara; when Jerott, commending his courage, could not disguise his disgust: at a nature so exigent, so governed by intellect as to be unmoved by the fate of a boy.

But that was before he had seen him with a cowed and beaten and terrified child, murmuring to it as it played with its shells. They were all wrong. But who among them now had the will and the inhumanity to take Gabriel's life, and sacrifice those of Philippa and the children?

One person, it appeared. Climbing out of the boat and up the ladder into Gaultier's house Jerott turned to face Marthe; ignoring Gilles; ignoring Gaultier sitting rocking, his hand to his shoulder. His voice was perfectly calm. 'You will take your brother's message to Philippa Somerville, and you will deliver it, correctly and fully, under guise of repairing the spinet. Or I shall bring the Janissary into the house.'

She had of course expected it. She had been afraid perhaps of worse: that he would hand her regardless to the Seraglio and attempt to use the treasure for barter. She did make one last attempt. 'You would throw Master Gilles to the wolves?'

'I would tell them the truth,' said Jerott. 'That he did only what he was forced to do, and for no personal gain.'

She did not say, *You would throw me to the wolves?* although she could have had no illusions about her own fate if he denounced them. Instead she gave a short laugh. 'So this,' said Marthe, 'is true love. I made my only error, I think, in Aleppo. A rape on the floor of the tekke would have avoided this nuisance. But to tell the truth, I judged you incapable.'

He took the flat of his hand across her face then: the hard, soldier's hand, which made an impact like the sound of the breaking of sticks, and left her fine skin staring livid; and then colouring fast with bruised blood. 'I hope,' said Jerott, breathing softly and hard, 'that you never meet those who will judge what you have done. How would you recognize love? Or compassion? Francis at least has learned that. You avaricious little slut . . . do I call in the Janissary; or will you do as I say?'

Her face was unflinching as a tablet of stone. 'I shall do it,' she said. 'Since I must, to be free of you. Go then and find you a whore-monger. What use to you—any of you—is a mind and a soul, when all you need is a body?'

There was a silence. 'You didn't ask,' said Jerott at length. 'But I would have forgone even the body for the sake of the mind. And I would have claimed neither body nor mind, had I discovered a soul.'

*

He informed M. Chesnau that day that Gaultier's niece was willing to adjust and rewire the spinet, assuming the Kapi Agha still thought it necessary.

It was, as he knew, entirely necessary; no one else having the proper thickness of wire. The following day one of the Chiausi arrived with a summons for Marthe, and, the following morning, she entered Topkapi.

She was unescorted, save for the Janissaries who were commanded to fetch her. Gaultier had refused point blank to associate himself with a folly he considered she had brought on herself, although what she could have done to stop Jerott he was unable to suggest. He remained in his house with Pierre Gilles, who had now received, from Jerott, an outline of the quest which had brought him and his friends to Stamboul.

'Then of course,' Gilles had said, 'the girl must go to Topkapi.' And to the vociferous Gaultier: '*Tacite*, little man.'

Nevertheless, the outcome mattered to Gilles no less than to Gaultier. If Jerott found Marthe had failed him, he might do as he threatened and denounce them and their treasure. And if anything happened to Marthe, how would he ever recover his papers?

Jerott took no chances. Having discovered that neither Gaultier nor the old man could swim, he removed the boat to another part of the cistern. The swim back through dark, ice-cold water was more exhausting than he had expected, but he accomplished it; and set someone he could trust to keep a watch on the house. No one after that was allowed out or in but the negress, for food. Until Marthe came back, no one was going to smuggle that treasure away from under Jerott Blyth's nose.

Marthe wore her best dress for Topkapi, but made no other concessions to the occasion; stalking through to the ultimate splendours of the Ottoman Empire like a physician called in to bleed it. She made no comment on the magnificence of the room in the selamlïk where she was led to work on the spinet. It was one of Khourrém Sultán's chambers, although the Sultan's wife was not there. Marthe asked the black eunuch who brought her, presently, to request the presence of anyone who could play it; and Philippa appeared almost immediately.

Of all those who had set out on the *Dauphiné*, Philippa's lot had been the most solitary, and the separation from her own kind now very long. Her brown eyes were waterlogged, frowning to keep back the tears at the first sight of Marthe; but the blue answering gaze was unsmiling and even, in a curious way, angry. In French, which the eunuch understood, Marthe reeled off a number of questions on the spinet's performance; returned to the instrument and tinkered with it while Philippa stood, stupid and tentative, in the middle of the floor. Then Marthe called her over to hear some instructions.

It was timed with the efficiency she so scorned in her brother. Above their heads, as they bent over the spinet, the clock struck the hour. And under cover of its bells and its bustling automata, Marthe gave rapidly to Philippa the details she had been told to pass on.

When the frenzied activity stopped, Marthe was already bent over the wires, pliers in hand, while Philippa sat at the keyboard, her frightened body drowning her mind with primitive chemicals. Escape, with the child, was something she had never dreamed possible. She began, with cold fingers, to play a run in a difficult key, and said softly, in English, 'Is there another child?'

'Play middle G,' said Marthe. 'Yes. There are plans for him also.'

'Which——?' began Philippa, her brain beginning to function once more; but Marthe cut her off. 'No one knows. Thank you. Now D and C. Yes. I shall call the eunuch over now and instruct you both together. Is there anything more?'

'Only to thank you,' said Philippa. 'To thank you for coming.'

Marthe stared at her. Whether she saw the fresh skin and bright hair; the straight shoulders and thin, pretty hands, she gave no indication. 'I came,' she said, 'because I was forced to.' And turning, called over the eunuch.

She left shortly after, having exchanged no more with Philippa than that. The Chiausi escorting her were waiting at the door of the selamlìk and walked with her up the slope of the third court, the grey light cold on their silver-tipped staffs. Straight and elegant in her stiff Turkish over-robe, a veil over her hair, Marthe this time had relaxed infinitesimally; her blue eyes observing in silence the marbles and gold and the deep-coloured tiles within the slim colonnades, and the square wrought shell of the Throne Room before the Gate of Felicity.

The Gate opened slowly, the doorkeepers standing impassive before it, their white plumes lifting and flickering in the sharp little wind. Within the porch stood a line of tall men, dressed not as Chiausi or Janissaries, but in elaborate coats, with tall hats of violet velvet. Beside her, Marthe's escort had halted. She glanced at them, her heart thudding suddenly; and then took a step forward alone, her head high.

No one moved. She stopped again, and in a firm voice addressed them in Turkish. They smiled and nodded, variously, in return, standing immovable from wall to wall of the porch, but none of them spoke, except with their fingers. Then, still smiling, they walked forward and began to surround her, edging her away from the wide golden gateway and back into the innermost garden. She turned then, quickly, to speak to her escort but they had gone silently, disappearing between the green pillars; and they did not turn back although she called sharply before trying again, her voice cutting, to order the men in her way to stand back.

They heard, she thought, and understood probably; but they did nothing to help her, but merely stood smiling around her, while the Gate of Felicity closed. Then, gently, they gripped her by the arms and guided her back into the secret, innermost court of the Seraglio.

Marthe was in the hands of the mutes.

24

CONSTANTINOPLE: THE HOUSE OF JUBRAEL PASHA

The Meddáh that day was in the Hippodrome, the ruins of the great coursing-ground with its pillaged horseshoe of arcades high above the Marmara Sea, where once lions fought and chariots raced for the Byzantine emperors and their courts. Ottoman palaces now had encroached on its great thirteen-hundred-foot spread; its stones had been used for Suleiman's splendid new khan, and its marble pillars for Suleiman's mosque. Long ago, the old statues from Greece and from Rome had been thrown down or stolen: Castor and Pollux; Hercules in bronze by Lymachus. The chariot of Lysippus with its four golden horses had stood on the Imperial Box until the fourth crusade, when the Venetians had taken and placed it in their own church of St Mark's.

Pillars still remained, of coloured marble, upholding the galleries beneath which were the cages and chambers and storehouses; and at the other end, near St Sophia, some tiered buildings and remains of wide shallow steps. In the centre, in a straggling line, there remained also what was left of the treasures brought to Byzantium from Greece and Asia Minor, and all over the civilized world. The obelisk from Karnak, set up by Theodosius on its plinth of deep bas-relief, was now nearly three thousand years old; its hieroglyphics still sharp and clear. Near it, the Column of Constantine still showed the marks where its plates of gilt bronze had been pinned, and between them, twenty feet high, were the three coiled bronze snakes from the Temple of Delphi, whose heads had once held the great golden tripod and vase before the shrine two thousand years earlier. A century before, on another site, water, wine and milk had flowed from the three serpent heads which now gaped at the winter skies, broken and dry. Now Suleiman used the waste ground between for sports and for festivals, and the Janissaries practised their archery and rode fast, dangerous games of Djirit among its broken pillars and fragmented marble, where flocks of goats rested in summer, and dogs roamed, and vendors of sherbet and sweetmeats set up their stalls in the shade of the galleries.

Today it was cold; and there were braziers among the pale stones, where you could take your pieces of meat straight from the butcher, and have them skewered and roasted: the smell of hot mutton, pushed by the sea winds, floated among the drift of idlers who were watching a company of seraglio Ajémoghláns on horseback taking part in a wild and dangerous game of Djirit, their four-foot white wands stabbing, vicious as spears. The story-teller had been placed in state near one of the braziers, and the crowd increased; for he was now well known for his marvellous tales in the ancient tradition as well as for new ones of his own, which, like the silk-moth, he spun strand by strand without effort, filled with delicate wonders.

A man, then, of poetic imagination. But could one reconcile that, thought Jerott Blyth, on the edge of the crowd, with a man who could kill as Lymond had killed in Algiers; who could plan and act without mercy? He shrugged, inside his long fur-lined coat, and sent his Janissary over to buy a skewer of meat.

Ishiq came up, bowl in hand, a few seconds later. Jerott dropped in his coins. 'Tell him,' he said, 'that the girl has not come back from Topkapi, and that according to the Seraglio she has been invited to stay longer to put the spinet fully in order. We have had no direct message from Marthe herself.' He grinned at Ishiq; a happy slave, who had no doubts about his master, and the boy, calling Allâh to bless him, also grinned and ran off. In the background, Lymond's voice rose and fell in its beautiful Turkish: behind hood and beard and blindfolding bandage, Jerott could make nothing at all of his face. Then the Janissary came back, and Jerott stayed, chewing, till the skewer was empty and the begging-bowl came round for the second time.

In the bottom of the bowl was a screw of paper, half buried by small silver coins. This time Jerott plaintively refused a second donation but, as the bowl was thrust at him a second time and a third, he fished reluctantly in his purse at length, and put in an asper.

The paper came up, neatly unseen in the palm of his hand. It held only one word in English: *Proceed.*

On the other side of the city a Geomaler with a lyre wandered sleepily into Constantine's Palace and serenaded the lions, until the assistant keeper turned him rudely out. He left behind him a menagerie of restless animals and a small twist of paper on the broken mosaic floor, which the under keeper picked up and kept. Untwisted, it also held the same word in English: *Proceed.*

Within the damp, inhospitable walls of Gaultier's house the owner passed his days nursing his suppurating arm and his useless well both, in a fury of impatience, awaiting his niece's return. Pierre Gilles, sitting philosophically wrapped in a blanket and endlessly writing up his blurred Latin inventories, had long ago given up reasoned argument; and was all the more glad to see Jerott Blyth's face when at last he called on them, his Janissary as always outside.

To Jerott's story, Gilles responded with a frowning concern: he stared back at the speaker, thinking, while Gaultier exploded into a frenzy of angry demands. The girl had gone to Topkapi; had carried out their part of the bargain. Now it was for Jerott to carry out his. Bring back the boat, so that they could obtain what was theirs. Did he realize how long it would take to empty that chamber and ferry its contents back into the house? If something had gone

395

wrong: if the girl was in trouble: at any moment the Bostanji Bashi's henchmen might come . . .

Gilles cut into it. 'How long has she been in the Seraglio?'

'Four days,' said Jerott.

Pierre Gilles looked at him. 'Four days without sleep will not improve your chances of aiding her,' he said dryly. 'If she requires aid. Does your Ambassadorial friend see something sinister in this delay?'

Jerott said, 'I don't know. He hasn't allowed it to affect his plans.'

'But you say there is no love lost between them, so he may merely be unmoved by her fate. Yet if he believed her to be detained because of the message she carried, he would surely have altered his designs? If, on the other hand, it was because they have guessed our discovery, we here should surely have been molested by now. There is a strong possibility, it seems to me,' said Maître Gilles, looking down at the white face of his former secretary, 'that the young woman has merely been detained, as they claim, in order to restore the clock-spinet?'

'It is possible,' said Jerott. He added, curtly, 'It was my fault. Mr Crawford had no idea until I told him that I had sent Marthe with the message. . . . We can do nothing but wait. I can't go near Lymond now in case I endanger him.'

'You are watched. Of course,' said Gilles. 'So you remain at the Embassy throughout all, fretting. You know, I take it, the expression, "*Alterius non sit, qui suus esse potest?*" What, for example, if the girl and the two children are rescued, leaving Marthe to suffer in the Seraglio in their place? Or do you agree this would be just punishment for her misdemeanours?'

'I know the expression,' said Jerott. 'At the moment I am another's, and not my own. What I think doesn't matter.'

'I see,' said Pierre Gilles, watching him. He said, after a moment, 'I believe I should like to meet your friend Mr Crawford.'

'The world is full,' said Jerott wearily, 'of people who might have wanted to meet Francis Crawford, and who are going to be disappointed. So, among other things, Marthe has to be expendable.'

'And the treasure?' said the usurer Gaultier. 'Is that expendable too?'

The eyes of Gilles the scholar remained on Jerott's dark face. 'Yes. Of course it is,' he said. 'We also are being required to wait, and to fret. He has forced you to think, has he, this friend of yours?'

Herpestes had jumped on his lap. Jerott stroked him slowly, without looking up. 'I suppose so,' he said. 'You and he between you.'

It seemed like virtue rewarded when, a day later, a page from the Seraglio appeared at the Embassy in the afternoon requiring M. Chesnau to send an official to escort home the Khátún adjusting the spinet, who had suffered a slight breakdown in health. There was no question as to which official should go. Jerott was out of his room, his lined cloak over his arm, as soon as Chesnau told him the news, and was halted only by Onophrion's great bulk on the threshold, his voice deferential, but his face lined with concern. 'If Mr Blyth would allow me to accompany him? The young lady may well need attention. . .?'

He had thrown together, even in that short space of time, a neat emergency roll including aquavitae and a thick robe, hood and rug. Jerott, his mind busied with confused thought and emotions, was thankful indeed to have conducted for him the practical side of the journey. None was better than Onophrion at obtaining a boatman quickly, or horses at the far side, for themselves and the Janissary, with mules for the two servants bearing his burdens. They left in a matter of moments, and were at the Imperial Gate, the Bab-i-Humayun, inside the hour.

Onophrion had been before, with Lymond. Jerott, whose first visit it was, had an impression of great spaces filled with men and horses and the tall white caps and blue robes of the Janissaries, walking in groups or marching in small, brisk detachments. Chiausi took them through the first court to the Ortokapi Gate and between the feathered files of the Kapici: in the Divan Court they were greeted by the Bostanji Bashi, who led Jerott alone to the Gate of Felicity.

They had an affable, if formal, conversation on the way, their voices sounding loud in the strange Seraglio silence. In the gateway, as had happened with the Ambassador, the Bostanji Bashi halted, and directing the way to the retiring-rooms, asked Jerott to wait. He hoped they were looking after Onophrion. Above all, he hoped they would be speedy. For what he knew and they did not was that, before darkness fell, Philippa and both children should be out of the city.

Only then did it occur to him, stupidly, that Marthe knew that fact, for of course he had told her the details himself, to pass on to Philippa. Which was strongest in that solitary soul: hatred or avarice? Greed, he had assumed, but perhaps he was wrong. Perhaps he was here because she had betrayed them.

*

The carpet-dealer called late that afternoon at the house of Názik, the nightingale-merchant, and tramped in without knocking to pick up the carpet he had bought earlier in the day.

Názik was busy and short-tempered, and the interruption was unwelcome. At the same time the dealer, who was new to him and most likely to his job, had offered him four times what he had paid for a Persian prayer-rug, already a little threadbare, under the impression that it was a good deal more important than Názik knew it to be.

It was a bargain not to be missed. On the other hand, the cage-maker at long last had sent round his man with the two cages Názik had long coveted, and he had just unwrapped the first to find that the door was weak in its hinges. It was in other respects so splendid: so ideal, one would say, for Khaireddin, for example, that Názik could have wept. He caressed the ebony base, inset with ivory and mother of pearl and small simply cut jewels, and hung with tassels of silver and scarlet, all the time he was shouting at the cage-maker's man, who insisted, wailing, that all cage-doors behaved so.

It was no use. Clearly the cage was unsafe. He had just ordered the man to cover up the warped thing and take it out of his sight when he had to go and deal with the carpet. When he came back, soothed by the sight and feel of shivering aspers, it was to find the second cage standing in all its glory, even more fine than the first. They haggled for a long time over the price, and then at the last moment Názik balked at handing over the money, and told the man that he would call at the cage-maker's and pay it. They were in the middle of a second argument over whether or not the cage could be left, if unpaid for, when Názik's assistant ran in to say that the boy Khaireddin had gone. And that, as Názik well knew, meant death. Then Názik remembered the carpet-dealer.

They followed the tracks of the cart, running, through the uneven streets, shouting questions as they went to passers-by who stared and called back. The dealer had talked of leaving for Adrianople, and in fact had started towards the Adrianople gate, before doubling back and through a network of streets which led his pursuers, slowly and surely, towards the Golden Horn and its shipping.

They found the cart, in the end, with all its piled carpets standing alone on the landing-stage with its mule sniffing at fish-heads: the swarm of small boys who had just reached it and were pulling off the top heavy roll jumped down and scattered at Názik's breathless approach. It was his carpet they had partly dismantled, and inside was Khaireddin's small cap; but no other sign of the boy or the dealer at all.

They searched the waterside till darkness, with the help of those silent men who, day in and day out, had watched every move by the child. Finally, whimpering, Názik went back to his nightingales and began to pack, hurriedly. Míkál, who had come over to buy a few hours of Khaireddin's time, stayed to comfort him; and also to make quite sure that it occurred to no one at all to follow the cage-maker's mule, plodding out of the city gate and along the road to the west with a warped silver cage wrapped in cotton and strapped to its pannier.

In Topkapi, Philippa also was following instructions. That they had come in the first place through Marthe had been an astonishment from which she had not yet recovered. But then, as she wisely concluded, Marthe's relations with Lymond might well have undergone quite a change in all the months since last she had seen them together. Marthe's feelings towards herself were still clearly cool. Philippa had watched her leave the selamlik with something very like panic, but she was used to overcoming that particular impulse. It did not cross her mind that Marthe had not immediately left the Seraglio for good.

Unable to sleep or eat for frightened excitement, Philippa had counted the hours until today. It had been hardest of all, she found, to act normally with Kuzúm. On her actions today depended his whole life and his future: a future of which he had no conception. For surely, no matter what Gabriel had hinted, this and this only was Lymond's son? She shut her mind to the other, unthinkable possibility and took in hand, firmly, a wet, loose-lipped yearning to smother the child with treacly emotion. She played with Kuzúm that afternoon; scolded him briskly when he blew his nose with his mouth full of yoghourt, and took him downstairs with the other girls of the harem to see the bears fed.

The elephants were kept at Constantine's Palace, and the wolves and the lions: the Sultana's rooms were above the pound at Topkapi, and the Sultana's sleep must not be disturbed. So there the keeper put the smaller, picturesque animals like lynxes and leopards and ermines in cages; and tethered a brown bear to a stake, with her two cubs humping about her; all upturned toes and high furry bottoms.

Kuzúm loved the bears. He watched them with a fierce adoration: 'I see two ones. Kuzúm show Fippy where is the bears. . . . Kuzúm have a see. Now Fippy have a see. Now Fippy lift up me to see all the pussy cats. . . . Oh, it's fallened.'

It was a leopard, and it had indeed fallen. Philippa took Kuzúm back to the bears, and said to the keeper, 'One of your leopards isn't well.'

The face under the turban was familiar, but he gave her no glance of recognition: only swore under his breath in what she understood to be Urdu, and hurried off to the cage, the chattering girls in their veils following, bright as finches. 'Is it sick?' someone asked.

The little mahout answered in Turkish. 'It is sick, Khátún. It can be healed in the Palace menagerie. I shall take it there later.' He answered all of their questions, but his gaze, as always, strayed to Kuzúm. With his blue eyes and thick silky cap of bright hair, the little boy in his Turkish jacket and slippers was as sweet as a peach; his swooping voice striving to fasten together difficult words and impossible phrases, his open laughter and quick, warm affection creating a climate of trade winds and sunshine in which they all basked.

His own view of the weather was rather more literal. After he had had his fill of the bears and the ermines, and watched the keeper push meat in to the lynxes, accepting a piece of animal biscuit from the mahout in the bygoing, Kuzúm announced suddenly, 'It's very too cold,' and yawned, his pink skin stretched like a carp's round the O of his mouth.

'You're tired. We'll go in a moment,' Philippa said; and, taking off her own heavy lined cloak, wrapped it round the small boy. The young bears, attracted by the trailing thing on the ground, scampered after him and pawed it, dragging it half off his shoulders, and he rocked and sat down with a bump, his legs stuck out before him. The mahout gave him another piece of biscuit and he held it out for the bears to nibble, absently, before cramming the rest unhygienically into his mouth. Philippa didn't restrain him.

When they came to go, climbing chattering up the stairs and through the series of courts that led them finally back to the harem, Kuzúm had succumbed, and the mahout turned the folds of the mohair more closely around him. Philippa climbed the stairs carefully, carrying her small burden all swathed in her cloak: it was not yet time to return Kuzúm to the head nurse so she turned into her own rooms instead and, laying her burden down, got out one of her books and sat looking at it until the bustle had all died down and the girls had gone off, as she knew they would, for their music.

From this class she was excused. Philippa waited until there was silence, and then, producing a hairpin, crept out into the corridor and proceeded to put into use all poor Hepsabah's training.

Khourrém's rooms were quite empty: today was a religious festival and, in the absence of Suleiman, his wife was at St Sophia, she remembered. Philippa met no one, although she had her excuse ready. She had been summoned by the Sultana to check the offending spinet once more. She saw it as she sped through the great room, stirring like a beast in its sleep, all gold and Badakhshan rubies: it burst into action behind her back as she left, her nerves tight as the wires on the soundboard. She was, she accordingly told herself briskly, precisely on time. She let herself into the small vacant gallery overhanging the compound, and walked to the edge.

As Archie had said, there was a rope hanging, neatly looped round a column. She was supple and strong, for a girl, and not all that many months distant from boisterous games with the stable-boys over Kate's farm-building roofs. She let herself down and ran like a cockroach for the back of the largest cage, while the mahout pulled down the rope.

Kuzúm was there already, where he had been asleep since she had left the garden carrying her empty cloak wrapped round a bolster. Then Archie joined them, his hand on her hair. 'Good lass. Are ye frightened?'

'I think so.' Philippa, incurably honest.

'It's natural. Well, ye've no call to fear. That beast won't wake up for eight hours, if that, and your wee boy maybe longer. I've given him a terrible dose, but it was the only way to be sure.'

'I know. Archie, we'd better get in.'

'Aye.' He opened the back of the cage. She had thought about it, but she hadn't expected the leopard to be so large, or so heavy, or so warm. He lay on two solid feet of clean straw, with more banked at the back, and it was there that Archie made a small hollow and laid in the sleeping Kuzúm, a fine net bound lightly over his face. Philippa fished in her sleeve and pulled out another. Straw made you sneeze, Archie said. Try to minimize all the risks.

It was more difficult to hide a fully dressed girl, however willing and thin. She was half under the leopard to end with, its sleeping weight on her legs as if a great wolfhound had chosen to slumber beside her. Except that if this one woke, it could tear her throat out with a single turn of its head. 'You've got pluck,' Archie said. He seemed reluctant to close the cage finally: standing, door in hand, he looked again at the leopard, and the little he could see of the girl, her brown hair mixed with the straw and already submerging. 'You'll need to trust me; but that you can do. I could put my mother in there, if she wasna stone deid already, and she'd come to no harm.'

'I've taken the leet oath, Archie,' said Philippa, her voice shaking slightly. *Ye shall be buxom and obedient to all justices in all things that they shall lawfully command you.* Archie, I'll always be buxom to you.'

'And cheeky,' said Archie grinning. 'Get your head down. There's a cart and a driver due here in a minute. . . . I think I'll fling a wee something over the cage. We don't want poor Victoria upset by the light and the noises.'

Half an hour later, with Archie walking solicitously at its side and one of the stable-boys cracking the whip over the mule-train, the cage with Victoria rumbled out of the Gate of the Dead, which had other and less picturesque uses, and, having passed the scrutiny of the heavy Janissary guard, rolled out and into the street, where it made its laborious way up and down the painful contours of the Abode of Felicity to Constantine's Palace.

The Head Keeper also, on Archie's solicitous insistence, was cleansing his soul in Aya Sofia. The leopard, still sleeping, was detached and placed in a side yard, where there awaited already fully loaded a fine cartload of dung.

'Oh no!' said Philippa, warned by the smell. She put out her head and, seeing a sudden, breathtaking vision of marble pillars and archways, of gardens and houses and even, distantly, streets and chimneys and trees, gave a sudden hysterical gasp.

'Aye: you're out,' said Archie. 'Now ye have my apologies for the next bit, but it'll be worth it, as ye might say, in the end. I've left a clean bit at the back end of the cart. If ye can slip out of the cage and up this side—I'll give ye a lift—I'll hand the bairn in beside you.'

401

'What is it?' said Philippa, tears pouring out of her eyes, as she lay at length, the sleeping child in her arms, under Archie's clean bit of straw.

'It's elephant muck,' said Archie. 'You get a fair price for that. Anywhere in the world. You'd be surprised at the demand.'

'Oh, Archie: I'm sure I should,' said Philippa. 'I'm not surprised you sell it, either. Archie, what a blessing Kuzúm's asleep. . . .'

She lay, her cheek in the straw and her arms round the small sturdy body of Kuzúm, and heard the hollow roll of the wheels as they passed through the Edirne Gate and out of Stamboul into the green fields of Thrace.

Because of the forthcoming Festival the crowd round the blind story-teller was small that afternoon in the Hippodrome and he was able to speak to everyone in the way they liked best; inviting their comment on his stories and talking gravely or lightly, as the mood took his audience. A smaller boy than usual brought round the bowl: Ishiq, he explained, had been called to a sick brother. If the Meddáh himself missed a still smaller child, who used to stand outside the Beyazit Mosque, his hand on his knee, no one could have guessed.

He stayed a long time, and his friends were bidding him rise to warm himself at their brazier and eat at their tables when Ishiq skipped lightly in and, taking the bowl, murmured in the blind Meddáh's ear. The story-teller smiled, and turning to the murmur of voices said, 'It is well. His brother is better: thou seest him shaking his shoulder-joints? Praise be to Allâh, the Knower of Subtleties. May Allâh the Bestower of Sustenance walk with thee.' Then, Ishiq holding his arm, Lymond rose, and walked for the last time in the robes of the story-teller to the house of Míkál.

He changed as he listened to Ishiq's long story, peeling off the coarse robes of the Meddáh, the wig and bandage and beard already dropped on the floor. Míkál, sitting crosslegged and silent, said nothing, but watched the way he moved; the unhurried fingers; the intent, constrained profile as Ishiq told how the child Khaireddin, safe in his cage, had been brought out of the city and taken well to the west before being placed, as arranged, in the big barn of a farmer who was anxious for money and indifferent about his method of getting it. There one of the Geomalers was awaiting him: a familiar face whom he would trust. Then, joined by Philippa, Kuzúm and Archie, they would continue their journey.

'And what of Philippa Khátún?' Lymond said. He had dressed European-style in dark tunic and hose, with fine Turkish buskins laced on for quietness and speed. Over a chest lay the loose, hooded surcoat he would wear in the street, and the staff, to account for his stooping.

'She is safe,' Ishiq said. 'And the child.' Again, he recounted the story, and, listening, Lymond ran his hands over his disordered hair and, bending, began transferring possessions quickly and deftly from one robe to the other. One supposed, thought Míkál, that he had spent at least some hours of tension, telling his tales and awaiting this news. But it might have been of no moment at all.

Míkál said softly, as the account came to an end, 'So you have achieved all you promised. The girl Philippa and both children are free.'

'They should be,' said Lymond. His pallor had become greater in these last weeks and was now marked: in it, his eyes now appeared of a deeper and more brilliant blue, their lids architectural in a spare structure of bone.

Old in the ways of the drug, Míkál had watched this man fighting it. Since he could order the measure for himself Lymond was no longer vulnerable to the violent changes in mood and in temper which had made him a tormenting companion ever since Malta. Under a high, steady intake of opium he was keyed up to a level of intense nervous activity: as capable of quick action and imaginative thinking as he had ever been: perhaps more so; and able, if he were called on, to sustain pain or intolerable effort without evident difficulty. It was the great virtue of the drug and, of course, the great danger. Míkál had seen a dromedary racing to Cairo on opium: it had travelled three days and three nights without halting or slackening pace; and on arrival had died where it stopped.

In small things, the drug made one careless. It was Míkál who cared for him physically: who brought food and saw that it was eaten, and who restored the clothes of which Lymond, so uncharacteristically, took little care. He saw too that he had regular sleep while he could, although its quality was now restless and full of turbulent dreams from which he woke silent and running with sweat. There had been times when to Míkál, too, it had seemed that this day would never come: the day set for release, when Archie and Jerott between them would guide the children to safety, and Lymond would be free to pursue his own fate, and Gabriel's. Míkál wondered what would become of the girl whom the man Blyth had compelled to go to the Seraglio without Lymond's knowledge. Lymond had sworn at him, but mildly, when he had come to confess it. They hadn't known then that the girl would be detained, nor had they made plans to free her. The Embassy, perhaps, would take care of that. . . .

Lymond was ready. By now, in the unlit farmhouse barn in the dark fields to the west of the city, Philippa and the two children should have met, and Archie would be setting out with them on the long, fast journey home, where bribery had already marked the stages and ensured them protection and shelter and food so far as was humanly possible in the time he had had to spare. Then they would be within reach of his own friends and thence from station to station until they reached France and Sevigny.

The planning was over: the meticulous arrangements with money running shorter and shorter; the talk and the listening; the making of a net out of cobwebs and a rope out of sand. His surcoat on, his hood still on his shoulders, Lymond turned to Míkál. 'Ishiq has what I can give him, and so have the others. What do you lack, that I may give it to you?'

Míkál's handsome, fringed eyes filled with a half-angry, half-affectionate scorn. 'Thou knowest too well,' he said sweetly. 'What I desire, thou dost not possess for thyself. How canst thou render it then to another?'

For a moment Lymond did not speak. Then he said, 'You have a tongue, have you not, which breaks backs? I have madness in many forms, but that which springs from the passions of the heart is not in my nature. That is all. We are all fashioned differently.'

'We are all alike,' said Míkál. 'But this thou hast not yet discovered. Give me then a piece of thyself. I will take a lock of thy hair. . . . It is unwelcome?'

'No,' said Lymond quickly. 'It is unwashed. But you may have it all, with pleasure, if you want it.'

A moment later Míkál stood with the brief ring of hair in his hand, watching while Lymond slipped through the door and out into the night, on his way at last to Gabriel's house.

*

Built by a dead Vizier from the limestone of Makrikeui and the marble bones of fallen Byzantium, Gabriel's palace was on high ground overlooking the Hippodrome and the Sea of Marmara beyond. The wind had dropped. Between the dark stems of the monuments sea and sky were a horizonless amethyst: small boats afloat on the water no more than a single pricking of light, set each on the quivering pillar of its reflection. And on the left St Sophia brooded, squat as a toad with its two slender minarets, smoke-grey against the veils of the sky.

The light waned. Lymond, standing motionless in the shadow of the high palace wall, had no need to reconnoitre: as Meddáh he had watched all the routine of Gabriel's household and marked all the gates and the windows, and the keepers who guarded them.

Gabriel would be in Aya Sofia, for worship. The call for sunset prayer had already gone out; the myriad voices rising each tinted by distance as the minarets held each their different tones in the fast-fading light. *Come now and worship the great God. Lâ illa Eillala, Mahomet Resullala. Olla bethbar: God is alone.*

The sea and the sky were now indigo; the twisted snakes of the Hippodrome and the arcaded buildings a dense brownish black. Round the dome and minarets of St Sophia there sprang suddenly a circle of small golden lights, then another, one tier above. All over the city, masked by roofs and cypresses and the pale blue haze of

404

woodsmoke in the dark, there hung pricked in the sky ring upon ring of lamps suspended like fireflies to honour the Prophet. Somewhere a cracker went off, and then another, in a burst of cerise fire above the Beyazit hilltop. Lymond turned and, making his way softly back along the dark wall, reached the place he had chosen and scaled it.

He killed the guard, quietly, as he made his rounds past the spot. It was not a time to take risks, or to be squeamish. Now he laid near him the drugged meat for the hounds which the other doorkeeper would shortly bring out and release. In half an hour the man lying at his feet would be due to report. Perhaps ten minutes after that, the alarm might be raised; and shortly after that Gabriel himself was due to return. He had forty minutes in which to do what he had to do. It was enough.

It had not been hard either to discover beforehand which was Gabriel's room. A travelling juggler, calling for alms in the kitchen, might well inquire the whereabouts of the master of the house. The servants too were proud of their new master, who was gentle and generous, and of the luxury fit for an emperor with which he had begun to surround himself.

There was an almond tree: the twisted grandchild of what had once been a hillside of blossom, near the wooden balcony, totally enclosed, which overhung the small herb- and water-garden at the side of the house. Lymond climbed it noiselessly, his eyes on the windows around him, and reaching the furthermost point, jumped for the balcony. For a moment he hung, securing his purchase; then with a swing of his body he was up and clinging against the brown intricate fretwork while he probed at the lock with a wire.

There was a click, and he was inside, and parting the cloth-of-gold curtains which led into Gabriel's chamber. Then he pulled them together behind him.

Complete darkness, and the scent of jasmine, mixed with the fading odours of incense. A woman's scent. Not surprising perhaps. Even when sworn to obedience and chastity, Gabriel had denied none of his appetites. Picking his way in the dark, Lymond made sure that the room had only one other door, and that it was locked. Then slipping out steel, flint and tinder, he struck a small spark and, with his spill, found and lit a fine taper.

The floor was carpeted, the pile deep as fur, and the walls were hung with silk chosen by a master expert in silks: cloth of gold with a raised pattern of velvet: a crimson velvet from Bursa, woven with leaves and cornflowers and roses in silver thread and white silk; a banded velvet and satin with the word *Arrahman*, 'The Merciful', within cartouches in olive and silver.

There was no Turkish mattress, but a couch in ivory inlaid with dark woods and outlined in gold: it was unmade, its coverlet half on the floor, and glimmering under it was a single earring: a pretty trinket made in the form of a tassel of seed pearls, its knot studded with rubies. Lymond looked at it for a moment, and then, scooping it up, slipped the earring into the purse at his belt.

The rest of the room was no less exquisite: the candelabra of silver, the Persian enamels, the storage chests of lacquer from Cathay, or of leather, bound with worked metal. In the corner stood a statue of Venus in white marble, signed by Praxiteles, a jade Mohammedan *tespi* slung round its neck. '*Cum fueris Romae, Romano vivito more...*'

There was no one to hear. Lymond knelt, and using his wire, forced open and lifted the lid of the first chest. '*. . . Cum fueris alibi, vivito more loci*. Loot, Gabriel? And gold. And some jewellery worthy of the grandest of Viziers—why not in your Treasury, I wonder? But no papers. Try again . . .'

There were very few letters. Lymond was both quick and thorough. Not only the furnishings of the room but the small shuttered cupboards were examined: the jewelled boxes meant for Gabriel's Qur'ân: the silk girdle-purses kept with his clothes. His robes and his furs were magnificent: after the briefest of hesitations, the flexible hands slipped among them and searched inside them, probing. Nothing again: nothing of consequence.

A pity. A pity that Gabriel also was thorough, and a veteran of guile. . . . There remained therefore only one task to be done. Perhaps Gabriel would return from the mosque before the dead guard and the drugged hounds had been discovered; but one could not be sure. Better to wait, therefore, knife in hand, where one might least be expected. . . .

Half an hour had gone by. Silence outside, and so far no noise of disturbance inside the house. Lymond snuffed out the taper, and sliding between the heavy gold curtains, stepped on to the balcony. The roof was strengthened inside, as he had remembered, with short wooden beams. It was the work of a moment to swing himself up and balance there, close to the ceiling, the shuttered balcony just below him, listening for the moment when Gabriel entered his room.

Five minutes passed, and ten. Inactivity was trying. His head on his arm, he found his mind slipping too easily from its shackles; drifting off into a limbo of fantasy until shocked awake by the shift of his weight on the beam. His mouth was dry with the pungent aridity of just-swallowed opium. . . . Gabriel would know of that: would be already aware of its effects and ready to play on them, given the chance. The worst which could happen to Gabriel was death. The worst which could happen to himself was to be deprived, he supposed of the opium he carried. A public degradation of body and spirit under Gabriel's eye would be less than inviting. But there was a simple way out of that.

Shortly after that he became aware that someone was unlocking the door from the house into Gabriel's room. It was done smoothly and quietly, but the door fell open after that with a whine, and he heard several feet quickly enter the room, and the muted chink of steel against steel. A voice said in Turkish, 'Empty. Search it.'

Not Gabriel's voice. And no one but Gabriel, surely, would issue orders in that room, had he been here. Lymond lay very still in the shadows, his knife lightly gripped in his fingers, and listened to the search coming nearer until suddenly a strong hand ripped the cloth-of-gold curtains apart, and a blaze of new candlelight flooded the balcony.

It was more than he had expected, but he was still in the shadows, and he did not move as they all came through in turn and examined the small shuttered room. There were four of them, and they were Janissaries. The tall white caps were only inches below him as they crossed to the shutters and tried them, expecting them to be locked.

They gave at once. Lymond saw the Odabassy open them fully and first peer outside, then examine the lock with a taper. The scratches on it were probably plain. . . . But if an intruder had clearly entered the house by this method, he might also by this time have left.

The four men came back, talking. It was pure ill luck that with the increased draught the taper flared suddenly high, so that the Janissary bearing it looked up, concerned lest the wood should have caught. He saw Lymond in the moment that Lymond launched himself at the unshuttered window and, sliding over the frame, swung himself hand over hand down and round the side, towards the leaning branch of the almond.

The men were shouting above him. He felt a knife shave the side of his arm as he jumped for the tree; and then there were answering shouts from below. As he landed he saw other white caps running towards him from the front yard of the house. He kicked the first one in the teeth as he jumped half the height of the tree, and drove his knife into the second, wrenching it out as he ran. The Janissaries above were climbing out of the balcony as he had done and were following him, scrambling and leaping: in a moment he would have no chance at all. Lymond turned on the run and set off swiftly and quietly for the wall by which he had entered. He reached it just before the pounding feet at his back, and hoisted himself without pausing up and over, his hands hardly touching. He landed on the balls of his feet; and snatching his folded robe, fled.

They came after him, shouting. Someone stepped in his way and he knocked him over: there was a shriek and a clatter and an appalling stench of cheap scent, followed as the Janissaries came up with a good deal more stumbling and some half-muffled grunts. It had been a pedlar's pack, he concluded; possibly even with pins in it. The contents of the pack stayed behind, but the contents of the spilled flask continued redolent as Lymond, running quickly and easily, led them up street after street to the biggest congested area he could think of: the covered bazaar.

It was open because of the festival: lane upon small twisting lane of low buildings of clay or of wood: three-sided boxes within which the merchants and craftsmen of Stamboul made and vended their goods, for Allâh had declared trade (by men) to be lawful, though usury was prohibited. Now torches smoked in their sockets outside all the booth doorways, and the smell of tallow fat rose to the awnings which closed out the sky, mixed with the sharper reek of geranium from Gabriel's Janissaries. With only a matter of yards between them and their quarry they plunged into the first smoky alley to find their feet treading on sawdust and their way barred by a puzzled man in a round cap and apron, a low wooden bench strapped broadside-on to his head. He turned this way and that, bewildered, as the Janissaries danced threatening before him, and finally revolved where he stood, admitting three or four, it was true, but felling three or four others as well. Behind him, someone had upset in passing a stack of small stools which rolled and oscillated on the uneven ground as the pursuers, stumbling and jumping, flung themselves after their vanishing victim.

In the next lane they were quilting: inoffensive craftsmen seated crosslegged with their curved needles and rolls of bright silk, the coarse sacks of cotton wool open beside them. Lymond darted through, smooth as an auk under water, and the air was dappled and dancing with cotton: the Janissaries ran full tilt into a blizzard of it, settling into their eyes and their noses, convulsing them with sneezes as they reeled on through empty sacks and furious quilters. '*Opus plumarium*,' someone said. They followed the voice.

They followed it through bright rolling copperware and the up-turned vats of the cloth-dyers, the wooden blocks printing their robes with small elegant flowers in bright colours as they slipped and slid in the pigment. They stepped moaning on bagpipes and were pierced with gazelle horns in the street of the knifehandle-makers; they slithered in linseed in the place of the oil- and soap-merchants and in the lane of the pastrycooks waded through a glue-field of dough scuttled in trayloads on its way between housewife and ovens.

It became a game in the thronged alleys; a game played in rough mime with much shouting and laughter by men of mixed races; who carried along for the length of a street and then dropped back to allow new faces to range alongside, pilfering, calling; grimly savouring the fun. No one laid a hand on the Janissaries; no one would dare. Until they came too close, and Lymond reached the place where daggers and scimitars were cheaply damascened, and furnished with sheaths of glass jewels. He took a handful of small knives in passing, and turning, studied and threw.

He killed one Janissary and wounded two others. If it was a game, it was one invented by a harsh and mischievous brain: a fertile brain which brought its owner finally out into the fairground before the Beyazit Mosque, pursuit now failing and farther behind. There,

Lymond threaded his way quickly through the performers, upsetting the man walking barefoot on scimitars and cannoning into another who was standing, his brow lined, transferring a three-hundred-pound vertical galley mast with infinite patience from one shoulder on to the next. By flinging themselves to one side, the remaining Janissaries contrived to avoid the slow, falling timber: they did not avoid the big Turk with the glass-headed arrows, who turned his aim towards them instead of the ostrich-eggs he was attempting to shoot without breaking. The arrows went through the leading Janissary's arm, clean as a whistle, and the trick would have made the marksman's fortune in alms, except that he threw his bow down and fled.

Lymond hadn't waited to see the outcome of that. A little before he had glimpsed, dimly lit by the torches, a tall swing of the kind common to Stamboul festivals, its seat at street level, its harness high in the rooftops. He reached it, still running lightly, and tipping out the hilarious occupier sprang on the seat. He worked it like a trapeze, twisting slightly and sending it hard and fast into the sky until, just as his pursuers rounded the corner, he let go.

He landed precisely as he planned on all fours on the rooftops and, sliding along, was three streets away while the Janissaries were still pelting in confusion below. Then, anonymous under his hood, he slowed up and, stepping down into an air free of all tinge of geranium, made his way through the dark streets towards the black arching aqueduct of Valens. There, he let himself quietly into the house of Míkál and, pulling off robe and hood, threaded his way swiftly through Míkál's cheerful companions and up to his room.

Míkál was there already, sleek as a fawn on his cushions, dreamily touching his lute, his brilliant eyes lighting with pleasure. 'Hâkim!'

Beside him was Gabriel.

'My dear Francis!' Gently ridiculing, the mellow voice spoke. 'What an expense of energy for a rather warm evening. If you had simply restrained yourself and trusted my Janissaries, they would have brought you straight here in the first place.'

He almost paid for his malice. The knife was in Lymond's hand before Graham Malett started to speak: quicker than thought his wrist rose to flick it and was caught, agonizingly, by a great fist from behind, followed instantly by the grasp of three or four men, crowding in through the doorway. Lymond twisted, his head down and using his feet, but although they swore at him and one fell back, moaning over his arm, the grip on him only intensified. They were, he saw, all Míkál's friends. The giant of the sheep-bone held his right hand and ripped the knife from it, drawing blood, idly, down his arm with the blade. Then he was dragged erect, to stand before Gabriel.

His clothes torn, his hair damply ravelled, his body and face marked with his handling, Lymond looked bright-eyed at the two on the cushions. 'Why, Míkál?' he said.

A shade of sadness crossed the wild, hollow face. 'It is laid on me by love,' said Míkál. 'As a cord of twisted bark bound upon the neck of each ploughing bull, I waded to thee through darkness, as though I waded through a full sea; but thou didst not receive me. I stood in darkness, with fear my innermost garment, and thou didst not warm me. Soon the devil thou dost swallow will claim thee, and where shall I be? I am a Pilgrim of Love, Hâkim; and thy soul is of rock.'

Lymond spoke quietly. 'One man who sells another, whatever the coin, is a traitor. Like the sons of Ghudáneh, you are not indeed gold, nor silver, nor pure silver, Míkál; but you are pottery.'

'If we have reached a breathing-space in your recriminations?' asked Gabriel amiably. He was wearing no turban; his short golden hair glittered bright in the lamplight and the spreading folds of his stiff Turkish robe were edged and lined with shining dark sables. 'I have some business elsewhere to attend to. I find it quite astonishing that you apparently had hopes of defying me, here on my home ground. They are waiting for you at the Seraglio. Míkál?'

'They are ready,' said Míkál, and clapped his hands, smiling.

With a force which pulled him off balance, Lymond was wrenched to one side by his captors. He regained his feet instantly and stood, his hands held hard at his back while someone with great deftness lashed both his wrists and his arms with first rope and then wire. Outside the door there was a brief bustle and another of Míkál's friends came into the room, followed by two Janissaries, scimitars in hand, who ranged themselves one on each side of the doorposts. Then through the door, her chin defiantly high, walked Philippa, with the child Kuzucuyum asleep in her arms.

Lymond said, '*Míkál!*' and then was silent, his face very white.

Philippa was greeny-pale too, with big circles under her eyes. She had seen Gabriel immediately and was staring at him, her nose pointing to the rafters, when she heard Lymond's voice and turned, her chest heaving.

'Hullo!' Lymond said lightly. 'The ancient and godly yeomanry of England. Come and join the club. Isn't he heavy?' His eyes, without expression, rested on the small bright head on her arm, and then returned to her face.

'It's all right,' said Philippa raggedly. The change in him paralysed her. He must have known it, because he smiled at her suddenly, his voice familiar and steady, and said, 'Don't worry. I'm sorry about the rats in the roost, but you can't always choose your——'

Gabriel shut his mouth for him, rising in a single smooth movement and taking the palm of his hand sharp as gunshot against Lymond's face, first on the one side and then the other.

'Control your nerves,' said Gabriel pleasantly. He added to Philippa, 'Do you know what an opium addict is like? Have you seen them in the street, foaming at the mouth like chafed boars and howl-

410

ing like dogs? You should learn what to look for: the diminished pupils, the slackened skin; the unsteady hands.' He caught Lymond's neck suddenly between iron fingers and, as he tried to fling himself free, fetched him another blow on the face which cut open his lip, blood running fast down his marked chin. His head turned away, Lymond had closed his eyes for a moment: opening them, he turned back and looked Gabriel again full in the face. 'Violence. The mark of a fool,' he said.

'One flavour sets off another,' said Gabriel calmly. 'You do not know what is still to come. Like Väinämöinen to Vipunen; I shall sink my anvil further into the flesh of your heart; I shall install my forge in a deeper place. You felt that blow? Then you must be in need. Shall I bring you what you crave? Where is it: in your robe? In the purse they have unbuckled?' Stooping, he picked up Lymond's satchel where someone had thrown it and, unfastening it without haste, opened it to the light.

'Alas!' said Gabriel. 'A seditious foreigner; and also a thief. Observe!' And putting inside his hand, he withdraw a sparkling fistful of jewellery. 'Purloined from my own chamber. It is known that you have spent all you have. Must you repair your own fortunes by robbing another?'

'I wish I'd thought of it,' said Lymond briefly. The accessibility of Gabriel's costliest belongings was thus simply explained.

There were other things in the satchel too: a box in gold leaf and some uncut stones, and a *tespi*, a prayer string of pearls itself worth all of three thousand pounds. Gabriel laid them aside, and at last found what he wanted. Philippa, all her strained attention on Lymond, saw his muscles harden, like a man expecting a sluice of cold water. Then Gabriel held something flat in his palm: a small marbled cake, tawny yellow in colour.

'How much do you want?' asked Graham Malett, his voice liquid with sympathy. 'Two drachms: three? You need a killing dose now, don't you, to keep your brain clear and your nerves steady and your purpose intact? A killing dose, often. How much would you like?'

Kuzúm had wakened. Empty with fright and exhaustion, he lay against Philippa's crumpled robe, his heavy blue eyes open on the incomprehensible scene. Lymond looked neither at Philippa nor the child. 'None,' he said dryly. 'Your concern breaks my heart.'

'This much?' It was close enough even for Philippa to smell: the pungent high-seasoned savour of it must have filled Lymond's senses. 'Between the teeth,' said Gabriel, gently insistent. 'Since your hands are not free.'

Seams of blood and sweat bright on his face, Lymond did not speak this time, but turned his head fully away; his lips shut hard; his breathing in spite of himself uneven and quick. Gabriel's face remained pleasant. 'You won't take a little? Then have it all, my sorry, hungering slut,' he said lightly; and as the men on either side of Lymond forced round his head, he stepped forward, the cake in his hand.

Philippa dropped Kuzúm. It was all she could think of to do, and her heart ached for the lost, bewildered child he had become in a matter of hours. But the movement and the wild, hoarse screaming he started brought all eyes towards her and gave Lymond a second: a moment's grace to postpone the sickening humiliation which Gabriel planned.

Lymond used the moment. His hands were tied, but he could wield the weight of his body: he could kick, and could bite. As their grip loosened he tore himself half out of the hands of his captors and flung his shoulder against Gabriel. The opium dropped, smashed on the floor, before Gabriel's hands, reacting instantly, came up to grip him; and the others, doubled up and grunting under the wild, sudden attack, pounced in their turn and threw Francis Crawford, still twisting and fighting below them till he lay half dazed, winded and bloody on Míkál's fine carpet.

Míkál, kneeling beside him, looked up at Gabriel with lustrous eyes. Gabriel, imperial in Venetian crimson and sables, stood and stared with distaste at the man on the ground.

'Violence?' he said. 'The mark of a fool. You are distressing the child. Perhaps you will have more care for the other when you reach the Seraglio. He should be there by now, along with Abernethy, your devoted mahout. You may even recognize others of those you have dragged to their damnation through your insufferable conceit. . . . Since you are so wild I think our friends should remove, for safety, whatever senses you may have left.'

Philippa covered Kuzúm's eyes as they delivered the blows which turned Francis Crawford over and over and left him unconscious at last at their feet. Prone on the bare boards, he shared the covered cart which took the Janissaries and herself to Topkapi, but he was far from waking, and Kuzúm sobbed all the way, afraid of the blood and the way his body was shaken by the jolt of the wheels. They stopped at the Bab-i-Humayun, and again at the Ortokapi, where she and Kuzúm were made to get down.

She did not see what happened to Lymond, nor would anyone answer her questions. Inside the Gate of Felicity they took Kuzúm from her. His screams and her own shaken voice arguing must have wakened that part of the harem until the child's voice was suddenly cut off by a hand over his mouth, and she was taken in turn by two of the black eunuchs she did not know, and thrust into a strange room, which was locked. From the noises outside, she thought they were taking Kuzúm to the nurse's courtyard, and prayed that it might be so, and that Tulip was there. Then, because she felt too sick and too weary to cry, she sat silent and wide-eyed by the barred window, and waited for dawn.

412

25

CONSTANTINOPLE: THE DIVAN

Lymond woke, shivering, while it was still dark, every muscle a stiff and separate pain. He was lying on matting; his own rolled kaftán under his head, and his wrist was lifted between someone's fingers, quickly removed. Then a weak candle flickered alight, and he saw Jerott kneeling beside him; and Archie's dark turbaned face in the background. He smiled at them both and said to Jerott, 'How in hell did *you*. . .?' He was overtaken before he finished by a convulsive yawn and, still smiling a little, put both hands up and over his face, shivering still. Archie disappeared into the darkness behind him.

Jerott said, 'We're in the Seraglio, I think in the Third Court. They sent word to the Embassy that Marthe was ready to come out, and asked for an escort. Then when I got here they locked me up on my own. Archie joined me a few hours ago. I don't know where Marthe or Onophrion are.'

Lymond said, 'Onophrion came with you?' He yawned again and said, 'Hell,' between chattering teeth; then, struggling, sat up and buried his head in his hands. Jerott, his face grim, looked over his head and said, 'Yes: he came with me. They've got Khaireddin too, but we don't know where. Archie says Míkál betrayed the whole plan. I thought perhaps it was Marthe, in spite of the treasure.'

Lymond said, 'What treasure?' through his hands, and Jerott told him. Archie was taking a hell of a time. But then of course he had the stuff sewn in the seams of his clothes, to be sure of it. Jerott finished what he was saying and was trying to think of something else when Archie's turbaned head loomed out of the darkness. Jerott got to his feet and moved away, as far as he could towards the high barred little window. He waited a long time, until Archie's voice stopped; and then turned and went back.

Lymond was asleep; and Archie, using the last light from the candle they had saved for this purpose, was stowing away again with care what he had carried inside his clothes. To Jerott's raised eyebrows: 'Ye can talk,' he said. 'He won't hear you. That's something else I've given him, because the poppy isn't quick any longer. But he's had a dose of that, too, I wouldna like to give to a beast. . . . If it's any comfort, he's very near the edge now. He couldna have gone on much longer.'

'He won't have to,' said Jerott. 'I imagine tomorrow will end it, one way or another, for all of us. He has enough now to see him through, and that's all that matters.' He paused, and said, in a detached voice, 'It's a pity we didn't mind our own business, isn't it?'

'Is it?' said Archie. He finished what he was doing, consulted

413

Jerott's face and, leaning over, pinched out the candle. 'I doubt, sir,' said Archie, 'if we had kept out of it, you could no more have lived with yourself after than I could.'

*

The two mutes who had locked her in brought Philippa breakfast next morning, and the wherewithal to make a rough toilet. She had just finished when the cell door opened and was shut and locked again behind Marthe.

Marthe, it was clear, was as bewildered as Philippa, although in a moment she had masked it; and, surveying the tray of half-eaten food, observed, 'I don't blame you; although, I advise you, it is easier to be bold if your stomach is full. You didn't escape?'

'I did. We were brought back.' She explained, and listened in turn, flushing, to Marthe's story. 'They kept you because you'd carried a message for me. I'm sorry. And it all went for nothing because Míkál told Gabriel everything.'

'Míkál,' said Marthe, 'who went with you to find the child at Thessalonika?' Onophrion had told her all they had learned on that journey, when he and Lymond had sailed on the same route with Míkál on board. She said, 'Weren't there accidents?'

'Where? I don't know,' said Philippa.

'On board ship with dear Mr Crawford. . . . It doesn't matter,' said Marthe. 'It isn't your fault. You had an outburst of philanthropy and I made an error of judgement, and it has landed us both in precisely the same spot.'

Untouched and slender, she seemed to Philippa's eyes quite unchanged: a little thinner perhaps; a little quieter perhaps, but that was all. It did not occur to Philippa to wonder how much she herself had grown in the last year or more; or how she had altered. She had seen herself in Lymond's eyes as the schoolgirl she had always been: an additional burden to be reassured. She did not see in Marthe's quieter mood a sober assessment of what the long imprisonment must have meant, and of the kind of spirit which had not only endured it but built on it. Philippa said, her hands hard one on top of the other, 'There was another child, too. I don't know if they caught him. Gabriel says one of them is his. I wonder what they'll do to the children?'

'Nothing, probably,' said Marthe. 'Mr Crawford, I suppose, stands to pay the full penalty for taking you and the children away against the Sultan's commands, and we shall be punished for helping him.'

'It's more than that,' said Philippa. 'They talked of sedition. They've even accused him of theft. You see, Gabriel is going to deal with him in his own way, and he must have full justification.' She said, hesitating, 'You said once that you were forced into bringing that message. If you could prove that . . . ?'

414

'I don't think,' said Marthe calmly, 'that it would do me much good.'

'You're beautiful,' said Philippa gently. 'He won't kill you.'

The glint of a cold surprise, so familiar from the early days on the *Dauphiné*, returned to Marthe's level blue gaze. 'You think I would scuttle into any man's harem? Would you?'

'Yes. For Kuzúm,' said Philippa. She hesitated, guessing. 'People help one another. Wouldn't . . . Mr Blyth perhaps do the equivalent for you?'

Marthe laughed, without amusement, deep in her long throat. 'Mr Blyth put me here. Mr Crawford and I owe each other nothing. My uncle I hate and you I do not know. No one, as far as I see, has endeavoured to engineer *my* escape.'

'I think . . . that was only because they didn't know you were a prisoner,' said Philippa. She was rather pale. She said, in a small voice, '*I* would do it for you.'

The colour left Marthe's face too, in patches; then flooded in, deep rose over her brow and cheeks and slim neck. She stood up. 'Because I look like my brother?' she said.

Philippa's dark brows had met in a straight line; her brown eyes opaque with a new self-control fighting with a faint and horrified understanding. After a while she said simply, 'No. Because I know what it is to need help.'

For a moment longer Marthe studied her; and Philippa rather bleakly wondered what amused rejoinder, what cutting remark she had called on herself. But Marthe in the end said merely, 'Then . . . when I need help, I shall have to call on you, shan't I?' in a voice whose coolness and impatience did not ring entirely true. There was a silence, and then Philippa said awkwardly, 'I didn't know. . . . Is Mr Crawford your brother?'

The blue eyes this time were both cool and amused. 'If he knew, he might prefer you to put it differently,' said Marthe. 'I am his bastard sister. We have the same failings. Didn't you guess?'

*

The tribunal before which they had all been arraigned was held without delay in the Divan Court the following morning. To Jerott, the former Knight of St John, who knew better perhaps than any of them the exquisite range of Saracen torture, the news was a relief. Lymond, to whom he said as much, did not reply, but Archie was blunt. 'He won't have us marked before all the pashas. It's afterwards, when we've been sentenced, that he'll have a free hand.'

Today, under Archie's ministrations, Lymond seemed completely himself; and although the marks of his beating were still plain on his face, the fresh robes they were given, according to custom, had covered the rest. Between waking and setting out for the court he had said very little: what was there indeed, thought Jerott, to say? An apology perhaps to Archie, for having trusted where he should never have trusted. But that was hindsight. Who could have suspected Míkál?

As for Jerott himself, he had brought his troubles on his own head. No one had asked him to compel Marthe to come, and no one had asked him to follow her. He waited, chatting with Archie, until they heard the tramp of the Janissaries outside, and Lymond said, 'Jerott . . .' and then stopped, his eyes brilliant; his face very white. He said, 'Surely they will let me speak to you both, before the end?'

'What is it?' said Jerott; and took Lymond's wrist. 'There is time. Tell us now.'

'I can't,' said Francis Crawford, an odd note of desperation in his voice. 'Archie, will this bloody stuff last out the morning, or shall I have to take more in the . . .?'

Archie's voice was steady as ever; comfortable as when he held converse with one of his lions. 'It should last. But you've more in your kerchief and in your purse, and I've supplies for several days after that.'

It was then that you remembered, thought Jerott Blyth suddenly, that Archie after all was a man in his fifties. And that Lymond was just twenty-six.

Then the door opened and Lymond, the balance back in his voice, said lightly, 'All right, gentlemen. Havoc and mount!'

*

Once before, as Ambassador, he had stood before the throne in the Divan Court, and Gabriel in white and gold had greeted him, his officials around him.

Now Gabriel was robed in purple and crimson, his turban girdled with rubies, and a brazier with great silver feet stood on the deep carpet beside him, where the robed figures ranged in their furred winter robes, their turbans and hats, round, conical, oblong, in every colour and shape describing as clearly as badges the ranks in law and security, holy teaching, administration and learning foregathered there. Gabriel sat, and they settled, each on his low stool, the clerks in a corner writing already, paper on knee.

It left Jerott feeling remarkably exposed, standing with Archie beside him near the door, a row of blue-robed Janissaries silent behind them. He wondered how Lymond felt, waiting alone before Gabriel, who, talking to his interpreter, had not even glanced at him. His back told Jerott nothing.

There was no sign of the children. None either of Philippa and Marthe, or of Onophrion. His gaze wandering round, Jerott caught sight suddenly of Míkál, his long hair freshly combed and a necklace of white salted roses over his purple silk tunic. Instead of bells, his wrists were banded with new bracelets of gold, and he had an anklet of gold on one slender arched foot. Rage flooding his veins, Jerott glared at him, and Míkál, lifting his head, saw him and gave a mischievous smile. Jerott looked away, just as Gabriel turned from the dragoman and said in his mild, golden voice, 'Lords: I beg your attention . . .'

The indictment was damning; inexorable. Gabriel himself conducted the case; recalling how the Scottish lord, Crawford of Lymond and Sevigny, had used his standing as Ambassador for France to persuade the lord Suleiman Khan to hand over a girl and a child from the Sultan's harem and, on being refused, had claimed even that the child was a son of His Grace Henry of France.

'This is untrue,' said Gabriel sorrowfully. He spoke this time in Turkish, the interpreter at his side, for appearances. He must have known by now, Jerott supposed, that their command of the language was as fluent as his own.

Gabriel was continuing. 'That it is untrue I can prove to you in a matter of days, when a courier will show you that the child this man claimed to be here is in fact safe in France. Therefore he lied to the Sultan, a lie which in his clemency the lord Suleiman overlooked, saying merely that he would hand over neither the girl nor the child without further proof from the Ambassador that the child was in fact the son of King Henry . . . Crawford Efendi could not prove such a thing. He therefore abducted the girl and the child. He further abducted a second child, the adopted son of Názik the nightingale-dealer, having already seduced him; and had caused both children to be taken out of the city, where they were discovered and stopped.'

Gabriel paused, his voice dropping. 'Why should he do such a thing? Because, lords, this dog of a Christian has fought for St John; held Tripoli against Sinan Pasha; did all in his power to prevent my leaving that vipers' nest of unbelievers in Malta, even to attempting my life in Zuara. His thoughts towards me are evil. . . . Learning then that I had a dear son, reared in the home of Dragut Rais in Djerba and Algiers, he took steps to capture the child, and because, moving from country to country in vain hope of eluding him, the boy's identity became confused with another, he took it upon himself to seize both children, and degrade them, and take them back to the West, where their souls would be wrenched like roses from Paradise and cast into the hell of the heretic. . . .'

Christ, thought Jerott. Míkál was admiring his finger-nails. No one interrupted, or asked any questions. He supposed the evidence would come along later: Názik and other bribed witnesses. The royal-bastard story had clearly been fatal. But it might have worked; and he supposed it had had to be tried. Now the mellow voice was going on about a theft from his house, which Jerott found outside belief, and a list of witnesses which was equally unlikely. . . . Assuming the

417

accusation was false, why had it been made? Perhaps because, thought Jerott, as that old satyr Gilles had once said, *Turcae non minus sunt insani quam nos circa aurifabrorum opera.* Turks were mad about gold. The theft of gold would strike home where a lot of abstract discussion about children would mean nothing at all. . . . And here was the third count.

The stirring up of sedition. Gabriel's voice, tinged with pain, was rolling over the phrases. How gross the guest, the diplomatic guest under their roof, who made profit from the canker within the host's flesh. All knew of the melancholy fate of the Prince Mustafa, his head turned with pride and ambition, who had thought to win the love of the army and ultimately the throne of the Shadow of God. Rustem Pasha, their well-loved Grand Vizier, had detected it. He himself, coming from Zuara, had seen it. Both had sent messages, urgent messages to Khourrém Sultán, the Sultan's beloved mistress and wife, that she might softly acquaint the Sultan with this his betrayal by the young man he loved.

So, with sorrow, the father had had to remove the undutiful son, and the Prince Mustafa had been killed. So, he had just heard, the Prince Mustafa's son of four years had been swiftly and mercifully put to his rest in the city of Bursa. . . . But far from accepting these things as the will of Allâh and allowing the bereaved and betrayed to be silent, mourning their dead, men had lent their ears to a vicious new rumour. A rumour that Mustafa Pasha had been innocent of plot against his royal father. A rumour that Rustem Pasha the Vizier, in guilty concert with the Sultan's wife Roxelana, had fabricated a plot against the Prince Mustafa, in order to place Roxelana's own son on the throne.

A cruel and malignant rumour, of which the man standing before them was author.

A rustle; a shifting of colour ran through the whole room. Lymond said clearly, in Turkish, 'That is not so.'

Gabriel turned on him. 'Is it not? Do you deny that since the death of Mustafa you have adopted the guise of a Meddáh and roaming the city have incited people to rebellion, talking to them of the innocence of Mustafa and the guilt of Roxelana, the Sultan's own gracious wife? Have you not entered and searched my home for papers the Sultana might have written proving her guilt? Have you not placed in the Sultana's apartments even a girl, an English girl who under the guise of knowing no Turkish could find and read the Sultana's own private correspondence, and could listen unseen to her talk? And when the Jewess who smuggled you out such information as you discovered was killed, did you not instal yet another, a French-woman, under the colour of mending the French King's clock-spinet?'

He paused, making a little space, and so the Grand Mufti, turning his white beard and great bushel-green turban, was able to ask his quiet question. 'Might it be known what information, if any, they discovered?'

What the Sheikh-ul-Islâm, the Ancient of Islam, inquired must surely be answered. Gabriel hesitated, but only for a moment. Then, with respect, he replied. 'Until Rustem Pasha is here, Hâkim, to answer for himself, it is not my place to divulge it.'

The white beard considered that. Then, gentle-voiced, the Grand Mufti supplemented his question. 'And the matter as it affects Roxelana Sultán. Were any new facts revealed about that?'

On his throne, Gabriel's fair face was lined. He moved a little, twisting his rings, his eyes on his fingers. Then looking up: 'I cannot answer that,' he replied.

'Then I can.' Lymond's voice cut through the whispering rustle. 'No papers have been found, in Stamboul or elsewhere, which support to the slightest degree the rumour you speak of, that Rustem Pasha and Roxelana Sultán together plotted to have Mustafa and his child killed.'

The green turban of the Mufti turned towards him, and the old voice was dry. 'Should thy tongue be so forthright? Had this been true, instead of the ganching spike, honour might have been thine as one who performs a great service.'

'With deference, Hâkim,' said Lymond, his voice equally dry. 'Had it been true I should be equally dead. Until it has set its own affairs to order, no nation can afford to have rumours such as these bandied abroad. I have nothing to gain either way, so I choose to tell you the truth. These stories are quite unfounded.'

'I think,' said Gabriel's rich voice softly, 'that we have perhaps slipped away from the point. The accusation is that Mr Crawford has spread certain rumours. That he has lent colour to them by certain actions. That he has incited the citizens, and not only the citizens but the Janissaries, the cream of our troops, to a point where very soon there will be an open demand for an inquiry. I ask him: does he deny it?'

Lymond glanced round the assembly. He looked, Jerott thought, undisturbed and quite self-sufficient, with no hint of the horror which had washed over him, briefly, before he came out. He said again, in that lucid, carrying voice, 'Do you know, I wonder, with your Western upbringing, the tale of the History of the Forty Viziers?'

Someone laughed. There was a rustle and Gabriel said smoothly, 'Of course.'

'You will remember, perhaps, its subject,' Lymond said. 'A king orders the execution of his innocent son, urged to it by the false accusations of his unhappy and desperate wife. Each morning the king is restrained from killing his son by fresh advice, framed in a tale by one of his forty wise councillors. And each evening he is

419

urged to it again by a tale from the queen. The stories are older than time, and told in many tongues: those I tell I had once in Persian. No, I don't deny earning my bread as a Meddáh. Attacks on the Embassy directed not at me but at my unfortunate household forced me to relinquish my post. As Jubrael Pasha has so eloquently told you, I had little money. I stayed in hopes of seeing righted an injustice concerning the children, and to stay I needed shelter and food. This I paid for with stories. And the stories, as I have told you, concerned a king far older than the present great Sultan Suleiman, and a queen long dead and far less beautiful than his wife. If men discuss these in modern terms, it is no fault of mine. . . .' He paused, and then added, a hint of laughter in the clear voice, 'Also, men were generous. I am not now short of money, Jubrael Pasha. The Forty Viziers in their day paid almost as much as your treasure-chests.'

Gabriel's face did not relax. 'You deny it now, but I have witnesses who can say that the History of the Forty Viziers was not all that fell from your lips in your innocent walks in the city. If you had no share in the rumours, why plant your spies? Why smear your suspicions in our very bedchambers, unless you wished it to appear that you were looking for evidence?'

'But I was!' said Lymond mildly. 'I was looking for evidence against you.'

In the Seraglio, all sounds were muted. The buzzing which ran round the chamber was no more than might have come from a nest-ful of wasps; but there was no doubt of the interest he had stirred. Gabriel rose to his feet. 'Dog and progeny of dogs! Is this proper language to me? . . . Take him away.'

Lymond did not move. 'And I found it,' he said. 'Is that why you wish to remove me? But how can you judge me when as yet you have produced no proof and no witnesses?'

'Witnesses?' said Gabriel. He sat down, smoothing his gown. He is not often crossed these days, thought Jerott. 'Since you ask, I will give you witnesses,' said Graham Malett, his rounded voice grim. 'I call him named Míkál.'

Amiable as a girl: lively as a fawn. Where had he read that? thought Jerott, watching the lithe figure unfold itself and walk slowly, with grace, to the brazier.

Lymond did not look at Míkál. Jerott, glancing from the Geomaler to the man he had betrayed, saw that Lymond's hands were folded loosely before him; his brows raised a little and his eyes on the carpet; like a man weary of excuses pitching himself to hear yet another. Gabriel said gently, 'Disguised as a story-teller, Crawford Efendi stayed in Míkál's house, and Míkál, of whose loyalty there can be no question, on my advice made himself privy to all his plans. Tell, Míkál, how as Meddáh this man was heard to speak to all about him,

420

inflaming them with hatred for Roxelana and Rustem Pasha. Tell how the English girl was installed by guile in Roxelana's own chambers, and told at all costs to find evidence against her. Tell how he fabricated a tale first of a son of his own and then of a child of King Henry's in order to wrest from me my only dear son. Tell how, maligning the Sultana, he has brought even the Janissaries to the point of open rebellion. . . .'

Míkál looked up at the Vizier and over his shoulder at Lymond's bent head. Then turning politely, he addressed the assembled officials. 'I would,' he said charmingly, 'if I could: but how can I say what is not true?'

Lymond's head came up at that, his eyes blazing; and Míkál looked into them and laughed, and against Gabriel's voice, beginning a sudden startled tirade, Míkál added, 'I regret to deny it when Jubrael Pasha has paid me so much; but while my conscience is clear I can conquer the world: the waterless desert fills me not with awe or with fear; I ride over it when the male owls answer one another at dawn, and I am not afraid. This I would keep. Therefore I say it is not true. The tales of the Meddáh were told, as you have heard, in all innocence, though many spoke of them afterwards who were not innocent, and these the Meddáh listened to, and questioned, for the truth he desired. Likewise in the rooms of Jubrael Pasha he sought what he sought for the sake of Roxelana Sultán, and not to her detriment. I have taken thy money, but in truth I must say it. He found at length what he had been seeking. That from Jubrael Pasha and none other had the rumours of Roxelana's complicity come.'

Gabriel's voice was no less threatening for its extreme softness. 'Whore! What has he paid you to lie? Or did he pay you in something other than gold? He found a cheap coinage, they say, for the Aga Morat in Gabès to prevent him from spreading his favours. . . . My lords, the boy is corrupt as the man.'

'Then you had better,' said the Grand Mufti against the hum of excitement, 'call another witness who is incorruptible? Or perhaps the prisoner should speak? What of this proof he claims, incredible though it appears, against the Vizier himself?'

'I would call,' said Lymond, his eyes on Míkál, '. . . I think I would call . . . the Agha of Janissaries.'

Then for the second time Gabriel rose to his feet. A big man, splendidly built, he stood in majesty by his throne, the rubies answering with their fire the dull fire of the brazier; his gold-sewn crimson sweeping the floor. He spoke, with all the weary charitableness of which he was capable. 'Lords: how can I stand, your Vizier, your appointed head of administration and supreme judge, your presiding head of Divan, and while judging find myself under attack? This court is no longer a court but a strutting-place for those who wish to be notorious. . . . I close the session. The case, if there is still a case, must be reopened and tried elsewhere. The accusations against myself, if anyone entertains such, must be placed in the proper way, in the proper quarter. The prisoners meantime will return to their rooms, the man Míkál with them. Make way.'

He had got to the door and the Janissaries in a sweep of blue had stood out of his way when the daylight was blocked by a massive figure: the person of the head of the black eunuchs, the Kislar Agha himself. Gabriel hesitated, and the eunuch, looking at no one else, addressed him direct.

'Lord, I bear a summons from Roxelana Sultán, for thyself and thy prisoners, together with the women and children and all concerned in this accusation today to present themselves forthwith in the selamlìk, in the Hünkâr Sofasi. There is an escort outside.'

There was, of eunuchs and Chiausi. Gabriel hesitated. The Mufti, his green robes rustling, rose gently and stood at his side. 'Pray do not hesitate on our account,' he said thinly, 'to do thy mistress's bidding. Thy ruling is paramount and the court is concluded.'

Then, his face set, Gabriel turned. He looked at them all: Jerott, Archie, Míkál and finally Lymond himself, still standing very still by the throne. 'Do you think it is finished?' said Gabriel, in English. Then he added, 'Bring them!' curtly to the Chiausi, and, flanked by the eunuchs, walked down the steps of the Divan and over the court to where the leaves of the Gate of Felicity had swung quietly open. A few moments later, the four men followed him through.

Half-way through the inner courtyard Lymond, who had spoken to none of them, suddenly met Míkál's eyes and said, *'But why bring back the children?'*

'She ordered it,' said Míkál. His eyes glittered with hidden excitement. He said, 'Tell me of the Aga Morat?'

'Oh, my God. . . . Another time,' said Lymond. He was still, Jerott saw, completely steady . . . refreshed somehow, perhaps, as they moved from the Divan. Jerott said perversely, 'Yes. Tell us about the Aga Morat. He formed an attachment for you, and you used him.' It was strange to be able to speak of it, almost in jest. He stared at Míkál, wondering how far anyone was trusting him. 'What did you use him for?' said Jerott.

'All the usual things,' said Lymond evenly; and, walking ahead, stepped through the wide door of the selamlìk. Archie, catching Jerott's abashed eye, took his arm grimly and walked him in after. Míkál followed.

*

Of her two identities, it was Roxelana the Ukrainian and not Khourrém the Laughing One who elected to hold her own tribunal that morning with every harness of power and magnificence owed to her as wife of Suleiman the Magnificent. For it, she chose the largest room in the selamlìk: the room used by her husband in winter for his entertainments and his receptions, in which girls from the harem played and danced, and musicians from the outside world performed blindfolded on strange instruments, and poets, blindfolded, recited.

Today it was filled with silence: silence from the mutes and dwarves, the pages and the black and white eunuchs ringing the walls: silence from the immense dome with its ring of coloured glass windows and the speckled tesserae of glass and of gold within, blazoned with the words of the Prophet. The words of the Qur'ân, in gold and enamel, also fretted the cornice; but from there to the ground the walls were tiled in pure white, flowered with blossoms in blue, in cerulean and light and dark ultramarine, the inner petals embossed with a bright coral red, shining like satin. Rugs hung over the tiles, and delicate hangings of silver and taffeta, masked by the long hanging chains bearing lamps of wrought silver and crystal and gold, each fashioned and domed like a mosque, its hanging pendant tasselled with seed pearls and diamonds and each cut from an emerald six inches square.

There was little furniture: open wall cupboards of carved wood and ivory; a marble fountain softly playing against one wall; a few low tables in mother of pearl and cedarwood and tortoiseshell, and some round stools of brass, scattered by the great braziers on the deep carpeted floor. The windows looked on the Bosphorus, and against them a carpeted dais filled the whole width of the room and was divided from it by a low rail picked out in gold, broken by shallow steps in the centre. At right angles to this, on a smaller dais and under the carved canopy and turban of state, sat Roxelana Sultán.

The throne was a network of gold, linked with small gold devices and set thickly with turquoises, interspersed with gold lozenges covered with rubies and pearls. Seated high on her cushions, her feet on a footstool, Roxelana looked stately and small; her face lightly veiled under her headdress; her carnation skirts spread wide around her. She wore peacocks' feathers, bound in gold thread and thrust in a socket of ivory, from which diamonds trembled over her brow. Jerott, all the levity of reaction struck heavily from him, stared at her numbly, only half aware of the Kislar Agha in his yellow robes deferential at one side, and on the other a woman, also veiled, in attendance.

On the carpet below the dais there were two velvet cushions, widely spaced; and on these, by her orders it seemed, Gabriel and Lymond both knelt in silence. In silence also, Jerott with Archie and Míkál were pushed into line a little behind the two cushions, the mutes at the back. Then, with a leap of his pulses, Jerott saw Marthe come in unveiled, her bright hair bound in a fillet, her brows raised; her walk graceful and careless, self-possessed and touched with contempt. He saw, as she walked, the blue gaze, without cordiality, find Lymond and stare at him, and Lymond's eyes in turn lift to meet hers, of identical colour. To Jerott's breathless fancy, a challenge, or something near it, for a moment seemed to pass from one to the other. Then Marthe was past, without glancing at Jerott, and had joined the black eunuch standing beside the Kislar Agha, to one side of the throne.

She was followed by another girl, whom Jerott did not at first notice; and then, startled, identified. It was Philippa Somerville, her glossy brown hair swept back from her high schoolgirl's brow to lie on her shoulders; her body slender under thick tawny silk, its new softness overlaid by a rope of gold and white jade, clasped with an infant tortoiseshell, high on her shoulder. It was indeed Philippa, although she walked as Jerott had seen women walk from the bathhouse with their servants, slim and straight as an *elif*. But the brown eyes under the thin dark brows were the same, anxiously searching; lighting with a small, relieved smile first on Lymond, then on Archie and himself; with puzzlement and a little hauteur on Míkál. Then they swept on, still searching, Jerott did not know for what, until he saw, on the big dais, a negress sitting, a child by her side.

It was Khaireddin, a fixed smile on his white, old man's face: the face Jerott had seen twice before; in the shed of the silk merchant of Mehedia and not long ago, playing with shells on a carpet while Francis Crawford lay, soft-voiced and motionless, trying to undo the damage which Gabriel had done.

Philippa's eyes fell on the child as a man groping in water might lift, flinching, what he had found. She stood by the Kislar Agha, her gaze on the boy, and as he watched, Jerott saw her lips open and then shut tight, her eyes very bright. She was still standing like that when the second child came in and was led to sit by the negress's other side. A round-faced boy, sturdily built, with a cap of bright yellow hair, whom he had not seen before. Unlike the other child he looked round at once, complete consternation printed on his plump face, saw Philippa, and screamed '*Fippy!*' at the top of his voice.

The negress gave him a small slap and he looked at her, his face crumpled, and then wriggled close and sat still. Philippa smiled at him, and then at the other child, and Jerott, looking at Lymond's impassive face, thought, My God: it's a bloody crèche . . . the ultimate humiliation. The last hand-to-hand fight with this man who can win empires with abominations and rot them with evil, all stickied over by babies in napkins. The last tomb, whoever should occupy it, furnished brightly with ridicule.

Then the doors closed. Roxelana Sultán made a slight movement, and, at a sign from the Kislar Agha, both Gabriel and Lymond rose to their feet. For a moment the Sultana studied them without speaking. Then she addressed them in Turkish, lapidary and precise.

'You are assembled here because it seemed to us that the good name of the State and the security of the Ottoman peoples are touched by the matters opened in the Divan Court this morning, and that the rest of the hearing should therefore be held and concluded in private.'

She paused. No one spoke. No one asked how she knew what had passed in her absence in the Divan Court: and although Philippa looked at Lymond he did not answer her glance. Roxelana continued, her voice firm behind the light veil. 'One of you has been accused of spreading lies which stain the honour of Suleiman Khan through me, his wife. For that, the punishment is torture and death. The other has replied with a counter-accusation, to the same effect. Both of you have cited as witness a Geomaler who appears to have borne allegiance first to one side and then to the other. You are here to prove to me each your case, in any way that you can, so that I may judge between you. First, Jubrael Pasha.' And Gabriel stood forward and set forth his charges.

Listening to the golden, persuasive voice, Jerott was carried a long way back: to a loch-side in Scotland, to a cathedral in Edinburgh, where the same beautiful cadences had spread falsehood and havoc through a small nation, until before the altar at St Giles it had come to a finish. This time Graham Malett fought under a handicap: he could not call on Míkál and dared not cite, as he had expected, Míkál's allies and friends with whom to bolster his story.

But he had other suborned witnesses: men who had heard Francis Crawford as Meddáh maligning Khourrém and Rustem Pasha, and stirring men's hearts to rebellion; those to whom the Jewess Hepsabah had confessed the Meddáh's command that all to the discredit of Khourrém should be sought out and, if need be, manufactured.

It was Philippa, then, no longer stricken by ceremony, and used to the ways of the court, who moved quickly round to the throne and bending, in a flutter of robes to kiss Roxelana's foot, said swiftly, 'Princess, may I speak? This is an untruth. The Jewess Hepsabah had been warned of a plot against you by Jubrael Pasha your Vizier, and how he had invented falsehoods in his secret writings to you, the better to colour it. Punish me if you must, for I confess I have opened your secret places, and read what is within. But this was done for you, not against you.'

The veil over Roxelana's face told nothing, but the voice was even and cold. 'Explain then,' said the Sultana, 'the fluency thy tongue now commands in my language, so recently gained?'

Philippa had not risen. She said, her brow on the floor, 'I believed that in this way I might obtain freer access to Your Grace's apartments. Forgive me.'

'It is the word of a lying English infidel against Hepsabah's dying confession,' said Gabriel. 'If what the girl claims was in fact true, why should she run away? Why not stay and claim the rewards of her faithful care for the Sultana's honour?'

'May I answer that?' said Lymond's voice pleasantly. Philippa rose and stepped back, her aching head bent; while Lymond went on. 'She was taken away, with the child, to remove her from Jubrael's vengeance. Only through his machinations were the girl and the child placed in the harem in the first instance; and, but for his advice, the mighty lord Suleiman would surely have freed them as he was asked. We hoped to expose the Vizier to Your Highness's judgement. We were afraid in so doing that these innocent lives would be destroyed. For they are innocent, Princess. The girl Philippa merely sought, as I have said, to detect what would harm you. The girl Marthe merely came, against her will, to deliver the message which would enable the others to leave the harem.'

The veil stayed turned on him for a long moment; then a ringed hand signed Philippa back to her place. 'Proceed,' said the Sultana to Gabriel; and listened in silence to the rest, which was uninterrupted.

It was a good case, thought Jerott. Not watertight, but circumstantially good. And Gabriel had the wealth and the standing and all the confidence of the Sultan behind him. He was glad it was possible to feel so detached. And Gabriel, of course, had made much of the weakest part of Philippa's statement: if they were purporting to search for evidence of Gabriel's sedition against Roxelana, why look for it in Roxelana's own rooms? The explanation did not really satisfy Jerott either; but Lymond had looked neither relieved nor concerned. Jerott, shifting his stance, began to worry, suddenly, about the length of time the whole thing was taking, with Lymond's own submission not even begun. One of the children said something in a swooping treble, and was hushed. Then Roxelana signed to Gabriel to stand down and, after a brief conversation with the Kislar Agha, called upon Lymond.

He stood facing the veil: looking at it, thought Jerott, as if he could pierce it; or at least in some fashion send his own mind close to the brain behind the plumes and the diamonds. He said, 'Princess, Míkál's testimony has been heard, and although the evidence of him and his helpers is true, doubt has been thrown on his integrity. You know perhaps of the history of your Vizier Jubrael Pasha, and of the changing allegiances of his recent years, which have closed Europe to him. You know perhaps of his ambition, which is not of the kind which easily acknowledges a master, whether this be the Grand Vizier or the Sultan himself. It seemed possible, to us who knew him well, that he would not be content as the wise servant and counsellor he seemed, and that his intentions were of a kind which would be tragic for Turkey. . . .

'It has not been concealed from you that my pursuit of the Vizier has been also for personal reasons. I cannot prove to you that my son is one of the two boys whose lives he has warped and commanded, any more than he can prove that his son is the other: the

426

trail is now too faint and too many who knew the true facts are dead. All I can say is that from the evidence both he and I know it to be so. One of my concerns therefore has been to remove both children and the girl Philippa, Durr-i Bakht, who became involved with them, out of his grasp. My other purpose was to destroy him; and if I could not do this myself, to bring him to receive his deserts from his masters. . . .

'Much has been spoken of evidence, but little has appeared. I think the time has come for witnesses, not hearsay; and words fashioned of ink and not air. I call on Kiaya Khátún.' And smiling, the woman beside the Sultana flung back her veil.

Gabriel cursed. Jerott could hear the words in English stream from his lips: words whose meaning he hardly knew, from lips which had gone purple. Lymond, who had inexplicably gone very white, in the sudden way that happened to him, gave the woman a faint smile in answer, the colour coming back into his face. Jerott's tongue came out, insensibly, between his teeth.

Kiaya Khátún. A bright, hot morning in Djerba, and a clear olive face with a Greek nose and black hair and brows. And a low voice saying teasingly, *I am Güzel, Dragut Rais's principal mistress. But I should like you, if you will, to address me as Kiaya Khátún.*

Jerott put his tongue in. Philippa, he noticed, savingly, was also staring as if she had been struck on the head. Míkál was smiling. And Marthe . . . Jerott looked again at Marthe's face. Marthe's face was filled with a strange, contemptuous anger.

Then Kiaya Khátún spoke, in her pleasant contralto; coming forward as Philippa had done, with the same low, pleasing obeisance. 'Princess, hear me; for I also have been your servant in these matters. By my agency the Geomaler Míkál set out to win the confidence of Jubrael Pasha, and undertook for him certain services, all of which he reported to me, or to Crawford Efendi, whom Jubrael has accused. All Míkál has told you is true. All Mr Crawford has said of Jubrael Pasha's designs on the children is true, and Míkál can vouch for it. I in turn, myself, can swear to you that the parts played by Philippa, Durr-i Bakht, and the girl Marthe were of no evil design, but merely to obtain evidence, again, about Jubrael's efforts to dupe you and those all around you. . . . Mr Crawford spoke of witnesses. These I have, and shall bring now before you. Among them, you will hear from the Agha of Janissaries himself how the Vizier has attempted to suborn him. He spoke of letters. These I have also taken from Jubrael Pasha's own house. In them you will see in Jubrael's own writing how the rumours were spread and how the so-called evidence against you and Rustem Pasha was to be used, to denigrate both you and your heirs, and leave Jubrael Pasha himself in command, in the twilight of our gracious lord's life. . . .'

Gabriel's mellow voice said, darkened with pain, 'Now Allâh protect us! That my enemies should share the same roof as my

427

Sultana: that the serpent should eject venom from its mouth into her dish. This woman is a creature of Crawford's, conspiring against this great empire at Djerba many months ago, when, escaping with her aid, he sought to help the infidel attacking Zuara, even to killing myself. Ask thyself, who in this Seraglio would obtain the most power on the downfall of Roxelana Sultán? This woman: this she-camel common to men, who will turn her back on Dragut and set her eyes even on Suleiman Khan, so great is her yearning for power. What punishment do these things demand?'

Kiaya Khátún looked at him, her perfect dark eyes astonished. 'I have had it,' she said. 'When you said on your knees, Be my bed-fellow. You did not question my honesty, that I remember, on your couch.'

A single trickle of sweat was running down the splendid framework of Gabriel's face. For a moment he said nothing at all. Then he said, quietly, direct to the Sultana, 'If these spies tell the truth, then they have what they should not have, and know what they should not know.'

And like an answering chord, Lymond's voice spoke equally quietly. 'You forget. There is nothing to know.'

Then the veil lifted, but the small pointed hands kept their grip of the letters. The precise, ringing voice said, 'Jubrael Pasha . . . I have to tell you, after reading these letters and hearing the evidence that I think your guilt is undoubted . . .'

Jerott closed his eyes. He opened them and saw how white Lymond was, and that his hands were laced closely together, to still them. Archie's head turned the same way, and back. The voice went on, '. . . and would beyond doubt merit the severest death in our power to bestow. On the other hand, it is also clear that others, accredited and without authority from western and infidel nations, have chosen to meddle in our affairs, have penetrated the Seraglio and attempted to enforce their own justice, even though the Sultan himself should give them welcome and be answered with falsehoods. . . . This also cannot pass unnoticed.'

Philippa also had gone very pale. In Marthe's face Jerott could distinguish no change: what was she made of, in God's name? He caught sight of the children, and felt sick.

'Between nation and nation,' said the even voice, 'such a matter might become war. For that reason this hearing has been held in private, where no diplomatic papers may return the result. It is a matter within the Seraglio, for the Seraglio to judge and the Seraglio to punish. . . . It seems to me,' said Roxelana Sultán, 'that this nation has become embroiled in a private feud between two masters: a feud which has been played like a game: falsehood within falsehood and guile within guile. I propose that what has begun as a game, entangling as puppets who knows how many innocent as well as the guilty, should end in like fashion. . . .'

The eyes behind the veil studied them all: Gabriel's face splendid even in anguish; Francis Crawford's still controlled: lightly closed like the chiselled face of one of Gilles's marble treasures, his eyes very dark. Roxelana said, '*I propose you a game of live chess*. You will return to your cells. When you come back, you will find this room your chessboard. You will each direct your own pieces and each play the part of your own King.'

Lymond said quickly, his voice surprisingly rough, 'And our pieces?'

'Will, of course,' said Roxelana, 'be culled from your friends, the two children included. I exclude only the girl Philippa. Her I shall present to the winner.'

'Princess . . .' Philippa's voice was stifled. 'The boys are too young.'

'They will be helped. Since it is not known to whom they belong, perhaps they will be safest on Jubrael Pasha's side——'

'*Safest?*' The sharp inquiry was Gabriel's.

The veil turned inquiringly towards him. 'Indeed. Do you think I plan for you a game any less lethal than the one you have both played, so discommodingly, in my city and court? The penalties in this game are death. Death to each piece as it is taken, and death to the King who is mastered. Those who are left on the winning side may go freely, and in peace. The others, at the winner's discretion, will die.'

There was a sigh: a sound which had no single origin, but floated over the heads of those watching and up to the ringed roof. In it, Gabriel exclaimed sharply, and started forward, but Lymond's voice spoke first, very evenly. 'The Sultana has spoken, and we shall obey. Jubrael Pasha, who is guilty, and I, who have been presumptuous, will play against each other and the loser will die. But since my sin perhaps is less than your Vizier's, may I put my head under your foot for a boon? Let the game be between us two only, with inanimate pieces, or men who will suffer nothing if taken. The others standing before you are not deserving of death.'

The veil studied him. 'Indeed, Mr Crawford,' said Roxelana Sultán. 'Then it will be for your skill to protect them. You may leave.'

The sun was shining when they came out, and there was even a bird trilling high in the bare branches of the plane tree, deceived by the promise of spring. In the harem, where Philippa and Marthe were marched with the two children, it was, surprisingly, the prosaic Philippa who exploded into angry tears like a rocket until Marthe, pale-faced, slapped her cheek hard and held her by the thin shoulders until her sobbing died down. Marthe said, 'The children. You're frightening the children'; and Philippa, breathing harshly, was quiet.

'Now eat,' said Marthe. 'Whether you want to or not. The children as well. . . . *Juste ciel*, don't you recognize yet that this is life, this two-sided trickery? There is hope, and here is brutality, to cancel it out. You think we should help one another. Why, when in a twist of an hour our lives can be turned into ashes, through no fault of our own? I told you once. I live for nothing, and I hope for nothing. I am not disappointed.'

The four men walked through the gardens too, between two files of white-helmeted Janissaries, and in their cell were given water and food. The sight of the food made Jerott want to vomit. He said cheerfully, 'Well, well. Thank God you're a dab hand at chess.'

'If you're going to be bright,' said Lymond, with a soft and frightening venom, 'I'll break your sweet little neck.' He put his hands back over his face and said half to himself, 'Oh, hell. Oh, bloody, bloody hell. . . .'

'She is a bitch,' said Míkál's musical voice. Of them all, he seemed least perturbed. 'A known bitch. Even to get the Sultan to marry her, she resorted to trickery. . . .'

Lymond said, his voice even lower, 'Why the *hell* did you bring back the children?'

'You asked me that before,' said Míkál. 'I told you, Kiaya Khátún required it. She said, when you betray Mr Crawford to Gabriel, you betray also the escape of the children. It will look natural.' His face brightened. 'Perhaps Kiaya Khátún will dissuade the Sultana.'

Jerott said, 'I notice Kiaya Khátún isn't among us. I take it she doesn't rank for this purpose as one of your friends?' He wondered how heavily Lymond was drugged. He knew the signs now: knew that Archie had given him a massive dose on his return and that he was fighting drowsiness at this moment; trying to build towards the level of self-control and command he would need in the afternoon. Archie, busy, thought Jerott furiously, as a bull-fighter's auntie, had no time, apparently, to feel qualms about what was going to happen that same afternoon.

He started to repeat his question but Lymond suddenly brought his own temper hard under control and said quietly, 'I'm sorry. I heard you. Look . . . Kiaya Khátún is Dragut's mistress and governess of the girls. She knows too much, and she's too powerful, and too well connected to have her neck wrung in a chess game. Roxelana will keep her, and do her utmost to buy her silence and friendship. . . . We are a different matter. Gabriel, too.'

'You did find something then?' Jerott asked.

'Of course,' said Lymond wearily. 'Do you think we made it all up? The rumour Gabriel was spreading was perfectly true. Rustem Pasha and Roxelana between them made Suleiman believe quite falsely that Mustafa wanted to usurp his throne. Roxelana wants her own son to succeed. Rustem pretty well does what she says and wants more power anyway. What Gabriel left out was that he was the third person in the plot, the go-between who carried messages from

Rustem to Roxelana. The letters Philippa found, and which we have not shown Roxelana, prove that. It was the first concrete information we had about the thing. Then we found that Gabriel was stirring up the city, discreetly, with hints in all the right quarters about Rustem's and Roxelana's guilt. Of course she couldn't let him continue as Vizier or anything else once she suspected and we proved that he was trying to betray her share in the plan. On the other hand, because of the letters we found here in the Seraglio, she knows that we are aware of the truth. The expectation beforehand was that, having found Gabriel guilty, she would swear us to silence and then kiss us on both cheeks and open the door. We were over-optimistic.'

'Or Kiaya Khátún was,' said Jerott. He couldn't leave it alone; not now. He said, 'Wouldn't a simple assassination have been easier?' He leaned over and shook Lymond's shoulder and Lymond said, his eyes opening, 'I know. I'm awake. . . . I tried that. In fact, name some way I didn't try it. He knew, you see. He was guarded from morning till night; even his food was tasted beforehand. Therefore the State had to do the butchering, and I had to get into the Seraglio to present my case to the State.'

'With Míkál's help?'

'With Míkál's help,' agreed Lymond.

It was not Jerott's moment for being magnanimous. 'What a pity,' he said austerely, 'we were all required also to assist.'

Lymond sat up, his eyes blazing. He said, 'Now, look . . .' and then cut it off, shutting his lips. But Jerott, his face flushed, was already saying quickly, 'I'm sorry. I'm sorry, Francis. I know it was my own bloody fault. You didn't mean the boys and Philippa to be brought back and you didn't need Marthe to go to the Seraglio and you didn't expect me or Onophrion . . .' He stopped. 'Where's Onophrion?'

Lymond's face was still white, but at least he was now very awake. 'Yes. Where indeed?' he observed.

26

CONSTANTINOPLE: PAWN'S MOVE

The big room seemed much emptier when they were all taken back. The eunuchs had gone, and the dwarves; and the Kislar Agha's place by the empty throne had been taken by the Bostanji Bashi, the Chief of Security. The executioner. And against the flowering walls stood the silent ranks of the mutes.

Then Jerott saw that the Kislar Agha had moved down from the throne and was standing with Gabriel beside him and four other men: men whose faces were vaguely familiar, and whom Jerott recognized suddenly as having given evidence for their master. Gabriel's pieces ... but only five in all?

Answering the thought, the Kislar Agha paced over to Lymond, his bearing and dark fleshy face mantled in all the dignity of his African race. 'Mr Crawford? I need not tell you that in chess it is usual for each master to play sixteen pieces. In this game we restrict you to five, of which you yourself, playing the King, are one. You will be permitted a Queen, a Knight, a Rook and a Bishop, to be chosen from the friends now accompanying you with the exception of the boy Míkál, for whom a replacement has been put forward. On Jubrael Pasha's side, he will be permitted to play the same pieces and on opposing squares but for his Rook, which clearly must not confront his opponent's Rook at the start of the game with no Pawns intervening. He also has two extra pieces: the gift of two Pawns, to be played by the children. These will stand before his King and his Queen, thus preventing the Queens from opposing. Do you understand?'

'I think so,' said Lymond. 'You mean that we are to play five-a-side chess; but that Jubrael Pasha is to have seven pieces. I take it that it is beyond my powers to object. May I ask why Míkál is to be withdrawn, and who is to substitute?'

The Kislar Agha had a sovereign way with awkward inquiries. He said, 'He is not eligible. At the girl Marthe's suggestion, we have brought her uncle, the usurer Georges Gaultier.'

Christ, thought Jerott; and, in spite of the shivers in the small of his back, nearly laughed. Míkál, of course, would be preserved by Kiaya Khátún, if not Roxelana. No one could afford to antagonize that restless, moneyed race of strange children of love. And in his place, implacable to the end, Marthe had let them send for her uncle. Jerott wondered if they had searched the house when they found him and what else they had found. And what Gilles had said. . . . Then Marthe came in herself, very straight, and something almost a smile on her face as she walked up to Lymond and, meeting his gaze briefly, ranged herself at his side.

His gaze on the door, Lymond spoke to her. 'You were right, it seems, to fear and despise us. Man has brought you to a death which any woman could have averted. There is no reparation possible for what I have done to you.'

Marthe was looking at him still, a faint smile in her eyes. 'Relieve your conscience of me,' she said coolly. 'You have enough to answer for. Mr Blyth may go to the devil for me, as I shall for my uncle. What part shall I play?'

Then Lymond looked at her and said, 'The Queen: what else?' and Jerott knew he was giving her the principal piece and the most agile; the one which he could most swiftly move out of trouble. For to be taken was death. And it came to Jerott at last that while he himself had been carping and backbiting and quarrelling Francis had been bracing himself slowly and quietly for the most terrible rôle of his life: the rôle of God with seven lives in his hands, and two of these children.

To kill Gabriel, Lymond must take the King he represented. To do so he must use his five pieces, and use them better than Gabriel, who in turn would try to take Lymond's King. Not only that, but he must use them somehow without a piece being taken, for a piece taken by either side meant that the person playing that piece laid down his life. Lymond must therefore fight with this venomous handicap: that none of his pieces must be imperilled. And worse than that, must defend himself against Gabriel, who would care little, Jerott imagined, for his own men, but who could rely on one thing absolutely: that under no circumstances whatever would Francis touch his two Pawns.

Only half conscious of his surroundings, Jerott watched Gaultier come in, panic-stricken and pallid, stammering with anger and accusations aimed at Marthe and at Lymond. He saw Philippa enter, carefully groomed with her head held very high, and take her place by the throne as the Kislar Agha directed. Then, deaf to Gaultier's hoarse voice, he watched the negress bring in the two children and, walking over, leave them at Gabriel's side. Beside him, Lymond stopped speaking and Jerott, his fingers like fish-hooks, leaned over and dragged the old man, struggling and exclaiming, to his other side. In his softest voice Jerott said, 'Be quiet. Or the mutes have orders to throttle you'; and there was a sudden silence. The door opened and Roxelana Sultán entered with ceremony and, mounting the throne, was seated. Porters brought and unrolled over the carpet a painted cloth on which sixty-four squares had been laid out, coloured alternately in red paint and white.

The chessboard. Beside Jerott, Lymond closed his eyes, and Jerott's mind, once launched on its unaccustomed effort of imagination, tried to follow his thoughts. Every move was potential death for Jerott himself, for Marthe, for Archie or for Gaultier. Every move must be thought out twice over: once for its purpose and once for its risk to his pieces. If Lymond were too careful and keeping his players lost his King in the outcome to Gabriel, Gabriel could choose to kill not only Lymond but all his friends with impunity.

So this was no sport, no impersonal battle, no exhibition of vanity or childish adventure embraced out of pique. This was an ultimate trial of every quality all his life Lymond had squandered: of speed and wit and clean, objective intelligence. Move by move his decisions had to be right, for, if they were not, no anonymous ally would disappear to lie under some exiguous cross. Two mutes would cross the floor with a thin piece of hemp in their hands, and before Lymond's face, one of his players would die.

Then Lymond opened his eyes, and Jerott thought of Pierre Gilles and what he wanted to say, and moved to touch his silk shoulder. 'Francis.'

For a moment Lymond didn't turn, and when he did, the blue gaze, utterly detached, looked through Jerott. Jerott said quickly, 'Francis ... if there is any doubt: any doubt at all of the outcome, sacrifice anything and anybody so long as you take Gabriel. Do you understand?'

'Of course,' said Lymond. Jerott looked at him, his black brows painfully knitted, until Marthe, putting out her hand as he had done, drew him firmly away. 'Leave him,' she said. 'Leave him alone.'

The children would not stay in their places. Kuzúm cried; and Philippa finally, in desperation, got permission from the Sultana and walked across the bright squares to Gabriel's side, where she crouched, her robes spreading around her, between the two unhappy Pawns. Behind her, Gabriel laughed and said something under his breath, and the man playing Queen sniggered in return. To the left, also behind her, she could see out of the corner of her eye Gabriel's Knight and his Rook, and to her right his solitary Bishop, an unshaven lout in yellow. Then on the opposite side of the board Lymond, suddenly smiling, led Marthe to her place as his Queen, with Jerott his Knight on her right, and Gaultier and Archie playing Bishop and Rook on his left. They had tossed dice, Philippa knew, for the privilege of starting, and Lymond had lost. Then the Kislar Agha, looking at both sides in turn, said, 'Begin,' and stepped back off the board.

Gabriel had changed into white and gold, as befitted a King and the side he was playing. From him spilled a placid and mighty confidence: the ease of a brilliant mind which knows its own power. He looked at Lymond, smiling, as he called the move which, clearly, the Kislar Agha repeated. 'Queen to Queen's Rook's fourth.' And the man on Gabriel's left, grinning, walked down his line of white diagonals and stopped, turning round, to face a range of clear spaces at the end of which, exposed, stood Lymond's King. 'Check,' said Gabriel. It had begun.

By some coincidence, or perhaps by no coincidence, Lymond's high-collared robe was embroidered jet black on scarlet, matching the red of the squares. His arms, in his own lace-edged shirt-sleeves, hung relaxed below the short sleeves of the robe and his face, in a curious way, although concentrating, was also relaxed; as if with the onset of this one cosmic problem a thousand others had somehow dissolved. He saved himself with a move of no importance: 'King to King's Bishop's second!' and, walking one square diagonally to his left, escaped Gabriel's check. Gabriel's voice answered him, amused, 'Queen to Queen's Rook's eighth.' And as Jerott was still working that out, Gabriel's sniggering Queen walked up and stood just beside him.

Jerott looked round. Behind him was Marthe. Behind her, Gaultier and Archie still stood in line. In all the blank squares of the board there was no piece of Lymond's which could prevent Gabriel's Queen from taking himself, Jerott, at the next move.

Looking at the mutes, Jerott wondered if they understood, or if the Kislar Agha would have to tell them. . . . He wondered, in an academic way, what he would do if Lymond ordered him to move, exposing Marthe to his neighbour and thus saving himself at Marthe's expense. He didn't think Lymond would. Then Lymond said prosaically, 'Queen to King's Rook's fifth. Check,' and he was saved.

Marthe, the proud Marthe's knees were shaking as she walked down the straight path towards Gabriel's King. Jerott saw her robe trembling and was grateful, for his own hands were wet and wanted to quiver: he clenched them hard. Gabriel, a shade of a frown on his face, was preparing to move as King out of trouble and in the next move, Jerott supposed, he himself would be moved safely out of the way. Then, if Gabriel wanted blood, it would mean also the sacrifice of his Queen, for Gaultier, in his path, was safely covered, as Marthe had not been. . . . And Gabriel, Jerott thought suddenly, would have taken great pleasure in removing Lymond's Knight from the board, at almost any expense, whereas he was unlikely to spend a Queen on poor Gaultier. Which was why Lymond had done what he had done.

Jerott let out his breath very slowly as the two moves were accomplished and stood, his heart like a drum in his chest, for Gabriel's following move.

His next ones were also attacking, and Lymond's defensive. Gabriel's Rook moved up the board, harmlessly, and Jerott himself moved down, towards Gabriel's end of the files. It was while he was there that, suddenly, he found himself under attack from an unexpected quarter. Gabriel had moved up one of his Pawns.

It was the Queen's Pawn, Kuzúm. He had no wish to go, and stood crying in the middle of his square until Philippa lifted him and carried him bodily to the one next to Jerott. Where, thought Jerott, he threatens me, if he only knew it, with death. And looking round for his succour, saw suddenly, standing guard at the end of the line, Lymond's Queen Marthe looking at Lymond.

He had only to order the move, and Gabriel's Pawn would be swept off the board. Lymond smiled at his Queen and said, 'Rather a drastic way to end two-year-old tantrums. . . . Jerott, you'll have to get out of it. Knight to Queen's Bishop's fifth . . .' and the moment was over.

For the time being, Jerott found himself left alone after that. There was a move by Gabriel's Queen which forced Lymond on to a white square but otherwise didn't do any harm. Then there followed some play between Marthe and Gabriel's Bishop, which brought Archie also into the game and gave the Bishop an anxious time until Gabriel sent his Queen over and, next to Archie, the Rook. Lymond's answer was to send Archie straight down the board to check Gabriel's King.

There was only one move Gabriel could make, and he made it. Lymond moved Jerott on one of his staggered moves forward, and said, 'Check.'

Gabriel couldn't resist it. By moving up, he threatened Jerott as well as moving out of check. Lymond let him do it, and then removed Jerott, neatly exposing Gabriel to attack by his Queen. Gabriel had a choice of two squares, and he chose the wrong one. On the eighth square Archie the Rook, alone and forgotten, confronted Gabriel's Knight over four empty spaces, and Gabriel's Knight was no longer protected. 'Rook to Queen's Knight's eighth,' said Lymond's voice quietly. 'Rook takes Knight.' Except for Archie, everyone stood very still. Archie Abernethy walked along the four empty squares and, on reaching the fifth, laid his hand on the shoulder of the man standing there.

Even then, Gabriel's Knight did not quite understand. When he did, he made the mistake of trying to run for it; and the mutes, surrounding him near the door, were not able to exercise their usual skill. He made a queer noise, within the circle of men, and the carpet rucked where his falling foot dragged it. The Kislar Agha said, 'Take him away,' and the mutes returned to their places, while the Janissaries saw to the body. They all stared after it, thought Jerott, as if no one until now had really believed it would happen. . . . It had happened. Philippa, he saw, was kneeling talking, her arms round the children. Lymond said, 'Your move,' his eyes very bright. Gabriel, his jaw firm, brought on his Pawn.

It was a little time before Jerott realized what he was doing. Until that, he saw the two pawns as a bitter obstruction. He had watched Lymond forgo move after move where he might have taken a piece except for the infinitesimal risk that Gabriel might attack first, throwing away his own man in order to make sure of Lymond's. The lines of attack open to Lymond were therefore not many, and made even fewer by presence of the two sacrosanct Pawns. Whenever he made an opening, it seemed a Pawn stood in his way, a Pawn belonging to Gabriel, which could take Lymond's pieces quite freely but which Lymond himself could never remove, because the part was played by a child.

Khaireddin had recognized Francis Crawford by now. White and docile under the fingers of Philippa and the other strangers who pushed him about, and told him when to stand still, he paid no attention to the other child or the woman, but set himself gamely to please and pacify the men, the dark circles under his blue eyes, which smiled starkly on, although his mouth visibly trembled.

He smiled at them until in the seventh square he came face to face with Francis Crawford: so close that in a normal game, he would have been lost. Then Lymond, looking down at him, said conversationally, 'Hullo. A strange game, isn't it? I don't enjoy it much either. But we have to finish it. Then *you* choose what we play next.' And a smile broke over Khaireddin's face: a genuine smile; the first one, thought Jerott, that anyone there had probably seen. Then he said something in the little voice, so much less fluent than Kuzúm's; and Lymond said, 'Of course, your shells are still there. Supper first, and then you shall play with them. Goodbye. I have to move, now.'

And indeed he had, for Gabriel's Rook had moved up to threaten him, and there was no one to mask him who would not instantly be taken. Then Gabriel moved his Pawn to the eighth square and said coolly, triumph barely concealed in his voice, 'I claim the return of the Knight.'

It was, of course, the rule. Take your Pawn, step by step, from one side of the board to the other and you receive a commensurate privilege: you may replace the Pawn with any missing piece that you wish. For a Pawn, slow, restricted and vulnerable, such a journey was not normally easy. For Gabriel's two untouchable Pawns, it was the simplest series of moves he could wish. Lymond, turning to the Kislar Agha, said only, 'May we have the Sultana's ruling?' And the Sultana's articulate voice in return said briefly, 'The move is permitted.'

So Khaireddin, who had been a Pawn, became a Knight, and Gaultier, suddenly threatened, had to be moved, allowing Gabriel's Queen to put Lymond in check, from which he could escape in only one direction. It cleared the way, as Gabriel intended, for the advance of the other Pawn, Kuzúm. Jerott said, 'Francis . . .' and then stopped, for there was nothing he could say that Lymond did not already know. And in any case, a moment later, he was on the move, for Lymond sent him, in one simple move, to check Gabriel's King, and Gabriel, escaping and threatening at once, moved into the next square to Jerott.

The most nightmarish aspect for Jerott of the whole brutal game was this proximity. Enemies and friends passed one another in silence or stood side by side, as he and Gabriel were doing, awaiting Lymond's next words. You stood in silence because dignity forbade you to canvass. You stood with your eyes elsewhere in case, catching Lymond's eyes, you found yourself signalling, *I am in danger. I am in danger, and unless you abandon your design and help me, in the next move I shall die.*

Then Lymond's quiet voice said, 'Knight to King's Bishop's fifth'; and Jerott was saved; and whatever plan Lymond might have, had again been obstructed, for Gabriel used the freedom of his next move to shift Kuzúm one square nearer the eighth. And Jerott wondered again, as he had wondered all through the game, what would have happened if, reaching out, he had seized Gabriel and, before help could reach him, had managed to kill him. But they had no weapons, and Gabriel was a powerful man, and the mutes very near. He risked failure, and he risked death then, he supposed, for them all. Jerott thought, then, that if Lymond lost and he himself were still alive, between them they might manage it before they were halted. It gave him, in a way, a little fugitive strength.

Philippa stood between the two children. The one she did not know, the boy called Khaireddin, stood, smiling still, without really looking at her: she wondered when he was going to break, and what they would do with a blindly hysterical child on their hands. On her other side, her own Kuzúm was quiet and a little tremulous, but she knew now that he would manage, unless the game went on too long.

She had explained as much as she could in her friendly voice, and her warm, firm clasp of his shoulder, helping him from one square to the next, had steadied him: when she moved him, he pulled her head down for a kiss. She had looked at the other child then, smiling, and touched his bright hair with her hand and felt him flinch like an ill-treated horse. The desperate smile did not alter. Marthe's eyes were on her then, Philippa found. And across half the board, Marthe sent her a smile like her brother's: light and cool and encouraging. Philippa, her hands shaking, smiled back.

There was a long pause. In a moment, thought Jerott, Gabriel's remaining Pawn would reach the eighth square and would be exchanged, as had his first, for a piece of infinitely greater power. Thus Gabriel would have not merely two Pawns, but two attacking pieces played by the children which could not be taken. And one piece more on the board than Lymond possessed. Then Lymond said, 'Rook to King's Bishop's sixth: check'; and Jerott knew he was going to try and prevent Kuzúm's reaching the eighth square by attacking Gabriel's King and engaging him until somehow check-mate could be achieved. Jerott moved; and so did Gabriel, threatening

Archie; his face expressionless, who stepped forward and put Gabriel for the third time in check.

Then Gabriel escaped, as he had done before, by threatening Jerott; and, as had happened before, the manœuvre had to cease so that Jerott might be saved, lifting the pressure from Gabriel's King for the one necessary move. Gabriel, smiling, said 'Pawn to Queen's eighth;' and Kuzúm made his last move as a Pawn after all, with little gained for Lymond, Jerott thought, but the repositioning of his Rook. Jerott put up his hand and moved his fingers slowly over his brow, which contained a ringing headache such as he had never experienced before in the whole of his life. He had stopped wondering what Lymond felt because he could not conceive him at the moment as flesh and blood: a man of frivolity, who had outraged the fat bathers of Baden; a man who had slept at his side on the *Dauphiné*; a man he had drawn from the waves at Zuara: a volatile exhibitionist who had shared with him that crazy display of trick riding in Djerba. For all of them now, even Gaultier, grey-faced absorbing the moves, Lymond was only the disembodied voice of a disembodied intellect, the last Fate controlling their lives.

Kuzúm had become, unsuitably, a Bishop. For a moment Jerott wondered why, until he realized that by his position Lymond himself was now in check and, having to move, was presenting Gabriel with yet another chance of free action.

Gabriel took it. He put Lymond in check to his Queen. He turned him down the board, using Bishop and Rook and, all the time, his two invulnerable pieces: his Knight and his second Bishop, which could take any square with impunity, for no one would touch them. Once, Lymond was able to move Marthe to the eighth square and for a moment to challenge Gabriel's King, forcing him to move up the board. A little later Gabriel in turn brought down his Queen, and for an instant both Queens confronted one another, and Gabriel's seemed at Lymond's mercy. Then Jerott saw that Archie stood in the next diagonal to Gabriel's King, totally vulnerable, and it seemed instead that Marthe or Archie must be lost. Lymond moved his Queen quietly to the square behind Archie, shielding him; and Gabriel abandoned it, and returned to his smooth and brilliant game.

One would imagine, thought Jerott, that in any case they were well matched: Francis Crawford and Graham Reid Malett. They both had the capacity, the imagination and the concentration which this game of all games demanded. Gabriel, the older man, perhaps possessed more experience; but Lymond's sharp-witted mind Jerott had seen sometimes take logic and soar without explanation beyond it, on what power of intuition or inspiration or guesswork Jerott had never decided. And because the two men were on the whole evenly matched, and because of the unusually small number of pieces, it now became obvious what should have been clear all along: that the handicap for Lymond had always been incredible; and that with the transformation of the two Pawns, it must now be too great.

None of Lymond's team had yet been taken. But pursued by Gabriel, Lymond's King was now driven too easily from his consorts, and the breathing-spaces he could snatch out of check in which he might make some move other than one of defence came along less and less often.

From Lymond's voice and manner, no one could have told that the tide against him had turned. Archie's face was unreadable but Jerott thought Marthe knew it, walking silently, straight and steady when she was required, her eyes often on Philippa, moving gently from one child to the other. Once, when Khaireddin came near her, Marthe guided him instead.

Gaultier had begun to breathe heavily. To himself, Jerott made a calm promise that if the old man broke into supplications or sobs, he would kill him with his own hand. Then he caught Archie's eyes on the clock.

The afternoon was growing old. The mild sunlight outside the bright-coloured windows would soon drain away; and so would the strength of the drug on which all their lives now depended. Suddenly all Jerott's fears pooled in a moment of suffocating anger with Lymond, that he should have harboured and failed to conquer by now this essential weakness; and he began to watch Francis Crawford for the first time, with deliberate scrutiny, as with angry pain a woman might watch her false lover for the first signs of a plague.

He saw nothing. Lymond's voice was unchanged. His hands, tucked into his over-robe, were quite invisible. His face, shadowed against the dimming light from the windows, was the colourless etching it had been from the start: pure emotionless lines drawn by needle and acid. At rest for the moment, Jerott stood between Archie and Gabriel's Rook and watched Lymond from two squares away until, feeling it, Lymond turned. For a moment, he looked at Jerott and Archie. Then, too quietly to be overheard, he said, 'Pray now, if you want to pray. And don't look round.'

Don't look round at what? Guarding his eyes, Jerott tried frantically to compose the board in his mind. Behind him was Gabriel, in the red corner-square, with one of the children, Kuzúm, just taking a new place before him, and the other, the Knight played by Khaireddin, in the Queen's place a few squares along. Lymond, Archie and he were together, and one of Gabriel's Rooks had shifted behind him, he remembered, to the same side as Gabriel. There was a Bishop of Gabriel's in the same region, and his Queen somewhere there in the middle. On the far side Marthe was standing alone, where she had been for some time at the edge. He had an impression that Gaultier, playing Lymond's Bishop, was in a corner too, not far from Marthe and opposite that occupied by Gabriel himself.

The impression was right. Just as the thought struck him, Gaultier screamed, and Jerott whirled round. At first he thought it was perhaps checkmate, the final disaster; the locking of Lymond's King by Gabriel so that no escape was possible and the game therefore lost. Instead he saw, face to face in opposite corners, the figures of Georges Gaultier's Bishop and the newly arrived Kuzúm, Gabriel's Bishop, ready to take it.

Don't look round, Lymond had said. Don't look round, Jerott thought, so that Gaultier might not notice his fate; might not observe death about to cross the long line of squares there towards him. But Gaultier had observed; and Gaultier screamed and, swinging round, began uttering hoarse protestations and demands to the calm veil on the throne, which surveyed him in its turn and then lifted to look at Graham Malett. And Graham Malett laughed aloud, and said in his beautiful voice, 'He's a pretty sight, isn't he? Calm him, dear Francis. Tell him that it is your move to follow, not mine. You have liberty, this time, to lead him away from the slaughter.'

The mocking voice; the cruel, pointless move were more than Jerott's lacerated nerves could stand. His anger rose and this time exploded, not against Gabriel but Gaultier, of the loud, high-pitched voice, fastening on to his reprieve; demanding of Lymond the move which would take him away from that threatening Bishop. Jerott started to move; whether to rush at Gaultier and to fell him, or merely to shout, he hardly knew yet himself. But Lymond's hand closed on his wrist, and held it with a pressure which squeezed it, bone to bone and muscle to muscle, as if a machine had opened and snapped shut its jaws. Then Lymond said, his voice very soft, 'Don't hurt him. He's only a goat tied to a rock, to occupy our attention until Gabriel makes his next move.'

'What move?' said Jerott.

'The last move,' said Lymond, and he smiled at Gabriel as he spoke. 'King's Bishop to King's fourth: checkmate in one.'

'. . . You can avoid it,' said Jerott.

'This time,' said Lymond. He was speaking, it seemed, less to Jerott than to himself, or to Gabriel or to some bodiless interrogator, combing his mind. 'Next time, no.'

'And so?'

'And so,' said Francis Crawford; and for the first time he lifted his eyes and looked full at Jerott. 'Look at the board.'

Jerott turned. So did Archie and Philippa, but Gaultier did not look. He was intent on Lymond: willing Lymond to utter the words which would take him to safety, and he sighed, from time to time, in his anxiety: a sigh caught with a sob. Presently even that died away, and the profound silence in the room made itself felt: a silence which continued until Jerott himself could have shouted, or fallen down on his knees, with the ache of it. The cool triumph on Gabriel's handsome face faded, and a shadow crossed the magnificent brow. Then he looked at Francis Crawford, and Lymond said, 'You were too intent on your own slaughter; too ruthless; too greedy. You have pushed me until I have no alternatives left. You must take the consequences of that.'

Gabriel did not speak. But Philippa made a queer sound, suddenly, on a too-sharply intaken breath, and beside Jerott, Archie the phlegmatic, the stoical, said in a high sudden whisper, '*Oh, Christ!* Oh Christ, the bairns.'

Oh Christ, the bairns. When the orphan weeps, his tears fall into the hand of the beneficent God. Gabriel had planned it, this delicate checkmate, with Lymond's King locked in his place, with no possibility of escape; with every possible route filled or covered by an enemy piece, or by the two children.

Or by the two children. In his next move, the move he was never to make, Gabriel would have put Lymond's King in check so that Lymond could free himself in one way only: by taking a child.

So Gabriel had intended. So, with all the power in his hands, he had made his delicate, malicious moves to this point, and so all the pieces around Lymond were there in position, except the second locking Bishop, whose move Lymond had forestalled.

Graham Malett had forgotten one thing. Far off, unregarded on the edge of the board, stood Lymond's Queen, and Georges Gaultier, his own Bishop, still there in his corner. And in a straight line, from Queen and from Bishop there ran a free, shining path to each child.

In three words, Lymond could direct Marthe, his Queen, down that path to the death of Khaireddin. Or instead, he could send Gaultier, square by square, to take the Bishop played by Kuzúm. Either move would free him from all fear of checkmate. More . . .

Either move would checkmate Graham Malett instead.

Oh Christ, the bairns, thought Jerott flatly. Oh Christ, one of them; Kuzúm or Khaireddin, who must now pay for the life it had never had; for the happiness it never had; for the stranger's sin which begot it, and the stranger's quarrel which brought it here. One life to save seven, and the horror facing Philippa as Gabriel's mistress. One life pinched out on a harpstring, and Gabriel's King would be locked in checkmate, as Lymond's was to have been. One life, and Gabriel had lost for ever; had forfeited his existence and that of his men. One life, and Gabriel, here and now, in this hour, was dead.

Changeless; like the machine Jerott had felt him to be, Lymond turned in the long silence to Roxelana Sultán; and the Queen, facing him, put back her veil. A narrow, vigorous face, a small mouth and arched nose and shrewd, painted dark eyes studied him, from the fair orderly hair to the rich scarlet robe. Lymond said, 'High and mighty Princess . . . thy rules have been obeyed; thy burdens borne without protest. The game is now mine. In one move I shall claim the life of Jubrael Pasha, as you have promised, and of all those on his side save the children. I beg thy highness's word that this will be permitted, and that my friends and I may then go free.'

'It is so,' said Roxelana; but Gabriel's smooth voice, a thread of discord somewhere in its honey, said strongly, 'Princess, what are you thinking of? Let them free, to bandy your letters from court to court, from gutter to gutter? Might they not go to the Sultan himself in the field? What tale will they tell him?'

'A tale of a traitrous Vizier,' said Roxelana calmly. 'And some forged papers. . . . Make thy move, Hâkim.'

But Lymond did not turn away. Instead he said, in the same level voice, 'Once, Princess, you returned, out of the delicacy of your spirit, what you could not accept without granting a favour. That which you returned is again in the care of your Treasurer and I have to beg you, a second time, to take this gift in your hands. . . .'

From Lymond to Roxelana, a bribe. Jerott, following every syllable and the sense of nothing, wondered bleakly what the gift was; and then saw Philippa's face and wondered again. It would be, he supposed, with Kiaya Khátún. Roxelana said, 'Thou art foolhardy with thy wealth. What now is the wish of thy heart?'

'Only this,' said Francis Crawford. 'That when I make this move, I may let the child live.'

'That is not the rule,' said Roxelana Sultán calmly. 'The rule is clear. Break it, and you lose.'

The blue eyes, searching met hers; but the dark gaze gave back nothing. Lymond said, in the same prosaic voice, 'Then allow me to take the child's place. I have no objections, and you might find it . . . convenient.'

'Thy persistence does thee honour,' said Roxelana blandly. 'But the answer is no. Make thy move, or forgo it. Had a pestilence seized them this summer, the children would have suffered no less. Now you need lose only one. Choose, and move.'

From her place by Kuzúm, the light of her life, Philippa stood up. She did not say goodbye, nor did she kiss him or touch him, but moving slowly backwards she withdrew from the chessboard and stood still, her eyes on Lymond, leaving Kuzúm alone. *The shepherd clutch thee fast. O my lamb; O my lambkin . . .*

Khaireddin had been alone for a long time, in the square next to that which Lymond had vacated to go to the throne. His smiles, which no one returned, had run dry now; and through his courage a whimper broke loose and a single tear, escaping, slipped down his cheek.

Lymond didn't come back to the board. He stood by the Kislar

Agha, looking before him; his brightly lit face and hair an un-
familiar intaglio of highlights and unexpected sharp shadows. Still
as the clock-spinet, thought Jerott, marking the hours, its case rimed
with spectacular jewels; its inner wheels blindly spinning, awaiting
the impersonal touch on the lever to trip it into a mechanical cascade
of action. Which child to use for his checkmate? Which child to have
killed?

Gabriel, rousing minute by minute from his paralysis of disbelief,
cut through their thoughts. 'Give up, Francis. How can you know
what you're doing? You don't make decisions at low ebb. Not
decisions you'll live with in after years. Leave the children alone.
I won't checkmate you. I'll give you stalemate in a handful of moves.
Stalemate. . . . A draw, neither winning. You go free, and so do I.'

'No,' said Lymond.

'Your vow?' said Gabriel. 'That means nothing either? You
would have your son strangled?'

'I don't know,' Francis Crawford said steadily, 'which is my son.
I do tell you this. If you are a Moslem, make your prayers. If you
are a Christian, make your peace with that God. I have reached my
decision.'

Jerott looked at the children, his heart in his throat. Which? The
one who had experienced love and a modicum of happiness, or the
one who had not. The one whose life had been innocent, or the one
who had been earliest corrupted and whose first uncertain steps had
just been taken towards his birthright of friendship and joy. To
which would he offer the gift of survival . . . and how had he chosen,
knowing nothing? Knowing that the dead child might be his own,
and the survivor the child of Gabriel and his sister?

Lymond said, '*Marthe.*'

The end of a baby's life in two syllables. The direction to Marthe,
his Queen, to take the Knight in her path.

And the Knight was the child who had not yet known happiness;
the child Lymond had drawn to himself. The little boy called
Khaireddin, with the bruises still on his body from the nightingale-
dealer's house.

The word broke Philippa, as an iron smashes a lock. Air rushed
into her throat and tears blinded her eyes, running over her fingers
as she pressed them fast to her lids. She moved then a little way on
to the board, towards the light of her life, and then stopped, her
lips trembling, as Marthe began her steady walk, a trifle stiffly,
towards the small boy at the end. He noticed her coming and Marthe
smiled at him faintly, still walking, and said to Philippa as she
passed, quietly, 'Leave him to me.'

So Philippa turned and knelt by Kuzúm, but gently, so that the
other child would not see and be hurt, and gathering the child's
bright head in her lap, covered his eyes.

444

Marthe had almost reached Khaireddin when he became frightened and, his face crumpling, suddenly made towards Francis Crawford. Half-way there he halted, bemused by the look on Lymond's face and after a moment said in a small voice, 'I've 'topped being a bad boy. I've 'topped. . . . *Mo chridh* is a good little boy now. . . .'

And at the Gaelic, Jerott said, 'Dear God in Heaven,' and looked away from Francis Crawford, whose face was that of a man tortured with thirst, or lack of air, or the bitterest hunger. Then Jerott saw that the mutes were closing in, and that in a moment the child would reach Francis's arms, and he began to run, to spare him the last terrible betrayal.

But Míkál got there first, and swept the child into his own embrace, all carnation and jasmine and soft hair and bright tinkling jewels. 'Come, my love,' said Míkál, 'and say goodnight to the dark.' And held him close, full of a sweet young compassion, as the little boy died.

Francis Crawford, who had commanded it, watched the killing take place. His belly heaving, Jerott kept his eyes there as well, for what Francis saw he must know, although he hardly knew why. They had used a knife, so the child's face was not distorted: Míkál, when it was over, laid him down and wiped a trace of blood from the small lips. Then he lifted Khaireddin again, gently, to carry him out; and Lymond moved swiftly from Jerott's side to where the fine hair, curling like silk, lay on the Geomaler's arm; and bending his head, kissed the dead child, as he had not kissed the living, full on the mouth.

Then he turned, Thanatos of the dark underworld claiming his chosen; and walked straight to Gabriel.

Gabriel struggled. He talked and shouted and promised glory and riches, and finally cursed as men seldom venture to curse, the malevolence dripping on to them all as he twisted and rolled in the hands of the mutes. His men did not help him. He spat in Lymond's face as finally, every limb pinned, helpless as a baron of beef, he stood, his white and gold silk grating against the smooth white and blue of the tiles, while the Kislar Agha, without a word, gave Lymond his sword. It was a good weapon, about four feet long, with the hilt set in perfect gold fish-scales and the sheath sewn with coral and diamonds. There were even a line or two of the Qur'ân engraved on its blade.

Lymond got the mutes to free Gabriel just before he killed him; partly, thought Jerott, because he could not bring himself to execute a motionless man, and partly to manhandle him. He did, laying aside the sword, and Jerott looked away from that. He thought, towards the end, that Gabriel had reached the end of his wits, for although he fought, it was without conviction, and the promises and threats he was shouting were gibberish. Then Lymond flung him against the wall and drove the Kislar Agha's sword into his chest up to the hilt, and again four more times. He stopped himself at that, with a strength of will as great as any he had shown that afternoon, and flung down the sword. The red silk robe showed nothing, although it glistened stiffly, where it caught the new lamplight. Gabriel, in a stained heap on the ground, was quite dead.

*

Silence fell. Breathing very fast, his yellow head bent, Lymond remained looking down at the dead man, his hands flat on the blood-stained tiles at his back. Jerott retreated; and did not know Marthe was watching him until her dry voice said, not unkindly, 'If you are going to be sick, get it over with outside and come back. We're going to have a full-scale collapse on our hands in a moment. . . . How much opium does he need?'

Looking at her, Jerott forgot the agony in his guts for a moment. He said, 'Your cheeks are wet,' and when she shook her head impatiently, the single deep line like Lymond's between her fair brows, he took hold of himself and said soberly, 'Archie will do it. How did you know?'

'That he was an addict? I know the Levant,' Marthe said. They were pulling Gabriel's body away: the eyes, the blue of Kuzúm's or the blue of Khaireddin's, were open and vacant. His men had long since been dealt with, the mutes filing out. Lymond hadn't moved and Jerott, hesitating, turned to the throne.

Roxelana had gone. Marthe's cool voice said, 'She left a command with the Kislar Agha. Tonight, we are to have the hospitality of the selamlik, with all they can offer. Tomorrow we shall be escorted from the Seraglio; the child and Philippa also.'

Jerott looked round. The room had emptied itself but for the Kislar Agha and the black eunuchs waiting there by the dais, and the Janissaries on guard at the door. Three men in leather jackets had taken hold of the painted chess cloth and were rolling it up. The patches of blood had not yet dried on the paint, and their fingers were red. They jerked it a little under Gaultier, who had sunk down, spent with relief, his head on his knees, and he looked up and rose, stumbling out of their way. Philippa had already moved, her face bone-white, fiercely protecting Kuzúm, who had broken down into tears; and locking out everything else. Archie had gone over to Lymond.

Lymond didn't look up. But when Archie's brown hands, fumbling, tried to unfasten his surcoat he looked down and said, 'Why . . .?'

Archie said, 'It's stained, sir. They want to give you another.'

Then Lymond lifted his head and said flatly, 'But I wasn't anywhere near him. . . .' And Jerott, listening, realized that it was

Khaireddin of whom he was speaking; and that the death of Gabriel had already gone from his mind. After so much toil and effort and agony, Gabriel's end had made no impression; had meant nothing compared to what had happened before; had been only an intermission in the acts of a tragedy. Jerott said harshly, 'Let's get home; and to hell with selamlìk hospitality. . . . Archie, what can you give him?'

The surcoat was open, but Lymond ignored it, standing still, his hands spread on the wall. Archie said, 'He's had all he can take. He carried it with him. I can't give him any more.' Archie paused, and then said to Jerott, 'We can't leave the Seraglio, sir. Not if it's a command. Mlle Marthe has already told the Kislar Agha we'd prefer to go out tonight, but they say it must be tomorrow. He's waiting now, sir, for us to follow him.'

Marthe's voice said quietly, to Jerott and Archie. 'You go. Take the others. I'll bring Mr Crawford.'

Archie hesitated only a moment. Then turning to Jerott he made up his mind. 'She's right. Come, sir. Let them be.'

Marthe watched them go. Then she turned to her brother.

Quiet and firm, her light voice addressing him made no concessions to tragedy. 'You are not going to fall. This is shock. Put your hand on my arm.'

There was a long pause; then without really seeing her Francis Crawford did remove one hand from the wall and stretch it, groping, before him. Marthe took his palm then in hers and, drawing him from the wall, supported him lightly. 'It's all over now. Leave it. You can change nothing by staying.' The voice, so like his own, was quite even. 'The moment is past. The chessboard has gone; and the people. You must let me take the room from you too.'

Outside, it was dusk. On the way to the threshold she had slipped off his stained surcoat and he stood beside her now in the European clothes he had worn at Míkál's house, torn a little where Gabriel had manhandled him, his face still bruised and his lip cut and swollen from it.

But Gabriel was dead. And beside her, the man Gabriel had so scornfully challenged now stood, wit exhausted and self-command fallen away: all consciousness reduced to a single lens projecting, over and over, a small boy running; and stopping, frightened, to beg; and Míkál's voice saying, *Come, my love. . . . Say goodnight to the dark.*

Archie would give no more opium: not yet. Lymond was too near the edge: too near the limit of the drug: the place where, driven beyond their means, first the body relinquished the race; and then the mind. *Madness cometh sometime of passions of the soul, as of business and of great thoughts, of sorrow and of too great study, and of dread.* Marthe said, thinking aloud with that austere, sexless mind, 'Would madness be kind?'

They were waiting for the Kislar Agha to return and conduct them to their quarters. Lymond shook his head slowly, his eyes looking at nothing, and Marthe said again, watching him, 'Would it be kind? The spinet is there. Shall I play for you?'

And the calculated cruelty of it stung him awake. Within the dead wastes of his mind she struck a spark: a spark of new shock, which must have glimmered, for the first time, on the days and months and years still lying ahead. Lymond looked at her, his eyes open and living, and said, 'Leave me here. Please go and follow the others.'

Blue eyes stared into blue. 'No,' said Marthe. 'Such things will not last. Music makes you a coward because you have no other key for your passions. One day it will come. And you forget. You have one child to see still to safety. I think you owe that to him, and to Philippa. Think . . . when Philippa goes back home from this, what will become of her? Will a convent accept her? Or will she become as Janet Fleming, the courtesan she is now trained to be? She has not considered these things. You must do this for her. Escape into self-destruction by all means; but not until your duty is done.'

The Kislar Agha was coming. Francis Crawford stood beside Marthe and awaited him, drugged and dizzy in his torn clothes, and said nothing more.

The day appointed had come. And in it he had indeed received, as Gabriel promised, the anvil sunk in his heart.

When the time came, he walked collectedly enough by Marthe's side through the garden to the rooms set aside for their quarters. Then the head eunuch left and Lymond, groping, put both hands on the doorpost and rested his wet brow on his wrists. Marthe said, 'Yes. You are going to faint. But it will be more comfortable here than in that death-chamber. And here we shall see that you wake.'

*

They had put a blanket for Kuzúm in Marthe's chamber. She watched Philippa settle him, fussing; before observing with faint and familiar irony, 'I don't intend to eat him, with lettuce. If he's a quarter as fatigued as I am, he will sleep until morning.'

Philippa pushed back her hair. The moment when Kuzúm was asleep and she had no more to do was one she had tried not to think of, ever since leaving the Throne Room. She said, 'I'm sorry. It must be so irritating. I know he'll be all right, of course.' She hesitated, and then said, pallidly cheerful, 'Have you heard what they've done? I'm the prize in the chess game. They've put me with Mr Crawford in the same room.'

For a moment Marthe stared at her. Then she said pleasantly, 'I'm sure Mr Crawford will have no objections. But if you want it changed, I imagine you have only to ask the maids, or the eunuchs.'

'I have,' said Philippa. 'They won't. I've even seen Kiaya Khátún. She says if we move, Roxelana will be offended.'

'I see,' said Marthe. After a moment she said, 'By all means then; we must not offend Roxelana before morning. What does Mr Crawford say to an odalisque in his bed? Is it a bed?'

Philippa laughed a little. 'It's a European four-poster,' she said. 'He's awake now, I think; but I haven't seen him. They're bringing us supper soon in the other room.'

'Then you can break the news to him then.' Marthe studied the other girl for a moment. 'Will you take advice?'

Philippa's brown gaze was direct and her answer as simple. 'About Mr Crawford? I think you know him much better than I do.'

Unexpectedly, the thick fair lashes fell. 'In some things. For example . . . he will not, I think, find it logical to live with what he has done today. I have told him that you are his responsibility. While he believes that, he will continue to protect you. I tell you this, so that you will understand what is happening. He will measure his life by your helplessness.'

Philippa stared at Lymond's sister, the circles black under her eyes. 'According to Kate,' said the Pearl of Fortune, 'I am the very nadir of helplessness. So is Kuzúm.'

'Good. It is perhaps academic,' said Marthe. 'Soon the drug will. kill him unless he stops; and if he stops he will not be fit to travel. . . . And I have a feeling that, when we go, we should go very quickly.' She smiled. 'I shall look after your Kuzúm. Go and eat, and sleep. He will be kind to you.'

27

CONSTANTINOPLE: THE FRENCH EMBASSY

He was kind, for a man who had nothing left but a violent longing to be alone. From the moment Lymond wakened in the silver four-poster bed which some sycophantic Doge had sent long ago to some Sultan, his companions hovered about him, brushing him with their silent solicitude until he brought together all his self-command and addressed Jerott, an edge in his voice. 'Tell Archie I'm getting up. It's like being host to a sheep tick.'

He had had two hours' rest. Because of that, and the febrile stirring of the drug, he had recovered a flickering shadow of vigour: a nervous temper which Jerott, puzzled and anxious, could not rightly interpret. He saw only that Lymond had thrown off some of his exhaustion and was thankful. But he still would not leave him; escorting him doggedly into the larger room where they were to eat, and where Philippa had now joined Abernethy and Gaultier.

Philippa watched them come in. She had already heard their voices: Lymond's cutting in anger, and Jerott answering. It was obvious what was happening. She even began to say, 'Archie . . .' and he had turned his broken-nosed face and answered her quickly. 'No. We can't leave him alone.' Then they were in the room, Jerott breathing hard, his lips straight, and Lymond beside him, his eyes blazing, his voice soft and detached. '. . . Be a father-figure by all means if you must. Protector of the Poor and father of Orphans; the refuge of widows and the mirror of honesty and shamefastness accompanied by Modesty. Acquire a harem. But kindly *don't meddle with me . . .*'

Then he saw Philippa and Archie and stopped; and after a moment crossed and dropped on the cushions Archie indicated beside him. Jerott walked straight past and went to stand at the window.

Philippa sat, crosslegged and silent, her bent face masked by the fall of her shining brown hair, and gripped her hands, knuckle to knuckle, until her fingers went white and the bones cracked. Dear Kate, how understanding we were about funerals: how we shared in the weeping beforehand and the lightheartedness, the unsuitable laughter which followed. We've had a victory. We've won a battle whose importance perhaps no one yet knows, after a year of effort which has changed every one of us. Gabriel is dead; and we are free and alive, except for one small boy, a stranger to whom we were strangers too. And tonight there is hardly one of us who does not wish, in his remorse, that he had died in his place. She said, 'Do we want to eat, Archie? Marthe and Kuzúm are in bed.'

'Could you sleep?' Archie said. She was going to answer when

Lymond said suddenly, 'As alternatives, they leave a lot to be desired. Could no one bring us some raki? If we must have a wake let us make it a happy one. *Heureux qui, comme Ulysse, a fait un beau voyage*. Let's have Jerott's form of decadence for a change.'

Jerott said, 'Francis, shut up.'

Lymond went on, ignoring him. 'Can you recite? Tell us six dirty stories. Let's have a sing-song, like the brave old days round the campfire. Why not be cheerful?'

'Why not,' said Gaultier viciously, 'play chess?'

It silenced Lymond. His head went back as if he had been struck, the indrawn air caught in his throat. He said nothing more.

Archie Abernethy got up and, bending, wrenched Georges Gaultier to his feet with the arms accustomed to tigers. Then he slung him, protesting, out of the room into the bedchamber and turned the key in the lock. Jerott said, 'Has anyone got any money?'

No one had. Philippa thought of the diamonds now lying in Roxelana's silk coffers, a fortune squandered for nothing. She said, 'Would this help?' and, undoing the tortoiseshell clasp round her neck, held out the jade. She saw from Archie's eyes that he guessed what it cost. Jerott said, 'It might,' and, pocketing it, made for the door, his courtly manners struck from him; reduced, as they all were, to the basic humanities. Archie said, 'What? Raki?'

'If I can bribe someone,' Jerott said. 'He's right. I'd rather be decadent than mad.' Archie said, 'I'll come and help.' The door closed. And Philippa found herself with Lymond, alone in the room.

No one spoke. In the silence filling the room she could feel the blows of her heart in her ribs: her breathing made a queer noise, like the sound of weak bellows in a poor state of repair. Lymond's arms rested on his updrawn knees and his head was bent over them, the long fingers deep in his hair. Next door, she could hear Gaultier move about, muttering; perhaps going to bed.

Five minutes passed. The wall was just behind her. She learned back, softly, stretching her cramped limbs, the tawny silk spread all about her; and, as if in answer, slowly the tense fingers opposite relaxed, and without looking up Lymond spoke to her. 'Temperament. I'm sorry.'

'You have nothing to apologize for,' said Philippa; but she had stirred some thought in his mind, because he dropped his hand and said, commanding his mind with an effort that could be felt, 'Don't wrest from me my repentance. A whoremonger, a haunter of stews, a hypocrite, a wretch and a maker of strife. . . . Kate is going to think I have a great deal to apologize for.'

'Luckily,' said the new Philippa calmly, 'we aren't talking about what Kate thinks. I don't regret anything. Except, perhaps, all that training and I never did wriggle up from the bottom of the bed. I always wondered how one got past his feet. And my philology is superb.'

It was the faintest of smiles on his lips; but it was there. He said, 'I'm sure of it. But it all poses certain problems in ordinary life.'

'This isn't ordinary life?' said Philippa; and he shook his head, and said, 'It's all right. You don't need to clown. I'm speaking of going back home. No more peacocks, but eating the milk of buffaloes and cast-down melon skins.'

'Do you think,' said Philippa helplessly, 'that they'll try to stop us?'

He looked at his hands. 'I shouldn't be surprised. It would suit Roxelana for one thing. But at least they'll let us get out of the Seraglio, I imagine, and back to the Embassy. Don't worry. I shall get you back home. With Kuzúm. . . . Philippa, have you given a thought to the future, once you *are* home?'

Kuzúm. Philippa said, her throat tight, 'You'll want him, of course, at Midculter. But if I could stay with him until he gets to know you all better . . .' And saw by his face that she had read him quite wrongly.

He said, 'Kuzúm? But he is yours, of course, for as long as you want him. I was speaking of other things. They have broken to you, I imagine, the exciting news about the Venetian four-poster. Don't worry about that either. Think of it as a camp, with Míkál and his friends. You shall lose as little privacy as possible. What I am trying to point out is that, once you are home, you will find that to some people innocence doesn't exist side by side with experience, and adventure is a limited thing. It will be known, long before we get there, that you have been a concubine in Suleiman's harem; that you journeyed alone through Greece with Míkál, and that you were given to me and that we shared this room together. And men are conventional beings, even the best of them.'

Philippa's brown eyes suddenly danced. 'You mean my reputation is ruined? No wealthy gentlemen suing for my favours?'

'No *respectable* wealthy gentlemen suing for your favours,' he said. She had made him half-smile again.

It seemed such an extraordinary thing for him to be concerned about that Philippa stared at him owlishly while she considered the matter. Then she said, guessing his main preoccupation, 'Kate won't be troubled. I don't know any gentlemen, anyway.'

'Thank you,' said Lymond. 'You mean that when you left home you were too young for the marriage market. Or uninterested, at least. Such are the ways of nature, I must inform you, that one day the situation is likely to change.'

He stopped abruptly, and rising to his feet, walked to the wall and then turned, looking down on her. 'You were ready to spend the rest of your life safeguarding that child,' he said. 'You faced God knows what dangers and devilment tracing him. You will no doubt in due time collect your just award in the Heavenly Kasbah, daily visited by seventy thousand angels. Until that time, so far as I am able, I intend to see that nothing which has happened to you here interferes with your happiness or prospects. I can't say you're being very helpful.'

Philippa looked up at him, her narrow face grave. 'I have helpful intentions,' she observed. 'Actually the Kislar Agha is the man for these assurances. Do you think he would give me a written guarantee, dated tomorrow?'

'Philippa?' said Francis Crawford. And this time, the tawny silk unrumpling slowly, she rose to her feet.

She had grown. Kate's vicious friend, once so elevated, was taller by little more than a head. She drew her brows together, and studied the circles under his eyes. He said lightly, 'My dear girl; it's Almoner's Saturday. With six frails of figs and a sackful of almonds, I am offering you my name.'

Philippa's lips parted. The smith in her chest, changing a wooden mallet for a small charge of gunpowder, pulverized brain, lungs and stomach and left her standing, wan as a blown egg. She said shakily, 'How would that help?'

Round his mouth, the curled lines deepened, and his eyes, very blue, lit suddenly with something like the flame she had seen struck in them at other times, by other things and other people. 'Stout Philippa,' he said. 'Sit down and hear. . . . There is no guarantee for you now except marriage. Do it now, and you go home a respectable matron of fifteen . . . sixteen——'

'Nearly seventeen,' said Philippa.

'Yes. Well: with no money but a good many friends and enough property to keep a roof over your head and Kuzúm's. Then, as you choose, you may divorce me.'

She cleared her throat. 'On what grounds?'

He looked at her directly, his voice level. 'On very obvious grounds. We shall find another Kislar Agha, if you like, to give you a guarantee. . . . You must have no fears that this will be anything but a marriage on paper. But I want it done now. Tomorrow, if the Embassy chaplain can do it.'

Philippa's gaze was also direct. 'You think there is a chance we may not all get home?'

'There is a chance some of us may not,' he said quietly. 'I want to do this very much. I have very little to offer you . . . an irresponsible past, and a name which is . . . in some places questionable. But it will shelter you until you can do better.'

'And you?' said Philippa. 'With a fifteen- . . . sixteen- . . . seventeen-year-old titular wife? What will Sybilla say? It isn't a practical method of founding a dynasty.'

'My brother has founded the dynasty.'

Cool and curt. It ended any attempt to discuss his affairs. And yet what less could she do, when offered this prodigious bounty? He had foreseen a difficulty, which was undeniable, although she could not see it as pressing. He had further felt he owed her a duty. He had talked of the benefits to her; he had not spoken of what he might be sacrificing. Was there some woman waiting, at home or in France, who might be mortally hurt by this gesture? What indeed would his mother, Sybilla, say? And what, oh, what, would Kate? . . . *Dear Kate. You will be pleased to learn that my hand in marriage has been sought and received by Mr Crawford, and I am happy to inform you that you are now his . . .*

Philippa said abruptly, 'I'm sorry. I think it's a magnificent gesture, but the situation really calls for nothing nearly so drastic. People would think we were crazy.'

He was not smiling now. He said in the same quiet voice, 'You are afraid?'

'No,' said Philippa angrily. 'My goodness, after all those interminable lectures? I understand what you're trying to guard against. But I don't see why, even at the worst, it can't wait until we get home.'

Lymond was angry too. He said, '*Oh, God in Heaven,*' furiously, and got up again to prowl to the wall where he stopped, running his hand through his hair. Then he dropped it, and drew a long breath. 'All right. Let me spell it all out for you. I am doing this now because I almost certainly have no future. If I escape Roxelana, I shall see you all into safety. If the opium lets me down, Jerott and Archie will see you the rest of the way. If it doesn't let me down, I shall take it until you are all out of danger, and then I shall cease taking it and leave you. What happens then will be interesting, but I am told the chances of a complete cure are not very high. In any case, I have no intention of going back to Scotland, then or at any time in the future. Therefore I ask you to marry me tomorrow. There will be no other chance. It may matter to you. And it matters to me not at all.'

She had asked for it; and she had got it. She stared at him, breathing hard to keep back the tears, and knew suddenly and finally why Marthe had warned her. Philippa said, 'I shall do it if you give me a promise.'

He said, 'How kind of you. What is the promise?'

The stability of her chin became a matter of moment. She said hardily, 'That . . . even married to me . . . you do nothing, ever, to arrange your own death.'

There was a little silence. Then he said, 'Whose idea was that? Jerott's?'

'I think,' said Philippa carefully, 'it was an inspiration of my own. . . . If anything would damage my chances of a good second marriage *that* would.'

This time, there was no pause. Francis Crawford said merely, 'These things have nothing to do with you. Think again.'

'I have thought,' said Philippa stubbornly. 'No promise, no bride.'

It was not pleasant waiting. Nor, when he spoke, was it better. 'You bloody little dictator,' he said. 'You're exactly like Kate.'

But he gave her his word.

*

In the end, all the raki Jerott and Archie brought back was in Jerott and Archie. They were quarrelsome and maudlin by turns, and Lymond turned them into the same room as Gaultier and left them alone, without trying to install either information or planning into their oblivious heads.

By then, Philippa, aching as if she had been beaten, had slipped off her outer robe and climbed into the Venetian bed in her body linen, which was embroidered and not very long, her combed hair tidied back with a ribbon. After a moment she got out again and, pulling off the exquisite quilt, made a sleeping-bag of it on the carpet and wondered whether, as one of the underprivileged young, she should occupy it herself. Then she decided that if she were to have a new status forced upon her, she might as well learn to live up to it; and, climbing back into bed, fell astonishingly and profoundly asleep.

She awoke an hour or two later shivering, and recalled with a great drop of the heart where she was sleeping and why. It had become very cold. Craning over the edge of the bed, she saw on the far stretch of carpet the dark shape which must be the quilt; and then, straining, the gleam of Lymond's hair in the faint moonlight streaming through the high window. She did not realize that he was awake until his head turned, his eyes dark as a lynx in the night, and his voice said quietly, 'What is it?'

All Kate's maternal instincts and her own common sense rose and drowned Philippa's qualms. She said, 'I'm cold. And if I'm cold, you must be freezing. Put that quilt back on the bed and come and sleep on the other side. I don't mind. And who's to know?'

There was faint amusement in the low voice. 'My dear girl, there isn't a soul in the Seraglio who doesn't believe I'm there anyway.'

Philippa had forgotten. She recovered, and said, 'Well, put it back anyway. You can't sleep without it, and neither can I. Heaven knows, the bed's big enough.'

It was: a remarkable object running to cherubs, with a great deal of pendulous drapery. The quilt, homing back to its blankets, fell over her with a comforting sigh: laying it straight, Lymond's hand for a second touched her. Philippa sat up. 'You're frozen!'

455

He had moved to the far side. 'I'm tired, that's all; so I feel it. Look, you're sure you don't mind?'

'After *Míkál*?' said Philippa. 'Anyway, it's almost legitimate. We're going to be joined in holy wedlock tomorrow.' She rather liked the terrible phrase. 'Did you enjoy your bachelor party?'

'Archie and Jerott both did,' he said drowsily. The mattress had hardly moved to his weight, but she knew he was there, lying still, with the furthest extent of the big bed between them. The cold must have kept him awake a long time, for once there, he slipped almost at once into sleep.

Silence. With warmth once more enfolding her, it was strange that she was content just at first to lie awake, thinking in peace, the moonlight slowly searching the bedchamber; the quilt, the crystal cherubs; her partner.

Frightening, that Fate should so turn that Francis Crawford of Lymond, the source of her earliest terror, the hated intruder in her mother's calm house, should be here, alone and asleep in her bed. How many women, one wondered, had lain adoring that fair head at rest on the pillow? *Why, everywhere he goes*—down through the years came her own hoarse, childish voice—*he has hundreds and hundreds of mistresses.* And Kate's voice, not quite as amused as it seemed, *Do learn tolerance, infant.* Then Philippa herself fell asleep.

She woke much later because of a movement of the bed and this time lay still, remembering at once where she was. Then the man on the other side of the bed moved again, blindly abrupt in his sleep, and she realized that in the restless slumber of opium he was not an easy bedfellow; hard on her, and harder still on himself. For a while, still half asleep, she drowsed and woke and drowsed again through the disturbance, sometimes aware of his voice. Once he said, clearly enough to be distinguished, 'Tell me. I can't understand. *Why did you do it?*' And added, after a moment, in a queer voice, 'Poor Eloise.' Another time he said only, 'O mill. What hast thou ground . . . ?' Philippa knew that reference. Her impulse was to move to him as she would to Kuzúm, and put her hand on his arm, but she was afraid of both his pride and his temper.

But in the end it was he himself who, flinging over in some great gesture of escape and despair, touched her body. He recoiled like a spring; like someone who had received his bane-blow, torn half awake by the shock, his expressive body hard with revulsion. Shocked herself by his reaction, Philippa sat up, and in that second he became thoroughly awake; aware of the flurry of movement, and of her alarm. He said, '*What have I done?*' And as, confused and distressed, she did not at once speak, he said wearily, 'Oh, my God;' and leaving the bed, crossed the carpet to the furthest corner of the room, and, dropping by the stool there, covered his blind face with his hands.

456

Sitting rigid, Philippa heard him draw in his breath; and then again; and knew by the sound what he was trying to subdue. She lay back, tears running down her face, and covered her ears with her hands.

When she removed them a long time after he was perfectly silent, his head on his arms, but it was not over, for he spoke, as he had once before, hearing her movement. 'Philippa . . .?'

Philippa said fiercely, 'Look: nothing happened. You only thought it did. You moved in your sleep, that was all.'

He didn't lift his head, and his voice, muffled by his hands, was not familiar at all. 'I know. I thought it was somebody else. . . . Philippa . . . release me from my promise.'

She put her hands over her mouth, and then took them away. 'I can't. I can't.'

He had pulled his own hands down, looking still at the stool, his face quite turned away. 'You can. *Philippa. Please let me go.*'

Her refusal this time was a whisper; but he must have heard it, for he didn't ask her again. The rest of the night Philippa passed lying awake, without moving; without speaking; and keeping to herself all the untoward weight of her grief and her pity. In her diary no entry ever appeared for that night, in which the light-hearted hoyden of Hexham vanished altogether.

Towards morning she thought perhaps Lymond slept, but he didn't stir, and she could not harass him with the quilt, although the intense cold had gone. Then, weary as she was, she must herself have fallen asleep, for when she next opened her eyes, the corner on the far side of the room was illumined with daylight, and empty.

*

He had gone to the room Jerott shared with Archie and Gaultier. Shaken unwillingly awake, Jerott heard the cool voice, not quite in its familiar tone. 'Drunk and in a state of legal uncleanliness. Wake up. We have a lot to discuss.' Jerott opened his eyes.

Lymond was standing back, waiting for him in his stained hose, his torn shirt pulled off and thrown over one shoulder. His back was to the light. But even so, Jerott was suddenly quiet, and he heard Archie beside him say sharply, 'Have you had any sleep at all?'

'I have had delightful dreams,' said the soft, roughened voice. 'Fawns in the shape of fairies with musk-fragrant hair. And I have breakfasted on opium. Will you listen, or are you anxious to do all the talking?'

Jerott held down his permanent nausea. 'Philippa?'

Lymond said, 'Those who gather frankincense are dedicated unto divine honours, and use no carnal company with any woman. Philippa is well, and deep in blameless slumber. We now have to decide how best to get her and you safely home.' And this time they listened.

At the end, Jerott said after a long pause, 'Must you marry her?'
Lymond shrugged. 'What else? Maidens despoiled, men-children defiled; children brought up in impious abominations. Kuzúm will get over it, but her integrity has gone.'

Jerott said, as Philippa had done, 'And you?' And Lymond stared at him, his brows delicately lifted. 'I shall gather frankincense,' he replied.

*

Escorted by Chiausi, they left the Topkapi Serail of the Sultan Suleiman by the sea gate, spared the long procession back through the great courtyards; spared too the curiosity of those who might concern themselves too closely with Roxelana's affairs. The Sultan's barge awaited them by the crystal kiosk, rowed by the long line of the mutes. They took their places, four men, two girls and a child, silent in new flowered silks; who had been made to taste in Paradise the chastisement of Hell. The day, thought Philippa, white-faced with the child Kuzúm on her knee, on which men shall be as scattered moths, and the mountains shall be as loosened wool. The day which makes grey the heads of young children . . .

The words now had meaning. All poetry had meaning, and sorrow she had never envisaged. Behind, veiled in soft rain as the dragon-prowed barge slid across the grey water to Pera, she saw for the last time close at hand the soft, frescoed height of the Seraglio, heart of the Ottoman world, its domes and chimneys and towers, its tall cypresses and gardens picked out in grisaille and gold.

Today, perhaps, the Gate of the Dead would perform its true office for a small boy whose heritage no one knew; who had lived in squalor and perished in fright. A sacrifice to diminish the soul. A sacrifice to colour all the rest of one's days.

In silence they crossed the water and, hardly speaking, they landed. Philippa carried Kuzúm. Lymond had come for her before leaving, his eyes steady, and she had returned his greeting, her face and voice equally peaceful. A well-governed exercise. Except that you could see still, about his eyes and his brow, the marks of the murderous thing which had touched him when Khaireddin had died.

They disembarked, and found horses waiting to take them up to the Embassy.

Chesnau was waiting, ignorant of everything save for the news that they were all returning that morning. One deduced, from his face, his relief that no diplomatic intervention was necessary: no international incident had taken place. Lymond said nothing about Gabriel. He merely asked for their boxes to be packed and arrangements made for them to leave as soon as the *Dauphiné* could be provisioned.

Their most unexpected welcome, dislocated with emotion, came from Onophrion Zitwitz. Onophrion the unregarded, who had been sent back to the Embassy on Jerott's detention and had remained there ever since, consumed with anxiety. Activity of all things was the emollient he desired: he flung himself into the preparations for departure; the monumental architect of other men's projects; and Lymond asked for the chaplain.

In the plain and pungent philosophy of Philippa's life, bridal visions had never intruded. Flaw Valleys with Kate and Gideon, their laughter and music had been all she had ever desired. She remembered the wedding in Greece, all sunshine and dancing; the crowned girl and boy with tinsel in their dark hair; and how she had pitied them. But now, preparing for another wedding with a table for altar in a damp Turkish study, and the smell of ink and expediency instead of incense and roses, Philippa thought again of the bride, blushing, receiving her shoe-buckles; and the Pilgrims of Love, giving their hearts and their laughter and the moonlit song of the lyre. And Míkál's beautiful voice: *The fountains make thee thy bride's veil; the lyre spins thee thy ribbons; the mallow under thy foot is the hand of thy bridegroom. . . . Sometimes, one must travel to find what is love.*

She let her mind go just so far; and then, with gentle hands, closed the door she had opened. Then, wearing not her Turkish robe but a plain woollen dress of her own, her hair unbound; with no paint and no jewels but a small silver brooch long ago bought by her father, Philippa walked with Onophrion to the place of her wedding.

Lymond was not there. He came a little late, quickly, changed too into his own doublet and hose, neither too elaborate nor too discourteously simple. They both, thought Philippa flatly, knew all the nuances that etiquette demanded. He gave a comforting smile, and then took his place by her side.

The priest was old. Philippa could hear the witnesses, Jean Chesnau and his chief secretary, shifting a little behind her, impatient with the slow voice. Outside, Onophrion was keeping the door. Of Jerott and the others there was no sign. . . .

Marthe had no interest in marriage. Marthe was in brief and competent charge of Kuzúm, who was worried by Fippy in a strange dress which fitted her middle, and no *kohl* on her eyes. Philippa thought suddenly, with a frisson which ran like wind through her nerves, *Now she is my sister. . . .* Then she felt Lymond glance at her swiftly, and forced herself to forget it.

The words of the Mass went over her head. She made her mechanical responses, and heard his voice, sealing his pledges. Other people married young, to men they didn't know, and had no dispensation such as she had. To sleep alone; to plan her own destiny. A virgin married, with a son not her own. . . . Kate always said, thought Philippa, blinking, that the Somervilles were mad to a man. Then

Lymond's hand on her arm guided her to her feet and then dropped. 'It's all over,' he said.

Etiquette was silent on the answer to that. He did not offer to kiss her. Philippa said, to the scandalization of priest and secretary and chargé d'affaires, 'I think I'd like to get drunk.'

They all called her *madame*. There was no wedding-feast, but a dinner now preparing, to be laid out for them all in an hour or so's time. Onophrion, his mind on his ovens, spread before them his deferential good wishes and fled. Lymond said, 'Come out for ten minutes.' Then as she studied him with sober brown eyes he had said, smiling a little, his eyes tired, 'It isn't a command. You must do as you please. But I thought a little air might help us both.'

Philippa said, overwhelmed with repentance. 'I'm sorry. Kate always said I'm a lout. Are you feeling all right? Can't *you* go and get drunk?'

He picked up her cloak and held it for her, his teeth white as he smiled. 'You have still some things to find out about me. I don't drink. In any case, think of the example to Kuzúm.'

She took a little time working that out, as they walked down the hill through the morning traffic of Pera, their Janissary following behind. Certainly, there had been no raki last night on his breath, last night of all nights when one would have expected it. She thought of him, unwillingly, as he had looked in the shadows, his arms crossed, his head buried between them, and compared it with another memory, sharp in her mind. They were threading their way down to the Golden Horn, past the burial-ground and tekke of dervishes, when Philippa suddenly said, 'Was it *Jerott* . . . Jerott who drank too much on the *Dauphiné*?'

He did not quite know what she meant, but he said mildly, 'Jerott, I suppose, has certainly been known to drink too much, on board ship or off it. So until last year have I. He'll stop, no doubt, when he has resolved his trouble with Marthe.'

'Why did you stop?' she asked. Someone had engaged their Janissary in heated argument. Lymond didn't look back.

He shrugged. 'One escapes; but one always has to come back. I found too I disliked not being in command of myself.'

She did not put her next question. He raised an eyebrow and said, 'What restraint! Will you do something for me?'

'What?' said Philippa warily.

'As we pass, slip into the tekke. Someone will speak to you. If they say, '*Aşk olsun*,' answer them, '*Aşkin cemal olsun*' . . . can you remember that?'

'I heard it all the way to Thessalonika,' said Philippa. She had gone very pale. 'Then what?'

'Follow wherever he takes you. He is a friend.'

For a moment longer she stood, looking at him. Then she said, 'You gave me a promise. I have done what you asked.'

'And I shall keep my word,' Lymond said. 'So far as fortune will let me. . . . *Now!*'

The dark door of the tekke opened up on her left. In a moment, Philippa was inside. '*Aşk olsun*,' said the soft voice of Míkál.

28

CONSTANTINOPLE AND THRACE

Ten minutes later, decidedly changed in appearance, Philippa walked again into the street.

She had no idea where she was going; only that, robed in veils once more, Moslem fashion, she was to follow the slender robed shape of Míkál just ahead, keeping her head modestly low, trying only not to lose sight of him as he threaded his way down to the boats and across the Golden Horn, back to the city they had just left with such pain. There a donkey was waiting for him, its panniers full of red earthenware, and he mounted it and sat, his dirty feet stuck out on either side, while she trudged at its side.

She had never before walked in the city: never seen this from the straw of her cage when she bumped through with Archie, or when the Janissaries brought her back, veiled and chained, on their horses. She climbed the hill to Suleiman's great new mosque, the monument to his glory, still unfinished, the marble columns from buried Byzantium being levered still into place, the tomb waiting for its magnificent master. Mustafa now would never come to worship there in the robes of his father. Of Roxelana's sons, the fragile adoring disciple of Mustafa was already failing: the other two eyeing and circling, prepared to fight out the succession perhaps over all their father had erected.

Perhaps she had seen Ottoman power at its height at this moment, in this city lying under its uneasy winter, awaiting the flowering season when the sharp lilac-pink of the Judas tree would cloud the gold of the cupolas, and the tulips bar the short grass in the Seraglio gardens, where the gazelles came to graze and later the soft wind would be filled with the smell of carnations.

Past Suleiman's Mosque and the high walls of the Old Seraglio, with the house of Názik the nightingale-dealer at its foot, now shuttered and closed, the birds silent and gone. The covered market, the channelled chords of its commerce vibrating with sound: a bright-winged aviary like Názik's of deep-throated men. The pigeons, before Beyazit's Mosque, where another story-teller sat, telling the tale of the Forty Viziers, but not as the Meddáh used to tell it who had now joined the First Story-teller Suhâib Rûmi in Paradise, where the ground is pure wheaten flour mixed with musk and saffron, its stones being hyacinths and pearls, and of gold and silver its palaces. Or so the boy Ishiq said.

Ignorant of these things, Philippa followed Míkál until the donkey stopped before a stone house set in waste ground where a dog nosed in a courtyard full of sour rubble and weeds, and the door was fast locked.

Míkál tapped while she stood by the donkey; and presently, the warped door creaked open, and the frightened face of a negress, peering through, retreated to allow Míkál and Philippa to climb the steps and slip in. Then they walked down a passage and into a room full of people.

'Enter, children of sloth,' said Lymond pleasantly. 'My God, I thought you were never coming. Míkál . . .?'

'They are watching the house. You say there is only one boat? For nine people?'

Nine people. Philippa, pulling the veil wide-eyed from her face, saw with a leapfrogging heart that they were all there, Jerott and Marthe, Archie and Gaultier. A large old man with white hair whose extreme placidity struck an odd note in the feverish air of the room. And . . . '*Fippy!*' someone screamed, and flung himself into her arms.

'Dear, dear,' said Philippa, hugging him, weeping. 'You can't get rid of some people; no matter how much you try.'

'Actually,' said Lymond, 'we've one boat and a raft. While we were in the Seraglio, Master Gilles has been busy.'

'*A raft?*' said Gaultier. He turned round, his fingers closing on air, his face ashen. 'A raft? My God, the thieving old bastard. . . . *He's taken the treasure!*'

The old man's bushy eyebrows reared in his big face. 'Quiet yourself, Pharisee. *Turpe est Doctori, cum culpa redurgit ipsum.* One set of thieves is enough. I have merely completed my inventory.'

Míkál was peering through a crack in the shutters. 'More are coming. There is little cover, were one to shoot. There are no muskets?'

'There are no muskets,' said Lymond. 'Don't be blood-thirsty. . . . We have two vehicles. Suppose we employ them.'

It was not easy, climbing one by one down that vertical ladder into the small rocking boat at its foot. Jerott took the small raft, with Philippa and Kuzúm, while the other six crowded into the boat. Lymond, closing the cupboard and bestowing the trapdoor neatly up above, was the last. Then they were afloat in the great underground cavern, in the world of green water and dim drowning pillars, the roar of the fall in their ears.

To Archie and Lymond himself it was no great surprise, after Jerott's description. Míkál clearly also knew what to expect. But to Philippa, holding Kuzúm still at her side, it was like the last mysterious station, dark, enchanted and cruel, of some terrible Odyssey. Ahead, the light of the boat slid between the black pillars and sank green into the waters, filled with flickering fish. Jerott, lightless, poled his silent way after until, distant from the thundering inflow, he was able to answer her questions. Her last was a natural one. 'When did you all come?'

Jerott said, 'We've been coming all day nearly, in different ways. Francis had it arranged early this morning, first with Míkál and then with the rest of us. Then he got the Embassy preoccupied, you see with . . . various . . .'

'I see,' said Philippa. 'It would have been awkward, I suppose, if I'd had a nerve-storm and stopped the wedding just as you were all climbing out of the window, or whatever you did. But I really would like to have been told.'

Jerott cleared his throat. 'He didn't like doing it.'

'I'm sure he didn't,' said Philippa. They didn't speak the rest of the way.

She was persuading Kuzúm into the darkness of the tunnel when they all heard, far across the dark cistern, the sounds of a fierce hammering, muffled by distance.

'They're breaking into the house.' Lymond, leaning down, his hand on her arm, said, 'Philippa, there's no time to coax him. Hand him to Marthe, and jump up yourself. We have to get rid of the boat.'

Then she was in a black, reeking conduit, just high enough to let them walk stooping, and when Kuzúm stood suddenly still, frenzied rejection on his white dirty face, she helped Marthe tie her handkerchief over his mouth.

Lymond scuttled the boat, sending the small raft first spinning into the darkness; and then quickly and silently rebuilt the entrance with bricks. Jerott, the dim lamp in his hands, looked at him for a moment in question, and then without speaking pushed past to Gaultier and Gilles and led the way forward. For good or evil, their retreat was cut off.

On the long, scrambling journey to the treasure-chamber, none of them spoke. Míkál, sure-footed and slender, helped Marthe and Philippa through the narrow, rubble-blocked openings, and Jerott, his teeth on edge with his slowness, walked behind the old man. Gaultier, the least agile of them all and the most desperate, thrust painfully through, battering himself and colliding with others, with Archie a noiseless shadow behind. Last of all Lymond picked his way bearing Kuzúm, the little boy's face in his shoulder, the second lamp in his hand.

There was no noise behind. There was no sound ahead, but the slithering crunch of their feet scaling the uneven landslides of limestone and brick, and the sudden rattling fall of small gravel disturbed by their weight. Scrambling on grimly, hot and dirty in her long robes, Philippa wondered about Marthe and her uncle, and the secret they seemed to have kept from them all. She was not clear, from what Jerott had said, exactly what part in the business Pierre Gilles had played. On other points, too, Jerott had been exceedingly brief. When she had asked what would happen now to the relics, Jerott, on the other hand, had given an unamused smile. 'You weren't present at the interview between Marthe and Francis this morning. He called her one of nature's bloody little hermaphrodites. Then he told her she was a mercenary bitch and could pay for it.'

Philippa said, 'When did he say that? This morning? Not last night?'

'Look, he wasn't in any state to command language like that last night,' Jerott had said. 'Anyway, he hardly saw her except at the chess game. No, this morning. Why?'

'She doesn't hate him,' Philippa had said. 'Last night she wanted to help.'

And Jerott had paused before saying, 'Well, I'm damned sure she won't want to help now. We're using this conduit as a means to get through to the Hippodrome and out before Roxelana traces and stops us. She and Gaultier and Gilles can all take from the chamber in passing such small relics as they can put in their sleeves or their purses. All the rest must be left. The master has spoken.'

He sounded disenchanted and angry. Philippa had said, 'Do you think Roxelana would really be interested in pursuing Gaultier and Marthe? Gilles wasn't even at the Seraglio.'

'You have put your finger,' Jerott had said blandly then, 'on the point at present exercising M. Gaultier. On the other hand, the only way to be sure is to stay behind and see whether they kill you or not.'

The path had begun to drop steeply. There was some kind of aperture, heavily barred, on their right, and then the tunnel plunged ahead into darkness. She thought she could detect some distance ahead a cleared fork, with a passage running off to the right while the main channel went on, steadily climbing. Behind them, Lymond's voice said softly, 'Stop.'

They all halted but Gaultier. It was Gilles who wound his powerful fingers into his arm, and holding him, gave a short, curious whistle.

There was no sound. But a shadow detached itself from other, different shadows and, racing towards them, flung itself on Pierre Gilles. Philippa swallowed. It was a cat. No, it was a long-bodied grey beast like a cat, with a small, pointed black muzzle, and whiskers and little round ears. It sniffed round the anatomist's face and beard, apparently in affection, and then slipped down his body and stood before them on the path, head tilted and one paw upraised. Then, silently, it ran backwards and forwards into the depths of the tunnel, pausing every third or fourth time to look up at its master.

They all stood where they were, thought Philippa, bewitched as if the beast had been one of Archie's pet tigers. Then Gilles bent, and scooping the animal up, turned to Lymond and jerked his great head. Jerott saw it too. Arms outspread, in silence he began pushing them all back, up the hill of the tunnel, and blew out the torches.

Lymond's lamp was still lit. He transferred Kuzúm to Philippa's arms and turned again down the passage, his voice muted but clear. He said, 'No, I was wrong. We hadn't gone far enough. It's there, just to the right.' And swinging the lamp, he walked on downhill, making a lot of quiet noise. Behind him, they all stood in the dark in their places, Archie's hand this time on Gaultier's shoulder. Marthe stood quite still. It was Jerott who, after a moment, swore under his breath and, leaving them, moved off after Lymond, talking in the same kind of voice. Philippa saw Lymond's one angry gesture, waving him back, but Jerott walked on downhill, ignoring it. He got to the bottom and smiled; and Philippa saw Lymond smile in return. Then Lymond's voice said, 'Hell. The light's gone out.'

The lamp had indeed vanished. For a moment nothing more happened, then Philippa heard Jerott's voice say in the blackness, 'Look, let's go round to the room. We can relight it there. Put out your hand to the right. There's the wall. . . .'

The footsteps in the darkness started again, going slowly. Behind Philippa, with the smallest of chinks, Archie Abernethy got out his sword.

It must have been only seconds after that that she was aware of someone coming towards her: two sets of footsteps, crushing the small stones in spite of their stealth. Not Lymond or Jerott, but men of heavier build, whose hoarse breathing they could all hear. Then she felt Archie move, and then Míkál, and there was a trampling, covered by the greater noise made by the two men walking ahead. The breathing became wild and was cut off: someone made a noise in his throat. Then she felt Míkál, breathing lightly, slip back beside her, and after a moment Archie came too. Of the two strangers there was no sign at all.

Silence fell, disturbed only by the footfalls of Jerott and Lymond, out of sight far ahead in the short passage leading, she guessed, to the treasure room. Then the sounds came to a halt and she heard their voices, arguing evidently about relighting the lamp, which was clearly giving some trouble. In the end, it stayed unlit, for no bloom of light reached them from the arm of the passage, and indeed there came a brief silence, presumably as they let themselves down to the chamber. Gaultier jerked, and Archie's hand dug into his arm.

The second set of hurried footsteps, much lighter than the first, made themselves heard just as a greater noise erupted suddenly from the far rising end of the conduit. The noise this time of many men with lanterns, rushing downhill towards them and turning along that same junction where the treasure room lay. The sound reverberated against the low roof: the tumbling of rubble and swearing of colliding bodies running hard and stooped in the dark, and then the echoing sound of many voices in differing keys: question and answer, a puzzled trampling about and a swinging of light, reaching

466

out from the short arm of the passage and illumining the long conduit rising uphill ahead, now perfectly clear.

It illumined also Lymond and Jerott, running noiselessly back to the flock, and waving them on. '*Now*,' said Francis Crawford, and, as Philippa snatched up Kuzúm, he put a hand on her elbow and raced with her down to the dip and towards the uprising ground.

Georges Gaultier got there first. He must have known that the trap had been sprung; that believing them all to be in the chamber by now, or at least round and in the short passage, their adversaries, whoever they were, had swept round into chamber and passage, hoping to trap them. But if he knew, it made no real difference. All that mattered was that Lymond was leading the way on through the main channel, and past the way to the treasure.

So Georges Gaultier ran. He ran past Jerott and Lymond and Philippa, down into the flickering light of the junction, and swung round to face the short passage, arms upraised, the light full on his face. 'Don't take it!' he shouted to the anonymous faces, staring at him behind the massed torches. 'Don't take it! It's mine! I'll pay you for it! I'm not with the others: I can prove it. I found it all, and it's mine!'

He didn't even see the arrow that killed him. It flew arching from the bright lights and took him full in the chest, so that he stumbled, his knees sagging, and fell forward, his hands raking the rubbish, without hearing the sonorous voice which addressed him. 'Come then, M. Gaultier,' it said. 'Come and get it.' And added, still rich, still soft, still deferential even in its smooth cadences, 'I really should not advise you now, Mr Crawford, to lead your friends through past the junction. There are six bows trained on the opening where poor M. Gaultier stood, and the light is now excellent.'

'*Onophrion Zitwitz!*' said Philippa.

The unseen speaker had heard her. 'Ah, the bride. How many of you are there, I wonder . . . ? I need not tell you, madame, that your groom is a master of trickery. But for poor M. Gaultier, I believe he might have escaped, for the moment. And I had made up my mind that twenty-four hours more of life was all that M. le Comte de Sevigny should have.'

'Twenty-four hours more than Graham Reid Malett?' said Lymond softly. First in that headlong rush down the passage, he had stopped dead as Gaultier darted out past him, Philippa swinging against him; and slithering to a halt in turn, all the others behind him had stood still, concealed in the shadows, and watched Gaultier's murder take place.

'Twenty-four hours more than the greatest man who ever lived,' said the hard voice of Onophrion Zitwitz. 'It is more than I promised myself. But you will die the death he would have wanted for you, and your assorted friends with you.'

'Gabriel sent you to join me at Baden?' Lymond's voice, coolly interested, told nothing of the speed with which, turning the assorted friends round, he was in process of dispatching them to safety, back along the long path to the cistern.

Onophrion's voice halted him and them. 'If you go back, you will meet still more of my friends. It will have taken them a little time to find a new boat, but when they have found it, they know what to do. I paid a call on M. Gilles while you were all in the Seraglio, didn't I mention it? He wasn't at home, although my watchers knew he hadn't emerged. What were you doing, Master Gilles? Making an inventory? At least the house was quite vacant when I got in, and I could search it at leisure . . . the secret was not hard to find. . . . Yes, Sir Graham asked me to join you at Baden, and to tell him all that you did. I would have laid down my life for Sir Graham. . . . Alas, I could not prevent you from killing him. . . .'

'The mutes were good at it too,' said Lymond pleasantly. 'He made himself unpopular, you know, with Roxelana. Even without me, she couldn't afford to let him survive.'

'He could have survived anything,' said the rich voice, suddenly roughened. '*Anything*, but injustice and double-dealing by those whom he trusted. You . . . Leone Strozzi . . . de Villegagnon—all tried to besmirch him. At Zuara, you tried to kill him.'

'Hence the accidents between Malta and Thessalonika,' said Lymond. 'Until you got news from Egypt in the Beglierbey's house, you thought as we all did that Gabriel was dead. Gabriel living had told you not to harm me: I was to be preserved—am I right?—for a more painful fate. Gabriel dead meant that at last you could take the joys of revenge. And whether living or dead, there was a revenge you had already taken, for which I was hoping to pay you in very particular coin.'

'It seemed to me,' said the disembodied, gratified voice, 'that you might presently realize that the opium was reaching you through your food. It hardly mattered. You did not understand until too late, as it happened, that you were receiving opium at all.'

'Or Salablanca might have lived,' said Lymond evenly. 'If not Khaireddin. What a great deal, I'm afraid, you must answer for.' He was looking after Marthe, who had laid a hand on his arm, and then disappeared. After a moment the old man Gilles followed her. Archie, consulting Lymond with his eyes, stayed where he was, and so did Jerott, Míkál and Philippa, clutching Kuzúm. Then Philippa saw Jerott give a great start and, staring at Lymond, bend to pick up the extinguished torch from the floor. Lymond said aloud, 'Where did you meet Graham Malett?'

'I was a Serving Brother on Malta. A humble Brother, but he allowed me to care for him as if I were worthy. It was Graham Malett who trained me.' Lymond was working with flint and steel and paper. There was a spark. The torch, shielded by Archie, flared into light. Lymond said suddenly, light-heartedly, 'I always thought your urchins in ginger were bloody appalling. Did he give you the recipe?'

Onophrion's shadow leaped on the wall. Onophrion himself was more circumspect. Hurt in his tenderest spot, he moved a mere two feet forward, but it was enough for Lymond, slipping down the passage quietly, to emerge for a second so that he and Onophrion were in full view. The marksmen behind in the short passage had hardly time to swing round and aim when Lymond's knife, thrown very hard, entered Onophrion's leg at the groin. And in the same moment Jerott, dodging round the same corner, threw his torch, equally hard, at the rampart of straw. Onophrion screeched and fell like the trunk of a tree to the ground. And the straw stacked against the wall of the short passage, the wall opposite the chamber of treasure, began to crackle and blaze.

The glare of it and the first of the smoke came round the corner and back up the conduit to where Philippa and the rest were all standing. Jerott with Lymond behind him came with the smoke, fast up the incline, and Philippa found herself retreating; pushed gently by Jerott with the rest of the party back up the hill: back the way they had come. She said, 'Once they get a boat, the other men will simply come up the conduit behind us?'

'Once they get a boat,' said Lymond. And to Jerott he said, 'Will he think of it?'

'He's busy with his leg at the moment,' said Jerott. 'You meant to miss?'

'I meant,' said Francis Crawford, 'to do just what I did. Maître Gilles, you know what will happen?'

Rose-coloured in the increasing light, Pierre Gilles's white-bearded head nodded. 'It's best. It was the girl Marthe's idea.'

Turning briefly, Lymond's eyes looked for and found the blue eyes of Marthe. 'As Master Gilles here would say, *Ars sine scientia nihil est*. It may bring down the roof. And you've lost everything, you know.'

'It will bring down the roof. *Moist Mother Earth . . .*'

He finished it for her: '. . . *engulf the unclean power in thy boiling pits, in thy burning fires. . . .* Or we shall suffocate.' He broke off, listening to the voices. It seemed to Philippa that Onophrion had called out his men: she could hear them beating on straw, with no results but to make the great light burn even brighter. Then, the rich voice ringing; sobbing with the pain in his leg, Onophrion directed that the straw should be moved. A flaring gobbet, thick with white smoke, was pitchforked suddenly into the dark conduit at their feet, and made them flinch back. It was followed closely by another. Blocks burnt and unburnt built up before them as they stood choking and watching; then Lymond with Jerott and Archie began to work with their swords. Not to put out the fire, or to turn it away: but to direct its full force against the dark wall on their right.

A trickle of water, trembling with vermilion lights, ran suddenly past Philippa's feet and dried up, hissing, on the hot stones. And Lymond, lifting his head, met Marthe's gaze once more and said with gentle inflection, 'And what a thing is an *intelligent* hermaphrodite bitch. I think we should get back. No one will try to leave yet. They'll want to save the stuff in that room.'

And so they backed, coughing and choking; Kuzúm's screaming face pressed on Philippa's neck, and Philippa looked down again at an icy touch on her ankles and found the whole passage was running with water, which rose as she watched and soaked the hem of her dress. She turned and ran properly, back up the hill after the others, and in passing, looked and saw the opening from which the river was issuing.

It was the aperture on which Gilles and Marthe had been working, hauling down the barred timber and pressing open the door on a glittering cave, creaking and seething within. It was then that she realized that the right-hand wall of the long passage and of the short enclosed a warehouse of snow.

Now the bricks of the wall were red-hot. Water poured through the door-hatch, followed by glistening slush and half-dissolved floes thrust through the opening by the increasing pressure behind. The framework of the hatch suddenly burst and they drew back as the torrent increased in size, thin jets of spray playing like mist through the brickwork adjoining, the mortar melting in front of their eyes. Pierre Gilles said, in his most practical manner, 'I should point out that if this wall collapses ahead of the other, the lower parts of the junction will be filled to the roof. It does not assist our escape.'

'You mean,' said Lymond, 'you think we ought to run for it now?' And as the old man's beard twitched Lymond smiled in return and said, 'I believe you are right. Jerott, take Marthe on your left. Míkál, will you take Philippa and Kuzúm? Then Archie and M. Gilles. . . . I'll bring up the rear.'

They ran down the slope as the fires, hissing, were giving way to white clouds of steam mixed with smoke: clouds like windblown feathers and streamers of muslin, which hid and enfolded them as they reached the bright junction, the water high at their knees, and stumbled through and began to struggle on uphill, out of the wet.

There was no one to stop them. The treasure-chamber was half full of ice water, the green streams pouring down over the bright painted frescoes and stirring and nicking and gouging chariots and charioteers from their strong ancient beds. The caskets, floating a little, became waterlogged and sank unregarded as men fought for the rope, and the water, brimming faster and faster filled up the room. In the short passage it was now hard to hold to one's footing:

the men already out with their plunder floundered, blinded with smoke, their bows laid down, their burdens grasped in their arms. Onophrion, the blood from his groin marbling the flame-rippled water, struggled and shouted in vain to be set on his feet, to be carried, to be helped up the dry road to safety.

At first, seeing Lymond come out of the smoke, he thought his prayers had been answered. Then he saw who it was, and put up his hands as the sword went through his heart.

Jerott's party heard the wall of the conduit collapse when they were far along the high passage, and a blast of hot air followed it, stirring their clothes and their hair. Then there was a greater rumbling: a movement of stone and of earth that went on for a long time and was still going on when Lymond joined them out of the darkness, sheathing his sword. He said, 'Let's go quickly,' and they turned and hurried, without speaking, up to the air.

They left the *Dauphiné* where Roxelana was guarding her. They slipped through the sea gate to Marmara where a fishing-boat rocked, its owner conveniently absent, its sail and oars not. Míkál went with them until they were past the confines of the city and some way along the coast, where horses were waiting. Míkál's friends were waiting there too, singing poems by Lisáni to the jasmine skin of their lovers. They got into the boat laughing, with a ripple of bells, and Míkál took Lymond's hands. 'The Dhammapada says, *The fletcher carves and adjusts the horn of which his bow is made; the pilot manages his ship; the architect hews his beams; the wise man governs his body.* I shall not keep thee. A man must hurry in twilight. Thy little bride has the soul of a lion.'

'My little bride has an extraordinary range of erotic Persian poetry,' said Lymond. 'What else did you teach her, on that journey from Zakynthos?'

'Happiness,' said Míkál simply. 'She has the key. She will open the door, in due time, herself.'

Pierre Gilles's farewell was less scented, but equally firm. From Marthe he knew now where to find his lost papers in Chios. They had come to terms with each other, these two: whether because of the death of her uncle or the gesture she had initiated which had saved them: the disappearance for ever of all she had dreamed of for sixteen long months. For Jerott, on the other hand, he had formed an inconvenient attachment, largely because of the excellence of his medical Latin. With great difficulty Jerott disentangled himself from an offer to pursue his career in his patron's palace in Rome, breakfasting on ancient Greek manuscripts and dining on dissected giraffe. The old man, disappointed, had left him with a warning. 'Watch that woman. She'll eat you alive.'

'You wouldn't like to *take* Marthe?' said Jerott, with malice. 'She has Latin.'

'She has too many ideas,' Pierre Gilles had replied. 'Women with ideas are a threat to the civilized world. Get an ichneumon instead. They have only one idea. It's the same one, but they're more open-natured about it.'

Thus there were six of them at last; travelling day and night: travelling with Kuzúm, hollow-cheeked asleep in Philippa's arms, until Lymond found them a primitive cart-coach in which Marthe and Philippa and the child could snatch an uneasy night's rest while he drove it steadily on. It was slow, but it was better than stopping. And in daylight they left it and rode on, fast again.

They were all young but Archie, and he was probably tougher than any. But as they travelled westward and south, snatching sleep, too tired to speak, even Jerott began to question the pace. The only opposition they had had was of Onophrion's making. What if Roxelana was quite content to let them away, and their haste now was for nothing at all?

Lymond answered curtly and, when Jerott persisted, lost his temper in spectacular fashion. They had long outpaced the gentle attentions of Míkál's fellow creatures, and all the organizing since had been Lymond's with Archie to assist, riding ahead to obtain food and fresh horses and provender. They dared not take guides.

Because of the searchers at Gallipoli they could not take ship there either. In any case, in that season the large trading-ships with their holds full of passengers were rarely found in these parts, and Lymond wouldn't trust to a small vessel, driven by weather to frequent and perhaps dangerous anchorages; easily overtaken by a single powerful galley. Once, when they could find no horses, he hired a boat they could row themselves and took to the sea, joining the road further on down the coast. With Kuzúm asleep at their feet Philippa and Marthe shared an oar, grimly in silence, until Jerott, turning, pulled it out of their hands and helped them to ship it, sweat streaming down his own face. Marthe, sitting swaying in the soft air, her blue eyes half closed, said, 'I forgot. Your friend is a professional.'

By the time they landed, the girls were asleep, lulled by the salty wind and the comfort after the jolting dust of the saddle. The man who pulled up the boat told them of the company of troops they had just missed on the way. They had gone to all the villages and taken the horses: there was no horse to be had for ten miles to the east, and troops strung out all over the road. 'But only to the east, Lord,' he said. 'If you are going west, you have missed them.'

His brother had horses, and some food. The price Lymond paid for them took more than half of their small stock of money, but at least they were mounted and again on the road. On the way, Jerott apologized.

Lymond said briefly, 'It seemed unlikely that Míkál was taking so much trouble purely to fend off Onophrion. . . . We shall have to use our wits. They have faster, fresher horses than we have and good ships if they need them. If the news about us has reached this point already, it'll be all over the archipelago in a matter of days.'

'So?'

'So we continue. What else do you think we can do? We want a Venetian ship trading with Malta, or a Venetian state where we can wait for one. For that we've got to go south and west. We take turns scouting ahead.'

Jerott was silent. The journey had been punctuated by weary quarrels aggravated by Lymond's impatience. The witty, intolerant tongue whipped them all on until, in the end, Jerott rode without answering, his eyes blazing, his mouth shut on his fury. Archie took it in silence.

The hell of it was, Lymond was right. Their hopes lay in Malta. There Leone Strozzi and the Knights of St John would give them shelter and rest, and when the time came a perfect escort for the rest of their journey. Once in France it would be easy to arrange Philippa's journey to Scotland with Kuzúm, a strong armed retinue and Archie perhaps to go with her. Marthe, one supposed, would return to that queer household in Lyons, or the house in Blois where the Dame de Doubtance sat in her web. Jerott himself . . . he thought little about it. Home to Nantes, perhaps, and then to join Lymond's company wherever it might be fighting. Or perhaps not to join Lymond's company. His tired mind could not decide.

What Lymond's own plans were, he had no idea. Discussion began and ended with hour-to-hour problems, and the all-consuming one of reaching a suitable ship. Meanwhile, travel became more and more difficult. Once they nearly ran into a patrol and had to split forces, Jerott hiding the women while Archie and Lymond drew off pursuit.

The next time, in the hills near to Volos, Archie rode off to scout and didn't return. Jerott, scouring the district in daylight, found him finally with a broken-legged horse, and taking him up on the crupper made his way back to the shack where he had left Kuzúm and the two girls sleeping, with Lymond on watch.

He saw the flames of its burning from two hills away, and heard Kuzúm screaming from closer than that. Driving the laden pony round the last ridge, Jerott saw before him the hut, burning bright as a taper with a group of men fighting before it. Closer, he saw Philippa running, Kuzúm in her arms, into the coarse grass and scrub. Then in the whirling group of battling men he saw Lymond's bright head, and beside it another as fair, her arm rising and falling, the glint of steel in her fist. Three assailants, and Lymond and Marthe.

Jerott shrieked, tearing downhill, and one man fell to Lymond's sword as he looked round. The other had Marthe's arm by the wrist, his blade lifted, when Lymond knocked it away and engaged him, Marthe falling back gasping. The third man wheeled and ran, and Jerott, dropping Archie by Lymond, spurred his foundering pony to follow.

The running man was a delly, the same breed whom Jerott had outfaced in the partridge garden at Chios. He turned, his eyes glinting, at the sound of the hooves, and then changing direction, made for where Philippa stumbled over the rough ground, the little boy in her arms. The delly got to her just before Jerott reached him, and snatching the boy from her grasp, turned round, his knife at the small throat. 'You move. I kill,' he said.

'Stay still, Kuzúm,' said Philippa. To Jerott, frozen on his horse she said, her voice steady, 'Tell him we shall pay him for the child, and he may go free.'

Jerott translated. Behind him, all fighting had stopped. He could hear footsteps running towards him which slowed and then, as the delly gestured, stopped altogether. Lymond's, he guessed. The delly said, broken teeth shining, 'No. You kill: you take money back. You give me the pony.'

Lymond's voice said, still half-winded, 'Get off and give him the pony.' He was closer than Jerott had thought. 'Tell him once he is on the pony, we shall pay for the child, alive. He can throw the boy down.'

'How much?' said the delly.

Jerott risked a quick glance behind. The building still burned. Before it, Archie stood sword in hand beside the spreadeagled bodies of the two other dellies, Marthe a little behind him. A few yards away Lymond was standing, still breathing quickly, the sweat shining bright on his cheekbones and inside the open neck of his shirt. As Jerott watched, he put his hand within the torn lawn and brought out the flat deerskin purse of Venetian zecchini, the last of their money. He shook it, so that the delly could gauge the weight from the sound, and poured a few coins into his palm, and then back. 'All of that. Get off, Jerott.' He added in English, 'Get the boy when he mounts.'

It was touch and go, but greed won. Jerott dismounted and the delly, stretching an arm, caught the reins and drew the pony towards him. Then eyeing them all, he set the child in the saddle and began to swing up behind him, knife in hand just as Lymond flung him the purse. It fell short, rolling jingling on the rough ground, the gold jumping and sparkling and the delly, aghast, stopped for a flickering second.

In the same second, Jerott threw himself at the horse. The delly's knife flashed and a line of red sprang across Jerott's right hand. Then he had Kuzúm's solid flesh in his hands, and ducking back, had

474

rolled with him out of reach. For one wistful moment the man hesitated, his eyes on the gold on the ground. Then, seizing the pony again, he mounted and threw it into a gallop.

Lymond, running flat out, flung himself at him. Trying to tear Kuzúm's sobbing stranglehold on his neck, Jerott knew only too well why. One man escaped would bring the whole pack down on them. And they were now two horses short. Jerott tore free and, side by side with Archie, raced after the delly.

Lymond's jump, a little misjudged, had been short. He had done what he could to redeem it, clinging with one hand to the back of the saddle, dragging the horse with his weight while, knife in hand, he tried to dislodge the rider. Steering with his knees, the delly had turned and with both arms was trying to hammer him off. At Zuara, Lymond had jumped like this and mastered his balance in a matter of moments but now, watching them fight, Jerott saw that, clinging one-handed, Lymond was not succeeding in bettering it and, indeed, would be forced to drop unless he used his knife soon. Then he saw a spark of silver jerk through the air, and knew that the delly had kicked the knife from Lymond's free hand.

There was only one thing left for Lymond to do, and he did it. Closing both arms like a vice round the rider's thick body, he dragged him with him out of the saddle, and between the horse's hooves to the ground.

Far behind, Archie and Jerott saw them roll over and over, and then Lymond on top stumble to his feet and, bending, seize the half-conscious delly by the hair. He had no weapons, but there was no shortage of rocks. By the time Jerott came up, with Archie racing behind, there was very little to see of the landscape, rock, grass, earth or straggling weed, which was not crimson with blood.

His brow stiff with difficult lines, Jerott looked up at Lymond. Unhurt, so far as he could judge, but splashed, shirt, doublet and forearms, with the delly's lifeblood, he had eased back to an outcrop of rock, and was half sitting, half leaning on one of the heavy pale slabs, his eyes closed, his head high on the stone at his back. He said, without opening his eyes, 'Is he dead?'

'*My God,*' said Jerott, and swallowed, the smell of fresh blood in his throat. 'Do you think he could be anything else?' Then Archie, standing still behind, put a hand on Jerott's arm and held it there, warning.

A long way behind, in the silence, Jerott could hear Kuzúm coughing and sobbing, and the murmur of Philippa's voice. Marthe he had seen already half up the small quarry, where the three other horses were hidden. The pony, its immediate fright over, had slowed down some distance away and was nervously grazing. Archie walked forward slowly and quietly and came to a halt close to Lymond. He said, 'Ye did that blind? Can ye see now?'

'No,' Lymond said.

Jerott's hands opened. Archie went on, his face hard as teak, 'Has it happened before? Is there pain?'

'It happened . . . after the chess.'

His quick, gasping breathing half stifled the words. Archie moved forward and, barely touching him, slipped his hand inside Lymond's shirt. 'Try to tell me. Is there pain?'

'Yes.'

'You damned fool . . .' said Archie under his breath; and Francis Crawford smiled and half-opened his eyes. 'But I got you . . . quite far.'

'You got us all the way,' Archie said. 'There's a Venetian ship in the harbour at Volos, with a cargo for Malta. My dear lad, we are home.'

*

They were probably the last words Francis Crawford heard in that place. Leaving him where he lay, Jerott walked back slowly towards Philippa and Kuzúm. He had no idea what to say.

Kuzúm, mercifully, was quiet, his head in her skirts. Philippa said, 'Is he badly hurt?'

'It isn't that,' Jerott said. 'It's worse than that.' He stared at Philippa, his face blank, thinking. *Christ . . . he married her . . .* From the morning of the escape, the circumstance had left his mind utterly.

Philippa said matter-of-factly, 'It's the opium. He is dying?' Marthe, her three horses hobbled behind her, had joined them swiftly, standing by Philippa's shoulder, watching Jerott's pale face.

Jerott said, 'We don't know. It *is* the opium . . . Archie's terrified to move him. His theory is that even if he recovers from this exhaustion we have to cut off the drug.'

'He won't stand that, surely?' said Marthe.

'I don't know. There doesn't seem to be an alternative. Archie says that to continue now would be tantamount to dying of poison.'

'He might prefer it,' said Marthe. 'He knew what would happen. He has laid wagers with himself, I imagine, for days: how many hours, how many miles towards safety before he has to drop out.'

It was then that Jerott told them of the ship going to Malta. And as they stared at him, silent, he said to Philippa, 'He would want you and Kuzúm to go on it. I know it will feel like desertion; that all your instinct is to stay; but think of him and not of yourself if you can. What he is paying for now is Kuzúm's freedom.'

'I could nurse him,' said Philippa. And: 'No,' said Marthe evenly. 'I shall do that.'

Jerott could not shake her. Immovable as she had been on the *Dauphiné*, so Marthe now had made up her mind. Archie should go on the Venetian vessel to Malta with Philippa and the child, and from Malta travel with them to Scotland. Jerott, the former Knight of St John, should stay at Birgu with his fellows. There, when Lymond could sail—if Lymond could sail—she would bring him.

It was a plan they followed with only one alteration: Jerott had already made up his mind to stay on Volos with Lymond and Marthe. He consulted briefly with Archie, and then set off to find lodgings, while the girls gathered together what was left of all their possessions, and with cloaks and half-charred timber constructed a stretcher of sorts.

In the end, they left it behind. Jerott was back in an hour, two small mules jogging behind him, bearing a fine horse-litter of hide piled with blankets. With him on a pot-bellied donkey came a priest, his black robe trailing the dust. On a little hill to the north-west of Volos he had found a small church with a whitewashed school and almshouse and hospital. There Lymond could be cared for in peace.

The priest and Archie between them lifted him into the litter. He had not spoken again and was quite unconscious, the blood stiff on his clothes, the cavities deep under his eyes. Shortly after that, having instructed Jerott with all he knew, Archie took the road to Volos city and harbour, Philippa with Kuzúm at his side.

She didn't cry. Her spirit felt scoured; her brain arid as if slaked in quicklime: she remembered with shame the doubts and vanities she had shown over that *mariage de convenance* whose conveniences, so humiliating at the time, were indeed a matter of life and death to so many, and whose lack of grace concealed a true grace she was only beginning now to discern.

Until their wedding eve in the Seraglio of Topkapi, Francis Crawford had been a friend of her mother's; an adult whose alien being she did not wish or pretend to interpret.

She could say that no longer. She was his wife in nothing but name: the privacies of his nature were not hers to explore and to analyse: she kept him as far as possible out of her thoughts, and conjecture out of his affairs. Leaving him was less like leaving even the most simple of her friends in Flaw Valleys, and more like losing unfinished a manuscript, beautiful, absorbing and difficult, which she had long wanted to read.

She saw him before she left; but it did not occur to her to give him any spurious parting embrace, any more than she had expected to receive one at her wedding.

Yet he himself had bestowed one, on Khaireddin. It was, perhaps, the most disturbing of all the things she had seen him do.

Kuzúm liked the boat.

29

VOLOS

They kept Lymond in the crowded ward of the hospital until he recovered consciousness. Then they moved him to one of the alms-houses, a small, self-contained building with a low common-room and, above, one small cell with a bed.

This became his. At first he lay there, his eyes closed, while the nursing brethren spoke in whispers to Jerott. Such stillness was what the overstrained body required. Pray God it would last.

Downstairs, Jerott unleashed his anxious irritation on Marthe. 'They know it can't last. Why don't they admit it?'

'They are kind. They are innocent. They believe God is merciful,' said Marthe.

From the moment of Lymond's collapse, the supply of opium had been cut off completely. This isolation and privacy were what Archie had advised, and the priest in charge of the sick man endorsed it, his wise eyes turning from Jerott to Marthe. 'Have you seen one thus afflicted when the drug is withdrawn? There is acute pain, intestinal and muscular, with intense weakness and tremors and nausea. That is in the body. In the spirit, there is also a peculiar anguish and isolation, a madness I can compare only with the frenzy of total bereavement. This young man has a strong and resilient body. Pray that this may be true of his mind.'

He was strong-minded enough, when the time came, to send the nursing monks packing. It was the first sign of trouble: the priest on duty descending the stairs from the sickroom, his robe dragging on the rough unfinished wood, and walking over to Jerott. 'I fear I and my brothers can be of no further help.'

At first Jerott believed they were abandoning Francis. Then he understood that it was the other way round. 'He does not wish us to attend him. It is not wise, but it is understandable,' said the priest. 'Indeed, there is nothing we can do that you, his friends, cannot now do better.'

One could not argue with that. Jerott was silent. It was Marthe, accepting it, who said, 'I shall sleep here then, if a bed can be made up in the common-room. I suppose one of us should be on call.' And Marthe who, when the arrangements had been made, walked upstairs with the first tray of bouillon and entered the sickroom for the first time.

There was little in the room but the bed, placed between the door and the two small windows pierced in the outer wall of the courtyard. And it was the bed, its clean, coarse linen in a rucked, disembowelled heap, which held her attention: that and the fair hair and twisted robe and claw hands of the man tangled within it, his face buried unseen. Then Lymond stirred, breathing sharply, and after a moment abruptly changed his position. His face came round, heavy-lidded: written over and over with desperate suffering; and his eyes opened full upon Marthe.

He had no more colour to lose. Instead, he took a short breath like a man hit in the face, and stayed where he was, with hauteur, in all that humiliating disorder. Marthe put down the tray with a small jolt, which she had not intended, and said evenly, 'There is soup for you. If you want anything, ask for it. Jerott and I will do what we can.'

'Thank you,' said Francis Crawford. His voice was cynical, and almost as steady as hers. '*The origin of pain, says Buddha, is the thirst for pleasure; the thirst for existence, the thirst for change. Destroy your passions as an elephant throws down a hut built of reeds: the only remedy for evil is healthy reality.* You are my healthy reality. I am indebted to you. But as I have already told the hospital brethren, I need no further attention.'

'You need food,' said Marthe. 'If we do not bring it, then the priests must. It is a time for logic, not vanity.'

His lashes were wet and the pillows sodden with sweat. He said, 'And a time, I suppose, for revenge.'

Her hair, drawn back in its shining silk coils, was the same gold as his: her face, pale and high-boned and controlled, came from the same mould. She said, 'I am not here to mock. Ring the bell if you want help. Jerott will come if he can. If not, you will have to put up with me.'

To Jerott below, she said merely, 'It has begun.'

Once under way, the illness gained weight like an avalanche, and the next time Jerott climbed the stairs he found the door locked and, listening, realized that Lymond was up somehow and roving the room, the light footfalls buffeting up and down, backwards and forwards, round and round. Jerott spoke through the door, and knocked, but received no answer then or later; nor did Marthe on the same errand. They alternated like clock weights, said Jerott with bitterness, through the entire dreary day until evening, when Jerott lost patience and threatened to kick in the door.

A moment later the key turned and the door crashed back open as Francis Crawford, turning back inside, sat on the bed, his head in his hands. He said, without looking up, 'Do what you have to do, and get out.'

Jerott banged down the milk he had brought. 'Look. If you are having pains, scream. If you are seeing thousand-pound elephant birds with reinforced iron nests, tell us and we shall believe you. If you want to climb up and jump from the roof, let me tell you that we feel exactly the same. Only don't lock your door like a maiden aunt with the gravel.'

Lymond moved suddenly, and then was still. 'I agree in principle,' he said. 'Only, if I did begin screaming . . . you wouldn't like it.' He added abruptly, 'I don't want Marthe. Send her away.'

His brows drawn, Jerott looked down on him. 'She could have gone with the others. She stayed behind to look after you.'

'Oh, Christ. *I don't* . . .' began Lymond and broke off, stopped by a long, shuddering yawn, the circles brown-black under his eyes.

'You don't need help?' said Jerott with desperate sarcasm. 'Or I don't need help?'

Like a man lifting a great weight, Lymond looked up. With the same terrible effort, he said flatly, 'Every time that door opens . . . I start counting. And I go on counting until it shuts again. Otherwise I should be on my knees, crying for . . . what I want. If you want to help me . . . keep out. If you want to shame me, send Marthe. She and I are . . . unmerciful adversaries.'

Jerott's breath caught at the top of his stomach; but this time he knew what must be done; and he did it.

'You and she are brother and sister,' he said.

Francis Crawford gave a small sigh. His face, already stripped to the bone by extreme physical stresses, looked suddenly as if it had been pushed apart, flesh and muscle, by some grisly, slow-moving stamp. He said, 'If she says so . . . she's lying,' and, raising himself with shaking hands from the edge of the bed, stood for a moment staring unseeing at Jerott. Then one of the great waves of cramping pain took him, and he turned and grasped at the window-ledge, gasping, his brow on the glass.

Jerott went forward and put his hands hard on his shoulders, but Lymond stayed there, his throat knotted, and would not turn round. After a long time, he spoke. 'If she comes in here again, I shall kill her.'

Jerott let his hands drop. 'She won't come,' he said curtly. 'And neither shall I, if I can help it. There is a bell, if you want me.' And he left abruptly, closing the door; leaving Lymond to face whatever was coming as he wanted, alone.

He did, in his own fashion; nor did he ring all that night. As the new day dragged its way on, the watchers below were able to follow, by sound, the steadily rising violence of the whole onslaught until as the sun reached its height a voice above joined the uneven footsteps; softly at first, and then in outbursts of noise, stopping raggedly and starting without warning and rising to strange rhythmic climaxes before falling to a murmur again.

Her eyes on Jerott, Marthe rose and went upstairs; and after a while Jerott joined her where she sat in the passage above, outside Lymond's room, her cheek pressed to the cold wall. When Jerott made to speak she held up her hand, and he took his place beside her in his turn, and, in his turn, listened.

If I screamed, you wouldn't like it, Lymond had said. And because the anguish could now no longer be borne, and because he would not scream, he was using the uncontrollable voice, the trumpet of suffering and conduit of impossible sorrows. And he had dressed it, as a burning ship sets out her fragments of bunting, with the trappings of poetry. Agony spoke in the ringing, uneven voice, but decently transmuted into the words of the poets, flowing onwards and onwards, verse after verse, tongue after tongue.

> *En un vergier lez une fontenele*
> *Dont clere est l'onde et blanche la gravel*
> *siet fille a roi, sa main a son maxele*
> *en sospirant son douz ami rapele . . .*

> *Still under the leavis green*
> *This hinder day, I went alone*
> *I heard ane mai sair murne and meyne*
> *To the King of Love she made her moan . . .*

> *I pray thee, for the love of God*
> *Go build Nejáti's tomb of marble . . .*

He spoke each poem through to the end, and beside Jerott, Marthe's lips moved, following. Sometimes the hard-pressed voice, uplifted, made no sense of the words it spoke. Then when the violence died would come relief, and the voice would pick its way again:

> *Unlike the moon is to the sonne sheen*
> *Eke January is unlike to May . . .*

Sometimes the voice trailed into silence, perhaps even into sleep for two minutes or five. Then it would leap into life, footsteps treading the boards back and forwards accompanying it, and a little thicker, a little more tired, it would go on with its recital, rising, holding and falling to a tide not its own.

Jerott stood half an hour of it and then left, suddenly, his face white, walking straight through the common-room and out into the faint golden sunshine where he sat, his hands over his ears.

Marthe stayed. She stayed until the voice, now roughened and slow, found trouble at last in sustaining that uneven flow of beauty and other men's wisdom and stumbled, spinning the fabric of poetry too thinly to conceal what was lying beneath. Then she opened the door, and went in to him.

Lymond was beyond attacking her now, and almost beyond reasoned thought. He stood between the two windows, his back to the wall, and his face was nothing but eyes, blue and lightless and dead. Staring at her, he looked like a man crossing a chasm on a fine skein of silk; who has seen its strands fray, and now watches an enemy untie the whole.

'Whom have ye known die honestly without the help of a pote-cary?' said Marthe. 'We can do better than this. Turn your back to me, and listen.' And paying him no further attention, she sat down on the ruin of his bed and recited, hugging her knees.

> *J'ay bien nourry sept ans ung joly gay*
> *En une gabiolle*
> *Et quant ce vint au premier jour de may*
> *Mon joly gay s'en vole . . .*

In the next verse his voice chimed in wildly, and because he was entrenched by the wall, his eyes closed, he did not see her eyes fill up, sparkling with tears, though her voice barely faltered.

Two voices ended the poem and started the next and the next, following Marthe's lead through verse half known and forgotten, kept fresh and exact in her strange, precise mind.

> *Hast thou no mind of love? Where is thy make?*
> *Or art thou sick, or smit with jealousy?*
> *Or is she dead, or hath she thee forsake . . . ?*

> *La Sphère en rond, de circuit lassée*
> *Pour ma faveur, malgré sa symétrie*
> *En nouveau cours contre moi s'est poussée . . .*

> *Ysonde to land wan*
> *With seyl and with ore*
> *Sche mete an old man*
> *Of berd that was hore . . .*

> *Mis arreos son las armas*
> *Mi descanso es pelear*
> *Mi cama, las duras penas*
> *Mi dormir, siempre velar . . .*

She stayed all afternoon and evening, and all through the night. Sometimes he couldn't keep up. Sometimes, when the attack was at its height, he broke off, the breath dead in his throat, and crouched gasping with pain by the bed until, girder by girder, he built up his courage again and, rising, wrapped the voice of his torment once more in the words Marthe brought him.

Throughout it all, she never attempted to touch him; even when, towards morning, he was so tired that he slept sometimes where he knelt until, driven upright again, unstrung and suffering, he would lift his eyes and, looking out of the blank greying panes, begin all over again.

But sleep, this time, was coming. Each spell of quiet had begun to last longer: the frayed voice, dropped to a whisper, told over its verses with less and less violence. At last, as the light slowly brightened and he stood, swaying a little, his back to the wall, he began, without her, a poem Marthe had not chosen.

> *I have a young sister far beyond the sea*
> *Many be the dowries that she sent me*
> *She sent me the cherry withouten any stone*
> *And so she did doo withouten any bone*
> *She sent me the briar without any rind*
> *She bade me love my leman withoute longing*
> *How could any cherry be without stone?*
> *And how could any doo be without bone?*
> *How could any briar be without rind?*
> *And how could I love my leman without longing?*

Somewhere in the white shell of his face, there was a lost spark of a smile, for Marthe. Speaking softly, Marthe answered it.

> *When the cherry was in flower: then it had no stone*
> *When the briar was unbred: then it had no rind*
> *When the doo was an egg, then it had no bone*
> *When the soul has what it loves: it is without longing.*

'. . . You see,' said Marthe. 'I am not here to mock. I have worn out my revenge. You have guided me into a world which has been closed to me all my life. You have shown me that what I hold by, you hold by and more. You have shown me strength I do not possess, and humanity I thought belonged only to women. You are a man, and you have explained all men to me. . . .'

His eyes were closed, nor did he give any sign that he had heard her. Marthe smiled and, moving closer, laid her hand for the first time on his. 'Francis. It is morning. Come and sleep.'

She had made the sheet smooth, and the pillow in its place was fair and downy and deep. She held the bedlinen back while he came to her; and when he lay still and delivered in its cool depths, she folded it round, barely touching him. He was already asleep.

The stairs were dark and uncertain, and she walked down them trembling, her icy hand gripping the rail. Below, in the grey light, Jerott was standing, his face white and strained and full of a queer and difficult grief.

He opened his arms and Marthe ran into them crying, and stayed there weeping as if she had just learned of madness; and been informed of the nature of death.

*

It was the turning-point. Lymond woke in exhausted peace, flat on the pillows, and allowed Jerott to do what he wished.

Later, when Marthe went to his room, he received her with un-clouded tranquillity, and quoted her own words back at her as she sat at his side. 'Whom have ye known die honestly without the help of a potecary?'

Marthe, searching his face, drew a breath. 'Last night you called me something else.'

His face was grave, but the smile had not quite left his eyes. 'I called you sister,' he said. 'Was I right?'

'Yes,' said Marthe. And hesitating: 'What made you sure?'

'The luggage of poetry you carry,' said Francis Crawford; and far down in the tired eyes the smile lingered still. 'Your other burdens I can also share.'

'I want no ties,' said Marthe. 'I need no help.' As an afterthought, she added, 'You have made free enough with your name.'

His thin-boned hands, lying loose on the counterpane, drifted slowly together and folded. He said, 'Are you sure it is my name you should bear?'

In the little silence that followed she could hear clearly the tick of a clock. Like him, she knew too much poetry. . . . Uncivil clock, like the foolish tapping of a tipsy cobbler. A blasphemy on its face; a dark mill, grinding the night. . . . A nerve flicked, like a thread, at the side of his mouth and was gone.

Marthe said, 'No, I'm not sure. I know the names of neither of my progenitors, nor have I any longing to know. To me, the matter is nothing. . . . My first recollection was of my convent at Blois: my only relations have been with the Dame and Georges Gaultier. And they answered no questions.'

Lymond said, 'Gaultier is dead,' his rising tension betrayed by his voice.

'So is the Dame de Doubtance,' said Marthe. 'Your meeting with her was the last one: did she not say so to you? Surely you felt her beside you when you chose Kuzucuyum? Surely you knew she was with us last night? She died when you slept, at daybreak this morning.'

He didn't ask how she knew. He accepted what she had said because he had reason to do so, and said only, 'She died, knowing your parentage?'

Marthe shrugged. 'The secret died with her. It would trouble her little. She had breathed life into her puppets: you and I to discover what in ourselves we still lacked. Philippa to be gilded as befitted her spirit. Jerott . . . to be taken from you. And my lover and I to be parted.'

For a while Lymond did not speak. Then he said, 'What do you believe she wanted for Jerott?'

Marthe's hands also were interlaced; her firm chin was high, her eyes dense and steady. 'Kindness,' she said. 'He will have it.' Then she rose, quietly because he had had more than enough, and said, 'You will rest and get well. Jerott tells me you will not go at once back to Scotland. What then will you do?'

His slow voice was wry. 'Earn my living. And that of my . . . new dependants.'

And Marthe turned at the door, her pale fall of hair alight with the sun from the window; the tired della Robbia face, so like his own, reflecting his irony. 'There is no need. You are a rich man, brother,' she said. 'All of which Gaultier died possessed was bequeathed to the Dame de Doubtance, his patron. And all she had in each of her houses was willed, so long as I have known her, to you.'

He looked at her, disbelieving; and then instantly answered. 'Then it is all rightly yours.'

'No,' said Marthe. 'Whatever my life holds, I have no wish to owe it to them. And wherever she is, even dead—don't you think she would know, if we frustrate her will now? What is there will keep you in luxury.'

'It will keep Philippa and Kuzúm,' Lymond said quietly. 'Like you, I have no wish to be further beholden.'

Staring down at his spent face on the pillow, Marthe's expression was wry. 'The wife who calls you *Mr Crawford*,' she said. 'The child you don't even know.' And as he didn't answer, Marthe said suddenly, 'How many souls on this earth call you Francis? Three? Or perhaps four?'

For a moment he looked at her unsmiling; and for a moment she wished, angrily that she could recall the question. Then quite suddenly he smiled, and held out his hand. 'Five,' he said. 'Surely? Since last night.'

*

He was slow to recover, but neither Jerott nor Marthe was impatient; and only Jerott latterly became angry at his total absence of plans. If a fortune awaited him in Blois or in Lyons, Lymond repeated, it would be used solely for the comfort of Philippa and Kuzúm. For himself, he had his own way to make.

Until Jerott, exploding ill-advisedly like a soldier and not like a former Knight of St John, said, 'Then when *are* you going back to see them in Scotland?' And Francis Crawford said, 'Never.'

He left the day after that, before Jerott or Marthe was awake, to keep his appointment. Before he went, he had taken leave in his own private fashion of each, though he made sure neither knew it. He had satisfied himself of their future, both immediate and distant, now slowly bonding together. And he had acknowledged, with all the generosity of which he was capable, the gift of his life and his reason.

The note he left required Marthe not to follow him, and Marthe, he knew, would force Jerott to honour it. He laid his plans well, choosing an hour when he was fresh, and able to ride, he believed, a measurable distance. He escaped from his room, left the precincts and acquired his prearranged horse with no incident at all, and merely the expenditure, as throughout his discreet dispositions from sickbed, of a modest outlay in bribes.

One may, however, be fresh as a rose in a bedroom, and by no means the terror of mules on the road. This, he acknowledged, gravely, after a mile or two; and after five was not acknowledging anything at all except a strong impulse to vacate the saddle. None the less, he reached the crossroads near his objective at precisely the hour he had planned and, leaving the hard-beaten, uneven track, picked his way between trees to a place where another road could be discerned, this time going west. Within sight of the road, but concealed from chance travellers by the low scrub and bushes, Lymond tied his reins and slipped from the saddle.

There was nothing to unpack. He had no saddlebags with him; no clothes and no money; no food and no drink. He had his sword in its sheath and his cloak on one shoulder, and somewhere a vestige of flamboyance, which led him to slap his horse on the rump, and to watch it canter, kicking, into the depths of the wood, saying, 'In the Name of Allâh, the Beneficent, the Merciful. Let there be love.' Lymond stood swaying for a moment, watching the road; and then subsided on to the turf.

When the heavy coach with its two horses and four armed out-riders came along and pulled up, in a trembling of dust, he was lying in the short grass, its shadows swinging over his face. A black-bird, feeding close to his hand, flinched and sped away chortling as the outriders dismounted, scimitars jolting bright in the sun, and after a little searching, bent and lifted him, his head moving loosely, over into the coach.

This was little else than a cart with a Gothic arched cover, but it was more than palatial inside, with benches ranged by the luggage, and cushions on the carpeted floor. The men laid him on these, at the feet of the one other person the carriage contained, and saluting, withdrew. A moment later, to the sound of whip-cracking and the yelling of voices, the vehicle groaned into motion again.

Lymond stirred. Above him, there was a slow smile on the lips of his companion. An arm lifted, removing a veil. And a small hand, fine and soft and exactingly jewelled, stretched out to touch Francis Crawford's fair hair in a light and pensive caress.

'It is well,' said Kiaya Khátún. 'You are here; and we have begun on our journey together.'